City of Darkness

City of Darkness

WILLIAM HEINZEN

Design by Standout Books

ISBN 978-1-7336479-0-8

Dedication

This novel is for my friends and coworkers at National Information Solutions Cooperative. We have a simple motto there: do the right thing, always. One of the fundamental questions at the core of this novel is whether or not people have the ability to choose to do what is right. The answer is that we do, and each of you at NISC proves it every day.

Acknowledgments

*T*here are a lot of great people who helped me turn this story into a reality. First and foremost, I'd like to thank my preliminary round of readers: *Rossina Gil, Mike Rothstein,* and *Dave Heinzen* (Dave is a guy who will help you with numbers). Mike, the many conversations we had on road trips between northern Minnesota and southern Alabama contributed greatly to helping me understand where all these characters ended up after Warrior of Light. Also thanks to *Rebecca Moesta,* who is an absolutely brilliant editor. When I tried to cut corners, you called me on it, and the story is better because of your help. Also, remind Kevin that he owes me a beer. A big thanks to the production team at Standout Books: *Euan Monaghan, Alex Hemus, Bronwyn Hemus,* and *Frederick Johnson.* As for *Sean Flory* at the University of Jamestown, you have always helped me discern between which ideas are good ones and which are, as you put it so delicately, bats—t crazy. Last but certainly not least, thanks to *Barb Heinzen* for a final proofread.

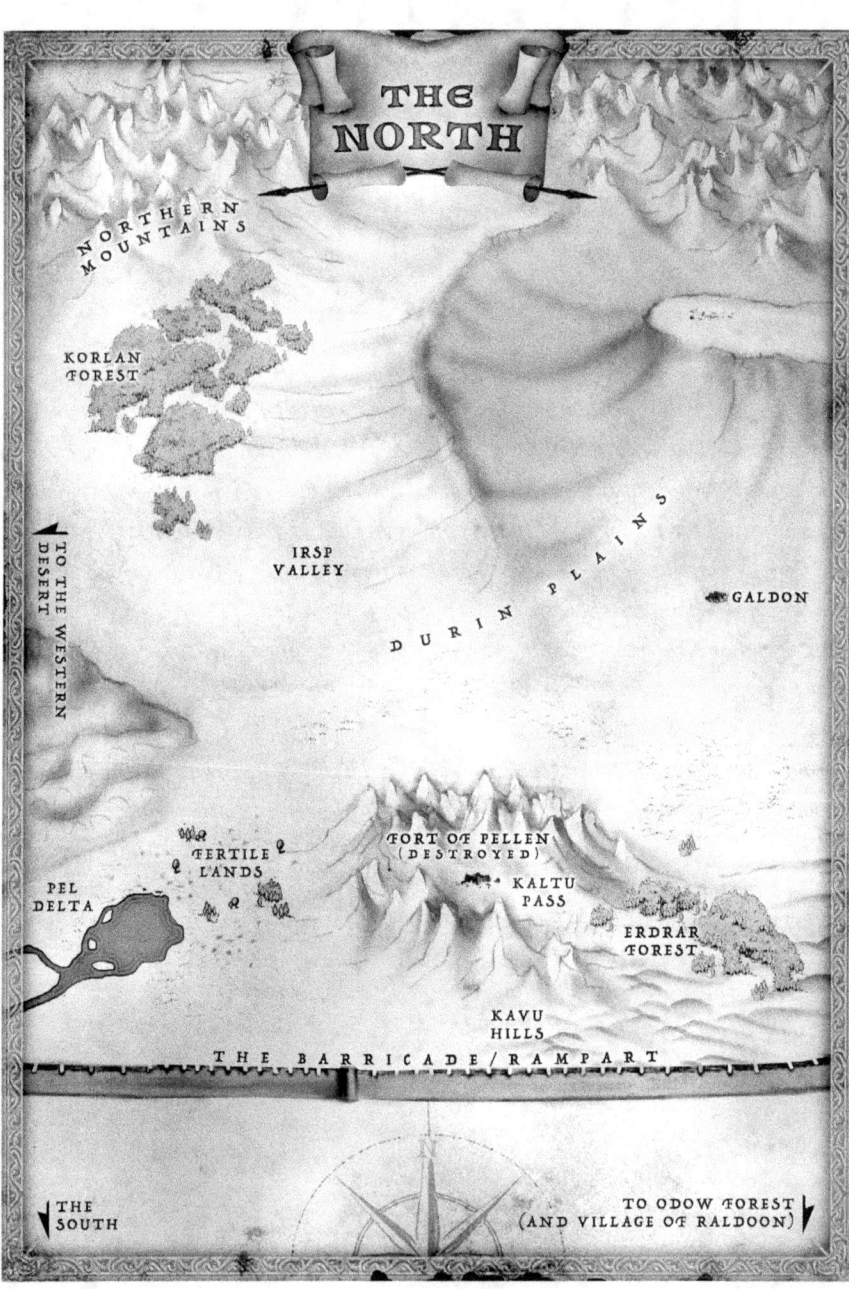

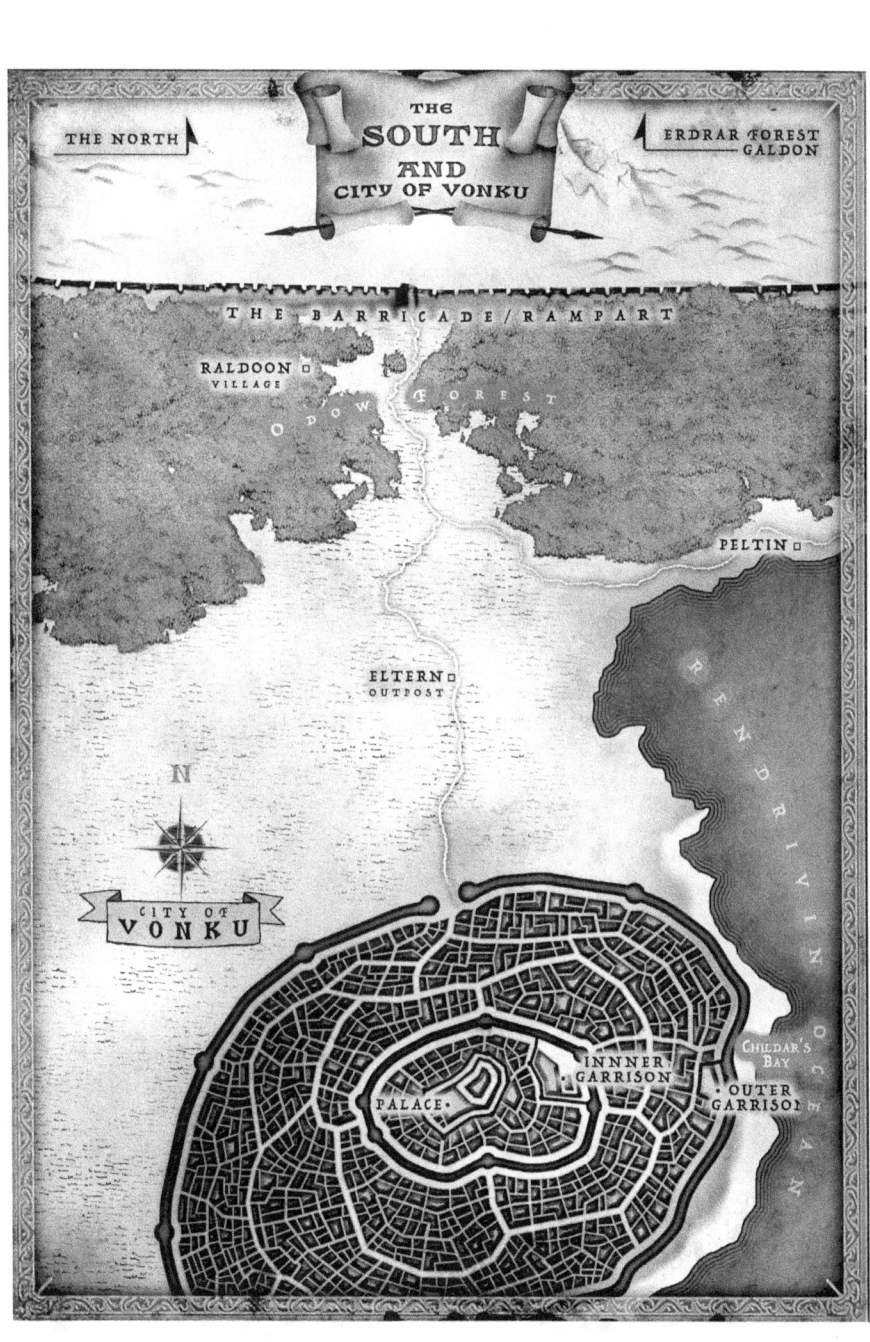

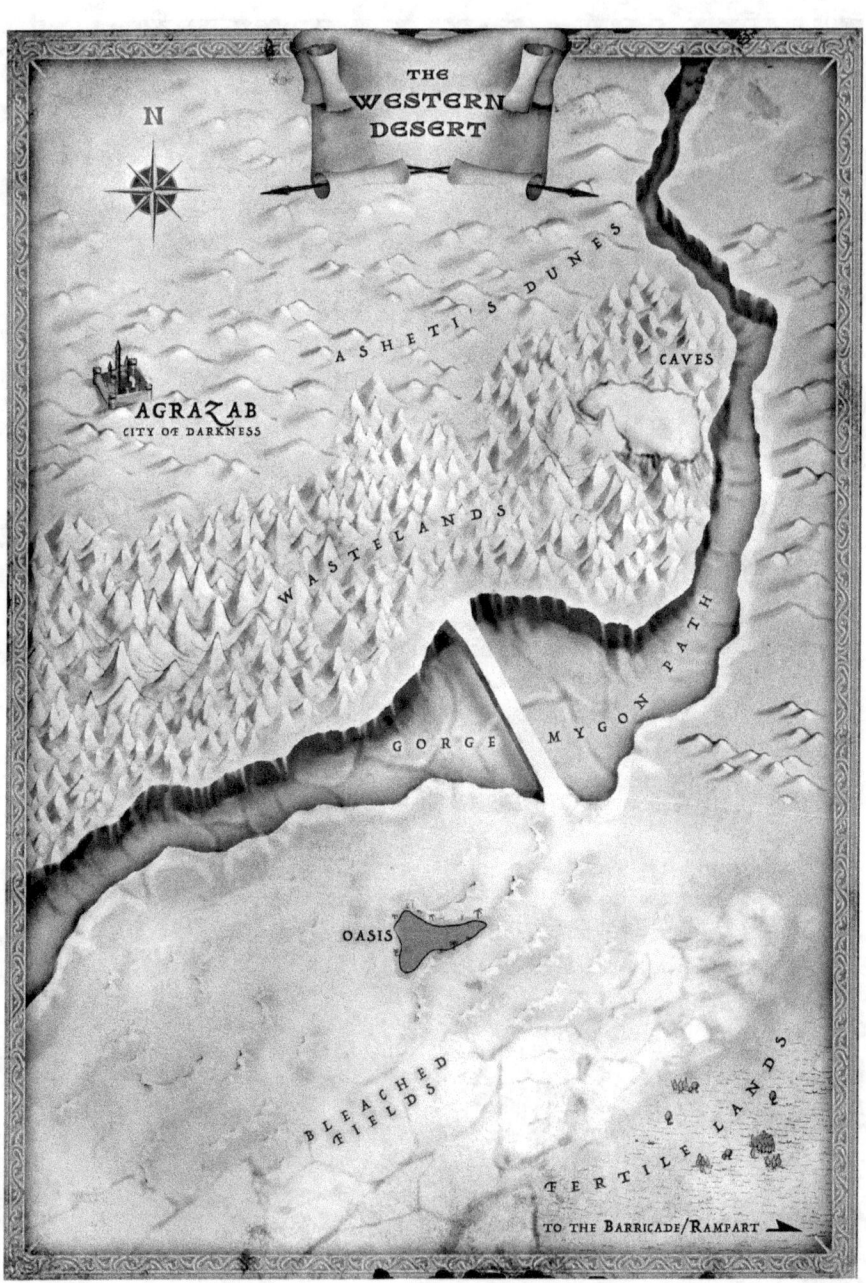

1

The elion opened his eyes. He lay in darkness, the earthen floor unyielding against his back. He did not know how long he had been here—hours? Days? Years? It mattered little, for he had long since surrendered his free will, and with such a change, time became meaningless. He'd had a name once, but he'd forgotten it. Names were temporary constructs anyway, and his master's business was with eternity.

The elion rose, stretching dormant muscles, smelling musty air.

IT IS TIME, the voice said. There had been another voice before this one; he'd hated it and needed it, feared it and loved it, gone mad in its presence and catatonic in its absence. This new voice, though, was life itself, and the elion did not know if he could draw another breath without its power coursing through his veins. Beside him, a root poked through the cracks of the wall. He grasped the root, rising to his feet, breath escaping from his lungs in a low whine. Needing no light to see, the elion stumbled across the tiny space and grasped the rail of a ladder before him. One step at a time, he climbed, silent save for the sound of his feet scraping against each successive iron rung. His head brushed against a cellar door, and with a single push he lifted it out of the way.

He placed a hand in front of his eyes, shielding himself from the resultant light that shone past him, revealing a man's body still lying on the floor of packed dirt below. The corpse's throat had been torn out, and stains of dried blood covered the neck. Free will or not, an elion still had to feed.

The elion emerged from the cellar and into the living area of a simple cottage. A table sat in the center of the living room, where furs lined the walls and the front door hung ajar. A trail of blood stretched across the floorboards, thick in some places, thin in others, stopping at the cellar entrance. The woodsman's struggle had been brief but violent. Fragments of dishes lined the countertop, furniture lay in several places, and windows had been shattered.

The elion reached the table in two strides. He picked up a knife and tested the edge with his thumb, feeling the bright prick of pain as blade sliced flesh. The folds of his skin peeled back like soft clay, and a droplet of deep red sprang from his fingertip. He raised thumb to lips, savoring the flavor. When he stepped outside into the setting sun, the glow of dusk hung heavy over the forest, but the otherwise-expected sounds of nightfall remained conspicuously absent. He supposed it had something to do with himself, and the thought made him smile. He looked west, facing the red orb as it slipped below the horizon. His destination lay somewhere in that direction. He did not know the way, but the voice would guide him.

Before he departed, one more task lay in front of him. The forest around him used to be desolate and barren, but now signs of life grew everywhere— short, healthy trees poked up from the ground, young and with much room to grow, while the formerly lifeless older trees bore every manner of leaf, branch, and flower. It had not been long since the darkness passed, but long enough for the earth to turn once more.

HASTEN TO THE TASK AT HAND, MY SERVANT. LEAVE THIS PLACE AND COME TO ME. YOU SHALL BE MY HAND, IN THIS LIFE AND IN THE NEXT.

"And what of the faithless?" he asked. The words came out of his mouth in a dry croak, echoing against the surrounding forest.

NAUGHT BUT UNENDING DARKNESS.

The elion swallowed, tasting the crust of the woodsman's dried blood at the corner of his mouth. "Of course, my Lord." He moved into the woods, as above him a sliver of moon replaced the sun. He would not fail his master; he'd given too much to accept anything other than success. By the time he departed from the forest and onto the plains, a light wind had picked up, wafting across his face. Once, winds had howled across this land, ceaseless and without mercy, but much had changed during these last eighteen months.

Yes, the Warrior of Light had been victorious, but when one door closed, another opened, figuratively and literally. As darkness descended, the elion continued his journey across the plain, making his way into the night.

* * *

Boblin Kule was getting married.

Tim Matthias thought back to when he'd first met Celia Alcion, right after he and Boblin fled the doomed Fort of Pellen. They had been taking shelter in the Kaltu Pass during the aftermath of the Fort's last stand when Celia slipped up on them, giving Tim neither his first nor his last lesson in elion stealth. Tim had known from that moment—the way Boblin looked at Celia, averting his eyes ever so slightly, a flush creeping into his cheeks—that his comrade loved her more than words could say.

Now Boblin stood before a mirror, fingers around his collar, pulling the cuff tight against his neck. The window outside revealed the streets of Galdon, many of its buildings still under construction.

"Are you nervous?" Tim asked.

"No."

"Well, that's the third time you've adjusted your collar. I don't think it's getting any straighter."

"*You* try getting married, and we'll see where your bravado is."

"Who would I marry?"

"I could care less. A three-legged goat, perhaps, or whatever stops you from distracting me with unhelpful feedback."

Tim nodded. "I think that Commander Boblin Kule of the Frontier Patrol is afraid of a public kiss. Not that this surprises me."

"Go boil your head."

"Go carve up a malichon."

"Thanks to you, there aren't any malichons *left* to carve up."

A loud cough at the front of the room interrupted them as Quentiin Harggra, dwerion of Raldoon, hero of the Pit, entered the room. Four feet tall, half as wide, Quentiin wore a long, red coat and leather boots turned down at the calves. "Are ye ready?" the dwerion asked.

"I am," Boblin said, at the same time Tim said, "He's not."

Quentiin shook his head, a wistful smile on his face. "Weddin's. It's always somethin', eh?"

"Look sharp and march fast, gentlemen," Boblin said. "On with it."

"Giving us orders?" Tim asked. "Do we look like members of the elion infantry to you?"

Boblin looked Tim up and down. "No. You're too ugly."

Tim acquiesced, tilting his head and gesturing to the door. "Lead the way, Commander."

With Boblin in the lead, the three companions walked the short passage from dressing room to chapel proper. Rows of oaken pews filled the worship hall, and shafts of sunlight filtered through the stained-glass windows that lined either side of the room, casting a dusky glow. Father Anelion stood at the head of the chapel, robed in white. During his time in Zadinn's Pit, Anelion had served as a spiritual guide to the slaves, nurturing their faith in that dark time. Now, as head of the chapel, he had conducted his fair share of weddings during the year and a half since Zadinn's downfall. Many of the liberated people had chosen to celebrate their freedom in the best way possible.

Anelion had performed a more solemn task when they laid Pellen Yuzhar to rest one year ago. And while the ceremony had not been without sorrow, all knew that Pellen's respite was long earned and long overdue. He'd led the elion for two hundred years during Zadinn Kanas' reign, gifted—or perhaps cursed—with an unnaturally long life by Nazgar of the Kyrlod. Pellen's duty had been to see the elion through their battle to freedom, and he had done just that, passing away only after laying the first cornerstones in their process of rebuilding the imperial city, Galdon, now situated in a new location on the Durin Plains.

Quentiin and Tim took positions by the door, prepared to usher guests in, while Boblin stood at the foot of the steps beside Father Anelion. Soon, the guests began arriving, first in trickles, then steadily gaining. Tim recognized every one of them, for the North had been a tight-knit community upon its liberation from Zadinn's reign. First he seated Mandar and Jess Kule, Boblin's mother and father, who had been a steady but quiet presence in the background of the elion refugees' travels across the former wastelands. After them came Boblin's cousins, Faldon and Tavin, who had guarded the company's camp on a many a cold, dark night. To the next row of pews Quentiin ushered Wayne Gendashar, who had been one of Boblin's early partners on scouting expeditions in the Frontier Patrol, alongside the twins Hugo and Ken Rindar, a formidable elion duo who had kept many a recruit alive during the long years of Zadinn's reign. Tim also seated Jend Argul, former—and legendary—commander of the Frontier Patrol, and the most highly respected elion in the Fort next to Pellen. All had participated in the refugees' perilous journey through the Northern Mountains in search of the Army of Kah'lash, after which they'd fought side by side on the slopes of the Deathlands against Zadinn's armies. Many had traveled into the Mountains, but few returned, and those who survived joined together to build this new city, ushering in the future they had fought and paid for so dearly.

Emperor Ladu Jovun IV soon arrived as well, a pair of elion guards flanking him. Ladu did not necessarily need protection in this place, but the Frontier Patrol took protocol seriously. During their quest north, the Fort's refugees had found Ladu in the Mountains, preserved in a block of sorcerous crystal from his time as Zadinn's prisoner, and following the Battle of the Deathlands he returned to his rightful place as ruler of the North.

After the guests sat, Celia Alcion arrived, radiant in her white gown. Her long, dark hair flowed over her shoulders, and she smiled at Boblin as she approached, the shine of joy in her deep, brown eyes. Boblin smiled back, and the two stood facing each other at the base of the altar, holding hands. Tim looked toward a stained-glass window, through which shafts of sunlight shone, adding a warmth and vibrancy to the room that reminded him of early spring days in the Odow Forest. The Odow had been his home at one point, but it was not anymore. The North was his home, the elions his people, and Ladu his monarch.

Outside the chapel, makeshift structures lined a street of half-finished cobblestone. Galdon had been the capital city of the old empire, and now it formed the centerpiece of the new. Its original location had been destroyed in Zadinn Kanas's invasion two hundred years ago, and Ladu wished to honor its memory by giving the new city the same name. Tim and Boblin had been working on the palace wall just yesterday, wrestling the last stones into place and sealing the chinks with mortar. It was tiresome work, sometimes progressing at great speeds, other times in painful increments, but Boblin swore they would finish the wall by his wedding day.

"I'm an elion of the Frontier Patrol," Boblin had said, "and I'll burn in Malath before I wed in sight of an unfinished garrison."

There were no malichons to fight, no threats from without, but Tim suspected some things would never change. For the elions, vigilance was as much about tradition as protection. They'd survived two hundred years because of the Frontier Patrol, and the Maker willing, would survive for many more.

As silence fell over the assembled group, Father Anelion cleared his throat.

"Love and sacrifice," the elion said, "are the two reasons we stand together today."

Sacrifice. Tim thought to a night not quite two years gone, when he knelt in the shadows of the Kaltu Pass beside his father Daniel. *There are many things I would like to say to you, but a lifetime is not long enough for a father to tell his son the things he must.* For the elions, Daniel and Rosalie's sacrifice had by no means been the first, but it had been for Tim. Tim's parents bought the refugees their freedom that night, giving the elions the means to escape into the Fertile Lands while Daniel and Rosalie held back the entirety of the malichon pursuit.

"They are forever intertwined, love and sacrifice," Anelion continued. "Each reinforces the other, for what is love but sacrificing our needs for another? What is sacrifice without love to give it purpose? Eighteen months ago, we fought on the slopes of the Deathlands, buying freedom with our blood. Those who do not possess the capacity for love are incapable of sacrifice, and those who cannot find cause for sacrifice have lost their ability to love. We must cherish both, remembering that they are what brought us together. Whether elion, dwerion, or human, these two fundamental gifts unite us all, and they are the foundations that separate Harmea from Malath."

Tim did not think Father Anelion actually enjoyed speaking in front of groups. Every time he began a service, his voice came out thin and reedy; an occasional gulp, or extra breath of air—only noticeable if one knew to look—indicated a nervous tension within him. Without fail, as the elion continued speaking his words became clearer, his confidence more pronounced, his message more assertive. He had been born in the Pit, what guidance he gave the slaves often provided under cover of dark, hidden from malichons more than eager to snuff out any essence of hope. *Or maybe they knew about him all along, but let him be, for how better to torment than to dangle the unattainable in front of a persecuted people?* If torture had been the slavemaster's intentions, they had underestimated their captives, for Father Anelion stood in front of a liberated people, his voice stronger than ever.

"The elion people have always sacrificed," Anelion concluded, "always given blood. And with this union, we join Boblin and Celia together, their blood one blood, their commitment absolute."

He presented them with the cup of union: Boblin and Celia each pricked a finger, letting three droplets of blood spill into the wine, and drank from the cup. Truth be told, Tim thought it an odd custom, but the elions were an odd people, and he supposed it *did* fit their history, which had seen more than its share of bloodshed in the name of community.

"Thus, you are joined," Anelion said. He bade the two elions turn and face the assembled group, who rose to stand in acknowledgment.

Tim did appreciate the ceremony's brevity. It was in keeping with elion culture. *No time for extended tradition when there are battlements to patrol.*

Just then a dark, oily presence flared at the back of Tim's mind. A window on the left side of the chapel shattered, sending jagged fragments of glass tumbling to the ground. Tim turned, hand going to the hilt of his sword. It was not *his* blade, not the one with the focusing point—that was currently mounted in a cairn in the Kaltu Pass—but it served him well enough. A man came through the window, sending more crystalline splinters to the ground. He wore rags, and lines of dirt streaked his face. He opened his mouth, revealing crooked teeth and flecks of spittle, and though he looked like a man possessed, when Tim reached toward him with the Lifesource he sensed more a presence devoid of sentience than a presence mad.

As Tim stepped toward the intruder, another window erupted, a second man—every bit as feral as the first—crawling through. Even as Tim faced the threat, his subconscious began asking questions. Galdon was a small city, most of it unfinished, its citizens comprising survivors of Zadinn's slave empire and settlers from the south. True, there *were* homeless folk—some former slaves found had themselves adrift, afflicted by a sickness of the mind following years in captivity—but they were few and far between. Where had these seemingly crazed people come from?

Jend Argul, battle instincts sharp as ever, beat Tim to the first attacker, flowing forward and closing the gap toward his opponent. The man growled, a knife appearing from beneath his rags and into his hands, but Jend slipped into a traditional ailar stance to block the blow. Ducking underneath the crazed attacker's guard, Jend delivered an elbow strike to the ribs, dropping him to the ground.

A mere span of heartbeats had passed since the first man's arrival. Two additional windows shattered, and a man and woman appeared, joining the others in a space that was starting to remind Tim of a seedier section of Vonku he had been well advised to avoid as a child. He cleared his mind and sought the Lifesource, even as more intruders arrived, some through the gaping windows, others from behind a door in the upper-right corner of the worship space. One had the distinct misfortune to come through the main entrance, directly into Quentiin Harggra's vicious defense.

Tim hooked around a pew, facing three of the attackers. They could not have been more different, two men and one woman, the first man big and bearded, the second short and scrawny, the woman well beyond her youth. The big man raised his axe, teeth bared in a snarl, and directed a blow toward Tim's skull.

Right hand on his still-sheathed sword, Tim opened his left palm and the Lifesource surged through him. An invisible shield of air knocked his attackers backward. The big man flew the farthest, crashing into the chapel wall, while the woman struck the edge of a broken window and tumbled back outside. The scrawny man slammed against a pew, but this last turned his momentum into a roll, coming back up with sword in hand.

Boblin Kule slid past the pew on one knee, striking his hand against the man's temple. He rose back into a standing position, taking the scrawny man's sword in time to drive the blade through the chest of another attacker who had clambered through the window overhead. All around them pandemonium reigned, the assembly under assault from close to twenty crazed folk wearing rags and bearing crude weaponry. Most of the wedding's guests were well acquainted with combat, and all but a few had weapons upon them.

At the head of the chapel and from behind Father Anelion, a ragged woman rushed forward with dagger in hand. Sensing the danger, the old elion spun, and the dagger which would have landed square in his back instead caught him in the shoulder. Celia came to Anelion's aid, placing herself between the elion and the woman. Tim heard Celia utter a curse, no doubt because her ostentatious wedding gown hindered her movements. Nonetheless, she managed to deliver a palm strike up and into the woman's chin, causing her mouth to slam shut and head to snap back. She dropped to the ground, instantly unconscious, and Celia seized the woman's dagger.

Beside Tim, Boblin spun, blocking a blow from the side as yet another assailant came at him with an axe. Two more, one elion and one dwerion, surged toward Boblin from behind, but Tim raised his hand and knocked them back with the Lifesource. As Boblin dropped his opponent to the ground, he and Tim turned toward the altar, where Celia held her unconscious opponent's dagger in a reverse grip, hilt in hand.

"She's going to—" Boblin broke off as his wife of less than two minutes turned the dagger on her wedding dress. "Yes. She's doing it. She's cutting her dress."

Celia used the blade to create a vertical cut down the center of the fabric and between her legs, effectively dividing the dress in the same manner as a riding skirt, so that she had the mobility of her legs to run and jump.

"Two hundred gold Jovuns," Boblin said faintly, impaling another opponent from the side without shifting his gaze. "Two hundred."

From the front of the chapel, four more people came forward, bearing a motley assortment of weaponry. Tim curled his fingers and a ball of green fire appeared above his right hand. His mentor, Nazgar, had instilled into him the necessity of using nonlethal force as often as possible, but their assailants' numbers were growing. He flicked his wrist and the ball of flame zipped through the air, striking the first attacker in the chest. The man screamed and fell to the ground, flames wreathing his body. Celia, proceeding with further wardrobe adjustments, tore another section of fabric from the bottom of her dress and pressed the wad against the wound on Anelion's shoulder.

"At least she's being resourceful," Tim said.

"I'll be a sun-baked lizard," Boblin said. "Is this what marriage will be like?"

On the far side of the chapel, Quentiin, the Rindar twins, and Jend had their hands full as still more attackers crawled through the window. Ladu's guards held several at bay, while few guests not trained in battle had fled the chapel, not so much from panic as to give those remaining more room to fight. It remained crowded enough that Tim could only use the Lifesource in a contained, targeted manner. He let loose another stream of fire toward a pair that had come through the windows, driving them back outside. He flowed forward, raising his sword and blocking a blow from the flank. Lifesource or not, sometimes there was no substitute for good, ordinary steel.

With Anelion stabilized, Celia leapt away from the altar to join Tim and Boblin in the fight. She whipped her knife through the air with deadly precision and buried it into a burly man's neck in a spray of blood. With a concentrated effort, the friends slowly but steadily turned the wave of opponents back. Tim weaved magic in and out of the combatants, Boblin and Celia worked in tandem to pin opponents between them, Quentiin let fly with an axe obtained from one of his felled enemies, until but one man remained. Upon seeing himself alone, the man turned toward the nearest window, hands scrabbling for purchase in his haste to escape. He managed to get midway through the opening before Tim caught him in a hook of the Lifesource, pulling him back into the room. Tim wrapped the captive in cords of air and held him suspended in the center of the chapel, facing the loosely assembled group.

"Yield," Tim said.

In response, the man spat. Like all of the intruders, a fierce zeal burned in his eyes. This created a stark juxtaposition against the fact that, through the Lifesource Tim felt *nothing* from him.

After a moment, Emperor Ladu waved his guards aside and stepped forward. "It is the highest order of treason to launch an assault on the emperor, so tell us: who sent you?"

The man looked from Tim to Ladu, licking his lips and twisting his mouth. He began to convulse, and at first Tim didn't understand what this meant, but then a laugh bubbled from the captive and Tim realized it was mirth.

"Bloody crazy," Quentiin said in his gravelly voice, "that's what he is."

One crazy man certainly isn't out of the question, Tim thought. *But where did over twenty come from?*

After a span of heartbeats, the man ceased his laughter and settled his gaze on Tim. In another instant, his body locked rigid and he began to speak, but the voice that issued could not have been his, for it was deep, cold, and dark.

"WARRIOR."

Tim froze. He drew upon more of the Lifesource, feeling the power tingle in his veins as he braced for a possible attack. He gestured with his hand toward those in the room, urging them to step further back from the man hanging in the center of the chapel.

"AT LAST, I SEE YOU," the voice continued. *"LONG HAVE I WISHED FOR THIS MOMENT. THE TIME FOR SURROGATES IS PAST."*

"Leave this place," Tim said, placing the tip of his sword at the man's neck.

"I THINK NOT, WARRIOR. I ENCOMPASS YOUR BEGINNING AND YOUR ENDING. FIND ME AT THE END OF YOUR WORLD, AND I SHALL BRING YOUR WORLD'S END WITH ME."

The prisoner's head snapped to one side with a resounding *crack*, his body going slack and dropping onto the flagstones. The temperature in the chapel had dropped noticeably, almost to the extent that Tim could see fog in the air before his breath. *Once, the North was always this cold*, he thought. *A memory of the past, or a harbinger of what's to come?*

"What in Malath was that?" Quentiin asked.

"There's someone else who can use the Lifesource," Tim said. "He's playing games."

But he knew that Uklith, Demon-Lord of Malath, did not play games.

* * *

The elion stood in one of Galdon's alleys in the dark of night. Overhead, the stars spun in the sky, perhaps the only observers to that which transpired far below. The wheels had begun turning, set in motion by the elion's hand. Kule's wedding had served its purpose—to what exact end, the elion did not know, but his job was to obey rather than question. His master would be pleased that the opening moves had been executed, and now, it was time to proceed with the next task.

In Galdon, half-finished streets crisscrossed between buildings in various stages of construction. No doubt these citizens thought they would have many more years to complete that which they had begun, but their time was much shorter than any could have imagined. The Demon-Lord had designs, and they would not wait.

The elion waited until the moon neared its zenith and ventured forth, slipping between Galdon's structures. Ladu and his followers had such grand designs for this world, all of which would be for naught. Whenever he glimpsed the occasional passersby, the elion slipped into the shadows and remained still until they passed from sight. It would not do for him to encounter people here. It would not have presented him any great difficulty—he'd just kill them—but Uklith had specifically commanded the elion keep his presence as secret as possible, and leaving a trail of bodies in his wake would do little to accomplish that purpose.

For the most part, the streets remained silent. And so the elion continued forward, shrouded in darkness, leaving neither sign of his arrival nor trace of his passing. When he disappeared from the city of Galdon, slipping into the shadows of the North, it was as if he never existed in the first place.

2

"I'll give you twenty-five Jovuns," the man said. "Copper, obviously."

Tim sighed. *You can always tell the Southerners from the Northerners. The first group is better at haggling, but the latter is catching on. Some things never change.* "I need to repair three arrowheads."

"And?"

"And that costs me money."

"Doesn't make your venison any more valuable to me, does it?"

Tim landed a backstrap on the counter. "Thirty-five. It's the best cut, too."

The hawker picked up the slab of meat, hefting it to test the weight, narrowing his eyes as he inspected it. Wrinkling his nose, he dropped it back on the table. "The sun's addled your brains. I can maybe give you twenty-eight."

"Thirty-two."

"I've got expenses of my own to cover."

"And I've got other customers." *Okay, that was close to being a lie. There's not that many people in Galdon.*

"Thirty, and my daughter's going without a name-day present."

"Deal." They shook hands, and the hawker pushed a pile of small copper coins across the counter toward Tim. *About that present, though…*

Tim peeled off two of the coppers and slid them back across the table. "For your daughter's name-day."

The hawker hesitated, as if trying to figure out if this was still a part of the barter. Eventually he gave an awkward bob of the head and pocketed the returned coppers. "Come back as it pleases you."

"I'd be glad." Tim turned to depart the market square, but before he'd taken his first step the man called out.

"You're him, aren't you?"

That certainly cemented the man as a southern immigrant. Anyone who

had been here when Pellen laid the foundational stone of Galdon recognized
Tim Matthias on sight. Tim looked back over his shoulder, giving the hawker
a brief smile. "Have a nice day, sir."

Tim left the square, passing through a crowd of elions, dwerions, and humans alike. In its first weeks, Galdon had numbered just shy of a thousand individuals, most of them newly liberated slaves from the Pit, but as time passed
others emerged from hiding throughout the North. While the Fort of Pellen
had been the only true community to remain free, other scattered homesteads
had existed, many to the east, eking out a living as far from Zadinn's eye as
possible. The largest influx of people had been settlers from the South. The
recovering soil of the North was potent and fertile, as if making up for time
lost under Zadinn's sway, and once Tim opened passage through the Barricade,
citizens began coming through. Many settled on the Durin Plains outside the
city, but others found the opportunity for business and enterprise in Galdon.
The first formal census was still under way, but Tim imagined the city of Galdon housed two thousand people, with perhaps half that number scattered on
farmsteads across the Plains. It was a tiny population for a new country, but a
far cry more than the three hundred elions that had once inhabited the Fort
of Pellen.

He stepped to one side of the street, closing his eyes and taking a series of
measured breaths. He reached out with the Lifesource, heightening his senses,
immersing in the bustle of citizenry about him. His early instruction in the
Lifesource had been focused on combat, but in the past year he'd learned that
the Lifesource was more than just a blunt weapon, it was also a means of es-
tablishing a deeper connection with the world about him. He hadn't mastered
all possible skills—healing, for one, still eluded him. The one time he'd tried
to fix a minor cut on himself, he only bled more. He'd made strides in other
areas, though, and when he reached out to the crowds of Galdon, he sensed
something *fresh* about this place, an atmosphere of opportunities and promises,
of hopes and ambitions.

Of course, not everything spoke of optimism and goodwill. *Were it so
easy.* Individuals were complex—they harbored regrets and worries, doubts
and envy, and Tim sensed all of it: tension between family members, disputes
with neighbors, fear of the future, and scars from the past. All of these emotions, both the good and the bad, enveloped Tim Matthias in a myriad blanket,
swirling, fluctuating, changing. Today, he probed deeper than normal. Usually,

he moved like a mayfly upon water, skittering across the surface, experiencing only a small part of what it offered, but now he plunged into the depths with the entirety of his being—

—and there it was: the rot, a cold, dark vein running beneath a world that would otherwise have been idyllic. A scent of decay rose to his nostrils. Tim hadn't sensed any of this before a few days ago, but he also hadn't been looking. Only after Boblin Kule's wedding had Tim reached out in such a manner, attempting to see if something was awry in this new kingdom. Even if he had discovered the rot prior to the attack, he might have dismissed it as a lingering effect of Zadinn's dark touch, which had blighted all the lands and from which vast portions of the North still recovered.

He didn't know what it meant, and for now, he simply checked it to see if had grown any more, or become less, than that which he'd sensed on the previous day. So far, it seemed to hold. He didn't like that it existed, but it also hadn't worsened. *So, we'll see.* He had some ideas on what it meant, but he needed time to think upon them. Tim opened his eyes, relinquishing the power. The Lifesource left him in a rush, leaving him feeling winded and a dizzy. As the noise and commotion of Galdon returned to normality around him, his other tangible senses came back to the forefront, and he found himself standing in front of Pellen Yuzhar's tomb. A rectangular slab of white marble lay beneath a leafy canopy, set in a semicircular nook beside the palace's front steps. Visible to those approaching the palace, yet far enough apart from it, the memorial served as a peaceful resting place for the Fort's leader.

A pile of roses lay before the tomb, ranging from newly fresh on top to dried on the bottom. The elions of the Frontier Patrol took meticulous care in keeping the area around the marble slab clean, but left the flowers alone save to remove the occasional excess.

Boblin Kule stood in the shade of the canopy, hands clasped behind his back. He turned at Tim's approach. "Well?"

"There's something here, but it feels suppressed. It's almost the inverse of how things used to be—the land was dead, but a fragment of life still hovered beneath it. Now, the land is alive, but death lingers beneath."

"Well, I have heard that marriage turns one's world upside down. This might be an example."

"You've been married three days, and now you're an expert?"

"I didn't say I'm an expert. I just said it makes things different."

"You know what else is different?" Tim reached into his satchel and tossed one of his arrowheads to Boblin.

The elion caught it, frowning. "You know how to stop this from happening? Hit the deer next time, not the tree."

"You know I'm capable of setting you on fire with a single gesture, right?"

Boblin tossed the arrowhead back. "Nazgar taught me how to dodge those kinds of attacks. Come on, if it makes you feel better, I'll pay the repair bill."

They went to Vinsor Dalin's shop in a city section west of the palace. The fletcher sat behind the counter, spectacles on the end of his nose, examining the edges of an obsidian arrowhead. Quentiin was there, too, on a stool adjacent to the entrance, mug in one hand. *Swapping old stories from the Legion, no doubt.*

Seeing Tim, Vinsor looked up, a smile creasing his face. "Matthias. What have you discovered in the Erdrar of late?"

"That he shouldn't shoot trees," Boblin said, closing the door.

"It happens to the best of us, I'm afraid." Vinsor reached beneath the counter and produced a spare shaft. He took the arrowhead from Tim and placed it beneath a magnifier. "As for you, Kule, how goes marriage?"

"It's different."

Quentiin snorted so hard that Tim expected to see ale spew from the dwerion's nostrils. "That's all ye can say, laddie? It's *different?*"

"Well, it is. And good morning to you, too. How long will you be with us this time?"

"I'll stay the week, an' then it's back to Raldoon." Quentiin held up a scroll. "Aras has new terms he'd like Ladu to consider."

Tim wasn't sure that Quentiin used honorifics except when addressing either the King of Alcatune or the Emperor of the North directly. The dwerion wasted little time on formalities, not out of disrespect but simply by nature. Quentiin Harrgra called folk by their names, whether a beggar in the streets or emperor of a land.

"What does King Aras propose?" Tim asked.

Quentiin replied with a noncommittal grunt. "Yer guess is as good as mine, laddie. I didn't read it."

"You're fulfilling the role of diplomat between North and South quite admirably, my friend. I always suspected the people crafting the rules didn't understand them, but now I have proof."

"I ain't a diplomat, Matthias, I'm a *liaison*."

"Only because you threatened to gut anyone who called you a diplomat," Boblin pointed out. "At that point, Emperor Jovun had to call you something else, and I hope the king of Alcatune showed similar concern for the well-being of his court."

Quentiin took another long swallow. "They're reasonable men, unlike either o' you, eh?"

Reasonable or not, Aras and Ladu were leaders of separate nations and therefore harbored a degree of caution—*distrust* would be too strong a word, but close—toward each other. Neither allies nor rivals, each man represented the interests of his own country. Farmers leaving Alcatune meant less in crops for Aras's kingdom, and farmers remaining in Alcatune meant less hands to till the North for Ladu. The parchment Quentiin carried no doubt addressed some limitations on the rate of emigration from Alcatune to the North, the details of which would only be of minimal interest to the friends in Vinsor's shop. Because of situations like this, Tim did not envy Ladu his position, nor did he regret having turned down the crown of the North when it was offered to him.

"I can't speak for the state of affairs between my king and Ladu," Vinsor said, setting Tim's arrowhead down, "but *this* cannot be salvaged. I can, however, offer a replacement."

"Your best pick. Boblin's paying." As the elion rolled his eyes, pushing several coins across the counter, Tim turned to Quentiin. "To the palace?"

"Aye, Aras's proposal ain't goin' to deliver itself."

Side by side, Tim, Boblin, and Quentiin proceeded toward Galdon's center. The morning crowds had grown in size, and the companions navigated around shoppers, merchants selling wares, inns serving refreshments, and the odd pair of Frontier Patrol elions walking the streets. They passed Pellen's tomb once more, following a cobblestone path to the front of Ladu's palace, though *palace* was a strong term at the moment. Several partially completed turrets rose from different locations, and many of the upper levels were only half-finished. Men and women worked upon a scaffolding at the construct's northernmost face, lowering stone slabs into place. By the next spring, this place would be well on its way to doing justice to the new, free kingdom of the North.

Faldon and Tavin Kule stood guard on either side of the entrance, shielding their eyes against the light of the sun. The elions wore light leather jerkins, swords strapped to their waists. The casual observer might have thought them standing idly, but the more experienced eye noted a slightly tensed posture: outwardly loose, inwardly ready to spring into action at any sign of a threat. As the companions approached the steps, the two elions straightened, backs going rigid as they saluted Boblin. "Commander Kule," they said.

Boblin waved a hand. "Gentlemen."

"So, Commander," Tavin began, "how's marriage?"

"It's different."

Faldon cocked his head. "Interesting choice of words, sir."

"If you want flowery speeches, talk to the emperor."

"Listening to speeches might be better than standing around here all day," Tavin replied.

"It's not *that* bad," Faldon countered. "Remember the southern parapet?"

The three elions shared a look. Boblin had told Tim that the Fort of Pellen's southern parapet had a reputation for being exposed to the wind. Once upon a time, the men of the Frontier Patrol had drawn lots to see who took the duty of manning that portion of the wall, especially during the morning when the winds blew strongest.

"As you were," Boblin said, nodding at his cousins before following Tim and Quentiin up the steps. Just past the doorway, they walked in front of a small niche where Hugo and Ken Rindar sat at a small table, taking their ease tossing dice, no doubt serving on a rotation shift with Faldon and Tavin at the front gates. At the sight of Boblin, the two elions stood and snapped salutes, crisp and identical to those which Faldon and Tavin had delivered.

"Commander," Ken said. "How's—"

Boblin cut him off before he could finish. "It's different."

"Fair enough, sir." Ken sat back down, shaking the cup of dice.

"You should ask them how your wife describes it," Tim said. "She gets here earlier than you, doesn't she?"

"Yes, she makes the recruits do their ailar training early. She says it gets them ready for the day."

"I have to agree, laddie," Quentiin noted. "Mornin' is a time to be up."

"I don't disagree, but I'd rather not spend mine getting kicked in the head by my wife."

Inside the front hall, a tapestry of the elions setting themselves against the malichons on the slopes of the Deathlands hung on one wall. Along the other side of the passage, glass cases of ancient weapons stood at intervals, an arrangement reminiscent of the Floor of History in the Fort of Pellen. Indeed, some of the relics came from the Fort. The Patrol had salvaged what wreckage they could over the summer and brought it to Galdon to adorn the new palace.

Tim, Boblin, and Quentiin zigzagged through several corridors, stopping to acknowledge the occasional guard, until coming to the spacious but modest throne room, where Emperor Ladu sat upon a dais at the center of a circular space. A broad skylight allowed the sun to illuminate most of the room by day, while a chandelier suspended beneath provided lighting after nightfall.

A man and a woman stood on the dais next to Ladu, holding a conversation with him. Tim suppressed a grimace. Endar and Raisha Varuc had come out of hiding in the past year. The brother and sister identified themselves as descendants of a house once allied with the Jovun dynasty, and during the years of Zadinn's reign they had lived with a group of people in caverns far to the east, upon the borders of the ocean. It had been as far from the Death-lands as one could travel, and Tim doubted Zadinn's malichons ever bothered patrolling that far.

Endar and Raisha stepped away from Ladu, halting whatever conversation they had been holding. Tim knew Ladu well enough to see he was grateful for the interruption, evidenced on the emperor's face by a slight relaxation at the corners of his mouth and a slight brightening of his eyes. Ladu tolerated the Varuc siblings—distant relatives to the Jovun family, but only in royalty did one trace lineage that far out—giving them their due because of the allegiance their predecessors had shown Ladu and his father. Ladu was much older than he appeared, having remained in the enchanted block of crystal for two hundred years before Nazgar and Boblin released him.

"Ah," Endar said. "What news have you for us, dwerion?"

"Last I checked, I had a name," Quentiin growled. "*Nobleman.*"

"Gentlemen," Emperor Ladu admonished, raising a hand. In spite of his tone, the look in his eyes suggested he would gladly buy Quentiin a fresh pint of ale every time the dwerion spoke so bluntly to the Varuc siblings.

Endar bowed. "Please accept my apologies, Quentiin Harggra. I meant no offense." Rather than call Endar a liar—Tim suspected the phrase hung on the dwerion's tongue—Quentiin nodded. "None taken, Lord Varuc." He drew a parchment from his knapsack, seal unbroken, and held it toward Ladu. "Here ye are, yer Majesty. Direct from King Aras."

"Thank you, Quentiin." Ladu waved Raisha and Endar to move back. "My lady, my lord, some space." He produced a silver blade, sliced the parchment open, and began to read. He paused upon reaching the end, face expressionless. He appeared to read it a second time, after which he looked up at the group. His gaze was solemn, and his eyes held a touch of hardness. "I cannot allow this."

"What is it, your majesty?" Raisha asked.

Ladu did not respond to her, but instead looked at Quentiin. "I am sorry, my friend. Your king wishes for us to halt all immigration into this country. He makes the case that these people have sworn allegiance to his crown, to his country, and that they cannot take oaths to a foreign land without a formal transference of allegiance."

Tim had little interest in politics, but he understood the fundamentals, and they were simple enough: the issue at heart was that the rapid emigration into the North was causing a depression in Alcatune's economy. Vinsor was a prime example: a retired Legion soldier, who excelled in his profession and had provided an essential service to the kingdom, was now gone and working in the North. *How many Vinsor Dalins have there been over the past year?* Ironically, Tim had been on the brink of serving in Aras's Legion before events changed and he discovered the North. Daniel and Rosalie had held the king in the highest regard; Aras was not an unkind man, and he only wanted what was best for his people. In truth, he probably only needed more time to better assess the impact of emigration upon Alcatune's economy. On the other hand, Ladu's kingdom needed resources—hands to till the land, builders to construct the city, citizens to help govern—and they would struggle mightily without an influx of assistance.

"They ain't my words, they're his." Quentiin paused, then took a breath. "But I stand by my king."

The room grew silent. The words could not have been easy for Quentiin to say. He had been there when Ladu was crowned, had shed blood beside those in this very room, and he was personally responsible for the survival of many of the North's first citizens. His oaths to Aras, however, went back much farther, to the days when he served in quelling the Icor Rebellion. Tim suspected Quentiin might disagree with the content of Aras's proposal, but the dwerion's allegiance to his country, and his duty as liaison to the king, superseded any personal opinions.

"And what right has your king to prevent these people from living where they wish?" Ladu asked.

"None, but he does have a right to protect those he is sworn to lead, an' that's what he's doin', yer Majesty."

"This is preposterous," Endar interrupted. "This land was founded by those who fought for freedom. If others wish to join us, no man should stop them. Our people fought and died for that right."

Quentiin stepped toward the nobleman, a low smolder in his eyes. "You forget who ye're speakin' to, laddie. You'll preach to me about what 'yer' people fought for? I was there in the Pit while you sunned yerself on the beach. What blood did *you* shed in that war?"

Ladu raised his hand yet again, forestalling further comments from either side and turning to Endar. "Choose your words better, Lord Varuc. I myself take offense to the implication that Zadinn Kanas and King Aras are oppressors of the same variety. Regardless, we have a problem. Your king wishes to understand how this migration of his population may have adverse effects on his kingdom. This I understand—and I could agree, perhaps, to a limitation on the number of people who move between our countries, but I cannot allow an absolute cessation of movement. That would only fester ill feelings between both sides."

"So do ye suggest an alternative?" Quentiin asked.

"No. I will not propose what number is best for King Aras and his country. That, I must leave to him. My reply is simple: I will not accept these terms as proposed. Should he wish to ban his subjects from leaving, that is a decree I have no control over, but that will be between King Aras and his people. I will not honor it, and those who come to this land will be welcomed."

"But ye *would* agree to a limit?" Quentiin asked.

"I would entertain a proposal within reason, if King Aras presented one. Until then, I have no more to say on the matter."

Quentiin nodded his head with the slightest air of stiffness. "Of course, yer Majesty."

"Please accept my apologies, friend," Ladu said, voice softer. "I will never forget what you did for our people, and I count you among the few individuals I would wish to have at my back when the odds are against us. But in this matter, I must act as Emperor, not as a comrade. We have, of course, prepared quarters for you in the palace. You are welcome to take your leisure in the city before returning to the South—because, all other matters aside, it is good to see friends again." Allowing himself to smile, he stepped down from the dais and embraced the dwerion. "I must take my leave, but do not hesitate to let me know if you are in need of anything."

"Indeed," Quentiin replied, departing from the throne room, Tim and Boblin beside him.

"Un-karfing believable," the dwerion said after they entered the corridor. "I don't understand monarchs."

"It's Tim's fault," Boblin said.

"Oh?" Tim said.

"You did that thing after we beat Zadinn. You know, the land."

"Ah. The 'nudge.'" In all fairness, Boblin might be onto something. After defeating Zadinn, Tim had delved into the land with the Lifesource. It hadn't been much, but he had *pushed* it on its way toward healing, accelerating a process that might otherwise have taken decades.

"Why do you think the land is so fertile?" Boblin asked. "Now all your farmers want to come here. If you'd just left things alone, nobody else would want to be here. It would be great."

"Great?"

"I don't like crowds."

As they passed a side corridor, Quentiin grumbled. "Well, this is where I leave ye for the time bein'. If I don't have good news to bring back to Aras, at least I'll take the time to enjoy Ladu's accommodations and drink his ale."

After the dwerion left, Boblin and Tim returned to the palace gates. "It's good to see him," Boblin said. "I can only hope our respective leaders take their heads out of the sandhill and start talking. You were wise to avoid that crown, my friend. Hopefully they don't decide to solve this issue with swords and crossbows."

Tim doubted it would come to that, and he didn't think Boblin believed it either. Wars had indeed started over less, but it would take more than this disagreement to set the men of the North against anyone. A debate over agriculture paled in comparison to the tyranny they had lived with for two centuries.

At the guardhouse, Faldon and Tavin had departed from their post, and in their place stood Jend Argul, scanning the horizon. "What's a retired soldier doing here?" Boblin asked. "Technically that means this post is abandoned. The troops will do body-raisers for this."

Jend turned at Boblin's voice and raised a hand in greeting. "Ah, Commander Kule. You'll understand the joys of retirement someday. It's...*different,* as they say."

Boblin arched an eyebrow. "As who says?"

"Just a saying going around the garrison: 'it's different.' We've found it useful for describing a number of scenarios."

Boblin's eyes narrowed. "The number of body-raisers everyone's doing just doubled."

* * *

Taking his leave of Boblin at the Patrol training grounds, Tim left the city on horseback and headed south. As his mount galloped across the Durin Plains, Tim raised his face into the breeze, and above him the sun neared its peak. Ahead of him, the Plains, once bare and stony, had turned into fields of green and brown. In some places, the grass grew waist-high. He rode down a dirt path through the fields, every so often passing a homestead. Some of these places had fields of crops stretching behind them, and others had herds of cattle on acres of gated pasture. Tim waved to people whenever he passed them, still marveling at the signs of life where before there had been nothing but death. Some patches of rocky landscape did remain, but healthy vegetation, pushing up from cracks in the ground, had replaced the cragged, withered scrub-brush. While the landscape of the Plains was mostly flat, when Tim looked toward the horizon he saw the gentle rise and fall of the fields in the distance.

Ahead and to the right—southwest of the path—lay the foothills of the Kaltu Pass. While these jagged stone outcroppings retained their former appearance more closely than other areas of the North, even the Pass had changed at least a little, with the occasional evergreen growing in areas that had received favorable amounts of rain and sun.

At times the wind gusted across his face, but such bursts were no longer the savage gales that had once torn over the landscape. They felt gentler, more natural, and no longer carried the same chill. Directly ahead a line of trees marked the start of the Erdrar Forest, where the once-withered trunks had expanded into leafy boughs, creating a canopy of green. During Zadinn's reign, animal life had been reduced, but now it flourished—deer, rabbits, birds, squirrels, and insects. Tim found this change most fascinating of all, for while he could attribute the reappearance of vegetation to the awakened soil, he could not say the same for the animal life. It had been gone and now was back, and while he didn't understand it, he supposed he didn't *have* to, for it was both right and good.

When he reached the fringe of the forest, he dismounted from his horse. Though Tim was silent, the Erdrar was not; as he made his way across the earthen floor, he heard the wingbeats of birds fluttering from one tree to the next, the pattering of animals in the undergrowth, the scratching of branches from the summer breeze.

His cottage stood not far past the borders of the forest, a small log-and-thatch structure with a single chimney through the roof. In the South, he'd once lived in such a place with Daniel and Rosalie. Much might have changed in the time since the malichon attack on Raldoon, but Tim Matthias's love for the peace and quiet of the wilderness had not.

Tim was one of very few who had settled in the Erdrar. Boblin and Celia lived in Galdon—not that either preferred the city, but they had duties in the Patrol that kept them there. Quentiin, meanwhile, had returned to the South, for Raldoon was the place of his people. Tim, on the other hand, had made his place here. The forest had been good for him in many ways. His last battle with Zadinn had left scars visible and not, internal and external, and this quiet place allowed him an opportunity to heal in peace. And yet, as he ate his meal at the kitchen table, gazing out the window into the forest, he could not help but feel the weight of solitude. When it came down to it, few in the North truly *knew* him. True, there were the elions he had been with on the journey north through the Mountains, but to most of the rest, he knew he remained an enigma—a man to be respected and admired, but always kept at arm's length. For he was the Warrior of Light, the one who had led them out of the darkness into freedom. There were those that loved him for it, but not with the kind of love that existed between Boblin and Celia. Tim had never experienced that kind of closeness with another person, and because of the enigma between himself and the citizens of the North, he feared it was something not easily within his grasp.

Yes, he was the Warrior of Light, but at the end of the day, in his cottage in the Erdrar, he was no more than a man alone.

3

Boblin crouched in the Erdrar Forest, back against an oaktree trunk, a shrub concealing much of his body. The overhead sun shone through the leafy canopy, creating pools of golden light on the ground. In front of Boblin's hiding place, a whitetail buck moved with soft, cautious steps, tail twitching as it approached a ravine. Boblin nocked an arrow to his longbow, controlling his breathing and his motions.

Ears perked, the deer looked about. It began to drink. Its antlers were magnificent, broad and sweeping, six tines to each side of its head. Water gurgled over the rocks in the ravine. Boblin raised the longbow, drawing the string back. The fibers grew taut in his hands, sixty pounds of pressure holding fast, waiting to be set loose upon release of his fingers. He sighted along the arrow, pinpointing a spot just above and behind the deer's front shoulder blade. He held the draw for a count of five, exhaling at the end to settle his aim.

Killing shot all but assured, Boblin relaxed, pointing the tip of the arrow toward the ground, removing shaft from string. He wasn't hunting today, only mapping territory. He had presumed this spot, next to a streambed and heavy with foliage, would be ideal for deer. He felt better that he'd verified his theory. When the supply of venison grew scarce, he could return here at his leisure, short as it might be, when he wasn't conducting drills with the elions in the Frontier Patrol.

The Patrol's function had shifted from the days of Jend Argul and the Fort of Pellen. True, they patrolled Galdon, but other than breaking up the occasional drunken fight, their skills in peacekeeping hadn't exactly been taxed. Instead, they devoted to most of their resources to building the palace and completing the census.

Boblin remained in silence, watching the buck. It perked its head back up, sniffing the air and stamping its hooves. *It senses something's not quite right, but it doesn't know what.* Each time, Boblin thought the deer would eventually fit the pieces together and register his presence, but without fail the buck simply returned its business at the ravine. Eventually it finished drinking, sniffed the air one last time, snorted, and trotted back into the undergrowth. If there was a finer parallel to demonstrate the purpose of the Frontier Patrol, Boblin couldn't think of it. *The deer sensed the wrong in the air, but each time did nothing. Easier for it to think that all was well than to acknowledge the presence of imminent danger. That's why the Patrol must keep the watch, so that we never find ourselves caught unaware.*

He shook himself. *This is hunting, not philosophy.* He rose and stretched, a handful of birds fluttering as he did so, and glanced at the sun. It was nearing noon, which meant it was time to go and meet Tim. He began walking north, moving in the general direction of the Erdrar's border, passing through the undergrowth quickly and lightly, leaving no hint of his presence.

The summer before last, he'd led Tim and the other Southerners—Daniel, Rosalie, and Quentiin—through this very forest, when creatures dark and unseen had prowled through the shadows at night. There was another forest, the Korlan, to the northwest, and it was much worse than the Erdrar. Where the Erdrar's dangers might befall a hapless traveler in the wrong place at the wrong time, the Korlan actively *sought* to ensnare its victims. It had been a thing alive, and even now, the North's citizens stayed away from it. Shreds of evil would linger longer in some places than others, the Korlan chief among them.

At the summit of a small knoll, Boblin shouldered his arrows and squatted on the ground, waiting. It had been upon this very knoll, in fact, that he and Tim's companions spent a night during their journey, eerie sounds rising about them. Therefore, it was with a twist of dry humor that Tim had selected this to be their regular meeting place when scouting the surrounding area.

Boblin heard his friend long before he saw him. The man was getting better at controlling the noise he made, and was probably considered stealthy by human standards, but Tim was no elion. Still, Boblin had hope that he'd learn one day. *He's gone from snapping every fifth twig to every tenth, and it's fair to call that progress.*

Several minutes later, Tim appeared from behind a pair of yew-leaf trees, raising a hand in greeting. "How many deer did you get?"

"One," Boblin replied. "Big buck. I can imagine those backstraps, wrapped in pork and roasted over the fire."

Tim shook his head. "You must be losing your touch. I got *three* deer."

"You're lying."

"The Warrior of Light doesn't lie."

"Then excessive use of the Lifesource has addled your brain and you're seeing triple."

Tim gave a noncommittal shrug, spreading parchment on the ground. He produced a stick of charcoal, making notations on the locations he'd visited, and handed the charcoal to Boblin to do the same. They'd been at this for the last month, mapping the Erdrar one day at a time, Boblin splitting his time between the Erdrar and the Patrol, Tim splitting his time between the Erdrar and whatever served as training in the Lifesource for an Advocate. Boblin supposed the man juggled fireballs, proclaimed it a successful expansion of his esteemed abilities, and then took an afternoon nap. It's what Boblin would have done if *he* was an Advocate.

Tim stuffed the newly marked parchment back into his knapsack. "Come on."

The two companions set off down the hill, traveling in silence. When they reached the northern quadrant of the woods, however, Boblin paused. Something felt off. He couldn't pinpoint anything other than a gut sensation, but he'd learned long ago to trust such things. He held a hand up, and Tim halted behind him.

"Do you—"

"Yes," Tim said. "I feel it."

The forest was quieter than usual, for one—no rustling of the surrounding brush, no birdsong, and there was a strange scent in the air. They moved forward more slowly.

Boblin saw a dark patch on a leaf before him. He plucked it from the branch and handed it to Tim. "Blood."

Several more splotches formed a trail leading forward, each fuller and thicker than the last, until he came to a large stain at the base of a tree. Blood in the woods wasn't unusual—animals got their fair share of scrapes in the underbrush, not to mention predators making a kill—but not this much. Boblin examined the dried pool, running a hand across its surface to test for freshness.

"What do you think?" Tim asked.

"Not a squirrel."

Tim placed his hand on the trunk and closed his eyes. Boblin knew how to recognize when the man was seeking the Lifesource, so he sat back and let Tim concentrate. Eventually Tim stood back up. "Fox," he said.

"You can really tell that?"

Tim nodded. "The Lifesource connects all living things."

"I'm going to have to start calling you Nazgar."

"Except Nazgar never pulled your leg. I have no idea what it is, Boblin. It could have been anything."

Boblin stood as well. "I'll be a sun-baked lizard. Here, there's a trail."

Just beyond the tree, a trampled swath of bushes indicated the wounded creature had stumbled into the undergrowth. The friends pushed through the forest, noting increasingly larger and darker patches of blood as they did so. Soon enough, Boblin noted a rank smell and grimaced. "Keep your meal down, mate."

They came upon the doe's body in a patch of brambles, tufts of white hair poking from her underbelly, a marked contrast to the darker brown fur on the rest of her body. She lay with legs splayed, neck outstretched, and eyes glassed over. A cluster of flies dashed to and fro over her corpse and over the puddle of dried blood on the leaves.

Boblin approached the deer and looked down. This was by no means a predator kill. Wolves and other predators ate nearly all the remains, leaving barely a sign that a corpse had even existed in the first place. Here, except for the hole in her chest, the doe's body was almost completely intact, with only a few entrails leading from the cavity. Boblin peered into the wound, holding his breath so as to not smell any more than necessary. He thought of the buck from earlier in the afternoon, and wondered if this doe had sensed anything untoward before her demise. After a minute, he stepped back a few paces and allowed himself to breathe the relatively cleaner air.

"Her heart's gone," Boblin said. "Something reached inside her and tore it out." *Certainly not normal woodland activity.*

"That makes no sense," Tim said, looking at the deer, then back at Boblin. "Crazed folk at your wedding, dark currents in the Lifesource, bodies in the forest…getting married sure does make things different doesn't it?"

Boblin glanced at the heartless corpse. "Yes, mate, it does."

* * *

"Mela and I been here six months," the man said to Celia. "We had a home-stead in western Alcatune, and we grew a proper radish crop when the season turned right. But things weren't the same these past years. Folk crowding in, land getting scarce, people in town getting sod-angry at each other—"

"The mayor's wife found herself with another man's baby," Mela said, and the tone in her voice left no doubt as to what she thought about *that*.

"Anyway, we decided it was time for something different."

"You're farmers, but you settled in the city?" The question came out before Celia could stop herself. *This isn't an investigation. You're just here to tally the numbers and leave it at that.*

"Galdon ain't a city. Our village had more people than all of Galdon. Be-sides, I'd had enough of tilling fields. We thought we'd try our hands at a bakery, eh? Always someone in need of fresh bread in the morning."

"I have no disagreement with that." Celia made a notation on a piece of paper. "So, it's just the two of you?"

"Aye, me'n Mela. Our eldest serves in the Legion, and the younger manages an arbiter's accounts in Vonku. We'd like to show them this place someday. I think there's opportunity here for them, if they want it."

Your king might have something to say about that, from what I've heard. Still, not my concern. "I wish you the best of luck. Thank you for your time."

Celia's Patrol recruit, Hanqar, opened the door for her, giving the couple a polite smile before he and Celia turned to leave. Once outside, she handed Hanqar the parchment. "And that is how you conduct a census. You've got the next house."

Hanqar replied with a wry smile. "Yes, ma'am."

She had to admit, Hanqar's duties as a new member of the Frontier Patrol were a far cry from what hers had been. Shortly after her sixteenth birthday, she'd been in the hills of the Kaltu Pass guarding against malichons. Hanqar, on the other hand, was helping conduct an onerous tally of every person in the city. *Different times indeed—but better to be a soldier in a time of peace than a refugee in a time of war.* Besides, it was important and necessary work, and the Patrol had the hands to make the task light. They numbered three hundred soldiers—and the fact that the Patrol alone was the size of the former Fort continued to amaze her.

Leaving Hanqar to his task, Celia returned to the palace garrison. In the training yard she passed lines of recruits holding practice weaponry. Hugo and

Ken Rindar stood before one group, Faldon and Tavin Kule in front of another, ensuring that each and every last one would be trained to perfection against the Frontier Patrol's standards.

The first recruit Celia ever trained had been Ana Teldin, an elion with the best of potential. Ana had died on the quest to find the Army of Kah'lash, killed by the sarchons in the darkness of Malath's Teeth. Were she still alive, Ana would no doubt be here training recruits as well, passing on the guidance Celia had given her, just as Celia had taught others what she had learned from Jend Argul and the Rindar brothers.

Nearby, two elions grappled on the ground, practicing the basics of ailar, the art of hand-to-hand combat that had been intrinsic to the Frontier Patrol since the days of its inception. Commander Jend had held numerous times that, even if deprived of all other weapons, an elion would still possess hands and feet with which to fight. In fact, ailar was Celia's favorite form of combat; Boblin preferred the sword, but to Celia there was nothing like the subtle art involved in understanding the balance of her body and the way in which she could use it as an extension of her mind to defend herself.

When Celia reached the far side of the grounds, Hugo and Ken fell in alongside her. Both elions' skin bore the sheen of sweat, and Ken had a slight bruise on his jaw. She suppressed a smile; a recruit must have gotten in a good hit. *Or, it happened by accident.* One of the best-hidden secrets of any trainee was that sometimes he or she succeeded only by a complete and utter mistake that turned lucky. The trick, she had found, was to turn such lucky mistakes into actual techniques.

She stepped inside the interior garrison and sat at a long table, Hugo and Ken taking the opposite side. "How goes it today?"

Ken spoke first. "They'd do against malichons in a pinch. But…"

"It's not quite the same for them. We see it in their eyes." Hugo finished.

Celia nodded. She'd seen it as well, *felt* it. These new soldiers lacked the sense of urgency Celia and her companions had felt underneath Zadinn's oppression. They did not fight with the absolute commitment those of the Fort had shown, and while Celia didn't like it, she also didn't know what they could do about it. As she and Boblin had discussed, when an elion knew his or her freedom or livelihood was at stake, it changed the way they approached things—then, they trained to fight with every last fiber of their being, because they knew they risked losing everything otherwise. The new recruits were good, no doubt about that, but they didn't have the same pressure to perform, and while Celia would never trade this newfound freedom, she had dwelt too long in the shadow to feel comfortable growing lax.

"Maybe we could send them to Malath's Teeth to train with the sarchons," Ken said. "*That* is a fine idea."

"Speaking of Malath," Hugo asked, "what of the attack at your wedding? That was dark magic, without a doubt. Have you learned anything?"

"Not yet," Celia said. Tim had publicly implied that the prisoner's message meant there was someone else who could use the Lifesource—perhaps a Dark Advocate—but in private, he'd told Boblin and Celia this was unlikely. It would have been impossible for another Advocate to remain in secret during Zadinn's reign, and in the eighteen months since Zadinn's downfall, it was also unlikely a new one had risen to power so quickly. Furthermore, the man had very clearly been possessed, a mere Advocate could not do that. It had to be Uklith, of that Tim said he was certain.

The histories in the Fort provided little information on Agrazab, the City of Darkness where Zadinn learned his craft from the Demon-Lord. They'd had only had a few texts from Galdon's original libraries, and of them, a single manuscript mentioned Agrazab, stating that over a thousand years ago the Demon-Lord of Malath entered the mortal world and manifested himself in human form there. This dark city supposedly lay to the west, beyond a vast desert. Uklith could not leave Agrazab, bound there by a spell using magic from the ancient tongue of Homdee. Celia wondered if other people lived in the City. Had Uklith exerted his influence on a new Advocate, possessed him, and sent him east?

"I don't like it," Ken said. "It stinks of foul things afoot, and I've had enough of those to last a lifetime."

"Agreed," Celia replied. "I don't like it, either."

The bell sounded the hour, and the three elions returned to the yard to work with the recruits. As Celia stepped into the ring, assuming an ailar stance with the trainee in front of her, she raised her eyes to look at the sun.

For a moment, a cloud passed over it, leaving the courtyard in shadow. Celia felt a sudden chill, one she knew had nothing to do with the shade. The darkness buckled around her, causing her vision to shimmer. She blinked, flexing her fingers before her, trying to bring the world back into clarity. Next, she felt a tug from the south and looked over her shoulder. The *pull* had not come from the courtyard, or even from within Galdon. Then the cloud passed, gone as quickly as it had arrived, and she found herself standing before the recruit once more.

"Is everything all right, ma'am?" the elion asked.

As far as Celia could tell, the recruit had neither noticed the cloud nor felt any untoward sensation. "Yes, my apologies. Proceed."

It hadn't been her imagination. Celia knew herself well enough to acknowledge that much. It had been very real, and besides, this was the North. If the last two years had taught her anything, it was that nothing should be taken for granted here.

* * *

Tim followed Boblin through the woods, pursuing the bloody trail left by the deer's passing. As he'd done in Galdon, he reached out with the Lifesource, immersing himself in the surrounding world, seeking any sign to indicate the natural order was out of balance. He felt the loam of the earth below him, breathed in the scent of leafy vegetation around him, and heard the whisper of wind. Beneath it all, though, a rot lingered, subtle but apparent, a trail of evil running parallel to the path of blood on the ground. They moved through the brittle, thin trunks of an aspward swale, where twigs blocked their way and brambles tore their clothes, before arriving at a small clearing. Here, the sensation was stronger than before, no longer hovering below the surface, but instead present and palpable. After a glance and a moment of unspoken agreement, he and Boblin traded places, Tim taking the lead. They crested a hill and saw a small cottage before them. Even from here, they could see broken windows and a front door askew. A dark sensation radiated from the place.

Boblin drew his sword. "Of course, an abandoned house in a formerly haunted forest. I should have known."

They approached with caution. Tim suspected that the evil he sensed was no more than residue, that no active threat remained in the house, but whatever *had* been here had left behind a strong footprint indeed. After stepping into the dim interior, they stopped and allowed their eyes to adjust. They observed signs of struggle everywhere—broken furniture in the corner, shattered dishes on the counters, and splinters of wood littering the floorboards. More spots of blood, some large and some small, all dry, covered the walls, floor, and ceiling.

They passed from the living area and into an adjoining bedroom, where the mattresses had been torn apart and a bookshelf lay upon the ground. Scattered volumes and torn pages spoke of someone searching for a specific object or text, but without success. The next room held little more than a washbasin and a shattered mirror. Several panels were missing from the wall, leaving behind gaping holes and tufts of dried mossgreen for insulation between outer and inner frames. Boblin poked his hand into one of the empty sockets. "What do you suppose they were looking for?"

Tim just shook his head in the negative. He'd noticed something when he left the living area, and, just to confirm his observation, re-entered and exited it once more. "Whatever I'm feeling, it's strongest in the main room. We need to look closer."

The cottage's sparse, minimalist nature did not make for a long search, and on their second circuit they didn't notice anything they hadn't seen the first time. Eventually, Tim stood in the center of the living area, while Boblin examined the edges.

"Okay," Boblin said after a period of silence. "Step to the right."

After Tim obliged, Boblin flipped back the lip of the rug upon which Tim had been standing. This revealed a trapdoor set into the floor, with a single iron ring in its middle. "Well, then," Tim said, and pulled it open. A dark shaft led underground, rungs of an iron ladder marking the way.

Boblin gestured toward the hole. "When I was a young elion in the Patrol, I'd have leapt at such an opportunity to prove my bravery, but today I say Warriors first, my friend."

Tim snapped his fingers and a globe of green light leapt into existence above his head, providing illumination. He descended the ladder, grasping its rungs one at time, each well-worn and free of dust, indicating the cottage's owner had used this cellar quite frequently. Musty air wafted up. As Tim continued down, the sensation of evil grew stronger than ever, indicating that the cellar had recently been used for something more malevolent than preserving jams.

When he reached the ground, Tim saw the body immediately. Its throat had been torn out, and the now-familiar sight of dried blood covered the earth beneath it. Tim touched the corpse's arm, but while the Lifesource had many uses, it did not make one omniscient, and this time it didn't tell Tim any more than he already knew: that this man was dead, and only recently so. Tim's nose could have told him as much—though the stench of death was not as strong as it might have been, given that the cellar's cool, dry air had at least slowed the inevitable decaying process.

Behind him, Boblin reached the bottom of the ladder, taking in the entire scene from the body on the ground to the shelves lining the walls. "Do you know him?"

"Tarvil. A settler from the South."

"Did he ever give any sign that he enjoyed practicing dark magic on weekends?"

"I doubt Tarvil ever practiced dark magic. I think he was just in the way of somebody who wanted something very badly." Tim stood to examine the tiny cellar. After looking more closely at one of the shelves, he pointed at the ground. "See: there."

A soft depression in the earth indicated the shelf had been moved several inches to the left, then perhaps back again, but not to the same spot. Tim and Boblin seized either side of the shelf and dragged it away, revealing a hole in the earthen wall behind it, two feet in diameter, within which a small, leather-bound book rested. Tim reached into the hole.

Boblin touched his arm. "Wait. What if it's a trap?"

"It probably is," Tim replied and picked up the book.

Above them, the daylight filtering through the cellar door dimmed as a cloud passed over the sun. A chill rose, and the world seemed to waver before Tim's eyes. The manuscript had no markings upon the cover, and yet the evil Tim sensed through the Lifesource had grown strong. When he opened the cover, it came as no surprise that the words on the first page had been penned in blood.

It is here in the City of Darkness that I, Zadinn Kanas, set pen to paper and transcribe the words of my Master.

Tim had no time to wonder how and why a text from Zadinn Kanas came to be in the cellar of a woodsman's cottage within the Erdrar Forest. As soon as he read the first sentence, the dimming world whirled. He recognized a powerful spell and attempted to back away, but the vortex caught him, pulling him forward, locking his eyes onto the page. A roaring rush of air filled his ears.

"Tim?" Boblin asked, Tim could not respond, for he felt himself falling forward, the cellar filling with absolute darkness. He lost all sensation—he could not hear, see, or feel, and was dimly aware, as if an observer outside his body, of falling to the floor of the cellar with book in hands. Boblin reached down, as if to knock the book away. Tim tried to warn Boblin off, to tell him that the darkness was too strong, but he could not speak.

And then—

4

Tim hung over a city nearing nightfall, an invisible observer without form, yet able to sense the glare of the setting sun and feel the heat of the fading day. Below him, two men stood on a parapet, facing east over an expanse of sand and dunes. Dry air, hot and still, hung over all.

The guards remained silent, backs to the setting sun as the shadows lengthened. Tim shifted his focus to the city behind the battlements, seeing buildings of clay and streets of dust. The citizens went about their tasks with inherent slowness, a tendency borne of living in the desert's merciless heat. As darkness descended, the people's movements grew both more subdued and more hurried. They kept their gazes to the streets, hoods over heads, those already inside closing curtains and barring doors, those outside hastening to do the same.

"Times have changed." Tim looked back at the guards on the battlements, one of whom had just spoken. "No word comes from the east. Nights grow longer, and days grow shorter. Small disputes become fights, we spill blood over minor transgressions, we lie more than we are honest, and each day it grows worse."

The second guard nodded. "It's as if there's a restless undercurrent in the streets, a low simmer on the cusp of boiling over. More and more, we fear the dark—and why?"

The first guard looked to the sky. "I think we all know why, but none are willing to say so aloud, for to speak it would be to acknowledge that which we know to be true. He is coming."

"Will it happen again tonight?"

"Of course it will. It's happened every month on the full moon, for the last six, and tonight will be no different."

Tim followed the men's gaze, looking up to where the stars had begun poking gentle, white holes in the sky's velvet blanket. He could see that the moon was round and full, and he felt a chill steal into the air. Next, he heard laughter, and the guards turned toward a third man upon the battlements, who approached them with one hand on the hilt of a sword. A manic light showed in the newcomers' eyes, the self-same gleam Tim had seen from those attacking Boblin's wedding.

"Mardrin," the first guard said, "you should not be here. You have been removed from the guard."

"Ah, but what will that matter by this time tomorrow?" Mardrin asked, looking from one man to the next. The grin on his face bore no sign of any actual humor. "Do you feel it coming, Keldor? Do you deny it, Remiel? I think not."

The guards remained quiet, until Remiel—the one on the left, Tim supposed—stepped forward, leveling his spear. "You must leave the battlements, Mardrin. Only members of Agrazab's guard are allowed up here after dusk."

Agrazab. Tim was not surprised; he'd suspected as much since the vision began.

"He will break all of you," Mardrin said. "That which you guard against cannot be stopped. My friends, you can either resist inevitability and suffer, or embrace it and rejoice."

Keldor joined Remiel, facing Mardrin square on. "Leave. We shall deal with this upon the morrow."

The light in Mardrin's eyes grew fiercer. "By then, it will be too late, I'm afraid. He comes tonight."

After Mardrin left, Remiel spat. "He's gone mad."

In response, Keldor shook his head. "I fear the whole world is going mad."

The moon rose into the sky, filling the landscape with its ghostly hue. Mardrin and Remiel returned to their watch, holding themselves with more than a slight presence of unease, gripping spears with knuckles that had grown a shade too white. A wind gusted across the nearest line of dunes, raising a swirl of sand into the air. The last ray of sunshine disappeared, and night reigned supreme. At the interior base of the battlements, Mardrin slumped to the ground, back against the wall, looking at the sky with a face of devoted expectance.

Movement caught the corner of Tim's eye, and he looked toward the moon in time to see a black sliver appear at its edge. Hardly noticeable at first, the shadow moved forward with increasing pace, creating a steady eclipse of the underlying orb. A cold cackle came from Mardrin's throat, and his voice shattered the stillness. "It begins!"

From the guards' reactions, the eclipse was no surprise. They had expected it, this monthly phenomenon that had occurred for the past six. In the city below, the few inhabitants who remained outside fled behind closed doors, slamming them shut with desperate urgency.

When the moon had all but disappeared, a series of strange, multihued lights streaked across the sky and a prism of colors unfolded, shades of red and yellow, green and purple, orange and blue clashing. Those in the city wailed in fear, for the sight was strange, majestic, and terrifying. In the desert the wind picked up, whipping the dunes into a frenzy, sending cyclones of dust toward the battlements.

At this, Keldor and Remiel exchanged looks of surprise and stepped back. Tim suspected this part, at least, was new to them. He heard a rushing sound, and the colors in the sky grew more frantic as the entire world tilted. Tim heard an awful, gigantic, tearing sound as the sky split down the middle, and from the recesses of this crevice in the heavens an inky cloud billowed forth, reaching forward with tendrils to consume the world in a darkness more absolute than Tim had ever experienced. The citizens of Agrazab shrieked in despair, all save for one voice that cut above all others.

"He comes! He comes!" Mardrin shouted, a mix of pain and ecstasy infusing his voice.

Everything around Tim grew so cold, he half-expected to see ice crystals forming on the air, except that he could see nothing at all through the encroaching blackness. Though he still had no form, he nonetheless had the sensation of his breath rushing from him, as if he were suffocating.

Moments later, the world righted, and the heat of the desert came back in a rush. Air flowed into Tim's nonexistent lungs, while below him Keldor and Remiel straightened from where they'd been writhing against the battlements, hands clutching their throats. In the sky, the cloud of darkness retreated to form a singular ball of shadow, hovering over Agrazab's center. It stopped over the roof of the tallest building, spinning in place as the returning light of the moon shone upon it. The cloud elongated vertically, and the wisps of smoke coalesced into the shape of a young man, tall and pale-skinned, with dark hair and even darker eyes. Tim could see the stranger's features with clarity, even from a hundred paces away. The man had a familial resemblance to Zadinn Kanas, as if he might be an uncle or cousin to the dark sorcerer, and Tim knew without a doubt that he had just witnessed the arrival of Uklith, Demon-Lord of Malath, in Agrazab.

"Greetings," the man said. His clear, cold voice carried across the city. "My name is Uklith. I am one." He raised his hands. "I am many." He flicked his wrist, and a hundred Ukliths appeared in locations all over the city, in the streets, on rooftops, in houses, along the walls. "I am young." Another flick, and the many Ukliths transformed into young boys of the same appearance, perhaps eight or nine years in age. "I am old." Another flick, and the boys became old men, supporting themselves on canes, with drooping hair and leathery skin. One last flick and the old men disappeared, replaced by varying monsters of all shapes and sizes, full of fang, claw, and drool. "I am your worst nightmares, and I am eternal."

The citizens of Agrazab moaned, even as the monsters disappeared and only a single Uklith remained, the same man as he had first appeared, standing atop the tallest point of the city. Tim caught movement on the far battlements, where a guard from another wall threw himself from the parapet. Tim's invisible stomach twisted in revulsion as he heard weeping and screaming. In the streets, another man drew a knife and cut the throats of his family before turning his blade upon himself. On the battlements, Keldor fell to his knees, clawing his eyes out, leaving bloody sockets behind. Remiel slumped to the ground, covering his ears, shaking his head.

"Master! Master!" Mardrin screamed in the streets, prostrating himself.

Uklith raised his hands once more, face filled with ecstasy, and a leaden weight pressed down on Tim. The entire city fell silent, every single inhabitant growing still. "Worship me," Uklith said. The citizens of Agrazab, men and women, young and old, all turned toward him and bowed.

* * *

Images flashed before Tim, years passing in the space of heartbeats. He watched the city of Agrazab grow darker and more macabre: men murdered women in their homes, children stabbed one another over scraps of food, and blood ran in the streets. All the while, Uklith's presence hovered over the city, driving the folk to every form of depravity imaginable. On occasion, travelers happened upon Agrazab, where they, too, fell under Uklith's sway—no matter how noble or kind they were upon arriving, Uklith corrupted.

Tim rose above Agrazab, vision traveling to the east, where he saw a man in dark robes crossing the desert. Tim had encountered this man but once before, and yet Zadinn Kanas's face would be forever etched upon his memory. The would-be Dark Lord did not look a day younger than when Tim had faced him, for he had found a means of preserving his youth in the dark, unnatural magic he practiced. While studying as an Advocate at the Academy of Naxish, Zadinn had learned of the City of Darkness from ancient texts that chronicled the very same history Tim had just witnessed. Those words had intrigued Zadinn, promising him a power far beyond that granted to other users of the Lifesource, and thus he sought the City and Uklith.

Tim floated beside Zadinn as the young man's journey continued across crags and gullies, peaks and ravines, sand and stone. The desert might have killed an ordinary human, but Zadinn channeled the Lifesource without restraint, using it to protect himself from the unforgiving elements. This excessive use of power caused his skin to turn pale and his veins dark, and still he walked on. When vultures landed near him, thinking they had a potential victim in their midst, Zadinn snapped his fingers, and they collapsed into throes of death.

Eventually, Zadinn came within sight of Agrazab's squat, rectangular walls. The heat of the day shimmered about him. When he arrived at the entrance, where a pair of gates barred against the outside world, two guards stepped forward with spears at the ready.

"Abase yourself, commoner," the guard said. "You have entered Uklith's realm, and you must subject yourself to his wishes."

"His wishes, certainly," Zadinn said, the familiar sound of his cold voice raising unpleasant memories for Tim. "But never yours."

Zadinn waved his hand, and the guard's head spun to the side with an audible crack. The second guard hastened back, spear-hand trembling, looking from Zadinn to the gates behind himself.

"You're asking yourself if you fear me more than you fear him," Zadinn said. "You ask, is it better to avoid certain death now at the risk of punishment later? It need not be so, for your master and I share a singular purpose. To obey me is to obey him, of this I assure you. Still, I will make the decision easy for you."

He waved his hand again, and the second guard collapsed, dead before he struck the ground.

Zadinn continued beneath the archway and into the City of Darkness, where overturned carts, refuse, spoiled food, and human waste littered the streets. Flies buzzed over corpses, treating themselves to a feast of human flesh. As Tim's gaze followed Zadinn's passing, he glimpsed people in the shadows of side alleys. Occasionally one of the people would venture into the open, just long enough to seize a trinket or scrap of food before retreating. They wore little more than rags, and many were missing limbs or covered in sores. Even the healthiest appeared emaciated and worn. The lucky ones—if they could be called that—lived in squat buildings with curtains drawn shut, while the less fortunate lay moaning in streets and alleys, on the cusp of death.

In his disembodied state, floating alongside Zadinn, Tim continued to feel the heat of the day. Zadinn peered into the shadows of the alleys he passed, and at one point laughed when he saw two men clawing each other over a husk of bone. When Tim had lived in Vonku, if even a pair of dogs had fought over a scrap such as that, the Royal Legion would have put them down in an act of mercy. These poor, tortured people lived a cursed half-life, sustained only by the Demon-Lord's power, serving no purpose other than to fulfill Uklith's entertainment.

As Zadinn neared the city's center, the signs of outright depravity lessened, and while Agrazab remained far from civilized, here the citizens showed at least some degree of nourishment. They still watched each other with narrowed eyes and obvious distrust, but their clothes were whole and their homes intact. Several wore the same breastplates as the guards at the outer edge of the city. When an urchin from outside dared to venture forward, the guards warned him or her back with spears.

Zadinn entered the city's inner ring without challenge. He'd been stopped as a newcomer at the outer gates, but the guards farther in didn't appear to have a reason to halt him. They eyed him with as much distrust as they eyed anyone else, but otherwise let him be, and Zadinn gave them even less notice than they gave him. He approached a building with a fortified gate, and though its walls did not have the ornamentation one might normally expect of a palace, Tim knew this had to be Uklith's seat of power in Agrazab. He recognized the guard: Keldor, standing upright, breathing, with only empty sockets where his eyes had been. As Tim's incorporeal body drew closer, he saw Keldor stood almost *too* stiffly, as if invisible strings held him upright, and he realized that the man was not breathing at all, but was merely a reanimated corpse, deceased but kept upright by Uklith's dark magic.

Keldor turned to Zadinn as he approached, a hissing sound in his throat. Zadinn watched with idle curiosity until Keldor eventually stepped away from the door in a clear invitation to enter.

Zadinn pushed the door open. Once inside, Tim found himself with Zadinn in a long hallway filled with silks on the walls, lavish rugs on the floor, and ornate vases on pedestals. Wealth might not have any real value to Uklith, bit he hoarded it anyway, keeping it from the people and reducing them to fighting over bones in the alleys.

"Welcome."

The air in the hallway flickered, and Uklith stood before Zadinn. The former Advocate stood still and met the Demon-Lord's gaze, his eyes betraying no expression.

"Well," Uklith said. "This is unexpected."

When Zadinn did not reply, Uklith raised a hand. Zadinn dropped, crying out and writhing. Uklith let it last for an entire minute before lowering his hand. Zadinn's screams stopped, but he lay on the ground panting for a handful of heartbeats before regaining the strength to stand back up. He faced Uklith once more, this time breathing slightly heavier.

"I am the master," Uklith said. "Do you understand?"

"Yes," Zadinn said. "Master."

Uklith grinned. "Then let us begin."

* * *

After yet another flicker, Tim found himself in the same hallway, this time with two new men and one woman. He suspected some time had passed, for the tapestries on the walls had faded and the ornaments had lost their luster. The trio wore the same ragged clothing as Agrazab's citizenry, but their straight-backed postures spoke of confidence rather than desperation, and a keen light of determination shone in their eyes. One man was tall and bearded, with broad shoulders, while the other two people were short and lean.

"Zadinn left today," the woman said, "traveling east."

The bearded man had a grave demeanor about him. He reminded Tim of Jend Argul, muscles tensed to spring into combat, eyes prepared to spot the nearest threat. "They've succeeded in their plan. They've torn the veil to Malath and summoned its demons."

"Aye, the malichons. Those creatures are evil incarnate, filled with lust for blood."

Tim knew who the three must be. Nazgar had told him of these people, just as he'd told him about Zadinn's journey to Agrazab. The big man's name was Gardellin, the other man was Amalar, and the woman was Shelendel. They were legends among the Advocates of old, not only because of what they had achieved, but also what they'd sacrificed.

"We must depart," Amalar said. "We have to prevent Zadinn's invasion."

Shelendel shook her head. "The empire must wait. Uklith and Zadinn did great damage to the barrier to the underworld when they released the malichons. Before, Uklith's strength was tethered to remaining in Agrazab, because he had to stay near the portal where he first entered our world. With the veil torn, he may be able to draw on his power from Malath untapped."

"We cannot leave Uklith unchecked," Gardellin agreed. "If we combine our powers, we have a chance of success before he grows stronger."

Amalar nodded. "Let us prepare ourselves."

The three Advocates turned to face the long hallway. The flickering torches cast shadows upon the walls. They walked side by side, marching as one toward an oaken door at the corridor's far end.

"Strike without hesitation," Gardellin said, and the other two nodded. He placed his palm in front of the oaken door and it slammed open. They entered a large, domed room with a dais and chair at its center. A quartet of black-armored guards stood in front of the dais, spears raised. Uklith sat in the chair, eyes closed, fingers gripping the armrests. The air about him shimmered, and his slow, steady breaths spoke of concentration.

He's drawing on the portal, Tim thought.

The guards rushed toward the three Advocates. Gardellin gestured, a thunderclap sounded, and the first guard dropped dead. The remaining guards went flying, slamming against the nearest wall.

Amalar and Shelendel raised their hands simultaneously. Uklith's throne blew apart, disintegrating into fragments of shrapnel. Meanwhile, the three guards were picking themselves back up, preparing to resume their attack. Gardellin opened his palms, hands splayed to either side of his midsection, and bars of blue fire shot from his fingers. Each found a target, and the guards landed on their backs once more, this time with smoking holes in their chests.

In the resulting silence, Gardellin, Amalar, and Shelendel faced the mound of jagged, broken stones that had once been Uklith's throne. A pair of heartbeats passed, and a slow, cold laugh pierced the air.

"Kill," a voice said.

The Advocates spun toward one another, streaks of multicolored magic lancing between them. Gardellin dodged and rolled, an explosion sounding above his head. Shelendel grabbed a spear from the ground, thrusting it at Amalar, who retaliated with a wave of fire.

"Stop!" Gardellin shouted. "We cannot let him control us!" Immediately thereafter, his body jerked rigid, a marionette dangling from someone else's strings. He waded into the fight, even as his eyes revealed a man wildly trying to stay in command of himself. Shelendel got past Amalar's defenses, driving her spear into his shoulder, pinning him to the ground. Shelendel pulled the weapon free and raised it above her head before bringing it down to strike repeatedly, not to kill but to maim, as Amalar began shrieking.

Gardellin's hands leapt ablaze with blue fire, but instead of directing it toward the others, he clapped his palms against his cheeks. He fell onto his knees, screaming, and Tim suspected he was using the pain to regain control over himself. Sure enough, Gardellin's movements become more regular, less strained, and he managed to tackle Shelendel, tearing her away from Amalar. Gardellin clapped another hand of fire to Shelendel's skull, holding firm while Shelendel lurched beneath his grip. After a moment Gardellin let go; Shelendel's gaze refocused, and she was herself again. Amalar still lay on the ground, writhing from numerous wounds but alive.

At the front of the throne room, the rubble shifted and Uklith floated into the air. He smiled down, but the Advocates merely returned his gaze, two standing, the third on his back, defiant to the last.

"We *will* stop you," Shelendel said.

Uklith looked to them. "To the contrary, my friends. You thought to catch me off guard, and yet look at what I bade you do here in the matter of a few seconds? Oh, I could make you commit all sorts of depraved acts." He gestured toward his slain guards. "One morning I made them eat their tongues. It was quite entertaining."

The Advocates struck again, the combined force of their power causing cords of magic to wrap around Uklith's body. On the floor, Amalar began chanting, face set in concentration as a series of obscure words rolled from his tongue.

"You fool," Uklith said. "You absolute *fool*." He pointed toward Amalar, and the air rippled around the Demon-Lord as he pushed back. The cords began to dissipate, but when Shelendel and Gardellin added their voices to Amalar's, the bonds returned at full strength.

Uklith froze in place, immobilized. "The tongue of Homdee cuts both ways," he said. "Do you know what this means for the three of you?"

Gardellin paused while the other Advocates continued chanting. He leveled his gaze at Uklith. "We do."

"And you are willing to pay this price?" the Demon-Lord hissed.

"A thousand times over."

As Gardellin added his voice back to that of his companions, Uklith's eyes shifted from one Advocate to the next. He began laughing, but there was no mirth in it. "So be it."

Smoke floated from all corners of the room, accumulating to form a dark cloud that rolled past the three Advocates and surrounded Uklith. Muted lights flashed within the depths of the darkness, along with the sounds of Uklith's laughter. Either he could not fight back or chose not to, but Tim suspected the former; spells of Homdee were incredibly powerful. According to Nazgar, there was no defense against a spell of Homdee, but this power came with a steep price, for the caster always had to suffer what he or she inflicted.

An invisible force pressed against Tim, pushing the Advocates and him across the length of the room and out of Uklith's chambers. In front of them, the doors slammed shut with an unmistakable sound of finality, leaving Uklith trapped inside.

Gardellin and Shelendel collapsed, their magic vanishing in a shimmer. Amalar remained upon the ground, his blood pooling on the flagstones. "It's done," he said, and yet Tim knew it wasn't. They had a price to pay. Wisps of black smoke were seeping through the doorframe, creeping toward the Advocates.

A voice echoed in the hallway. "You have taken my freedom. And in return...I am now permitted to take yours."

Amalar was the first to expire, body shuddering, eyes going sightless. Shelendel and Gardellin followed suit, muscles slackening as they died. Soon after, however, Gardellin's limbs twitched and he came back to his feet, facing Uklith's prison. His eyes had lost all color, becoming orbs of pure black. Behind him, Amalar's wounds sealed over, and he too rose, followed by Shelendel. They joined Gardellin in front of the closed door, faces blank, eyes black, waiting with unquestioning servitude.

"You cannot go far, my friends," the Demon-Lord's voice said. "You are bound to this City, the same as I, but that does not mean I cannot make use of you. Your first task is simple: kill them all."

As Tim watched, the three Advocates marched through the city, fire and shadow blazing from their fingertips. They laid waste to everything in their path: humans, dwerions, and elions alike, young and old, male and female. Lightning shot from the heavens, striking those who tried to flee. It was a horrible, all-out slaughter, and the sight churned Tim's nonexistent stomach. True, many of these people had been living depraved half-lives, on the verge of insanity and worse, but they were still people, and they still deserved a more dignified ending than this. The Advocates themselves might have been the most unfortunate, for now and again Tim caught a flicker of their former selves in their eyes, an acknowledgment that they had become unwilling marionettes dancing on Uklith's strings.

When nobody remained alive in Agrazab, the undead Advocates returned to the hallway outside Uklith's chambers, standing side by side in their robes, unflinching, unspeaking, awaiting their master's next command.

"And now, my friends, we wait," Uklith said.

The vision flashed once more, and Tim saw a new scene, one he knew quite well, for it was the North. Two hundred years after Uklith's imprisonment, Zadinn Kanas's citadel erupted during the Battle of The Deathlands, a column of green fire shooting into the clouds as the Cauldron of Souls, containing Zadinn and those within it, exploded. This had been the day that Tim defeated Zadinn, and the Dark Lord's soul had returned to the depths of Malath alongside the remnants of the malichon armies.

The scene changed a final time, and Tim saw an elion in the cellar below Tarvil's cottage, hunched over the woodsman's body. Bloodstains ran down the elion's lips and chin, and a pink chunk of human flesh hung from the corner of his lip. His face showed a blend between Mardrin's outright zeal and the cursed Advocates' unquestioning obedience, and it rattled Tim. Who needs malichons, he thought, when one can twist the living into such as this?

In the cellar, a voice resonated. *You have done well, my servant. Open the manuscript.*

In response, the elion held up the book from the cellar niche, raising it to the flickering candlelight, and the voice continued speaking. *Zadinn Kanas left a piece of himself behind—a reservoir, a shred of power to be used in a time of need. A pity it did not serve him—but it shall now serve me instead.*

The elion opened the book. He stiffened, and a green light similar to that which had erupted into the clouds on the day of Zadinn's death leapt out of the pages. It illuminated the man, causing his hair to stand on end. He screamed as the power washed over him.

Good, the voice said. *You have what you need. Set forth and let us break the spell.*

The elion's eyes went black, just like those of the Advocates within Uklith's citadel. He turned from Tarvil's body. He dropped the book and began to climb the ladder.

And Tim knew that they were all in grave danger.

* * *

Tim sat up with a gasp, eyes opening. He was soaked in perspiration, one finger of his hand still on the book.

Boblin stood over him, tense and poised to react. "What happened?"

"Nothing good," Tim replied. "Do you remember the day Zadinn's citadel erupted?"

"It's not something I'm likely to forget."

"Did anything come from the book when I collapsed? Green fire, like the spell that returned the malichons to Malath?"

"No."

Tim looked at the manuscript, wary of further traps. "I don't know if *that's* good or not, but it does explain why the manuscript is still here. The elion who found it absorbed the power within—power that Zadinn had left behind. The book was of no further use to the elion, so he left it."

"An elion? Did you recognize him?"

"I can't name him. But … he did look familiar."

Boblin sighed. "Great. And what is he going to do with his newfound abilities?"

"I think he's going to free Uklith."

5

Admiral Vila Kaarst watched the horizon from the bow of *Innocent's Blood*. Ahead of him, the setting sun cast golden light across the waters of the Rendrivin Ocean, while beneath his feet, the pitch and yaw of the brigantine's deck moved in cadence with the rhythms of the sea. The Rendrivin was both fair and cruel: smooth and glassy on the best of days, raw and stormy on the worst of nights. Its waters—opaque blue under a clear sky, steely gray under an overcast sky—could either provide a man with hours of tranquility or serve him a brutal death. He viewed the ocean as a worthy foe; men's lives came and went, but the Rendrivin remained. Many a corsair before Kaarst's times had met his fate on these waters, and many after him would do so as well.

"Adm'ral!" a voice called from the mainmast. Kaarst looked up to see his first mate, Grizzlen, lowering his spyglass.

"Aye!" Kaarst called back.

"We be close, Adm'ral! I see Aras's walls upon the horizon!"

Kaarst smiled. "Good."

Two schooners, *Night Predator* and *Dagger's Thrust*, flanked *Innocent's Blood*, and four additional brigantines sailed an hour to their rear. The calm waters had provided easy passage this afternoon. Around the admiral, the crew hauled lines from the water, lashed cargo to the deck, and adjusted the jibs. The corsairs caroused as often as they cursed, and were as likely to deliver a congratulatory slap on the back as to slide a blade between the ribs. Kaarst embraced it all. If one wasn't celebrating with another man, he might as well as be killing him.

He entered his cabin, Grizzlen climbing down from the mainmast to join him. Inside, charts and navigational instruments lay across a table. A map of Vonku hung on the wall, a dagger pinning it in place.

"How many years, Adm'ral?" Grizzlen asked, looking at the drawing of the city.

"Twenty-six." *A lifetime, and then some.*

"Do ye think it's changed?"

"No." Kaarst pulled the dagger free and laid the map flat. He placed a handful of figurines, denoting the ships in his fleet, upon the parchment. "Vonku doesn't change. Aras doesn't change." *I served the throne once. My entire family did. Yet that service of ours mattered little to you, Aras, on the day you stripped me of all titles and sent me into exile.* Well, Kaarst had never liked the nobility in Vonku, anyway. He was better off without them. Still, Aras's betrayal demanded a response. Twenty-six years might be a long time, but Vila Kaarst did not forget, and he most certainly did not forgive.

"We'll be on the Bay by midnight," Grizzlen said. "Be it time to send word?"

"Soon," Kaarst replied. He'd heard from Crazvin and Aldris today; the former in position in the north, the latter in the south. He placed Crazvin's figurine on top of the outpost of Eltern, and Aldris's near Sevilin. "Isolation, Grizzlen, that be the key here. We must cut the king off on all sides." At this time of year, many of Alcatune's ships would be out to sea, completing coastal supply runs, leaving Childar's Bay ripe for the taking.

"Do ye think Crazvin an' Aldris be ready to face the Legion, Adm'ral?"

"*We'll* be facin' the Legion, my friend, an' we are well equipped to do so. Crazvin and Aldris, though … Vonku has grown fat on peace, an' it be an ill-kept secret in the Legion that the outposts of Eltern an' Sevilin ain't manned with the best. When a man ain't got what it takes to serve in the city, they send him to either Eltern or Sevilin. Crazvin an' Aldris won't be fightin' the Royal Legion, lad, they'll be fightin' its rejected recruits."

Grizzlen returned the smile. "That, Adm'ral, is somethin' I can get behind."

"Send the pigeons at nightfall, an' be ready to swim in nobles' blood." The pigeons would deliver orders for Crazvin's and Aldris's crews to strike the outposts in the early hours of the morning, at the same time as Kaarst's fleet struck Vonku's seaward walls. *With the Eltern and Sevilin under our command, and the sea ours, Aras will be without aid, alone. Then, your majesty, we will see what you remember of Vila Kaarst.*

After Grizzlen exited the cabin, Kaarst opened a trapdoor leading below-decks. He clambered down the short ladder and hopped onto the planking, pausing to let his eyes adjust. Shortly after his exile, he'd found himself in the country of Icor, where he'd discovered he was not alone in his spite for the aristocracy. He'd plucked at these strings of unrest, fomenting discord. He might despise the political courts in which he had been raised, but he had learned from them, and he put these skills to good work in Icor. Soon the country was in open rebellion against its king. King Aras had sent his soldiers, along with other monarchs in the South, to help quell the resistance. Toward the end of the conflict, as other leaders in the rebellion were being rounded up and sent in chains to the gallows, Kaarst—ever one to know which way the wind blew—decided it was time to leave dry land behind.

He had started as a deckhand on a lowly schooner to avoid being recognized as a leader of the rebellion, but that hadn't needed to last long. Once they were far enough out to sea, he murdered the captain in the fat idiot's cabin, and the ship was his. Well, it hadn't *entirely* been his, as some of the crew remained loyal, but they fed the sharks in short enough order. Those had been intriguing years upon the early seas, living from one conquest to the next, far from the country of Alcatune. In the distant Threa Ocean, his command had grown from that of a single vessel to a fleet of them, thirteen vessels and twenty-five hundred men. After many long years, the day had come when Vila Kaarst decided it was time to return home.

Vonku was a city of thousands, but most were common folk, and the Royal Legion housed in the city numbered an even thousand. Those soldiers would soon have their hands full protecting the walls to the sea as well as defending against attacks from outposts no longer belonging to them. And, while sieges *did* often favor those behind the walls, Kaarst had one more card to play.

Thoughts returning to the present, he crossed the ship's mid-deck, floorboards creaking. A long tube of iron, eight feet in length, sat before the nearest porthole. The entire structure was mounted on wheels and lashed to the deck many times over, keeping it securely in position. Kaarst laid a caressing hand on the device, one of six, which waited ready to roar upon their unsuspecting victims.

King Aras had no such weapons. His men possessed only steel and arrows, and his seaward catapults might be capable of wreaking devastation upon the corsair fleet, but Kaarst had no need to come within range of such defenses. He'd discovered the secret of black powder in the lands beyond the Threa Ocean, guarded closely by its owners. To acquire it, Kaarst had found the proper connections, called in his debts, and most importantly, betrayed when the time was right. And so Admiral Vila Kaarst had acquired the mystical power of the cannon, and from that point forward none could withstand him.

Alcatune's people knew little of black powder or the of damage it could cause, but they would learn soon enough. With his cannons, Kaarst could fire from beyond the range of the king's catapults, chipping away at Vonku's walls until they crumbled. Sooner or later he would have to take his battle to the streets, but not before he had broken the brunt of their defenses and left the Legion's best men rotting at the bottom of the bay.

Even if King Aras had three times the ships in his harbor—which he didn't—it wouldn't have mattered, because with these six weapons of cast iron, *Innocent's Blood* was the deadliest warship the South had ever seen.

* * *

"Wake up."

Sendalion Danris sat upright. Horatio stood nearby, pulling a jerkin over his head. "It's time for our turn at watch."

Sendalion stifled a yawn, swinging his legs over the side of his bunk. *Five years in the Royal Legion, and it's still no easier getting up at four bells past midnight.* Nighttime watch on Vonku's seaward battlements was far from pleasant. Even in the barracks' dry interior, he anticipated the spray from waves crashing against the wall and soaking his rubii-spun cloak. There would be a steady breeze over the waters, and come sunrise he'd be wet and shivering, eyes stinging from saltwater, numb fingers gripping the haft of his spear. *At least it's only midsummer,* he thought. During the winter, the air carried a dampness like no other, leeching into one's bones with all the mercy of a wounded redpike.

Sendalion followed Horatio down the garrison hallway, where flickering torches cast shadows on the walls. They passed several other soldiers of the Royal Legion, those who had the good fortune to be ending their shifts, and stepped outside to take position on the parapet. As they faced east, standing in silence, Sendalion reflected it wasn't *all* bad serving in early morning. The rush of surf, the caress of wind, and the smell of brine could be quite soothing. On nights when a full moon rose, a man could see all of Childar's Bay, and beyond it the full breadth and majesty of the Rendrivin Ocean. This morning, the clouds hung low as fog rolled in, a sight which carried its own majestic quality.

"It's going to be a thick morning," Horatio said.

Sendalion nodded. "Aye, we won't have much to show for our watch today."

"Have you heard anything from Vinsor?"

"No, but I expect he's doing well. He always knew how to come out ahead." It was hard when a fellow soldier left the Legion, but Sendalion supposed the North was right for Vinsor. The man had always been the roving type. Personally, the North made Sendalion uneasy. It was a new world, with a ruler they understood little and a history they understood even less.

"Do you believe the stories that come from there?" Horatio asked.

"Those about Tim Matthias?" Sendalion paused. "Captain Yastlin says the boy's father, Daniel Matthias, served in the Legion during the Icor Rebellion. First swordsman, even."

"Where is the elder Matthias now?"

"They say he died early after crossing into the North. I don't know if it's all true, but the younger Matthias claims to be an Advocate of the Lifesource."

"Isn't that what started it all up there? One Advocate went bad, and he put everyone else in chains?"

"That's what they say." It was hard to separate truth from myth, though.

Horatio shuddered. "The last thing we need is somebody like that coming south. I have little desire to go to war with those who use magic."

"I doubt it would come to war." The Rebellion was still young in Alcatune's memory, and it sounded like the Northerners had also experienced their fair share of bloodshed this past year. As the two men returned to silence, the fog continued its steady crawl, thick and undulating in some places, thin and vaporous in others. Sendalion felt the first telltale signs of a shiver stir deep within his being. The crumbs of salt upon his lips had become full-fledged crystals. Below them, the waters rippled as the ship *Steadfast* sailed through a parting in the fog, making its patrol of the bay. Waves lapped against its hull.

"I never liked being on a ship myself," Horatio said, grimacing. "The waters aren't easy on my stomach."

They heard the creak of jibs as *Steadfast* disappeared behind the fog once more. Then a sudden *boom* split the night, cracking across the waters. Sendalion started, snapping his gaze toward where *Steadfast* had vanished, hand curling around his spear. He'd never heard anything so loud in his life.

"What in the name of Malath was that?" Horatio asked.

"I have no idea," Sendalion replied, right before another *boom* sounded.

This time, he also saw a flash of light from within the fog. He shifted from spear to longbow, nerves taut, senses tingling. "Sound the alarm."

As Horatio took off running, a cacophony arose from the bay, that of men yelling and steel clashing. Soldiers on the battlements drew forward, bows in hand, peering into the gray light to discern what was going on.

They heard a third *boom*, and Sendalion's stomach roiled. He held an arrow nocked between thumb and forefinger, ready for anything to indicate the presence of an enemy upon whom he could fire his weapon. From the western tower of the battlements, a bell rang as Horatio pulled the cord, alerting the Legion that the garrison was under attack. By whom or what, Sendalion surely did not know, but those questions could be answered later.

In the bay, several Legionnaires piled into longboats, standing by to assist *Steadfast*. They did not depart immediately, instead waiting to ensure that the current conflict was not a diversion to pull defenses away from the gates. As the minutes passed, no further explosions sounded, but Sendalion could hear the increasingly pitched sounds of battle carrying across the waters. After a quarter hour, a horn sounded, *Steadfast's* call for aid, and three of six longboats launched.

Horatio returned to Sendalion's side, holding a longbow. "Any sight of the enemy?"

"No. We've precious little information to go on, I'm afraid. All we can do is trust those on the waters."

A fourth *boom* sounded, and Sendalion heard splintering. Water splashed, men cried out, and he feared a longboat had met a swift fate at the hands of whatever made such an awful noise. That may very well have been the apex of the battle, for the sounds of chaos soon dwindled.

After the silence settled, the *Steadfast* reappeared, listing to one side. At first Sendalion thought its sails had been torn to shreds, for he saw fluttering in the breeze from the height of the masts. But when the ship drew closer, he realized the dangling objects were not sails at all, but bodies of the crew, hanging from ropes. Several heads had been placed on pikes across the front bow in a macabre lineup of death.

Chainmail clinked as Captain Yastlin joined the men lining the battlements. At the sight of the approaching ship, the big man called out, voice echoing across the bay. "Who goes there? Show yourself, and answer for your crime!"

Long seconds passed before the first stirrings of motion on *Steadfast's* deck. A lone man emerged, striding past the dangling bodies. "First mate of *Innocent's Blood*, Grizzlen Beltin, at yer service," the man called back. He offered a sweeping, exaggerated bow. "I be deliverin' a message from Admiral Vila Kaarst, who politely requests ye surrender to him."

Vila Kaarst? Surely it can't be.

If Yastlin felt the same surprise as Sendalion, he concealed it well. His face darkened. "The name of Vila Kaarst is well known, corsair. You have launched an attack on a vessel of the king, an act which demands swift justice." He lifted a hand. Sendalion and Horatio, along with the other men on the battlements, drew their bows. "At my word, men, send these rats to the seabed."

Grizzlen raised a hand. "Ay, the Adm'ral said ye might need some convicin'." Behind him, a score of men assembled, wearing the unkempt clothes and crooked weaponry designating them and their brethren for what they were: pirates. "Don't let those arrows fly, boys. Do so, and ye'll be regrettin' it soon."

"Mayhap," Yastlin replied, "but you'll still be dead." He dropped his hand, and a volley of arrows flashed across the bay. Almost all found targets, but Grizzlen ducked, seizing one of his comrades and shoving the man in front of him. Grizzlen's human shield dropped dead with an arrow between his eyes, while other corsairs either collapsed on the deck or toppled over the side.

"If the Admiral has sent you," Yastlin called, "where is his fleet?"

Grizzlen stepped out from hiding just long enough to show a toothy grin. "*Everywhere*," he said, and jumped over the far side of the ship.

Perfectly in time with Grizzlen's words, the fog in the bay rose, revealing no less than seven corsair ships. A volley of flaming arrows flashed forward from the deck of Kaarst's leading brigantine toward the *Steadfast*, which floated halfway between the attacking ships and Vonku's walls. Fires flared into existence as the arrows *thudded* into its hull, sporadically at first, then with increasing frequency once the corsairs launched a second volley. Soon the ship was completely ablaze. Sheets of dancing flames illuminated the harbor, casting its gray waters in an orange glow, and thick plumes of smoke climbed into the pre-dawn clouds.

As Kaarst's lead brigantine drew closer, Yastlin signaled the archers to draw once more. Legionnaires from the garrison below swarmed upward, adding their strength to the walls, while several crews hoisted catapults into position.

In the bay, Kaarst's ship turned, exposing its broadside. Sendalion watched the corsairs that lined the side of the vessel filing into position and preparing to launch arrows of their own, but it mattered not. The corsairs had neither the reach of the experienced longbow archers, nor the strength of the catapults. Their arrows would clatter harmlessly against the unyielding stone of the garrison's walls. As the attacking fleet closed the gap, for the moment still out of bowshot range, Sendalion saw a series of six tubes poking from the corsair ship's middeck. He narrowed his eyes to get a better look. He'd never seen such things before, and he had just enough time to wonder at their purpose when the first tube flashed with fire. The now-familiar *boom* sounded, and a section of wall just to Sendalion's left blew outward. He staggered, partially from the impact and partially from the shock, as chunks of stone from the battlement rained into the harbor below. The blast left a large divot in the wall, and while it hadn't compromised the structural integrity, a succession of such blasts would surely demolish the defenses.

Horatio saved him next, grabbing Sendalion from the side and pulling him away as a second *boom* sounded. A chunk of shrapnel shot skyward, right where Sendalion had been. Through ringing ears, Sendalion heard Yastlin yelling commands, ordering the men to form a new line. In the harbor below the remaining longboats surged forth, but a third blast split the lead boat in two.

Sendalion peered over the ledge, seeing a new divot in the wall not six paces below where he'd been standing. In the bay, Kaarst's weapons found their mark on the next longboat. It erupted, sending wood, screaming men, and body parts in all directions. Those who survived the initial blast landed in the bay, yet when they bobbed to the surface, arrows *whisked* from the corsair ships and struck them as they treaded water. On the fringes of the conflict, several of Vonku's defending ships swept into the bay from the south, aligning themselves against the corsair ship. As the king's fleet at last had a chance to return fire, corsairs began falling to their deaths under the onslaught of retaliatory strikes. Two final explosions sounded. The first missed its mark, and the second struck a defending ship, doing signification damage to its starboard gunwale. Following this, the weapons went quiet, and Sendalion wondered if Kaarst needed time to prepare the devices for a subsequent volley. As the battle in the bay dissolved into chaos, Sendalion and his comrades could do little but watch. This was the biggest attack the harbor had seen in years. Sendalion Danris looked to the bay beyond, watching his comrades fight and die. Sooner or later, the corsairs would draw close enough for him and those on the walls to do their part, but the odds were not good—not against whatever Kaarst had on that ship.

And all the while, the *Steadfast* burned.

6

King Aras of Alcatune paced the empty halls of his palace. The older he grew, the less he slept, and this morning had been no exception. At this hour, the servants left him alone, and for this he was grateful. A king had precious little time to himself, and Aras was glad for the opportunity to think on matters without interruption. Though, some on his court claimed Aras had *too* much time for himself, for Queen Salise was long dead and Aras had no heir.

Returning to his bedchamber, the king stood in front of a window, facing north, the direction from which a new crop of troubles contributed to his increasingly sleepless nights.

When Quentiin Harggra, formerly of the Royal Legion, and Billian Briiga, mayor of Raldoon, had arrived in Vonku the previous summer to tell of the North, Aras had received the dwerions with no small degree of skepticism. The villagers brought with them a tale of lands beyond the Northern Rampart, of a sorcerer named Zadinn Kanas and Advocates of the Lifesource. Captain Yastlin had confirmed Harggra's honorable service to the Legion during the Icor Rebellion, but it did not make the tale any more believable. When Aras sent scouts to the Rampart, they confirmed the dwerion's claim that a passage between the lands was indeed open. Even then, Aras did not fully believe until the day he stood at the Rampart, gazing upon the tunnel to the North. Later, Aras met Tim Matthias—son of another Legion soldier from the Rebellion—and the young man had used the Lifesource to raise a goblet into the air before Aras's eyes.

But there was the matter of this new land to consider in the aggregate. Though Aras held no outright misgivings about any of these people—be it Matthias, or Harggra, or the self-proclaimed emperor Ladu Jovun—they had nonetheless managed to upend his entire world in the matter of a few weeks. Throughout the South's history, the impenetrable Rampart had been the one constant: nations rose and fell, monarchs came and went, but the Rampart remained. True, Matthias and Ladu delivered a message of goodwill—they wished this new country to be open to all, and Alcatune, with a robust population and increasingly limited acres of tillable soil, suffered for good farmland. Yet there was simply so much they did not *know* about the North. Its violent and troubled history was but one of many uncertainties, and while Aras showed Ladu and his people the same goodwill that they had shown him, he would not risk exposing his subjects to the darkness that had enslaved the other country for so long. Zadinn Kanas might have been defeated—all accounts were clear on that—but Aras wondered if Matthias might one day present a similar threat. The High Chaplain said that touching the Lifesource was sacrilege, a blasphemy to the Maker. What if Matthias succumbed to the same temptations that had corrupted the former Dark Lord?

Still, the way was open, and Aras could not keep those who wished to depart from doing so. True, he *could* use force to impose his will, but a king did not take such a path lightly. Many a monarch had miscalculated the benefits available via a course of strength. Most recently, Aras had sent Harggra north with a delaying tactic in hand, but as of yet he did not know how it had been received. The "formal transfer of allegiance" had been Lord Prendil's idea, a way to temporarily halt emigration. Publicly, Aras communicated this under the pretext of mitigating a recession from an exodus of farmers, but in truth, it was to allow him and his advisers to prepare plans for defending against an invasion of Alcatune by the North. Aras's gut told him that Ladu would not respond favorably to the request for halting emigration, but Aras *owed* it to his people to protect them. If these measures failed…well, they would man that parapet when it came to it.

"Your Majesty?"

Aras turned his head as a servant entered the room. The king received his visitor with some surprise; it was much too early for the palace staff to be speaking to him, unless something was gravely amiss.

"Yes?" Aras asked, waving his hand for the man to rise from his bow. "What is it?"

"Captain Yastlin, your Majesty. He requests you come to him at once to address a matter of urgency."

Aras's chest tightened. Something was indeed wrong. The Captain of the Royal Legion did not request the king's presence upon a whim, least of all before dawn. Aras put on his royal cloak before leaving his bedchamber, allowing the servant to lead the way. He walked down the wide halls of his palace, the arched ceiling high above him, torches in sconces lighting the way. Only on occasion did they pass another individual. Some were nobles afflicted of the same early-hour inclinations as the king, others were servants beating dust from tapestries and sweeping the corridors. Each one bowed to Aras as he passed, and he always waved a hand for them to rise. The last thing those folk needed was the king's presence disturbing them from their duties. The palace already asked much of its servants, and the least they could receive in return was the ability to perform their tasks in peace.

In his throne room, Captain Yastlin stood at attention, three soldiers behind him. The big, bearded man's face looked tense, and his eyes were troubled. The sight made Aras's chest constrict further; not all was well in Vonku tonight, and the Captain was here to tell him of it.

"There has been an attack on the seaward garrison, your majesty," Yastlin said.

Aras started in surprise. He might have expected trouble on the streets themselves—not that Vonku was particularly dangerous, but mercenary groups had caused civil strife in the past. While such events were rare, an attack on Vonku's exterior was even more so. It spoke of foreign action, a prelude to war, and since the end of the Icor Rebellion, there had been precious little of *that* in the South, thank the Maker.

Unless... Aras swallowed. *Is it the North? Have Ladu and Matthias determined our lands shall be theirs?* "What do you know, Captain?" he asked.

"It's him, your majesty. Admiral Vila Kaarst."

Aras felt surprise as well as an odd sensation of relief. *It isn't the North.* His kingdom faced only other men, not a mad agent of the Lifesource. As for Kaarst, Aras knew the name quite well. Many years ago, the man had been charged with the murder of doctor in the outer city. Kaarst's family had wished for mercy, but exile was the most leniency Aras could allow in lieu of death. Because Aras believed in fate, and because he knew the Maker brought life full circle, he always suspected he might cross paths with Kaarst again. Nonetheless, he found himself wondering how this attack had come to pass. Vonku's seaward walls were mighty, capable of withstanding a sizable enemy fleet, and for such an action to be anything more than folly, the Admiral would have needed to amass a considerable force.

"Tell me more," Aras said.

"We've counted seven vessels in the bay, but there may be more. The outposts of Eltern and Sevilin have gone quiet, and I believe Kaarst may have taken them unawares."

Aras furrowed his brow. Seven vessels were not a trivial force by any means, but they didn't present a serious threat to Vonku's well-fortified walls. At most a vessel held two hundred men, meaning less than fifteen hundred corsairs in the bay. True, that was more enemies than they had seen in a long time, but the Royal Legion was better trained, held a superior position, and had more resources.

Yastlin had clearly anticipated his ruler's thought process, because he spoke again after a pause. "There is more you must hear, your majesty. Kaarst possesses a weapon of sorts. We don't know how it works, but it destroyed several of our vessels and damaged the outer wall. When the attack began, we heard a noise like a clap of thunder multiplied tenfold. When the fog lifted, we saw Kaarst's ship armed with a series of iron constructs that spat devastation against anything in their path."

Aras tightened his lips. It sounded similar to Harggra's account of the weapon used by Ladu's elions during the Battle of the Deathlands. The northerners claimed it was a combination of herbs which, once lit on fire, was capable of a devastating and deadly explosion. He didn't fully understand how it worked, but it was said to be a regular part of this Frontier Patrol's arsenal, and it was yet one more reason Aras felt he must tread carefully when dealing with these strangers. Considering Matthias's command of the Lifesource and the elion's command of a superior weaponry, Aras was well and truly outmatched against these strange folk.

Could Kaarst have obtained this weapon from the North, or is Ladu in league with the corsair admiral? There was simply too much Aras did not know here. Many things were coming to a head, and too fast: he bordered a nation he did not understand, and now he faced a shadow from his past, a nobleman come to seek vengeance against the throne that had cast him out.

His first instinct was to send word to Icor. Two decades gone, Icor had requested Aras's aid when the rebellion grew too big for one monarchy to contend with, and Aras had obliged, building an alliance that had contributed to a foundation of peace ever since. Though his brother nation would not have hesitated to repay such a debt, many miles of mountain passes separated the way between them. It would take weeks to even send word and months for troops to arrive. Vila Kaarst often mocked the noble culture, but there was one matter the young man had studied assiduously and gained an aptitude for: battle. He'd devoted himself to learning a commander's tactics—the maneuvering of troops, the superiority of position, and the ability to apply proper leverage. Aras would dispatch a man to Icor nonetheless, because he would rather have the option in play than not at all, but they would need assistance more quickly than the other country could provide.

Aras directed his gaze to the commander of the Legion. "What do you suggest, Captain?"

"A runner, sir. He'll have to go across country, of course. I fear the corsairs control the outposts, and through them, the roads."

"It's a long way to Icor, Captain."

"Aye, your Majesty, but Raldoon is much closer."

Aras cocked his head. "Raldoon?"

"Quentiin Harggra lives there, your majesty. The oaths he swore to serve the throne still hold. I know—he is but one dwerion, and yet he is the same dwerion that rallied the oppressed slaves from these supposed Deathlands in the North and freed them. We can have a man in Raldoon in a quarter of the time it takes to reach Icor."

"Once you have contacted Harggra, what would you ask of him?"

"We must liberate the outposts. With that, passage in and out of Vonku becomes ours once more. If it comes to a protracted engagement on the coast, we can clear the city of citizens, and the Royal Legion can make these streets our fields of killing."

The thought of turning streets into deathtraps for incoming corsairs was a grim proposition, to be sure, but it might well be the best defense they had. And in the matter of Quentiin Harggra, had not the citizens of Raldoon proven themselves? In the North, they had passed through a time of fire, death, and blood that few, if any, of Aras's men had experienced. Last, the matter of timing was of no small import. One could only guess how long the walls might hold against Kaarst's superior weaponry. Better to give the Legion avenues into and out of the city, granting them control of their terrain.

Aras glanced at Yastlin and saw a strange look in the man's eyes, a train of thought half-finished. "What else, Captain?"

"There was something unusual about this attack, your majesty, beyond what I have told you already. Perhaps I've spent too much time listening to tales of this North, but I sensed forces beyond our knowledge at work this morning."

So there it was: Yastlin had observed the same similarities Aras had seen. "And you think Harggra may be better equipped to fight this battle because of his knowledge?"

"Yes, your majesty. It goes against all reason, but it's what my gut tells me, and if I've learned one thing in my time with the Legion, it's that I must trust my gut."

Aras allowed himself a smile. *Soldiers and their instincts.* They trusted such things to the point of superstition. Still, many a fighter had survived the battle-field by intuition alone, and Aras could not disregard it. "And what does your gut tell you of Harggra, Captain? If the North is involved, can he be trusted?"

"I don't know that the North *is* involved, your Majesty, only that the methods and weaponry used here may be similar to those that are used beyond the Rampart. Regardless of whether Ladu and Matthias are involved, Harggra is a man of the Legion first. He swore an oath. He can be trusted, on that I would stake my life."

"Our lives very well *may* depend on it, Captain," Aras replied. "Nonetheless, I shall follow your lead. This is your Legion, and it is your fight. We do as you say."

Yastlin bowed. "As you command."

"Do you have a runner in mind?"

Yastlin nodded, gesturing toward the soldiers who had stood behind him in silence this entire time. A tall, wiry man stepped forward. Upon closer inspection, Aras saw soot and abrasions on the man's face and arms. He must have been on the parapets when Kaarst's strange weapon unleashed its bite this morning. The soldier took a knee before his king, keeping his eyes on the ground.

"Your name, Legionnaire?" Aras asked.

"Danris, your Majesty—Sendalion Danris."

"How long have you been with us?"

"Six years, your majesty."

Aras looked at the dark-haired soldier. The Rebellion had been before this man's time, meaning he hadn't seen hard combat yet. Nonetheless, six years of service was nothing to scoff at. "Do you understand your mission?"

"Yes, your majesty." Danris raised his face. The look in his eyes was all Aras needed to see. The man possessed a quiet resolve and was stronger for it. A willow to Yastlin's oak, where Yastlin was all raw strength and brute force, Danris would endure and outlast. This soldier would make it past the enemy lines, Aras had no doubt about that.

"Very well, Legionnaire," Aras said. "Captain?"

Yastlin drew his sword, offering the weapon hilt-first to the king. Aras touched Sendalion on the shoulder with the flat of the blade. "I charge you with this mission in the name of the king of Alcatune," he said. "May the Maker light your path."

After Aras gestured for him to rise, Danris thumped a hand against his breastplate. "I shall not fail, your majesty."

At a nod from the king, the lone soldier turned from the throne room and departed, vanishing into the early dawn to complete his task.

* * *

Jolldo Graff knelt in the dirt outside his cottage. Rows of tilled earth stretched before him, planted with beets, potatoes, carrots, onions, and beans. He took a deep breath, looking at the sky and relishing the midday sun upon his face. He massaged the arch at the base of his neck where the muscles had begun to ache. Gardening was difficult work, though not as difficult as mining chunks of stone above a pit of flames.

Several dwerions had taken up gardening upon returning from the North. Their time in the Pit had changed them, and the act of tending to the earth proved soothing at a fundamental level. During their imprisonment, they had been surrounded by so much death and destruction that their only recourse was to cultivate and nourish. *I'm gettin' philosophical,* he thought. *Quentiin always said I was the thoughtful one.* Jolldo supposed Quentiin was philosophical enough in his own way, but it would snow in Malath before Quentiin ever admitted it.

He stood, hearing and feeling his joints protest, and bathed in the peace of the surrounding forest. The air hung heavy with the warmth of early summer, comfortable enough to be outdoors without a cloak, but not so hot as to drive one indoors toward the nearest cask of ale. Above him, a handful of birds flew from one tree to another, while farther along, two squirrels raced across the mossy ground, spinning in circles and chattering in fierce tones.

Jolldo's homestead was located at the village's western edge, near a dirt road running south through the Odow Forest, connecting the dwerion village to the rest of Alcatune. To the east, Raldoon still bore the odd sign of the malichon attack from the summer before last. Some houses had scorch-marks running along their wooden foundations, while others had been relocated or reconstructed. From his homestead, Jolldo could see the rooftop of the rebuilt inn, which served as a common area in the evening. The only stone building was the village hall, which was also one of the very few to withstand the original attack.

Being outside village limits, Jolldo's cottage had fared better than most. Returning to his porch, he took a long, grateful drink from a glass of water. In the background, insects buzzed. Unlike Quentiin, he'd never returned to the North since Zadinn's downfall. He simply could not muster the willingness to cross the Rampart again. Doing so would have brought back too many memories; he'd made an awful mistake in the Pit, and he wasn't sure he could ever rectify it. If not for Quentiin, they might all be dead, blown to dust in the massive blast that had wiped out the citadel after Tim defeated Zadinn. Instead of being in the Pit during that cataclysmic event, however, they'd been free, fighting on the slopes of the Deathlands alongside the elions and the Army of Kah'lash.

Jolldo remembered when Quentiin had first arrived in the Pit. Quentiin had spoken of escape, but Jolldo silenced him, told him to never mention it again. That was the rub: Quentiin had needed him, and Jolldo had let him down. He supposed he'd have to face this truth someday, but for now it was easy enough to pretend such hard facts didn't exist.

Something thumped in the distance, the steady drumming of hooves, and Jolldo turned toward the road. Two years ago, travelers to Raldoon had been infrequent. At the time, the only other village of import sat on the shores of the Rendrivin Ocean a week's journey east, but now that the Rampart had been opened, Raldoon experienced more regular traffic. Some folk came to see the tunnel in the wall, whereas others intended to settle in the North. As the hoofbeats grew louder, a rider galloped from the woods. He was hunched over his horse, hands clasped to the saddle. Upon seeing Jolldo, the rider dug his heels into his steed, pushing the mount forward, dust rising in his wake. The horse thundered into Jolldo's yard, flanks heaving, skin glistening, and when the man dismounted, Jolldo saw the glint of a sword in his saddlebags.

"I'm Sendalion Danris of the Royal Legion," the man said. The jagged line of a recent wound ran across his jaw. "I come at the behest of King Aras. Is Quentiin Harggra in the village?"

Jolldo looked at the soldier. He certainly had the bearing of a Legionnaire, but...

"Where's your sigil, laddie?" he asked.

Jolldo had not served in the Legion, but Quentiin had, and this stranger was not wearing the Legion's characteristic purple emblem over his right breast. *No use on the left breast,* Quentiin had explained once. *That would be too fittin' of a target over one's heart. An enemy archer might thank ye, but that's about it.*

Danris nodded. "Of course." He reached toward his saddlebag. Jolldo tensed, taking a step toward one of his gardening rakes. Two summers ago, his danger sense would not have kicked in so quickly, but after the Pit, he suspected more and trusted less. *Yet another demon behind yet another door.*

Danris did not draw his sword, though. Instead, he simply produced the familiar sigil of the Legion. "I could not wear it on the road. The king needs help. Where is Harggra?"

"He ain't here. He's already on the king's business."

Sendalion's face tightened further as he looked beyond Jolldo toward Raldoon. "Of course he is," he murmured. "I don't suppose you expect him soon?"

"I simply can't say, laddie."

"Can you send for him?"

Jolldo looked the soldier up and down. "It's urgent, ye say?"

"The kingdom needs him," Danris replied, giving the dwerion an appraising glance. "Might I speak to your mayor?"

"I'm right here, laddie," a new voice said. Jolldo and Sendalion turned to see the mayor standing at Jolldo's doorstep. Jolldo gave Briiga a nod, suppressing a smile at the Legion man's surprise. Briiga often stopped by; those who had suffered underneath the whip of Veldor the Slavemaster had forged strong bonds, and often sought out each other's company. *A timely visit, friend mayor.*

Danris took a deep breath. "The corsair admiral Vila Kaarst has barricaded Vonku's seaward borders and holds our outposts. The royal city is under siege, and Quentiin Harggra is hereby recalled to the Legion in service of his king."

"What of reinforcements from Icor?" Briiga asked.

Sendalion shook his head. "We've sent for them, but the journey from Icor to Vonku is not quick. We *must* send for Harggra."

Briiga nodded. "We'll do what we can, laddie. Follow me."

Jolldo looked at Briiga, raising an eyebrow, and the mayor gave a slight nod. Well, Matthias had given them the object exactly for such purposes—though this would mean revealing its existence to a member of the king's guard, and Jolldo did not know how well *that* revelation would sit with King Aras.

As Jolldo followed Briiga and Sendalion, he rumbled deep in his throat. He didn't like the position the villagers of Raldoon found themselves in of late. They owed it to King Aras to be forthcoming with all that they knew of the North, and yet they had a unique friendship with Emperor Ladu and the elions, as well as with Tim Matthias. Before the passage to the North ever opened, Tim and his family had been the first to help, serving the people of Raldoon in their darkest hour. Divided loyalty, even if for the right reasons, was never a good thing. They shouldn't have to be in this position, protecting the secrets of their friends in the North while still accountable to their monarch of the South, but here they were nonetheless. Aras and Ladu needed to resolve their differences soon. It wasn't good, not for anyone.

But King Aras was in trouble, and a dwerion served his king. Jolldo had seen what became of a subjugated people, and he would not let the same happen to the citizens of Vonku.

7

"So, now what?" Emperor Ladu Jovun IV asked.

Tim stood in the Emperor's throne room, the book from Tarvil's cottage on a table in front of him. Boblin, Celia, and Quentiin were there, too, but no one save Tim had dared touch the manuscript. So far, it didn't appear to contain any lingering traces of dark magic. Zadinn described many evil deeds within its pages. Tim might have witnessed the Dark Lord's cruelty firsthand the previous year, but what he'd seen paled in comparison to what Zadinn had written in his journal. In Agrazab, Uklith had nurtured the rot within Zadinn's heart, watching with glee as his protégé became more of a monster and less of a man.

"It's quite obvious," Quentiin rumbled. "We have to stop Uklith. Seems simple to me."

In spite of the seriousness of the situation, Quentiin's direct nature made Tim smile. *Always charging ahead to save the world. We could use a few more like him, I suppose.* "Without a doubt, my friend, but there are more fundamental questions we must answer first. I'm not sure how the book ended up below Tarvil's house, or who took it. I saw an elion in the vision, but little more than that. We need to start by finding out these things."

"Do we?" Ladu countered. "I don't suggest we disregard those questions, but regardless of who the elion is, he found Zadinn's journal and absorbed a latent reservoir of his power. We *know* what the elion intends to do; as Harggra said, I think we might be better off focusing on how to stop him than on how he came about the journal."

This time, Tim suppressed his smile. *Quentiin and the emperor just agreed on something, even if it did take the gates of Malath opening to make it happen.*

Beside him, Boblin spoke up, ticking off his fingers. "Summarize what we know. One: a group of possessed folk attacked our wedding. Two: a voice spoke to Tim through one of the prisoners, indicating Uklith's power was growing. Three: an elion discovered Zadinn's journal in Tarvil's cellar. Beyond that—"

"We have our assumptions," Tim said. They'd discussed this beforehand. "We assume the voice that addressed me was Uklith, we assume that the individuals at the wedding and the elion in Tarvil's cellar are serving Uklith, and we assume this elion intends to free Uklith. While these *are* assumptions, I see nothing to indicate they're false. I'd also suggest we would risk more by disregarding these assumptions than by accepting them—so for the time being, I believe we should proceed as if they're accurate."

Boblin finished the thread. "Last, there's what we don't know. We don't know how the journal ended up below Tarvil's house, we don't know how the elion plans to free Uklith, and we don't know when the elion left the Erdrar. Most importantly, we don't know *where* Agrazab is."

Ladu tilted his head in acknowledgment. "Therefore, making the first order of business to discover Agrazab's location. How do you propose we do this?"

"I'll start by reading the entire journal," Tim said. "It might have clues I haven't discovered yet."

"And the rest of us?" Quentiin asked.

"Boblin and I will return to the chapel," Celia said. "We'll look it over one more time."

Quentiin grunted. "I could ask around about Tarvil. He was a Southerner, and mayhap some folk in town knew him. I can't see how he came by the journal of the evilest man in the world." He shook his head. "Zadinn. *Writin'.* Seems so..."

"Mundane?" Ladu asked. "Most leaders are mundane, when it gets right down to it. As for myself, I'm the only one who was around when Zadinn actually invaded the North. My memories of that time are hazy at best, but I'll visit what remains of Pellen's archives." He stood. "We have work to do, my friends."

* * *

"I've heard some couples renew their vows, but I'll admit, this is sooner than I expected." Boblin said. He and Celia stood at the front of the wedding chapel. The windows had not yet been replaced, though the stained-glass shards had been cleared from the floor. Summer air floated in through the jagged holes, providing a surprisingly comfortable reprieve from the permeating heat of summer. Boblin wouldn't go so far as to *encourage* rabid attacks by crazed citizens, but the breeze sure made worship hours more pleasant.

"Well, I am told our marriage is 'different,'" Celia replied. "Have you heard that phrase anywhere?"

"No."

"Wise answer." Celia and Boblin separated to investigate opposite sides of the room. The Frontier Patrol had already inspected the chapel forward and back again, so Boblin was not optimistic this new research would return anything of value. Still, wisdom dictated one more search was in order. He stopped at a long, bare rectangle on the floor where a ruined pew had been removed, revealing a few dried spots of blood on the flagstones.

"Still nobody saying they recognized the attackers?" he asked Celia.

"No." That was odd as well; while the population in the North was far larger than it had been, it was still small enough that *somebody* should have recognized the attackers. On top of that, shouldn't a member of the Frontier Patrol have encountered at least one of these individuals during the emperor's census? Giving up his examination of the floor, Boblin stood and looked at the broken windows. He closed his eyes, trying to recall specifics from the fight.

Celia and I were facing the altar, Father Anelion before us, Tim and Quentiin at the back of the room. Boblin had sensed something was wrong right before the windows exploded. *They came through the holes, men and women, howling. They had no coordination, no leadership, merely an instinct to kill.*

The spot upon which Boblin stood marked the location where he'd thrown his knife into one of the attacker's throats, dropping the man then and there. Afterward, the group had gone over the bodies, looking for any sign of purpose, identification of names or allegiance, but found none. They'd scoured the chapel's exterior, looking for indications of where the attackers had come from. The small signs they *did* find indicated that the strangers may have come from several different directions in the city, converging on the chapel before attacking. Tim had reached out to the bodies using the Lifesource and felt a black, oily taint, which he said indicated a malevolent presence upon the attackers' minds, an external influence driving them forward.

Boblin opened his eyes, turning his gaze back to the bloodstain. For some reason, his thoughts kept returning there. After the Patrol members conducted what they felt was their due diligence, they cleaned the chapel, removing the wreckage and mopping up the blood with soap and water, but they must have missed the small droplets near this bench. That didn't surprise Boblin, given that there had been a fair amount to clean away. He crouched and ran his finger across the stain, feeling the faint grime on the floor, a few coarse grains of dirt. There was something—

There. He felt an indentation in the stain, a pockmark of sorts in the stone. Assuredly, these flagstones had minor imperfections from the passing of feet, yet this pitting reminded Boblin of the way a sarchon's blood had eaten through the walls of the caverns in the Northern Mountains. True, sarchon blood had been black—decidedly different from the natural red of the attackers at the wedding—but still...

"Celia," he said. "Can you find any bloodstains the Patrol missed when we cleaned the first time?"

He walked along the edge of the pews, looking for additional markings. Most of the stains had indeed been cleared, but every so often he saw additional spots of minor pitting at locations where bodies had fallen and blood had pooled. He examined the wall beneath the windows next, running his fingers over the sills. This was where the people would have crawled in after shattering the glass. No doubt shards had cut them on their way through...and yes, there they were, pockmarks upon the stone wall where blood had run from their hands and knees, leaving these strange markings.

If I look closely enough, though, I may find pockmarks all over the chapel, including in places where there have never been either blood or bodies. Stone pits over time, so what does it really mean? Nothing except a reminder of a place aptly named Malath's Teeth. Eighteen months ago, Boblin had fled through those nightmarish tunnels, the sarchons behind them hunting the elions through the twists and turns of stalactites. He'd had his share of unpleasant dreams regarding *that* particular adventure.

"Found some," Celia said.

Boblin met her next to the opposite wall. There was a crusted brown spot near the base of the wall, and sure enough, he saw more shallow divots. "See how the stone's been eaten away?" he asked her.

"You've seen that somewhere else?"

Boblin nodded, showing her the spot he'd found by the missing pew, and next the markings near the windowsill. Celia ran her hand across the markings as Boblin had done, testing the feel.

"Remind you of anything?" Boblin asked.

"Sarchon blood."

Boblin nodded. "It was the first thing I thought of, too. Pattern, or coincidence?"

Celia stood back up. "Pattern, my love. Normal blood doesn't burn stone."

So we have a connection, if even a vague one, between the creatures in the Northern Mountains and the attackers at our wedding. But what does it mean?

Well, there had been that *one* rumor. "Do you remember what some of the older elions used to say about the malichons?" he asked.

She nodded. "Yes, I do. It occurred to me the first time I felt sarchon blood burn me, in fact. Do you know what I'm thinking?"

"Being married doesn't allow me to read your mind, much as I might wish otherwise."

Celia tapped him on the side of his head. "You'll learn. I'm thinking, dear, that we talk to someone who was here when the malichons and sarchons first arrived."

* * *

"Vinsor," Quentiin said, entering the fletcher's shop. "How be ye, laddie?"

Vinsor had an arrow set before him, mounted upright on a stand. With a magnifier in one hand and a tweezer in the other, he was carefully adjusting the feathering at the base of the shaft. It was a delicate process, to be sure, but Quentiin had known Vinsor long before he came north, and the man was the best.

"I think this will have twice the range when I'm finished," Vinsor replied. "What do you think?"

I don't doubt it. "Laddie, ye should see some of the weaponry those Frontier Patrol blokes use. They wired the Fort o' Pellen with their powder, strung it up in the walls an' used kegs full o' the stuff as breakpoints. Later, they got an idea from the Army o' Kah'lash on how to make it more mobile. They've started packagin' it in birchbark tubes with a fuse at one end. If they had *yer* mind at their disposal, let me tell ye…"

"I like my work, Quentiin. Arrows and fletching suit me well, and it's where I belong. Nothing against your Northern friends, let me be clear, but this is what I've put my mind to."

"Aye," Quentiin acquiesced, "I won't begrudge ye that, laddie. Ye've earned it."

"Ever courteous, my friend. How can I help you today?"

"What did ye know of Tarvil?"

Vinsor arched an eyebrow. "What *did* I know about him?"

Quentiin grunted; he hadn't meant to do that, but it was an easy enough mistake to make. *Out with it, then.* "He's dead."

"Dead?" Vinsor's question must have been reflexive, since he didn't wait for a response. "How?"

"I can't say, laddie. It's the emperor's business."

"Ah. Well, I didn't know Tarvil per se. He lived out of town, and only came in on occasion. He was a pleasant enough fellow, but I know little more than that."

"Did he ever speak o' his time in the South? Talk about what brought him here, or why he decided to live in the Erdrar?"

"I can't say he did. But—" Vinsor's brow furrowed. "He came in the week before last. Aye, that time was a bit odd."

"What d'ye mean?"

Vinsor ducked beneath his counter and returned with a crate. Sheaves of paper filled the box to the brim, spilling over its edges. Any good shopkeeper viewed record-keeping as a necessary evil, Quentiin knew. It wasn't pretty, and it sure as Malath wasn't fun, but it was important.

Vinsor wet a finger and flipped the papers, which he had arranged by date. Every so often he pulled out a customer's order, only to shake his head and put it back. Quentiin scratched an itch on his thigh. It was getting hot in here; as a general rule, the North was cooler than the South, but that didn't mean it couldn't get uncomfortable in the summer. It hadn't always been that way—when Zadinn Kanas ruled, it was almost always cold, the cumulative result of many years of his touch poisoning the land, but now that the Dark Lord had been defeated, natural weather patterns had slowly but surely reasserted themselves.

"Here," Vinsor said.

Quentiin leaned over the counter and examined the records. The frequency with which Boblin and Tim left arrows for repair made him smile. After a minute, he came to Tarvil's name. "Three dozen arrowheads?"

"Enough for a small patrol. It's not much to go on, but it *was* an order for an unusually high amount, and given that he's dead..."

Quentiin itched his thigh again. By Malath, that was irritating. *Tarvil was afraid of somethin'. Mayhap he thought his place was bein' watched, an' it probably was. Pity the arrowheads he bought didn't keep him alive.*

Vinsor was looking at him. "What does all this mean, Harggra?"

"Emperor's business." Quentiin wiped a brow. It shouldn't be this hot. It *couldn't* be this hot. And that itch on his thigh was about to make him— "Ah!" A bright, burning pain flared in his pocket. *By Malath, that hurts!*

"Are you okay?" Vinsor asked.

"Fine, laddie, fine," Quentiin grumbled. "It's no matter." If he hadn't been so distracted, he might have recognized what was happening sooner. "I beg yer pardon, I need a moment. May I?"

Vinsor spread his hands. "Please."

Quentiin stepped outside the shop, squinting in the sun. He walked around the edge of the building and into the shade of an alley. It hadn't been the summer heat in the shop at all; the focusing reservoir in his pocket had been activated, and it came with unpleasant side effects. No matter. The reservoir was valuable and worth the discomfort. Besides, how better for it to draw his attention?

Quentiin took a marble from his pocket. It still felt warm to the touch, but thankfully it did not have the scorching heat that had seared his skin moments ago. As he held it before him, the reservoir flared into a green glow. Quentiin stepped further into the shadow of the alley, hoping to remain out of sight.

"Quentiin?" Jolldo Graff's voice came crackling and faint but audible. "Are ye there?"

"Aye, laddie, I'm here."

The device had been Tim's idea. He'd spent three months working on it. Quentiin didn't pretend to understand the Lifesource, but as near as he understood, anything natural—untouched by man—could become a focusing point for the power. Tim's sword held such a stone in its hilt, and when Tim used the Lifesource, he funneled power into the stone, transforming the blade from an ordinary sword into a truly formidable weapon. In the case of Tim's focusing point, he had to actively maintain a hold on the Lifesource to keep the power funneled into the stone, and when he released the Lifesource, the sword lost the magic. This past year, Tim had spent time investigating whether he could infuse a focusing point into a true reservoir of Lifesource power, something that could retain magic independent of an Advocate's control. At first, he succeeded on a limited basis using his sword. Tim had filled the blade with power and handed it to Boblin Kule, and the sword retained its power for few heartbeats before dying out. The success had been short-lived, but it proved the theory.

Quentiin's focusing reservoir had been Tim's second test. The lad had decided to attempt creating a useful but nonviolent reservoir, as he did not wish to inflict potential injury upon the bearer. Quentiin had suggested a communications device, given his travels between North and South. Tim searched a quarry a half-day to the east and eventually found two stones suitable to the task. Jolldo Graff currently held the second stone in Raldoon, and he had used it to hail Quentiin.

The reservoir was just that—a reservoir—and as such only held a limited amount of power. Once drained, Tim could re-infuse it, but the process would leave him weakened for days. The dwerions had concluded they would have to use it sparingly, and Quentiin knew it would be a long time, if ever, before such tools were commonplace. Still, in the interim, it allowed for a way to communicate during urgent situations. The individual wishing to use the reservoir had to concentrate, much as an Advocate did. The task had not come easily to Quentiin, and Boblin continued to fail quite miserably at it.

"What is it, laddie?" Quentiin asked, wondering what had necessitated Jolldo to reach out.

"It's the king. He's recalled ye to the Alcatune Army. Vonku is under siege from a corsair fleet."

"Corsairs?" Quentiin said. He was familiar with the fact that pirates roamed the Rendrivin Ocean, but he didn't think any would have been foolish enough to assault Vonku's hardened walls.

"Aye, laddie. A Legion man came to Raldoon to deliver the news. He says it's Vila Kaarst."

Ah. Quentiin's fist tightened. Vila Kaarst was a name well known to those who had served in the Legion, the infamous nobleman King Aras had banished, and who in no small part had subsequently contributed to the chaos of the Icor Rebellion. But still...

"Why me?" Quentiin asked. The king could indeed recall former soldiers to the Royal Legion at any time and for any reason, but there were numerous Legion veterans dispersed throughout Alcatune.

"It's because o' the nature o' the attack, laddie," Jolldo replied. "The corsairs have weaponry the Legion doesn't understand." There was a long pause from the other end. "Kaarst either used the Lifesource, or some manner o' explosive device that is similar in nature to what the Frontier Patrol uses."

In which case, Aras should have called on Tim or Emperor Ladu. He hadn't, meaning…

Aras thinks Ladu or Tim might be behind *the attack.* Quentiin felt sick. *He's worried the North is preparin' an invasion.* The king was flat-out wrong, of course; Ladu had absolutely no intention of invading the South, but suspicions were creeping higher and higher between the two monarchs, and Kaarst's attack would not help perceptions. *This whole stalemate between our nations is a karfin' mess.*

But what if the Lifesource truly *had* been a part of the attack on Vonku? That meant someone else with the power was loose in the world, and his or her designs appeared to be more harmful than those of Tim Matthias. *And can it be a coincidence, given what we've seen here? Strange things afoot in the North, strange things afoot in the South.* They could indeed be separate matters, but writing off such events as coincidence was the defense of someone unprepared to accept realities.

"Aye, laddie," Quentiin said. "Tell the king's man that I will leave for Raldoon with all due haste."

"Understood," Jolldo replied. "The Maker be with ye."

"The Maker be with ye, too." Quentiin let the focusing reservoir die, putting it back in his pocket. He'd said *with all due haste,* but he wouldn't be departing at once. No, he had to get back to Ladu's palace first. The others needed to hear about this.

* * *

Tim sat in a study of the palace wing, Zadinn's manuscript before him. He turned a page, the paper crackling in his hands. In the journal, Zadinn started by writing about the night he had murdered his mother and father before setting out west across the desert. However, Zadinn offered precious little information on how he actually reached the City of Darkness. He made several references to his journey, but none were clear enough to provide any direction on how to cross the hot, inhospitable wastes. Instead, most of the journal covered Zadinn's training, often in grim detail. Nothing had been forbidden in the study of dark magic, and when Tim read the passage relating the ritual to establish the portal to Malath, he nearly became ill. On that day, the streets of Agrazab had been filled with blood and the air with screams.

He found no clues to indicate a cause behind the strange happenings of the last few days, other than a section at the end where Zadinn noted he had intentionally established a reservoir of the Lifesource within this book. Zadinn had left the reservoir for *himself*, though, not Uklith, no doubt as a reserve for an hour of need. The more Tim read, the more confident he became that Zadinn never intended to release Uklith. After traveling out of the desert and defeating the old empire, he'd found himself in the position of unchallenged, absolute ruler. The Dark Lord of the North had no reason to set Uklith free, not when he could continue ruling on his own.

"What do you have?"

Tim looked up, seeing that Boblin had entered the room. "Nothing. Zadinn doesn't describe how he made it to the City, and I don't think Uklith even *knew* of this reservoir at the time Zadinn designed it. I think he discovered it more recently, and saw a way he could use it to help himself, but I don't have much beyond that."

Boblin leaned against the wall. "The sun rises in the east and sets in the west, right? So we put it at our backs in the morning and face it in the evening. Sooner or later we'll find the City, I suppose."

"It's an option."

"How did the journal come to be below the cottage?"

"Tarvil built upon the ruins of an old farmstead. Zadinn wrote that he hid the book in the Erdrar because he wanted to keep the journal separate from his palace in case he needed to retreat outside the Deathlands. I doubt Tarvil even knew it was in his cellar."

"That's truly bad luck for him."

Considering how Uklith had exerted his presence on the possessed folk at Boblin's wedding, and what he'd done to the elion beneath the cottage, Tim wondered if Tarvil's choice of location had actually been bad luck, or another of Uklith's machinations. *Or maybe I'm getting paranoid.*

"And that's all?" Boblin asked. "The journal just ends?"

"He continues for some bit after the invasion, but yes, he fills it to the last page. I suppose that's when he took it to the farmstead in the Erdrar and hid it."

At the sound of footsteps, Tim and Boblin turned. Jend Argul stood at the door. The tall, muscular elion was beginning to show the first hint of gray in his hair, but his eyes were as discerning as ever. "We might have something in that regard," the former commander said.

Boblin smiled at his onetime superior. "It's good to see you," he said. "The emperor must have called for you?"

Jend nodded. "He wanted to know if, during my time on the Patrol, I'd ever heard of a way for traveling west. And no, I never did. The truth is, we interrogated precious few malichons over the years. Not that I wouldn't have, but they were never ones for turning themselves in alive."

"So, what *do* you have?" Boblin asked.

"We've been leading other excavation efforts from time to time throughout the North. As Matthias said, I believe Zadinn made use of failsafes in the event his citadel fell." Jend held up a book. "And he had more than one."

Tim looked at the book. "Where did you find that?"

"On a different excavation, this one below where the citadel was in the Deathlands. There are quite a few texts there, and to be honest I didn't even know we had this one until this afternoon. We've been gathering them for some time. When I heard Matthias was reading a journal of Zadinn's, I went through the records and found this one. I think he prepared multiple reservoirs to be stored in separate locations, much the same way that we at the Fort prepared more than one avenue of retreat. At the same time, he used them to chronicle his deeds. This appears to be the one Zadinn was writing at the time the Fort fell."

"You opened the book?" Tim asked. "That could have been dangerous."

"So I hear, but I've done a dangerous thing or two in my time, and I'm still alive." Jend handed the book to Tim. "Read the page marked toward the end."

Tim opened the manuscript, recognizing Zadinn's scrawl from reading the other book. He turned to the section Jend had indicated, beginning at the top and stopping halfway down. He read the passage twice, and then looked at Jend.

"You never knew of this?" he asked.

"I had no idea," Jend replied.

"What?" Boblin asked.

Tim read aloud:

"*Isanam returned from the Desert today. That which I speculated has indeed proven true: my master remains bound to Agrazab, with no way to touch this world. Isanam also told me that a patrol of his malichons discovered a man wandering at the fringe of the Fertile Lands. It comes as no surprise that there is a group of villagers who long ago took shelter deep in the Pel Delta, which is barely navigable and offers opportune chances for hiding. I have often wondered why Pellen and his people did not seek shelter there, too. They remain in their Fort, perhaps as a gesture of defiance against me, and for that I shall have their blood.*

They brought the man to me in my throne room. He was raving, and so I probed his mind to learn about his village. This community relocates often, never staying in one place for long to lessen their chance of discovery. What I found most intriguing was unveiling the secret of how this man lost his sanity. I recognized Uklith's touch upon his mind immediately. The raving man—I learned he was called Darmet—had been to the City. There, he was exposed to my master's power. I could only ascertain fragments of what happened, for Uklith's touch is not gentle, but Darmet did not travel to Agrazab alone. Any others with him who survived have likely returned to their village. I have Darmet in the cells, but it will take some time to extract the location of his village from his broken consciousness. The matter must wait, for Elson Tulak is in position in the Fort. Once I deal with the elions, once I defeat the Warrior, these refugees in the Delta shall have their turn."

Tim closed the book. "So there were folk living in the Delta."

"We always knew it was a possibility," Jend said. "The Fertile Lands are thick, and there was a degree of wisdom in hiding there. We ourselves were often tempted to relocate into the Fertile Lands, but we knew that sooner or later Zadinn would come for us, so we thought it better to fortify in the mountain than to hide in the greenery. The Lands could be burned down around us, but the walls of the Fort could last until such time as we saw fit to tear them down by our own doing. At least, that's how we saw it."

Well, this certainly changes matters. "Get the rest of the group," Tim said.

After Jend left, Tim closed his eyelids and rubbed his brows. So they needed to travel south before going west. *It's fitting, after a fashion. Last time, we traveled north, so this time we will travel south. Sooner or later, though, we'll need to turn our sights west. When that happens, the Maker preserve us all.*

Soon Jend returned with Ladu, Tim, Boblin, Celia, and Quentiin. "There's villagers still in the Pel Delta," Tim said. "They've been to Agrazab, or at least some of them have. One man lost his sanity in the process, but the remaining survivors may have a different story. If there's a way to find the City, these people are the best ones to tell us of it."

"Who says they'll be willin' to tell ye where it is?" Quentiin asked.

"Nobody," Boblin replied, "but I'll ask nicely, and if they say no, I'll turn them over to you."

Quentiin rumbled deep in his throat. "Unfortunately, laddie, I may not be with ye. There's more at stake. Jolldo spoke to me through the stone, and I've been recalled to the Royal Legion. There was an assault on Vonku. King Aras believes the Lifesource may have been involved."

Tim took a moment to process this. "Do they know who attacked?"

"Vila Kaarst. He has a long history of bad blood with King Aras. I'll level with ye, laddie—because of the Lifesource, I'll guarantee Aras suspects that either you or Ladu, or both, are involved."

"Hence why he recalled *you*."

"Aye, don't stuff the messenger with arrows. Regardless, I have to go. Ye'll need to make for Agrazab, an' let me take care o' Kaarst." Quentiin narrowed his eyes. "An' I'll enjoy doin' it."

Tim looked at Ladu. "Your majesty, what do you say?"

The emperor exchanged a glance with Boblin and Celia.

"There's one more thing, mate," Boblin said. "It's about the blood."

"The blood?"

"It burned the stones of the chapel," Ladu said. "Not dramatically so, but the Kules noticed it when they returned to investigate. Malichons, I fear, were not the only soldiers that Zadinn drew from the underworld."

"Yes, he sent the sarchons too." The three-headed, winged demons, too monstrous for even Zadinn's army, had eventually disappeared into the Northern Mountains. There, they preyed upon many an unwary traveler, including Tim and the elion refugees.

"There was a rumor during the invasion," Ladu said. "Supposedly, Uklith had the power to infect a mind, to possess it and turn it into a tool of his will. In fact, I believe you said that he did this very thing to the Advocates who rose against him."

"Yes, but that was a consequence of a spell of Homdee, your majesty. I'm not sure they are the same thing."

"It was said, though, that when Uklith claimed a soul, the body shed burning blood."

Tim felt cold. "But what about the malichons? Sarchon blood burned, yes, but malichon blood never did." *In the chaos of battle, can I say for sure? Maybe it* did *burn, but so little that I didn't notice.*

"They had much more sentience and self-awareness than the sarchons, and therefore the effect would have been less noticeable. Even regarding the blood of those who attacked us in the chapel, the burning was only apparent after the Kules searched the area more closely."

Jend spoke up. "Emperor Ladu is right. At the Fort, we had to replace the occasional blade when it showed signs of deterioration after too many fights. It wasn't common, but it happened."

"That has to explain the dark touch I felt upon their bodies when I investigated them with the Lifesource afterward," Tim said. "They were quite literally possessed by Uklith."

"Some may not have been even alive at all," Ladu replied. "It was always said that the Demon-Lord could raise the dead. I *did* fight against undead in the invasion, rare as they were. Zadinn did not have the power to summon them, but given what you saw of Agrazab's history, I expect that Uklith sent some of the City's inhabitants out under Zadinn's command, albeit after they'd been murdered."

And now we have possessed individuals in Galdon, perhaps even undead. How can the Demon-Lord's reach extend so far?

"Ye need to go west," Quentiin said. "All of ye. I'll make my way to Raldoon, but I don't think any northerners should come—given the King's misgivin's, I'm afraid that would be the wrong move." He pulled the focusing reservoir from his pocket. "I'll bring Vinsor Dalin with me. He's a Legion man, an' he'll be a welcome presence back home."

"Okay," Tim said. "Your majesty, do I have your permission to find Agrazab?"

"You have more than my permission," Ladu said. "I order you to do so."

Tim looked at Boblin, Celia, and Jend. "Are you with me?"

Boblin rolled his eyes. "Quit asking dumb questions."

"All right," Tim said. "Let's go stop Uklith."

8

The elion stopped at the northeast corner of the Fertile Lands. He'd left the city of Galdon far behind him. It would still take several days before the landscape he traveled gave way to desert, but the delay failed to disturb him. Time had no meaning anymore. He breathed the night air, looking to the stars above, thinking of all he'd gone through to reach this point. He knew there were others like him out there, sworn in service to the same master, following the same path Zadinn Kanas had walked two hundred years ago. He wished he could have seen those days, when the former Advocate swept out of the west and descended upon the North in all his dark fury, claiming a victory unlike any before. In the end, though, Zadinn had failed Uklith, and that was a mistake the elion intended to rectify.

His service had begun when Uklith spoke to him in dreams, announcing that the world was to be made anew. At first the elion dismissed such experiences as nightmares, but over time came to understand that they were visions of a powerful, terrible time to come. In such a battle, there could only be one side—that of those willing to please their new lord—and so he'd sworn obedience, forsaking all earthly possessions in pursuit of this cause. Zadinn, the elion knew, had never inspired this degree of loyalty from his subjects. The Dark Lord had subjugated his people, ruling via fear and his power, but Uklith gained his subjects through pure bliss, showing them what they could become, promising them rewards beyond imagining. It was for such a loving master the elion committed himself wholeheartedly.

The Demon-Lord had followers everywhere, more than one might expect in a land recently freed from Zadinn's rule. Because the elion had been one of the first, Uklith's presence upon his mind revealed itself more forcefully than for others, but many of his master's other servants still walked among society, biding their time, giving their fellow citizens no indication of their true allegiance.

The elion longed for fresh blood. It had been some time since he drank from the farmer's neck, savoring the sweet trickle upon his chin, feeling Tarvil's life gushing out, seeing those eyes wide in surprise and pain. He'd captured a few rabbits and squirrels along his journey, taking what sustenance he could from them, but they paled in comparison to dining upon a living human being.

Beside him, the trees of the Fertile Lands rustled. The Warrior would soon travel these lands, as per Uklith's design. The elion knew of the folk living deep in the Delta; the Warrior would be seeking them out, for two years gone a hapless group of the villagers had journeyed west, seeking a home far from that ruled by Zadinn Kanas. They had instead encountered the Demon-Lord's domain in all its majesty, and only two returned from that journey, one man with his sanity, one without. The Warrior needed a guide, and he would request this man's assistance. Whether or not the man would grant his help was yet to be seen, for the villager had suffered greatly in Uklith's city.

Regardless of whether the guide rendered his assistance, Uklith had designs for this village. He saw all, anticipated all, and conquered all. Against the lord of the underworld, master of death, ruler of all things eternal and the Maker's antithesis, Tim Matthias had more than met his match.

* * *

The company set out from Galdon at dawn, the sun rising as they rode. The morning air felt crisp and cool, not yet elevated to the full warmth of a summer day. At this early hour, the horses' hooves clopped against largely-empty cobblestone streets, for most were still awakening. The group did see the occasional shopkeeper opening his or her doors for the morning—sweeping entryways, wiping windows, and laying out wares—and waved in passing.

They numbered nine in all: Tim, Boblin, Quentiin, Vinsor, Jend, Celia, Hugo, Ken, and Hanqar. After they left the city, the company made their way south on the road leading across the Durin Plains. They expected to reach the Kaltu Pass by nightfall, and would travel from there into the Fertile Lands the following morning. As they made their way across the landscape, a familiar wind picked up. Tim recalled when had first entered the North with his parents and Quentiin the summer before last. The North had seemed entirely foreign to Tim when he first saw it, a land of sharp gullies and deep ravines, lacking water and substance. They had met Boblin in the Kavu Hills, where the elion aided them in defeating a malichon ambush. Afterward, Boblin had taken them to the Fort, where they'd made a stand before fleeing into the Fertile Lands. *We're heading to the Fort again, only this time it's broken instead of whole, and from there we'll return to the Fertile Lands. Then, we traveled through a land once alive but dead; now, we cross a land once dead but alive.* Each blade of grass and crop of wheat they passed seemed a small victory, and every so often they entered a thicket from which they jumped a deer or flushed a bird.

They remained on the hard-packed road for the first part of their journey. With each passing hour, the shape of the Kaltu Pass grew more sharply formed upon the horizon. At midday, reaching the halfway point between Galdon and the Erdrar, the travelers halted.

"This is where we part ways, laddies," Quentiin said in his gravelly voice.

Tim nodded. "For now, my friends. Be safe. Remember, whenever possible—"

"Aye," Quentiin cut him off. He took the focusing reservoir from his pouch and handed it to Tim. "At nightfall every day, ye'll raise us if ye can, an' we'll answer if *we* can. Imagine if ye'd had this in the Mountains, laddie. Tools like this will change the world."

Tim did not doubt they would, and after seeing the use of Zadinn's focusing reservoir, the thought made him feel a little cold. *Do I actually understand what I've created?*

"Give Uklith my regards, eh?" Quentiin said, digging his heels into his mount. Vinsor followed suit, and the two Southerners' horses bucked forward and galloped down the road toward the Erdrar Forest. Already two members fewer, the group watched Quentiin and Vinsor disappear from sight. They left the path to ride across the Durin Plains, traveling in silence while the sun climbed into the sky, the only sound the whisper of the grasses in the breeze. Tim watched with no small degree of jealousy as his elion companions guided their mounts across the terrain with ease, anticipating changes in the landscape and shifting their courses accordingly. Certain skills came more naturally to Boblin and his people; the elions had relied on physical prowess for so long in their struggle against Zadinn that talents such as riding and fighting, bowshot and swordsmanship, were as much a part of them as the blood running through their veins.

"What do you think he'll find in the South?" Boblin asked Tim, looking toward the Erdrar, which had dwindled to a dark spot in the distance.

"I've been thinking about that." Tim placed a hand on the pommel of his saddle to keep himself steady. "I don't see the South having any strategic value for Uklith. We're more vulnerable to an invasion in the North. I think the attack on Vonku might be a diversion."

"Keeping us away from Agrazab?"

Tim nodded. "If I'd traveled south to fight a Lifesource user in the corsair fleet, we wouldn't be headed west to stop Uklith. I heard stories of Vila Kaarst when we lived in Vonku. He was legendary, the corsair that defied the king. Some say he singlehandedly started the Rebellion."

"Do you suppose this Kaarst actually did discover an Advocate?"

"That one's been giving me more trouble. It's conceivable an Advocate escaped the destruction of the old empire by heading overseas, but I don't see how one would have allied him or herself with Kaarst."

Boblin halted his mount, turning to Tim. "What if Uklith trained a *second* surrogate? A backup to Zadinn?"

The thought had occurred to Tim as well. Zadinn had ignored his master for two centuries as he ruled the north, and while two hundred years might be of little consequence to an immortal being, that didn't mean Uklith would permit outright disloyalty. Nor, for that matter, would he put all of his bargaining chips on the table at one time.

He cleared his throat. "That would be very bad." If such a possibility *were* true, Quentiin could be riding to meet a full-scale invasion force led by an enemy strong enough to rival Zadinn Kanas. *But if that* is *the case, we're still taking the best course of action. Somebody needs to stop Uklith, period, and that somebody needs to be me. We had to send someone south, and all the better it be someone Aras trusts, and someone who understands what we are up against.*

Boblin nudged his horse forward again. "I hope Quentiin knows what he's doing, because I'll be a sun-baked lizard if I have the first clue what *we're* doing."

"We're riding across the Plains, dear," Celia interjected. "That much is apparent to everyone else, at least."

Amazing, Tim thought, *she's managed to imitate his tone to perfection. There could be a scholarly study performed on this.*

Boblin stared at his wife, brain quite obviously spinning. "I've got a smart response for that. Just give me a minute, and I'll have it."

Tim chuckled, leaving the two of them to it and guiding his horse forward.

As they drew closer to the rise of the Kaltu Pass, his mind drifted back to the summer before last, when Boblin had brought Tim and the rest to the Fort of Pellen. Upon arriving, they had been imprisoned in the dungeons, Boblin framed for Pellen's apparent murder. That day, Tim had met Nazgar of the Kyrlod, learned the history of the North, been in his first true battle, and lost his parents. *Until that point, I hadn't really joined the elions in their cause. I hadn't experienced what deaths in battle could do to a person. Sure, I'd imagined, but imaginings are far from reality.*

Morning turned to noon, noon to afternoon, and the grass of the plains thinned into the rock and stubble of the Kaltu Pass. At the same time, the flat terrain gave way to a rise and fall that grew steeper as the elevation increased, taking them up and away from the Plains. A solemn silence descended upon the elions as they entered the foothills that had once been their home. This place carried far more emotion for them than the streets of Galdon. For two hundred years the elions had eked out a meager existence here, taking shelter in the Fort's walls, utilizing the landscape to their advantage. They had patrolled these hills day after day, night after night, vigilant against the ever-encroaching malichon army. The steep hills and narrow passages provided them a strategic advantage available nowhere else in the North, and the Pass had played no small part in allowing them to remain free. Disregarding the scattered homesteads that emerged after Zadinn's downfall, the Fort had been the one unified presence, the single community that persevered during those cold days and long nights.

Actually, that's not true, Tim reminded himself, because they were in fact traveling toward the Fertile Lands to find a second community that had persevered, albeit in a different fashion. The Fort had survived through the spirit and skill of its defenders, while the village survived by vanishing into the Delta.

None of that negated the solemnity of this moment. The elions of the Fort were returning home at long last, to a place that had sheltered them and served as a symbol of freedom to those languishing in captivity within Zadinn's slave pit. The sun dipped into the west as they rounded the last peak and came upon an eerily familiar sight: the sloping path that led uphill where the Fort's gates once stood. The hour of the day made the experience all the more profound for Tim, because when Tim came upon this path for the first time, Boblin Kule had led the way with the sun setting in the west.

The Fort's main gates had faced east, with battlements on three sides and its back set against the stone of the mountain. Of these battlements, only partial sections remained, thrusting up from the ground like jagged teeth, while the sections between lay in rubble. During its construction, the elions had lined the walls of the Fort with fuses and explosive power, devised as a last resort and final means of escape. The Frontier Patrol destroyed the Fort by their own hand the day Tim arrived and the malichons invaded, striking a final, vicious blow against Isanam and his forces.

The somber group rode their horses up the pathway toward the ruins of their former home. Jend Argul had lit the fuse of destruction himself, causing chaos and killing scores of malichons while the elion refugees escaped into the hills of the Pass. At the crest of the trail, they navigated their horses past rubble and wreckage. The grass inside the ruins had grown long and wild, poking up at intervals between chunks of stone and shattered glass. Every so often they came across a fallen weapon or piece of armor, the steel rusted from exposure to wind, rain, and snow. A breeze drifted through the wreckage, bringing whispers of the past. The tower that once stood in the center of the Fort had collapsed inward, leaving only portions of the upper levels intact. The breeze became a gust, lifting the shreds of a tapestry from the Floor of History into the air.

As the group dismounted, preparing to make camp for the evening, Jend raised a hand. "This place was once our home, and this evening it shall be again. Do not regret what was lost here, for it made us into the people we are today."

Tim patted his horse before draping a bag of feed over its snout. The creature nickered and stomped its hooves. The group was near a half-standing section of wall, next to a slope of rubble that had been the former parapets on the Fort's northern perimeter. As Tim set about the task of putting tent stakes into the ground, something in the wreckage caught his attention: the curve of a grappling hook, partially set against a crenellation in the grass. The rope attached to the hook had frayed and rotted away. Tim picked up the hook, a smile coming to his face. "Boblin," he called. "I've got something here."

The elion looked up from the beginnings of a campfire. His mouth twisted in distaste upon seeing what Tim was holding. "Don't remind me."

"It was *your* idea."

"That doesn't mean I liked it." Tim and Boblin had been trapped inside the uppermost room of the tower, malichons on the opposite side of the door pounding their way through, and the only way free had been to climb out a window and descend to the battlements via rope and the grappling hook in Tim's hand. "Still, it was better than when I almost fell off a cliff in the Northern Mountains. Do me a favor, Tim—this time around, keep the whole journey on level ground, okay?"

"I make no promises," Tim said, tossing the hook to Boblin. "Keep it. You're more sentimental than you let on."

"You're more annoying than *you* let on."

After the camp was set up and the fire lit, Jend took out his fiddle—now that he was no longer in command, he had more time for the instrument—and played a slow, mournful tune. As flames danced over the assembled company, Tim turned away from the snap and crackle of the fire. With smoke curling into the air above the ruins, Tim left the camp and walked outside the Fort's boundaries. On the horizon, the sun slipped away, replacing the bloodred hue of afternoon with the soft gray of dusk. Tim climbed into the Pass slowly but steadily, keeping his breath even and his movements efficient. The gravelly landscape crunched under his boots as the air about him cooled. The world had a fresh, wholesome smell, occasionally marked by the stronger scent of the freshly grown evergreens on the hillside. Tim supposed this area might one day become heavily forested, but not in his lifetime.

He retraced the steps he had taken with Boblin, Celia, and Ana when they had escaped to the refugees' rendezvous point in the wake of the Fort's destruction. He remembered feeling raw panic as the group fled through these hills, Isanam's malichons behind them in earnest pursuit. It had been a dark, desperate night, full of fear and pain.

This evening, Tim's journey ended when he reached the base of a mound of stones, marking the spot where the walls of the Pass had once stood—a location he knew well. So it was that Tim Matthias came to the graves of his mother and father beneath a sky of full stars and the light of a partial moon. The landscape around him was bathed in a white hue. At the peak of the mound, a sword had been placed into the crest of a cairn, point downward. Tim climbed toward it, pausing to glance up as he progressed. The realm of Harmea was out there, beyond the sky above him, and Tim did not doubt that two souls watched as he reached the cairn and knelt.

He closed his eyes, speaking aloud. "We've come a long way, and we wouldn't have made it this far—*I* wouldn't have made it this far—without you." He wrapped his hands around the sword's leather-bound hilt. "It seems I have farther to go, because Zadinn Kanas was only a puppet, and I must now face the puppetmaster."

The pommel stone in the sword's hilt began glowing with a faint, pulsing green light, following the cadence of Tim's heartbeat. "It won't be the same without the two of you. It's *never* been the same. I'd feel much better with you here, but that was not in the Maker's design. And so, I do what I must."

He rose to his feet and pulled his sword from the cairn in a single, smooth motion. The blade came free without resistance, and when the full length of the weapon was free, it erupted into a green, blazing fire. Tim turned west, where the sun had vanished and left only darkness in its wake. Somewhere out there the City of Darkness, and the Demon-Lord in his palace within, waited for him.

"I'm coming," Tim said.

9

Quentiin Harggra and Vinsor Dalin stood before the Barricade. At over two hundred feet high, this massive wall of seamless stone—called the Barricade by northerners and the Rampart by southerners—had divided North from South, Dark Lord from Warrior of Light, for countless years. Quentiin had been there with Daniel and Rosalie Matthias the day Tim opened the Barricade. He had awakened in the middle of the night to see sheets of coruscating light rippling over the wall, forming the outline of an arch that folded inward to create a tunnel. They had passed through, only to be trapped on the far side when the passage closed behind them.

Tim later told Quentiin the truth of what had led to their small company's crossing on that night. Zadinn Kanas, in his search for the Warrior of Light, had unsealed the Barricade using the blood of a Kyrlod. By design, once Tim crossed into the North, the passage had sealed once more, a mechanism planned by Nazgar and his Kyrlod brethren to keep Warrior and Dark Lord on the same side of the wall until one defeated the other. *The Kyrlod planned this all, every one o' them from Nazgar to Ragzan, from the time they raised the wall until Tim and Zadinn faced one another. They pulled strings from the shadows, a nudge here, a prod there, assurin' their machinations would bear fruit.* Quentiin did not doubt Nazgar's altruism in serving the refugees—the prophet's every move had been designed to protect the world from Zadinn—yet he could not help feeling a twinge of unease to learn that much of what had appeared to be happenstance had actually been orchestrated from out of sight.

Quentiin looked at the tunnel before him. The passage was only wide enough for a few to travel abreast, a small route for such a significant journey. Tim intended to create additional tunnels in the future to facilitate simultaneous crossings, but he wasn't making it a priority. In light of the current tension between South and North, one tunnel presented enough challenges, and they had no need to create more. The elions of the Frontier Patrol had built a gate-house near the tunnel's mouth, and having traveled this way plenty of times, Quentiin knew the sentries by name.

Upon Quentiin and Vinsor's arrival, Wayne Gendashar stepped out to meet them. "Back on through?" the elion asked.

"Aye," Quentiin replied. "It's time for me to be returnin' to Raldoon."

"Best of luck." Wayne paused for a second. "How goes it in Galdon?"

"Nobles. What can ye say? A bit o' bickerin' between them. Nothin' they won't sort out. Meantime, it keeps me busy."

"That it does." They shook hands. "Safe travels."

"Always." Dismounting and leading his horse by the reins, Quentiin en-tered the arched tunnel, where a guttering torch marked the opposite end. The distance was a mere twenty yards, and once more Quentiin marveled at how such a small distance had divided the two lands. Prior to the tunnel's opening, countless adventurers had tried finding ways over, beneath, or around the Bar-ricade, but they had always failed.

Upon reaching the far side, the two travelers came to a similar guardhouse, this one managed by soldiers of King Aras's Royal Legion. The sentry here, a man named Olen, gave them a nod upon arrival. "Harggra," he said. "And Dalin? It's been some time, friend."

"It has indeed," Vinsor answered. "I figured it was high time I visited Vonku once more." Neither he nor Quentiin said more than that; they didn't know how much the guards knew of the city's current troubles, and didn't want to compromise Aras's position by sharing more information than the king might desire. After Olen waved them through, they mounted and con-tinued into the Odow Forest.

As always, upon entering the South, Quentiin observed changes in his surroundings. The air was warmer, the smells more robust, and the sounds of life more prevalent. The forested terrain was thicker with undergrowth, and the ground beneath the horse's hooves had seen the passage of far many more travelers. There was also a touch more humidity, though not enough to be un-pleasant. The dwerion village of Raldoon was two days away by foot, but they should cover the distance more quickly on horseback. They wouldn't make Raldoon by nightfall, but these were good roads and they intended to press on long after sunset. In the North, Quentiin wouldn't have dared ride in the dark, for the landscape was still treacherous in many places, with no formal road south of the Erdrar Forest yet. Here, they could make up for lost time on Vonku's much better-maintained roads.

Afternoon passed into evening, and evening into night. They pressed heels to mounts, taking respite only to care for the horses as needed. Once the moon passed its zenith, Quentiin and Vinsor halted and slept by the roadside, alternating the watch. When the first cracks of dawn showed they resumed their journey, arriving at Raldoon at midmorning. Quentiin always felt a rush of warmth on seeing his village, though this time around, the tension of the moment dampened his usual sense of elation. They skirted the northern side of the community, bypassing the center of the village and any obligatory conversation, and made straight for Jolldo's homestead.

"Ever spent time in Raldoon, laddie?" he asked Vinsor as they rode.

"I only passed through on my journey north. I suppose the inn gets a fair amount of business from travelers these days."

"Aye, it does." Quentiin had been in the inn when it burnt down during the malichon invasion, burying him in the process. But for the timely arrival of the Matthias family, Quentiin might have died under the rubble.

"Aras did send members of the Legion to help rebuild, but I wasn't among them," Vinsor said. "It was hard for fletchers to get duty outside of the city. They liked to keep us fairly busy."

"Why *did* ye move north, anyway?" Quentiin asked.

"I wanted to try something new. I'd lived in Vonku my entire life, and as I said, they didn't allow us much time for getting away. I loved the Legion, but it was time to move on. The Rampart was all but a myth to us, and the idea of actually stepping on the other side, of breathing the air, feeling the soil between my fingers...well, I had to see it."

Quentiin grunted. "The North ain't a bad place, I have to admit. The Emperor's a good man, an' he does right by his people."

"As does Aras."

"Aye, as does Aras. That's why we're here, after all."

They reached Jolldo's homestead, riding their horses into the yard. Quentiin dismounted and tied his horse to the hitching post, patting it on the neck before turning toward his friend's cottage.

"Jolldo Graff!" he called. "Let's get on with it, laddie!"

The door opened. Behind Quentiin, Vinsor had to stoop to make it through the entryway, and once inside, his head brushed the ceiling. Dwerion homes were not made for full-sized men and women. The cottage was quite simple, and few dwerions would have preferred anything else. A small, circular table stood in the center of the space atop an oval rug, a counter and sink ran along one wall, and a window provided a view of the garden outside.

Jolldo nodded when Quentiin entered. When he saw Vinsor, Jolldo paused, looking the man up and down, but said nothing. A second man, tall and lean, sat at the table wearing a leather jerkin with the signet of the Royal Legion. The soldier had a sword buckled at his waist.

Jolldo stepped forward, gesturing from Quentiin to the man at the table. "Quentiin Harggra, meet Sendalion Danris."

Quentiin clasped Sendalion's hand, eyes darting toward the purple insignia. "Second swordsman of the Legion, I see." It was a rank accorded to those who displayed a high level of proficiency with the blade, and only the rank of first swordsman, which few had earned, signified a higher competence.

By way of response, Sendalion tilted his head. "And you were?"

"Second as well, laddie. We can't all be Daniel Matthias." Daniel's expertise explained why Tim Matthias was so karfing good with a blade. "An' this is Vinsor—"

"Dalin, I well know. *Somebody* finally managed to get you back on this side of the wall, I see."

"The king's in trouble, and I'm still a Legion man," Vinsor said.

Sendalion relaxed slightly, a slightly observable loosening of his muscles, and he smiled. "It's good to see you, friend."

"True, but I'll admit the circumstances could be better."

"Aye," Quentiin agreed. "Let's get on with it, eh? I was enjoyin' the Emperor's finest ale when I received yer message. What of Admiral Kaarst an' the siege?"

"You already know most of what I know. Kaarst has seized the outposts and blockaded the coast. I escaped on foot, with instructions from King Aras to obtain your assistance."

"Fair enough, but let's clear up on one matter immediately. This ain't Ladu Jovun's work, and it ain't Tim Matthias's. Neither o' them would so much as lift a finger to harm King Aras. Matthias is an Alcatune native by birth, an' Emperor Jovun just fought one war an' ain't keen to start another."

Sendalion tensed once more, just enough for Quentiin to notice. The soldier shifted his glance away for a moment before returning the dwerion's gaze.

"That's a message for the king's ears, not mine. As it stands, I have one objective: end the blockade on Vonku. Everything else is secondary."

"On that we agree, soldier. What's the plan for the three of us?"

"Four," Jolldo said.

Vinsor and Sendalion turned to Jolldo, but Quentiin had stated their number aloud to give the dwerion an opening. He'd suspected this might be coming.

"I never served," Jolldo continued, "but that doesn't mean I'm leavin' my king out in the cold when he needs the help."

Sendalion looked at Quentiin, and the dwerion waved a hand. "He ain't sworn, I know, but I'd say the regulations can go to Malath."

Sendalion paused before nodding. "I suppose they can. We'll need all the help we can get. Let me show you the maps." He withdrew two rolls of parchment from his saddlebag, placing them side by side on the table. The papers crackled as he placed weights to uncurl and hold them in position. One was a detailed portrayal of Vonku and its seaward garrisons, the other a map of Alcatune with Eltern and Sevilin marked.

"Kaarst's primary advantage in taking the outposts was to cripple Aras's means of communication," Sendalion said. "It also restricts supplies into the city, but there are enough resources within Vonku to make it self-sufficient for some time. As a secondary point, we expect Kaarst to use the outposts as staging locations for striking the city, but we have little knowledge as to when that might occur. The admiral's armada is formidable, but he can only stretch himself so thin. The east side will take the brunt of his attack once he launches a seaward assault on the garrison."

"Tell me about these weapons he has," Quentiin said.

"They lay waste to everything in their path. When I was on the walls, I saw them on Kaarst's ship. They are giant tubes of iron from which the admiral can direct a targeted explosive. The blasts shredded one of our ships in a matter of minutes and did considerable damage to the outer garrison."

"Aye, an' as ye already noted, I've seen similar weaponry at work in the North." Quentiin did not understand the elion's devices nearly as well as Tim or Boblin, since he had been unconscious beneath the Fort the first time the explosives were used, and the second time, he had only entered the Battle of the Deathlands after most of the weaponry was detonated. He'd had more exposure to it afterward, including participating in some of the tests Boblin and

Celia conducted with the Patrol. The elions used handheld projectiles that had range as far as one could throw them, but it sounded as if Kaarst had acquired something larger and with more devastating potential.

"The weapons do have limits, though," Sendalion continued. "Once a projectile is fired, it takes time to prepare a second discharge. If my count is accurate, Kaarst has six aboard his flagship. I don't know if the other ships have any, but I speculate they don't. Ordinarily, Kaarst times his shots at intervals so that he always has one of the iron constructs at his disposal."

Vinsor crossed his arms. "So, if one could force his hand into firing all at once, we might gain ourselves several minutes of advantage."

"I've been thinking much the same, assuming someone is crazy enough to draw all of that attention."

"Crazy is Quentiin's middle name," Jolldo said.

"So I've heard, but we aren't on the water yet." Sendalion pointed back to Eltern on the map, positioned north of Vonku on the main road. "Captain Yastlin's first order was to liberate the outposts."

Makes sense. If they took Eltern back, the advantage was two-fold. One, they would liberate the soldiers held there and increase their numbers by a fair amount. Two, they would end the northern blockade and King Aras could begin evacuating the city.

Vinsor grimaced. "I'm all in, but retaking Eltern is a tall order for four of us."

"More dwerions than just Jolldo an' I will answer this call," Quentiin said. "Those who were in the North will come; the Pit provided plenty of trainin' in its own way. That means Yagglem, Briiga, and Vellgo will be with us for sure, an' I expect Herrdra an' Yuulin may join as well."

"An even ten," Sendalion said. "There will be over a hundred corsairs at the outpost, of course. We won't take it by force, but we never expected to. We need to get someone on the inside.

Quentiin grinned at that. "I may have something, at that. D'ye think Kaarst has any dwerions in his fleet?"

* * *

Kaarst had several dwerions in his crew, as a matter of fact. One such dwerion, named Grippla, had just incurred the Admiral's wrath.

"Avast ye!" Kaarst snarled, kicking Grippla to the deck and pointing to a torn mainmast. "Ain't ye ever adjusted a jib before? Because of yer idiocy, we be without steerage, ye worthless boat scum! How d'ye expect us to destroy the garrison if *we can't even point the cannons at it?*"

Grippla struggled to his knees, begging forgiveness, and Kaarst backhanded him across the face. The dwerion went sprawling once more, blood running from his lips.

Kaarst turned to the crew. "What say ye, boys? Ye all be workin' hard here, an' one o' your shipmates went an' snagged the whole thing up! So, what do we do when a mate botches our plans?"

"We keel haul!" the crew shouted in unison.

Kaarst pointed at Grippla. "Aye, we keel haul! Quartermaster!"

"Keel haul! Keel haul!" the corsairs chanted as the quartermaster stepped forward. The big, burly man pressed Grippla to the deck by kneeling on the dwerion's back. He bound the hapless corsair's wrists and feet with a length of twine, then dragged him to a standing position. The assembled corsairs whooped and hollered, eager for the sight of blood. Kaarst also observed a hint of fear in their eyes. Well they should fear, for they knew that if any of them showed sympathy toward Grippla, it would only earn them the same punishment.

"Let's make it happen, boys!" the quartermaster roared. Sunlight glinted off the silver in his teeth. Several crewmembers stepped forward, dragging a long, massive rope between them. Grippla struggled as the corsairs looped the rope around his waist, but he might as well have saved the effort. Led by the quartermaster, the crew hoisted Grippla above their shoulders and walked to the side of the ship.

"Keel haul! Keel haul!" those on deck continued shouting. The quartermaster tossed Grippla over the edge, and the dwerion let out a wail as he crashed into the water.

Kaarst turned from the commotion, leaving the crew to their amusement as he walked to his quarters. He'd been made to keel haul in his time; such was the mark of being a corsair. The rope Grippla had been tied to stretched from one side of the ship to the other. The crewmembers would use it to drag him across the entire underbelly of *Innocent's Blood*. Grippla would be submerged, raked against the ridged boards of the ship's underbelly and across the crusty shells of barnacles lining the hull. Kaarst had plenty of scars on his back from the experience, and Grippla would soon bear some of his own.

When Kaarst placed a hand on his doorknob, he felt his stride waver. Grippla's offense had been a minor one, when it came right down to it—working with the jibs was delicate work, and rife with potential errors. Kaarst had issued a punishment disproportionate with the crime. He was on edge, and not because the siege was at a temporarily standstill. No, much as he loathed to admit it even to himself, Vila Kaarst was scared. A man waited for him in his cabin, one whose presence and assistance Kaarst had concealed from the rest of his crew. He did not quite understand who, or what, the man exactly was; he'd never given a name, and Kaarst had not possessed the willpower to ask. He only thought of the stranger as *him*, a dark and mysterious figure to whom Kaarst owed no small measure of his success.

The admiral glanced behind himself, confirming nobody was watching, and opened his door. He felt his hand tremble as he stepped inside. The noise of the crew's laughter, and of Grippla's screams, cut off behind him. The resulting silence felt leaden and oppressive.

Kaarst's quarters appeared the same as he had left them: maps and charts strewn about, documenting Vonku with intricate detail, along with the position of Kaarst's ships and the assemblage of his men at Eltern and Sevilin. Most of the light came from wicks in lamps on the wall and a window on the far side of the room. His mattress and personal quarters lay in the farthest corner of the room, opposite the window.

Normally, the heat of summer and moisture of the sea hung heavy in this room, but now the faintest of chills passed through Kaarst's quarters, followed by a breeze of no origin, for the windows remained closed. The breath of air caused the maps on the tables to flutter and the lamps to flicker. Indeed, the lamps in the farthest corner of the room guttered out entirely, after which the shadows in their wake rippled with tangible substance. Kaarst smelled a dungeon's musty scent and felt the chill grow stronger as the writhing blackness in the corner coalesced to form the shape of a man in hooded robes. The newcomer kept his hands clasped and face bowed. Kaarst had never seen him eager to show his features, not even when they first met years ago. At the time, the man had lent his services to Kaarst and helped the corsair admiral obtain his coveted cannons. For a time, Kaarst had thought he'd never see the stranger again, but the hooded stranger had reappeared this spring, stating the time was ripe for Kaarst to make good on his debts. Well for this stranger that he had, for by that time Kaarst had resolved to make his move on Vonku, preferably sooner rather than later.

The stranger spoke first. "Would you know, I've never seen someone keel hauled before today?"

"The sea was never your domain, was it? You've been upon it, but you haven't *lived* it. It hasn't molded you as it molded me." Kaarst had dropped the corsair accent, speaking with the same cultured inflection he'd learned in Vonku. He wasn't in front of his crew, and didn't need to follow the pretenses they expected.

"No," the man answered. "I was molded in another fashion entirely."

Kaarst let the response hang. In any other scenario, he might have challenged the validity of such a statement, but not here and not now. He had no desire to know the story behind those words; indeed, he suspected the truth of it might drive him mad.

"How goes the siege?" the stranger asked.

"We've taken the outposts, and the sea is ours." Kaarst stepped toward his charts. "Vonku has an outer wall and an inner wall. While the exterior defenses are indeed formidable, the cannons will eventually get us through. Aras's men have seen our bite, but I doubt they truly understand what they're up against. The inner wall may be another matter, because at that point we'll be fighting in the streets and away from the coast. The cannons will not reach that far, so we'll need other resources."

The stranger waved a hand. "Leave the inner wall to me. Once you get past the outer defenses, I can deliver the rest to you in short order."

"We're almost ready for our next move. The jibs need repair, hence the screams you hear from the top-deck. I expect to be ready by nightfall. We shall attack under cover of darkness so that we can use the cannons to our advantage."

The stranger nodded, hands remaining clasped, face still concealed. "You've done well, Admiral. I'm pleased to see what has become of you since we last parted ways. I expected nothing less of the man I raised to admiralty."

His fear of the stranger notwithstanding, Kaarst could not abide such a statement. He curled his lips. "My *men*, not you, named me Admiral. You might have helped me obtain these cannons, but that was years ago, and the successes I have claimed since are rightfully mine."

He knew one did not incur this man's wrath lightly, but the hooded figure seemed to take little offense at the reply. "Noted, Admiral. Your achievements for yourself should be acknowledged, but do not forget those who stoked your potential in those early days."

"I haven't." *Cannons and ships for a promise; the ability to rule the seas in exchange for a debt I am only too happy to pay.*

The hooded man continued. "I never doubted your willingness to launch an assault on Vonku, and your promise to use these cannons to do so was as much to your benefit as mine. What was more important to me was your guarantee to *wait*—such that I would help you obtain these cannons, but only if you would attack Vonku at an hour and day of my choosing. Tell me, was it hard, Admiral? Once you built your fleet, was it difficult to wait, knowing you had the tools and resources to lay waste to this city, but holding fast until I returned to let you know the time had come?"

Harder than you will ever imagine, dark man. I most certainly did wait, but then I tired of doing so, and resolved to proceed of my accord. You are fortunate your arrival coincided with my decision to move forth, regardless of your desires. Instead of voicing such thoughts, Kaarst smiled. "One does not command a fleet this size without learning the virtue of patience."

The hooded man raised a finger. "A virtue indeed, and one I will ask you to exercise once more. Yes, the blockade is in place and outposts are yours. The matter of repairing the jibs is inconsequential, for I need you to maintain the blockade for one week before proceeding."

Kaarst opened his mouth, but the hooded man continued speaking. "There are matters at work here, Admiral—matters which extend far beyond this city and your quarrel with its ruler. Fear not, when the week is up, you are free to ravage Vonku at your pleasure. However, I have plans of a delicate nature, and the timing of Vonku's fall must be on my schedule."

"Is that so?"

"That is so indeed." The stranger clearly did not intend to explain further, and Kaarst almost told him to go to Malath, but thought better of it. He quite vividly recalled the first time he met this man; there had been a lot of blood. "Very well."

Not for the first time, he wondered what game this man was playing at. The enigmatic stranger had made use of strange, vicious powers to quicken Kaarst's rise among the corsairs of the Rendrivin and Threa oceans, and all for what? So Kaarst could use this fleet to launch an assault on his home city, something Kaarst longed to do in any event?

The shadows in the room shimmered once more, and the lamps flared back to life. The noticeable chill left the room, though that did not prevent Kaarst from shivering. It was too late to wonder if he'd stuck his fist into the redpike's net. He stepped to his window and looked to the west, where the walls of Vonku's outer garrison waited. In the grand scheme of things, he supposed, the delay didn't matter. He'd waited many years to claim his revenge, and he could certainly wait one more week.

10

"*Movin' south.*"

Boblin heard Quentiin's voice, hollow and tinny, emanating through the focusing reservoir in Tim's hand. The stone pulsed with green light. Boblin had yet to figure out how the blasted thing worked. It made sense that Tim, with his innate Lifesource abilities, could use the reservoir, but Boblin was no Advocate. Neither was Quentiin, but where Quentiin had succeeded in using the reservoir Boblin still failed. Tim had explained to him that he needed to maintain a meditative mindset, and Boblin thought it should have been easier for him, given that he used a meditative focus when practicing ailar, but every time he tried, the stone remained a stone. Among their company, only Tim and Celia could successfully use the reservoir, but that was good enough for Boblin. If neither Celia nor Tim were available to communicate back to Quentiin, the company would likely have bigger things to worry about. Boblin had his sword, and he had ailar. He'd leave abstractions of the Lifesource to others.

"Good luck," Tim replied. "Let's speak again at nightfall in three days."

"Aye, laddie." After Quentiin's response, the reservoir winked out. Tim placed the stone in a pouch hanging from a string around his neck. The small company stood in a circle around a campfire upon which logs popped and snapped, sending sparks skyward with a trail of musty smoke. They'd been in the Fertile Lands for two days, having traveled farther into the area than Boblin had ever come before. The last elion outpost, abandoned after the Fort's fall, stood a day behind them.

Strange as it might seem to others, Boblin had never liked the Fertile Lands. They'd always felt like a denial, an illusion of safety, an avoidance of the fact that Zadinn's presence had encroached ever onward. The Fort, at least, had stood tall and strong in the face of adversity, making no concessions, refusing to delude its occupants about the harsh realities waiting outside its walls. Ironically, those same realities had been inverted—instead of the Fertile Lands wasting away to resemble the former North, the new North would grow and thrive to resemble the Fertile Lands.

Boblin turned to Tim. "Quentiin's plan sounds interesting."

"It's *Quentiin*. I wouldn't expect anything less."

"Did you ever meet King Aras when you lived in Vonku?"

Tim chuckled. "Vonku isn't like Galdon. Over one hundred thousand people live there. It's the largest city in Alcatune, and the third-largest in the South. No, I never met King Aras. That being said, he was well liked. No monarch is favored by every one of his subjects, but King Aras probably got as close to it as any ruler could hope."

No monarch is favored by every one of his subjects. Tim's comment made Boblin think of Pellen, and of how every elion in the Fort had admired the aging elion—but no, that wasn't true, was it? Elson and Kaiel Tulak had, for one reason or another, eventually lost respect for their leader. They betrayed his trust, not to mention the trust of Jend Argul and of every other elion in the Fort. Even Pellen Yuzhar had not received universal loyalty from those he led. The Fort had housed little more than three hundred elions, and two out of those three hundred had betrayed their leader. By that math, in a city like Vonku, hundreds of individuals might hate and despise their ruler. Two thousand people, for that matter, lived in Galdon, and Emperor Ladu would not be able to please them all. He already found himself skirting uncertain territory in his dealings with King Aras, and though Aras and Ladu were attempting to do right by their subjects, a man could only make so many calls on divisive issues before making a choice the people he served would disagree with.

And where, Boblin thought, *does that leave me? I'm commander of the Frontier Patrol, and it has grown in numbers since Zadinn's fall.* At the Fort they had all known Jend Argul by name, and vice versa, but even now there were recruits Boblin had only met a handful of times. Many of them were former slaves from the Pit who'd been born into captivity and needed something new to devote their lives to, and there might be some who spoke of Boblin in the same way Tim spoke of King Aras. *Commander Kule means well enough,* they might say, *but he can only do so much when he leads the largest military force in the empire.*

"Don't overexert yourself," Tim said, interrupting Boblin's thoughts. "You look like you're thinking about something especially deep, and I know that taxes your brain."

Boblin shook himself. "I was just thinking of Jend." It was true enough, after a fashion. "Let's go talk to him and discuss our next steps."

They approached the elion warrior, who had taken up watch at the opposite end of the camp, Hugo and Ken beside him. They had been a formidable trio in the days of the Fort, and Boblin was glad to have them with him once more. "How much do we know about the Fertile Lands from here?" Boblin asked.

"Only fragments, sir," Jend replied. The last word sounded odd coming from Jend's mouth; even after a year Boblin wasn't used to the onetime commander addressing him as *sir*. Jend took a parchment from his saddlebag and drew it across the stump of a tree, using the flattened surface as a makeshift tabletop. "I've only traveled beyond our current location a handful of times, all of which were years ago. The waterways of the Pel Delta are constantly shifting, making it difficult and treacherous to navigate."

"It's why the area made such a good hiding place," Hugo noted. "As near as I can tell, we are a day's travel from where the Delta begins—or at least where it began the last time I came this way, eight summers past."

"Our best course is to make notations on the map as we go," Jend said. "Once we hit the waters, we begin making circles, starting small, going broad. A settlement has to leave signs, no matter its size, when it picks up and leaves. We *will* find them, sir."

They could be down there for weeks, and Boblin didn't like losing time, but they could either spend the time searching for the village in the Delta, or spend time searching in the desert for Agrazab. Boblin could guarantee which environment would be more hospitable.

Tim smiled, as if he could hear Boblin's thoughts. The man swore he *couldn't* read minds, but Boblin trusted Advocates about as well as he could use focusing reservoirs. "We could always get lucky," Tim said. "Find them sooner rather than later, right?"

Boblin tore a strip of dried jerky and began chewing. "If it helps pass the time, mate, keep telling yourself that."

* * *

Celia was lying on her cot when her husband opened the flap of their tent from outside. The night air of the Delta floated in, along with a faint wisp of smoke from the fire, as he entered. He sighed, sitting next to her and pulling off his boots. She noticed his sleeves were rolled back, his forearms streaked with dirt, and he had the faint mark of a bruise on his cheek.

"Hanqar wanted to practice," he said by way of explanation. "He should have gone with you. You're the better ailar instructor."

Celia propped herself up on one elbow, smelling Boblin's tangy perspiration. "But you're the one he looks up to."

"How well do you know him?"

"Not very," she said. "He was one of the first in the Pit to take up arms against the malichons after the dwerions saved Quentiin from execution. He was raised there. His mother died giving birth, and his father never identified himself." Concealing heritage was not uncommon in the slave pens; the malichons used any emotional attachment as leverage to cause pain and suffering. Since no father had stepped forward after the fall of Zadinn's citadel, he had most likely died long before.

Boblin ran his fingers through his hair. "What do you think of all this?"

"Better than working on a census."

Boblin *hmph*ed. "Censuses aren't so bad. They serve a useful purpose. The numbers are elegant, and nobody tries to stick a sword in you."

She arched an eyebrow. "Some have taken the adjustment to freedom harder than others. You weren't on the visit to Baarndle's. He frequently forgets who we are, and sometimes even who *he* is. I think he thought we were Zadinn's soldiers coming back to round him up again. It took some time to calm him down, and he cut Ken in the process. There aren't many that suffer as he does, fortunately, but even one is too many."

"Getting cut by Baarndle is still safer than trying to find a portal between our world and Malath."

She leaned forward, voice smoky. "I love it when you talk about dangerous things."

"You're a bad influence."

"Don't deny you enjoy it."

He cupped his palms around her face and kissed her. "Can I ask you something difficult?"

When he tried to draw back, she took his own face in her hands and held it there. "You can ask me anything, any time."

"How often do you think about Ana?"

Ah, she thought. *So that's it. I should have picked up on it sooner.* Ana Teldin had been Celia's protégé, smart and tough. When the Fort fell, Ana had been forced to graduate from training much too early. Everyone became a warrior that day, whether ready or not. Ana later died in the shadows of Malath's Teeth, her throat torn out by a sarchon twenty paces away from Celia. "I think about her nearly every day. She should have been around much longer. She should be here right *now.*"

"We lost two out of every three who tried to find the Army," Boblin said. "If those same odds hold true, only two of us will come back from this one."

Celia shook her head. "There's no reason those numbers should apply now. You're right, Boblin—this *isn't* a census."

He bowed his head and let out a deep sigh. "What would I do without you?"

She kissed his forehead. "You'd be much worse at ailar, for one."

"I don't deny that."

She wrapped her arms around him and drew him onto the cot with her. Outside, Hanqar stood lone watch by the fire, his back to the camp, facing out into the dark of the night with his sword at his side, while above them all, the stars slowly spun.

* * *

Tim wiped his brow as he pushed aside a vine. The Pel Delta was *muggy.* He found it oddly reminiscent of the South, and then reminded himself that they were for all intents and purposes *in* the South. They were at most a day's travel from the Barricade, due north of the country of Childar, west of Alcatune and opposite the Odtune Mountains. Childar had a rich, humid atmosphere. Its groves bore all manner of fruit, and had the Barricade not existed the travelers might be considered in Childar's groves proper right now.

It was slow going through these parts. They'd cut their horses loose near the northern border of the Fertile Lands. The animals knew their way back to Galdon, and they wouldn't be any good in the bogs and mire of the Delta. Tim was half tempted to cut through the thicker undergrowth in front of him with his sword, but he couldn't bring himself to use the blade in such a fashion. It didn't seem proper for a weapon that had once been wielded by the Advocates of old, so he used a hatchet instead. Beside him, Hugo and Ken Rindar did the same, hacking and slashing, while Boblin and Hanqar hung behind, having alternated from the lead position an hour ago. They rotated often enough so no one traveler bore the brunt of labor.

When Tim chopped through a tangle of brush and arrived at a small clearing, he found himself facing Jend and Celia. The two elions, who had been scouting ahead, were taking their respite on a downed tree. They raised their hands in greeting as the rest of the group arrived.

Celia held a stick, marking the ground to show what they had found. "We've scouted the easiest path to the waters of the Delta," she said, placing an *X* near where they had first entered the Lands after leaving the Kaltu Pass. She made similar markings to the east, denoting areas of the Lands that they had either already crossed or were familiar with from their time living at the Fort.

"The nearest waterway is less than a quarter of a league from us," Jend said. "Once we're afloat, we can make much better time." They assumed, as they had when searching the lands beyond the Mountains for the Army of Kah'lash, that the villagers needed to be near a source of water. The Maker knew there was enough water in the Delta to choose from, but the searchers nonetheless improved their chances of finding the village by staying close the streams.

After a quick rest, they followed Celia and Jend down a path the two elions had made. The ground gradually declined and the undergrowth thinned until they found themselves on the bank of a passage that was too wide to be a stream and too narrow to be a river. In the center of the tributary, water swirled around rocks and boulders, indicating a mild but steady current. Beside Tim, Boblin narrowed his eyes, looking at the downed logs along the banks. After a moment, the elion took lengths of thick, sturdy twine out of his knapsack.

"You can use the Lifesource to do this, right?" Boblin asked. "I'd rather not be here for the next half day."

"Technically, yes."

"What do you mean, *technically*?"

"I mean I can use the Lifesource to build a raft, but it won't be any quicker than by hand."

"What good are you?"

"Levitation *was* the first thing I learned," Tim said. "Actually, the very first thing that Nazgar taught me. I can't count opening the Barricade or roasting two malichons in the Fort's dungeons, since during both of those instances I didn't really know what I was doing."

Boblin squatted by the logs. "Okay, tell me what you *can* do."

"I can put the logs into position on the ground, and I can lay other logs on them crosswise. I can even lash them together with the twine you've got there—but that's the same thing any of us would be doing by hand, and therefore it would take the same length of time."

Boblin held up a finger. "You're telling me you can obliterate an entire horde of vrawl with one spell, but you can't build a simple raft?"

"No, I *can* build the raft, just not quicker than you. It doesn't equate to defeating vrawl, in any case. It's much easier to destroy than create, young one."

"Profound words, but words won't make my back less sore, and I'm not any younger than you."

"If it helps, I can sit on the bank and *use* the Lifesource while you do the handiwork."

Boblin handed him a length of rope. "Go kiss a three-legged goat. You'll be partaking in the same misery as the rest of us."

The group set to work, dragging logs from the water, estimating sizes and spaces, and laying them in the river. They started at noon, and by the time dark fell they had made significant progress on two rudimentary rafts. Neither was suitable for extended use, but that was not their objective. They'd be on the waters of the Delta for a week at most. By midmorning of the next day, they were ready to push off. Jend, Hugo, and Ken took one raft, and Tim, Boblin, Celia, and Hanqar the second. They used long aspward poles to steer their crafts away from the banks into the current. Their best guess had them on the Delta's northernmost tributary, which would ultimately join with several other waterways in a growing confluence before reaching Lake Pel, the largest body of water in the Delta. Lake Pel's position had been charted in the Fort's early days, but rarely returned to, and Jend was the only one in the group who had even seen it.

All members of the Patrol had spent enough time in the Fertile Lands to learn rafting and swimming as necessary, and as expected they crossed territory more quickly while rafting. Best of all, the current did most of the work for them.

While the first and second days on the waters passed without incident, Tim turned his thoughts to Agrazab, unconsciously rubbing his thumb on the pommel stone of his sword as he did so. Nazgar had told Tim little about the City of Darkness; Zadinn had been too immediate a threat and too formidable an adversary for Tim and Nazgar to spend time on peripheral matters. Still, the Kyrlod had given him an outline of Agrazab's history.

Uklith had not picked the city in the Western Desert for arbitrary reasons. The City had the singular misfortune to be located where the veil between Malath and the physical realm was thinner than usual. The Demon-Lord had exploited this location, creating a momentary hole in reality to enter Agrazab, where he manifested himself in human form, though he needed to remain in close proximity to the portal to draw on his strength from the underworld. That was why he had required an Advocate, someone he could send east to rule in his stead. In the physical realm Uklith was limited to a fraction of the power that he had in Malath, but with a new servant headed west, holding the last fragments of Zadinn's powers, Tim suspected Uklith would be able open another portal to Malath that allowed him to draw on his full power.

But all these ruminations were secondary to a fundamental fact: in Tim's final battle against Zadinn Kanas, the opponents had found themselves equally matched, neither one possessing a shred of power more or less than his nemesis. This gridlock of equal, opposing strength in the Lifesource resulted in a stalemate that caused the surrounding terrain to reverberate and tear itself apart. In Tim's vision, Uklith was *stronger* than Zadinn, which led him to an unavoidable conclusion: *Uklith was stronger than Zadinn, and Zadinn's powers were equal to mine. Therefore, Uklith is stronger than I.*

Of course, it would have been hubris to assume otherwise. Zadinn had been a man—an extremely powerful man, but still a man, while Uklith was an entity as old as time. He was the Maker's opposite, ruler of the underworld. True, while in human form in the City, his powers had been reduced, and yet he had destroyed three Advocates without any outward indication of exertion.

Tim could not allow himself to get drawn into a direct confrontation with Uklith. If things progressed to that point, the world was lost. His only hope was to catch up to the elion and stop him before he could break the Demon-Lord free. *But what then? If we succeed in stopping the elion, can I really turn my back on the west?* The threat of the Demon-Lord would exist for as long as he remained imprisoned within this realm. If Uklith's current servant failed, he would simply call another.

Not for the first time, Tim wished Nazgar was here. But the Kyrlod had given his life in the Dark Lord's citadel, and Tim had nobody to provide him guidance, nobody to give him the answers. It was not a comforting thought.

When they pulled onto the bank the evening of the third day, Jend called out from ahead of them. The former Commander's raft banked first, Hugo and Ken jumping ashore to pull it in. As the second group arrived Tim saw what had caused Jend to alert them: farther up the bank, right before the undergrowth grew thick again, a cluster of charred logs indicated a former campsite. Tim leapt onto the earthy bank, hand on his sword, as Jend bent over the remains of the campfire. Tim joined him, running his hand over the logs. He felt no heat, so some time must have passed since the site's occupants departed. He tried to make sense of the markings on the ground, but scant evidence remained other than a few sparse scuff-marks and the odd sign of disturbed vegetation. "What do you think?" he asked.

"Scouts," Celia answered. She inspected a scuff mark as if attempting to determine if it constituted a trail or not. "The village moves often, as we already know. It stands to reason they'd send advance groups to determine potential locations beforehand. They still believe they need to be on guard against Zadinn Kanas, and they didn't remain hidden this long without being careful. I'd suspect at any given time they have at least four alternate locations already prepared, each at a different point of the compass. If they need to move quickly, they already have options, and if they find themselves cut off from one or even two directions, they have other places ready."

Jend nodded. "We did much the same at the Fort. The location we fled to in the Pass was but one of several. We always had to be prepared for contingencies."

During his watch that evening, Tim probed into the Delta with the Lifesource, immersing himself in the flora and fauna of the Fertile Lands. The earth had its own heartbeat, a subtle cadence underpinning everything that lived and breathed. In some places it was more noticeable, such as when a deer found itself flushed by a fox. In those instances, the earth's natural beat matched that of both the deer in its panic and the fox in its hunt, a perfect balance between hunter and hunted. In other places the natural beat was far fainter, such as when a yewbark sapling thrust up from the soil, reaching for the sky in increments, soaking in the first minutes of what would be a long, steady life. It would be much the same when that yewbark died in many years, returning to the loam that had given it birth, a final gasp when it gave way and permitted others of its kind to rise. *There is neither good or evil within the Lifesource*, Nazgar had once told Tim. *It is the choices of the men who harness it that make it what it is.*

The following afternoon, the travelers on the two rafts arrived at an intersection of three tributaries, which increased the width and depth of the passage, forming a proper river with a stronger current. They were likely coming closer to Lake Pel, and Tim felt certain their chances of finding the village would increase. He scrutinized the banks, making note of every disturbance in the brush or markings upon the ground, using the Lifesource to sharpen his vision and strengthen his hearing.

As the group traveled, another truth about the Delta became apparent: the Fertile Lands had in many ways been the ideal location for staving off the wastelands of the North during Zadinn's reign, but they were by no means a paradise. As Tim swatted what felt like the hundredth mosquito from his neck, he simultaneously shooed a fly from his wrist. He'd managed to avoid this one, but plenty of flies before it had delivered piercing bites. They came in groups, dancing in with quick, needle-like landings, drawing droplets of blood before retreating.

"Good call on not building Galdon here," he said to Boblin. "Half the residents would have left."

"Or gone mad," the elion replied. "Then again, as of my wedding, a fair share seemed to be going mad anyway."

"You can't blame them, dear," Celia said. "I suspect for most people, even the *thought* of marrying you would cause their sanity to crack."

"I love you, too."

Shortly thereafter, a rushing sound filled Tim's ears and the river picked up speed. *At last, a proper pace, and the breeze might even keep the insects away.* The raft veered toward a bank, but Hanqar pushed them away and re-centered their course. Ahead of them, Hugo performed the same maneuver on the first raft.

"All else aside," Hanqar added to the conversation, "this place is something else, when it gets right down to it. When I was in the Pit, I'd have never thought so much water or green could exist in one place."

"You should visit the South, Hanqar," Tim said. "Have you ever seen the ocean?"

"I have not, but I hear it is majestic."

"It's a sight you'll never forget." *Or the groves of Childar, or the evergreens of the Odtune.* It pulled his thoughts away for a moment, to Quentiin and Aras and the challenges between the kingdoms. *They have to end this dispute. Our two worlds have so much to offer one another, and we can't squander it on border conflicts.*

"What about a waterfall?" Boblin asked. "Have you ever seen one of those?"

"No, sir."

"Well, you're about to." Boblin spun and picked up a pole. "*Move!*"

The raft picked up pace, the swirling current creating tiny eddies beneath the platform's corners. The wooden planks beneath their feet pitched to the side, only righting when Boblin plunged a pole into the depths and kept them on course. Ahead of them, the waters grew frothy and violent. The lead raft, with Jend and the Rindar brothers aboard, tilted at a precarious angle.

They came upon a rock in the middle of the river, and Boblin pushed with the pole one more time, veering them away from the obstruction. The current spun the raft in a half-circle, causing their supplies to heave against the lashings. It was all Tim could do to keep his balance. In the space of seconds, the river had transformed into a winding and dangerous beast, with rocks and logs rising from the water on all sides.

Between Boblin and Hanqar, they could only control so much. A spinning log came up beside them, striking at such an angle that Hanqar lost his pole as well as his balance. He almost tumbled over the side, but Celia grasped his forearm and pulled him to safety. Mist filled the air, and the roar of the rapids drowned out all else. Spray soaked their clothes, the lashings snapped free, and their supplies tumbled over the edge. Tim grasped the strap of his knapsack, barely keeping it aboard.

Ahead of them, Jend's raft disappeared beneath a wall of raging foam. Before Tim or his companions could react, their own raft slammed into a boulder, and that was the end of things. The logs splintered in a shower of wooden fragments, and the jarring impact knocked Tim onto his knees. As he scrambled for purchase on what remained of the slick surface, he looked for the others. Hanqar, almost fully in the water, clung to a splintered log with one hand as the current dragged them along. Boblin had landed on his back and wrapped one wrist through a loose lashing to keep his purchase, and Celia was nowhere to be seen. They slammed into yet another boulder and Hanqar disappeared as the last remnants of the raft disintegrated beneath Tim.

Cold, fresh water flooded his mouth and nostrils as he submerged. Tim waved his arms in a swimmer's stroke, coming back up and breaking the surface, trying to simultaneously tread water and gain his bearings. Beside him, Boblin broke surface, too, only to collide with a pair of broken logs from the raft. The impact sent him back under.

Tim dove, feeling about for his friend, and grasped a fistful of Boblin's tunic. He wrapped his arm around his friend's waist as they slammed into a rock. He used the stone to his advantage, bracing against the obstruction and tearing Boblin free. They surged back to the surface together, wiping their eyes and sputtering water.

"What now?" Boblin shouted above the current's roar.

"We go over," Tim shouted back, for they had reached the waterfall's edge. He felt the current tug at him, as if it had tied a rope around his waist. He surged backward, catching a glimpse of a steep drop set against a sheet of continuously descending water. Then he was spinning, sliding, and falling, out into the open air and toward the turbulent chasm below.

11

Celia had just pulled Hanqar to safety when the next pitch of the raft tossed her over the side. She inadvertently swallowed a gulp of water, tasting the river's muddy silt as she slammed into a rock. Hot pain lanced her side. Celia scrabbled at the obstruction, hoping to pull back above the surface, but the force of the current tore her away. Moving her arms in an upward stroke, she emerged in a gush of water, where waves and froth surged. Celia as she spun her head, trying to catch sight of—

She glimpsed the raft right as it slammed into a boulder. Mist obscured her vision. Celia went under again, and when she forced herself back up a second time, she saw neither the raft nor any of her companions. The river pulled her forward, and she knew it was only a matter of time before she reached the waterfall. The churning world of violence around her indicated the drop was growing closer.

With the roar of water filling her ears, Celia struck out for the bank, hoping to beat the current, but it was no easy task. She used an overhand stroke to make her way forward with as much effort as she could muster, navigating around rocks and other obstacles along the way. Downstream of her, Jend Argul's head bobbed into view. He appeared to be senseless. Celia shifted direction, letting the current carry her forward, passing the scattered pieces of Jend's raft swirling in the current. As she neared Jend, he went under, and she dove beneath the surface to retrieve him. Groping about by feel, she seized his collar and surged back up, tilting Jend so he lay on his back with head above the surface. Next, she veered toward the shore once more, but it was all but impossible to make any progress with the leaden weight of Jend's form dragging them downstream.

As the cusp of the waterfall came into view, she swam with renewed urgency. Behind her, Jend's body snagged to a halt, and she would have uttered a curse if she'd had the breath to do so. She jerked Jend toward her, *hard*, but to no avail. Celia inhaled deeply, diving beneath the water yet again and feeling about to find the source of the obstruction. *There.* The heel of Jend's boot had snagged in a tangle of submerged branches. Celia wiggled Jend's foot, but it remained stubbornly stuck in place. Under other circumstances, freeing him might have been quite easy, but with the continual pull of the current threatening to tear her away, it took half her strength just to hold on to Jend. With the waterfall perilously close, she had little margin for error.

Lungs protesting for air, she surged above the water and took a deep breath. Diving once more, this time she used the momentum of the river to her advantage. Rather than trying to free Jend by pulling crosswise against the current, she shifted his boot *with* it. After a moment, his boot popped free. The river gave its strongest tug yet, and as Celia broke the surface she knew they were almost surely going over this time. She straightened her body and positioned herself at a diagonal angle toward the shore. With luck—

They struck the bank only a handful of paces from where the river shot over the edge. Celia reached out, grasping at twigs, a tuft of grass, *anything*, and at last dragged herself and Jend free from the water. Behind her, the falls descended into a furious white inferno.

Celia rolled over on the bank, facing skyward and sucking in gulps of air. Her muscles burned from the exertion of fighting the current. Though she could hardly move an inch of her waterlogged body, she knew she couldn't remain still for long. Beside her, Jend remained unconscious. She rolled onto her knees and raised up over the former Commander. First, she felt for a pulse, and next she lowered her ear to his chest to detect a breath.

It did not take long for Jend to stir. His eyes fluttered, and he coughed up a stream of water. She rolled him to the side, allowing him to spit out several more mouthfuls before his hacking subsided. Celia closed her eyes in silent thanks; she'd already been more than exhausted, and performing chest compressions would have undone her.

"Where are the others?" Jend asked.

"Gone."

Jend looked at the raging waters, raising a critical eye over the quickly moving current and debris. "We'll have to move downstream. Perhaps others have washed up farther along. What about weapons or supplies—gone as well?"

Celia nodded. "And I *liked* that sword." She did not dwell on what else might lie at the bottom of the waterfall—broken bodies, lost comrades, *Boblin*. No, she couldn't think like that, and besides, she was absolutely confident her husband was still alive. She'd *know* if he wasn't.

Celia stood, adjusting her clothing as best as she could. The Delta's cloying humidity would make it harder to dry off than she would have liked. With Jend behind her, they made their way along the river, eyes open for any sign of their comrades. The bank became too steep for them to remain adjacent to the water, forcing them to higher ground and deeper into the woods. They stayed as close to the ridge as possible, surveying the river where they could, but it was slow going.

After several hundred paces, Celia stopped and held up her fist. Behind her, Jend halted, too. They'd come upon another abandoned campsite. The pair of smoldering logs in the middle of the small space indicated that this camp had been vacated much more recently than the previous one they'd found. "What do you think?" Celia said.

Jend swatted a bug on his neck. The creatures didn't seem to mind if the elions were soaked or not; they bit and stung as always. "The fire is fresh. I think we should wait it out. They might show themselves."

Celia stepped back out of sight of the campfire, keeping low to conceal her presence. "Do you suppose they are in the middle of scouting for a new location?"

Jend remained silent for several long moments. At first Celia thought he was considering the possible reasons for the campsite before responding, but the silence stretched much longer than she expected. Eventually she turned to glance at him.

Jend lay on the ground, eyes closed, unconscious once more. She had not so much as heard him fall. Nor had she caught site of any attacker. But—

His hand remained clamped to his neck, right where he had slapped at the insect. Celia lifted his palm and saw a small dart embedded in his skin. She tensed. *Not an insect at all.* She raised her eyes to survey the surrounding territory. *Get to better cover!*

She felt a stinging sensation in her own neck, and even as she raised her hand to strike it away, she knew she was too late. Celia pulled the dart out and cast it into the underbrush, wondering how much time she had left. She wished once more for her sword, which no doubt lay at the base of the waterfall along with all the other wreckage.

In her final thoughts, she had enough foresight to check Jend's pulse. She felt a mild rush of relief upon feeling his heartbeat. *Whatever this is, it won't kill me.* It was a small consolation, but she'd take it. The wooziness struck her and she tumbled to the ground. The world around her gelled to slow motion. At first her heartbeat quickened, a pace that contradicted the way in which everything else around her seemed to be moving slower. As time stretched, the cadence of her pulse subsided, and her nervous tension began to dissolve in a slow trickle. This wasn't so bad…she was tired, but that was understandable given everything she'd just fought through. She just needed to rest…to close her eyes…

As the world faded into darkness, she used the last of her strength to roll onto her back. She felt the soft earthen floor of the Fertile Lands beneath her, heard the roar of the river nearby, and saw wisps of smoke from the campfire trailing into the sky. Around her, leaves rustled, and she knew people were emerging from the woods, but she couldn't muster the strength to raise back up and see who it might be. She wondered one last time about Boblin. *He has to be alive, right? I'd know if he was gone.* It was the last coherent thought she had before the darkness took her.

* * *

Boblin felt his stomach climb into his throat when his raft flew over the edge of the waterfall. Blinding, roaring spray filled his vision as he descended into a raging, thunderous sheet of white. Below him, a cataclysmic vortex rose to meet him—

He tensed, steeling for impact by tucking knees to chest and wrapping his arms around them in a somersault position, protecting his vitals. When he struck the surface of the river, he submerged, realizing as he did so that he'd be out of luck if the water proved too shallow. He half-expected to feel his bones shatter against the stony bottom, but he felt no contact. Boblin did not know how deep he sank before he managed to spread his arms, swim back to the surface, and tread water. Logs and other wreckage from the raft spun about him.

He struck out for shore. Tim and Hanqar bobbed into view, likewise making for the bank. As the current carried them away from the waterfall's point of impact, the river's violence dissipated, allowing them to swim toward the bank with increasing ease. When his feet touched ground, Boblin seized a knapsack floating beside him and tossed it onto dry ground. He and Tim climbed ashore, and Boblin appraised the soaked rations with a doubtful eye. *Well, soggy bread is better than no bread.*

Boblin looked downstream, scanning the horizon for Celia and the others, but saw no one, and felt an unwelcome tightening of his chest. Celia had vanished from the raft before the rest of the company went over, and he could only hope she'd made it to the bank somewhere above them. Jend's raft was similarly unaccounted for. At the moment that left only Boblin, Hanqar, and Tim.

Farther down the shore, Hanqar had also reached dry ground, and was sorting through more wreckage. Beside the remnants of several more knapsacks, Boblin saw the gleam of a familiar sword. He picked it up and showed it to Tim. "This is Celia's blade. Did you see her after we went over?"

Tim shook his head. "This is a fine mess of things, isn't it?"

Boblin nodded. "Come on. Let's collect what we can and get moving."

They found one of Jend's crossbows in the wreckage, indicating that the first raft had indeed gone over the waterfall. They recovered less than half of their supplies, the remainder either missing or destroyed. As for weapons, they only managed to gather one more crossbow.

"Between the three of us, it would not be a good time to run into a malichon patrol," Boblin said. He narrowed his eyes, seeing that Tim still had his own sword strapped across his back as if nothing were amiss. "You've got to be kidding me. How did you manage to hang onto *that* this entire time? We lost two rafts, but no, you've still got that karfing thing."

"Secrets of the Advocates. You can't separate us from our blades."

"Of course. You couldn't have done that for *my* sword, could you?"

Hanqar joined them, his inspection of the nearby area complete. "If I might suggest, Commander, let's split up to see if we can find the others. I'll climb back to the higher ground above the waterfall and retrace the way we came. Meanwhile, the two of you continue forward along the bank. That way, we can cover two directions at the same time."

"That works as well as anything," Boblin agreed. "When the sun is half past noon, we turn around and meet back at this location." He handed Celia's sword to Hanqar. "Take this. If Tim and I run into trouble, he's just going to show off with *his* sword anyway."

Hanqar took the blade and delivered a crisp salute before turning away, vanishing into the foliage on his way to climb back to the top of the ridge.

"All right," Boblin said, "follow me, Matthias. Just make sure you don't get lost."

"You know I was raised as a woodsman, right?"

"You were raised in the *city*. You told me so. Just humor me; if you get the magic sword, I get to be the guide." Boblin pushed ahead into the foliage, noting that his sense of humor was even more biting than usual. The tightness in his chest had not lessened one bit, and he did not expect it to until he confirmed Celia was alive and well.

The first hour of their search proved fruitless, and Boblin figured they had about the same amount of time left before they needed to turn around and make their way back to reconvene with Hanqar. "Something's been bothering me," he said as they walked. "When we lived in the Fort, we scouted the Lands often enough, even if we only stayed on their periphery. That said, I would presume these villagers scouted *outside* the Lands just as often as we scouted into them. It's the first rule of proper defense: patrol your borders. They would need to know if malichons were getting close, or at least judge the pace at which the Lands were decaying from Zadinn's blight. But Zadinn has been gone for close to two years, and anyone who was familiar with the North would almost certainly recognize the signs of change that have occurred since. Which makes me wonder—"

"Why the villagers haven't left hiding yet," Tim finished the thought. He paused, as if pondering further. "You know, that's a good point. If they'd done any scouting at all in the last two years, they'd have seen plenty of indications Zadinn no longer held sway."

"What do you suppose that means? They never scouted?" *No, that can't be right. They* had *to have scouted.*

"Unlikely," Tim said. "Look at that." He pointed toward a break in the trees ahead.

Boblin saw what Tim had seen and fell silent, to a defensive posture as he advanced. He moved lightly, aware of every leaf and twig on the ground, allowing himself to blend into the background of the woods. This was the way of the elion scout, merging into the surroundings to keep one's presence unknown. Tim followed suit, though he did not move quite as adeptly as Boblin. *Still,* Boblin thought, *he's not bad for a man.*

At the edge of the trees, Boblin lowered into a squat. In the middle of the clearing, a dozen tall poles stood in a circle, each painted white. This unnatural hue created a sharp contrast to the greenery of the surrounding vegetation. Even more shocking and out of place were the bleached white skulls mounted on the poles. A mound of ashes had been left in the center of the circle. From this distance Boblin could see they were many hours, or even days, cold. Around the bases of the poles, the passing of many feet had pounded the dirt floor of the clearing flat.

Beside Boblin, Tim loosened his sword. Boblin saw the pommel stone glowing, a tiny indication that Tim held the Lifesource.

"Should we check it out?" Tim asked.

Boblin nodded, rising and stepping into the clearing. The site was obviously abandoned, the surrounding forest empty. Though he sensed no peril, he was not foolish enough to think this precluded the possibility of danger. *The Fertile Lands are seeming less and less welcome, if I do say so myself.*

Upon closer inspection, the white painted poles also bore brownish-red streaks of dried blood. The pile of ashes in the center of the site revealed the charred remains of human skeletons among the logs.

"I'll be honest with you," Tim said. "I thought you elions were crazy for sheltering in the Pass all those years, but I'm now convinced you were the North's saner residents."

"You have no idea."

"This was a sacrifice of some sort," Tim said, kneeling. "But for what?"

Boblin turned in a circle, scanning the site as well as the surrounding foliage. The movement of a bobbing branch caused him to twitch, but it was only a squirrel hopping from one tree to the next, oblivious to the brutal scene near its nest.

A moment later, Tim tensed. "Someone's coming."

The Lifesource had alerted Tim first, but only a second after he spoke Boblin also heard the telltale *crack* of underbrush. Whoever it was moved quietly enough, but they were drawing close. From the campfire Boblin picked up the sharpest stick he could find. It was crude and rudimentary, but it would do in a pinch. Side by side, he and Tim started to back away from the camp.

He recognized his mistake a second after he placed his foot upon a trampled swath of grass and felt the noticeable lack of resistance from the ground underneath. Without further warning, the false flooring gave way and the two companions tumbled into the pit below.

* * *

Her head *hurt*.

Celia opened her eyes. The resulting light stabbed into her retinas, causing the pain in her skull to increase tenfold. Wincing, she squeezed her lids back shut and reached out with her other senses instead, trying to gather as much information as she could about her situation. She could feel her hands and feet tied around a thin pole. From the way she bounced up and down, she suspected two of her captors were walking in single file, sapling held on their shoulders, Celia dangling between the two like a prize catch from the day's hunt. In addition to the pounding pain inside her head, she felt an uncomfortable scraping sensation as her wrists and ankles chafed against the bonds holding her prisoner.

She risked opening her eyes a second time, slowly and incrementally, until she adjusted to the light enough to see without pain overwhelming her. Her captors remained mostly silent, save for the sound of their footsteps and labored breathing as they moved through the forest. She swayed to the left, bumping against Jend Argul, who was tied to a pole as well.

She worked her slightly swollen tongue around the inside of her mouth. It had been some time since she'd consumed any water other than unintentional gulps after going overboard into the river. The earthen scent of loam filled her nostrils, along with the faint tang of blood. She did not enjoy thinking on what *that* foreboded, but didn't find it unsurprising. Those with peaceful intentions did not knock out unsuspecting travelers and tie them to aspward saplings.

The pole she was lashed to was an aspward sapling. Her back occasionally struck the ground as those carrying the pole walked through the forest. Their captors had ash smeared upon their bodies, likely to create camouflage so they could blend more easily into the shadows of the Fertile Lands. She twisted her head to glance at the man carrying the rear of the pole and saw a red bar of blood streaked across his forehead. *So that's where the smell comes from.*

She looked at Jend Argul on the second aspward limb beside her. The elion met her eyes with his, raising an eyebrow, and she responded with a tiny nod, telling him all he needed to know: she was conscious, she understood the situation, and she was ready to fight as soon as possible.

She rotated her head in each direction to count what they were up against.

Two people carried Celia's pole, two carried Jend's, and two more walked at the front and at the back of the party. All had a streak of red on their foreheads. *So it's eight against two—not bad, all things considered. I've faced worse odds.* Of course, she'd need to address the matter of obtaining a weapon from her kidnappers. The man carrying the head of her pole was smaller and leaner than the rest, so she selected him as her most obvious target. He wore a long, dark sword at his belt. At some point she anticipated their captors would set down the poles, either to rest or to move her and Jend to another spot. That would be her opportunity. While most prisoners' natural inclination would be to loosen their bonds, Celia let them be, planning to use them to her advantage. The rope binding her wrists was tied in a solid knot, and any efforts to free herself would be futile and exhausting. Better to use the rope as a weapon: she could spin her captor into a headlock, wrap her arms around his neck and press the knot into his jugular, causing unconsciousness. At that point, his weapon would be hers.

Jend, she surmised, would go for the sword belonging to the woman carrying the base of his pole. Celia considered if there would be a possibility of taking hostages for leverage, but decided this would present only a temporary advantage. It would cause the others to hesitate, but in the end she suspected these people would gladly cut their comrades down if necessary.

They soon emerged from the brush into space that had much less undergrowth and more room to move around. The massive trunks of redbark trees rose on all sides of them, reaching overhead and forming a canopy that blocked most of the sunlight and left the forest floor in shade. Above her, wooden bridges stretched from one tree to the next, some ending in platforms that wrapped around the uppermost portion of a redbark's trunk. She spotted archers on the platforms, sentries patrolling the grounds, and gritted her teeth in frustration. She'd seen a steadily increasing number of villagers—too many to guess at, but she counted at least twenty on the forest floor and figured there were at least the same number on the walkways above. And those were just the ones she could see. A quarter hour ago, the odds had been favorable at eight against two, but not anymore.

Their captors carried them to what could only be the settlement's center, an enormous redbark with a wide platform forty feet in the air. Before them, Hugo and Ken Rindar sat with backs lashed against the massive tree, hands and feet bound together, watching the newcomers arrive while a sentry stood guard. Without a word, their captors dumped Jend and Celia on the ground next to Hugo and Ken.

"Where did you find them?" the sentry asked, teeth showing as he spoke. He kept his eyes narrow, and like the rest he bore the same red streak of blood on his forehead. Celia thought of Ladu's comments regarding possession and undead and wondered, for an instant, if the blood would burn when she touched it.

"Near the riverbank," the man at the head of Celia's pole answered. "Same place as the first two."

The sentry leaned over Celia, clamped a hand on her jaw, and twisted her face to look at him. "How many of you are there?" His hot, rank breath assailed her nostrils.

Celia said nothing, steeling herself to resist further questioning. Torture resistance was a regular part of Patrol training, although not an aspect she enjoyed. Still, it had been provided for the sole purpose of enduring a situation such as this.

"I didn't think so," the sentry said. "Your friends are just as quiet. Still, it will make it that much more enjoyable once you start screaming."

As if on cue, another pair of villagers approached, pushing Hanqar between them. It appeared that he, at the very least, had managed to land a few blows before they took him: one of his captors had a cut along the side of his jaw, and the other had a blackened eye. As for Hanqar, his nose had been thoroughly bloodied. The sentries shoved the elion onto his knees.

"It's been a long time since we saw anyone other than Keldurians," one of the women said.

Keldurians? The word meant nothing to Celia, though she could make a few educated guesses. She and her fellow prisoners had clearly been brought into a community of sorts, albeit one that appeared to have little in the way of peaceful intentions. One might have thought at first that they'd been captured only as a precaution, a way for the villagers to determine the strangers' intentions, but innocent refugees didn't paint their foreheads with blood. Zadinn's journal had only spoken of one village in the Fertile Lands, but the woman's comment indicated there were at least two communities in this wilderness. *Which begs the question, who has captured us, and who are the Keldurians?*

Another sentry approached the group, hailing his companions. "Taazvin sends word," he said. "We are to prepare the prisoners for trial."

Celia spoke for the first time. "Trial for what?"

The messenger turned to face them. Like the rest, he had a smear of blood upon his forehead. "For the murder of Zadinn Kanas."

* * *

Tim landed on his left shoulder, holding his sword away from his body to prevent impaling himself on his own blade. A jarring pain shot through his shoulder as he struck the dirt of the pit floor. Boblin landed a few feet away, uttering one of his telltale curses.

Through the Lifesource, Tim counted six distinct individuals moving toward them from above. He rolled from his fall back into a standing position, hand wrapped around the hilt of his blade. He filled himself with the Lifesource but did not infuse the blade with any power yet. Best to let this scenario play for a moment before showing his hand.

"I should have seen this coming," Boblin said. "Don't ever let me talk us into investigating any more abandoned sacrificial campsites. It only stands to reason they'd have pits for captives."

Tim held his sword in the en garde position, scanning the upper edges of the pit for any sign of their enemy. "Lessons for the future."

"Are they going to show themselves?"

"I'd say they will pretty soon."

As soon as Tim spoke, a man came into view above them, covered in camouflaging ash, with a red smear across his forehead. *An indication of rank, perhaps?* Upon seeing Tim wielding a sword at the bottom of the pit, the stranger lifted a long reed to his mouth. Tim caught a glimpse of a black-tipped dart at the end of the tube.

Boblin saw it, too, and sucked in his breath. "That can't be good. It's either going to knock you out or turn you into a lizard."

"Or just kill me."

"That, too."

Tim did not have enough room to maneuver away from the shot. The man puffed his cheeks and blew through the reed. Tim felt a sharp sting in his neck and pulled the dart free, casting it to the earthen floor. Above them, the man lowered the reed and drew a second dart from a pouch at his belt.

Tim began to feel woozy. A telltale numbing sensation started spreading from where the dart had struck his neck, into the rest of his body. His legs wobbled, and he fell over. "I'm going with knocking me out," he said.

"How long do you have left?"

"I'd say a count of thirty." Tim pointed to the figure above them as the man fit the second dart into the reed. "You've got thirty-five."

"Please tell me Nazgar taught you how to counteract poison."

"That would be healing, something I never learned."

"That's *great*."

"He did teach me something else."

"What's that?"

The man above them lifted the pipe to his lips and blew.

"You're not going to like it," Tim said as the dart sprouted in Boblin's neck. Boblin brushed it away. Above them, the other people gathered around the edge of the pit, waiting for their captives to pass out.

Boblin fell onto his knees beside Tim, pupils dilating as the poison took hold. "Any time, Tim."

Tim waited for the darkness to take near-complete hold. His sword slipped from nerveless fingers. He had no idea if this would work, and it wouldn't do for him to try *too* soon. He wanted to be on the cusp of unconsciousness—

Just before oblivion struck, he reached deep within himself and brought the Lifesource forward. He *pushed*, sending a spike of pain along every one of his nerve endings. His back arched and spasmed. He avoided screaming out-right but could not prevent a guttural grunt from escaping his lungs.

Tim's eyes flew open, bringing him to a state of full wakefulness as agony blazed through his limbs. He allowed it to course through his body for a count of five, and then, assured he would not lapse back into sleep, he clapped a hand on Boblin's shoulder. The elion had keeled over, eyelids closed, oblivious to all around him. Drawing on the Lifesource, Tim sent a similar jolt of pain into his friend. Boblin went rigid, his back arching as Tim's had, and let out a cry. His eyes snapped open, irises wide, and his hair stood on end.

"I said you wouldn't like it," Tim said.

He had to act quickly. Above them, their captors reacted in startled surprise, unsure of why their tactics had failed. The first man was already lifting the reed back to his mouth. Tim waved a hand, using the Lifesource to jerk the man over the edge and into the pit. At the same time, Tim leapt upward, using the Lifesource to boost himself out of the pit.

Below him, Boblin was in motion, too. As their captor landed on the floor of the pit, the elion spun, knocking the reed from the man's hands. Boblin next used his leverage to spin the man into an arm-bar hold and pin him to the earthen floor of their small prison.

Tim landed between two of their kidnappers. Though nowhere near as proficient as Boblin in ailar, he still knew some things. He elbowed the first man in the ribs and aimed a kick at the back of his knees, causing the man's legs to buckle and sending him into the pit as well. Tim turned to the second man, who had drawn his sword and was in the act of striking. Tim summoned his blade, which flew up from the floor of the pit and into his open palm in time for him to block the attack. Tim's opponent looked at him in shock as the steel of their blades clanged.

On the far side of the pit, one of the last two woodsmen placed a reed into his mouth and blew a projectile toward Tim. Tim spun underneath the arm of his current opponent, ramming his shoulder into the man's body and knocking him into the path of the incoming dart. The man staggered as the projectile hit him. Tim waved his hand yet again, and with the power of the Lifesource knocked the second dart-blower into the pit.

"Not so fast!" Boblin cried out from below. "I've got three of them! Slow it down a bit!" In spite of his comments, the elion had the situation well in hand. His first opponent was already unconscious, and the second was thoroughly incapacitated in a corner of the pit. When the third attacker tumbled in, Boblin merely took it in stride, closing the distance and pulling the weapon from the man's hand.

Tim's current opponent fell over as the poison took hold. Their last attacker, seeing his company defeated, turned and ran for the woods. Unwilling to let him raise an alarm, Tim took up pursuit, dodging to the far side of the pit and giving chase. The soft, earthen floor of the Fertile Lands tore in furrows under his feet as he ran from the clearing and into the thicker vegetation.

Ahead of him, the man dodged tree trunks and branches, moving through the undergrowth, hoping to minimize his profile as a target. Tim reached out with the Lifesource. If he could maintain line of sight for long enough, he should be able to—

There. He snagged the man's ankle with invisible cords, bringing his captive crashing to the ground. Tim was reminded of the time he had fled from the Hunter in the Korlan Forest. In that situation, the positions had been reversed, for Tim had been the one running and the Hunter had caused him to fall. Of course, that particular scenario ended with Tim overpowering the Hunter, so he moved forward carefully, not allowing himself to make a similar mistake by underestimating his own captive.

The man spun and scooted backward, reaching for the sword at his waist. Tim flicked his wrist and the blade flew a dozen paces away, out of reach. Vines curled up from the ground, holding the prisoner in place. "Who are you?" Tim asked.

"He won't talk," a new voice said. "They're too zealous for that."

Tim turned and saw another man, lying on the forest floor where Tim's captive's sword had landed. This man, whose hands and feet were bound, struggled into a sitting position and inched toward the blade. "A little help, perhaps?"

"Don't move," Tim said. The man did indeed stop, raising his bound hands in a gesture of appeal. Unlike the woodsmen who had attacked Tim and Boblin in the pit, this man did not have ashes smeared on his body or a red smear on his forehead. He wore a leather jerkin and sturdy trousers.

"Relax, friend," the man said. "As a starting point, I'd hazard to say we have a common enemy. At the very least, I've seen some of our skills, so rest assured I would not be foolish enough to take up arms against you."

Tim's captive eyed Tim and the bound man with a look of pure loathing. When Tim glanced at him, the man spat on the dirt at Tim's feet.

"I don't spit, either," the new man offered.

"Who are you?" Tim asked.

"Wurit Deslin," the man said. "I'm from the village of Keldur. The unbecoming gentleman in front of you is one of Taazvin's followers. They aren't an agreeable sort, and they've made a practice of killing my friends and family."

"Who is Taazvin?"

"It's a long story. Suffice it to say one of our former villagers took it into his head to worship something very evil, and his followers are the result."

"Is he a follower of Zadinn Kanas?" Tim asked.

Wurit scoffed. "He actually imagines himself Zadinn's equal, though from what I hear, that's far from the truth. No, Taazvin claims his god is the one who sent Zadinn forth."

Tim squatted beside the ash-streaked man. The prisoner bared his teeth and lunged forward. Tim pulled back from the man's snapping jaws as his incisors closed inches from Tim's forearm. He smelled rotting breath. The man struggled against the vines wrapping him, but they held him firmly in place.

"They bite, too," Wurit said. "Usually they're kind enough to kill you before they start *that* part."

Tim thought of the rotten smell on the man's breath and his stomach twisted. *Human flesh?* "For what it's worth, Taazvin's claim about his master is true." He returned to stand before Wurit, picked up the sword and leveled it at him. Wurit shied back, wincing as the blade passed close to his skin, but Tim only used it to slice through the bonds around the man's wrist.

"Here you go," Tim said. He flipped the sword in in his hand and passed it to Wurit, hilt first. "Do you know where Taazvin's people are?"

"They're how I ended up like this." Wurit sawed through the ropes around his ankles. "Taazvin's people move often, just as we do. It's the best way to remain concealed in the Delta. I'd been tracking their village for some time, and eventually found it. I was on my way back to alert Keldur when they caught me. I think you kept me out of their bellies, and for that I'm quite grateful."

"Can you take us there?"

"Just you and me?"

Tim nodded toward the clearing. "No, I've got a friend with me, too."

Wurit gave him a long look. "I don't think a third person will make a difference."

"Well, I have a hunch that at least three or four of our friends are also in the village, so that doubles our numbers."

Wurit shook his head as he stood. "I'm afraid you're crazy, but I *do* owe you. Yes, I'll point you in the right direction. It would be better if I returned to Keldur. I'm not abandoning you. I can bring back a fair number of my fellow villagers to help. Trust me, you'll need it."

Tim took the man's proffered hand and shook it. "I suppose that will do."

"Just so you're aware," Wurit said, "you'll be fighting against a village of a hundred lunatics until I bring reinforcements."

"We'll make do."

12

Celia gritted her teeth against the pain as a villager hauled her up the side of the tree by a noose wrapped about her waist. The man stood on the platform above her, pulling the rope hand over hand. At the top, Jend already lay on the platform, while Hanqar and the Rindar brothers waited their turn below.

The platform was at least fifty yards in diameter, encircling the entire tree, supported by struts running to the ground. When Celia reached the top, where a trapdoor provided access, the man with the rope grabbed her by her tunic and pulled her through. He dropped her onto the platform beside Jend.

In the center of the large area a space had been cleared, with a semicircle of five white poles erected adjacent to a rectangular dais. Behind her, the man proceeded to drag Ken upward. Another pair of sentries watched over the elion prisoners. Celia kept her bound hands against her back, one clenched into a fist to conceal the rock she'd picked up as her captors dragged her across the forest floor.

Once all five elions were on the platform, the villagers hoisted them to their feet and marched them toward the white poles. Around them, preparations were under way as a separate group of villagers brought logs and tinder up from the ground. The lead sentry tied each of the elions to a separate pole, facing the center of the semicircle. Into this space the villagers deposited the firewood they'd gathered, building a large pyre on an iron base. Celia did not like the looks of that at all. She rolled her shoulders and flexed her limbs, doing her best to keep the blood flowing so that she would be ready to move when necessary. She slipped her rock between thumb and forefinger and sawed it against her bonds, going slow, stopping every time a villager came near. It wouldn't do to have them spot her actions and raise an alarm.

The pyre complete, their captors next placed lighted torches in iron baskets, creating a ring of sconces around the group. As the dancing torchlight stood out against the fading dusk, a villager tossed his torch onto the firewood. As the kindling leapt ablaze, Celia and the rest winced from the searing heat. Smoke wafted into Celia's eyes, and she blinked to clear them.

"Commander," she said to Jend, using his former title to avoid actual names. The less the villagers knew about them, the better. "Be ready." She resumed slicing he ropes around her wrists.

"How much time?"

"Soon. Perhaps a quarter hour."

Jend passed the message to Hanqar, who sent it down the line to the other two. Celia assessed the crowd assembling before them, looking for weak points to attack first. Once the villagers had gathered into uneven rows, their conversations increased to a steady buzz. There were some striking similarities between these people and the strangers that had attacked her and Boblin's wedding. While not *quite* as feral as those in Galdon, these villagers nonetheless had an air of savagery about them. The ones who had captured her and the other elions were by far the most well-kept, but plenty of the rest in the crowd had neglected to properly care for themselves. They were unwashed and they stank, as if they cared for little other than the singular purpose that united them.

To her left, twelve robed figures appeared, mounting the platform that stood beside the prisoners. The crowd fell quiet as the twelve took their places on the rectangular dais and stood facing outward.

"Things appear to be moving forward," Ken murmured. "Do you suppose you could be ready any quicker?"

"I'm working on it," Celia said, voice terse.

Once the buzz of conversation ceased, a man in the center of the dais stepped forward and lowered his hood. He was young man of nineteen or twenty, with blond hair, piercing eyes, and the telltale bar of dried blood across his forehead. The man looked over the prisoners, eyes fanatical, and raised his hands. The villagers faced him intently, hanging on his every move.

"Name yourselves, trespassers," the blond man said to the elions. "I, Taazvin, bid you speak in the name of Uklith."

Well, that seals any doubts I might have had about their affiliation. None of the elions responded, and for the second time that day, Celia steeled herself to resist any unpleasant means of questioning that might await them. Surprisingly, Taazvin dismissed their disobedience with no more than a wave of his hand. "Fear not, my friends. It is your choice whether or not to witness on your behalf. Uklith gives all a fair chance to serve him, and we shall let it be known you rejected your opportunity to do so." He turned back to the crowd. "We found the unbelievers on the banks of our river, but they are not from Keldur. They come from outside, from the wastelands of our master's Advocate. It is they who conspired to rebel against the Dark Lord Kanas, and though Kanas strayed far from perfection, he was still Uklith's advocate. A crime against him is a crime against our god."

The crowd rustled at his words. A villager at the front broke forward toward the elions, pulling a dagger from his robes, but a guard restrained him.

Taazvin smiled. "Uklith appreciates your ardor, Ildor, but we must wait to dispense justice. Tell me, outsiders, do you have any defense? Do you claim innocence, or guilt?"

Celia spoke for the first time. "I'd hardly associate the notion of guilt with overthrowing Zadinn Kanas."

The villagers rustled once more, and Taazvin held out a hand. "So be it. Note that the unbelievers have come into our midst and refused to give witness. Let us proceed with the trial, and after that, the judgment."

* * *

As night fell, the forest around Tim and Boblin grew darker. They followed the trail Wurit had set them on before departing, promising to return with assistance from Keldur. Tim held his blade, keeping it dim to avoid giving away their presence. Boblin had armed himself with a sword and crossbow procured from their former captors. Side by side, they advanced beneath the shadows of the canopy, wary for sign of their enemy.

Every so often, they came across signs of others: a trampled swathe of grass here, a footprint there. They'd found lapel pins from Jend and Celia on the ground. Tim suspected the elions were bound with rope, but that wouldn't have stopped them from tearing the pins off with their teeth and leaving them to mark their passing. Tim not only assumed the rest of the party had been taken—he went so far as to *hope* they had been, because for one, it would mean their group would reunite shortly, and for another, he'd rather walk into a village of zealots knowing he was on the right trail.

He heard a steady *thump* from within the woods. At first, he dismissed it as either his imagination or wildlife—perhaps a grouse—but when the noise grew in volume and cadence, he and Boblin exchanged a glance.

"Perhaps Taazvin's musically inclined," Boblin murmured.

In any case, the sound meant they were drawing close. Tim steeled himself, reaching out through the Lifesource to see if they were coming near any sentries yet. He and Boblin continued following the trail, placing their footsteps with increased caution, muscles loose and ready to fight. Wurit had told them that Taazvin and his followers lived in the trees, an oddity related to Taazvin's desire to worship the setting sun—west, toward Uklith's city.

Soon Tim saw lights flickering in the distance. The trail in front of them widened, changing from a rugged route through underbrush to a more readily identifiable path. Here the trees grew farther apart, making Tim uneasy about how visible their subsequent approach might be to any guards. The lights he had spotted were torches in the treetops. Tim could see the first platform in the redbarks, not a hundred paces away.

The Lifesource flared with sudden, impending danger as a pair of branches rustled above them. Tim dove to one side, Boblin to the other, right before a quivering arrow landed in the loam where they'd been standing. *Apparently, the villagers are opting for a more lethal form of defense than darts.* Tim tracked the branches, looking for their assailant, but Boblin was ahead of him. The elion's crossbow twanged and the dark shape of a sentry's body fell from its perch, twigs around it snapping, and landed in a crumpled heap.

"Nice shooting," Tim said.

They resumed their progress, Tim keeping his senses on alert as they made their way to the tree with the first platform. There, a ladder of studded pegs in the redbark's trunk led into the heights of the village. Tim climbed first, Boblin standing guard on the forest floor below him.

When Tim reached the top, he nearly bumped into an ash-smeared villager. The man, clearly another sentry, had a longbow strapped across his back. Tim did not allow him any time to react. By the time the man's eyes widened in surprise at seeing him, Tim had driven his blade into the man's chest. As he lowered the sentry's body to the floor, Boblin reached the top of the platform behind him.

The companions appraised a bridge leading across the gap between their tree and the next, surveying the scene to ensure the way was clear. In the far distance, they saw a bonfire at the center of the aerial village with a mass of shapes gathered around it. They crossed the bridge to a new platform without incident, but after making their way to a third tree, they stopped upon seeing a pair of sentries entering the platform from a bridge connecting to the next tree. Tim and Boblin ducked behind the cover of the redbark's trunk, keeping low.

"Did you hear what Taazvin said?" one of the guards asked as they neared Tim and Boblin's hiding spot. "These people aren't Keldurians. They're *outsiders*."

The second guard made a sound of disgust. "Keldurians or not, I could care less. They all burn the same."

"Aye, that they do."

Boblin spun around the tree, crossbow leveled toward the guards. They stopped in their tracks, and one man's hand went for his sword. "Don't," Boblin said, and the man stopped.

"Tell us about this burning," Tim said. "Has it started?" The sentries remained silent.

"Fine," Boblin said, and pulled the trigger. The first man dropped. The second reached to draw his own arrow, but Boblin had already plucked a knife from his belt and whipped it through the air. The dagger landed between the second guard's eyes and he fell backward, toppling from the ledge.

"Come on," Boblin said to Tim. "I think we need to hurry."

Tim glanced toward the bonfire, which he could see more clearly. It was a broad iron fire pit at the center of a large platform, upon which stood a crowd facing a semicircle of five white poles. He heard chanting, accompanied by the sound of beating drums. "Yes. I think we'd better."

* * *

The trial was a sham, not that Celia expected anything different. Zealots rarely concerned themselves with facts. This "trial" was simply one of their many delusions, a way for the community to convince themselves that they still clung to the norms of a civilized society. However, she had little time to focus on the philosophical aspects of religious fundamentalism; as Taazvin listed the many transgressions for which the five elions deserved to be burned, she focused her energy on freeing herself from her bonds. Soon enough, the ropes fell free. She held them in place with her fingers to retain the appearance of still being a prisoner. *An illusion of captivity to complement the illusion of a trial,* she thought. *How poetic.*

Once freed, she bided her time, waiting for the proceedings to finish, listening to Taazvin's litany of charges.

"Not only did these people conspire to overthrow Kanas—already a crime deserving of death—they succeeded!" The man said. "Uklith showed me a vision of their treachery. They bathed in the blood of our allies, and showed the ultimate hubris in raising an emperor of their own. And now they have the audacity to come *here*—to enter our domain, to defile us with their unholy presence!"

The crowd surged, a tidal wave waiting to descend, and Taazvin raised his hands to hold them still. "Yet all individuals serve Uklith's design, even if they know it not. The Demon-Lord delivered these elions into our hands, where they will not only receive his judgment but also escalate his release. Lord Kanas's downfall was Uklith's triumph, and our master grows stronger than ever. He is on the cusp of breaking free, and when he does, he shall cover the land in his glory, rewarding the faithful and punishing the faithless!" He looked over the crowd. "What does Uklith demand, my followers?"

"Blood!" they shouted.

"And who gives it to him?"

"We do!"

"It is so, my people! These traitors shall pay for their sins with their lives, and thus the blood of their sacrifice shall be one more step in weakening the shackles holding the Demon-Lord!"

Taazvin drew a knife from his robes. He ran the blade across his palm, clenched his fist, and held his hand high. Dancing flames lit his manic expression, and his eyes glinted with reflected torchlight. Bright red droplets of blood ran through his knuckles, splashing onto the wooden platform one at a time.

In a single, uniform motion, the assembled crowd pulled daggers from their belts and ran the blades across their palms as Taazvin had. They raised their fists, hands running red.

"Blood! Blood! Blood!"

Taazvin faced the prisoners, eyes burning, teeth glistening. "Your time has come. Your judgment is at hand." He opened his palm and drew it across his forehead, adding to the existing smear of blood. "Let the burning begin."

* * *

Overhead, Tim and Boblin stood in the shadows of another platform, watching the proceedings below. A pair of dead sentries lay behind the two friends; they'd dispatched the guards before moving into the position of their new vantage point.

Celia and the other four elions, bound to the semicircle of white stakes, faced a raging fire. Even from this high, Tim could feel waves of heat rolling against his skin. Down there it had to be much worse, and he hoped the elions were holding out okay.

They'd listened to Taazvin preach about Uklith. As the man spoke, his motions grew more frantic, his tone more fervent, and he pulled the crowd right along with him. "You know," Boblin said, "I always felt we needed more community events at the Fort—healthy, fun activities. We could have taken a page from Taazvin's book, I think. He knows how to keep a group engaged."

"What do you suppose the smart play is?"

Boblin hoisted the crossbow. "I'm considering just shooting him."

Tim took a quick look over the group. "Wurit said Taazvin had over a hundred followers, and I'd guess half of them are down there."

"How long before our friend arrives with reinforcements?"

Tim shook his head. "Too long. Our friends will be nice and crispy by that time."

Boblin pursed his lips. "Fine. You take the big crowd on the far side of the fire. I'll take the small one on the raised platform."

"That works for me. What about Celia and the rest?"

"I'm not worried. She's already free."

Tim narrowed his eyes, looking at the five elions. "They look fairly well tied up to me."

"Trust me. She's free."

"Okay." Tim peered down and his stomach gave a momentary lurch. Their platform hung a good twenty feet above the next, and forty feet above the ground. A short gap separated the two structures—nothing they couldn't cross with a healthy jump, but still...

"You never got over your fear of heights, did you?" Boblin asked.

"Neither did you."

"No, I didn't."

Below them, Taazvin had stirred the crowd into a frenzy. They had their fists raised in the air, chanting as a set of robed figures stepped down from the platform and made their way toward the captives.

"I think that's our signal," Boblin said.

In a single smooth motion, the two comrades stood up and vaulted over the ledge.

* * *

Celia waited for the robed figures to cross the distance between them. As one came to her side, she saw his robes shift, revealing a sword's hilt protruding near his belt. Good, she could make use of the weapon. The man reached for her, and—

Now! Celia flung the loose cords away and jumped forward, catching the man's wrist and spinning him around to reverse their positions. Moving behind him, she drew his sword and held it across his neck, using his body as a shield.

In front of her, the robed executioners paused in the act of drawing their weapons. "Back!" Celia ordered. Beside her, the flames of the raging bonfire crackled, casting the entire confrontation in an angry light. For a few tense moments, the only sound was the snapping of burning logs. She checked her periphery. Only a handful of seconds had elapsed since she made her move. The assembled villagers had been in the act of coming forward when Celia attacked, but they, like the robed figures on the platform, stood in tense uncertainty.

This place is a lit fuse, ready to explode. Celia knew she had to choose her next move carefully. There were only two people on this platform who could dictate what happened next: Taazvin, who had control of the crowd, and herself. Whichever of them took command in the next handful of heartbeats would tip the balance of power in their favor, and she did not think it would take Taazvin long to decide Celia's sole prisoner was expendable. She pressed forward, moving as close to Jend as possible, and flung her captive toward the bonfire. The man stumbled away in a flutter of robes, and Celia slashed the ropes holding Jend prisoner.

"Kill them!" Taazvin screeched. Everything erupted into chaos. Celia leapt toward the robed executioners, turning her momentum into a roll that brought her up before one of the figures. As she came to her feet, she raised her sword

at an upward angle and into his chest. Behind her, Jend took on another opponent, coming around in a turning side-kick, delivering a blow to the would-be
executioner's midsection and knocking the man back several paces.

Celia pirouetted away from her latest opponent, landing beside Hanqar
and slicing him free. Ken burst from his bonds as well, moving to his brother's
aide, a pilfered knife in the palm of his hand. The five elions came together in
the center of the platform, standing in a loose circle, backs against each other,
and braced themselves as the rabid, howling crowd surged forward.

* * *

Boblin landed in the shadows at the side of the platform. On the dais, Taazvin
screamed for the mob to slaughter the prisoners.

I thought that might happen.

For a split second, Boblin turned toward his wife and the others, intending
to lend them aid, but at the last moment he changed direction. Celia and Jend
had their situation well in hand, while Boblin stood only a handful of strides
from Taazvin's dais. He caught a glimpse of Tim landing farther down the
platform, ready to deal with the masses.

*Taazvin is driving all of this. His rage fuels everyone else. I need to take him
down first.*

Sword in hand, Boblin leapt onto the dais and swung the blade toward
the zealot's neck. One of Taazvin's followers interjected himself between his
leader and Boblin. The man carried no weapons and was therefore defenseless,
but such things mattered little to a man in the throes of religious fervor. He
slammed into Boblin, tackling him around the midsection.

Boblin fell onto his back, landing on the wooden platform and rolling.
Above him, the man's eyes were wild, and he opened his jaws as if to bite
Boblin's neck.

Well, of all the things—

Boblin did not have full range of motion to strike his attacker with his
blade, but he did have enough room to slam the hilt of his sword into the
man's head. The zealot snarled, stumbled to the side, and slipped off the platform. Unfortunately, he still had a hold on Boblin's tunic as he fell. Boblin had
just enough time to utter an oath before he, too, tumbled away into the dark,
empty night.

* * *

As Tim landed on the platform, feet square on the planking, he filled himself with the Lifesource. He saw the fight with Celia and the elions erupt on the far side of the bonfire, but he had no time to give it thought. A mob of crazed villagers stood before him, on the verge of tearing his comrades apart, and he had to act fast.

He held his blade crosswise in front of him. A tongue of green flame enveloped the steel, burning fierce as he infused the focusing point with his power. The crowd shied away for a second, wary of this new threat, but at the sound of Taazvin's cry they charged forward anyway, brandishing an array of daggers, axes, and swords. The steel of their weaponry flashed in the light of the bonfire's flames.

Tim rose on the balls of his feet to gain momentum before dropping, coming in low and fast between a pair of villagers. The crowd enveloped him, striking from all directions. He whirled from one sword-form to the next, slicing left, then right, felling an opponent with each stroke. He sensed three more coming toward him from behind and pushed *out* with the Lifesource, knocking them back several feet. A fourth opponent slipped past his guard, and though Tim managed to twist away in time to avoid a fatal blow, the villager's dagger pierced his left shoulder. A searing pain shot through him. Tim moved his left hand in a circular motion, trapping the man's forearm in his grip, and brought his knee forward into the man's stomach. Tim's opponent doubled over with a wheezing cough.

Tim didn't dare remove the dagger from his shoulder. At the moment, it would do more damage on the way out. He pushed his opponent into the crowd, where the man's body collided with others, hindering their movements. Pain pulsed in Tim's mind, causing his control of the Lifesource to waver. He needed to end this quickly.

Another group of villagers came at them, and he pushed them back with yet another buffet of the Lifesource. Sustaining such a massive push took energy, and Tim's reserves were fading rapidly. He stumbled, noting the crackling of the fire behind him and the smoke curling up into the sky above him. *Strange, the things we notice when we're moments from death.* Before him, the flames lit the villagers' expressions, allowing him to see every nuance. They had seen his powers, and for that they feared him—but they also hated him, and Tim held no illusions regarding which sentiment would prevail in the end.

The heat of the fire washed over him, and that was when the answer clicked into place. As the villagers rushed forward yet again, Tim closed his eyes, exhaled, and reached out with the Lifesource one more time. *Whoosh.* He extinguished the flames with a mere thought, and in the bonfire's absence, the entire platform plunged into darkness.

* * *

Boblin and his assailant landed in a rope net suspended beneath the platform. The net twisted and spun as they made impact. Boblin's foot slipped through a gap in the cross-hatching, and his sword-arm slipped through another. He lost hold of his weapon, which tumbled free and spun end over end to land on the ground. From this height, a fall wouldn't kill him, but it would most certainly be painful and result in a broken bone or two.

Boblin quelled his immediate instinct to struggle, knowing such action would only tangle him further in the net. He'd landed beneath his attacker, so Boblin slammed his free elbow into the man's stomach. The villager grunted. His hot, rancid breath filled Boblin's nostrils.

This is just wonderful. Here he was, fighting face-down in a net, having lost his sword, and his opponent literally stank of having eaten human flesh. *Finding the villagers was supposed to be the* easy *part. It wasn't supposed to get hard until we entered the desert. On the day I come face-to-face with the Maker, he and I are going to have a long, hard talk about his sense of humor, and how I often find myself at the wrong end of it.*

Boblin sensed rather than saw the man pull a knife free and prepare to thrust it into Boblin's spine. *Great.* As the man came in for the blow, Boblin elbowed him once more, this time managing to regain his balance enough to spin halfway and catch the man's wrist. Rather than resisting the man's downward momentum, Boblin leveraged it to his advantage, allowing his assailant to complete his stroke, but directing it toward the net's cross-sections. The man's blade sliced through the ropes, causing the bottom of the net give way beneath them. Both combatants tumbled free, but Boblin grabbed a dangling section of the rope and clung to it, while his assailant fell to the ground below, landing with an unceremonious *thump.*

And good riddance to you.

The next thing Boblin knew, a hand reached over the edge of the platform, seized his tunic, and dragged him back up to where the bonfire raged and his companions fought. Boblin found himself lying on his back yet again, this time facing Taazvin.

The man bared his lips in a snarl, pressing a blade to Boblin's throat. "You will pay for this. I've dined on my share of unbelievers, and you will be next."

"That is absolutely disgusting," Boblin replied.

He felt a rush of air, and the bonfire at the center of the platform winked out.

* * *

Tim knew he had to act fast to take advantage of the villagers' surprise in the darkness. Their disorientation would be temporary, and they would regain their bearings soon. He rolled to the opposite side of the extinguished bonfire, past the wafting ashes and into the small semicircle where Celia and the elions fought the robed priests. He slammed his palm on the floorboards, releasing the power of the Lifesource into the wooden planking. The platform cracked down the center, gigantic splinters of wood shaking free in the wake of the sudden rift. Tim *heaved* outward, pushing the two halves of the platform in opposite directions and creating a large gap. Each section, bereft of central support, sagged down toward the middle, and some of the villagers descended into the newly formed crevasse before the rest gained purchase. Behind Tim, Celia and the rest remained far enough away from the incline to keep stable footing, though the sudden disruption had caught them off guard as much as anyone else.

Tim came to Hugo and Ken's aid first, sword ablaze as he cut two of the robed priests down. At the same time, all three companions pushed their opponents back and paused, breathing heavily.

"Where's Commander Kule?" Hugo asked.

* * *

Boblin felt the platform *crack* from Tim's blow. The world rocked, upsetting Taazvin's balance. Boblin pushed his knee upward, which gave him just enough space to throw Taazvin off him. Coming to his feet, Boblin struck Taazvin with yet another blow, tearing the zealot's sword from his grasp.

He risked a glance across the space. Tim, Celia, and the others stood on the opposite half of the divided platform, engaged in battle with a mere handful of the villagers. Though Boblin had no doubt his companions would make short work of their opponents, he did not have the same optimism for himself.

He stood alone, facing not only Taazvin, but at least forty other crazed fanatics.

"You've got to be kidding me," Boblin said.

* * *

Tim saw Boblin standing over a disarmed Taazvin. The religious leader lunged toward Boblin, while the surrounding villagers cheered in expectation of an easy kill. Boblin dodged back, his curse audible even across the distance separating the groups, and several things happened at once. Tim rushed toward the gap, summoning his power, as Boblin feinted left and then drove his blade through Taazvin's neck. Blood sprayed.

The noises from the mob turned into screams of rage. Without a moment to spare, Boblin ran away at full speed and launched into the air. He only made it halfway across the gap between platforms, but Tim caught him in a net of the Lifesource and pulled him the last few feet to safety. Boblin landed on both feet, glaring at his friend and pointing toward Taazvin's body on the other side. "He wanted to *eat* me."

Tim shrugged. "At least I caught you."

"It was the least you could do, you son of a three-legged goat. Next time, leave me on the *same* side as everyone else."

"What now?" Ken asked as the group gathered on the platform. The elions had dispatched the remainder of their opponents, and the villagers on the opposite half had lost what little cohesion they once had. Some wailed over Taazvin's body, others spat at Tim and the elions. One man tried to make the jump but fell short and plummeted to the ground.

In answer to Ken's question, a volley of arrows flashed upward, claiming targets from the opposite platform. The villagers shied away from this new onslaught, pulling back from the edge as a score of newcomers streamed into sight on the forest floor, led by Wurit. From below, the short man caught Tim's

gaze and gave him a friendly wave. Beside him, the reinforcements began securing the remainder of the camp in a quick, efficient manner.

"And this is...?" Celia asked.

"A friend of mine," Tim said. "Come on."

They hopped from their platform down onto a smaller one, making their
way to the ground by increments. Once on firm earth again, Tim led the group
to where Wurit stood with a cluster of men and women. The man from Keldur
gave Tim a crisp salute and clasped his hand.

"I said I'd be back," he said with a smile. He glanced at the platform. "I
admit you appeared to be holding your own somewhat well. How in the name
of Malath did you accomplish *that*?"

"Don't fluff his ego," Boblin grumbled. "He left me to get eaten, and I haven't received so much as an apology from him."

"Harmea save me from this drama," Celia said. "I'm sorry, Tim. It's all you
and I will hear about for the next week."

Wurit looked from one elion to the next. "You are an interesting group, I'll
say that. I'd also be lying if I didn't say I was in your debt. *All* of us are. Taazvin and his followers have threatened us for some time, but as of this evening,
he is no more." He bowed. "So thank you."

"Don't thank us yet," Tim said. "We're likely to call in that debt sooner
rather than later."

Wurit eyed him warily. "And what form of payment might that be?"

Tim met his gaze. "We need you to lead us to Agrazab."

13

Trivian Seltor knelt next to his comrades in the dirt. The men were arranged in a row with hands bound behind their backs, faces turned toward the earth. A bead of sweat trickled from his nose, landing on the ground with a minuscule explosion of dust upon impact. The captives on either side of him breathed heavily.

A palpable tension hung over the group. The time for the drawing had arrived. It had been one week since Eltern fell, the corsairs catching Trivian and his companions unawares and unprepared. It was an ill-kept secret between the soldiers of Alcatune that the outposts of Eltern and Sevilin were a punitive assignment. If a man couldn't cut it during his regular training assignments, or botched a field command, those higher up the chain of command would send him to the outposts. Many of the soldiers here were very young, with a few slightly older men like Trivian among them. Eltern and Sevilin had little strategic value in and of themselves; Eltern served as no more than a stopping point on the way to the dwerion village of Raldoon, and as for Sevilin, well, Trivian suspected it only existed because folks decided that if Vonku had an outpost to the north, it also needed an outpost to the south.

Trivian's father had been a man of the mines, and had told him of how he and his companions carried a julian bird with them into the caves at all times. If the julian bird died, the men knew poisonous air was building up, and it was time to clear out. Similarly, Trivian always thought of Eltern and Sevilin as King Aras's julian birds. There was no way they'd been made to actually *protect* the royal city—that's what the Legion was for. The outposts existed as a trigger alarm; if they fell to invading enemies, Aras's *real* soldiers knew it was time to stand a little straighter and keep the weapons sharp.

So it had been that Kaarst's corsairs descended upon some of the least well-equipped soldiers in King Aras's army. Trivian had been lounging in the barracks when the alarm sounded. Their commander had looked to Trivian for guidance, *then* of all times. The man treated Trivian like a leper when he first arrived, because while it was bad enough for an ordinary soldier to be sent here, a man who once commanded an entire *division* within the Royal Legion had to fall far indeed to deserve such treatment. It had not surprised Trivian that the chain of command shunned him—perhaps rightfully so, because Trivian held no illusions regarding his worth—and relegated him to the dirtiest of tasks. It was only after the corsairs came pouring in, burning what they could and cutting every throat in sight, that the man turned to Trivian Seltor in despair.

It hadn't saved him. Every time Trivian closed his eyes, he saw the commander wailing in fear, begging for someone, *anyone*, to save him as a corsair dragged him across the ground.

"We surrender!" Commander Betlin had screamed, the chaotic firelight of burning buildings illuminating his face. *"For the love of the Maker, we surrender!"*

"Hush," the corsair said, drawing his blade. *"Crazvin be in charge, and you be knowin' it."*

"But we've given up! We've yielded!"

"Aye," Crazvin concurred, *"ain't that a pity."* He slid his sword into Betlin's stomach, yanking it out and letting the man scream his way to an awful death. Stomach wounds did not kill quickly.

When the poor man's misery ceased, Crazvin mounted his head on a pike and paraded it before the remaining captives. At the time, Trivian wondered why the corsairs bothered taking any of them alive. Captives had little strategic advantage for the crew, but the corsairs nonetheless rounded them up, stripped them of weapons, and tossed them into the barracks. After he came to his senses awash with the pain of a pounding headache, he learned the answer to his question soon enough. The corsairs had kept them alive for the drawing. For *entertainment*.

A line of prisoners knelt in the dirt, faces to the ground, as Crazvin passed in front of them. "Draw, me hearties," Crazvin said, holding a leather pouch before them. *"Draw."*

The first captive reached a trembling hand into the bag and drew a small, white stone. He let it fall with a gasp, his entire body shaking with sobs of relief.

"Easy, laddie, easy," Crazvin said, patting the youth's head. "Ye've made it another day. Next!"

The corsair continued down the line toward Trivian. In the week since his capture, Trivian had often considered simply refusing to draw. It would have ensured his execution, but he was too tired to care. Besides, although he might have lost most of his honor in the streets of Vonku five years ago, enough remained to convince him it was better to face his death with back straight than to engage in Crazvin's games. And yet, when the bag came before him, he reached into it just as he had done these last seven days, wondering if today would be the day, and felt a twinge of mingled relief and guilt when he drew a white stone. He tossed it to the ground without further reaction. Crazvin grabbed his chin, twisting it to face him. Trivian met the corsair's gaze, and Crazvin let out a chuckle.

"This one has some backbone yet, eh?" He patted Trivian's cheek. "Ye're a fun one, laddie! I like ye!"

The bag was five soldiers down from Trivian when it happened. The boy—his name was Pieder—drew a red pebble. He let out a whimper, falling forward as Crazvin broke into a big, toothy grin.

"We have a winner, mateys!" Crazvin shouted. He grabbed Pieder's wrist and raised the prisoner's arm into the air, as if celebrating the victor of a fencing match. "Let's give him a hurrah!"

"Hurrah!" the assembled corsairs said, breaking into a round of applause and laughter, a few slapping hands with one another. "Hurrah! Hurrah! Hurrah!"

"Name yerself, me hearty!" Crazvin said to Pieder, who was weeping openly. "Name yerself!"

He always asked their names. While Trivian had not yet convinced himself to skip the drawing outright, he swore to himself that if he did draw the red stone, he would at least refuse this request. He did not owe these men his *name*.

Pieder did not appear to share Trivian's convictions on the subject. "Pieder," he answered, the name coming out in a stutter.

"Ahoy, me matey! Pieder it is! Ye be a fine pick for the drawin' today, so ye be!" Crazvin said. "Well, me lad, let's get it on with, shall we?"

He pressed Pieder to the ground and drew a long blade from his belt. Trivian saw some of his comrades avert their eyes. Most shook in fear, and not a few shared Pieder's sobs. *Untrained boys, every last one of them.* This was not fair to them; they had not asked for this, had not been tested on the front lines of such battles as those in the Icor Rebellion. Outpost duty was supposed to be safe, a way to earn coin to send to your family. It asked little and demanded nothing. Battle-hardened Legionnaires knew what they had been signing up for, but these youths, half of whom only shaved once a week, did not.

Trivian continued watching. Pieder deserved such respect, deserved knowing his comrades—his *men*—stood with him at the end.

Crazvin drew his dagger and sliced Pieder's jugular. A fountain of blood spurted as the corsairs cheered, breaking into another round of applause and laughter. As the young soldier's body thrashed in death throes, Crazvin proceeded with the grisly task of severing head from body.

"Look on this, me 'earties!" Crazvin said, turning to the assembled prisoners and holding Pieder's head before them. He pushed it into their faces one at a time, moving down the line. Many turned away, tears in their eyes. "This be what awaits ye, my lovely boys! The fun comes in askin' when *yer* turn will come—be it tomorrow, or the day after? *We* don't know, only the stone knows!" He picked up the red pebble and held it aloft, his laughter turning into a sharp cackle while the corsairs rounded up the prisoners.

As they shuffled back to the barracks, the young men around Trivian did not resist. They walked with faces numb and voices mute, allowing their captors to herd them forward. Crazvin tossed Pieder's head to one of his corsairs, who placed it upon a pike near those who had also fallen victim to the drawing. "Come back tomorrow! We play again!"

They made their way in single file back to the barracks, the sobs of a few still reaching his ears. Then Trivian heard a new, gravelly voice rumble in over that of the other corsairs.

"Be this what passes fer entertainment here, laddies? Fine sport ye make!"

Trivian paused in mid-step, hands bound behind his back. The man behind him bumped into him, and the entire line halted. This ordinarily would have earned a sharp reprimand from their captors, but Crazvin and his men had also turned toward the newcomer.

A dwerion, one arm bound with the red sash of Kaarst's fleet, stood flanked by two of Crazvin's sentinels. Behind him stood a tall man bearing the purple sigil of the royal legion on his breast, hands and feet in shackles, head bowed. Trivian caught the faintest hint of cuts and bruises upon the man's face. His captors had clearly been rough with him, not that Trivian would expect otherwise.

"Aye," Crazvin said, eyes narrowing as he sized up the dwerion. "We be passin' the time, me friend! An' what did ye bring for us?"

The dwerion smiled, showing his teeth. His voice bore that peculiar mix of dwerion brogue combined with a corsair accent adopted by the dwerions in Kaarst's fleet. "We have ourselves a runner here, a real guest o' honor! Me and my crew were scoutin' the southern border o' Raldoon on the Adm'ral's orders when this one come to us! He rode his horse right into our camp, a gift on hooves!"

Crazvin's eyes filled with wicked glee. "Aye, a guest o' honor indeed! It ain't often we find ourselves acquainted with one straight from the Royal Legion!" He drew his cutlass and waved the dwerion aside. The newcomer moved with obvious reluctance, uneager to relinquish his prize.

Crazvin placed the tip of his blade beneath the Legion man's chin and raised his head, forcing the prisoner to look at him. The man stared back with a spirit of defiance that none of Trivian's fellow captives had managed to muster. *And this is the difference, Crazvin, between capturing a boy of Eltern and capturing a man tested in Aras's most elite unit. What do you think of this? What do you think of staring into the eyes of one who knows how to stare back?*

"What be yer business north of Alcatune, matey?" Crazvin asked. "Interestin' direction for the king to send a runner! What does Aras hope to do—raise Raldoon against us?" He let loose a throaty laugh. "I don't expect half o' those villagers know how to lift a sword!"

The prisoner said nothing, and the dwerion spoke again. "He be a tough one, matey, but we helped him talk soon enough. All it took was a wee bit of encouragin'. He was headed north, all the way past the Rampart. It seems Aras seeks the aid o' the emperor in the North."

"Aye, so it seems indeed!" Crazvin said with a bright smile. "As it happens, the emperor will have to wait another day!" He sheathed his sword and stepped away from the prisoner. "Ye'll be housed in the best of accommodations, matey! Ye're here with *us* now!" He shoved the Legionnaire into line with the rest of the prisoners. The man stumbled, but righted quickly enough.

Crazvin turned to the dwerion. "An' what be yer name, laddie?"

"Blaggo," the dwerion replied. "I serve under Grizzlen's command."

"Under Grizzlen!" Crazvin said, slapping Blaggo's shoulder with respect. "We be hostin' famous folk all around, me hearties! A man from the Royal Legion *and* a guest from Grizzlen's crew. Take yer rest, me matey, throw your boots up an' share a pint! It be a good day in Eltern!"

As Blaggo accepted Crazvin's hearty handshake, the corsairs on either side of the captives prodded them back on their way toward the barracks which had become their prison. The tall Legion man joined them, keeping to himself with eyes focused on the ground.

The corsairs shut the doors of the barracks with a hollow *boom*, leaving them in the musty dimness with only the light coming through the windows to illuminate the room. Dust motes danced in the shafts of sunlight as the former soldiers of Eltern separated, many leaning against the wall and sliding to the ground in apparent defeat.

Trivian kept his eye on the Legion man, somewhat curious to see what the new captive would do next. Now that the guards had shut them in, the soldier surveyed the room, his gaze piercing and discerning. *Aye, that one won't miss a bit.* The Legionnaire looked first at the door, then at the windows, and last upon the prisoners themselves. *He's sizing up the situation, just they are trained to do—as I was trained to do. Know your exits, know your weapons, and know your allies.*

The newcomer stood by himself, to all outward appearances disregarding most of the prisoners—not out of scorn, but because he was looking for the third element, the ally, and none of these boys were ready to be the ally he needed. He met Trivian's gaze, where his glance lingered just a little longer. Trivian returned the look, and after a long moment, gave the subtlest of nods. The Legion man's head twitched, a bare acknowledgment of an acknowledgment, and he continued with his assessment of the room.

Trivian stepped to the side, beneath a window where the sun streamed in. He kept himself upright, back against the wall, whereas most of the prisoners either sat or lay down. A few wandered without purpose or direction, only passing the time. Trivian supposed the act of repetitive physical motion was their only respite from the strain of wondering whom the drawing would claim next.

The tall man joined Trivian by the side of the room, similarly placing his back against the wall and watching the prisoners.

"How long has it been?" the Legion man asked.

"Seven days," Trivian replied. "They take one each day. Most here never saw a real battle before last week." He gave a humorless laugh. "This is where you end up when you can't prove yourself. No one expects Eltern to actually *test* them."

The new prisoner looked at Trivian, his assessment going unspoken—for one, because it would have been unnecessary to do so, and for another, out of courtesy. The man seemed to understand that Trivian, unlike most of the others, *had* seen battle, but for the Legion man to inquire further would mean broaching the taboo subject: how a trained, hardened man ended up in Eltern. It was a point of honor that one man did not ask another how and when he had fallen from grace. Instead, the soldier offered his shackled hands. "I'm Sendalion Danris of the Royal Legion."

Trivian accepted the greeting with his own bound hands. "Trivian Seltor. Of Eltern."

Recognition dawned on Sendalion's face, but he said no more. As they clasped hands, Trivian felt a long, thin strip of metal fall into his palm. He started, looking up into Sendalion's eyes. He opened his mouth to speak, but then closed it. Sendalion nodded, releasing his hands and leaving Trivian holding the lockpick.

"Stand ready, my friend," Sendalion said. "It's the corsairs who've drawn the wrong pebble this time around."

* * *

Inside the guardhouse, Quentiin downed the mug of grog Crazvin offered him in one gulp. The liquid burned all the way down his throat, sending a tingling sensation through his sinuses and causing his eyes to water.

This ain't ale. It's swill.

He resisted the urge to cough and splutter it back up, instead embracing it with a grin that was half grimace. He raised the empty glass and pounded it on the table, letting loose a loud belch for effect. Around him, the corsairs roared their approval, one slapping him on the back in congratulations.

"An' now ye be one of us, Blaggo!" Crazvin said, slamming his empty mug on the table beside Quentiin's. "Ye've brought us a prisoner an' partaken in our grog. Well met, laddie, well met!"

"Aye!" Quentiin called back. "Well met indeed!"

What I wouldn't give to run him through right here. Quentiin had seen the end of Pieder's execution as he approached with Sendalion in tow, much too late to interrupt Crazvin from his sickening game. He took solace in knowing the prisoners would have a chance to deliver retribution soon.

As the afternoon wore on, he gambled with the pirates, tossing dice and playing cards. They passed mug after mug of grog around, and though Quentiin took a swig when he had to, more often than not he took advantage of a timely dice toss to drain the mug behind his back. So much other filth had already accumulated on the floor he doubted any would notice a few extra puddles. He threw daggers at the wall, roaring in laughter with the rest when a corsair—Quentiin thought his name was Urgil—took a poorly aimed throw in the shoulder. Urgil snarled and drew the blade free, whipping it back at the offending corsair, Nezlin. The blade landed quivering in the seat of Nezlin's chair, right in front of his groin. This increased the crowd's mirth, and of course they had to pass around another mug of grog to celebrate.

Quentiin eyed the sun outside the guardhouse as it sank, fingers of dusk reaching across the land. Meanwhile Crazvin's crew continued their revelry, growing bleary-eyed and red-cheeked as the evening wore on. Some stumbled out the door of the guardhouse and into the night, others simply passing out in chairs or on the floor. Crazvin was among the former, not quite as off-kilter as some of his companions.

Quentiin adopted a feigned stagger, purposefully slurring his words and blinking his eyes. At last a mere handful remained, tossing dice onto the table with no apparent objective other than to keep the game going, having lost all count of the score. Quentiin wondered whether there would be any sliced bellies over the pile of coin on the table. He even considered starting a debate over the ownership of the pot, as this might mean one or two fewer corsairs to deal with when the next phase of the plan went into motion, but decided it would raise one too many variables. If he started an altercation in here, he might never slip outside.

Late into the night, Quentiin stood and stumbled his way to the door. Behind him, Urgil managed a farewell before a sequence of hiccups overtook him. As Quentin stepped into the night, he saw a few dark mounds sleeping on the ground. Apparently, the corsairs who'd left the gatehouse had decided to make the lawn their bed for the evening. He looked for Crazvin, but did not see him anywhere, and supposed the corsair chief had retired to a more solitary section of the outpost. While Quentiin would have preferred to know where the man was, in the end it was irrelevant. He'd deal with Crazvin when the time came.

He staggered to the gates proper, where two corsairs stood beside the door. Even as he approached, Quentiin could tell neither was in the best of moods, perhaps irritated they had been stuck with guard duty while their shipmates gambled the night away. He provided a loud belch to signify his arrival, swaying in the middle of the dirt road as they turned to face them.

"Look, this be our guest," the first guard said, the sarcasm evident in his voice. "What do ye be needin, *mate*?"

"Aye," the second guard said. "It better be summat good. If ye be here to relieve us, get on with it, otherwise ye'd best be goin' on yer way. Not all's us can afford to get saucy drunk, much as we might wish otherwise."

"I be headin' to the road," Quentiin said, pointing beyond the gates. "Back to my postin' south of the Odow."

"Ye ain't makin' it *half* that far tonight, matey. Ye be tippin' faster than a broken mainmast. Get back inside an' put yerself to sleep."

"I ain't that bad," Quentiin replied with a hiccup, taking a step closer. "Had a few sips, s'all. This be a normal night for me."

"If that be the case, I can't tell whether to feel sorry fer ye, or to envy yer good fortune in havin' that much grog at yer disposal every day," the second guard said. He spat on the ground. "Get outta here. Nobody leaves without Crazvin's orders. Find yerself a nice comfortable corner to hole up in, an' ye can leave tomorrow with the commander's blessin'." His smile was tinged with malice. "If yer headache ain't too bad, that is."

Quentiin stopped before them, leaning to look to the road beyond, swaying as he extended his midsection. "Well—if ye say so—"

"I *say* so," the first guard said. "On with ye, unless ye want a dagger betwixt yer eyes." Quentiin acknowledged with a sloppy salute, dropping a casual hand to the pommel of his sword as he began to turn away.

And then he struck.

All pretense of stupor gone, he spun back in full circle, drawing his blade and slamming it against the base of the second guard's skull. The guard dropped instantly, out cold in the dirt. The first guard went for his sword with a muffled curse, but Quentiin already had the tip of his sword at his throat.

"Not another move, laddie," Quentiin said. "Nor a peep, if you value yer life. D'ye ken?"

The guard nodded, mouth clamped shut. His eyes burned with malice, but he would do as told. Heroism didn't exactly run in the veins of such men as these. They could be counted to act out of self-preservation above all else, and the good of their comrades could go to Malath. No chance this one would raise the alarm, not when Quentiin's blade was at his throat. Still, Quentiin had to do *something* about him. He gave the guard a nice, firm rap on the head with the hilt of his sword and the corsair joined his companion in the sweet sleep of unconsciousness. "I think ye'll be the one havin' the headache on the morrow, laddie."

The dwerion stepped around the fallen corsairs and lifted the pins holding the gate in place. It swung outward with a *creak*, opening to the night beyond and revealing a dirt road that stretched north into darkness. Rolling green hills and fields marked the eastern and western edges of the path, which wound on its way toward the Odow Forest and the lands beyond.

Quentiin took one look around, assuring himself that none were in sight, and imitated the whistle of a night-trill. Moments later, forms stirred in the darkness of a nearby ditch, and a single file of dwerions appeared from the darkness. Jolldo came first, followed by Yagglem, Vellgo, Briiga, and the rest. They numbered twelve plus Vinsor, who took up the rear. While their number certainly did not constitute an army, there were few other folk Quentiin would rather have standing at his side when his back was against the wall.

"Follow me, laddies," Quentin rumbled in a low tone. He led them into Eltern single-file. For the moment, he kept the red sash on his arm. He'd managed to procure it from a captured corsair, one of Grizzlen's actual crew they had caught roaming the countryside. He had sorely hoped Crazvin was not well acquainted with Kaarst's right-hand men, as this would have ruined his charade, but he'd known the odds were in his favor. The Admiral's fleet was big enough that one corsair could not be expected to recognize all the others.

After dragging the unconscious guards outside of the city walls and leaving them in the ditch, the twelve dwerions dispersed at Quentiin's direction. Some stationed themselves near the entrance, others by the guardhouse, and a few climbed the battlements. Sendalion estimated that Crazvin's crew numbered just shy of a hundred. With an expected fifty prisoners in the barracks, the people of Alcatune would still find themselves outnumbered, but not dramatically so.

Quentiin had known what to expect regarding the caliber of soldier they'd find here. He'd served his time in the Legion, and knew the truth about those sent to Eltern as well as the next man. Still, with Quentiin, Sendalion, and Vinsor to coordinate them, he had to trust these boys would revert to their training, and while they would not be Legion recruits any time soon, they were a far cry from the average farmer. The corsairs' inebriated states, combined with the prisoners' element of surprise, would work further in their favor.

Quentiin made directly for the barracks, Jolldo and Vinsor behind him. They stayed low, clinging to the shadows along the wall, and only stood to the fullness of their heights upon reaching the door.

He heard a voice behind him. "What be this, mate?"

Quentiin turned to see Crazvin lounging against a nearby barrel, a smile on his lips. The corsair had an unhealthy gleam in his eye, the gaze of a predator that had waited for its prey to enter the snare. "Be ye payin' the prisoners a visit?" Crazvin asked. "I'll tell ye one thing, matey. I don't know that I've ever had a shipmate who dislikes dice and drains grog behind his back." Moonlight flashed against steel as Crazvin produced a dagger and started pruning his fingernails. "I be watchin' ye, mate. I be watchin' ye *real* close. So tell me—what's this about?"

Behind Crazvin, a half-dozen corsairs gathered upon their leader's cue. They were large, even for humans, dwarfing Quentiin as they stood with hands on weapons. He looked over their tattooed faces and corded muscles. He shrugged, dropping his corsair accent and reverting to his natural brogue. "I don't know how to frame it, laddie. I suppose it'd be what ye call…a rescue?"

And then he flung the door of the barracks wide open.

* * *

Sendalion had been waiting on the other side, watching the exchange between Quentiin and Crazvin through a crack in the wall. Trivian Seltor stood behind him, tensed and ready for action once the signal came. That one would do well enough in a pinch, and as for the rest—well, they'd do just fine, too, as long as he managed to get some blades into their hands. They knew they were fighting for their lives. Also, after watching their comrades executed over the last week, they were ready for a healthy dose of retribution.

When Quentiin flung the door open, Sendalion sprang forward, Trivian beside him. Crazvin cursed as he saw the tall man coming for him. The corsair raised his dagger and Sendalion ducked, jerking to the side to take cover as the blade spun through the air. Trivian was not so quick. He took the dagger in the ribs with a muffled grunt, tumbling to the ground. Sendalion spun to help the fallen man, but Trivian waved him away.

"I'll be fine," the soldier said, pulling the knife free. "Fight!"

Crazvin faded behind his men, letting them surge forward to engage the flood of prisoners streaming from the barracks. The leader of the corsair crew raised a horn and let loose a blast that pierced the night air. "To arms, mateys! To arms!"

Sendalion went for the nearest corsair at the same time as the man came for him. Beside him, he was aware of Quentiin taking on another. But the remaining four—

They attacked the weaponless captives, blades swinging through the air. Sendalion saw the first man fall, cut down before he could so much as defend himself. He grimaced, but could do nothing to help, for his own opponent was upon him, sword snaking toward his midsection. Sendalion dodged the first strike, coming in low and close, depriving the corsair of room to use his weapon. He swung his fist, two knuckles hitting the notch in his attacker's throat. The corsair stumbled and gagged, momentarily off-kilter. Sendalion elbowed the man in the ribcage, dropping him to his knees, and delivered a turning sidekick. He felt the *crunch* of bone beneath his boot as the corsair's face exploded in a spray of blood. The man's weapon clattered to the ground, and Sendalion picked it up.

"You!" Sendalion shouted to a soldier who had just rolled out of reach of another corsair's strike. "Take this!"

He tossed the blade through the air, and the young man caught it, eyes coming alive with hope as he spun and met the corsair's attack head-on.

Around Sendalion, the camp erupted into chaos as more corsairs swarmed into the battle. Many of them moved sluggishly, courtesy of their earlier carousing with Quentiin, and as such presented a greatly reduced threat. On the periphery of Sendalion's vision, the dwerions from Raldoon attacked, axes and swords flashing through the air as they came to the prisoners' aid. A small volley of arrows descended from the battlements, skewering some of the pirates where they stood.

Quentiin felled his opponent, driving a sword through the man's heart. He turned to acknowledge Sendalion with nostrils flaring and teeth bared. At the sight of the battle-rage flowing through Quentiin's veins, Sendalion thought of the oft-mentioned adage that there was nothing greater than a dwerion's wrath. For such a gentle folk, they transformed into the most terrifying of opponents during battle. Together, the two warriors engaged the remaining corsairs from the original group. The corsairs stumbled under the collective might of fifty stampeding men. Sendalion and Quentiin caught a single pirate between them, cutting him down on the grassy lawn.

In a moment of reprieve, Sendalion turned to where he'd last seen Trivian Seltor kneeling on the ground with Crazvin's blade between his ribs, intending to bring him aid.

But Trivian was gone.

* * *

Trivian staggered through the night, side throbbing, listening to the sounds of the fray behind him as the captives rallied against the remnants of Crazvin's men. Trivian, however, had thoughts only for Crazvin. The corsair leader had vanished when the skirmish began, allowing his men to engage the newly freed captives while he fled into the shadows. At the sight of Crazvin running away, Trivian rolled free of the conflict and took up pursuit. The wound in his side spiked pain afresh with every step, and though it was hardly mortal, it still hurt like Malath.

The darkness enveloped him as he ran into a portion of Eltern that had been abandoned since the corsairs captured the outpost. A grassy area held a series of tents, some of which had been used by Eltern's soldiers for stocking weapons, others for meals, and others for official business. Upon reaching the first pair of tents, Trivian paused and listened for any sounds to indicate Crazvin's location. The moon shone down, illuminating the area. His sides heaved as he regulated his breath. Blood seeped through the fingers he placed over the wound on his side, dripping into the dirt. He tore a strip from his shirt to form a makeshift bandage, wrapping it around his side to stem the flow. Hearing nothing, he took a step forward, then another, before emerging from between the tents into a more open area.

A rush of air was the only warning he had. He dodged the incoming blow as Crazvin attacked from the side, cutlass passing through the air where Trivian's head had just been. "What have we here, laddie?" the corsair captain asked. "Come to avenge yer mates?"

Trivian held only the knife that Crazvin had thrown into his side. His reach with the blade was short, and he had to economize his movements. He dodged Crazvin's cutlass, stepping from one side to the other, pushing the pain in his ribs to a distant corner of his mind, focused solely on survival.

"I must say," Crazvin continued, "I don't know I ever met such a craven bunch o' untrained whelps. One woulda' thought they'd have accepted their fates with some dignity, rather than showin' themselves to be spineless cowards."

Trivian ignored the taunt, dropping to the ground and rolling in a backward somersault toward the corner of a tent. He came back up, weapon in front of him, as Crazvin advanced. At the last moment, Trivian moved into the tent's interior. It had been built to allow three or four people inside, with a table at its center, and he pushed the table toward Crazvin as the corsair entered. As Crazvin stumbled over the table, Trivian sliced a slit through the far flap and retreated back outside.

Still inside, Crazvin laughed. "Shy, laddie? Don't worry yerself, I'll end it quickly enough. Ye had some spirit—I saw it, and I owe ye an honorable finish."

Trivian slashed the ropes attached to the tent's stakes. The structure collapsed, fabric ballooning outward. As the tent engulfed Crazvin, Trivian tackled him from the side, bearing the corsair to the ground. He lost hold of his knife, though, and Crazvin surged back up, knocking Trivian to the ground. Crazvin shrugged free of the tent. Trivian almost made it to his feet, but halted when he felt the tip of the corsair's cutlass against his throat.

"Last words, laddie?" Crazvin asked.

Trivian met his gaze. "You talk too much."

Crazvin swung his blade. Trivian fell to one side, using gravity to his advantage as the blow missed, whisking so close to his head that he felt a breath of air ghost over his scalp. Crazvin brought the blade around for another strike, but Trivian had grasped a tent stake from the ground. He slammed it into the flesh of Crazvin's thigh, and the corsair shrieked in surprise and agony, letting his cutlass fall to the dirt.

"Does that hurt?" Trivian asked. Crazvin wavered, and fell forward onto his knees. *Just like we knelt for the drawing.* "Here. Let me help." He pulled the stake free. Blood sprayed as Crazvin's cries echoed off the walls of Eltern.

Trivian staked Crazvin in the heart, cutting off all further sound. Trivian let his gaze linger on the pirate's corpse. He spat on it before turning away, limping back to the center of the outpost.

* * *

Quentiin surveyed the gathered survivors. They numbered close to forty, in addition to himself, Vinsor, Sendalion, and the dwerions from Raldoon. *A fair number. Enough to perform the task that needs doin'.*

"Do you think they're up to it?" Sendalion asked him.

Quentiin nodded. "They have to be. They swore the oaths."

At the edge of the group, Trivian Seltor appeared, shirt torn and bound over the wound in his side. He waved away an offer of assistance, made his way forward, and extended a hand to Sendalion.

"I owe you thanks, Danris," he said. He turned and shook hands with Quentiin, too. "As I do to you. And—" he stopped upon seeing Vinsor. His eyes narrowed for just a second, and then his face smoothed back into a flat expression. "Captain Dalin. I trust you're well."

Vinsor stepped forward, looking Trivian up and down. The men exchanged a long glance, but Vinsor broke it first. "Just Vinsor, Trivian. I'm no longer a captain."

Quentiin observed the exchange but said nothing. It wasn't hard to add up. Trivian was better trained than any of the other men at Eltern, which could only mean one thing. *He's a former Legion man.* But it took quite a bit to send a member of the Legion to Eltern, and of that, it did not bear fruit to ask.

"What of their leader?" Sendalion asked.

"He won't be leading anyone anymore," Trivian said. He looked from Quentiin, to Sendalion, to Vinsor, and back to Sendalion again. "What next, friends?"

"Ask Harggra," Sendalion said, nodding toward Quentiin. "He's the one in charge."

"Harggra?" Trivian asked. "As in Quentiin Harggra?"

"His Majesty saw fit to recall me from my duties in the North to attend Kaarst's barricade," Quentiin said. "Are ye up for breakin' it?"

"My life for the king," Trivian replied. "Nothing more, nothing less."

"Very well," Quentiin said. "Let's talk about what we're going to do from here. Are your men willin' to join us, too?"

"They're not my men," Trivian said. "Commander Betlin led them."

"And where is he?"

Trivian gave no response, though his eyes flickered toward the pikes that held the heads of the deceased Eltern guardsmen.

"I figured as much," Quentiin said. "I guess that means ye're up, Commander Seltor."

* * *

The elion paused, facing the setting sun.

Before him stretched the Western Desert, a vast plain of yellowish-brown stone. Cracks ran across the parched landscape, which was flat in some areas, marked by crags and gullies in others. The ground looked like a skeletal husk devoid of any life, a choked and inhospitable wasteland from which lashes of heat rolled in waves. In his mind, the elion thought he could hear the earth itself begging for just a single drop of water, anything to ease the pain of its tortured existence.

The sun slid over the lip of the horizon, casting a dim red-orange glow over the desert, creating a hue that spoke of blood. And blood there would be, the elion knew, once he reached his destination. When the armies of the Demon-Lord poured out and claimed this earth, the corpses would pile high as mountains. The elion had been told he would sit atop a throne of bodies, foes and friends alike laid low at his feet in return for his devotion.

Though he'd come far these last few days, his true quest was just beginning. The sands of the Desert held horrors beyond imagining—from monstrosities beneath the Cliffs of Desolation to creatures that prowled the Wasteland— and he needed to pass through all of them before he could reach the gates of Agrazab. As darkness descended, the man waited. One final task awaited him before he could leave the North behind. Far to the south, the Warrior of Light roamed the Pel Delta in search of those who had come this way before, and he must not succeed. The winds around the elion picked up, and with them came a swirl of dust from the sands of the desert, a foreshadowing of the long, hard path awaiting those who would venture into its depths.

They arrived from afar, their cloaked shapes illuminated against the dusk. There were two of them, each seven feet tall, wearing robes that undulated with currents of darkness. The Master had sent them to the elion, one serving as his right hand and the other as his left, ancient beings that existed do his bidding. They were Uklith's Assassins, and they came to the elion, for they had been given to him as tools to serve their master's bidding.

They wore hoods but had no faces. The only physical forms visible to the elion's eyes were their pale white hands, hands with fingers long and pointed, hands that could grasp and choke, hands that served one purpose: death.

"You must travel to Keldur," the elion said. His voice came out in a rasp from his raw throat. He hadn't spoken in some time. There was no need, when all communication with his master occurred inside his head. "The Warrior seeks the one who visited Agrazab and returned, and their paths must not cross. Kill either or both of them—it matters not, so long as the Warrior's quest does not come to fruition. Go and do our lord's bidding."

Uklith's Assassins gave no outward acknowledgment, other than to turn from the elion and face south. Side by side, they started out once more, making their way toward the Fertile Lands and into the Delta beyond. The elion watched them go, the darkness absorbing them as if they had never existed in this world to begin with.

* * *

Hieb the woodsman was drunk. There was nothing unusual about this. Hieb was drunk most days, and it suited him fine. He sat on a stump outside his cottage, a forgotten hatchet at his feet, flask in hand, and took another swig.

When evening came on, the scars on his back would throb as always. He'd received them in the Pit, where his life had consisted of naught but hauling gigantic chunks of obsidian rock—up the path, down the path, across the bridge, above the flames. Oh, how those fires had danced and called to a man. Hieb had never known anything other than that Malath-cursed place. From the day he crawled screaming from his mother's womb until the day Quentiin Harggra led his fellow slaves in an uprising, the Pit had been the sum of Hieb's existence.

Quentiin's uprising had been fine and well for *them*, Hieb supposed as he took another sip from his flask. Quentiin and his companions had only lived in the Pit for a matter of months. They hadn't known what it was like to *truly* live there, to know nothing but the lash of the whip and the grind of the stone-carts. Looking back, Hieb wondered how long it would have taken Quentiin to learn what it truly took to survive in the place—how long it would have taken the dwerion to become like *him*.

It was easy for Quentiin to play at resistance, to make himself the martyr and serve as figurehead for the cause, but Quentiin had been enslaved in fortuitous circumstances—at a time when the count of slaves in the Pit increased following the Fort's fall, and the guards decreased as Zadinn Kanas focused his attention toward the Warrior of Light. Quentiin hadn't been in the Pit when the majority of the slaves were weak and old, or when the malichons had little else to do but devise new means of torment. Hieb recalled Quentiin's speech about how the slaves outnumbered the malichons, but for most of Hieb's life, the numbers had not been in the slaves' favor at all.

Over the years, Hieb had done what was necessary. The first time had been the hardest. It was during an especially brutal winter, when the slaves had been placed together into cells so they could eke what small warmth was available from each other's bodies. The malichons didn't care if an individual slave lived or died, but they couldn't have half their work-force freezing to death overnight. Hieb had been hungry, *so* hungry, for food was in short supply, and he'd seen the old man holding a husk of bread. The man had already been on the cusp of death, a day or two from his demise. Hieb knew the husk of bread would do the man no good, not when he had so clearly progressed along the inevitable march toward oblivion. He had his misgivings, but he overcame them quickly enough. It wasn't like this was a *child*.

He was as good as dead, and I needed his bread. As Hieb sat on his stump, swaying from intoxication, a laugh bubbled from his throat. *Dead, bread. It rhymes.*

It hadn't taken much. Just a pinching of the nostrils, a hand over the month. The man didn't even struggle. On the contrary, he seemed peaceful. His eyes opened after Hieb covered his airways, but he never showed a moment of panic, only a gentle acceptance as his body relaxed beneath Hieb's grip. Later, Hieb had thought of the man's simple passing, and envied him for it.

Other nights, other winters, came after that one. And then there were the times the guards needed information and paid for it with the best currencies of all: food, rest, easy duty. Hieb profited from those who were foolish enough to attempt escape, and from those like the old man who had but little left in them. Was there any shame in that? Neither the would-be-escapees, nor the elderly, would have survived anyway. Hieb merely used such timing to his advantage.

Then that dwerion arrived, acting as if he knew or understood the half of what it took to survive in the Pit. Oh, Hieb had helped in the revolution well enough, once it became clear where the tide was headed, but afterward, Galdon was not for him. No, far better for him to make a new life in the Fertile Lands, away from the judging eyes of those he had once lived alongside. Out here, he could live his life in peace, and drink, and think of the way the old man's body had slackened beneath his grip while his life slipped away.

The bushes rustled.

Hieb looked up, the world around him swirling as he did so. He'd be paying for his excess in the morning, but for now the sensation felt quite nice. He looked toward the noise, expecting to see a deer—the sound had been much too big for a rabbit or squirrel—but instead saw nothing, except…what was that? A shadow? He squinted, trying to make out the form more clearly, but saw only ripples of unending darkness.

Hieb felt a cold hand touch his heart and shied away. The old man, the first one, had returned after all. Hieb saw him in his dreams often. The alcohol kept the man at bay, kept him from whispering at the edges of Hieb's thoughts, but Hieb had known it was only a matter of time before he arrived in the flesh.

A tall figure emerged from the bushes, draped in flowing robes darker than the surrounding night. A pair of white hands stretched from its open cuffs, and Hieb thought he heard a whispering accompany this new arrival. At the sight of the robed figure, the cold hand around his heart clenched even tighter, shooting tendrils of pain deep into his chest. Hieb doubled over, the flask falling from his hand and landing with a muffled *thump*. He staggered back to his feet, pushing off the stump. His breath came in wheezing gasps. In front of him, the tall, awful figure merely stood in place, watching events unfold in utter silence.

A low moan escaped Hieb's lips, and he felt wild terror clawing up into his throat. He ran, stumbling past the corner of his cottage and into the woods beyond. He risked a glance over his shoulder and saw the robed figure walking toward him, taking its time, unhurried and unconcerned. It was as if it knew the woodsman's efforts at escape were futile, and though this thought made Hieb try to run faster, he felt time compressing around him as he did so. His movements grew awkward and hindered. It had to be the drink. Nothing else explained the strange way he seemed to be moving through jelly. Behind him, he heard the crunch of his pursuer's slow, deliberate footsteps upon the leaves of the forest floor.

Hieb reached a yawning cavern beneath an uprooted tree trunk and forced his way inside. *Yes.* This was it: the place where he could dig and crawl and hide, escaping further notice for all time. He fell to his knees and clawed at the dirt hanging over the cavern entrance, tearing at the soft loam with his bare hands, lodging dirt beneath his fingernails and covering his hands with soil. Or was it blood? He couldn't tell, and didn't have time to think about it.

Behind him, the robed stranger moved ever closer. Hieb dug faster, offering up prayers to a Maker he had forsaken long ago, on the night he accepted damnation in exchange for a husk of bread. At last, the earth yawned open beneath him, dropping him to the pit of the cavern. Hieb landed on hands and knees, oblivious to the jarring pain of impact. He'd made it—he was safe, and no one could bother him here.

He looked up and saw a second robed figure standing before him. This one had been inside the cave. *Waiting.* Hieb screamed. He tried to move but had lost all power of doing so. The creature reached toward him, its white, bony hand protruding from beneath its robes.

Its touch was cold and eternal.

* * *

Some time later, Hieb's body lay on the floor of the cavern, the forest silent and unmoving for miles around him. Uklith's Assassins had long since departed, headed south on their inexorable journey toward the Pel Delta and the village of Keldur.

Above, the moon reached its peak, shining into the cavern and illuminating Hieb's body in a pale pool of white. After a few moments, barely perceptible to the naked eye, Hieb's hand twitched. Any casual observer would have thought it nothing more than a trick of the light, but moments later, in a decisive matter that was certainly *not* a trick of the light, Hieb sat up. His eyes opened, but there was nobody behind them: no personality, no thought, no soul. This soulless corpse, an automaton once known as Hieb, looked left and right before rising to its feet. It stepped out from the cave, standing tall in the moonlight and surveying the forest before it. The usual nightlife had vacated this vicinity, steering well away from the area ever since Uklith's Assassins had passed this way hours ago.

The once-Hieb turned south, toward Keldur, and sniffed the air. Its fathers had gone that way, on a mission given them by *their* father, but undead Hieb did not have business that way. No, its business lay elsewhere. Its father's father had many plots in play, threads of planning stretching all the way from his prison in Agrazab to the lands on the far side of the Barricade. As its purpose grew clearer in its mind, the undead turned away from the Fertile Lands and faced north. It began making its way through the woods.

Toward Galdon.

14

The company entered Keldur in the dark of night. As Wurit escorted the group through a pair of sentinels, past a row of torches, Tim surveyed the guards. They stood poised on edge, alert and tense, displaying a level of acute awareness that, contradictory as it might sound, was unusual during guard duty. Such a task was ordinarily long and boring, and even the most highly trained of individuals succumbed to the monotony of long hours. *Not tonight.*

Upon seeing Wurit returning, many of the sentinels relaxed, their tension lessening visibly. Tim also observed an occasional glance of surprise, which he expected had something to do with the fact that Wurit's people were coming back largely unscathed. The villagers had left to engage in a conflict in which they held the lower hand, and now they returned with a group of strangers—who *did* bear the marks and scrapes of battle, while Wurit's group showed nary a scratch.

They'd left Taazvin's village an hour ago, after Tim requested that Wurit lead them to Agrazab. "You ask much to repay the debt we owe you," Wurit had replied to Tim after a silence. "Perhaps too much."

"I know," had been Tim's response. "I must ask, but I will not hold you to it."

Wurit barked a laugh. "You *can't* hold us to it. There is but one in the village who could repay such a debt, and even if you held him against his will, he might opt to cut his wrists rather than accede to your demands."

"We only ask as one ally to another. I do not wish for conflict, my friend."

"I only speak in hypotheticals, and besides, the decision is not mine to make. It's not even Sheel's to make. I will do this much, outsider: I will bring you back to Keldur, and from there we will see what comes next."

And so Wurit led them through the woods and waters of the Delta until they arrived at Keldur, walking past the wary sentinels into the village proper.

Here, rudimentary huts lined a crude street. As expected, the buildings had not been constructed with any degree of permanency in mind.

"We move every half-year," Wurit said, noting Tim's gaze upon the buildings. "We establish basic shelter and stay in one place long enough to maintain a semblance of normalcy, but then we move. It's been this way ever since Zadinn's rise."

Tim didn't miss Wurit's use of the present tense. *So Taazvin knew of Zadinn's downfall, but these people do not.* Tim shivered at the implication; Taazvin's knowledge of the outside world lent credibility to the idea that this information had indeed come from Uklith. It was hard to believe a man in the woods could communicate directly with the Demon-Lord—not even Zadinn had done that, as far as Tim was aware. Tim considered telling Wurit of Zadinn's demise, but for the moment left it alone. He would tell them soon enough, but it would be prudent to first discern the hierarchy within this village. He still wasn't closed to the possibility that the people of Keldur might pose a threat. He doubted this very much, and he had every reason to believe they would find common cause as allies, but he didn't want to make assumptions too quickly.

As if in parallel to Tim's thoughts, he saw Boblin and the elions surreptitiously surveying their surroundings: counting sentinels, identifying avenues of defense and counterattack, determining routes to safety. *No offense intended to our hosts, either. It's how the elions operate, how they succeeded for two hundred years where so many others failed.* As they entered a ring of buildings, a quartet of soldiers approached the group. A woman of lean build and blonde hair led the other three, carrying a long sword at her waist. As she came forward, Tim also caught a glimpse of two daggers, one hidden under each of her sleeves.

"What of it, Deslin?" she asked Wurit as they met in the street.

"It's done," he replied, and Tim saw the same slight expression of relief flow on her as he'd seen from the other sentinels. "Taazvin's people are no more."

"And Taazvin?" she asked.

"I put a sword through his neck," Boblin said. The woman turned to him, and the elion shrugged. "He tried to *eat* me."

The woman looked over the newcomers, her blue eyes appraising them with the same guarded assessment the elions themselves had made of the village.

Nobody knows who are friends and who are enemies yet.

"What now?" she asked, returning her gaze to Wurit.

"We take them to see Sheel. At the very least, we owe them a debt of gratitude. Besides, he'll want to hear what news they have of outside."

The woman nodded and stepped aside, the three soldiers at her back letting the group pass.

Once they moved out of her earshot, Wurit waved one of his men close. "Find something to distract Hamur," he said. "The last thing we need is to have her in that room."

"I understand," the soldier replied. He hung back a second, letting the group continue.

Tim and Boblin exchanged a glance. *Oh yes, there are indeed layers to decipher within this place. These villagers have their secrets, just as we have ours.* Behind them, Wurit's soldier joined the woman and her companions, speaking to them in low tones before turning and walking down a side street together.

Wurit led Tim and the elions to a building that stood apart from the rest. It was larger than the others, indicating it held some import or status. Lamplight flickered from one of its windows. Most of Wurit's group had dispersed by this time, leaving only the short man and two others. When they reached the building, Wurit waved his companions off.

"This is Sheel's council hall," he said. "He's our leader, or the closest thing we have to one. He has kept us alive while Taazvin harried our flanks during the last two years, and he succeeded because he's more suspicious than most. It's not my place to ask what business you have in Agrazab, but he'll want to know, especially when it concerns the well-being of one of our own."

Tim nodded. "Thank you for your assistance."

"Thank *you*," Wurit replied. "Without you, I'd probably be a charred corpse on one of Taazvin's poles." He pushed open the door of the council hall and stepped inside.

Two men and three women sat at a table, lamps around the room providing complete light. One of the men stood when Wurit entered. He was aging—well into his seventh decade, Tim guessed, which was no mean feat of survival in a place such as this. According to Boblin, in the days of the Fort few of those in hiding lived longer than five decades. The rest around the table were younger than the man who stood, but not by much. Tim suspected the youngest was the other man, at perhaps five and forty years, while the three women ranged somewhere between the ages of the two men.

"Wurit," the man said. "We received word the moment our scouts sighted your return. As they tell it, you and your people come back to us looking haler than we expected. A fortuitous turn of events, it seems."

"We did not lose a single man, and that's not something I would have postulated twelve hours ago. Taazvin is no more, Sheel." Wurit gestured to Tim. "This man and his companions helped. Truth be told, much of the fight was over by the time we arrived."

The old man faced the outsiders, his eyes narrowing as he looked them over. "I count but seven of you," he said. "You mean to tell me you dispatched over two hundred of Taazvin's people by yourselves? Speak: what of you? Where do you come from?"

"We are the elions of Pellen Yuzhar," Boblin said. "We come from the North."

Sheel folded his arms. "Pellen Yuzhar? Some around here consider him a myth, though I know otherwise. We crossed paths once when I was in my teenage years. I asked that he keep our encounter in confidence. Since you are here, I suspect he broke this oath, but I will tell you what I told him: we have lived here well enough these past years, and we have no desire to partake in your war."

Tim saw the elions stiffen at that. Celia's gaze alone could have cut stone, but Jend Argul was the one who spoke. "Pellen Yuzhar kept every oath he ever took, villager, and we did not learn of Keldur from his lips. You may disregard our struggle if you wish, but I will not suffer ill comments about our Fort's leader. While you remained safe in your homes, we risked our lives to hold the malichons at bay. Think long and hard on that, my friend. You may not have participated in our war, but you have certainly benefited from our sacrifices. If not for the elions of the Fort, Zadinn would have razed these lands long ago."

Sheel remained silent for a long time, locked in a gaze of wills between himself and Jend Argul. Eventually it was the man of Keldur who relented, the leader of those who had hidden giving way before the commander of those who had fought.

"And how do you fare in your struggle?" Sheel asked.

"We won," Celia said.

The previous silence was nothing compared to this one. The slightest noise would have sounded like an explosion as the villagers of Keldur exchanged glances. Wurit shifted his stance, first toward Sheel and his councilors, second toward Tim and the elions.

"How long has it been?" Sheel asked.

"Eighteen months," Tim said.

"And Zadinn Kanas?"

"Is no longer a part of this world."

Sheel expelled a pent-up breath and closed his eyes. A weight seemed to lift from the entire room, rising up to fade into the night sky. Muscles relaxed, tensions lessened, and in the corner, Wurit leaned against a beam, his hand falling away from the pommel of his sword.

"One night," Wurit said. "In one night alone, you have relieved the burden of both threats facing Keldur." He was the first to smile, and though other council members did so as well, when Sheel opened his eyes once again, his face remained grim.

He knows. The others don't realize it, but there's still an axe suspended in the air, and Sheel's waiting for it to drop.

And it would.

"The how and why remain, do they not?" Sheel said, more a statement than a question. "How did you come to know of us, if not for Pellen? Why have you come this deep, if the lands beyond are free?"

"Because we need your help," Tim said. "Zadinn might have fallen, but the Demon-Lord still reigns to the west. We found word of you in Zadinn's archives, and we know some of you have traveled to the City. Uklith's shadow grows. We must head west to stop it, before it grows beyond our means to resist."

Wurit tensed again, standing a little straighter. "Zadinn had word of us, of Keldur, in his archives?"

"No more than fragments. He recorded this not long before his downfall. He found one of your men who had gone to Agrazab and took him to his cells. He had planned to seek you out, but he wanted to launch his attack on the Fort first. This proved to be his undoing, and he never had time to turn his sights on you."

"Zadinn was the most powerful Advocate to ever walk the land," Sheel said. "Pellen told me the people of the Fort numbered little more than three hundred. How did you manage to stand against the Dark Lord?"

"We had aid from the Army of Kah'lash," Jend replied.

"They are a tale of the Kyrlod."

"They are real."

Sheel turned to Tim. "Pellen had no humans at his Fort. He told me that they died when a sickness took them."

"I come from elsewhere. The South."

"Through the Barricade?"

"Yes."

Sheel remained as suspicious as ever. "Yet one more impossible feat? You are withholding something, are you not? It's the crux of the matter, the truth behind your victory, and you have yet to voice it. *How did you win?*"

Might as well come out with it. Tim snapped his fingers and held his hand out. A small, green flame leapt into existence over his palm, dancing and flickering for all to see. "I was trained in the Lifesource by the last Kyrlod," he said. "I am the Warrior of Light. I faced Zadinn in his citadel, and I won, but now I need your help. I seek Agrazab, the City of Darkness."

Sheel shied away from the flame, fear evident in his eyes. All of the council members appeared threatened, and Tim wasn't surprised. The last Advocate to walk the North had enslaved every living being in sight. Wurit alone remained unperturbed.

And therein, Tim thought, *lies the difference between a soldier and a politician. A soldier knows what makes an enemy and what makes a friend, but a politician only knows whether he or she is the most powerful one in the room.*

"Leave us, Warrior," Sheel whispered.

"We mean you no harm. We only seek help in defeating the evil that gave rise to Zadinn. The self-same evil gave rise to Taazvin, and if we do not stop it, it will give rise to another."

Sheel regained some of his former presence, his spine straightening and his voice growing firm. "You can fare just as well without us. There is but one in our village who knows the way to Agrazab, and far be it for me to speak for him. Zadinn, Uklith, it doesn't matter—I had no wish to draw the former's eye upon my village, and I dare not tempt the latter. Ride west to your conflict, but leave us out of it."

"If we fail, it will *become* your conflict, whether you wish it or not," Boblin said. "If Uklith breaks free, his shadow will cover all."

"Pellen Yuzhar said much the same of Zadinn's encroachment," Sheel said. "Yet sixty years after that encounter, the Pel Delta remains as it always was. In any case, as I already said, we could contribute but one man to your quest, and I doubt it would make a difference." He turned an eye to Wurit. "Hamur said she would escort you back here, yet she is noticeably absent. You kept her from this conversation. Leave, soldier. We shall speak on this later."

Wurit returned Sheel's gaze. "I believe we shall." The wiry man gestured to the travelers. "Come with me, friends. I fear there is no more conversation to be had here."

As they turned to leave, Celia moved in a fluid motion, hands a blur. Tim caught the flash of a dagger in her hand right before she whipped it through the air. It spun end over end, burying itself in the wall against which Sheel stood. The hilt quivered a mere hairsbreadth from the villager's neck, and if it had landed one inch to the right, it would have killed him. Sheel's eyes went wide with shock. The councilors scraped their chairs back, rising to their feet.

"We bought your safety by spilling our blood on the slopes of the Death-lands," Celia said. "We bought your safety by standing against Taazvin in his followers. Once a weapon is loosed, *someone* has to stop it." She pointed to the wall, where the dagger still held. "How long will you continue to let others face the danger in your place?"

They stepped out into the night, Wurit leading them. "Please accept my apologies," the small man said after they made it a few paces from the building. "Sheel has always been protective, but he rarely tends toward outright idiocy."

"He only wants what he thinks is best for his people," Tim said.

Wurit shook his head. "That's no excuse for cowardice. The elion said it best: you stood against Zadinn Kanas, you stood against Taazvin, and Sheel has done neither. Come, follow me. I will do what I can to meet this debt."

He led them away from the council hall and to the center of the village. It was well into the evening, and most folk were indoors. The homes were arrayed in rough lines on either side of the street, most comprised of mud exteriors and thatch roofs. Wurit led them to a larger structure, one built of logs and comprising two levels.

"Some families have given more than others," Wurit said by way of ac-knowledgment as the others looked upon the size of the cottage. He knocked and a lantern flared inside, followed by a scraping sound. Moments later, the door swung inward, revealing one of the biggest men Tim had ever seen. The stranger, easily six and a half feet tall, matched the elions in height, but pos-sessed much greater physical bulk than the lithe Patrol members. None of the man's weight was wasted, either; he was all slabs of muscle topped by chiseled features and broad shoulders. His entire frame filled the doorway, a lantern glow outlining him from behind.

"You should have brought this one along for the visit to Taazvin's place," Boblin murmured.

"Wurit," the man said, nodding. The difference between the two was almost comical; Wurit's head reached only the middle of the other man's chest. "Word has it that you've brought Taazvin's reign to an end."

"These folk did more than I," Wurit said, gesturing to the group behind him.

The big man nodded. "So I've heard as well. Tell me, my friends, what can I do for you?"

For a moment Wurit appeared to lose his voice. As the silence stretched out, the big man crossed his arms and looked from Wurit to the group, then back to Wurit again. "What is it, Deslin?"

"They need your help, Eklan," Wurit said at last.

"I'll give it if I can."

"Sheel doesn't know we're here—"

Eklan grunted. "The list of things Sheel doesn't know is far greater than the list of things he *does* know."

"It's—"

Tim cut Wurit off. "We need to find Agrazab."

Eklan's face grew dark, his features hard. "Oh," he said. "Is that all?"

He slammed the door shut with such resounding force that Tim could swear the very foundations of the house shook. A *boom* echoed down the empty street.

"This village is very accommodating," Boblin said.

Tim stepped up to the door and raised his hand to knock, but it swung open once more before he could do so.

"I felt it necessary to make a point," Eklan said.

Tim let his hand fall to his side. "I realize I am asking much of you."

Eklan snorted. "Do you? Have you ever walked into Malath and back out again?"

"Yes."

"He defeated Zadinn Kanas," Wurit said.

At this, a degree of Eklan's animosity appeared to fade, and though some ire remained in his face, when he spoke again he did so with added respect. "I see."

"As we speak, an elion travels toward Agrazab," Tim said. "He means to free Uklith, and we mean to stop him. But we do not know the way, and we need someone who does."

Eklan looked to the side, as if lost in his thoughts. "After all these years," he murmured, not to Tim but to himself, "its hooks remain." He looked at Tim again. "You might have cut your teeth on Zadinn Kanas, but that man was nothing compared to what awaits you on the far side of the Western. The Demon-Lord is immortal. Eternal. Unstoppable."

"And that's why we don't dare fail."

Eklan looked over the group. "Seven is a motley number indeed. I traveled with twelve, and but two of us returned."

Two returned? But they've been telling us there is only one who could lead us. Now was not the time for this question, though. Tim saw Eklan's mind teetering on the edge of a knife, the horrors of his previous visit vying against the needs of nothing less than the world. It was not a decision Sheel understood, but Eklan grasped it well enough, and such great need was not something a man easily dismissed.

"Come back on the morrow," Eklan said at last. "I will draw you a map, but I can do no more than that. It was only by the Maker's grace I returned from such a place. No man receives such grace twice."

Tim bowed his head. "Thank you. We will be in your debt, friend."

"I'm no friend of yours, Matthias. A true friend would slit every one of your throats, here and now, to spare you from the horrors awaiting you in the west." He stepped inside and closed his door, more softly this time.

"Come," Wurit said to the group. "I've done as you asked, and you shall have what you need. My roof is yours for the night."

He led them four houses down the street and ushered them inside. The space would be tight indeed for the seven travelers, but after nights spent on bedrolls atop roots in the Pel Delta, it seemed a palace. Wurit's home had a basic interior. Where Eklan's house had been made of logs, Wurit's was the mud-and-thatch variety like most of the homes in Keldur. Aside from a stove and a modest living area, he had a loft for sleeping, reached via ladder.

As Wurit began cooking a stew dinner, they passed the time with light conversation. Tim was tempted to ask how Sheel had risen to his position of prominence in the village, but decided it wasn't the time for such a question. The small man had done much for their company this evening, and it was best not to prod for unoffered information.

After the elions and Wurit retired, Tim stepped outside once more. He needed time and space to think. He sat on a crude bench by Wurit's front door, unbuckling his sword and laying it across his knees. The focusing point at the hilt glowed once, an acknowledgment of his presence, and dimmed.

Tim closed his eyes, letting the night air of the Delta run over him. It was ever hot and muggy down here, but with nightfall came a lessening of both, along with the blessing of faint, cool breezes.

He wondered how Keldur had first come into being. Sheel was not Pellen Yuzhar—Pellen had been over two hundred years old, a feat only made possible by Nazgar's magic after Pellen fled the battlefield of the North in the wake of High Advocate Herrdrar's fall to Zadinn. Nazgar had tasked Pellen with leading the North's people over the long centuries into the eventual fight for freedom, but Sheel had received no such longevity. He held a normal lifespan, born perhaps seventy years ago. In his sheltered life, Sheel might never have needed to lift a sword in his defense, since he had folk such as Wurit to do so for him. Taazvin had been a minimal threat; all Sheel had to do was move the village and the conflict went away—at least until they had to move again. *He's survived by avoiding threats, not facing them. It stands to reason he would treat this current situation the same way.* And what of Eklan? What had first sent the big man to Agrazab, and what was this apparent grace that had allowed him to return?

Tim looked toward the solitary man's house. The lamp which Eklan had lit upon their arrival still shone through the window. Sleep would not come easy for that man, not tonight, and Tim felt a twist of guilt within his stomach. He knew nothing of what Eklan had gone through, what horrors he'd endured, and Tim had knocked on the man's door without so much as an introduction and asked him to return to the City of Darkness. It had been an unfair request and an unfair choice. *I've asked him to relive his worst nightmare so that the world might be saved. For a man of conscience, is that even a choice to begin with? Or, if a man perceives it to be a choice, does that give him cause to doubt his own conscience?*

The shadows near the corner of Wurit's house rippled. Tim tensed—hand twitching for the hilt of his sword—before he saw it was only another villager, the woman who had approached them at the edge of the village before they went to the council hall. She stepped into view, moonlight illuminating her features. She had a hard face, with jaw set firm and one hand on the hilt of her sword. She approached and stood over him, looking down. Her clear, blue eyes flashed with controlled anger.

"I hear you visited my brother this evening," she said.

He might have wondered which one was her brother, Sheel or Eklan, but her eyes answered the question for him. Eklan possessed the same piercing, intelligent gaze. Though she was lean where Eklan was massive, there was no mistaking the confidence with which both carried themselves.

Some families have given more than others, Wurit had said outside Eklan's house. Keldur had not remained free simply as a result of Sheel moving the village every six months. No, it was people like Eklan and the woman before Tim who had done their part in keeping these people safe.

"We needed his help," Tim said. "I have no wish to bring anything unpleasant upon him, but there is much at stake."

"And you think that gives you the right to come here and lay such a burden upon him?"

"No, it doesn't."

She looked him up and down. The cold fire had not left her eyes. Finally, she straightened and stepped back. "Follow me, Warrior."

He did as she asked. This time they walked to the far end of the village, away from Wurit's and Eklan's homes, almost reaching the outer ring of torches where the sentries patrolled Keldur's perimeter.

This woman's home was even smaller than Wurit's. A thin wisp of smoke curled from her chimney, reaching far up into the night sky beyond. She said nothing, didn't even offer her name, until they reached her door.

"They tell me you're an Advocate," she said. "Can you heal people?"

"No," Tim replied, "I never learned."

"I thought not." She pushed the door inward. "Step inside, Warrior. It's time you learned the consequences of what you ask."

He followed. Inside the room, a small table stood next to the hearth. Much like Wurit's home, a loft at head level held a sleeping mattress. A rocking chair sat in front of the hearth, and in it sat a man with head nodded forward. He had been big once, like Eklan, but now his skin hung loose upon his bones. His hands were folded in his lap and a blanket was drawn up to his chin. Like

Eklan and the woman, the man had blond hair, but many strands had fallen out, and those that did remain stood in disarray. At first glance Tim thought the man was asleep, with head tilted forward and a trickle of drool running down his chin, but then the man's eyes opened and he looked toward them. His expression was so simple, so plaintive, that Tim could not help but feel a wrench of agony in his heart.

"Meet Reidell," the woman said, "the third Hamur sibling. I'm Bria, by the way. It seems fitting you know the names of all those you will hurt." She nodded toward the man in the chair. "Reidell returned from Agrazab strapped to my brother's back. Agrazab paralyzed him in body and in mind. Reidell was the only other survivor of their journey to that Malath-cursed place, and you have the gall to ask Eklan to return."

"I'm sorry," Tim said.

She scoffed. "Sorry? Those are weak words, Matthias, from one who thinks he can walk into this village and tear my family apart once more. Leave. I have no further words for you. I just wanted you to see the truth behind what you ask."

Tim acquiesced, ducking through the doorway. As he stepped outside, Bria closed the door none too gently in his face. He remained standing in place for several long minutes before turning and walking back into the night.

15

Eklan Hamur sat at the table in his cottage, a single lamp providing all the room's illumination. Hands folded, head bowed, he closed his eyes and thought of the past. The journey had been a fool's errand from the start. It began three summers ago, after the old man arrived in Keldur. The stranger, dressed in robes and bearing tales of the lands beyond, spoke of a place in the distant west, far outside Zadinn Kanas's realm, a city once inhabited but abandoned. The man had shared other legends, too, of countries south of the Barricade and islands east of the seas, but it was the city in the west that remained in Eklan's mind long after the wanderer departed. Eklan and his fellow villagers had lived all their lives in Keldur, on the run, hiding from Taazvin and Zadinn alike, always at the mercy of those who persecuted them. So Eklan asked for volunteers to join him in finding this city; they planned to chart the way first, and later return to Keldur to lead their companions out of the Fertile Lands and into the Western Desert. They would make this abandoned city their new home, a place where they no longer needed to live in fear, where they could begin anew.

The quest had been long and dangerous. They lost half their number by the time they reached Agrazab, and yet the horrors of the Desert paled in comparison to what Eklan and his companions faced in in the City of Darkness. *Uklith, in all his awful might.* Eklan did not doubt this Warrior had faced Zadinn Kanas and emerged victorious, but a victory against a mortal man, no matter how powerful, meant little compared to facing the Demon-Lord. Any person that ventured into the City was accepting a fate worse than death.

I will draw a map to show him the way, and in doing so I will cause his death. Eklan did not want to draw the map, did not want to so much as set quill to paper, but he could see that this Tim Matthias intended to find Agrazab one way or another. Tim saw it as his duty, and Eklan Hamur understood duty.

Furthermore, if what Matthias said were true—that plans were in motion to set Uklith free—Eklan supposed Tim had little choice. The Warrior needed to travel to the City, and therefore Eklan needed to chart the way. What transpired next would be beyond his conscience or control.

At times, Eklan thought back to the old man and his tales. He wondered what had become of the ancient stranger. In spite of his age, he had been spry and energetic, his eyes filled with the light of life. His gaze had been knowledgeable, but also cunning, perhaps even devious.

He'd never told them his name, though.

Eklan stood, his bulk filling the room and casting shadows against the door. He doubted sleep would come. Since his return, sleep was difficult most nights, and after speaking with Matthias this evening, it would be all but impossible. He would still go through the motions of attempting rest, though. No need to leave his lamp burning all night, sitting at the table.

As he reached forward to pinch out his light, the front door opened of its own accord. Eklan paused, fingers inches away from the lamp's flame, and looked toward the entryway. There stood a hooded figure, taller than Eklan. It had no face distinguishable within its hood, and the only visible body parts of its body were the cold, white hands that protruded from its sleeves.

Eklan had seen the like before, of course. It was one of Uklith's Assassins. The first time he encountered one, the sight had frozen him in place, rendering him unable to move—and not just because of his fear. The thing exuded power in waves, quite literally trapping its victims in the terrifying box of their minds. He recalled standing in the street in Agrazab, watching the creature lift Yoric into the air. Yoric had screamed once, but it had been a long, awful scream, and Eklan had been quite sure that he'd seen the man's very soul being ripped from him.

Eklan sensed the creature in his house reaching out with its powers, trying to ensnare him in the box of fear once again. Eklan had broken free of such a box the last time, escaping into a nearby alley as Yoric died, and tonight he would not allow the same box to imprison him again. He *pushed* back, and while he was unable to prevent the sensation of frigid cold from settling upon him, he could still command his limbs to move, which was all that mattered. Eklan stepped back from the entryway, overturning a cabinet to delay the creature's inexorable advance, and ripped open a door to his closet.

The Assassin stepped into Eklan's house, ducking its head to make it through the arch of the doorway. Eklan seized a sword from his closet, one hand about its leather-bound hilt, the other hand upon its scabbard, and pulled the blade free with a rasp of metal. He faced the awful thing standing before him, and though its presence compelled Eklan's muscles to tremble, he nonetheless willed them to be still. *Not again. I survived you once, you Malath-cursed spawn of Uklith, and I shall survive you again.*

It was as if the creature heard Eklan's thoughts. From the depths of its hood, a dry, rasping laugh issued, accompanied by a sound that made him think of bone-chimes striking one another. "This reckoning has been long in the coming, Questmaker," it said. "The Demon-Lord does not abide trespassers, and his reach is long."

Eklan held his sword in a defensive stance. "Reaching for the wrong throat is a good way to lose one's hand."

The Assassin moved with whip-like ferocity, robes fluttering as it whisked around the table and came for him. It was almost too easy for Eklan. As the creature opened its arms wide, Eklan drove his blade straight into its chest. He felt resistance, not exactly that of flesh and bone, but enough for him to know he had made contact, and the creature hissed. At first Eklan thought it was making noises of pain, but he soon saw the error of his ways. Uklith's Assassin was not making noises of pain, but of *amusement*. It looked upon him from within its faceless hood. "Do you believe mortal weapons are of any use against me? Your time has come, Questmaker."

It seized Eklan around the throat with hands so cold they burned. It lifted him, leaving his feet dangling, and slammed him against the wall. Eklan felt wood splinter beneath the impact of the blow.

This was how Yoric died.

But it was not how he would go. *Not tonight.* Eklan looped his thumbs around the creature's grip, attempting to tear it free from his throat, and threw his body against the Assassin. His momentum carried them to the floor. They landed with Eklan on top, but the Assassin soon rolled to reverse their positions, straddling his body. Through it all, its grip on his throat remained firm—cold, burning, and deadly.

Eklan felt numbness spreading through his body. Shadows grew at the corners of his vision, enfolding him in their embrace. He could not leave it like this; he looked toward the table above him, seeking anything that could serve as a weapon, and his gaze settled upon the lantern.

Lantern. Flames. Will attract attention.

As Eklan clung to the remaining shreds of consciousness, he reached out. The tips of his fingertips touched the lantern's handle. He strained, dragging it firmly into his grasp, and with the last vestiges of his strength hurled the lantern against the floor.

* * *

Tim had just returned to Wurit's house when he felt it—a ripple within the Lifesource, the barest sensing of a presence not just unfamiliar, but also *wrong.*

There was evil afoot in Keldur.

He spun, looking into the darkness of the street, trying to trace the source of the sudden, cold sensation. Though he saw nothing amiss, he nonetheless knew with undeniable certainty that something was awry. Placing a hand on the pommel of his sword, Tim stretched out with all his senses, pinpointing the source of his discomfort—and heard a crashing sound from Eklan Hamur's house. He whipped his head toward the noise. A dark, cold warning rolled toward him through the Lifesource. Tim broke into a run.

Behind him the door of Wurit's house opened, and the villager poked his head into the street. "Matthias?"

Tim paused just long enough to acknowledge him. "Get Boblin and the others!" He ran toward Eklan's house, just as flames blossomed on the opposite side of Eklan's window. The front door hung askew, and by the time Tim reached the steps, smoke was billowing out the entryway and into the street. He stepped into the midst of an expanding conflagration, with waves of heat blasting his face.

The attack came in a flood of miasmic energy. Before it could engulf him, Tim slammed down a shield of the Lifesource, creating a bubble of protection around himself. His assailant's powers washed off the shield, spilling harmlessly away from Tim and slamming into the floorboards and walls of Eklan's home. He felt his enemy's efforts redouble. The force of the creature's magic caused Tim to slide backward, but he planted his feet firm to hold his ground. In the next second the bubble popped as Tim's magic won out, and he heard a crashing sound from within the inferno.

Flames danced in front of him. Tim stayed low to keep the smoke from stinging his eyes, peering through the haze in search of his attacker, and caught a glimpse of two large figures locked in combat. Hungry fire raced across the floorboards, licking the walls, curling toward the ceiling, while fumes and smoke pumped skyward. Holding his breath, Tim rose and took a lurching step toward the opponents.

And then a burning timber fell from the roof to crash down onto him.

* * *

Uklith's Assassin moved through the streets with quiet, deadly grace. After its partner entered Eklan Hamur's house, the second had continued on a separate assignment. It had only come across one villager in the night—most folk were inside, asleep and unaware of that which prowled outside their homes. The villager had not had time to raise the alarm; one quick stroke of the Assassin's dagger, and the man lay in the shadows, his sightless eyes staring skyward, a pool of blood beneath his neck.

The Assassin approached the house of the man named Sheel. It waved a hand, and the door opened. The creature stepped over the threshold, little more than a wraith in the dark, and surveyed its surroundings. The interior of Sheel's home was sparse; it, like Hamur's house, was one of the few wooden structures in the village, a symbol of the man's status as leader of his people. And yet, even having been in this village for little more than a quarter hour, Uklith's Assassin could smell the difference between Sheel and Hamur. The big man was everything the village leader was not. At a different time in a different place, Eklan Hamur might have been the leader, not this cowering bureaucrat.

It sniffed the air. Smell happened to be one of an Assassin's most potent weapons; a man's scent was his spoor. Sheel's scent spoke of insecurity, of a need for power and the willingness to do whatever was necessary to keep it. This was a man who wrapped himself in complacency, who thrived because of it. It was no wonder he eschewed the outside world, for to participate in it would only lessen his status. If this man joined Ladu's empire, he would lose his worth, becoming little more than another citizen serving the dynasty of the North.

Stepping into a side room where Sheel slumbered in his bed, the Assassin stood at the foot of the mattress. It patiently waited for Sheel's eyes to open. Though it could have completed the deed much sooner, the Assassin wanted to see the look on the man's face when it delivered its killing blow.

Sheel bolted upright, eyes going wide as he scuttled back against the headboard of his bed. He froze as they all did, mouth opening to cry but no sound coming out. The Assassin closed the distance, the blade of a knife appearing in its hand, and sliced Sheel's throat. A dark current of blood gushed from the man's neck. Sheel fell to the side, his life ending in a manner as insignificant and immaterial as the way in which he'd led his people during these past decades.

The Assassin left the house, waving a hand again as it did so. The structure burst into flames behind it, forming a fitting parallel to Eklan's home burning at the far end of the street. Around the creature, people streamed from their houses as Keldur awakened to the commotion. One of the villagers saw the Assassin and cried out. Those who were armed unsheathed their blades, flocking to confront the creature. From within its hood, the Assassin would have smiled if it had a face to do so.

* * *

Boblin looked up as Wurit opened the door of his house and rushed inside.

"Trouble," the man said.

"Of what sort?" Hanqar asked, but Boblin was already in motion. Drawing his blade, the elion leapt out the door and into the street.

Rising flames were on the verge of consuming Eklan's house. Boblin ran toward the fire and charged through the building's shattered entryway. Once inside, he saw nothing but flames and a towering black figure. It flicked a hand toward him, and though the movement was casual, almost negligent, Boblin felt an invisible force slam into his chest. He flew backward from the house into the street, where he landed in an unceremonious heap.

At the sound of a cry farther down the road, he looked toward Sheel's house, only to see that the home of Keldur's leader had also caught fire. Outside the burning structure, another tall figure in robes stood before a closing semicircle of villagers.

Celia touched his shoulder. She looked into his eyes and nodded toward the commotion at the end of the street, where in front of Sheel's house the slaughter had begun. The robed figure slipped in and out between the village folk, dodging their blows, dealing calculated strikes. Wherever it moved, men died.

Boblin cast one last glance at Eklan's house. "Let's let Tim handle that one." He climbed to his feet, sword in hand, and ran toward the cyclone of death at the far end of the street.

* * *

As half the second floor collapsed onto Tim, he wrapped another shell of protection around himself. The falling timbers slid harmlessly away from his shield, but that didn't stop them from obscuring his vision.

He didn't recognize the opponent he faced. Was this creature some kin to Isanam, the Malichon Overlord, who could also use the Lifesource? He did not see how such a creature could exist in the wake of Zadinn's defeat, but now was not the time for deliberation. He had to act first, survive first, and fill in details later. He used the Lifesource to push the rubble away from himself, emerging from the wreckage. Before him, Eklan Hamur lay on the ground, the robed assailant atop him. The big man fought with lip curled and a growl in his throat.

Tim rejoined the fight and saw Eklan's eyes roll back into his head as the man succumbed to the creature's grip and fall into unconsciousness. This time it was Tim who struck, lifting his hand and sending the robed assailant flying across the room. It slammed into the wreckage of a cabinet which had already seen its fair share of damage tonight.

The creature was back on its feet in an instant, hands outstretched, cold power radiating outward. Standing twenty paces apart, the two combatants clashed in a will of sorceries, Tim's power against the creature's power. Any outward observer would merely have seen the two staring at each other from across the room, each straining against an invisible force, while in truth a maze of Lifesource energy hung between them, vying for supremacy as the flames of the burning building raged.

Tim saw a flicker of motion, and half-turned as Bria Hamur entered her brother's house with blade drawn. The distraction proved to be his mistake, as the creature's attack slipped past his guard and delivered a crushing blow to his ribcage. He crumpled, throwing up a defense against a subsequent strike that could very well have torn him half.

Bria ran her blade into the creature's chest. Though it did not appear to be outwardly affected by the blow, Tim felt its attention waver just enough for him to stand again. He grabbed Eklan by his arms and dragged him through the flaming wreckage toward the door. The Assassin could not afford to intervene, as it refocused its efforts on Tim.

As Tim moved, he caught a glimpse of his sword on the floor. He shifted his attention to the remainder of the second floor, *pushed*, and brought it crashing down on the Assassin. The creature cleared the wreckage away from itself, the delay giving Tim the opportunity he needed. He dove for his weapon and rolled back into a standing position, blade blazing to life in his hands.

The Assassin attempted a final, futile attack before Tim brought his sword around in a whirling circle, delivering a blow to a neck that was not there, feeling resistance nonetheless. There was a cold, explosive *whoosh* as the creature's life winked out, and its robes collapsed in a loose heap.

With the battle done, Tim's senses returned to the present in all its flaming intensity. The very foundations of the house were about to collapse, and he had no time to lose. Tim sheathed his sword and escaped the building at a run.

* * *

Boblin launched himself into the fight just as the robed attacker felled a trio of soldiers before him—one, two, three, all with clean and deadly strokes. The tall figure's robes swirled, its blade flashing in the moonlight as it flowed from one victim to the next.

"Fall back!" Boblin yelled. He and the elions would operate best in a clear area, unhindered by the movements of any well-meaning but potentially ineffective villagers. His request, of course, went largely unnoticed, and one more man died before Boblin made his way into the conflict.

He jumped high, swinging his sword downward, already anticipating the robed assassin's retaliatory move and planning ahead. Their blades met with a ring of steel against steel. Boblin had ascertained that this attacker was not human; in the light of fire from Sheel's cottage, he could see the unnatural hue of its skin and the lack of a face within its hood.

Wonderful. Just karfing wonderful. Earlier tonight it was religious zealots who also happened to be cannibals. Now it's some Malath-cursed creature that Uklith decided would be more intimidating if it didn't have a face. Dramatic effect is vastly over-rated.

Celia and the other elions were close behind. The creature struck at Celia, not with its sword but with its apparent Lifesource abilities, and she landed on her back from the attack, skidding across the ground in a scuff of dirt.

Twice Boblin had fought against an opponent who could use the Lifesource. The first time, he had faced Tim in the Northern Mountains, and the second time, he had fought Isanam during the Battle of the Deathlands. Prior to these encounters, Nazgar had taught Boblin techniques for defense, showing him how ancient students of ailar used their martial skills as a means of combating Lifesource-capable enemies. The subtle practice, by no means perfect, had saved Boblin's life on both occasions. To use it effectively, one had to observe things like the expression on a face, the direction of a gaze, and the tension in an opponent's body muscles to predict where they would strike. The rub in this particular situation was that Boblin's attacker *had* no face. This limited Boblin's ability to read his opponent but didn't inhibit it completely. When the creature raised its hand in an obvious gesture of attack, he rolled to the side, and the ground erupted where he had just been standing.

The remaining elions entered the fight, Jend and Hanqar coming at the creature from one side, Hugo and Ken from the other. The Assassin moved in a blur between them. Within an instant Hugo was on the ground, bleeding profusely from a shoulder wound, and it was a testament to the elion's skill that he was even alive at all. Jend and Hanqar dove to either side next, dodging an attack similar to the one the assassin had directed toward Boblin. A column of earth exploded between them, raining rock shrapnel down. Ken managed to drive his blade into the creature's neck, but it had no obvious effect, and the robed figure kicked him onto his back.

As Boblin came up from his roll, Celia rejoined the fight. He purposefully placed himself between the burning cottage and the attacker, hoping that the heat of the flames and roiling smoke would distract the creature and make it harder for the assassin to focus its attacks directly.

Celia shot a crossbow bolt into the creature's face. The quarrel disappeared into the hood, the far end of the shaft poking out the back of the cowl, but once again the weapon had no effect. Still, it gave Boblin an idea. As the creature went for Celia, Boblin unhooked his own crossbow and dipped the tip of the quarrel into the rising flames behind him. The arrow quickly caught fire. *Let's see how you do when we burn your robes right off your body,* he thought, then raised his crossbow and fired.

* * *

Tim hit the street. He saw Bria Hamur kneeling over her brother, attempting to revive him. She glanced at him as he stumbled to her side, smoke billowing out of the building behind him. Several other villagers also approached to help, but she waved them away.

"What in Malath was that thing, Matthias?" she asked. The glare in her eyes suggested she harbored no shortage of blame toward him regarding this night's events. To be completely fair, she was likely correct in doing so. The attackers had obviously come here to prevent any further journeys to Agrazab. Had Tim not brought his companions to the village, Uklith may have left well enough alone.

"I have no idea," Tim replied. "It was something of Uklith's."

He expected some reply from her, but she just looked at him for a long moment before returning to tend to her brother. Tim glanced toward the far end of the street, where he saw Sheel's house also in flames. In front of it, Boblin, Celia, and the rest squared off against a second one of the tall, hooded creatures. Around the scene of combat, bodies lay strewn in the street, all of them Keldurians. *How many of these creatures are in the village?* No time to count. Tim unhooked his blade from his belt once more and took off at a run.

* * *

The bolt landed in the creature's robes, setting it afire. Boblin heard a sound halfway between a hiss and a screech, and as he seized a second crossbow bolt, the assassin struck with a wave of its hand. A slug of compressed air punched Boblin in the gut, dropping him to one knee and causing him to drop the arrow.

The creature stepped toward Boblin, fully ablaze but otherwise unimpeded. Keeping his gaze focused on the creature, Boblin reached for the arrow by feel alone, wrapping his fingers around the shaft where it lay in the dirt. The assassin gestured again, and Boblin dove forward in a somersault, the ground where he had just been detonating in a fountain of death. He came out of his roll, arrow in one hand, crossbow in the other, and fit bolt to weapon as he reached his feet. The creature struck again, and this time the entire crossbow exploded in Boblin's hands.

He jerked back in time to avoid fragments from spraying into his face, knowing he'd only narrowly escaped being blinded. A wooden splinter buried itself in his chest, and another few embedded themselves in his forearm. Boblin cursed, tumbling back onto his knee, the pain and surprise momentarily disabling him.

He turned toward the creature, which closed the distance rapidly. Boblin moved his numbed hand toward his sword, knowing even as he did so that he was moving more slowly than he should, his freshly sustained wounds hindering him, that it would only be a moment before—

The creature exploded in a ball of green fire three steps from Boblin, the blast so bright it blinded him. He blinked to clear his eyes, and saw tatters of the creature's robe floating away on the wind. He took another moment to regain his footing, the street quiet in the absence of combat. The rest of the elions also picked themselves up from the ground, having either dived out of the way of the attack or been knocked down by it.

In front of the elions, Tim lowered his sword, its green flames dying out. "Was that all of them?" he asked, stepping up to join Boblin and the rest.

"Do I look like I have that kind of information?" Boblin replied. "My arm hurts."

"It was all of them," Eklan's voice said. The big man pushed through the crowd of villagers, his face haggard and weary, red marks around his throat. No doubt they would turn to bruises on the morrow. "They always come in pairs," he continued. "They killed three of us the last time."

Boblin looked around. The two that had been in the village tonight had done their fair share of killing. At least a dozen Keldurians lay dead in the street, and Sheel was well on his way to becoming a charred ember in the house behind them. "Uklith brings nothing but death," Eklan said, looking at his fallen comrades. "Do you still intend to go west?"

"I don't see that we have a choice," Tim said.

Eklan remained silent for a long moment. "No, I don't suppose you do. If the Demon-Lord's reach has truly extended this far, terrible things are at hand. Rest tonight, Warrior. You'll need it."

* * *

In the morning, the mist hung low to the ground. Tim stepped outside of Wurit's cottage, walking through the mostly empty village toward Bria Hamur's house. He passed the remains of Eklan's home, an ashen ruin like Sheel's on the far side of Keldur. The group had remained awake for some time the previous evening, first occupied with reducing the fires to a manageable level, next clearing the streets and paying respects to the fallen. Through it all, Tim felt Bria's eyes on him, still holding him accountable for all that had transpired. *And she is probably right to do so.*

He hoped she would not be at the house when he came to get the map from Eklan. He didn't want to face that accusatory gaze again. His hopes were validated when, instead of reaching Bria's house, he came upon Eklan in the street, already making his way toward Wurit's home.

Tim and Eklan stood in the low-lying mist, facing each other for a period of silence.

Eklan broke it first. "You say you don't have a choice, but you do. We *always* have choices. You could cross back to the opposite side of your Barricade—seal it off, hope for the best. Couldn't you?"

Tim said nothing.

"It's what Sheel would have done," Eklan continued. "I don't know if it's right to speak ill of one who has recently died, but I'll say it as I see it."

Tim let the silence stretch, and then nodded. "Yes, you're right—about choices, that is. This *is* a choice. I'm going, and the elions are coming with me. Do you have the map?"

Eklan tapped the side of his skull. "It's in my head, Warrior. I don't know how Sheel died, but I'm guessing he did it in his bed, defenseless. Or, if he was awake, he wouldn't do anything to stop it. Last night, it became clear to me that Agrazab is coming for us, whether I wish it or not. I'm not going to die as Sheel did. I'll go to Agrazab with you, Warrior. I'll show you the way to that cursed place, where it sits at the very edge of the earth, and we will face the end together there."

16

Emperor Ladu Jovun IV stood on his balcony, watching the sun set as a breeze fluttered over him, the rays of daylight casting their last warmth. He'd located his balcony here on purpose, in order to watch the sunsets and listen to the city's sounds.

During the past hour, Galdon's daytime buzz had faded as people finished their tasks and retired indoors. Below Ladu, a hawker had begun putting his wares away for the evening. The elion, a former slave who'd been freed from the Pit during the Battle of the Deathlands, did leatherwork on the same street corner each day within view of the palace balcony. Another merchant, a woman from Galdon who'd been in the city three months, tossed the last scraps of her cart's meat pies to an aging dog, which wagged its tail and attacked the meal with gusto. Over the past months, Ladu had watched these two merchants interact often, sometimes helping each other prepare their stands at daybreak, and he'd also seen them frequent the nearby tavern together. In this, a relationship between two individuals who would have otherwise been strangers, the two vendors provided a singular representation of a broader dichotomy: that of North and South, come together after many years on opposite sides of a continental barrier. Ladu suspected that neither merchant cared one way or the other for the disagreements between himself and Aras; they simply wanted to live as they saw fit in this land of new opportunities.

Aras's call to halt any further exodus of his subjects was unsustainable at best, and both monarchs knew it. The King of Alcatune was clearly working toward a position of negotiation, starting with an extreme expectation in the hopes Ladu would meet him halfway. *It was so much simpler,* Ladu thought, *when all we had were the swords in our hands and the quest before us.* Truth be told, Ladu had never enjoyed the intricacies inherent within the monarchy, and he was envious of men like Jend Argul and Boblin Kule, who led a tight-knit group of soldiers united in a single purpose. Serving as the head of a kingdom was another matter entirely. He had mouths to feed, affairs to govern, laws to manage, and Galdon, a city of two thousand, was a far cry from the hundreds of thousands his father had ruled.

Though Ladu had indeed lived during that time two centuries gone, his memories of those days were foggy. He'd only lived because he had spent the better part of those two hundred years sealed in a sorcerous block of crystal for his protection. When Nazgar set him free, Ladu hadn't even known his name for the first few heartbeats after awakening, and much had come at him in a rush. He eventually recognized Nazgar as the one who had sealed him inside the crystal in the first place, but seeing Pellen Yuzhar had been a total shock. Ladu had a hard time reconciling the appearance of this ancient leader with that of the same young elion he'd stood beside on the battlefield during their last defense against the malichon armies.

He missed Pellen's companionship. To say the elion's rest was well deserved would be an understatement, and Ladu did not begrudge him this, yet Pellen had been the only link to the world Ladu once knew. Besides, Pellen had been a mentor to Ladu as much as he'd been a friend. Few folk could have kept a community like the Fort together during the long, dark centuries of Zadinn's dominion, and Ladu respected Pellen all the more for it. During these days of frustrated negotiation with Aras, Ladu would have welcomed the aging elion and his words of wisdom.

"Your majesty?" a voice asked, interrupting Ladu's thoughts.

Still looking over the balcony, Ladu allowed himself a grimace before smoothing his face and turning toward Endar Varuc. The short, fat nobleman had a narrow face, with a slight hook in his nose. Long, greasy hair spilled down his shoulders. He wore ostentatious robes, which no doubt contributed to the constant sheen upon his face, as well as his distinctly unpleasant odor of armpits saturated in perspiration. Not for the first time, Ladu wondered when the man would give up appearances for function. *Then again,* he thought, *given what I've seen of the Varuc family so far, such a day is far off.*

"Lord Varuc," Ladu said, acknowledging the man with a nod of his head.

Endar returned the gesture with a sweeping bow. "I trust I am not disturbing you?" He had a thin, reedy voice, every bit as pinched as his cheekbones.

Lord Varuc, you always *disturb me.* "Never, my friend. How may I be of service?"

"Your majesty, you are too kind. It is *I* who serve you."

When the Varuc siblings left hiding the spring after Zadinn's downfall, they had brought with them a small band of people. The Fort had claimed to be the last free dwelling in the North, but there had been other small communities that came out of hiding after the Dark Lord fell. None were the size of the group that had lived at the Fort of Pellen, but over time they had contributed to the rising population of the new kingdom.

Ladu retained a few memories of the Varuc siblings' twice-grandsire Ultin Varuc, a loyal follower of the Jovun dynasty. Ultin had led the very first charge against Zadinn's malichons during the original invasion, dying a brave death. Ultin's descendants, it appeared, did not possess the same moral fiber as their ancestor. After learning of Zadinn's death, Endar and Raisha left the caves they had been hiding in far to the east and came to Galdon, expecting to find a kindred spirit in the new emperor. Ladu acknowledged their claims to lordship, much as it grated on him to do so. Blood lineage was blood lineage, and it would have ill served him to show disrespect to this man and woman in front of his new subjects. Endar and Raisha had been the leaders of a small band of survivors, and Ladu did not wish to slight them in front of those they had protected. It had been one of his first and most unpleasant lessons as emperor: sometimes you had to grant power to those you disliked in order to please those you served.

"And what thoughts do you have to share with me this evening?" Ladu asked.

"On the matter of Houses, your majesty," Endar began in his nasal voice.

Ladu drew a breath to calm himself. *Dear Maker, save me from this talk of Houses again. Uklith is preparing to tear apart the very fabric of our existence, and all this man has thoughts for is how to best assuage his sense of self-worth.*

"Creating a formal charter of those with noble blood would allow everyone to serve you better, my lord," Endar continued. "The minutiae of running Galdon day to day need not be the first thing on your mind. A Council of Houses could better attend to these matters, leaving you free to focus on the broader task of rebuilding your kingdom."

Truth be told, the Varucs had the right idea. If Ladu could delegate some of the tasks to a council of nobles, this fledgling empire might grow more smoothly. The rub was that Endar and Raisha were not the right ones to head such a council. *I have three Houses for you, my Varuc friends: House Matthias, House Kule, and House Argul. Those are folk I could trust to do right by my subjects.*

"I appreciate your suggestion, Lord Varuc," Ladu said. "It holds merit, but the time is not right. The people need their emperor to be visible and active; we are yet young in this endeavor, and I cannot appear to abdicate my responsibilities, however beneficial you and I know it would be. We must be patient. The council will come, but not yet." *And the time won't be right until I figure out how best to reduce your involvement.*

"Brother, you aren't bothering our emperor again, are you?" asked a new voice—smooth and sultry, much unlike Endar's. Raisha Varuc stepped onto the balcony, giving Ladu a smile that made him think of a cat sizing up a mouse.

This one plays with her food before she kills it.

Her silk robes clung to her tall figure, and somehow the heat that so poorly affected Endar's complexion did not even appear to touch her. She had long, dark hair, immaculately kept, and a gaze that could either seduce or destroy—or perhaps do both at the same time. Ladu had known those like her in his father's court. They made a man feel he was the most important thing in the world to her, so long as she needed something from him, and woe to him when his usefulness was up. While Endar's attempts at subterfuge were so obvious as to be amusing, Raisha sought to subvert Ladu in ways the emperor had yet to fully ascertain. It also didn't help that she made his breath catch every time she stepped into the room. *Which is exactly what she wants it to do,* he reminded himself.

"The Council of Houses, sister—"

She waved a hand, her lacquered fingernails glistening in the sunlight. "The Council, the Council. The emperor has heard your piece, I assure you. Until such time as he sees fit to proceed—*if* he sees fit to proceed—I suggest you let the matter rest."

Endar opened his mouth to reply, but something resembling a squawk came out. She drummed her fingers on the railing of the balcony, letting Endar wilt under the resulting silence. Raisha's ploy was simple enough—let Endar be Endar, and the man would undermine himself more with each passing day, leaving Raisha to step in and seize power.

Ladu felt a pressure building behind his temples. He almost raised a hand to massage the oncoming headache, but stilled the impulse. It would draw Raisha's attention in the same way a wounded deer drew a wolf. "No request is without merit," Ladu said, mostly to keep her off guard. Raisha was yet one more reason

Ladu allowed Endar to hold as much power as he did; the more time she spent trying to siphon control away from her brother, the less time she spent attempting to do the same to Ladu. "Your concerns have merit, Lord Varuc, but the day is closing, and I wish to take my respite in solace. I bid you farewell."

Endar replied with another of his sweeping bows. Ladu noted, with a subtle tug of amusement, a droplet of sweat flew from the nobleman's brow to splatter on the floor. "It is we who thank you, your majesty." Drawing himself up, he turned and faced Raisha.

She curtsied, dipping low, her elegance forming a stark contrast to Endar's almost comical nature. When she came back up, Ladu saw the hint of a gleam in her eyes. "Indeed, your majesty. The honor is ours." She left the balcony, hips swaying, Endar shuffling in her wake. As the siblings disappeared into the palace, Ladu caught a hint of Endar's piping voice providing Raisha a litany of the days' proceedings, along with a healthy dose of his opinions thrown in.

Ladu collapsed in his chair, free to massage his temples. *I wish those two had never come here.* It was bad enough contesting with King Aras to the south; the last thing he needed was a pair of power-hungry nobles more concerned with outdoing each other than with providing anything resembling valuable service to the citizens of Galdon.

As Ladu rubbed his head, his thoughts turned to the west. Matthias didn't have enough focusing reservoirs to leave one with Ladu. It made more sense to give the reservoir to Quentiin Harggra, as Matthias and Harggra each needed to know what the other was up against. The attack on Vonku made Ladu very uncomfortable: it had the smell of dark magic upon it, which was as disturbing a development as any of them. The activities of the possessed folk in Galdon spoke of dark magic as well, but the North was used to such things, whereas the South had been largely isolated from such powers. Matters taken for granted in Ladu's kingdom—the Lifesource, the Advocates, Harmea, Malath—were matters of legend on the southern side of the Barricade, or at least they had been until Matthias opened the way. If Uklith's reach could cross the Barricade, it was an unprecedented display of strength.

Tangential to this train of thought, if Uklith was mighty enough to reach the far side of the Barricade, how was it that he remained imprisoned—or was he in fact already free? *Is Matthias walking into a trap?* It didn't add up. If Uklith *was* at full strength, he had no need of a trap. He'd simply come out of the west and obliterate everything in his path. Subtlety served him little purpose.

Ladu was still musing on these matters when the flutter of curtains announced someone else stepping onto the balcony. *May the Maker preserve me*, he thought; if either of the Varuc siblings had returned, Ladu just might throw himself from this ledge and consider it a fair trade, for himself if not for the folk of Galdon.

When he turned toward the new arrival, Ladu started in surprise. A man dressed in rags stood before him. The stranger's face bore cuts and scrapes, his skin was bruised, and his hair in wild disarray. He panted, as if he'd run a long distance. Ladu had no time to wonder how the man had made it past the palace guards, much less onto the balcony. The man radiated the menace of a rabid dog, and every fiber of Ladu's being caused him to spring into action. He wore no sword, having done so less and less as his duties became increasingly bureaucratic. Now, he cursed his lack of foresight. *I can't become soft like Endar Varuc. A man needs his sword at all times, no more, no less. Let this be a lesson.*

He came to his feet as the man lunged. He saw the glint of a dagger in the stranger's palm, flashing in the light of the setting sun. Ladu tore the curtains from his balcony, leapt forward, and flung them onto his attacker. From within the curtain, the man hissed and spat, making unintelligible noises of rage. Ladu shouted for his guards with all the breath he could muster, using the rest of his energy to keep his attacker subdued.

Ladu had half a mind to end his attacker's life by smothering him with the curtain, but he needed information. While he could hardly expect a city of two thousand to unanimously love him, an outright assassination attempt was another matter entirely. As his muscles began to tire from holding his thrashing attacker in place, Ladu wondered if Raisha Varuc had hired this man.

Pounding footsteps announced the arrival of Faldon and Tavin Kule as the elion brothers swept onto the balcony, no doubt having heard Ladu's cries from the garrison below. Together, they wrested the curtain-enshrouded attacker away from Ladu, using their sword-points to hold the man under guard. Eventually, the prisoner struggled free from the curtain, his sides heaving in and out, face red from the struggle, clothing in greater disarray than before. He stood with his back to the balcony, Faldon and Tavin on either side of him, each with a sword to the man's neck. He looked from one to the next, then focused his gaze on Ladu.

"Who sent you?" Ladu asked. In response, the man broke into a fit of giggles. *This one is far from being in his right state of mind.*

Without warning, the man jumped onto the ledge of the balcony. He tottered for a moment before gaining a tenuous balance. "He comes," the man breathed, his eyes wild, his face lit with passion. "He comes! And there is nothing you can do or say that shall stop him!"

Ladu swallowed. So there were more like the ones who had attacked at Kule's wedding, and one had made it inside the palace. *But what draws them out? Where do they hide?* "We do not fear your master," he said.

Another giggle bubbled from the man's throat. "Oh, you should. Your dynasty is short-lived, son of Jovun! The time of his arrival is nigh, and all that lives under the sun shall be his!"

"Move carefully," Ladu said to the Kule brothers. "Let's get him down and bring him to the dungeons. We may yet be able to make sense of this."

As Ladu stepped forward, the man shook his head. "Oh, no," he said, voice a whisper. "I serve my master. And he promises...deliverance."

Ladu saw it coming and lunged, but he was too slow. The man spread his arms wide and fell backward, tumbling from the balcony without a sound. A mere span of heartbeats later, he struck the pavement below. He looked like a fly struck by parchment, limbs twisted at odd angles and pools of blood spreading beneath him. Ladu stood looking over the balcony, the Kule brothers beside him.

"Thank you for your quick action, captains," Ladu said to the elions.

In response, Tavin shook his head slowly. "Something is wrong here, your majesty. I believe that man was more than simply mad. I fear he was possessed. Uklith should not be able to hold this much sway in Galdon, though, not unless his prison is far weaker than we thought."

The captain is right. Uklith is getting through to our citizens, and that means he is far stronger than he was a year ago. "Double the palace guard," Ladu said. "And bring me my sword." It had been a mistake to stop wearing it in the first place.

And Ladu did not like mistakes.

17

The sun beat down on Quentiin and Trivian as they led the soldiers from Eltern toward Vonku's coast. They'd left the outpost two days ago, and aside from a minor skirmish with a roving band of corsairs the afternoon of the first day, the journey had been without incident. Quentiin thought it might be better for them to have faced more enemies. He'd prefer these men have more experience to cut their teeth on before they reached the sea.

Most of the soldiers, along with Quentiin and the dwerions, rode horses from Eltern. Trivian hung close to the men at the head of the group, out of earshot of the dwerions. A line of men stretched behind them, while beside them a small cluster kept pace on foot.

Jolldo caught Quentiin looking toward the soldiers. "A motley crew," he said. "What d'ye think of them?"

"They carried themselves well at Eltern. The weaker ones have been culled, cruel as it may sound to say aloud. Besides, we were all green once. We survived."

Instead of replying, Jolldo continued looking at the line of marching men. Quentiin studied his friend, observing subtle but conflicting emotions on his friend's face. Jolldo clearly had some skepticism regarding the skills of the soldiers riding alongside them, but it was more complex than that. He also showed a twinge of...*regret? Uncertainty?*

Quentiin had the answer to his question when Jolldo spoke. "I suppose so," the dwerion said. "Many of us were more than just green, too."

Guilt. The matter had gone largely unspoken of between the two friends. Quentiin believed the words were unnecessary, but as for Jolldo...well, Quentiin's friend had to decide what was necessary and what was not.

When they were prisoners in the Pit, Quentiin had sought the other dwerions' aid in escaping, but they had refused, fearing the malichons too much.

They'd seen the malichons perpetrate too much cruelty to muster the courage to rise up. On the last day, when Quentiin stood against their captors, Jolldo and the others allowed the malichons to overwhelm Quentiin and take him to the caves for execution.

As Quentiin watched Jolldo riding beside him, he knew Jolldo was wrestling with his conscience, telling himself that even as he questioned the bravery of these young soldiers, he had also failed not long ago when Quentiin needed him most. Except, as far as Quentiin was concerned, this wasn't true. Jolldo *had* indeed saved him, raising the dwerions and sweeping into the caverns, rescuing Quentiin from his grisly fate and turning the tide against the malichons.

The psyche was a funny thing, however. From today forward, Jolldo might rise to Quentiin's aid a hundred times, yet his mind would always latch on to that one time he hadn't, the one time he gave in to fear, rather than focus on the numerous times he'd been strong. Quentiin couldn't break through that wall for his friend, only Jolldo could, and it was something the other would have to learn on his own. The irony of it all, as Quentiin saw it, was that only through overcoming debilitating fear—as Jolldo had done—did one become brave. *We cannot understand true success unless we fail first, and we cannot understand true courage unless terror has overwhelmed us first. It's easy for a dwerion to stand tall when he's only ever been victorious, but it's defeat that gives us an opportunity to rise again.*

Jolldo would have his chance to show bravery soon enough. Kaarst and his fleet awaited them, and Quentiin knew they were sailing into the teeth of a battle for which they were vastly underprepared. Not only were the numbers against them, they also had to face these strange weapons Kaarst had at his disposal. *Aye, we will all be tested in that which comes next—Jolldo, these Legion men, me. The one named Trivian is atoning for some failure of the past, as we all are, and he may well have to answer for it before the end.*

As the group rode across plains near the southern edge of the Odow, Quentiin shifted his thoughts to the forest's great, green expanse. This was the home he'd known his entire life. They'd left the main roads long ago, knowing Kaarst's corsairs used them while roaming and pillaging the countryside. Even now, they passed an occasional ransacked homestead or farmhouse, some with the ugly sight of bodies out front, others blissfully barren and offering hope that the owners might have escaped the carnage. The company rode at a surreal peace, as if nestled in the eye of a storm. They might have violence ahead and behind of them, but for the moment they had a reprieve. The breeze rustled through the oaken border of trees to their north, while the air hung still over rolling fields to the south. A wisp of smoke on the horizon spoke of another raid, too far away to offer either cause for concern or opportunity to aid.

Quentiin intended to take the group to Peltin, a small coastal village that served as a supply point for ships coming to or from Vonku. Quentiin had never been there, but some of Eltern's folk hailed from the town. Quentiin did not doubt corsairs held the village—in fact, he was banking on it. Peltin was likely to be manned lightly, with the brunt of Kaarst's attack being focused on Vonku and its outposts, and from there, the group could commandeer one of Kaarst's smaller vessels and take to the waves. The Admiral's teeth were in his weapons, and so to weaken the sharpness of Kaarst's thrust, Quentiin had to deprive the man of his tools. *Oh yes, all of us will have the opportunity to prove ourselves, perhaps sooner than we might wish.* It was already bad enough for the soldiers facing Kaarst's attack from behind the walls of Vonku, but it would be far worse for those challenging him on the open seas.

They made camp at dusk, keeping their fires low and subdued. Kaarst's corsairs in these hills numbered companies of two dozen at most, none of which presented a serious threat to the men under Trivian Seltor's command, but getting into unnecessary skirmishes served no purpose. *Better to save ourselves for the fool's errand awaiting us upon the waters of the Rendrivin Ocean.*

Quentiin cast a watchful eye over the camp's northern perimeter. Two sentries had taken up post, facing outward into the forest. A cicada buzzed past them, emitting its telltale sounds while the group hunkered low, making food over concealed firepits. With a sword at his waist, Quentiin stepped past the guards, giving them each a nod of acknowledgment before he disappeared into the undergrowth. Once out of sight of the encampment, he stopped and sat on the trunk of a fallen tree. Here, he took moment to do nothing more than simply rest: all the world might be crashing down, but the peace of the Odow remained.

At the sound of a snapping twig, Quentiin did not start or reach for his weapon. Instead, he merely spoke aloud. "How are the laddies under yer command doin'?"

Trivian snorted in response. "They aren't under my command. Not officially, at least."

"I don't see that 'officially' matters at the moment. Ye're the one they're followin', ken?"

"They'd do well to follow someone else."

Quentiin stood, turning toward Trivian, hand on the pommel of his sword. "Stand straight and look at me, soldier."

Trivian narrowed his eyes but did as told, and the two companions faced each other beneath the dark canopy of the Odow's trees, their features illuminated only by the moonlight filtering through the branches above.

"It doesn't take a great deal of intellect to know ye've got somethin' on yer mind," Quentiin said. "Either out with it or leave it behind. The fact is, ye're the only reason those boys stayed alive as long as they did back there, an' they look to ye because of it. You can either shoulder that burden like a good soldier, or feel free to leave. We'll lose more than a few good people before this all shakes out, an' the last thing they need is a leader focused more on his struggles than theirs, d'ye ken?"

In response, Trivian's eyes narrowed further, his jaw grew tight.

Good. I need backbone, not self-pity.

"They aren't boys, they're *men*," Trivian said. "They're up to the task."

Quentiin grunted. "Aye, laddie. That's what I needed to hear. Come along. We're goin' to scout the perimeter. It won't do to have a drunken corsair stumble in upon the lot of us and upsettin' the onion cart, eh?"

* * *

On their return to camp, Trivian halted. The cicadas were loud as ever, and yet Quentiin found their noise more soothing than bothersome. In front of him, he saw a glimpse of low light flickering through the trees as a soldier in the camp tended to a muted fire. Revealing oneself in such a manner was a glaring mistake, but Quentiin had already assured himself that the surrounding forest was well and clear. They had bigger game to skin, and such lessons could be saved for another time.

"I was sent to Eltern two years ago," Trivian said. "Before that, I served under Captain Yastlin in the Royal Legion as a troop leader. I had twenty men under my command. The Legion isn't the same as during the Icor Rebellion. Back then, the entire Icor Peninsula was at war, and men of the Legion were battlefield soldiers, leading at the front lines. Today, the Legion is as much a peacekeeping force as anything else. But two years ago, a merchant's guild hired a team of mercenaries in a bid for power."

Aye, I'd heard about that. Engagements for the Legion had been few and far between since the Rebellion ended, but there were ever those who wished to hold the throne themselves. The merchant's uprising had been considered the most serious conflict in recent years, though Quentiin supposed that perspective would change in light of Kaarst's siege. The merchant's uprising might soon seem a bar-room scuffle in comparison.

"The mercenaries had taken the southwest quarter of the city and barricaded themselves in," Trivian continued. "Three separate Legion troops were trapped on the inside when the mercenaries took command. It was nigh impossible for us to break through the blockade to get our soldiers the help they needed. Captain Yastlin doubled my force and sent us into Hrethlin's Alley in the southeast quarter, adjacent to the blockade. We were meant to break through and bring aid to our men on the inside."

Trivian sat on a stump, leaning forward, forearms on his knees. In the moonlight, he looked like a weary man ten years his senior, with grooves of regret in his face. "We'd almost made it when I heard a pair of children crying within Hrethlin's Alley. I found out later they were the family of a merchant who had left the guild to remain loyal to King Aras. He had been escaping when the other merchants trapped him and his family and his building.

"I abandoned my orders and took my men toward the building where I heard the children crying. That's when the mercenaries sprang their trap. They had captured the family as bait, and the next thing I knew, the enemy had boxed us in, burying us in arrows from all sides. Legionnaires began dying, painting the streets with their blood. Our attackers set fire to the alley. Of my forty men, any that survived the arrow died by the flame, and I alone lived. Meanwhile, the soldiers trapped on the opposite side of the blockade lost half their number before a new force relieved them." Trivian raised his eyes. "My actions caused the deaths of over a hundred soldiers in the Royal Legion."

No Legion soldier would have done differently. Surely you understand that, do you not? Aloud, Quentiin asked, "What about the children?"

"I dragged them out of the building they were held in, past the bodies of their mother and father," Trivian said. "As far as I know, they still live—two young children and myself, the sole survivors of Hrethlin's Massacre. Afterward, the captain sent me to Eltern. One hundred lives lost, all because I heard two children crying."

"Aye," Quentiin said. "But do you think any of those who lost their lives would have had it any other way? Because now those two children will grow old."

A breeze rustled through the branches above, casting shadows on Trivian's face and concealing his expression. "Maybe. If Kaarst doesn't get them first."

* * *

Sendalion Danris wiped his blade on the grass. His limbs trembled from exhaustion. The last few days, he and Vinsor had been crossing the scarred and ravaged grasslands between Eltern and Vonku. Before them lay a trio of dead scouts. He and Vinsor were but two men, and they could hardly afford to get caught by one of Kaarst's larger bands of roving corsairs. This last encounter had been a very near thing; a scout had almost gotten away before Sendalion cut him down. Had the man managed to escape, it would have been only minutes before a score of corsairs descended upon the two Legionnaires.

They kept as far from the main road as possible, skirting farmhouses and other signs of human habitation, avoiding anything that might draw corsair attention. They stayed low during the day as they journeyed, and alternated watch at night. In spite of these precautions, this had been the fourth time they came across a corsair company. The constant strain of travel and lack of sleep was beginning to take its toll. Sendalion had a healthy gash across his thigh from a skirmish against seven corsairs the previous afternoon. He wore a bandage about the wound, and he could tell from its increasingly foul odor that it would need a Healer's attention soon.

They'd just made it to the final stretch. They could see Vonku's outer wall, but in front of it was yet another corsair camp. Sendalion's weariness built to a pressure point in the center of his forehead. He guessed there were near to a hundred corsairs in the camp, and while this was a far cry from presenting any threat to the folk behind the city walls, it would be more than a problem for him and Vinsor. They had no choice but to go around the camp, adding several more hours to their journey. *We're so close, and we must still endure well into one more evening.*

Beside him, Vinsor appeared just as tired. His clothes hung from him in shreds—Sendalion expected his own looked much the same—and he had a jagged cut across his left cheek. It would no doubt leave a scar, when all was said and done. "The Demon-Lord's laughing at us, mate," Vinsor said as he looked at the corsair encampment. "Either that, or the Maker has one dark sense of humor."

"I'd say both are true. We needed a stroke of luck, and we didn't get it. We'll just have to make our own."

"Legion soldiers always do."

They drew back together, putting a knoll between themselves and the corsairs. There, they took what rest they could until the sun set. On this last stretch, they would use night as their ally, remaining concealed more easily in the darkness.

Sendalion wondered how Quentiin Harggra and Trivian Seltor were faring. It took serious nerve to undertake the task Harggra proposed, but from the stories he'd heard, Sendalion expected nothing less of the dwerion. As for Trivian, well, the story of Hrethlin's Massacre was well known. Someone had to pay for the largest catastrophe suffered by the Legion since the Icor Rebellion, and Seltor had been the only man left breathing. Disregarding the notion that this experience made Trivian perhaps the most grizzled veteran of all, the grinding wheels of justice did not care. Sendalion speculated that Captain Yastlin had not wished to impose the exile, but it was one of the hard facts about the cold, logical structure governing the military: orders were orders. Trivian had them, he'd disobeyed them, and men died as a result. Allow for one exception, one *crack* in the vast hierarchy of the chain of command, and the whole thing tumbled down. Trivian Seltor had been sacrificed for the good of the Legion's legacy, not for what he'd done, and it seemed he was the only man who did not understand the truth of it.

Once dusk descended, Sendalion and Vinsor set out once more. Each time Sendalion placed his weight upon his leg, it grew weaker. He hoped they did not encounter any more corsairs, as he doubted he had the strength to face even another pair of scouts. The body had its limits, and he knew his had been met. *Just a few more hours, dear Maker. Give us that.* With the moon as their guide, they kept the hills between themselves and the corsair camp as much as possible, venturing closer only to gauge progress, and then retreating. Once they traveled as far west as they deemed prudent, they hooked south back toward the wall.

The lights within Vonku appeared impossibly distant, and for the first half of their journey the dots of torches remained the exact same size, refusing to provide any indication the two men were getting any closer. It was only during the second half of their journey, when the moon reached its highest point, that Sendalion felt they were making any significant progress.

Every so often, sounds of carousing came from the corsair camp, carried on the wind. Sendalion was fine with that; the more time the corsairs spent in revelry, the less attention they spent watching their perimeter. Even so, the camp's continued presence was an uncomfortable indication of how poorly things were progressing within the walls of Vonku—the fact that a platoon of Legion men had not been sent to snuff out a relatively small band of corsairs meant all their efforts were instead going into defending the coastal walls. At long last, with limbs aching, heads pounding, and throats dry, they came within touching distance of the city wall. Sendalion placed his hands upon Vonku's stones, closing his eyes. When he leaned against the wall, he did so not only in momentary relaxation but also in gratitude for the fact that he stood within the shadow of safety once more.

He faced east, right shoulder adjacent to the wall, and began making his way toward the nearest gate. The light flickered in the distance, teasing salvation, and when he and Vinsor drew within sight of the guards, they held weaponless hands over their heads, Sendalion with his Legion insignia visible in his palm. The soldiers took them under guard, and it was all Sendalion could do to remain standing as they waited while word was sent to Captain Yastlin.

"Water," Sendalion said to a sentinel after the messenger left. "Please, in the name of the Maker."

The man looked Sendalion up and down, eyes narrowed as he tried to assess the ways in which the tall man, should he prove to be a corsair imposter, could turn a water skin into a deadly weapon.

"Give it to him already," another guard said. "He doesn't have the strength to so much as throw it at your head."

Sendalion accepted the skin with thanks and took what felt like his first drink in the past week. As he handed the skin to Vinsor, hoofbeats announced Captain Yastlin's arrival. The big, bearded man waved a hand at the guardsmen as he dismounted. "At ease, soldiers. Give these men their weapons back. You've come a long way, Danris." He looked at Vinsor, face impassive. "But *you've* come even farther, Vinsor Dalin. You might have left the Legion with the king's blessing, but I'm half-inclined to throw you in the cells for desertion anyway. Lucky for you, I need all the help we can get."

Vinsor replied with a wry smile. "It's good to see you again too, Captain."

Yastlin turned to Sendalion, eyebrow raised. "Where's the dwerion?"

"He's gone east," Sendalion said. "Toward Peltin."

"And what in Malath does he intend to do there?"

"He's of a mind to steal a ship and sail it to Kaarst."

Yastlin cursed. "That's a fool's errand. You were supposed to bring Harggra *here*, not leave him to die on the Rendrivin. I'll need an explanation as to why sending you north wasn't a complete waste of time."

"Dwerions are stubborn folk, and Quentiin Harggra more so than most," Sendalion replied. "We liberated Eltern, which gives us back control over our northern routes once we deal with Kaarst's men camped outside our walls. Harggra made a compelling case, Captain. If we can take out Kaarst's flagship, we may find ourselves able to gain a stronger position against this blockade."

"We already tried. A lot of men died."

"Haargra's methods are…unique. He freed Eltern while significantly undermanned. He might have a chance here, and I was of a mind to let him have it."

Yastlin grunted. "We'll see. For the time being, let's get you taken care of. That leg of yours looks ready to fall off. I need you healthy—both of you—so that you'll be strong and fit when your turn to die comes."

* * *

Sendalion gritted his teeth. The healer's poultice seared him like a metal brand straight from the fire as she applied salve to the open gash on his thigh. The initial application was bad enough, but the fiery sensation spread and built until it felt like it was consuming his entire leg.

"You'd have lost the limb if you went much longer," she said. Talladora was well known by the soldiers of the Royal Legion. Many of them owed their lives to her skills at healing. "The infection was advancing quickly."

"And now?" he asked.

"You'll keep it. But bed rest for two days, minimum."

The Captain will love that. "Two days it is. I don't have time for any more than the minimum."

"It's bad out there, Danris. If you don't let yourself heal properly, you'll only be a liability to yourself and others. *Rest.*"

It might be bad out there, but it's bad in here, too. Rows of cots stretched on either side of Sendalion, bearing soldiers with an assortment of wounds. Some had been fortunate, like Sendalion, whereas others would never be the same. "How many have we lost?"

"Thirty from behind the walls, but that doesn't count the ships that went down. Those numbers are in the hundreds." Talladora shook her head. "They call this a stalemate, and I suppose it is. The Admiral hasn't advanced beyond a few probing attacks, and I think those are only so he can bleed the Legion's resources. Other than that, he's simply held position, and yet soldiers are dying from it anyway. If this is the stalemate, I shudder to think what it will be like when the real fighting starts."

"The good news is that we'll be clearing the city soon," Sendalion said. "Now that Eltern's been freed, the Captain will send a contingent to remove the corsair camp north of the city."

"I wondered why he was letting the camp stay there."

"He couldn't afford to do otherwise, not while there was so much activity on the seaboard side of the garrison. It will strain our resources to send the Legion to attack the camp, but with the roads to Eltern cleared, it will be worth it so that we can evacuate citizens."

Talladora wrapped bandages around the poultice, securing it against Sendalion's skin. "I suppose that should be a good thing, but I don't like what it implies."

"No, I don't, either." *It means fighting in the streets. It* will *happen, sooner or later. We hold the outer walls, but once they fall, we'll have to pull back to the inner quarter. That's when things will begin to go badly indeed. Your gambit better be worth it, Quentiin Harggra. Much rides on you.*

"Is it true, what they say?" she asked. "That Kaarst has dark magic at his disposal?"

"He has *something* at his disposal, but whether magic or otherwise is not for me to say. As far as I'm concerned it doesn't matter. The Legion will fight him the same."

"Did I ever tell you the name of the woman I served under during the Icor Rebellion?" Talladora asked.

"Rosalie Revier." Sendalion had heard Talladora speak of her before. The way she told it, Talladora owed her not-inconsiderable skills to Rosalie's mentorship.

"Yes, that was her," Talladora replied. "She was among the best. She married a Legion man, and though I don't recall his name, he had a wound much like yours. Those were dark days, but in a different way. We were far from home, and though our lives might have been in danger, *Vonku* never was. It may not seem like it makes a difference—one battle is the same as another, as I see it—but it *does*; it's different when it's your home, and that's the Maker's truth."

Sendalion looked up as Vinsor entered the room. The man wore his Legion attire, complete with insignia over his breast and sword at his side. Unlike Sendalion, he had been cleared for duty right away, albeit with a healthily padded bandage over the scar on his cheek.

"The prodigal soldier returns," Sendalion said. "Back in uniform again, I see."

"You know, I thought I'd be leaving these clothes folded in my trunk for good—"

"But when Alcatune calls, we answer."

"Always have, and always will."

Sendalion looked his friend over. "So, what now?"

"I've been tasked with clearing the corsair camp, seeing as you've seen fit to make plans for staying in bed these next few days. After that, we can begin getting the people out."

Sendalion clasped Vinsor's hand. "Save some of them for me, my friend. Preferably the ones you can't handle. I'll make short work of them, one-legged or not."

Vinsor grinned. "Bold words for a man on a cot. We'll see if that extends to the battlefield."

"The Maker go with you, friend."

The reappointed Legionnaire gave a firm nod and walked out of the room. Sendalion saw a group of healers rolling in six more cots, all of which bore wounded soldiers. *Casualties from the front. Hurry, Quentiin Harggra. We can only keep this up for so long.*

18

The company gathered in Keldur's streets in the gray light of early dawn, saddling horses from the village stables as they prepared to leave. Though the group's supplies had been wiped out when their rafts overturned in the river the prior afternoon, Keldur's villagers had been more than willing to provide them with mounts, food, and water for their journey. Following Sheel's death, everyone had looked to Eklan for guidance, and his proclamation that he would assist the group had in its own way earned the company more goodwill than they'd been able to garner by defeating Taazvin and Uklith's Assassins combined.

Fog hung low over the ground, the heat of the day still in its infancy. Tim tightened the straps of his saddlebags. The horse, Rookwind, had rich, brown skin and strong flanks. The stablemaster had done his work well, ensuring the horses in his care were well fed and well cared for. Tim caught sight of Wurit leading his own horse, laden with pack rolls and water skins, toward them.

The short, wiry man gave a half-hearted shrug. "I don't have anything better to do with my time, now that Taazvin's gone," he said. "I might as well spend it doing something useful. Besides, last winter the stablemaster fell ill and I stepped in for him. I know these horses."

"If you're crazy enough to join us," Boblin said from behind Tim, "I suppose you'll fit right in. Here, start stocking the water. We'll need it." He swung up on his mount, Dapple, which had gray skin and patches of white as the name implied. Once they entered the desert, water would be their most precious resource of all, and they'd brought along two additional horses to carry the extra supply alone, in addition to the skins each individual would carry. While Tim, Boblin, and Celia inventoried weapons, Jend, Hanqar, Hugo, and Ken focused on the most interesting task of all, fashioning crude tubes of birchbark and placing them into canvas bags alongside an assortment of herbs from the woods.

"What's that for?" Eklan asked, watching the elions in their preparations.

Boblin patted the big man on the shoulder. "We'll show you when we make camp tonight, mate. I think you'll appreciate it."

Tim sheathed a dagger on either side of his belt. The group had gathered an assortment of swords, knives, and crossbows from the village's armory, and though he'd never gotten quite as proficient as any of the elions at throwing a blade, Tim could hold his own when necessary. He'd already placed his sword in his saddlebags, and took a spare should it be needed, as well as a crossbow. *One can never have too many sharp objects,* as Boblin was fond of saying.

Tim had one more thing to do before they departed, though he didn't relish the thought of it. As the rest of the company finalized the assembly of their supplies, Tim led Rookwind to the far end of the village, walking in silence until he reached Bria Hamur's home. There, he raised his hand to knock, but the door swung open before him. Tim stopped, knuckles in midair.

Bria stood in the open doorframe, wearing a large knapsack on her back, with a saddlebag on one hip and a sword on the other. "Don't look so shocked, Matthias," she said. "Agrazab already took one of my brothers, and I'm not letting it take a second one."

"You're coming with us." He made it a statement, not a question.

"Yes, I just said as much."

"But what about Reidell?"

"The Council will see to him. I've already spoken with them. It wasn't really a matter for discussion, anyway."

Tim paused, but he didn't see any purpose to objecting. For one, he doubted Bria Hamur was the type to change her mind, and for another, they could use the help. "Okay," he said. "We're getting ready outside Wurit's house."

Eklan Hamur had a much different reaction upon seeing Bria returning with Tim. He met them in the middle of the street, raising a hand to forestall his sister. "Absolutely not," he said. "No way in Malath you're coming."

Bria replied with a long, hard stare. "No way in Malath you're stopping me."

Well, Tim thought, *at least she's using that look on someone else. I was beginning to think she'd reserved the expression exclusively for me.*

"I'll tie you up and lock you in your house first," Eklan said.

"Try it."

Brother and sister faced each other. Behind them, the rest of the group turned to watch the confrontation, and the silence stretched until Jend stepped forward to tap Eklan on the shoulder. "I'd let her come, lad. She's as much right to go on this quest as you."

Eklan held his sister's gaze for another moment before relenting. He stepped back and lashed his sword to his saddlebags. "As you wish. Get your horse, sister."

And so the three from Keldur joined the seven from Galdon, and the group became ten. Shortly afterward, the company mounted their horses. On the way out of the village, they passed the wreckage of Sheel's home, where three villagers sorted through the blackened ruins. A woman from the council stood in front of the meeting hall, clutching a shawl about her shoulders. She raised a frail hand as they passed, acknowledging the company's exodus in silence.

In front of the riders, the greenery of the Fertile Lands beckoned, the last wisps of fog dissipating beneath Rookwind's hooves as they entered the wilderness. The gelding had an easy, steady manner, dipping its head every so often as he walked, occasionally shaking his head when a fly landed upon his snout. Tim took one last glance toward Keldur, where a villager dragged a fallen beam away from a larger piece of rubble. The pile shifted, sending a swirl of ash into the air.

The travelers set their sights to the west, using the Pel River as their guide. The first day passed easily, though everyone was well aware the conveniences of the Delta—plentiful food and water, and smooth travel—would not last.

When the group stopped at nightfall, Tim removed the focusing reservoir from his knapsack. He and Quentiin were due to speak this evening. They had been waiting longer between communicating lately in order to conserve energy. He moved away from the camp to better clear his mind, holding the stone before him and closing his eyes. The Lifesource came naturally to him, much more smoothly than when he first learned to use the power. It flooded into his body in a rush, heightening his senses, and he became aware of every aspect of the natural world around him—the way Rookwind's hooves sank into the loam of the forest floor, the rustle of breeze through the leaves, the myriad of scents upon the air, the presence of creatures near and far.

The stone glowed a low, pulsing green, steadily increasing in radiance as Tim sought its power. Though Quentiin had made significant progress in being able to use the reservoir, Tim was the only one who truly felt the nuances of the Lifesource when the connection opened. He felt the bridging of a gap across many miles, and into the vacuum rushed the sudden linkage, as if the world were bending between him and Quentiin, closing the distance between them. Though he could not actually see Quentiin, he sensed the dwerion's presence before him.

"It's been some time, laddie," Quentiin's voice rumbled. "What have ye got for me?"

"We've had an interesting few days," Tim replied. "We went over a waterfall, and Boblin almost got eaten. The way he keeps moaning about it, I suspect he's actually quite proud of the experience."

"Ay, the laddie will never admit it, but he likes the attention."

After Tim told Quentiin the remainder of their encounter with Taazvin and his people, followed by the attack on Keldur and the group's subsequent departure, the dwerion paused. "Well," he said at last, "it sounds as if Uklith's tryin' his best to keep you from gettin' to Agrazab."

"He's trying, that's for sure. Whether it counts as his best? I'm afraid we haven't seen his best yet, much as that concerns me."

"Aye, that's true. Well, we've had a time of it ourselves; Kaarst's people captured Eltern when they first invaded. We managed to take it back, but now I'm in Peltin. We're gatherin' a means to capture one of Kaarst's ships, an' we mean to take to the seas. I have to see this weapon of Kaarst's from up close, I'm afraid. I've been thinkin'—I don't suppose how it could be, but do you think Kaarst is...?"

"An Advocate?" Tim finished the sentence for Quentiin. He shook his head, though the dwerion could not see him. "The thought did cross my mind, but no, I have to think I'd have felt his power."

"Are you sure?"

Tim hesitated. "No, I'm not."

The dwerion went silent again for a few heartbeats. "I thought as much. I'll let ye know what I find out, laddie." They bade each other farewell, and Tim let the connection terminate.

"Fascinating," Bria Hamur said. Tim turned and saw her watching him from astride her horse Menindara.

"We have a friend in the South," Tim said as the glow faded. "This helps me speak with him."

She cocked her head. "How often do you use the Lifesource, Matthias?"

He paused. "I don't exactly keep track."

"I presume you used it in Taazvin's village."

"Yes—"

"And I saw you use it when we were fighting the Assassins, obviously. Both of those instances, of course, don't surprise me. It's your weapon, and it stands to reason you'd make the most of it. This morning, though, I could have sworn I saw you tie your laces with it, and it made me wonder."

Tim mounted his horse. "About what?"

"About you, Matthias, and about this power of yours. Did you even know it existed before you came to the North?"

"Our religious leaders spoke of it, but no, I never understood it to be something I could use."

"But then you crossed the Barricade and the Lifesource became a part of you. It allowed you to defeat Zadinn. Now, you seem to use it every day, and it makes me wonder."

"About what?" he asked.

"I find myself asking if you remember what it's like for those of us who have never held it. And *that*, Matthias, makes me wonder who you'd be without it." She kicked her heels into Menindara's ribs and galloped forward, leaving Tim alone as night descended.

* * *

"All right, here's how this works," Boblin said, handing Eklan the knapsack.

The group had reached a rock quarry near the western edge of the Fertile Lands, one of the first indications that they were drawing near to the Desert. The quarry, a bowl-shaped depression devoid of vegetation and with a safe backdrop of rock wall at the opposite side, would be an excellent place to test the weapons the elions had constructed before leaving Keldur.

Sixty paces to Boblin's left, Celia had partnered with Jend, and the same distance to the right, Hanqar had joined the Rindar twins to do the same. Tim, Wurit, and Bria were a safe distance away at camp, the latter likely still using her eyes to spear daggers into Tim's skin. It was clear she blamed him for this whole mess, and though that anger might be rightfully placed from her perspective, Boblin saw it as stuffing the messenger full of arrows. *Then again, the messenger rarely shows up to drag one's brother back to Malath.* Well, it was

Tim's problem. Bria treated the rest of the company civilly enough, and Boblin didn't doubt they'd be glad of her sword before all was done—as long as she didn't stick that very sword into Tim's bowels first.

Eklan opened the knapsack, revealing an assortment of herbs the company had collected from the Fertile Lands, knowing full well in advance they would have a lack of suitable ingredients once they entered the Western Desert. Boblin produced a mortar and pestle, took a handful of leaves from the bag, and placed them in the bowl. "This will keep us occupied for evenings to come," he said, "and it will be well worth it. This is a mixture we used at the Fort, and later when we joined the Army of Kah'lash." The elions had refined the process over the past year, building upon what they learned after the Army showed them a more portable means of use during the Battle of the Deathlands.

As Boblin begin grinding leaves under the pestle, Eklan watched closely. "I presume it's a weapon."

"You presume correctly."

"It's just ... *powder*," the big man said with evident confusion.

"That's what I thought at first, too. It's not sharp like a blade, and you can't shoot it like an arrow, so what use is it, right? Commander Jend first discovered it, a few years before my time. The Rindar brothers tell me he almost died when it first happened."

"Is it poison?"

Boblin next took a birchbark tube from the knapsack. "Poison to whoever is standing in the wrong place, I suppose. The Army carried this in pouches upon them, and what you see here is our latest variation." Boblin poured the powdered mixture into the tube, ran a string through the tube, and sealed the top with more bark. He handed it to Eklan. "Hold this—but be *careful*, by the Maker. Let's take a few steps away." It had proven stable enough in transportation so far, but Boblin didn't plan to test this more than necessary.

He produced a thin stick the length of his finger from a pouch at his belt. "The Army used juice from an oaktree root, but we've always found fire to be best." Boblin held the stick over a strip of porous stone, which he had overlaid across the right-hand side of his belt. All members of the elion infantry wore such belts, which had been produced as quickly as the smiths and leatherworkers in Galdon could make them.

He took the tube back from Eklan and held it out at arm's length from his body in one hand, while with his other he ran the stick across the strip of porous stone on his belt. He used a quick, flicking motion, and the end of the stick blossomed into flame.

Eklan's eyes widened. "That's handy."

"Oh, just wait. You haven't seen anything yet."

Boblin touched the end of the flaming stick to the birchbark tube's fuse. He reached his arm back before throwing the tube as far forward as possible. It landed a good forty paces away and exploded. The resulting detonation shook the ground as a spray of dirt and stone erupted. Boblin shielded his eyes from the blast, and it was a few seconds before his hearing returned. The called the birchbark tubes "boomers," for obvious reasons.

"That was amazing," Eklan said. "We didn't have those the last time we went to Agrazab."

"Do you think we'll need more?" Boblin asked.

"Oh, yes. A *lot* more."

Boblin nodded. "I thought as much." As he turned to leave, he paused. Every time he used these, the blast brought back memories of that day in the Deathlands, of the fateful first charge against Zadinn's armies, of the subsequent skirmishes—and of Hedro, lying on the ground with malichons all around, Hedro bleeding, Hedro dying. He looked toward Celia, almost inadvertently, and thought of Hedro's last words. *Keep her safe.*

He'd done that, all right. Not that she needed it; half the time *she* was the one keeping *him* safe. But there had been times—in the Korlan, in the Mountains, facing Isanam…

I hope I've done well by your last request, my friend, he thought. *For her, and for those under my command.*

"Are you coming?" Eklan asked, his voice cutting through Boblin's thoughts.

Boblin shook himself. "Yes, indeed. These boomers don't make themselves."

* * *

By the following evening, Tim observed the vegetation of the Fertile Lands thinning, changing from lush green to subtler shades of red and brown. Trees gave way to scrub brush, and then to stone. All sign of water and tributaries had long since vanished. Their horses' hooves crunched against a brittle, rocky terrain, the only sound in an air that had otherwise grown dry and still. When dusk fell, the travelers topped one last rise and saw the place Eklan had called the Bleached Fields before them. It was a vast plain of unnatural white stone, standing out in contrast to the backdrop of the darkening horizon. Thin cracks ran in jagged streaks across the open ground in much the same way one's skin cracked and peeled when exposed to dry, unforgiving air.

This night, the company did not make camp. From here forward they would travel in the dark and sleep during the day, giving themselves a reprieve from the worst of the sun's fury. As they continued into the Bleached Fields, a half-moon rose. The pale landscape reflected back the natural light, allowing the travelers to see the path before them with relative ease. Even in the dark, Tim felt heat radiating from the stones, which had soaked in the sun's rays during the day and reflected the retained warmth upward. He imagined the landscape would cool as night wore on, the temperatures dropping to a more bearable level, before the cycle began anew the next morning.

Tim watched Eklan as they rode. Eklan's horse, Grendalar, was a tall black stallion with a flowing mane. The big man predicted they would reach Agraz-ab in two weeks, after the moon had reached full strength. Their guide sat astride Grendalar, shoulders square, facing forward. Over the last few days, he had seemed to accept his role in this process with a growing inevitability. Every time he spoke of the City of Darkness, he did so with an air of cynical fatalism. *He does not expect to return this time*, Tim thought. *He does not expect any of us to make it back.*

In turn, Tim looked his other companions. Boblin and Celia rode side by side, hands clasped together across the space between their mounts Dapple and Yestara. Tim and Boblin had come a long way since the day they first met, the day Tim had first killed in battle, the day he truly learned what it meant to be a soldier. Before that, Tim had only *thought* he understood the responsibility he had taken upon himself. He'd seen the raw, ugly reality of true battle as he stood before the dead malichon, his blade dripping with blood.

In those early days, Boblin had been new to the Frontier Patrol, his two years of service nothing compared to the experience of Jend Argul, or of Hugo and Ken Rindar. Even so, it had been Boblin who faced Isanam during the Battle of the Deathlands, Boblin who won. And here they were today, Tim the leader of the expedition, Boblin the commander of the Frontier Patrol. This realization jarred Tim every time he reflected upon it. *The last time around, we were the followers—we had Nazgar and Pellen to guide us. This time, we are expected to be the leaders, to be the ones with the answers, and I'm afraid we have none.*

Next, he turned his thoughts to Celia. She was, without a doubt, the bedrock of Boblin's existence, and while Boblin guided the overall strategy and mission of the Patrol, Celia served on the ground with the soldiers, leading by example, taking the recruits under her wing and serving as the unifying element that kept them tied together. Tim knew it was much the same way in her relationship with Boblin—she was the one with the inner strength, the fortitude to persevere and the determination to succeed, and they were each better because of the other. Celia's direct, uncompromising focus allowed her to succeed where others failed, to remain calm when others faltered, and to stand tall as others wavered. *She would take on Uklith alone, if she had the opportunity.*

Tim shifted his glance to Jend Argul, riding alongside the Rindar brothers. Jend had been commander before Boblin, but he'd chosen to relinquish the duty in the wake of the Battle of the Deathlands. As Jend described it, the war against Zadinn had been his war, much as it had been Pellen's war, and he was due for rest afterward. It had been trying for him to see so many of his elions fall in the final hours of the Fort, and still more during the subsequent quest that culminated in the Battle of the Deathlands. Jend, no doubt, had little desire to be drawn into another conflict—*none* of them did—but he'd chosen to come regardless, because retired or not, he'd spent too much of his life fighting the ever-encroaching tide of Zadinn Kanas to let this new threat jeopardize everything. So there he was, riding alongside the Rindar brothers, ready to serve again.

And, for their part, Hugo and Ken had often been considered Jend's right and left hands, the two most skilled and respected soldiers in the Patrol. Like Jend, they understood the stakes in front of them, and those three together—Jend, Hugo, and Ken—were practically an army in their own right. Tim slept better, knowing they were in this with them.

Hanqar rode to the rear of the group. Every so often, Tim caught a glance of the scars upon the elion's back, and he winced at the thought of the lashes that had caused them. For this reason alone, Tim wondered if Hanqar understood more than anyone what they faced. The other elions and Tim might have gone on the quest for the Army of Kah'lash, but Hanqar had experienced the cruelty of Zadinn's regime firsthand, and he *knew* what awaited them should they fail.

Then there was Wurit, who had become a fast ally in just a few days. Tim had quickly ascertained that not all the soldiers in Keldur possessed true combat skills, but Wurit certainly did. Having neither wife nor children, no family to fight for, he travelled with them on this quest anyway. Tim supposed this might be in part because Wurit felt he owed Tim and the elions a debt, but he also suspected that Wurit knew, just as Eklan did, that the task simply had to be done.

Tim's gaze settled on Bria last. Each and every one of her conversations with him had been terse, tinged with a sharp edge of hostility on her part. She focused her ire solely upon him, and did not treat the others in the group in the same manner—but Tim had, after all, coerced her brother into returning to his worst nightmare, back to face a horror that had crippled their other sibling. Tim supposed she was right to be angry, because he'd presented Eklan with an unfair choice: return to the place of your worst fears, or suffer the fate of the world.

I'm sorry, Bria Hamur. I will do my best to protect your brother.

It was as if she heard the thought, for she turned to look at him even as he looked at her. They faced each other from across the group, her accusing glare upon him, he returning her look with resigned stoicism, while around them the company continued into the night, across the desert and toward the City of Darkness.

19

Boblin sat with his back to the camp, which the group had erected using supplies from Keldur. Though the shelters were no more than crude lean-tos with tarps stretched across the top, they would nonetheless provide shade from the fiery orb climbing over their heads.

Last time, we made our way across a wasteland of cold, where the sun's rays brought no comfort. This time, we make our way across a wasteland of heat, where the sun's rays bring death.

Tim told Boblin that young men in Vonku often read stories of daring adventures, tales featuring heroes riding across lush and vivid landscapes, slaying evil creatures and rescuing ladies while sustaining nary a scratch. In those tales, the heroes never got tired, hungry, or thirsty, and they certainly didn't spend their days crawling into the shade in order to simply survive the next twelve hours. No, Boblin supposed a mind-numbing ride across the Western Desert would not hold any appeal for those who wished to experience such idyllic action and adventure.

Behind him, the group slept while Boblin kept first watch. Around him the cracked plains stretched in every direction, and in the distance, haze shimmered where the sky's faint blue met the earth's yellowish tint. The air, devoid of all moisture, held no clouds save for the faintest wisps of white far overhead. The ground beneath him was hard and unforgiving, and only the most resilient of insects crawled across it, emerging from fissures in the earth and quickly returning to the depths moments later. *If I had a crevice of shade,* Boblin thought, *I'd hide in it, too.*

Eklan had pushed them hard during that first night. Boblin wasn't personally in any rush to reach the site of a portal to Malath, but he supposed they had to arrive sooner or later. While keeping guard, he unsheathed his sword and laid it across his knees, one hand on the hilt and the other on the flat of the blade. He leaned against a pole from his lean-to, a skin of water at his side. Though they had packed skins upon skins of water, Eklan nonetheless encouraged them to use their supplies sparingly. Everything the big man did, from bringing materials for lean-tos, to sleeping during the day, to the way he rationed the water, was calculated toward ensuring the group's survival in these elements.

Eklan had spoken little of his first journey to Agrazab, and Boblin wasn't about to pry. The man had been deceived regarding Agrazab's true nature, though to what end Boblin could not yet say. Perhaps—*perhaps*—the old man who had spoken of the City had been truly delusional, as unaware of its identity as the villagers in Keldur, yet Boblin did not think this was the case. More likely someone—perhaps Zadinn?—had wanted the villagers to seek the City, and had sent the old man to sow the seeds of an idea in Eklan Hamur's mind.

Except it couldn't have been Zadinn, Boblin corrected himself. *According to the journal Tim read, Zadinn was unaware of Keldur before finding Darmet.* There must have been another player involved, maybe one of Uklith's other servants trying to free his master. Had the Demon-Lord thought he could lure the Keldurians to his will and entice them to free him?

There was another possibility, and it did not sit well with Boblin. The twin brothers Nazgar and Ragzan had roamed the North until just recently, members of the ancient line of prophets known as the Kyrlod. Both had died in Zadinn's citadel at the Dark Lord's hand; the former when he'd been there with Tim, the latter prior to Zadinn's assault on the Fort of Pellen. What if the stranger was another Kyrlod? Though far-fetched, Boblin wouldn't rule the possibility out, because Kyrlod were nothing if not good at remaining hidden when it suited them—and of being very visible when *that* suited them, too.

From the way Eklan had been led to the city years ago, to the attack at Boblin's wedding, to the mysterious invasion of the South that Quentiin had ridden away to forestall, Boblin had begun to feel like everyone was merely reacting to the circumstances around them, as if they were puppets dancing on someone else's strings. *Who is the puppetmaster? Is it Uklith, another Kyrlod, or someone else?*

He especially didn't like dwelling on the people who attacked his wedding. Zadinn's armies of malichons had been disturbing enough, but they had been from the underworld, demons clothed in physical flesh, and it only made sense that they would be in the service of their master. Those that had attacked at

Boblin and Celia's wedding had been *people*, and the one they pursued across the desert was by all accounts an elion. If Uklith could twist ordinary men, women, and elions into mindless automatons serving his cause, Boblin worried about what hope any of them would have. Would they simply fall under Uklith's influence upon crossing the gates into Agrazab?

Anelion would say we will need the Maker with us—protecting us, shielding us. But what if—

Boblin hissed sharply. A new, even more uncomfortable thought had occurred to him. Some time back, Tim had told Boblin of his conversation with Zadinn in the Dark Lord's citadel. Zadinn claimed they were part of an ancient war that stretched back to the beginning of time. In this battle, the Maker and Demon-Lord waged war between the realms of Harmea and Malath using human surrogates. Zadinn told Tim that victory would only mean the start of a long path in which the Warrior faced one challenge after another until the Maker discarded him in favor of a new surrogate. *What if the puppetmaster isn't Uklith or a Kyrlod at all, but the Maker? Did the Maker send Eklan to Agrazab in the event that the Warrior might someday need a guide?* If Uklith could twist humans to be mindless servants, was that any different than what the Maker was doing with Tim, Boblin, and the rest, albeit in a subtler manner? Their thoughts and limbs might be under their control, but were they *truly* on this quest of their free will, or was a mightier hand guiding their actions to a time and place not of their choosing, all so they could wage the war of one eternal being against another?

A chill ran through Boblin, creating a strange contrast against the heat of the rising sun. Father Anelion might tell Boblin his thoughts bordered on blasphemy—but no, to wonder at one's place in the cosmos was not blasphemy, and neither was being accountable for one's choices.

The old man might well have been Nazgar, meaning he'd deliberately withheld the information about Keldur from the elion refugees. Nazgar, though, had walked the earth for millennia—he and his companions *raised* the Barricade in an age long past—and it would be naïve to think he had not brought other designs to fruition during his long service to the Maker.

Are we but leaves blown onto a river, riding a current that takes us where it pleases?

Boblin shook himself. These were deep thoughts, and not exactly suited to a day sheltered from the sun's withering heat. *Perhaps the rays have addled my brains. Enough of this. Regardless of whose hand guides us toward Agrazab, it remains that Uklith desires to be set free on this world. If I have the ability to stop it, I will.*

The crunch of steps behind him announced Hanqar's arrival. "May I join you for the watch, Commander?"

"It certainly beats looking at grains of sand on the ground," Boblin replied.

Hanqar had shown promise early on. After Zadinn's defeat, when they began building the Patrol back up, he was the first to swear service. *I lived in servitude to another from the moment I was born,* he'd said, *and I now take up this sword so that no one else ever need suffer in the same way.*

Hanqar pushed himself twice as hard as the other recruits, never settling for less than his best, always first to volunteer and last to back down. He was only seventeen years old, barely of age to join the Patrol, but he'd proven himself time and again. *This will be his true test, his crucible. Everyone else here is a veteran, but this boy is a novice, and it's up to me to make sure he's ready for what might come our way.* In that light, Boblin knew this was his test as much as it was Hanqar's—a test of Boblin's skills as commander, leader, and mentor. *I hope I do well by him.*

"What do you suppose we'll find when we reach Agrazab?" Hanqar asked.

A faint breath of air slipped over them, just enough to be called a breeze, the only movement Boblin had felt in the time since they had made camp. It brushed across his skin like a faint caress, gone before he knew it, blissful in its immediacy. He ran his fingers across the ground and scooped a small palmful of coarse grains, rubbing one between thumb and forefinger. "If we're lucky, only dust and stone." He let the sand slip back through the cracks in his fingers, falling to the ground. "I don't think we'll be lucky, though."

"There was no such thing as luck in the Pit, sir," Hanqar said, "but we made our way to victory nonetheless."

And thus, the recruit teaches the commander a lesson. "Well put, soldier," Boblin acknowledged.

"Thank you, sir."

They continued sitting in silence as the sun climbed.

* * *

When the sun reached its zenith, Celia took Boblin's place at watch. She leaned against the same pole, surveying the surrounding desert. According to Eklan, the company had little to fear in the way of threats during these early days of travel—that would come later. But no self-respecting elion of the Frontier Patrol would set forth on any expedition, no matter how safe, without keeping watch during the sleeping hours. Furthermore, Celia supposed that the last time Eklan came this way, there hadn't been a madman racing ahead of them toward Agrazab. If one madman existed, there could very well be more, like the ones at her wedding. Celia didn't fear any attack, but it didn't hurt to remain prepared.

Hanqar retired along with Boblin. Shortly after the two elions left, Bria Hamur rose from her bedroll and joined Celia, who acknowledged her with a nod and made room for her in the shade of the lean-to. She took a sparing sip of water from her flask and handed it to Bria.

"How much do you know about the path we travel?" Celia asked.

Bria shook her head. "My brother didn't tell me much about it."

"I've been wondering something, if I may ask."

"By all means." Bria took another sip.

"Why didn't you go to Agrazab the first time?" Celia had been thinking about this ever since they set out. The other Hamur siblings had gone to Agrazab, and Bria had been as much of a protector of Keldur as they, so why had she remained behind?

Bria grimaced. "Those were the days after Taazvin made his early split from our village, and he was striking against us often. It probably wouldn't surprise you to know Sheel was against Eklan's expedition for this very reason, because Eklan took some of our best fighters with him when he left, and did so at a time we faced a growing threat. I can't say I fault Sheel for his side in that disagreement. He had the best interests of the village at heart, in the end. Eklan and I made an agreement: Wurit and I staged a diversion that allowed Eklan and his group to slip away. I stayed behind to defend Keldur, and my brothers set out to find a better home for us. Neither of us succeeded, though. Eklan lost his entire party, and Taazvin grew stronger. Truth be told, we were on our last legs against Taazvin's people when you arrived. Sheel never acknowledged it, of course, but you arrived at a time when we needed help the most."

Celia nodded. It made sense—two siblings set out, one stayed behind, but all three served their village. And now they had been called to serve again, in a way that neither wanted but each accepted. She supposed that was the way of things; it had been like this for them when they first set out to defeat Zadinn, and as it was today, and as it would likely be again in the future.

"When we lived at the Fort," she said, "we foraged often into the Fertile Lands. I always questioned whether or not we should just disappear into the forests. I think a lot of us asked ourselves that at one point or another."

"Why didn't you?"

"We knew such an escape would only be temporary. I'd already seen the barriers of the Lands retreat during my time, and my parents had seen it diminish during theirs. We saw the inevitable, but the real reason we remained at the Fort is much simpler: Pellen. I think he knew the Kyrlod wanted us there, and so we stayed."

Bria nodded. "Many of us *did* understand the futility of what we were doing in the Lands. Again, though, it came down to Sheel. Several of us contested whether we should leave and seek others in hiding—we *knew* they had to be out there somewhere—and we might have done so, had it not been for Taazvin. Once he started his uprising, we had our hands full, and any other concerns became secondary."

"What do you think will happen when we come back?" Celia asked.

Bria raised an eyebrow. "*When*? If?"

"*When*."

Bria shrugged. "Galdon sounds nice. I don't think Sheel has much to say on the matter anymore, and to be honest I'd rather be done with the Fertile Lands. We might have existed there, but we were never happy."

They lapsed into silence after that. For a long time, the only sound was the *scritch* upon stone as the occasional insect scraped its way across the surface of the Plains, alongside the rare but welcome swirl of wind. The air had a stale smell, and every time Celia licked her lips, she felt coarse grains of sand upon her tongue from where they'd accumulated on her face.

Over an hour passed before Bria broke the long quiet. "What about you? When you lived at the Fort—were *you* happy?"

Celia gave the question some thought before responding. Surviving at the Fort had been grim at best. Her life consisted of preparing for the Patrol, joining the Patrol, serving on Patrol, before it all came crashing down one fateful night. At times, it seemed there were only malichons, and survival, and nothing else. Except there *had* been other things, hadn't there? They had the Midsummer Festival, held on the lawn. They had times when they stood on the battlements and watched the sun set with smiles upon their faces. She'd had close friendships with Ana and Triste, with Boblin and Hedro. Though there had been little more than three hundred elions at the Fort, they had nonetheless stood together and weathered the darkness, side by side, backs strong as they faced the night, refusing to be vanquished.

"Yes," Celia replied. "We were happy."

Bria nodded. "That's something many in Keldur don't realize. Too many have been content with leaving well enough alone, and like it or not, that kind of denial puts a bad taste in one's mouth. That's why Eklan and Reidell set out to find the City, and that's why I stayed behind to defend our people. We'd decided we couldn't ignore it any more, that we were done with denial. Some like Wurit understood, but many didn't. When all is said and done, perhaps some will want to remain in Keldur, but I'm finished with that place. I'd rather make a new home, one that I'm proud of."

And that, Celia thought, *is as admirable a goal as any of us have.* She hadn't been sure about Bria to begin with; Bria's open hostility toward Tim notwithstanding, Celia didn't know if she could relate to a woman who had spent the same time under Zadinn's reign as she, but in a markedly different fashion. Now, sitting underneath the shade of the lean-to, Celia thought she understood Bria Hamur just a little better.

Aye, this is one I'll be proud to stand by. And I do not doubt for a second that she will learn to stand by us.

* * *

At the end of the third night, they came upon their first oasis, arriving with the moonlight reflecting across the harsh landscape. Eklan had warned such sites would be few and far between, especially the deeper they traveled into the desert. Around them, the terrain had begun to change, transforming from what Eklan called the Bleached Plains to what he simply referred to as "the sands." The flat ground gave way to a valley, running southeast to northwest, and stone shifted to softer, grainier sands. The horses did not seem to like it, and Tim didn't blame them. The going became much tougher when the ground had a tendency to shift under their hooves rather than remain firm. It was taxing, and it slowed their progress.

Thus, the protected area of vegetation at the bottom was a blissful, welcoming sight. Ken, who was scouting ahead, caught sight of it first. He called out, pointing toward the place where the first spots of greenery appeared. The group turned toward the oasis, moving none too slowly toward the low-growing trees and the telltale shimmer of water. Tim supposed that the valley's natural shape allowed rainfall, rare as it may be, to accumulate and bring life to the surrounding area. The water formed a narrow channel twenty yards across and less than a hundred yards long. Trees and bushes grew along either side, their vibrant colors contrasting with the otherwise drab backdrop of the desert, the juxtaposition apparent even in the moonlight.

After dismounting, they immediately watered the horses, which nickered as they lapped the refreshing liquid. Tim filled one of his skins and drank deeply of it, relishing the temporary reprieve of excess. He refilled his skin to the brim as the party around him did likewise, replenishing their supplies in full.

Afterward, Boblin was the first to pull off his boots and wade into the waters of the oasis. Tim followed suit, closing his eyes as the velvety moisture enveloped his body, slicking away the dirt and grime of the last few days. It was a simple, basic pleasure that had been denied them since entering the Desert.

"Change of plans, mate," Boblin said. "I think I'll just stay here while the rest of you make your way to the City. What do you think?"

Tim immersed his head and body, then resurfaced. "You and me both, friend."

Soon enough, the rest of the company joined them in the waters. For a few blissful moments Tim relaxed and floated on his back, looking at the stars spinning above in the far distance. He pushed himself away from the rest, enjoying temporary solace as the sounds of laughter and conversation carried across the surface of the water toward him. He heard the pattering of feet in a shrub near him, probably a lizard pushing its way through the brush.

Near the bank, Rookwind stamped his hooves on the ground, raising his nose and snorting. Tim only caught the movement at the corner of his vision, but the motion had the look of unrest about it, and it gave him pause. He stood upright in the water, which rose to just above his waist. Rookwind and the rest of the horses were looking toward the same spot where Tim had heard the lizard in the bushes. He studied the greenery, second-guessing his assessment. *Snake, perhaps.* Moments later, Dapple bucked and reared, issuing a loud *whinny* that caught the rest of the company's attention.

"What's got them spooked?" Boblin asked, coming to his feet as well.

"Probably a snake," Tim said, making for the bank. After his second step, though, the leaves in the rustling underbrush parted and he caught a glimpse of brown, leathery skin as *something* bipedal darted forward. The horses scattered, but Hugo's gelding Quarrel was too slow, squealing in terror as the oncoming creature knocked him to the ground.

"Krevurs!" Eklan shouted, wading through the water behind Tim and Boblin. Now that Tim could see it fully, it *was* a kind of lizard, except for the odd fact that it was bipedal and reached a height of about four feet. It had a long tail that no doubt allowed it to remain upright. The front of his head formed a long snout, with serrated teeth that glistened in the moonlight. The creature—krevur, Eklan had called it—opened its jaws in a snarl, tearing into Quarrel's flank in a spray of blood and gore. The poor gelding gave a scream of agony, legs kicking futilely into the air. The krevur had a pair of short, stubby arms ending in three-fingered claws, which it used to press Quarrel against the ground while proceeding with its ghastly meal.

Two more krevurs emerged from the brush, making for the other horses, but Jend Argul reached them first, sword in hand. Tim got to the bank next, eyeing the hilt of his blade in his saddlebags. He reached his hand out, summoning the Lifesource, and his sword flew from the bag into his hand. It blazed alight into green fire.

Something struck Tim, a blow so forceful it lifted him off the ground and threw him clear across the bank. He landed far from the conflict between the rest of the company and the krevurs, but he did not have the time or ability to process what was happening. A wave of liquid darkness consumed his entire mind, pouring over him. His every limb seemed to be on fire and his back arched with pain. The sword slipped from his fingers and winked out. Tim had only an instant to become aware that a presence was *inside* him before it spoke.

WARRIOR—

Had Tim been able to do more than simply process the voice in his mind, he would have recalled the time in the Northern Mountains when he reached out with the Lifesource toward the Deathlands. That had been the first time he encountered the presence of Zadinn Kanas, and for a few moments the Dark

Lord had been inside Tim's head before Tim pushed him out. What happened now was similar, but only in the way that both a candle and the sun provided light. Tim had been able to repel Zadinn with great effort, but this time he had no such recourse available.

The voice spoke again. *I SEE THE DESERT HAS PROVIDED YOU WITH ITS FIRST TEST. BE THANKFUL THESE LANDS HAVE GONE EASY ON YOU THUS FAR.*

Try as he might to resist, Tim could not stop the power that twisted his body, forcing him to sit upright and look at the group. He knew something other than himself was using his eyes to watch the company on the bank. The elions' blades flashed in the night as the krevurs darted around them, trying to find a weak spot. One of the lizards appeared to be down for good, but the other two remained in motion, slipping between Ken and Celia as they turned to face the attack.

YOU HAVE BUT NINE OTHERS WITH YOU. DO YOU TRULY THINK TO ASSAIL MY HOME WITH THIS SMALL COMPANY? MAN'S HUBRIS IS HIS GREATEST FLAW, WARRIOR.

Tim clenched his teeth and *pushed*. A river of the Lifesource surged through his body, striking with every fiber of his being against the all-encompassing force of darkness that threatened to consume him. Uklith merely laughed. *THAT MIGHT HAVE WORKED AGAINST MY SERVANT. ZADINN KANAS WAS STRONG, BUT IN THE END HE WAS AS YOU ARE— SIMPLY A MORTAL. NO, WARRIOR, SUCH EFFORTS WILL AVAIL YOU NONE.*

Leave this vessel, Tim managed to say through his mind. *I serve the Maker. You have no place here.*

AND YOU THINK THE MAKER HAS ANY SAY IN THESE LANDS? YOU ARE IN MY DOMAIN, MINE TO DO WITH AS I PLEASE. LET US WATCH.

On the bank before Tim, Celia and Ken caught the krevur between them on their swords, driving it to the ground. As it writhed in death throes, Boblin lured the last lizard along the bank, diverting it until Hanqar came into position. Hugo raised a crossbow and fired a bolt straight into the krevur's heart.

I SEE YOU HAVE A CAPABLE COMPANY, LED BY THE ONE WHO CAME INTO MY CITY BEFORE. A PITY MY ASSASSINS DID NOT COMPLETE THE TASK I SET BEFORE THEM. YET PERHAPS NOT SUCH A

PITY, FOR NOW YOU WILL BE MINE, WARRIOR. REMEMBER THIS, EVEN AS I RELEASE YOU.

With an awful, tearing sensation, the presence lifted from Tim, leaving him weak and trembling as he lay in the sands. An overwhelming urge to vomit rose in his stomach, but he pushed it back down. He knew his body and mind were wholly his own once again, but it still took some time to command his limbs to move. His hand shook as he curled his fingers around the hilt of his sword, drawing it back to him. He rolled over and took deep breaths, one, two, and three, looking at the stars above before at last rising back to his feet. His skin felt flushed and feverish.

"What was that?" Boblin asked as Tim approached. Quarrel lay dead, a crossbow bolt of mercy in his head. Blood and entrails stretched across the ground.

"That," Tim answered, "was Uklith."

The group turned toward him. "How so?" Boblin asked.

"Do you recall how Nazgar avoided using the Lifesource when we first set out to find the Army of Kah'lash? He did so because accessing the power also opened his mind to Zadinn." Tim swallowed. "I think the same thing happened here, only this time it's Uklith. I touched the Lifesource, and because of it he found me—found *us*."

Tim didn't add that, during their quest in the Northern Mountains, his presence in the Lifesource had eventually grown strong enough to protect Nazgar from Zadinn's influence. This time, Tim was the victim, and he had no such illusions that there would be another presence around to protect *him*.

"He let me go," Tim said, "but if I touch the Lifesource again, I will likely open my mind to him again."

"Which means—"

Tim reached into his saddlebag and grasped the focusing reservoir he used to communicate with Quentiin. The focusing point in the hilt of Tim's blade was safe enough—he simply had to avoid drawing on the Lifesource through it—but the reservoir was different. Not only did it contain a latent source of the power, but Tim had no control over if or when Quentiin would attempt to hail them. If they discarded it, they would lose all communication with their friend, but better that than allowing Uklith a means of prying into Tim's mind once more.

Tim threw the focusing reservoir into the oasis. It landed with a soft *plunk*, sinking below the surface, leaving a set of small, concentric ripples in its wake.

"It means using the Lifesource puts us at risk, and it's a risk I need to avoid." Tim looked at Bria. "You asked who I am without the Lifesource, Bria. It looks like you're going to get your answer."

20

Admiral Vila Kaarst stood at the front of his ship, looking upon the waters of the Rendrivin Ocean. The sun rose behind his back, casting rays of gold upon the blue waters—which would, he suspected, run with blood before long. The brigantine sailed toward Vonku at full speed, flanked on either side by the ships of his fleet. As the waves rushed by beneath him, Kaarst turned to face his crew, wind whipping the tails of his jacket.

"Men!" he called. "It be time at last! We've let Aras hide meekly behind his walls for too long. Today, though, we bid the folk of Vonku a rousin' good morn!"

Kaarst was well aware that attacking in broad daylight held little strategic value, for his enemy would be rested, awake, and alert. However, when he unleashed the fury of his cannons upon Vonku's defenses, the Legion had no hope of prevailing, and for this reason alone he *preferred* to attack in the daylight, just so Aras would know how soundly he'd been defeated. And, with the early sun slanting in from the east, the defenders on the walls would be staring into a blinding glare when the first salvo landed.

The previous night, the dark man visited Kaarst once again, giving the attack his blessing before vanishing. Though it irked Kaarst how this stranger in robes dictated events—for one, because Kaarst was beholden to no man, and for another, he couldn't shake the feeling he was merely a string threaded into a much larger scheme—at the end of the day, he decided it didn't matter. His men knew nothing of the robed stranger's existence, and scheme or no scheme, the throne of Vonku would at last belong to Kaarst. He had only ever wanted to see Aras kneel at his feet, to have the king's eyes plucked out and fed to the pigeons, and in light of this prospect all other concerns became secondary.

In the bay, Aras's pitiful handful of ships surged forward to meet the advancing corsair fleet. As instructed, Kaarst's other ships split to attack the defenders, engaging them in battle so the way remained clear for *Innocent's Blood* to continue into firing range of the walls. Bells rang out over Vonku, sounding the alarm of attack, announcing the city's impending doom. As battle cries echoed over the waves, arrows began flying between the ships, and some vessels came within close enough proximity to launch grappling hooks. Soon the boarding parties would start, men fighting axe to axe and blade to blade, bathing the floorboards of the vessels with blood and death.

Kaarst saw men bristling with longbows and other weaponry on Vonku's walls, flocking to the defense. Next came the ratcheting of gears as the Legion cranked their catapults into position. Within minutes the first boulder launched into the air, performing a graceful arc before crashing down upon one of Kaarst's brigantines. The force of its impact clove the ship down the middle, spraying wood in all directions. Foaming, angry water rushed over the vessel as the sea devoured its first prize. Corsairs leapt overboard to save themselves, and Kaarst gave a grim smile. The Legion could have their victory. *Innocent's Blood* remained out of catapult range with no need of coming closer. The cannons could do their work from here, so let Aras lob all the stones he wished. Men and ships were easy to come by, as far as Kaarst was concerned.

He turned away from the battle and made his way belowdeck. There, Grizzlen oversaw the preparation of the cannons, corsairs rushing between the cast-iron tubes. They had lined the decks with a series of shot balls, preparing to stuff them down the barrels when ready.

"All be well, Adm'ral," Grizzlen said. "Might ye wish to do the honors?"

"But of course," Kaarst said. "Avast ye!"

The men separated, standing crisply at attention, save for the pair directing the first cannon out of the firing shaft, aimed straight at the outer wall of Vonku. As Kaarst stepped forward, Grizzlen handed him a torch. "This be our victory, men," Kaarst said. "And it tastes good!" He touched the torch to the fuse running from the cannon. "*Fire!*"

* * *

Sendalion stood up from his cot, placing a hand against the wall to steady himself and flexing the muscles in his leg. *There.* He liked what he felt. While the muscle still felt tender a few layers deep, he walked with only a slight limp, and that would go away soon enough. He was, more or less, fully functional, and it was time to get back in the fight. He'd heard that Vinsor's group had cleared the northern camp in short order, and though he wished he could have helped them, there was no way he'd have gotten past Talladora. Besides, he had to admit that his rest had been for the better. His two days in the infirmary had allowed him to return to true mobility, rather than hobbling on an injured limb and tearing it down further.

He slipped on his chainmail shirt and buckled his sword about his waist. He intended to go find Vinsor, and from there slip back into the ranks to begin serving his city once more. He had only just left the healing room when the first alarm bell rang, loud and clear from the seaward garrison. Sendalion leapt into a run for the first time in several days, and as he moved, a portion of his mind gauged his stride and the impact on the ground, checking for any indication that his leg might collapse beneath him. Not only did the limb hold, it felt like it grew stronger with each stride. *Good.*

A part of him wondered why it had taken Kaarst so long to get around to this attack—but what did it matter? The Legion had known it was coming all along, a matter of *when* and not *if*, and now that the attack had arrived, it was time to meet it with all they had.

* * *

In his throne room, eyes red from yet another sleepless night, King Aras raised his head at the sound of the warning bells. *The time has come, Admiral Kaarst. Well enough, for I have tired of your games. Let us be on with it.* He looked out the window, which provided him a view of the streets of Vonku below. During the past few days Vinsor Dalin had performed an admirable job vacating as many of the citizens as possible, and though some of the city folk remained— more than Aras would have liked—the Legion had done their best in the time allotted. At the very least, they had cleared the outer city and moved those who remained to a position of relative safety behind the inner wall. If Kaarst's cannons worked as Aras's commanders described, the streets of the outer city would soon become a slaughterhouse, a veritable maze of butchery after the corsairs came through and the Legion began a retreat of attrition.

Aras squinted against the rising sun. Vila was far from incompetent, and Aras knew full well that the former noble had been well trained in military tactics before his fall from grace. At the edge of his vision, he saw shadows moving as the soldiers of the Royal Legion manned the walls, good men all. The catapults began their defense, lobbing boulders high and far, and Aras prayed every stone might find an enemy target in the waters of the Rendrivin. Supposedly Quentiin Harggra was out in the bay, perhaps on a ship, according to Sendalion Danris's reports. Aras hadn't expected this plan for Quentiin—he'd wanted the dwerion *here*, to answer questions about the dark magics at the heart of Kaarst's fleet—but he'd been king long enough to know that what one expected and what occurred were often two very different things. In battle, up was down and left was right, the unexpected became the norm, and a ruler simply had to trust in his people and in the chain of command. Quentiin Harggra had served his kingdom well in the Icor Rebellion, and he had served it well representing them to the North. The best Aras could do was pray the Maker remained with Harggra in his current endeavors.

"Your majesty?"

Aras turned to see Captain Yastlin standing behind him.

"It's begun, my king," the captain said.

"That I see, Captain. Thus, we are put to the test."

"My men need me, your majesty. Do I have your leave?"

"Aye, Captain Yastlin, you have your leave. Let your blade sing true."

Yastlin bowed, one hand on the hilt of his sword, and proceeded from the room.

Aras longed to close his eyes, to sleep. Whenever he looked in the mirror, an old man stared back at him. He was not young anymore, far from it—but one's kingdom did not care if its leader was young or old. A king's country demanded nothing less than absolute loyalty and absolute sacrifice, from the day the crown was placed upon his head until the day he was laid to rest. It was not right that this battle should be Aras's legacy, perhaps his last, but the world turned as it would. At the back of the room, his own sword hung on the wall, and though it had been a long time since he had held that weapon in his fist, Aras nonetheless suspected he would indeed need to hold it one more time before all was done here.

* * *

Quentiin stood upon the deck of a galleon they had commandeered in Peltin, Jolldo and Trivian beside him, riding the waves beneath the rising sun. It had been an easy enough task to seize the ship in the village; the corsair captain had left behind only a small detachment to guard it while he and the rest of his men roved the countryside in raiding parties. Trivian's soldiers, still full of fire and vengeance from the wrongs visited upon them at Eltern, had swept upon the small crew guarding the vessel, taking it quickly and without casualties. That had been two days ago. In addition to the obvious benefits of a bloodless victory, Quentiin was thankful for the psychological boost it gave the men. Such a win bolstered their confidence, giving them something to be proud of and allowing them to stand with backs a bit straighter. They would have need of that mettle, too, because what lay before them would not come without a cost.

They flew the flag of Kaarst's fleet from the foremast, a necessary deception for the next phase of their plan as they entered the waters east of Vonku. With each passing minute, the city grew larger in Quentiin's view, while in front of the outer walls he saw Kaarst's ships bearing down on the city. Aras's fleet had already engaged the corsairs, arrows flying over the waters. One enemy ship had been destroyed by stones catapulted from the battlements, another damaged, but Quentiin feared the defenders' early success would pale once Kaarst unleashed his weapons. He willed their ship to go faster; they were still out of reach of the battle and so for the moment he could only watch the events unfolding before him. The corsairs ignored the approaching galleon, as they no doubt presumed their comrades were simply moving in to join the fun, and Aras's ships were too preoccupied to start a new fight.

That was when it happened: the largest ship of all, a brigantine sailing square in the middle of the fleet, turned broadside to reveal a dark shaft protruding from its middeck. As the brigantine drew parallel to Vonku's outer wall, a *boom* resounded across the bay. The men and dwerions aboard Quentiin's ship shied back at the noise. The effect on Vonku's defenses was immediately apparent; a section of stone wall blew outward, raining fragments down upon the bay.

"What in the name of Malath was that?" Trivian asked.

Quentiin hadn't been conscious when the Fort of Pellen blew itself to shreds, but he imagined the sight had been similar to what unfolded here. A series of no less than five additional iron tubes emerged from the side of Kaarst's brigantine, firing in quick succession. The combined might blasted away at Vonku's walls, causing gigantic fragments of stone and the bodies of soldiers to descend into the bay.

"Ready yer men, Commander Seltor," Quentiin said. "We must strike quickly. Those walls can withstand only a handful of volleys before they crumble."

Sendalion had told him that the tubes—Kaarst apparently called them "cannons"—took a while to prepare again after firing, so this gave them a gap of time, and Quentiin intended to make the most of it.

"The plan holds?" Trivian asked.

"Ye better believe it," Quentiin replied. "The plan holds."

* * *

When Sendalion reached the battlements, sword in hand, the first explosion sounded. He felt the stones shake under his feet from the impact, as in front of him fragments from the wall tumbled into the bay. Though ranks upon ranks of archers filled the parapets, they could do nothing about Kaarst's flagship, which remained situated outside the reach of their longbows. The archers *could* reach some of the smaller ships attacking the defenders, thereby lending assistance to their comrades on the water, but Sendalion knew as well as the rest that Kaarst only intended those smaller ships to divert the Legion from the greater threat in the bay. A trio of galleons flanked *Innocent's Blood*, keeping Vonku's forces from engaging Kaarst's brigantine, and all the time Aras's vessels spent trying to clear a path toward it just gave Kaarst more opportunities to unleash his devastating firepower. Crews on the battlements hurried to load stones into catapults, the better to break down Kaarst's ships. Upon seeing Horatio at the head of the nearest crew, Sendalion sheathed his sword and rushed to greet his friend.

"Well met," Horatio said. "Rumor had it you were out of the fight until further notice."

"Further notice is now. Come on, let's send this scum to the seabed."

In response, Horatio grinned—and then his face exploded. Sendalion cried out in surprise, lifting a hand to shield his face from the sudden shrapnel flying in all directions. The impact of the cannon blast lifted him off his feet, throwing him against the far side of the battlements. He saw the catapult's wooden frame disintegrate as the same shot ball which had killed Horatio plowed into the structure and wrecked it beyond repair. Horatio was not the only casualty, either. Two more men tumbled over the seaward side of the battlements, knocked off balance by the impact, and from this height the water would shatter their bones on impact. In front of Sendalion a boulder slipped from its catapult bed, rolling toward the break in the parapet and following the two fallen soldiers over the side.

Ears ringing, Sendalion struggled back to his feet, knowing he had to move away from the point of impact before the next blast—

It lifted him off his feet yet again, and this time Sendalion fell down the steps on the interior of the battlement. As painful and disorienting as it was, he knew he was much better off than the men who had been in the way of the hit. *Kaarst will knock these walls right out from under us.* Beside Sendalion, another Legion man rolled down the stairs, colliding with him, and Sendalion grabbed man by the shoulder.

"Gather your company!" he shouted, his voice sounding tinny and distant to his ears. "We can only do so much from here—we need to be ready to meet them in the streets when they come through."

The man gave him a blank look, clearly taking a moment to process the information, but at last nodded his understanding. He stood back up, waving a hand at the men still collecting themselves on the battlements.

"Let's go," Sendalion said, drawing his sword and leading the way toward the streets below.

* * *

Captain Yastlin, as it happened, was a few steps ahead of Sendalion. After leaving Vinsor in command atop the parapets, the captain gathered a core of his soldiers and led them to the ground level gates. On the other side of the walls, the battle in the bay continued, while above their heads the battlements shook under the assault of Kaarst's cannons.

"Stand fast!" Yastlin called. At his signal, a pair of men rushed forward and heaved the gates open to reveal the sandy shore beyond. At the water's edge, the first of Kaarst's ships was coming to ground, and though a handful of arrows descended from the tops of the walls to meet the incoming vessel, most of the men on the parapets had their hands full reacting to the cannon fire, leaving the corsair crew unchallenged. Yastlin flexed his arms. *So be it.* Though Kaarst had the advantage of his cannons, Yastlin knew one thing for certain: man to man, blade to blade, his soldiers were far superior to the best of the corsair crews.

Ragtag battles on the seas were no match for the rigorous training and excellence required to serve in the Royal Legion. Here, his soldiers would face this rabble on solid ground, and Kaarst's men would know the wrath of the best-trained troops in the realm. As the first wave of corsairs disembarked from the ship, surging forward across the sand, Yastlin raised his sword. *"Charge!"*

The Royal Legion ran out of the gates, meeting the corsairs of Vila Kaarst's fleet on the shores of Alcatune. Above the heads of the two clashing forces, arrows flew through the sky, while behind them another salvo of cannonballs struck the battlements with devastating force. All along the parapets, catapults launched boulders in retaliation, some of which struck targets in the bay while others fell short, landing on the company on the beach to crush friend and foe alike. In the distance, several of the embattled ships had caught fire. Flames jumped from one vessel to the next, and soon the entire sea appeared ablaze.

Against this backdrop of smoke and carnage, Yastlin ran full tilt, skewering the first corsair he encountered, throwing the man backward with the force of his blow. As the corsair's body landed in the ankle-deep waters, Yastlin roared with fury, pulled his blade free, and spun to face his next assailant. The waters around his calves soon ran crimson, and while Yastlin's troop numbered less than that of the corsair crew, the tide of the first clash turned almost immediately in the Legion's favor, training and skill winning out over violence and barbarity. Soon enough, a second ship pulled in beside the first, lowering its gangplanks.

Even with the odds nearing four to one, the Legion soldiers might very well have beaten Kaarst's crews.

Until the cannons joined the fight.

Yastlin heard a resounding explosion nearby. In the midst of an erupting spray of water he saw no less than four of his men fall, the corsairs sweeping in to dispatch the wounded. When the second blast came, Yastlin felt a fragment of stone strike the side of his face. Pain like never before blossomed in his eye socket, and half the world went dark. As blood streamed down his face, Yastlin knew he'd lost the eye. In front of him, a dwerion came forward, bearing a battle-axe and a toothy grin, doubtless thinking he'd found an easy victim. Yastlin ducked the blow, and when he returned to full height, he plunged the length of his sword through the dwerion's face. He reflected that he might have gone for the heart, but that grin was too karfing snide to let be. Better it be removed from the dwerion's face for good.

"Rally!" Yastlin yelled, voice hoarse. His men came to him as they always did, the wounded and the whole gathering into a phalanx formation that bristled with weaponry and skill. Above them, Yastlin was dimly aware of the additional cannonfire slamming into the walls, and for the first time he saw a section of Vonku's mighty seaward defenses begin to buckle. *Not much longer. Let's buy them what time we can.* Yastlin let loose a final cry, the last command of a long, dedicated career, and led his men into the jaws of death.

* * *

As their galleon swept alongside *Innocent's Blood*, Quentiin saw the first portion of Vonku's wall crumble. Kaarst's cannons barked a final blast for the time being, and the tubes pulled in as the crews set to work reloading.

"Now!" Trivian ordered, and his men fired their grappling hooks into the sides of *Innocent's Blood*. The ruse had worked perfectly; they had gone unnoticed in the battle, assumed to be yet another member of Kaarst's armada. They had closed the gap, and it was time to end this. The cannons had already fired several successful volleys, and this last salvo had been the worst yet. Trivian was the first onto the lines between the vessels, a pair of soldiers following behind him, hanging suspended and moving hand over hand. Quentiin seized a cable, pulled it taut to ensure the hooks held against Kaarst's ship, and leapt over the open gap between the vessels. The waters danced below him, while upon the decks of *Innocent's Blood* a score of corsairs swarmed to meet this unexpected challenge.

From the deck of the galleon, the archers unleashed their first volley. Many arrows missed, reminding Quentiin that those on their side were not of the same caliber as full-fledged Legion soldiers. However, enough bolts found targets to provide the boarding group the cover they needed, and though Quentiin and the dwerions made slower progress than the men, their arms being shorter and able to cover less distance, they soon reached the lip of *Innocent's Blood*.

When Quentiin pulled himself over the ledge and into the tide of battle, a corsair came at him almost immediately. Quentiin rolled, his opponent's blade *whisking* through the air above his head. Without time to unsheathe his weapon, Quentiin punched the corsair in the stomach. Quentiin had never quite understood the elion's fascination with ailar—and not just because he was too short and stout to be an effective practitioner of the art—but some-times a good punch was all one needed. As the corsair doubled over, Quentiin wrested the cutlass from his grip and beheaded the man. He tossed the cutlass over the ship's edge—he had no reason to use something stained by corsair hands—and drew his own blade.

Around him, more of Trivian's men joined the fight. As the soldiers went to work, Quentiin waved Jolldo and the dwerions to him. Trivian had his or-ders—*keep the corsairs occupied*—and from the looks of things he was doing an admirable job of it. The dwerions had their own task to complete.

"All right, laddies," Quentiin growled. "Follow me."

It was time to see what these cannons were truly made of.

21

Sendalion hit the pavement of the streets, looking through the open gates to the battle on the beach. He saw Captain Yastlin's company disappear beneath the onslaught of the corsair horde, the Legion killing three pirates for every soldier. Had it not been for the cannons and the enemy's sheer numbers, the battle would have been a rout in Vonku's favor. Yastlin had six arrows protruding from him, and it still took four corsairs charging in concert to force the captain onto his back in the waters while a pair of them drove their blades in tandem through Yastlin's torso.

Sendalion and his band might have been too late to save the captain's company, but not too late to avenge them. He led a score of men forward from the gates, yelling a battle cry as they splashed into the waters of the bay and slammed into the enemy's flank. Sendalion swung his blade left and right, up and down, leaving bodies on all sides. From the corner of his eye, he saw yet another brigantine sweeping into position beside the other vessels, minutes away from disgorging another corsair crew. In the distance, the cannons withdrew into *Innocent's Blood* to begin the process of reloading. Though this gave the defenders a temporary reprieve, Sendalion feared his company was on the cusp of suffering the same fate as Yastlin's. Just then he caught sight of a new ship, a galleon swinging alongside Kaarst's flagship...

Harggra. Sendalion stepped back as a corsair swung a pike toward his chest. The blade passed a hairsbreadth from his skin. Sendalion parried the thrust and took the corsair's head in one sweep, flecks of blood spattering as the pirate's body sank beneath the waves. It was difficult to keep his footing out here, ankle-deep in the waters with the sands shifting beneath his boots. Behind Sendalion the walls continued to waver, their support undermined by the previous cannon volley, and more chunks of stone slipped from their sides to land on the beach.

Sendalion risked a glance toward the waters, where grappling hooks had been fired from Harggra's ship to Kaarst's. Men and dwerions were crossing the gap to board the brigantine and assault the corsair crew. Meanwhile, of more immediate concern, pirates had begun to swarm forth from the newly arrived vessel on Vonku's shore.

"Fall back!" he called. His troops would do better by returning to the momentary safety of the garrison and regrouping with the rest of the Legion. The soldiers about him pulled away, giving inevitable ground to the invaders, as behind them Vonku's great walls began to flex and buckle in their death throes.

* * *

Kaarst was belowdeck with his cannons, watching the walls through his spyglass. With this last shot, the irrevocable damage was all but assured. The sight of the crumbling defenses provided him no shortage of pleasure.

When he heard the first sounds of commotion above him, he experienced an unpleasant ripple of surprise. He turned toward the noise as the door to the topdeck flipped open. Grizzlen, who'd since returned to the duties of commanding the ship, poked his head through. "Adm'ral! We be under attack!"

What in Malath?

Kaarst climbed the ladder and saw a combination of men and dwerions surging over the sides of his ship, boarding from a galleon that had docked beside them. The admiral cursed, coming onto the deck and drawing his blade. "What do ye be waitin' for, me hearties? *Kill!*"

The corsairs swarmed to the attack, some taking the soldiers on head to head while others set about slashing the grappling lines. Kaarst would have liked answers to a good many questions, not the least of which was how Aras's men had managed to get this close to his ship, but he had little time for wondering as a soldier came straight for him. The fighter looked quite young indeed, and the admiral stepped easily to the side, drawing his sword in a flicking motion across the boy's stomach. The youth clamped hands to his waist in a futile attempt to prevent his entrails from spilling onto the deck, eyes wide in pain and fear. Kaarst left him to die. If the boy had any decency, he'd pitch himself over the side for the sharks and avoid making a mess, but Kaarst wouldn't count on it. Something for Grizzlen to clean up later, as punishment for letting things come to this. At the very least, there would be a swift flogging for whoever who had let the galleon come close. And that was the thing, Kaarst thought as he waded into the battle—no matter how busy things got, there would always be time for a proper flogging.

* * *

Jolldo and Yagglem covered Quentiin as he led the dwerions from Raldoon across the topdeck of *Innocent's Blood*, moving around bodies of the fallen, engaging in conflict when they had to, but otherwise heading straight for their goal: the belowdeck hatch. As they neared the trapdoor, Quentiin caught sight of a tall, lean man with a hook-shaped nose twenty paces away. His flowing black hair and piercing eyes made him appear every inch the corsair commander, and Quentiin did not doubt he was looking at Vila Kaarst. The man's blade flashed among his victims as they fell before him, but at the moment he remained much too preoccupied with Trivian's men to bother the dwerions—which was exactly the plan, of course.

Upon reaching the hatch, Quentiin flipped it open and leapt down the ladder with a growl, Jolldo and Yagglem close behind. Though there were plenty of corsairs on the lower deck, most were too fixated on the task of manning the cannons to notice the sudden appearance of three dwerions in their midst. Only when Briiga, Vellgo and the rest arrived did the first corsair take note, and by then Quentiin was already upon him, plunging his dagger into the man's jugular and causing a fountain of blood to spurt onto the floorboards. The dwerions took the first cannon crew by storm, descending upon their enemy before the pirates knew what was happening, hacking and slashing with swords, axes, and any other manner of weapon at hand. The cry of alarm at last went out, and the corsairs turned toward them. At the far end of the line, one group pushed their cannon back out the open porthole, setting fire to the fuse. It boomed in response. Through the slim hole Quentiin caught sight of Vonku's walls beginning their final collapse, and then all Malath broke loose in the hold.

The corsairs outnumbered the dwerions by a fair margin, and though Quentiin knew that he and his companions could use these tight quarters to their advantage by minimizing their need to defend against multiple directions of attack, he nonetheless realized they had to make short work of this situation. He approached the nearest loaded cannon, noting the pins and ropes that held it in place on the decking, and estimated it took at least three men to move it into position. Well, Quentiin supposed, the pitch and roll of the sea might accomplish what a lone dwerion could not. As one of Kaarst's crew—a dwerion, in fact—attacked, Quentiin pulled the first pin from the cannon's base. He snarled at the corsair, taking particular affront to the fact that one of his kind served in Kaarst's crew. As Quentiin's opponent drew a dagger, Quentiin responded with an elbow to the dwerion's face. Quentiin struck the deck and rolled to the far side of the cannon, pulling the opposite pin as he did so, coming back to his feet with the iron bolt clenched in his fist. When the corsair came back around, Quentiin was ready for him, using the bolt as a bludgeon to knock him onto the deck.

"Good riddance," Quentiin said, and stabbed his sword into the dwerion's heart. Beneath his feet, the ship pitched on a wave. Quentiin was heartened to see the cannon slip back against its bonds. With the pins freed, only ropes held the massive weapon in place. Quentiin raised his blade and slashed once, twice, thrice. The ropes fell away, and the next time the sea pitched, the cannon rolled from its slot and across the floor of the deck. It crushed one corsair with a sickening *crunch*, the man screaming in agony as his bones snapped. In the space left by the cannon's absence, the rest of the corsairs came at the group, bristling with blades and weaponry.

"Push, laddies, *push!*" Quentiin roared. The dwerions leaned against one side of the cannon, straining with all their might to swing the barrel around to point inward, straight at the rest of the cannons and the oncoming corsairs.

"All right," Quentiin said, pulling a torch from its sconce. "Let's hang this scum with their own rope."

He touched the flame of the torch to the fuse.

* * *

The exterior wall's final collapse came just after Sendalion pulled his men back into the outer city. The brick and mortar structure shuddered with a massive, eternal groan that built in might and cadence until the wall crumpled inward, sending up an enormous cloud of dust that rose as gravity overcame strength. While most troops had already vacated the parapets, a brave few had remained behind to man the catapults, and they died in the collapse, massive stones tumbling down all around to bury them.

Ironically, the destruction helped the surviving Legion soldiers. Before the wall descended, Kaarst's corsairs had drawn back toward the beach in order to avoid the devastation, and the heavy dust created a haze so thick that none could see more than a few paces, protecting the Legion soldiers from any immediate attacks. Peering through the dim glow, Sendalion held a rag over his mouth with one hand and shielded his eyes with the other. He led his men away from the site of the collapse, the dust cloud dissipating with every step, changing from a thick mass in which he could barely see to something resembling a low-lying fog, until at last the small company reached a rise in the city streets where they could stand in the clear. As the soldiers came together at the top of the hill, they turned and looked back the way they had come. The walls' monstrous collapse had left a gaping hole behind, looking like a giant's mouth that had lost its front teeth.

Next Vinsor's soldiers began emerging from the fog. Sendalion supposed his troops looked just as bad as these newcomers, every one of whom was covered in soot and grime and bore no small assortment of cuts and bruises. At this point, they had no count of how many had been lost. The group on the hill numbered perhaps two hundred, and at best two hundred more remained scattered around the garrison. Six hundred additional men waited in reserve behind the inner walls. *Our position would be more than enough, considering our inner walls, but Kaarst has his cannons. These foundations of brick and mortar will do us little good when he brings his weaponry onshore and takes aim again.*

Vinsor approached from his company, one eye heavily bruised, a deep gash across his forearm. "What of Captain Yastlin?" he asked.

Sendalion shook his head.

Vinsor sheathed his blade, giving a weary sigh. He looked toward the ruins in front of them. "I suppose that makes you *Captain* Danris. Your orders, sir?"

I'm not ready for this. I suppose that doesn't matter, though. "We need to retreat behind the inner wall. From there, we can bolster what defenses we have. It should be more than enough, except—"

"For the cannons. We knew that coming into this, though."

Sendalion nodded. "Aye, we did."

Beyond the hill upon which the Legion soldiers stood, the dust remained thick and cloying. It would not settle for some time, but that did not stop the men from observing the periodic flaring of lights within the murk.

"They've started the burning," Vinsor said.

It was an obvious move, serving to the corsairs' advantage and the defenders' detriment. Kaarst's men would systematically raze the outer city, creating a ceaseless barrage of smoke and flame that could last for days. Not only would it conceal the corsair's movements and wear the defenders down, it also worked as a psychological weapon. Plenty of men in the Legion had homes out there, and though all of their families had been evacuated thanks to Vinsor's efforts, seeing their city slowly burnt down would weigh heavily upon the soldiers' psyches. *It will also make magnificent cover for those cannons. They could be aiming right at us from behind a cloud of smoke, and we'd never know.* It all rested on Quentiin Harggra now.

* * *

Quentiin would have been flattered by such sentiments being directed his way, but he had little time to consider more than the immediate task in front of him. When the cannon detonated, the entire barrel recoiled. The impact threw him backward across the lower deck. He lost all hearing for an instant, only to have it return with a rushing sound and ringing, the noise of the surrounding world penetrating only in muted tones, as though he had cotton stuffed in his ears.

Before him, he saw that the cannon shot had ripped through the contingent of corsairs, shredding those in its immediate path and wounding many others. The ball tore a gaping hole in the far side of the ship, leaving splintered wood in its wake, and through it Quentiin could see the waves outside *Innocent's Blood* in all their turbulent majesty.

He clambered back to his feet. Time was of the essence, for they were far from finished. One successful shot did not constitute a victory. Kaarst's crew could still overwhelm them unless the dwerions did more lasting damage in short order. For the moment, the corsairs were too scattered and disoriented to form any sort of meaningful resistance, so Quentiin and Jolldo set to loading the next shot ball into the cannon. Around them, other dwerions defended the perimeter.

"Stand back, laddies!" Quentiin roared as he set fire to the fuse once more. This time he directed his shot across the remaining cannons in the lower deck. The dwerions took cover immediately, as well they should, for the destruction sent deadly shards of iron flying in every direction. Some of the cannons detonated, the powder within ignited by the blast. Those corsairs who remained were killed almost to the last man, save for a handful writhing on the deck in throes of pain and death. Quentiin raised a hand to signal the next phase of the plan. With cannons down and corsairs down, one last task remained.

* * *

Trivian felt the first blast echo from beneath his feet, causing the entire deck to vibrate. His men had known it was coming and took the surprise well enough, but it caught the corsairs off guard. Trivian used this surprise to press their advantage, pushing a line of pirates back into the far corner of the vessel. For now, the men of Vonku held their own well enough, but he hoped the dwerions would hurry. The Legion soldiers could only delay, not defeat, these corsairs. Trivian saw Admiral Vila Kaarst in the opposite corner of the ship, cutting men down. Try as he might, Trivian had not yet been able to carve his way through the mass of fighting to take Kaarst on directly.

Quentiin had told him to expect three shots, and knowing the second was to follow, Trivian directed his men toward the edge of the ship in preparation for the final phase of the attack. As expected, the planking rocked with the sounds of the second blast. A portion of the deck erupted, no doubt from fragments below shooting upward. A corsair fell through the resulting hole with a cry.

"Steady, men!" Trivian cried. "Grappling hooks!" He brought forward a line of defenders to stand in a semicircle around his men, who gathered at the edge of *Innocent's Blood* and began firing hooks back toward the galleon below, securing passage for their retreat. One of his men fired an arrow with a red flag skyward, the signal for those still aboard the galleon to take their cue.

When the red flag reached the top of its arc, a volley of flaming arrows streamed from the galleon's deck, raining fire upon Kaarst's flagship. It was risky as Malath to burn the ship with so many of their people aboard, but Trivian was learning that risky plans were Quentiin's method. Besides, Trivian thought of how the corsairs had burned *Steadfast*, and he thought it quite fitting to visit such poetic justice upon the Admiral's fleet.

It's your turn to burn, Admiral.

* * *

At the first blast, Vila Kaarst uttered a curse. Upon the second he was livid, and when the arrows descended upon his ship he flew into a full-fledged rage. He seized Grizzlen by the scruff of the neck, threw the corsair down, and screamed for his crew to make a path toward the door leading belowdecks. They did so, but with great cost to their lives. Kaarst could not care less for the corsairs' deaths and thought only of vengeance as he hacked and slashed his way through the Legion soldiers. *No one* attacked his ship, and *no one* fired upon his fleet. Whoever was down there, they would pay.

* * *

"Are ye sure about this, laddie?" Jolldo asked Quentiin.

"No, but it's too late for second thoughts," Quentiin replied. The other dwerions had left at Quentiin's orders, climbing up the ladder to return top-deck.

Quentiin lit the third and final fuse. This time, instead of firing horizontally across the lower deck, he directed the blast down into the base of the ship, blowing away the ballast.

For a heartbeat, nothing happened. Then *Innocent's Blood* gave a deep, titanic groan and tilted starboard. What started as a soft creak grew louder and louder, accompanied by the sound of boards snapping as the brigantine's foundations splintered. It wasn't enough just to destroy the cannons, not for Quentiin. This ship had to see the bottom of the ocean, and now it was well on its way there.

"Let's move," he said to Jolldo. "It's time to get topside."

Climbing back up the ladder and entering into a pitched battle was not the most strategically sound option, but they didn't have any other choices available. He and Jolldo never reached the ladder, though. The floorboards heaved beneath them, the ship tilting dramatically and causing the dwerions to lose their balance. As Quentiin hit the deck and slid toward the far wall, he saw the boards cave inward against the steadily building pressure of the sea. After that, Quentiin saw only the angry rush of foam as water surged inward, devouring them all.

* * *

Trivian hit the deck as the ship pitched to the side. Having moved to the port gunwale, he found himself standing at the ship's peak as the far edge tilted toward the ocean. One of his soldiers fell into the bay, but the others managed to gain purchase with the grappling hooks. As the deck around them blazed into fire from the arrows, Trivian grasped the first of the ropes tethering them to the galleon and began to climb hand over hand toward safety.

In retrospect, the flaming arrows may have been unnecessary. The ship seemed to be meeting its fate quite nicely regardless of the fire. Still, it was a nice touch. Billows of smoke floated upward, stinging their eyes as they moved. Trivian's muscles strained from the ache of climbing from one ship to another. The only upside to the return journey was that this time the corsairs were too preoccupied to launch attacks on anyone making their way over the open water.

"Any sign of Harggra?" he asked as he reached the safety of the ship and climbed aboard. All of the other dwerions were accounted for, but as to Quentiin and Jolldo, no one had an answer. Trivian looked toward the sinking brigantine, praying the last two dwerions would make it through.

* * *

Quentiin sucked in a lungful of air before the turbulent wave hit, slamming his body with bruising force. All was chaos as his body spun in the sea's grip. He slammed against the side of a cannon right before an opposing force sucked him downward. Pain blazed through him as his body scraped against shards of wood. Engulfed in salt water as he was, the cuts on his body became an all consuming agony. Raw survival instinct took over. Quentiin kicked his legs and rotated his arms in a stroking motion designed to bring him to the water's surface. He knew it would be no good, because there *was* no surface, the entire lower deck of the ship had been flooded and the vessel was sinking. Soon his head would strike against the ceiling of the deck boards above him, and that would be that for him.

He was completely surprised when he indeed *did* break the surface, rising above the waves of the ocean. The rushing force of water must have propelled him through the hole in the ship's wall, popping him out from the interior like a wine cork from a bottle. The scraping he had felt against wood had likely been the edges of the gaping hole raking the length of his body. Moments later, Jolldo's head appeared, too.

Jolldo brushed water from his eyes and spat to clear his mouth. "Don't tell me, laddie," he said. "The hole in the side o' the ship was part o' your escape plan all along."

"No, but I'll sure as Malath take credit for it. Bloody good thinkin' ahead, if I do say so myself."

Beside them, the remnants of *Innocent's Blood* slipped below the surface.

"A victory for us, laddies," Quentiin said as the schooner with Trivian and the Legion men pulled alongside them. "The Maker knows we needed it."

* * *

Sendalion raised his crossbow and fired, covering the Legion's exit into the inner walls of Vonku. In front of them, the first of the corsairs emerged from the smoky, dusty haze consuming the city streets, pressing hard to cut down any who remained in the outer area. With the last man safely inside the walls, Sendalion stood down. The guards on either side of him dropped the gates, providing a momentary reprieve from the fighting.

Sendalion sheathed his sword and wiped the grime from his face. Things were grim out there, that was sure enough. He could not see the bay, but knew that Kaarst's corsairs could be rolling the cannons through the streets, preparing a second volley at the walls. Voicing a cursory thanks to the men manning the gate, Sendalion pushed into the inner garrison and climbed the steps to the wall, hoping it would present him a vantage point over the battle.

Vinsor already stood atop the parapet. He wore a taut smile as Sendalion approached, and he pointed at the waters of the Rendrivin. "They may have won the outer city, but their noses are sure bleeding for it."

Sendalion followed Vinsor's finger, mirroring the other's smile when he saw the ball of flame engulfing *Innocent's Blood*. Harggra and Seltor had come through, and the men of Eltern had proven themselves once again, bringing still more honor to a title that too often carried stigma instead of dignity. *Good for them.*

The galleon bearing Trivian and Quentiin shot away from the battle, as well it should, for plenty of Kaarst's ships remained afloat. The vessels were scattered far enough apart that they could not inflict immediate damage upon the dwerions and Legion men, but the soldiers would do well to make quick work of their escape. Sendalion supposed they would sail north to steer clear of the battle before coming onshore. Sendalion and his fellow soldiers would lend whatever aid they could to get the Legion men and dwerions back inside their walls, but the corsairs would soon occupy most of the inner city, so for the moment it was up to Quentiin and Trivian to determine how to maximize the strength of their position on the outside.

On the subject of the city…well, that remained to be seen. The cannons were no longer a threat, which was a relief to the defenders of Vonku, but cannons notwithstanding, Sendalion expected the corsairs to continue their burning, filling the land with smoke and haze to obfuscate their movements. The battle might be over, but now the siege would begin. With a salute toward Vinsor, Sendalion began seeing to the defenses.

* * *

Kaarst breached the surface of the water, spitting out the taste of the sea. *Gone. My ship is gone.* He would find whoever was responsible for this and hang him with his entrails. He would make the man eat his own fingers and feed his toes to the sharks. He would dig the offender's eyeballs out with a rusted spoon. He would—

A fist grabbed his tunic and hauled him from the water. He landed in the bottom of a small boat, staring at a pair of oarlocks on either side. Kaarst uttered an oath and pushed himself to his knees, ready to unleash his fury on whatever unsuspecting idiot had seized him without so much as a greeting.

He stopped. The robed man, still surrounded in shimmering darkness, sat in the middle of the boat with one hand upon each oar. Though Kaarst could not see the man's face, he knew the stranger was almost surely smiling.

"I see you've made interesting use of my gift," the hooded man said.

Kaarst snarled and drew his cutlass. Mysterious powers or not, he would not let this stranger mock him. He felt his arm freeze mid-swing, halted by an invisible force.

"Patience," the robed man said. "We have only just begun this endeavor, you and I. Much work remains from here."

"Let's be on with it," Kaarst said. "I have a king to kill."

"As I said, *patience.* Without the cannons, you will find yourself at a strategic disadvantage. Oh, it is easy enough to blow smoke and fire in the streets—I see you've already begun as such—but Aras has hundreds of trained soldiers behind those walls, and you know as well as I that it will take more than your rabble of corsairs to proceed from here." The man gestured toward Kaarst's arm, which still held the cutlass. "I will release you if you promise to be courteous."

"Of course," Kaarst said. A moment later his arm belonged to him once more, and he sheathed his blade. "What next?"

"Proceed with your siege and hold the outer city. In spite of this unfortunate incident in the bay, things are continuing according to plan. Rest assured, the inner walls will fall as did the outer walls. I have work to do, and it is time I was about it."

Beside the boat, Grizzlen surfaced, spluttering water. "Adm'ral!" he shouted. "We be alive!"

"Aye," Kaarst said, adopting his corsair nuances again now that his man had appeared. "We be alive indeed." He pulled his captain into the boat. "It be good to see ya, me hearty. I am needin' to have a talk with ye."

He struck Grizzlen across the face, knocking the man to the floor of the boat. Grizzlen sputtered in surprise as Kaarst drew his knife. "Ye—lost—me—my—ship!" With every word, he shoved the blade into Grizzlen's body. The corsair howled as Kaarst stabbed again and again, flecks of blood spattering the gunwales as well as Kaarst's face. He continued long after Grizzlen was dead, carving into the corpse, shrieking curses.

"Temper," the robed man said softly, watching as Kaarst unleashed his grisly vengeance. "Temper."

22

From the top of a hill Tim and Eklan gazed at the landscape before them. They'd been traveling through the sands for the past day and a half, having left the Bleached Fields far behind. Here, they approached the Desert's next transition, where the hills flattened and the sands tapered off, leaving the company to face a jagged expanse of stones colored in a myriad of ochre hues. Pale yellow, orange, red, and brown interplayed across the field of Tim's vision. In the distance, the land ended at the edge of a sheer chasm, and the only way for the travelers to cross the subsequent gorge would be to walk upon a thin ridge that led from one side of the abyss to the other. The haze of the distant horizon obscured the far side of the path. The breathtaking sight, equal parts terrifying and majestic, gave the entire group pause.

"We called it the Mygon Path," Eklan said.

"Who was he?" Tim asked.

"He was a friend of ours in Keldur. Mygon loved heights, and he was always trying new tricks the rest of us thought were crazy. It made perfect sense to name the crossing after him. It takes two days to get to the far side, and we'll want to move as quickly as possible. That drop is liable to make all of us queasy."

True enough. From here, Tim could see the path was easily twenty feet wide, more than enough space to traverse safely, but the mind was a funny thing. Those twenty feet would no doubt feel much narrower when it came time to set foot upon the ridge. Eklan took the lead, guiding the group down the slope of the hill and toward the gorge.

Tim had not touched the Lifesource since the attack. He didn't like being unable to use his greatest asset, but he couldn't risk it. He now understood how Nazgar must have felt during their quest through the Northern Mountains, but even at that, Nazgar had eventually been able to use the Lifesource once

Tim's presence grew strong enough to offer him protection. Tim, however, had no expectation of any such reprieve. For the time being, he had to rely on the sword skills his father Daniel had taught him so long ago.

What about when we eventually reach Agrazab? He *might* be able to use his powers. Plenty of dark magic ran rampant throughout Agrazab, and Tim suspected he would be only a whisper against the background noise. Of course, this would also mean he faced a figurative river of his enemy's power, which created a host of other problems to consider. But one thing at a time.

Several hours later, they reached the edge of the chasm. The bottom lay out of sight, the moonlight only penetrating its depths for the first several hundred feet. Even in the light of day Tim doubted they'd be able to see all the way down.

"Any idea what's down there?" Ken asked.

Eklan grunted. "If we're lucky, nothing. I don't put much trust in luck out here, though."

The horses bucked and scraped, nervous of the approach, but after some coaxing the travelers managed to guide them onto the path. As Tim had suspected, the crossing was indeed wide enough to accommodate them safely, but the very perception of a steep drop ten feet to either side was more than enough to give them all a lingering sense of unease. They wouldn't have much space for setting up lean-tos when it came time to camp during the heat of the day, but they would make do.

For the most part, the ridge cut a straight path across the gorge, southeast to northwest, though it did from time to time curve slightly in one direction or the other. In some places, it expanded to as much as forty feet—Tim thought such an area would be good for making camp—while in others it narrowed to less than ten. Those latter sections stretched by in strained silence, horses and travelers alike needing encouragement to continue, and Tim's skin prickled whenever he came close enough to an edge to appreciate the fullness of the drop.

As the first night ended and dawn rose, he began to make out what Eklan had termed the Cliffs of Desolation in the distance. Eklan gave most everything around here a grim name, and perhaps rightfully so. The Cliffs were still a day and a half distant, but for what it was worth, Eklan had told him that they more or less represented the halfway point on their journey to Agrazab. Tim had asked their guide if they might go around the canyon rather than across, but Eklan told him that he knew neither where the gorge began nor where it ended, and so the company plodded across the Mygon Path, moving with speed and caution. Tim wondered at Eklan's comments regarding the bottom of the abyss, but he wasn't keen to ask about whether any of the man's party had died here on their first trip to Agrazab. That was Eklan's affair, and he would share it if he wished. All the same, if any *had* died on the Mygon Path, it would be best to know how to prepare for any eventual threats. Tim also considered asking Bria, but decided against it. At best she did not know, and at worst she would consider such a question yet one more way in which Tim manipulated her brother into reliving his nightmares. Once again, Tim wished Nazgar was here to offer guidance. He was on his own, though, and he'd have to figure these problems out for himself.

* * *

Hugo Rindar had always been accustomed to scouting ahead for threats, and this journey proved no different. Most of the time his brother came with him, or on rare occasions Jend or Celia, but this time Commander Kule had opted to take a turn. Hugo liked that about the Commander. It hadn't been *too* long ago that Hugo had been teaching Boblin how to properly scout, and Commander Kule still clearly valued the opportunity to learn from an elion who was his senior in years and experience, if not in rank.

This "Mygon Path," as Eklan Hamur called it, was certainly interesting. Hugo wondered how such a thing had come to be. One might have thought that after Hugo had seen such things as the Barricade, the Irsp Valley, the Northern Mountains, and the Deathlands, he'd have stopped thinking about the origins of such landmarks, but this was not the case. He meant to *understand* the world, regardless of what strange forces moved it.

Hugo often felt out of his depth during these events. He'd never wielded the power of the Lifesource like Matthias, never led the Patrol like Jend, never faced Isanam like Commander Kule. All of that was perfectly okay with him. He and Ken had trained their fair share of recruits, a task Celia had taken over of late, and he'd turned out many a good soldier in his time. Hugo took solace knowing that no soldier who trained under him went into battle against malichons unprepared, and that was good enough for him.

He wondered what they would face in Agrazab. The strange folk who had attacked Commander Kule's wedding came to mind, but Hugo found it hard to feel truly threatened by them. They had been insane, which was disturbing enough, but they hadn't possessed the calculated skill of trained soldiers. Even if the Demon-Lord gathered hundreds of their ilk upon his doorstep, Hugo didn't perceive a mad rabble to be a much of threat. He doubted half of them would be capable of holding a blade straight in their frenetic insanity. On the other hand, he well knew that Zadinn Kanas had brought malichons into the land while living in Agrazab, and if such a portal could be opened once, it could be opened again. In that case, things would get interesting. Perhaps when they arrived in the city, they'd be facing malichons all over again. Hugo didn't relish the thought, yet he also couldn't deny that a part of him would enjoy setting his skills against those creatures once more. It was time for a proper challenge.

Hugo rode near Commander Kule under the moonlight, the pebbles of the Mygon Path grinding beneath their horses' hooves as they advanced. To the east, the sky began to show its first hint of gray. Soon the early light would turn pink, then from pink to full sunrise, and the heat of the day would begin once more.

After scanning the horizon, Hugo reined in his mount. "Might be time to reign in, Commander. Daylight's coming."

At the commander's nod of acknowledgment, the two soldiers halted and waited for the company to catch up. As they were taking care not to press their horses hard, they would have only circled back if they'd come across anything of danger that warranted alerting the rest of the group. They didn't like the thought of their quarry continuing to escape on his flight to Agrazab ahead of them, but they dared not risk causing harm to their steeds. Better to be more conservative in their travels than to strand themselves without any means of riding.

"What do you suppose we'll have to do once we reach Agrazab, Commander?" Hugo asked.

Kule grimaced. "That's the question in front of all of us, isn't it? Fight, I expect. Uklith will have some matter of forces marshaled against us, but we'll have to get closer before we can ascertain what they might be. I don't think even Eklan Hamur can tell us what will happen for sure. He's been there before, but once we reach the city, we play by the Demon-Lord's rules, and there's no guarantee he'll play the same game as last time."

"Do you think Matthias will be able to use the Lifesource before we get there?"

"I am hoping yes, but add that to the list of things I don't know for sure. It's getting rather long, I'm afraid."

"It's a long list for all of us, sir."

They sat in silence for a while, and Commander Kule spoke up. "Does it bother you, Hugo? The fact that none of us seem to know for sure what we plan to do out here?"

Hugo shrugged. "Truth be told, I can't think of a single time we knew *exactly* what we were doing. When Commander Jend sent us on patrols, we never knew if we'd come across two malichons or two hundred. The whole time we were searching for the Army, it was touch and go at best, like a game of hide-and-discover while blindfolded. Malath's Teeth, the Deathlands..." he chuckled. "I don't see any of those as an example of stalwart planning. We did what we could, I suppose."

Kule went silent, and Hugo had a fair guess as to what was going on in the commander's mind. *He's thinking it was a whole lot easier when he wasn't the one responsible for the decisions, when all he had to do was follow orders.* This was why Hugo never had any desire to be in command. Standing in line to charge the enemy was easy, but ordering *others* to make the charge was difficult. He'd seen how often Commander Jend wrestled with similar challenges, though Jend's unease at such things probably hadn't been obvious to Kule at the time, just as a fresh recruit like Hanqar probably had little inkling of Commander Kule's doubts. Hugo didn't voice his thoughts, though. If the commander wanted advice beyond what he'd already asked for, he'd say so. Otherwise best to let him process the thoughts himself.

Dawn broke as the rest of the travelers caught up. Hugo and Commander Kule had selected an area where the path widened enough for the group to place their lean-tos in a more comfortable arrangement. Upon arriving, Ken dismounted and approached Hugo, who was lashing a tarp against the side of a pole as he erected his shelter.

"Is the way clear of danger, brother?" Ken asked.

"For the time being." It was their usual response to one another, an un-spoken acknowledgment of the fact that a scout could never be sure he'd accounted for every possible scenario. Scouting covered only a point in time, and while helpful, this didn't mean a host of malichons hadn't cropped up in one's absence. "The krevurs seem to be long gone, at the very least."

Ken grunted. "According to Hamur, they avoid this ridge. I suppose they don't like the heights. But he said we might enter their territory again once we reach the far side."

Hugo nodded and set to work laying his bedroll. Commander Kule would take first watch, as was his custom, and Hugo and Ken would likewise take the last one. It was different sleeping during the day, and not always wholesome rest in the withering heat, but it beat slugging through high noon on horseback. Besides, any elion soldier worth his or her hide knew how to summon sleep at will. The Patrol covered terrain far and wide, fair and rough, and they did not always have the luxury of choosing when or where to rest. Lying down, Hugo closed his eyes, evened his breathing, and was fast asleep within moments.

* * *

Bria took guard duty in midafternoon, exchanging places with Wurit. From her spot in the shade, she watched the sleeping companions, expecting Celia to join her soon enough. Her conversation with the elion several days ago had been illuminating. Bria had never been content with staying behind at Keldur during the first mission to Agrazab, though she'd known it was necessary. When Sheel discovered that Bria had deceived him, he'd been furious but also been smart enough to realize there was nothing he could do about it. It was all Bria could do to keep the village together during those days, and most of what kept her going was the belief that the work she did to protect Keldur would come to fruition once Eklan returned with news of a safe haven. But Eklan and Reidell had returned with a tale of disaster, and all the pain, toil, and suffering of the previous weeks seemed to matter for nothing. Sheel's leadership over Keldur had been growing tenuous prior to that point, but after Bria and Eklan's failed gambit, he re-solidified his role as head of the village once again.

Now here they were, heading back into the same territory, only this time the journey hadn't been prompted by the stories of an old stranger but by Tim Matthias. After being tricked once, Bria's willingness to trust strangers from abroad had worn thin. If she could be assured that this quest *would* mean something for her fellow villagers, even if it meant laying down their lives at the gates of Agrazab, she would not hesitate to do so, but she feared instead this was yet another exercise in futility, one that would end in things being worse and not better. These Northerners seemed genuine enough in their efforts to make a difference, but Eklan and Reidell had been genuine, too, and it still mattered for naught.

A scratching sound brought Bria back from her musings. At first, she thought it was Celia, but upon glancing around she saw the camp remained still. The noise went silent as she looked about. At first she remained tense, but as time passed without the sound repeating, she relaxed. *It must have been the wind.*

The scratching sound returned, this time to her left, and Bria looked around once more. Again, she saw nothing save for the far edge of the Mygon Path where it dropped off into the canyon below. As she sat in a state of alert readiness, the noise grew louder and stronger, until she knew it was in fact coming *from* the canyon. Hand on the hilt of her sword, Bria rose and walked toward the edge of the path.

Naming this path after Mygon Tilin, with his penchant for daring and unusual stunts, had been more than appropriate. But when Eklan told the travelers about Mygon, he left out one key detail: Mygon had *been* one of those on the original quest to Agrazab.

The noise became very distinct, and it made her skin prickle. She reached the side of the path, peered carefully over—

—and pulled back almost immediately, uttering an oath. She drew her sword and looked once more to verify what she had seen. An enormous scorpion, the size of a cottage, climbed the vertical incline of the ridge below where she stood. It must have come from the depths of the canyon. Its claws upon the stone wall were causing the steady *scratch* she had heard. A buzz emanated from its shell, its tail twitched in the air, and though it was still a hundred strides from the summit, Bria expected it to reach them in short order.

"Scorpion!" she yelled, turning back toward the camp. Eklan was the first to rise, his expression telling her that he understood, but the rest of the company gave her blank looks.

"Scorpion?" Boblin Kule asked, drawing his sword despite his obvious confusion. These elions were smart enough to know that even if they didn't fully understand the situation, danger was danger.

Behind Bria, she heard a massive scraping sound. She turned to see the scorpion appear. First it reached its pincers over the edge of the path, grasping toward the sky, then the rest of its body followed. As the hulking mass came into full view of the party, a few chunks of stone fell from the cliff face, tumbling down and out of sight.

"I see," Boblin said. "That's very big."

"Spread out!" Eklan ordered. The scorpion held still at first, as if assessing its prey. As the companions fanned into a semicircle, steeling themselves for the fight to come, Hugo and Ken drew their crossbows. It was a good enough idea, Bria supposed, but she doubted that the arrow bolts would have any effect on the creature's chitinous armor.

At last the scorpion moved, darting forward with a speed that belied its enormous size. Sprays of pebbles and dirt flew into the air as its eight sharp legs hammered the ground. Arrows from the elions flew, and as expected, clattered harmlessly away after striking the creature's shell. The scorpion brought its right pincer around in a sweeping motion toward Jend Argul, who stood at the upper left portion of the semicircle of defenders. Jend hit the ground and rolled underneath the claw, avoiding it in a neat somersault before returning to a standing position.

"How do we kill it?" Bria asked her brother.

"We need to get underneath. Its belly is the only place that isn't armored."

Bria eyed the snapping pincers and scrabbling legs. "And how do we get there?"

"Best thing to do is distract it." Eklan stood as tall as possible, waving his arms over his head. "Over here!"

The scorpion made a buzzing sound and charged once more, its tail lashing in the air. Celia, noting Eklan's words, moved in toward its belly, but she had to back off as the tail came for her. The elion dove to the side, the stinger slamming the ground so forcefully that Bria felt the earth shake. Mandibles wide, the scorpion came for Eklan. The Rindar brothers, seeing this opening, fired arrows toward the creature's mouth. The shafts buried themselves into the fleshy interior behind the mandibles, and the scorpion made a sharp sound that could only be a noise of pain—or perhaps, more appropriately, anger.

Bria leapt underneath the creature, looking for the exposed areas Eklan had mentioned. Her first blow glanced off armor, as did her second, and then—*there*! Bria slid her blade upward into an exposed pink area. The next thing she knew, Tim Matthias was beside her, doing the same with his blade. It was the first time she'd seen him fight without the blade being a blazing beacon of green fire. Apparently, it served its function well enough as an ordinary sword, sliding into the scorpion's flesh just as hers had. A viscous, sticky substance flowed from the open wound in the creature's belly onto her and Matthias.

Bria made a noise of disgust and pulled her blade free as she rolled away, leaving a trail of ooze on the ground. Matthias pulled back as well, repositioning for a second attack, but rolled into the path of the creature's pointed legs. Bria grabbed him by the tunic and pulled him out of harm's way just before the scorpion's leg slammed back down, inches away from skewering him into the ground like a kebab.

"Watch yourself," she said. By this time, the scorpion had moved far enough forward that they stood beneath its rear, where the tail flickered in its quest for a new target. With an unspoken acknowledgment, she and Matthias rolled away in opposite directions, exiting the area beneath the scorpion's belly and clearing themselves from the dangerous tail. Bria came back up on her feet next to Eklan, the slime on her body causing dirt and stone to stick to her. "We got in two good strikes. How many more?"

"A lot," Eklan answered. "They're tough."

The party backed off, forming a circle around the scorpion but staying out of range of its immediate attack. The fighters remained in constant motion, keeping the circle closed at all times, presenting the scorpion too many targets for it to maintain a singular focus on any one of them. Bria ended up fighting beside Tim again as the group maneuvered positions.

The next time it charged, the scorpion went for Celia. She stood her ground, waiting until the last moment to dodge. As Celia went beneath the creature, Boblin leapt into the air, landing on its back and grasping for footholds to climb upward on its shell.

Bria risked a glance toward Tim, who shrugged. "Elions," he said. "They're all crazy, if you ask me."

* * *

Boblin grasped his handhold and pulled himself upward, using the nooks and crannies in the scorpion's shell to stay in motion. On the opposite side of the creature, Hugo and Ken followed suit, no doubt thinking along the same lines as Boblin. *If there are cracks in the shell in the underbelly, perhaps there are some on the top of its body.* If Boblin had to hazard a guess, he'd wager his coin on an exposed spot being near the base of its neck. Nature's armor often followed the same design as handmade armor—or probably the other way around, Boblin supposed, but that was a theological consideration for a less stressful time.

The creature shifted underneath him. Boblin moved lightly, bouncing from one section to another, while on the ground Celia rolled back into sight, dripping with the same slime as Tim and Bria. The scorpion spun toward Celia, causing Boblin to fall on his back and slide down the curve of the shell. He grabbed hold of a chink in the armor and hung on. Farther down the creature's body, Hugo and Ken likewise struggled to keep balance, Ken toward the middle, Hugo near the tail. On the ground in front of the scorpion, Jend Argul fired his crossbow. The arrow flashed forward, burying itself in one of the creature's six eyes. Boblin figured Jend had his work cut out for him if he was to rid the scorpion of its sight. Jend rolled out of way of the scorpion's retaliatory blow, ratcheting a second crossbow bolt home as he did so.

Boblin pulled himself back into a standing position on the shell, making his way forward once more. This time, he made it farther along the arch of the creature's back. As he neared the apex of the shell, he hoisted Ken atop the scorpion with him, while farther back Hugo leapt through the air with his sword in his hands, landed at the base of its tail, and swung his blade like a woodsman felling a tree. When Hugo struck the first time, his sword glanced off the armor of the tail, but the second time it bit into flesh.

About fifty more hits like that, and he might actually succeed in chopping the karfing thing off, Boblin thought.

Tim and Bria, appearing to take a cue from Hugo, went for the first of the scorpion's sweeping pincers, taking strikes at it one at a time, while Wurit and Eklan attacked the other pincer. Jend fired a second arrow into the scorpion's eyes, and Celia rolled back underneath it to stab its underbelly once more.

This creature is one tough monster, but it looks like we've given it something to think about. I just hope it doesn't have a friend climbing up the wall behind it. That would be too *much.*

"Here we are," Ken said. Sure enough, at the base of the scorpion's neck, Boblin saw a horizontal slit in the armor, which revealed vulnerable pink flesh underneath. Boblin raised his sword, holding it above his head to gain momentum before driving it point downward into the scorpion's neck. The creature reared upward in sudden pain, spun incredibly fast—and started to roll over.

"Oh, karf," Boblin said, right before gravity and momentum threw him from the scorpion's side. Boblin hit the ground, striking his shoulder and feeling a crushing pain. Ken landed beside him and they rolled together, using their momentum to stay out of the way of the descending body. They came to a stop right on the edge of the Mygon Path. Clouds of dust rose into the sky as the scorpion thrashed and kicked, limbs flailing. Farther down the line of the creature's body, Boblin saw that Hugo had leapt free, dodging the thrashing tail.

Boblin and Ken rose together, standing with the drop at their backs as the scorpion righted itself and came for them. Neither held a sword anymore, Boblin's still buried in the creature's neck, Ken having lost his when he fell. Boblin reached into his bag to pull out a crossbow quarrel, the crossbow still slung across his back, and came up holding a boomer instead. He looked at Ken, then at the boomer.

"Well," Boblin said. "I guess this is how it will be." He struck fire to the boomer, placed it into the crank of the crossbow, and fired. The boomer flew through the air, straight in between the creature's snapping mandibles, and exploded.

Without pause, Boblin fitted a second boomer to the crank of the cross-bow, this time aiming for the armor across the creature's back. The creature thrashed its head from side to side, chunks of gooey flesh from its gaping wound spattering the surface of the desert. At the scorpion's rear, Hugo came in close, blade held overhead in two hands, bringing it down toward the tail with the intention of finally separating limb from body—

The tail was quicker, though. It arced forward, stinger poised, and struck Hugo square in the chest. The impact lifted the elion from his feet and flung him away. Hugo crashed to the ground in the center of the Mygon Path, and even from this distance Boblin could hear a sickening *crunch*.

The scorpion presented him a full broadside. Boblin fired. When the boomer landed, the scorpion's shell blew outward, fragments of armor and flesh flying in all directions. The creature crashed to the ground with sudden finality mere feet from where Boblin and Ken stood.

There was a momentary silence as the group looked at the body of the monstrous behemoth before them, and then Ken said one word. "Hugo."

He took off at a run toward his brother, Boblin close behind. The fallen elion lay on his back in a shallow depression in the stone, face grimy with sweat and dust. A deep red stain covered his chest from where the creature's tail had pierced him all the way through from one side of his torso to the other. He still breathed, although weakly, and his face was pale.

"Brother," Ken said, falling onto his knees beside Hugo and clasping the elion's hand in his. "Be still. I have you."

Boblin reached the fallen soldier, aware of his companions rushing forward as well, Jend foremost. He saw Hugo shake his head. "I'm not long for it, brother. You know it as well as I."

"Herbs," Ken said, turning to the group. "As many as we have."

Boblin grasped a saddlebag and opened it. It was a gesture in futility— they *all* knew it was—but he had to go through the motions. The Frontier Patrol took care of its own, no elion alone, no elion abandoned. That's all there was to it.

As Boblin came forward to apply the poultice, Hugo waved him away. "Don't waste the supplies."

"It's not a waste when it's what we brought them for," Boblin countered. "Lie still, and that's an order."

Hugo managed a smile through the pain. "It was an honor to serve, Commander Kule." He shifted his eyes toward Jend, who had stepped forward. "Commander Jend."

"No," Jend replied. "The honor was mine."

Hugo, still clasping Ken's hand, looked into his brother's eyes. "Finish this one for me, brother. Finish it well."

He relaxed, falling back and closing his eyes. And there died Hugo Rindar, one half of the duo known as Commander Jend Argul's right hand, legend of the Frontier Patrol, survivor of the quest to find the Army of Kah'lash, survivor of the Battle of the Deathlands, lying on his back in the Western Desert.

Ken laid a hand on his brother's forehead.

Boblin rocked back on his heels. *I failed him. This was not Jend's command, it was mine, and one of our best is dead.*

In the distance, the sun set, throwing its rays on the company as they huddled in a small cluster in this place of sand, stone, and death.

23

The elion paused at the edge of Asheti's Dunes. The sun beat down on him as he gazed at the seemingly endless expense of sandy terrain, which rose and fell at irregular intervals from where he stood to the edge of the horizon. *So close.* On the far side of the Dunes, Agrazab waited, and though he could not see it, he imagined the city in his mind's eye, its walls dark and majestic.

The remnants of the Wasteland were at his back, and even farther behind, the Cliffs of Desolation, where the company from Keldur traveled the Mygon Path in earnest pursuit. When Matthias touched the Lifesource early on—a mistake the man was not likely to repeat anytime soon—he had broadcast his entire presence across the Desert and into the Demon-Lord's prison within Agrazab. Through his master's awareness, the elion possessed a general understanding of how the Warrior and his companions fared on their journey.

The creatures of the Desert did not plague the elion as they would Matthias and his companions. The Desert was Uklith's domain, and its denizens did not dare disturb this dedicated disciple's journey. The Demon-Lord's blessing had been especially necessary while crossing the Wasteland, for the elion had felt many hungry eyes upon him as he passed through the rocky hills and valleys. Matthias's group would face a dire test when they came to that rugged landscape.

The heat of the day seared the elion's skin, leaving it red and peeling, but he paid it no heed. Some of the splotches had turned a blackish color, indicating growths of a deadly nature, but he gave them little thought, for his body was merely a vessel in the Demon-Lord's service. Should he waste away, he would be granted further blessings as a reward. The elion traveled day and night, stopping when it suited him, proceeding when the time was right. His toes wore holes in the tips of his boots, and the blisters on his feet had scabbed over and re-blistered countless times. As hard as he pressed his body, though, it had limits. It had been some time since he last took in sustenance, and he feared he must stop. When he approached the dunes, his legs gave way and he collapsed. He rolled to the base of the nearest hill, leaving a winding trail of sand in his wake. A breeze blew over him, blissful in its immediacy, leaving a thin film of sand grains upon his face.

He lay on his back, motionless save for the rise and fall of his chest, while the sun's orb continued its arc. Hunger pangs seared his stomach, clawing from the inside out, and he wondered if he had waited too long. A pair of vultures, spotting the motionless figure below, began circling above. They sensed death and knew their time to feed was drawing nigh. They flew in concentric circles, drawing tighter and tighter as the afternoon wore on. At last the first one landed in a flutter of wings, perched next to the elion's body. It stretched its neck, cocking its head to one side and surveying its prey. After a moment, it took one hop, then another, and reared back in preparation for its first bite.

The elion struck first, seizing the bird's neck in a vicious grasp. With a squawk, the vulture tried to jerk back, but soon found its prey had a much stronger grip than should have been possible for one so close to corpsehood. The elion clenched his fist, dragging the bird toward him as its wings beat. Its hooked claws scrabbled across the sand, all to no avail, as the elion brought his second hand around and curled his fists around the vulture's neck. He twisted, and the bird's neck snapped with a sound *crunch*.

Still sprawled on his back, the elion brought the bird to his mouth and sank his teeth into the warm, moist flesh around its jugular. He tore into the bird, feathers and all, and swallowed the first morsels of his grisly meal. Blood spurted from the creature's veins as he held it over his mouth, drinking from the warm, red river as he would from a flask. He savored the hot liquid, which stained the corners of his lips. When he finished, his belly full and his thirst slaked, the elion stood once more and resumed his journey across Asheti's Dunes, commencing on the last stretch of his journey to Agrazab.

* * *

The hot sun bore down on Tim. Though nightfall had not yet arrived, the group nonetheless broke camp and proceeded along the Mygon Path, having decided it was not worth the risk to stay in the same location when one of the scorpion's broodmates might decide to make another attempt at the party. A somber silence hung over the companions as they rode, the loss of one of their own heavy on their hearts. Hugo had been a constant presence in the Frontier Patrol over the years, and his passing felt surreal, all the more so because it had been at caused by a creature whose existence seemed impossible.

Tim wondered where the scorpion had come from. Its size defied explanation. They had faced their fair share of unnatural opponents in the North, too, which Nazgar explained was the result of Zadinn's presence warping the natural manner of things. If Uklith's presence had a similar effect upon the Western Desert, then what else lay at the bottom of this gorge was beyond contemplation. *Perhaps the pit leads all the way to Malath.*

While fighting the scorpion, Tim had considered using the Lifesource, but discarded the idea. He had to stay away from the power. To summon the Lifesource would be to render himself unable to assist the party in any way, not to mention the broader implications of giving Uklith too much information about their progress. In that same vein, Tim realized he had been of little help during the fight. Boblin and the elions had taken the brunt of the task, and it had been the first time in a long while that Tim faced a conflict without his abilities. Even when he trained with the sword, he usually held the Lifesource, sculpting it into an extension of his fighting abilities. Deprived of the power, he'd felt like a man half blind, able to see only part of the world.

Tim had not learned the sword, or combat, with the aid of the Lifesource, though. He'd learned under Daniel's tutelage, holding practice swords in the Odow Forest. There had been no frills or nuances about it, only raw soldiering. It was for the same reason that elions trained in ailar. Though the Frontier Patrol always went into battle armed with any manner of weapons, be it swords, crossbows, staves, or axes, their creed nonetheless held that should they to find themselves in a situation without steel for defense, the elions would still have their hands and feet to protect them.

It's not enough to rely on the skills taught to an Advocate. I have to know the skills taught to every soldier, for those are the fundamentals that make all warriors. Tim took a swig of water, one hand on the pommel of Rookwind's saddle, and studied the horizon. The Cliffs of Desolation loomed in the distance, marking the horizon from left to right. In spite of everything, the Desert was beautiful in its own way, with its shades of brown, yellow, and red mingling to create a terrain as breathtaking as it was hostile. While the pebbles of the Mygon Path ground below Rookwind's hooves, Tim studied cliffs, the entirety of which shimmered in the sun's heat. The dry air sucked all moisture from his skin and lungs, and he sipped from the flask much more frequently than during their night travels. The horses drank more, too, and it was harder to ration water for the animals than for the elions and humans. The animals needed sustenance, working as hard as they did to transport the party across this unforgiving landscape. The company would stop within an hour or two, but at the moment they wanted to get as much distance as possible between themselves and the site of the scorpion attack.

Of course, there's no guarantee our next resting location will be any better.

One good thing to come from this—well, Tim supposed *good* was a strong word to use, so perhaps *useful* was better—was that the boomer performed quite well when Boblin attached it to the crossbow. They'd known all along that the boomer's efficacy was limited by the range to which an elion could throw it. Their newfound ability to launch a boomer from a crossbow tripled the distance they could send the projectile, which made for a more devastating ranged weapon. They'd be using the boomers in conjunction with the crossbows quite a bit going forward.

Bria interrupted his thoughts, nudging Menindara closer to ride alongside Rookwind. "I'm sorry for your friend," she said. "He was an honorable elion."

"They're all honorable," Tim replied. "It's in their blood."

Bria nodded. "Honor came and went in Keldur. I think Sheel had it long ago, but it became less and less important to him over time. He traded honor for survival, and I can't blame him for it, but still..."

"It matters," Tim finished for her. "It's all we have, at the end of the day. How is your brother faring?"

She stiffened slightly at that, but visibly forced herself to relax. "He doesn't like this, but *none* of us like it. It has to be done, and so we're here."

"I really am sorry for all of this."

Her reply was a hard, even gaze. "No, you're not."

He couldn't refute that, because he *wasn't* sorry, at least not for the fact that they'd sought Eklan's aid. It was no different than the expectations placed upon the elions in their quest to find the Army of Kah'lash. It had been *necessary*, though that was a word Nazgar had long ago cautioned him against using.

Tim had often wondered why Nazgar seemed so aloof, so *uncaring* about the fact that he drew others into impossible battles and expected them to measure up to the challenge. Yet here Tim was, drawing others into the world

Nazgar had brought him into. He must seem to Eklan and Bria as Nazgar had seemed to him. *If Nazgar had told me he was sorry for bringing me into this conflict, I wouldn't have believed him, either.*

Tim closed his eyes and expelled a long breath. *The truth, this time. They deserve more than fabricated condolences.* "You're right. I asked for help because I needed it, and I don't regret doing so. Here's the truth." He opened his eyes and pointed west. "The ruler of the underworld is out there. He's strong, and he's coming for us. A year and a half ago, the elions and I fought the Demon-Lord's servant. It took everything we had, and many lost their lives along the way. At the end, I went into Zadinn's citadel and faced him alone. It was the most terrifying thing I ever had to do. Now Zadinn's master is about to be set free, and I have to stop him. It's the hardest burden in the world, and no, I am not sorry at all that I have good people along the way to help. I'm *grateful* you're here, because it would be an impossible task to take on by myself. So thank you, Bria Hamur. Thank you for being here."

She stared at him for a long, hard moment. At first, her eyes grew so narrow he thought she might wheel Menindara away and ride off without another word, but at the very end her gaze softened. She even smiled. Then she *did* turn, but not before touching him on the shoulder.

"Very good, Matthias," she said. "That's all I wanted to hear."

* * *

Boblin rode alone, hands on Dapple's reins, lost in his thoughts. He stared at the horizon, an unbroken stretch of craggy peaks and gullies marking the Cliffs of Desolation.

He'd seen elions die before, many times. Death was a matter of course in the Frontier Patrol, and Boblin was no stranger to it. The most personal experience had been when Hedro Desh passed away in his arms on the slopes of the Deathlands, but that had been under someone else's command. Jend Argul, Pellen Yuzhar, Nazgar of the Kyrlod, General Algar of the Army of Kah'lash—Boblin marched into battle at *their* orders, had followed *their* plans. It was in them he trusted, and it was for them he fought. But today, Jend no longer led the Frontier Patrol, Boblin did, and Hugo Rindar's death had been on his watch.

There's a fine line between responsibility and hubris. Remember that. Hugo served openly, knowing the risks, as did Boblin, Celia, and the rest. For Boblin to assume his command would only ever result in bloodless victories would be a delusion of pride and naiveté. Yet none of these reflections changed the simple fact that Hugo Rindar was dead. *Who will be next—Jend? Hanqar? Celia??*

The sun set and the company continued riding into the night. They planned to make camp just before dawn, at which point they would resume their regular travel cycle. This was the last night they would spend upon the Mygon Path before making their way into the lands beyond. Boblin had never liked camping on the Path to begin with. It was not strategically sound, and it left them exposed. They hadn't had any other choice, though. There was no way around the canyon, and to travel across the bottom would have been at best laborious and time consuming, and at worst a descent into madness, especially given what they had just seen emerge from its depths.

While riding, Boblin gravitated toward Jend, who like Boblin rode straight-backed, staring at the path. Jend had always been an elion of few words, and of late fewer than ever.

"Commander," Jend said.

It was hard for Boblin to keep his voice steady. "We lost a good elion."

Jend nodded. "He was one of our greatest, and I do not say so lightly."

"When you were in command—when we fought Zadinn, and our folk died—how did you cope with it?"

"I resigned."

The direct nature of Jend's reply caused Boblin's mind to give a reflexive jerk. He looked at Jend once more, seeing as if for the first time the grooves and lines etched into his face. Jend had a warrior's face, weathered and scarred by years of experience. His deep-set eyes had seen much and survived much. More than anything, though, Jend had the face of one who was *tired*—of death, of loss, of it all. Jend's retirement from his commander's post always had the mark of a well deserved rest; he had served the elions faithfully for many long years, he'd seen them through the greatest battle of their generation, and was ready for someone else to take the lead. At the time, Boblin hadn't thought much more of it than that. Now, he realized there had *always* been more to it.

"Command an army, and those you lead will die," Jend said. "Some will be those whose names you barely know, but others will be lifelong comrades. The Maker cares little about who returns from one battlefield to the next. I trust in the Maker's hand—I always have—but a simple soldier can only do so much.

I saw us to victory against Zadinn Kanas, but at a terrible cost, and I fear the final bill has yet to be tallied behind the walls of this dark city we seek."

"I feel as though I failed Hugo."

Jend shook his head. "No, Commander Kule, you did not. Any fool can give orders, but the best commander helps those he leads understand the *purpose* behind those orders. Hugo Rindar needed to know the cause he served was worthwhile. You did not lead him to his death, you led him to protect his people, and he understood that. It's why he came with, knowing full well such a fate might await him. You asked me how I coped with my soldiers' deaths, and I gave an unfair reply. The truth is, you can give but two things to those you command: training and purpose. Some will live, some will die, and you must simply hope the world is better for their efforts."

Boblin took a deep breath, closing his eyes and feeling the slight cooling of the night air wash over him. "Thank you, sir. I do believe that helps."

When they made camp, he made a space away from the group and began moving through the forms of ailar, transitioning from one stance to the next. He found something beautiful about ailar's simple elegance. Celia soon joined Boblin, going through forms as well, until they stood side by side in the dawn light while those around them slept.

"You told me you think about Ana nearly every day," he said to her.

"Yes, love, she replied. "I do."

"Jend told me this is why he resigned—or a large part of the reason."

"I suspected as much."

"You always were the more perceptive one."

"*And* the better-looking one, but I'm not keeping track."

Boblin wrapped his arm around her and kissed her cheek. "More of us are going to die, aren't we?"

"Yes." Any other statement would have been a lie, and both knew it.

"I need you, more than ever. I can't do this alone."

She turned to face him, holding him close, nose to nose. By the Maker, how he loved the brown of her eyes and the curl of her hair. "You don't have to," she said.

He closed his eyes and held her for a long while, the only sound around them the whisper of wind and the snoring of their comrades. In the short time he'd spent in Galdon, he'd become accustomed to the noise of the city folk, even in the quietest hours of the night, and in the woods outside there was the soft but continual noise of wildlife. Here, though, they had around them naught save for sand, stone, and relentless heat.

"Why don't you get some rest?" he asked. "I can take watch by myself for a while."

She stepped back and winked before giving him a crisp salute. "As you say, commander. You *are* in charge."

Before she stepped into the tent, he caught her arm and pulled her in for one more kiss. "I love you, Celia."

She replied with the vow she had used at their wedding. "In this life and the next."

24

Ladu tried to conceal his weariness. Emperorship, he decided, was more tedium than anything else. As the last case of the day came before him, he thought once more that he really did need to grow the size of his court. One of the biggest problems in the budding city of Galdon was that they had not yet adopted a formal justice system. As such, all matters of dispute—large or small—lay at the emperor's feet.

Endar Varuc surely wouldn't mind being placed at the head of a high court, Ladu thought. He suppressed a wry smile; the thought of the short, nasal-voiced man deciding the penalty for a murder case was laughable at best. *Even Quentiin Harggra would be better, though I admit he'd probably start handing out executions left and right, more so on days he was feeling irritable.* A laugh tried to bubble up his throat.

In front of Ladu, the shopkeeper Teklin wrung his hands. "They were right there in the street, your majesty, tossing rocks. Any fool would have seen one was sure to go through my window."

"They're just children, your majesty," Shem protested. "They can only be faulted so much."

"I ain't faulting your children, Shem, I'm only asking that you pay for the damage they caused!"

Quentiin Harggra must have been lingering in Ladu's subconscious, because he found himself thinking it would be very un-emperorlike to stand up and punch Shem and Teklin in their respective faces; Teklin for being stupid enough to let a petty dispute rise this far, and Shem for not agreeing to a reasonable request.

Shem's face was growing red. "I paid for half, and that should settle the matter. A man shouldn't go broke over summat like this. I've got mouths to feed."

"You're telling me about going broke—what do you think a shattered window does to the quality of my goods? Nobody's going to want to come in and get my pies after flies have been dancin' away on fresh food all morning!"

"It's always about your business, Teklin, isn't it? I don't recall you asking any of the homeowners on the street whether opening a shop would have been a good idea in the first place, eh?"

Teklin jabbed a finger in Shem's face. "Who doesn't like a good pie, I say? *Who?*"

Their voices ascended into a cacophony of yells, the words soon unintelligible. Feeling his face grow hot, Ladu stood and raised a hand. Both men cut off midsentence, mouths open, turning toward the sight of their emperor on the dais above them.

"Shem," he said, "Did your children break Teklin's window?"

Shem swallowed. "Yes, your majesty."

"Then pay him. Not half the cost. All the cost."

"Your majesty—"

"A man must pay his debts, Shem. And Teklin?"

"Yes?" the man asked, face flushed and eyes bright, no doubt pleased with himself and what he supposed to be a righteous victory.

"This court is a place for discussing matters of grave importance. In the future, see to it you find another means of resolving your differences. I will be very displeased if you return to me with complaints about a broken window." It had only been fair to provide Shem *some* sort of validation. Citizens who felt the throne ignored even their most basic needs were dissatisfied citizens, and dissatisfied citizens made for a poor place to live in. This was *their* kingdom, and Ladu merely its custodian.

Teklin's flush deepened, and he bowed so low his nose almost touched the floor. "Of course, your majesty. Thank you, your majesty." He began walking out of the throne room backward, facing Ladu the whole time, continuing to bow at irregular intervals as he did so.

"Well done, Emperor Ladu," Endar Varuc said, sweeping into the room, wearing ostentatious robes as usual, the light of the overhead chandelier glancing off his greasy hair. The North had had its fair share of unpleasant monarchs even before Zadinn Kanas came to power, and for some dynasties, assassinations had been a matter of course. In a manner that would have earned him the severe displeasure of his long-dead father, Ladu nonetheless fantasized about the many accidents Endar Varuc might experience, and the ways in which Ladu's life would be better because of it. "You will long be known as a fair and just monarch."

And you will long be known as a pain in my posterior. "I appreciate your kind words, Lord Varuc."

"On that matter, your majesty, I wished to discuss the ceremonial nature of the midsummer feast."

May the Maker save me. "We're still tilling the land, Lord Varuc. We must develop prosperity before we celebrate it."

"It was long recorded as a Jovun family tradition, your majesty! The people need to—"

"I well remember the tradition, Lord Varuc. I was, in fact, there for the feasts." Actually, Ladu did not remember the specifics of the tradition at all, but he could be forgiven for telling a marginal lie.

"The people have tilled much, Emperor Jovun. I've seen them at work in the fields. They are happy, and the wheat is plentiful!"

On the count of wheat, Endar Varuc *was* correct. As to his claim of farmers happily tilling the fields, Ladu supposed that an afternoon of work alongside such men and women would greatly change Endar's rose-tinted perspective on the subject. "It would be a feast of bread, Lord Varuc?"

Endar blinked. "Your majesty?"

"You are suggesting we fill the grand hall with tables full of bread? As much bread as the eye can see? Loaves of plenty, shall we call them?"

"There is venison—"

"Boblin Kule tells me that Tim Matthias misses deer more often than he hits them, though I suspect there may be falsity in that tale. Regardless, neither of them is here to provide us with their well-honed talents. Are you suggesting that you are up to the task, Lord Varuc? Have you ever gutted a white-tailed buck?"

"We have butchers, your majesty, who excel at the craft!"

"The butchers are busy earning coin for their families, Lord Varuc. We shall assign the task to you. Pay close attention." Ladu pulled a dagger from his belt. He'd been wearing it in addition to his sword since the attack on the balcony. "When dressing a deer, you must remove the genitals first. It provides you with an opening at the base of the torso so that you can remove the intestines from the deer's body cavity. Begin by making a circular slit around the anus—"

Endar's face grew pale. "Your majesty—"

"It's an important task you will be in charge of, Lord Varuc, so I expect you to take heed. Once you've opened the body cavity, you will move your blade in a sawing motion from the base of the belly until you reach the notch of the deer's breastbone. At this point you will have exposed the entire contents of the stomach and organs."

Pale had become green. "Please—"

"The smell is difficult at first, but you will become accustomed to it. I suggest the first time you do this, you wear pincers on your nose. It will help. Before I forget, I must caution you that slicing the skin to reveal the stomach is a delicate task. You must keep the blade horizontal rather than vertical. If you go vertical, you will pierce the organs themselves. This can be very messy."

Endar was on the verge of vomiting on the flagstones, which would create a mess, but Ladu thought it might be worth it if it would stop the man from prattling on about some feast. "The first time my father's huntsman helped me do this, I pierced a doe's full bladder. It sprayed urine *everywhere*, Lord Varuc. I believe I even tasted some."

When the scream came, Ladu thought it was Endar at first, and it was full of such horror and pain that he wondered if he'd gone too far in his humor. He stopped, knife held midair in the act of demonstrating the proper cutting motion. He looked at the nobleman, but Endar appeared as surprised as Ladu felt. As one, they turned toward the doorway of the throne room. A second scream came.

Ladu leapt down from the dais, sheathing his dagger and drawing his sword, and made for the hallway.

"Your majesty!" Endar wailed, waddling behind him with arms outstretched. "Be careful!"

Ladu looked left and right as he entered the corridor outside of the throne room, noticing a lack of guards. They, too, must have raced toward the sounds of commotion, but as Ladu skidded around a corner of the passage, he saw two elions of the Frontier Patrol lying on the ground with sightless eyes staring upward. Raisha Varuc stood over the bodies, a dagger in her hand.

"Treason," Ladu said, voice hard as he pointed his sword at Raisha.

"Oh, yes," a voice behind Ladu hissed. He turned his head to see Endar Varuc standing with an uncanny light in his eyes. All signs of Endar's former foppishness were gone, melted away like ice in sunshine, and it took all of an instant for Ladu to comprehend that he'd been seriously and badly tricked.

The fat man moved with surprising speed. Before Ladu could spin to face him, Endar came up from behind and slipped an arm around Ladu's neck. He pressed a knife's point close to the emperor's throat. "Make a vertical slit in the belly, did you say, your majesty? I think I'd enjoy that."

Raisha had taken a step toward Ladu when the emperor first appeared, but now she halted. "What is this, brother?" Raisha asked.

"I pull the strings, and you dance," Endar replied. "So it was, and so it shall always be."

A snarl came from the hallway behind Raisha as another man lurched into view, holding two blades, clothed in tattered scraps. Eyes wild, he gave a screech and launched himself toward Raisha. She stepped to the side, avoiding the attack, and shoved her dagger into the man's stomach. She moved awkwardly, unaccustomed to fighting, and it came to Ladu that her blade had been bloodless until now. *She did not kill either of those guards. They died protecting her.*

But as for Endar—

All members of the Jovun dynasty learned ailar, for the martial art had existed long before Jend Argul and the elions of the Frontier Patrol perfected it. Ladu dipped his shoulder to the left, elbowing Endar in the gut and creating an opening in the man's armlock. With a palm locked around Endar's wrist to hold the dagger at bay, Ladu threw him over his shoulder. Endar should have landed on his back, but he slipped free again with a slyness that belied his frame.

How much of it was an act? But Ladu knew the answer already—*all of it*, from the man's stature to the way in which he fumbled his words.

"Your majesty!" Raisha shouted, just before a scrawny woman flung her arms around Ladu's midsection and bore him to the ground.

Ladu lost his grip on his sword, the blade clattering from his fingers as he landed on his back. The woman tried to bite him in her frenzied state, her hands wrapped around his throat as she leaned forward with snapping jaws. Ladu held her mouth at bay with his forearm, half suspecting she was rabid and fearing for himself should it prove to be true.

Moments later, Raisha threw herself against Ladu's assailant. The assistance was enough for Ladu to wrest his attacker off of him and knock her senseless against the wall. The emperor rose, sword back in hand.

At the far end of the hallway, Endar backed away. "The city will be Lord

Uklith's soon enough," he said. "If you kneel and swear fealty to him, we shall spare you."

"No," Ladu said, "but I will be glad to hear the terms of *your* surrender."

Endar let loose a high-pitched, keening laugh. "I think not, Ladu."

He stepped aside and pushed open a doorway. From the other side, a howling mob surged forth, filling the corridor with a mass of bodies, first a dozen, then two dozen, jostling one another as their cries echoed from the high ceiling.

Ladu discarded all notion that he was dealing with people that were merely homeless, or crazy, or otherwise possessed. Uklith's undead had come to Galdon in full strength, and it appeared Endar had let them in.

"Your majesty," Raisha said, voice faint, "I suggest we run."

* * *

Faldon Kule hadn't exactly been happy when his cousin Boblin left him and Tavin behind while he followed Tim Matthias in search of Agrazab. They would have much preferred to participate in the quest. They *were* two of a select few, including Wayne Gendashar, who had survived the quest to find the Army of Kah'lash and the Battle of the Deathlands. Commander Kule had given them a fair hearing on the matter. Their orders to stay behind had been as much of a compliment as a frustration, for it meant the commander had entrusted the entirety of the Patrol to them during his absence—even if, at the moment, this meant primarily overseeing a *census*, of all things.

Faldon wondered how the party was faring in their quest. It certainly had to be more interesting than anything they'd encountered here of late, though there had been that strange incident with the man on Ladu's balcony. They were investigating this to the extent possible, but had precious few leads. In the meantime, they always had chess.

"Your move," Faldon said. His brother furrowed his brow, staring at the board before him. Faldon was pleased; he'd boxed Tavin into a corner, that was for sure. Tavin was often the better player, but this time around Faldon was growing confident he would prevail.

"Time well spent, sirs," Querilt said, entering the room and leaning against the wall with arms crossed. He peered at the board. "The Aritlian Escape should do it, sir," he said to Tavin.

"Quiet, soldier," Faldon said with a piercing look. "You might find yourself doing extra body-raisers in the morning."

Querilt held up his hand in an appeasing manner. "As you say, lieutenant."

Eyes bright, Tavin moved his bishop into position to execute the escape. Faldon wanted to curse. *I was so close. Still, there may be an option to pull this off. The Elderpass Ruse?* It *might* be possible, given the formation.

Querilt dropped to the ground with an arrow in his head.

The Kule brothers leapt into action. Tavin ducked and rolled as another bolt hissed through the air and buried itself in his chair. Faldon pulled a crossbow forward and braced himself against the ground, propped up on his elbows, and caught the shadow of the killer moving into view. He pulled the trigger, and the dark form fell against the wall.

At the moment, the rest of the gatehouse was entirely empty. Sentinels manned the battlements above their heads, and several other soldiers patrolled the palace proper. The rest were out in the city, working on the census. Faldon covered his brother as Tavin crept toward the body to investigate it. Upon reaching the crumpled corpse, Tavin uttered an oath of shock. When Faldon joined him, the reason for his brother's surprise became apparent. The attacker was Pedrar, a member of the Patrol, albeit a relatively new one. He had been among the many recruits from the slaves in the Pit. Those elions were as loyal as any, and there were zero reasons Faldon could conceive of why Pedrar would have turned against them.

Unless it was some sort of mistake? But no, showing up at the wrong post for duty was a mistake. Firing a crossbow into a fellow soldier's head was betrayal, plain and simple. Faldon's brain tried to retroactively find some logical explanation outside of this obvious truth, but he cut off any further second-guessing. The evidence was plain.

"What in the name of Malath is going on here?" he said. *First the attack on Ladu, now this.* The two elions had little time to guess at the larger picture, though, because from beyond the gatehouse and within the palace, they heard the sounds of battle rising.

Drawing their swords, the two brothers raced out of the gatehouse and into the palace. There, they found themselves in the midst of complete chaos, where a small contingent of the Patrol elions clashed against a mob of ragged enemies. They saw the telltale signs of undead everywhere: half-rotted flesh, strands of sparse hair, vacant eyes. On their own, any undead would have been no match for the Patrol soldiers, but when scores flooded into the palace halls, they overwhelmed the elion guards with numbers alone. There was perhaps a score of Patrol members scattered within the palace at any given point in time, a token force at best. Faldon counted six elions as he and his brother rounded the corner, even as one of the six went down before the mob.

The how or why no longer mattered. One way or another, Uklith had managed to amass a frightening number of undead in a short time, and it was up to the elions to deal with it. Swords high, Faldon and Tavin swept into the group, slashing left and right, leaving bodies in their wake. Two more of their comrades fell before the elions turned the tide of the combat in the guards' favor. The corpses piling up on the floor helped most of all, delaying the undead from moving forward with any speed.

"Where did they come from?" Faldon asked a surviving elion as they pulled around a corner to gather their breath.

"I have no idea," she replied. "One moment we were standing on guard, and the next they came around the corner. We tried holding them back, but they pushed us farther and farther out here."

"Pedrar attacked us in the gatehouse," Faldon said.

"*Pedrar?*"

"Aye."

The other elion took a deep breath. "That could be very bad, sir."

She's right, of course. If Uklith has turned trained Frontier Patrol members against us, then we face a very different enemy indeed. It appeared their cousin would not get all the fun out west, after all.

* * *

Ladu and Raisha raced through the hallway, though Raisha's dress forced her to move more slowly than Ladu would have liked. They had no hope of standing their ground, not against so many. Ladu had procured a crossbow, and every so often he ducked around a corner to fire a few shots to slow the pursuit. Meanwhile, Raisha kept her gaze to the front, warning him whenever a new undead appeared from a nook or cranny. Ladu had given her his sword, but her weapons training was minimal. If they survived this, he wouldn't be surprised to see her in the practice yard more often.

In the midst of it all, Ladu's mind remained a confused whirlwind. Part of him watched Raisha from the corner of his eye, suspecting he'd seen only half of the ruse, and that Raisha was soon to lead him back into her brother's arms. *No,* he contradicted himself, *if Raisha and Endar were working together, they had their opportunity to make their move when that woman was on top of me. Raisha would not save me only to turn around and deliver me back into Endar's hands after a long, bloody battle in the palace.*

As for the rest of the people in the palace, they had come across another pair of elion guards, dead and likely overwhelmed by more of Uklith's folk. More than anything else, what surprised Ladu was that there seemed to be so *many* of the enemy. He could not comprehend where they all came from, or what had coordinated them—other than Endar. *How is Endar communicating with Uklith?*

Ladu had little time to ponder these questions. As he and Raisha neared the gatehouse, from which they could evacuate the palace, Ladu took careful aim at a new pair of men coming toward them. When they lined up, one in front of the next, he pulled the trigger of his crossbow and took them together in one shot. They fell to the ground, tumbling down the stairway they had come from. Ladu turned to face the horde coming at him. What had once been a mob of twenty had tripled in size, though it would have been easily half again as many if not for Ladu's well placed crossbow bolts.

Beside him, Raisha released another breath. "I fear we can't keep this up for much longer, your majesty."

They came around the corner and ended up in the middle of a fiercely contested fight between the Kule brothers and undead. Ladu stumbled over one of the many bodies littering the corridor, most of which wore the rags of the undead. Faldon and Tavin appeared to be the last of a band of defenders, having fought their way through a group easily as big as the one pursuing Ladu and Raisha down the corridor. They leapt to the elion's defense, Ladu taking a sword from a body. An elion—not a member of the Patrol, but an undead—lurched toward him, eyes wild and bearing an axe with a wicked curve. Ladu dodged first one strike, then another, as the elion came at him. He raised his blade to counter the third blow and kicked outward with his right foot. He caught the elion in the gut, knocking him backward. Ladu completed the attack by coming in close and driving his sword through the undead's chest.

Beside him, the Kule brothers managed to clear the corridor. Raisha even brought an undead down. The loose band stood together, each taking a moment to gain his or her bearings.

"We were attacked in the gatehouse, your majesty," Tavin Kule said. "And you?"

"They came upon Raisha and me outside the throne room," Ladu replied. "I fear the palace is overrun."

Immediately following his words, the sounds of pounding feet announced the arrival of their pursuers. A strange, musty smell wafted down the corridor ahead of them, making Ladu think of barrows open beneath a full moon. *Bodies from the Battle of the Deathlands. That's where they came from.* Soon the group came into view, bristling with weaponry, a strange and fearsome assortment of opponents of all races and ages.

"In your flight did you come across any other Patrol folk?" Tavin asked the emperor, one eye on his ruler, the other eye on the mob moving toward them.

"Only bodies. And you?"

"A group of us made a stand here, but we're the last ones left." Tavin nodded toward the oncoming group. "I have no wish to repeat that experience."

"Aye," Faldon concurred. "Back to the gatehouse."

They turned and ran, feet pounding against the flagstones. *Little more than a year, and I've already lost my throne,* Ladu thought. *Perhaps the Jovun dynasty is cursed.* When they entered the gatehouse, Ladu saw an elion lying on the ground with a crossbow bolt through his head, and another with a bolt through his heart.

"Pedrar attacked us," Faldon said, gesturing toward the bodies. "I find that most concerning of all."

Ladu did, too. Undead were bad enough, but if Uklith had his hooks into living Patrol members, it would mean those who remained were up against a well-trained enemy force.

The gatehouse could be barricaded from either side, as was standard defensive procedure, so Faldon and Tavin set to work closing the door and dropping a large oaken board through the hooks on their side. The massive iron-bound doorframe and the subsequent barrier could withstand a heavy assault indeed. Mob or not, such defenses would easily hold for the time being against those on the opposite side.

"I fear my brother is the cause of much of this," Raisha said. "He led the betrayal within the throne room."

Tavin looked at the noblewoman with a grimace. "I never liked you, Lady Varuc," he said, "though, truth be told, I liked your brother even less."

Surprisingly, Raisha managed a smile, a feat when considering the seriousness of the circumstance as well as the offhanded way in which Tavin delivered the insult. "I suppose I might have earned that. If it counts for anything, I never liked my brother, either."

"Then all four of us have one thing in common," Faldon said, using his shoulder to lock the barricade into position and stepping back. Almost instantly, the doorframe shuddered as the group pursuing them assaulted the defenses.

"Actually, we have *two* things in common," Ladu said with a glance toward the door. "In addition to our mutual dislikes, we are locked out of my palace."

"To the battlements," Faldon said. "They will give us a better perspective of the situation."

They followed Faldon along the edge of the gatehouse and to the winding stairwell. The pounding sound on the far side of the door grew loud enough to fill the room with a chorus of noises, but the mob would have to significantly increase in size before they had a hope of breaking through.

When the four came onto the battlements, they encountered yet another fight. Five elions matched themselves against an even dozen undead, with several more bodies lying against the crenellations. Though Ladu's arms ached from all the fighting thus far, he nonetheless unsheathed his blade and joined the latest conflict. This time they made short work of the attackers, who stood little chance against the coordinated training of the Frontier Patrol.

"Sirs," one of the elions said. He delivered a crisp salute to Faldon and Tavin. At the sight of Ladu his eyes widened. He bowed. "Your majesty."

"Stand easy, soldier," Ladu said, acknowledging the elion with a nod. "Well done."

"Your majesty?" Raisha asked, face grim. "I believe we have a problem." She stood near the edge of the parapets, looking over the side. Ladu noted with a touch of amusement that she was holding her dress by the sides, raising it just high enough to keep the hem clear of the blood from the surrounding bodies.

Understandable, but she has to realize it won't stay clean forever.

Ladu joined her, jaw tightening at the scene below. At the far end of the streets, perhaps a quarter mile distant, a mass of people filled the cobblestones, many undead, others living citizens caught in the throes of fervent devotion like Perdrar. They filled the alley shoulder to shoulder, jostling forward in a shambling gait, headed toward the palace.

An elion on the parapets raised a seeing glass to his eye and surveyed the crowd. His face darkened after a moment, and he handed the glass to one of his comrades. "Is that who I think it is?" he asked the other elion.

His companion raised the glass, and after a moment nodded. "Aye," she said, lowering the glass with eyes narrowed. "It's Jeb."

"Jeb?" Tavin asked.

"He was in the Pit with us," she said. "He killed more than one of his cell-mates, and sold out a fair number of other folk to the malichons. We bade him good riddance after the battle. It seems he enjoys serving our enemies."

Some in the mob appeared to be chanting, though it was another minute before Ladu could discern the words.

"He comes!" they shouted.

Ladu's stomach twisted as he the group continued their march. *He comes. Does this mean Matthias has failed? Did the Warrior fall, and now the Demon-Lord arrives?*

"We need to get out of here," Faldon said, eyeing the mob. "They will be here within the half hour, not to mention those already in the palace. Your majesty, we need to get you and Lady Varuc somewhere safe."

Ladu surveyed the group. They were eight in all. Hardly a force to be reckoned with compared to the hundreds marching on the palace. "Very well, Lieutenant Kule. Lead the way."

With a crisp nod, Faldon led them down the far side of the battlements to a small egress point built behind a false wall. It opened to an alley outside the palace, where it was blissfully quiet, at least for the moment. Faldon took the small group down the street, careful to check any crossing for signs of enemy movement. At last they arrived at a fletcher's shop, which Ladu recognized as Vinsor's. He'd boarded the place up before going south with Harggra.

Tavin stepped up to the door, rapping it with his knuckles. After a few moments of silence, the door opened first a crack, then all the way. Wayne stood inside, sword strapped across his back.

"Kule," Wayne said, nodding at the brothers and bowing to Ladu. "Your majesty."

"It's bad, isn't it?" Faldon asked.

"Aye, we took ambush in the eastern quarter. We made it here well enough, though not without losses." He stepped back to let them in.

"Vinsor Dalin was a soldier in his day," Tavin said to Ladu by way of explanation as they entered the fletcher's shop. "He understood the importance of having a refuge point near the palace."

When they were safely inside the shop, Wayne bolted the door behind them and the group moved behind the counter. Wayne peeled the rug back to reveal a trapdoor, taking them down into a surprisingly large room beneath the shop. Ladu saw perhaps a score of Frontier Patrol members gathered throughout the room, which also bristled with armaments hanging from the walls.

"I'm pleased to see you've been working on more than a census," Ladu said to Tavin.

"It was Boblin—Commander Kule's—side project. Living in the Fort, one thing was clear: we always need an escape plan. Just in case."

"Nicely done, lieutenant."

They gathered together for a council. "For the moment, we need to assume the city has been taken," Faldon said to the rest of the group. "The Patrol folk know to come here, and we'll gather as many as we can."

"What about the citizens?" Wayne asked.

"We need to hope that they stay in their houses and keep their heads low. For the moment, they're on their own, much as it frustrates me to say so."

"There are but thirty of us," Raisha said. "What are our options?"

"We can hope more will gather here," Tavin said, "but if not, we'll make do. We're the Frontier Patrol, my lady, and we've been here before. Facing the odds is what we were trained for."

Ladu nodded. "Well said, Lieutenant Kule."

At the back of the room, Wayne gave a grim smile. "Outnumbered? Fighting from a position of hiding? Why, it will be just like the old days."

25

As the company neared the far end of the Mygon Path, the ever-present Cliffs of Desolation loomed in front of them, closer with each passing step. Here the Path was at least forty feet wide. The horizon bled red as the sun reached its morning hours.

The arid air around Tim sucked moisture from his lungs with each breath, the pores on his skin long since empty and dry. When they reached a broad widening in at the very end of the Path, Tim saw a small cairn of stones, nestled against the spot where the ground met the vertical rise of the cliff wall behind it. Against the small monument lay a sword, and Tim noted the lack of rust. *There's no moisture in this climate, which means no rust.* Or at least, not enough moisture in the time since Eklan Hamur last came this way.

The party slowed as they approached the cairn. Tim glanced sideways toward Eklan, noting how somber the man's face had grown. Tim raised his hand for the rest of the company to stop. They acquiesced, leaving Eklan alone to approach the monument. The big man moved toward it slowly, and when he reached it at last, he placed a hand upon the sword's pommel.

"Mygon?" Tim asked.

Eklan nodded, face tilted away from the company.

"You've seen the scorpions before?"

Eklan shook his head. "It wasn't a scorpion that killed Mygon. *That* one was a spider. It came from the gorge, too. He was the first man we lost."

Given that Hugo had also met his demise upon the Path, the first companion they had lost thus far, Tim found the parallel troublesome at best. *Are we doomed to but follow in the exact footsteps of those who came before us? Will two return, one sane, the other crazed, and remain around long enough to bring yet a third ill-fated party west when their time comes? Is this merely a game Uklith plays?*

To reach the summit of the cliff face, the group would need to travel a series of switchback trails that led upward. It would take time, but at least they would have plenty of stable footing to do so. Instead of camping when the sun rose, they decided to attempt the switchbacks in the morning light to allow themselves and the horses a better view of the way upward. The ascent took the next several hours, during which the company spoke little, most of their efforts focused on reaching the summit. Behind and below them the broad, deep gorge fell farther and farther away. Rookwind and the other horses required encouragement every so often. The occasional wind gusted past them, and Tim was grateful for the way it brushed the heat and dirt off his body.

At last the travelers crested the final switchback and reached the top of the Cliffs, where Tim stared at the landscape. One at a time, the rest of the company joined him, until they all sat on their horses in a line side by side, gazing upon the second half of their journey toward Agrazab.

"The Wastelands," Eklan said in his gravelly voice.

It was an apt name. Where the Bleached Fields had been flat, empty, and white, and the subsequent sands marked by slowly shifting grains and gently rolling hills, the Wasteland was arguably the most inhospitable landscape they'd faced yet. It combined the rise and fall of the sands with the bare stone of the Bleached Fields, though this stone was shades of brown rather than white. Occasional crags and gullies crossed the landscape, nothing to rival the width or depth of the gorge they just crossed, but enough to twist an ankle or break a leg.

"One other thing," Eklan said. "This is krevur territory again. They are smart and savage, and we must tread even more carefully from here."

They rested during the day and set out again once night fell. Before long, they saw their first skeleton, the shell of a scorpion, which must have crawled up from the gorge and ventured into the Wastelands. The corpse lay on its side, its long tail stretching into the dust, eight legs poking skyward at awkward intervals.

"It was not an easy meal for the krevurs, but they make do with what they can," Eklan said as they approached the husk. It was difficult to say how long ago it had died. Dust caked the northwestern surface of the creature's shell, which had faced the prevailing winds and the subsequent deposits of blowing sand as time passed.

"How many krevurs did it take to kill it, do you suppose?" Tim asked.

Boblin, not Eklan, answered. "I'd say at least six."

Tim looked at his friend. "How do you know?"

"Actually, I have no idea how many killed this one. But six is the number that's been following *us*."

Tim turned his horse around and looked at the landscape. Though it appeared empty, he knew better than to second-guess an elion's observation skills. "For how long?"

"Ever since we broke camp at nightfall," Boblin replied. "They've been hanging back, so as near as I can tell they're simply sizing us up. My guess, they're placing bets on what elion tastes like."

"Keep moving," Eklan said. "They always come in groups of three, which means two pods have joined together. As Kule said, they aren't quite sure what to make of us yet. The faster we travel, the better. Any indication of weakness will trigger them to attack."

Following Eklan's lead, they quickened their pace, urging their horses to increase their pace from a walk to a trot. Not ten minutes later, Tim caught a glimpse of a krevur, easier since he was looking for it. The bipedal lizard poked up over a rise perhaps a hundred yards away to his left, sniffed the air, and then darted down to conceal itself once more. Tim shifted his saddlebags, keeping the pommel of his sword within reach. Rookwind gave a nervous whinny and shook his head.

Things continued this way for the next few hours. The creatures only made themselves visible upon occasion, one or two emerging from behind the craggy structure of the landscape before returning to concealment. By midnight, a third pod had joined the first two, and they began to get more assertive. Three of the krevurs emerged to stand at full height in the moonlight, only this time they did not retreat but trotted beside the mounted company in plain view, keeping a distance of thirty yards.

After it became obvious the krevurs did not intend to leave, Eklan cleared his throat. "Take one."

Holding her bow, Celia twisted in the saddle, drew the string back, and released. The arrow flashed in the air to strike the krevur broadside. It staggered and, as no less than four more arrows from the other elions struck it, fell to the ground with legs kicking. One of its partners turned toward the group and opened its jaws wide, bracing as if to charge. The entire group readied their bows yet again. Appearing to change its mind, the creature vanished into a gulley, followed by its surviving companion.

That left them alone for the next hour, until they heard a series of distant *hoots*.

Eklan cursed. "Faster," he said. "They've forced us well off course, and now they're calling other packs. We need to get to higher ground. There's a plateau northeast of here."

They urged their mounts into a canter, following Eklan's lead. As time slid by, every so often shadows flitted against the backdrop of the desert. Though Tim didn't have an exact count of how many krevurs pursued them, by the time the first fingers of dawn reached into the sky he expected they had five packs on their tail.

They came to the base of the plateau before sunrise, taking another series of switchbacks toward its summit fifty yards up, the moonlight illuminating their path. The route was steep, at times challenging though not impossible for the horses. However, with high ground and high visibility the top of the plateau would be a good place to make a stand. The circular-shaped tabletop surface was two hundred yards in diameter. The northern and western sides of the plateau—the group had climbed up the south face—descended back into the Wastelands, while the eastern section ended against a jagged cliff. After riding Rookwind to the eastern edge, Tim realized that the plateau abutted an extension of the gorge they had crossed while upon the Mygon Path. The vast canyon wound across the desert in a sinuous arc, with the plateau they stood on abutting the gorge's northern trajectory.

Boblin dismounted Dapple at the center of the plateau alongside the rest of the horses. Tim followed suit, leaving Rookwind with the group, and he and Boblin returned to the southern end of the plateau. They crouched behind a ledge of rocks, peering over the side to assess the situation on the floor of the Wastelands. Six krevurs were moving toward the base of the plateau in a V-shaped formation.

"Where are the rest?" Tim asked.

"No doubt preparing to attack from another direction," Boblin said.

"How do you see this playing out?"

"Arrows drop them, but not easily. They have thick skin. The ones we fought at the oasis were difficult enough, and at last count we're dealing with fifteen here. I don't expect the missing nine stopped to share a pint of ale. They'll show up soon enough."

Tim stepped away from the ledge. "We need to get the horses as far away from here as possible. We can't risk losing any of them to the krevurs."

"I know the Wastelands," Eklan said from behind them, "and my sister and Wurit know the horses. We'll find a place to hide them."

"If the krevurs spot you off of the plateau, they will be on you like rust on an ancient sword," Boblin said. "Is it really wise to split up?"

"Keep their attention focused here, elion, and we won't have to worry about that."

"I worry about everything."

Eklan waved Bria and Wurit over, and they began tethering the horses' lines to lead the animals single file off the plateau. Celia and the other elions joined Tim and Boblin near the ledge.

Boblin looked at Tim. "Do you feel like living dangerously?"

"Always."

"All right. Here's what we're going to do."

After Boblin explained his plan, the group got ready in tense silence. Celia, Ken, and Jend each took up position along the southern edge of the plateau, crossbows at the ready, covering the switchback that led back to the floor of the Wastelands. Below, the six krevurs stood looking upward.

What are they waiting for?

Eklan, Bria, and Wurit finished tying the horses together. At Boblin's signal, the Keldurians took off down the northern side of the plateau, away from the impending conflict.

"Let's go," Boblin said to Tim. He hopped over the edge of the plateau and onto the switchback.

Tim followed. Above them, the elions held firm with crossbows notched, covering him and Boblin as they began taking the path back down. From the floor of the Wastelands, the krevurs watched them. One took a step back, as if second-guessing why prey would be so accommodating as to walk down *toward* them.

Tim drew his sword, resisting the immediate urge to seize the Lifesource. The last thing he needed was to be overpowered by Uklith's presence at a critical moment. The switchback reversed direction several times, leading him and Boblin down the vertical trajectory of the plateau's side. When they reached the midpoint of their descent, they came to an area where the path widened, leaving room to take a stand.

Boblin stopped. Below them, a krevur looked up at the group, and issued three soft but distinct *hoots* into the night air. "If that's not a feeding call, I'll be a sun-baked lizard," Boblin said. "Get ready."

The krevur reared back on its haunches and *jumped*. It cleared at least fifteen feet, landing at a point perhaps ten feet below Tim and Boblin.

"That's new," Tim said. He did not have a chance to speak again, for with its second jump, the animal cleared the remaining height and landed on the ledge between the two companions, snarling. It paused, leaning forward on its hind legs, snout testing the air before settling its focus on Tim. The krevur sprang toward him with a hiss, jaws open wide to reveal glistening teeth.

Tim supposed the krevur had picked him because he was shorter than Boblin and potentially easier prey. He stood on the balls of his feet, sword in hand, and then moved to the side when it attacked. He dove away and rolled to his feet, flanking the krevur and slashing his blade across its skin. The sword glanced off the creature's leathery skin, drawing a spot of blood but no more, confirming the krevurs' resilience.

Boblin moved forward to aid him, but a second creature made its leap upward to join the group, landing on the path and coming for the elion in a blur. The krevur in front of Tim spun around and came back for a second strike, while a crossbow bolt fired by one of the elions from above buried itself in the creature's side. It staggered, and for a second Tim thought that might be the end for the beast, but it righted itself and came for him. Behind him, he heard three soft hoots from the Wastelands, and knew a third krevur was preparing to join the mix.

Where are the other packs?

Soon enough, he had his answer.

* * *

Celia raised her crossbow and took aim. The plan was simple: she and the rest of the elions would remain on the plateau while Tim and Boblin moved down the ridge to draw the krevurs toward them, forcing the lizards together to present a clustered target. The last thing the group wanted to do was fight the krevurs at close quarters, so Boblin's plan was for Tim and himself to act as bait, while the rest used their bows.

With Tim and Boblin on the ledge, they needed to be careful about placing their shots. It wouldn't do to hit one of their companions instead of a krevur. Jend had taken the first shot, striking the krevur that threatened Tim, but it wasn't enough to bring the lizard down.

Celia focused her gaze farther out, on the four krevurs still at the base of the plateau, one of which had just given a series of *hoots* as it prepared to join the two attacking Tim and Boblin on the ledge. The four lizards were not quite within range, but...

The krevur landed on the halfway point of the ascent, just as the two before it. Celia tracked it with her crossbow, finger on the trigger. *Not just yet. Closer—closer—*

The krevur jumped again, and as it ascended Celia released her shot. The arrow flashed through the air, burying in the creature's neck, and though the krevur landed on the path in front of Tim and Boblin with both feet, the force of the hit knocked it backward to the very cusp of the ledge. It scrabbled for purchase, the claws of its toes digging at loose rocks on the ground, but eventually gravity won and the creature tumbled back over the side.

Celia fitted a second arrow into place as the krevur landed on the lower ledge, once again midway between the ground and Tim and Boblin. It settled with surprising grace and stability, in spite of the fact that it had two arrows sticking from it.

Beside her, Hanqar gave a cry of alarm, and everything went straight to Malath. Celia saw a blur of movement from the side and spun to see a krevur leaping through the air toward her. She registered that it must be from one of the other packs, right before it landed atop her and knocked her onto her back. The claws of its feet pressed onto her chest, tearing through her leather jerkin and scoring her skin. She brought her left forearm up into the space between the creature's jaw and its neck, preventing it from opening its mouth to swallow her head. Her right hand still held her crossbow, but the krevur leaned forward and used its arm to pin her wrist to the ground, the heat from its nostrils blasting her face. She was dimly aware of the other members of the group turning on all sides to face an attack as well, and she guessed that at least six krevurs—if not more—were upon them. They must have ascended the plateau from the group's blind side, to the west.

The krevur's tail lashed, giving the creature balance and momentum to press forward. She strained to free her right hand, at the same time putting the remainder of her energy into the gridlocked position of keeping her left forearm wedged under the creature's jaw. She felt a thin trickle of blood roll down the side of her chest from where the creature's claws had torn her skin, but it was hardly a mortal affair. She just needed to—

Her right arm came free. She brought the crossbow around, pressed the tip of the bolt against the krevur's temple, and pulled the trigger. The arrow released with decisive force into the creature's skull, piercing through flesh and bone, killing it instantly. The body slumped forward, dead weight atop her. Celia took a moment to catch her breath, closing her eyes and taking gulps of air, and attempted to push the krevur's body away with her free hand. Its weight doubled as a second krevur jumped on the first. Each of the creatures weighed as much as a full-grown man, and the combined pressure left her immobilized. She could barely move her right arm, and her left was trapped between the first krevur's body and her chest.

And her crossbow was empty.

* * *

Bria followed her brother and Wurit across the Wastelands, toward a second ridge three hundred yards away from the plateau. There was a cavern nestled partway up the side of the ridge, a perfect place to tether the horses in temporary safety, and close enough for them to return to the main group to lend their aid. Behind them, a series of hoots rose in the air, and she met Eklan's gaze.

"It's begun," he said.

Bria risked a glance over her shoulder toward the plateau. She could no longer see where the group was gathered, but she knew Kule and Matthias were using themselves as bait to draw the lizards forward. The problem was, if the krevurs were as clever as Eklan indicated—and she believed they were—then the lizards had little intention of becoming hunted instead of hunters.

For the moment, she and her two companions had their own worries. Beneath her, Menindara balked and neighed, sensing the disturbance atop the plateau. Bria kept a watchful eye on the surrounding rocks, ever conscious that krevurs might strike without warning. Though they tried to be quiet as possible, the sound of the horses' hooves upon the ground and the occasional nervous whinny did not allow them to be completely silent.

She could feel the heat of the day coming on, and it didn't do much to help the perspiration that had already begun beading on her forehead and trickling down her back. After several more tense minutes, they finally reached the base of the ridge. The path upward was as steep as ever, but Bria supposed anything that might dissuade the krevurs from attempting to climb was for the better.

The problem was, Menindara and the rest of the horses didn't much care for it either. They dismounted and led them slowly up the path in single file, moving paintstakingly, cautious of unstable footing. Every now and then a rock would dislodge under their feet, clattering down the side of the ridge.

When they approached the mouth of the cave, Eklan held up a fist for them to stop. He pulled his crossbow free. "Let me check it first."

Bria also took out her crossbow, ratcheting a bolt into position. She kept a safe distance behind her brother, ready to swing in and back him up if need be, but not so close that she would hinder his movements if he had to react quickly. Eklan rounded the edge of the cavern and stepped inside, swinging his crossbow to cover the area. After a moment, he stepped back and let out a breath.

"All clear," he said. "Let's move the horses in."

When he tried to pull Grendalar forward, though, the stallion dug its heels into the ground. The narrow path had made Grendalar freeze, not realizing that safety waited just a few feet away.

"Come on," Bria said to the Grendalar, stroking his neck and feeling the tremble of nervous muscle beneath the skin. "You'll be okay."

With coaxing, Grendalar eventually dipped his head and took his first tentative step forward. Growing more confident, he walked the rest of the way into the cave, the others filing in behind him. The space was wide enough to fit the horses side by side, and deep enough that the back of the cave was not visible from the entrance, keeping them out of sight from the eyes of prying krevurs. They tethered the horses to the very back of the space, ensuring the lines were secured tightly to a series of protrusions in the walls and ground.

"This should do," Eklan said. He took out a water skin that had been modified with an opening wide enough for a horse to stick its nose inside and drink. He draped it over Grendalar's snout first. "One of us should remain behind with them. Wurit?"

"Aye," the short man said, drawing his sword. "If a krevur *did* come up here, it would be easy feeding if we left them unguarded. You two go back. I've got things in hand here."

Eklan turned to Bria. "Ready?"

"Let's do it."

A clatter of pebbles caused them to turn toward the cave entrance, swords in hand.

A krevur stood at the mouth of the cave, blocking their only exit.

* * *

Boblin feinted left, then dove right, landing at the edge of the path. This time his diversionary technique *didn't* work. The krevur facing him wasn't fooled, and it came at Boblin's landing spot in an all-out rush. This might have been fatal for Boblin if he hadn't been counting on it. As the creature's claws came within inches of his skin, Boblin flipped back to his original position, leaving the creature to shoot past him in a spray of pebbles. It wheeled to face Boblin, jaws gaping, and he caught it with a turning sidekick, striking the flat of his foot directly against the lizard's center of mass. The blow knocked the creature from the ledge, and it fell away into the morning light.

Above him, Boblin heard the sounds of the conflict on the plateau. *It seems the other packs decided to show themselves.* Meanwhile, Tim had managed to score several hits against the lizard attacking him. The creature had a few barbed shafts poking from its side, courtesy of Celia's shooting.

As Boblin regained his balance, Tim used his position to pressure the krevur into a corner of the path, its back against the stone wall. Though bleeding from several wounds, it looked lively enough.

When Boblin came forward to help, Tim waved him aside. "Go," Tim said through gritted teeth. "Get back topside. I've got this."

Boblin hesitated, looking between Tim and the group above them, but Celia needed his help. He took off at a run, ascending the ridge. Taking a shortcut off the switchback, he jumped—*I'm a krevur now*—and seized the lip of the ledge, pulling himself over the side. He drew a dagger from his belt and entered the fray, where he saw one krevur atop another, Celia below them. Boblin whipped his dagger through the air. When the blade sank into the creature's neck, the lizard turned toward him, making a sound halfway between a screech and a roar.

Boblin unsheathed his sword. "That's right," he said. "Come get dinner."

The lizard jumped toward him, the dagger sticking from the side of its neck in an absurd fashion. This time Boblin simply took it straight on, planting his feet firm and holding his sword level. The creature impaled its body on the blade as it charged forward, steel crunching through flesh and bone. It died on the end of Boblin's blade, jaws snapping shut mere inches from his face. He jerked his sword free, let the lizard's body slump onto the ground, and stepped forward to help Celia back up.

Around them, krevurs snarled as they engaged other members of the company. The elions had been holding their own, but the lizards began a concerted drive, first darting forward to force the company to take a few steps of retreat, then pulling away before the elions could retaliate with steel. In this manner, Boblin and his companions were gradually forced back to the center of the plateau. There were seven krevurs against four elions, and one was already calling out with its familiar *hoot*.

"Okay," Boblin said, "let's chop these things up before this gets out of hand. We're supposed to die in the City, not out here."

The elions gathered in a loose line, ready to face the inevitable charge, but the krevurs stopped without warning. The leader of the pack leaned low, hissing in what sounded like a blend of fear and anger, and they began to shy back.

What?

As the creatures retreated, Boblin heard a telltale scratching behind them, and with a growing sense of dread he looked over his shoulder. A giant limb reached up from within the crevasse, latching on to the top of the plateau. This time it wasn't a scorpion that came from the depths, but a giant spider. It dwarfed the party with its massive frame. Its pincered legs spiked against the ground, and its mandibles snapped in the air.

"Come *on*," Boblin said, rolling his eyes. *Life is so unfair.*

"Now what do we do?" Celia murmured, looking from the krevurs, to Boblin, to the spider.

"Same as always," Boblin said, flexing his grip on his sword. He kept his muscles loose and ready. "Try to not get eaten."

26

At last, Tim saw an opening. The krevur in front of him moved more slowly, hindered by an accumulation of wounds. When it lurched toward him, it swayed, leaving its neck exposed, and Tim cleaved the creature's head from its shoulders. Gouts of bright blood spattered the ground.

Tim breathed heavily from exertion, but he received no reprieve. Another krevur jumped up to the ledge, replacing the first, and Tim began a careful retreat up the path toward the plateau's summit. The new krevur moved more warily than its predecessors, apparently aware that this prey had teeth. Instead of rushing at Tim, the krevur hopped incrementally forward, assessing Tim, looking for weak spots.

A snarl behind Tim caused him to risk a glance over his shoulder. A second krevur had leapt onto the path behind him, effectively pinning Tim between itself and the first lizard. Tim froze, flexing his grip on his sword, tensing for the attack to come. The krevur behind him struck first, leaping onto Tim's back and sending him facefirst onto the ground. The breath rushed out of him as he struck the ledge's stony surface, and he felt his cheek scrape across a scree of gritty pebbles. He lost his sword in the fall, so when he felt the krevur's hot breath blast against his neck, he brought his right elbow up to land a blow beneath the creature's jaw. Momentarily stunned, the lizard wavered, giving Tim just enough space to flip onto his back and face upward. He grabbed a knife from his belt, wrapping his hands around the hilt as the krevur prepared to tear his head open. Tim shoved the blade between the krevur's open jaws, through the roof of his mouth, and into its brain. Drool and blood slathered Tim's forearms as the creature went limp.

He pushed the body off of himself, but he had no time to retrieve the dagger. When the second krevur charged forward, Tim moved into a sitting position, back against the wall. The lizard jumped, landing before him with legs splayed to either side. Tim saw open jaws coming toward his face, and he pulled the only remaining weapon from his belt.

He crammed the boomer into the krevur's mouth, forcing it into a vertical position that held the creature's jaws locked open. The krevur shook its head, trying to dislodge this unexpected object and making guttural noises of frustration. Sweaty, covered in blood, Tim struck a firestick across his belt and held the small flame before the creature's eyes.

"Eat this," he said to the krevur, and lit the boomer. With his remaining strength he pushed the creature away. It toppled over the edge of the ridge.

Halfway through its fall, the krevur exploded, filling the night with a ball of fire.

* * *

Bria stood still. The krevur at the mouth of the cave hopped forward, looking at the group before it, assessing which target to attack first. Behind her, the horses bucked wildly, pulling at their tethered lines.

"Hey!" Eklan shouted, waving his arms. "Over here, you three-legged goat!" The creature spun toward him, opening its mouth wide. He rapped his knuckles against the wall. "Come on," Eklan said, taking slow steps backward. The krevur trained its beady eyes on him, leaning forward, head cocked to the side in an inquisitive manner. "That's right—you aren't as smart as you think…"

Bria pulled the crossbow from behind her shoulder and nocked a fresh bolt. She stood on the right side of the cave, Eklan on the left. Wurit took up position in front of the horses, ready to protect them should the lizard charge them. The krevur kept its attention solely on Eklan, though it hadn't leapt toward him, still assessing the situation. Only after a prolonged moment did it take its first hop forward. The creature's tail flicked, keeping it balanced. Eklan continued pulling back, drawing it forward one hop at a time, baiting it into a position where it would present its unprotected flank to Bria.

Moving slowly, careful not to draw the creature's attention back toward her, Bria took aim. When the krevur took its next hop forward, she loosed her shot. The shaft flew through the air, striking the krevur's midsection and causing the lizard to stagger. It turned toward her, the object of its pain, and let out a screech of anger.

"Hey!" Eklan shouted again, trying to draw its attention once more. "Back this way!"

Bria dropped her hand to her waist and retrieved a fresh bolt, while across the cavern Eklan seized a rock and threw it with decisive force. The stone struck the krevur on the temple and it snapped back toward him, alternating its attention between Bria and her brother, unsure which threat to attack first. Bria fit her second bolt into the crossbow, at the same time as the creature made its decision and rushed toward Eklan, the closer prey. Her bolt hit the lizard in its kneecap, causing its leg to give way. By the time the creature hit the ground, she'd already nocked her third arrow, and fired her killing shot straight into its head.

Bria wiped sweat from her brow, feeling a tremble run through her hand. *That was close.* In front of her, Eklan retrieved the shafts from the krevur's body. "Nice work, sister."

"Get going, both of you," Wurit said. "I've got this from here."

Bria and Eklan approached the mouth of the cave together, awareness heightened lest another krevur should appear. They emerged onto the thin ledge above the Wastelands and saw two dark shapes, the remaining members of the krevur pod, at the base of the ridge.

"I expected as much," Eklan said, looking down toward the lizards.

Bria shouldered her crossbow and sheathed her sword; speed would be of the essence here. "We'll need to draw them away from the cave—back toward the other group. Do you think we can outrun them?"

"No," Eklan replied matter-of-factly, "but that doesn't mean we shouldn't try. Are you ready?"

"Ready."

"Then let's go."

* * *

On the plus side, Boblin thought, *the spider doesn't have the same near-impervious exoskeleton as the scorpion. Its skin looks soft and susceptible to the point of my sword.* Over the side of the ridge, he heard a boomer detonate. Tim must have decided to employ a more effective means of defeating the krevurs on the switchback. Boblin had considered using a boomer, too, but with the elions clustered tightly together and only minimal space between

them and the krevurs, he didn't want to risk injuring one of his companions.

As for the situation before them, the spider clearly had the upper hand.
The krevurs remained gathered in a semicircle, not ready to give up their hard-
earned prey, yet clearly unwilling to engage the beast in front of them.

Boblin had never really liked spiders, less so now that he faced one larger
than his home. The oversized arachnid moved quickly, skittering across the
surface of the plateau toward them, all eight of its eyes rolling as it assessed
the situation. The group pulled together, standing in a circle with backs to one
another, Celia and Boblin facing the spider, Jend and the other two facing the
krevurs.

"Any bright ideas, commander?" Hanqar asked.

"Yes," Boblin said. "Let's make *them* fight each other. Under the spider!"

They broke and rolled, moving toward the spider rather than away from
it. Boblin landed beneath the spider's hairy, bloated underbelly, gagging as a
stench wafted over him. Hairy fibers brushed his head. He emerged on the far
side from between a pair of legs, severing one of the appendages with his sword
as he did so. The blade came back coated in the same sticky goo that he'd seen
when fighting the scorpion.

The spider wavered, regaining balance on its other seven legs. As Boblin
had hoped, the krevurs had rushed forward at the same time that he and his
companions retreated. The first of the lizards jumped into the air, scoring gash-
es in the arachnid's side. Foul, green pus oozed from the wound. The spider
whirled, picking the krevur up in its mandibles and pulling the lizard toward
its open maw. The krevur writhed in resistance even as the spider's mandibles
sliced it in half, and the spider stuffed the two sections of body into its mouth.
The rest of the krevurs flanked the spider, leaping toward it one after another.
Some landed on the spider, digging in with claws to keep their purchase, while
others missed the target and landed back on the ground.

"Take the legs!" Boblin called, whirling and hacking a second limb. After
several strokes, the leg separated from the body in yet another spray of viscous
fluid. The other elions, having scattered to separate sides when they rolled underneath the creature, heeded Boblin's call and began slashing left and right.

The spider staggered as it lost its third and fourth limb. It took one more
krevur into its mandibles before attempting to retreat over the ledge. That
was where things went very wrong for everyone—the spider, the krevurs, and

the elions. When Ken took the spider's fifth leg, the creature's massive body crashed to the ground. The krevurs pounced, slashing, tearing and biting, but they had all moved so close to the cliff's edge that the spider's thrashing legs caught everyone up in the commotion. They tangled into a twisting bundle of limbs, and as the spider's dying momentum carried it over the edge, it dragged elions and krevurs alike with it, off the plateau and into the gaping canyon below.

* * *

Tim staggered up to the plateau's summit—fighting off one more on the way—and stopped upon seeing the scene before him. Boblin and the rest, along with several krevurs, had become entangled with an enormous spider near the edge of the gorge. He ran toward them, but had only closed half the distance when he saw everyone go over the edge, borne off the plateau by the spider's massive frame.

No—

He had no idea how far the drop was to the canyon floor below, or if anyone could possibly survive the impact. He was still running forward when another krevur jumped toward him, because there was *always* another krevur. Tim halted, then took a few steps back. Weary as he was, aching from every joint and bleeding from numerous wounds, he nonetheless resisted the urge to seize the Lifesource and turn the lizard into a crater right where it stood.

Perhaps the spider's body cushioned their fall—

The krevur screeched at Tim. It raised its snout to the sky and gave three soft hoots. To his surprise, it turned and darted away. *Or perhaps not so surprising. This batch of lizards might have had enough for one night.* The krevur disappeared over the edge of the plateau, down the path Tim had just come from.

The others—

Tim turned and was running toward the place where his companions had disappeared when he heard Bria cry out Eklan's name.

* * *

Bria placed one hand above the next, scaling the side of the plateau. It had been Eklan's idea, and it made fair sense. They had raced at breakneck speed across the stretch of Wastelands to the plateau, the krevurs in pursuit with jaws wide and drool glistening. Rather than take the path back upward, which would surely have resulted in the krevurs catching up to them, Eklan opted for an almost sheer vertical section of the wall, but one with enough handholds for them to make the climb upward, leaving the krevurs below them on the ground.

Except the things could *jump*, so it wasn't as easy as getting a few feet into the air. Even as Bria climbed, one narrowly missed her, colliding with the wall in a spray of rocks. It scrabbled for purchase but failed, sliding back down as its jaws snapped shut a hairsbreadth from her face. Below, it coiled, preparing for a second attempt.

"Just a few more feet," Eklan grunted beside her. "Go, go, *go*."

She nodded, saving her breath for the climb. Her next handhold broke loose, the surface rock coming free in one hand, which left her dangling from the cliff face by the other hand. The krevur jumped again, slamming into her body, but now she grasped the rock that had come off in her hand and smashed it into the creature's skull. Stunned, it slid away yet again. Bria strained with all her might, swinging her body back to the right and reaching for a new handhold. She found a nook in the stone with her fingers. *Good. Five more feet.* She pulled herself higher. *Four more feet.* Yet another handhold. *Three more feet.* Below, the krevurs prepared to jump again.

She saw it coming before her brother did. "Eklan!"

He was too slow to react to her warning. The krevur did not rise quite level with them this time, but it didn't need to. Its jaws closed around Eklan's boot and the man cried out. Eklan kicked once, trying to dislodge the lizard, but the krevur was already falling. The weight of its body pulling down on his booted foot tore Eklan away from the wall and bore him down.

* * *

Tim reached the ridge as Eklan fell away. Eklan hit an outcropping ten feet into his descent, colliding with the krevur. The two slid down a scree in a tangle of limbs, raising dust in their wake. Tim reached out, calling Bria's name, and she turned to look at him. Face taut with anger and fear, she grasped his outstretched forearm and he hoisted her onto the plateau.

"They took him, Matthias. They took my brother!"

"I know. I saw." Tim looked back over the edge. Eklan had reached the floor of the Wastelands and lay still. The initial impact must have knocked him unconscious. The surrounding krevurs, instead of devouring Eklan, looked up toward Tim and Bria. The leader let loose a hoot and seized Eklan's boots between his jaws. It dragged him westward across the Wastelands, the members of its pack close behind.

"Come on," Tim said. "Let's go get him." Returning to the center of the plateau, he picked up one of the group's sacks and slung it over his shoulder.

"Where are the others?" she asked, looking around the empty plateau.

"Gone. They fell over the edge."

"Are they dead?"

"I don't know. But your brother looks to be alive, so he's the one we're going after first."

Bria nodded. They raced side by side over the edge of the plateau, into the dawn on the trail of the krevurs that had taken Eklan.

* * *

Ten feet above the floor of the canyon, the group of elions landed on a massive spiderweb. Upon first impact, the strands dipped down from the sudden weight, then sprang up on the rebound. It did not launch them into the air, for the sticky netting held everything—elions, krevurs, spider and all—locked into place. Boblin twisted in the webbing, a krevur's snout three feet from his leg. The krevur, writhing in its newfound captivity, reached toward Boblin with its deadly incisors. Its teeth clacked together as it strained to close the distance between itself and Boblin's delectable chunk of elion hamstring.

For his part, Boblin tried to pull back, but found his efforts to escape the krevur as futile as its efforts to reach him. Farther down, he saw Celia with half her body trapped beneath the giant spider. The spider lay on its back, caught in its own web from which it had devoured many an unhappy victim. Its three legs wavered upward uselessly, and its mandibles opened and closed upon the empty sky above. The other elions had landed scattered across the web, each thrashing about. Hanqar was closest to Boblin, on the far side of the krevur. The elion had enough space to reach behind his belt and pull a dagger free.

"Commander," Hanqar said in a hoarse voice, looking up and beyond Boblin. "There's *another* one."

Boblin craned his neck and saw a second spider, this one with all eight legs functional, upon the web perhaps fifty yards away. It made its way toward them, legs springing easily off the silky fibers that had ensnared everyone else.

"Great," Boblin said. "Just *great*. Start cutting."

Hanqar nodded, slashing at the strands with his dagger. They sprang free, but with woeful lack of speed. Boblin reached for his sword and felt his fingertips make contact with the hilt. He lost hold almost immediately. The handle wasn't close enough—just a little bit more—he strained—*more*—and *there*. This time he grasped the handle fully within his palm and drew the blade. With considerable effort, Boblin worked his sword-arm free from the web and began slashing. Around him, the other elions did likewise, Celia from beneath the spider's massive, hairy blob, Jend and Ken from much farther down. One of the krevurs had wound into a cocoon between them and the advancing spider, a fact for which Boblin found himself very grateful.

Celia cut her way free first, the weight of the spider making the process easier. As the bottom of the web fell out from under her, Boblin caught a glimpse of her crashing to the ground a handful of feet below. Celia pushed herself out of the way right before the almost-dead spider landed in the same spot. It flailed weakly, and Celia came up to its side and plunged her sword into its brain.

Above Boblin, the second spider reached the krevur in the cocoon. It opened its mandibles and drew the lizard in. The krevur let out a final screech of anger, right before the spider bundled it into its mouth.

At last, Boblin slashed the final strand holding him and plummeted, Hanqar beside him. They landed with a soft *plop* on something spongy, settling into a strange surface that exuded a rancid, vaporous scent. Boblin rolled to his feet and looked around, trying to gain his bearings, and a shiver of disgust ran through him. *Eggs.* Dozens of them covered the canyon floor in rows. The pair Boblin landed upon lay splattered and open over the stony canyon floor, the crushed remains of a tiny spider—though in this case "tiny" meant the size of a small dog—jutting from the cracked membrane.

So this is where all the horrors come from. No doubt another area of the canyon contained infant scorpions, and still other areas held other oversized bugs—centipedes, grasshoppers, beetles, all from his worst nightmares. The thought made Boblin shudder once more. Around him, the remaining members of the party fell free from the web, along with the last of the krevurs, all of which landed upright, ready for another round. Boblin and Hanqar joined Celia, who was wiping her blade clean of the thick gray sludge from the fatal wound in the spider's head. Jend and Ken came over as well, and the group formed a line, braced against the backdrop of the beast's large body. Before them, the two krevurs gathered in a cluster of fuming, hissing bodies, jaws at the ready, as above them, the spider clung to the remains of its web, eyeing the party below.

To the group's left, an egg from the nest split open. Another dog-sized spider clambered out, breaking free of the oozing interior, testing the air with its fresh limbs. The company drew their swords, preparing once more to face the inevitable conflict. Boblin leveled his blade, tensing his muscles to react at the first threat to strike.

"This," he said, "just keeps getting better and better."

* * *

The krevurs had disappeared by the time Tim and Bria reached the floor of the Wastelands. In the east, the dawn grew brighter, allowing them better visibility over the terrain. After a hurried examination of the surrounding area, Tim at last found sign of the creatures' passing: a series of three-pronged marks in the dirt, denoting claws, alongside a long furrow which could only have been left by Eklan's body as they dragged him away.

"Why would they take him instead of killing him?" he wondered aloud.

"Pack mentality," Bria offered. "Bringing the catch back to the den."

The last thing Tim wanted to do was walk willingly into the krevurs' lair, but he had no choice. He crouched low to the ground, running his fingers over the prints to determine a direction. The trail had turned south. *This is the part where Boblin would joke about how, if we are bound and determined to walk into a krevur nest, then at least it's one that keeps us farther away from Agrazab.* "Okay. Let's go."

They proceeded across the landscape as quickly as possible, taking care to watch their surroundings for any indication of ambush. For the first time that night, they caught little sight of other krevurs; instead, the Wastelands appeared unusually empty. Tim supposed he should be grateful for the reprieve, but his mind remained on high alert, sensitive to the fact that this was probably a trap. As they traveled, he wondered about his comrades who had fallen over the edge. The thought of them lying in a jumble of broken bones on the cavern floor, food for the next oversized scorpion to come their way, made him feel sick with worry. The elions were survivors, though, and if there was any group that could find a way to live through such an incident, it would be them. For the moment he needed to focus on saving Eklan, and so he pushed the thought of his friends from his mind.

In short order they came upon another carcass, similar to the first they had encountered: a large mass, long since stripped of flesh. This one was half-buried in the sand, indicating it had been some time since its passing. The krevurs' trail ran along the massive spinal cord before turning back west. Tim saw his first spot of blood, an indication Eklan was bleeding, though the wound was probably not serious—at least, not yet.

Next they reached the cusp of a broad basin that reminded Tim of the Irsp Valley, except the Valley had been completely empty, and this place was full of carcasses. While most of the remains had nothing left but bones, the odd skeleton still showed shreds of meat or skin hanging from its ribcage. The distinct, rancid smell of death and decay wafted forward from this place.

Sure enough, the krevurs' path led right into it.

Tim stopped and scanned the horizon, Bria beside him. "He's definitely down there," Tim said, "but I don't see anything. Do you?"

"No," she said. "This feels wrong, Matthias. It's too quiet."

"Yes." *But it only makes sense*, he thought. *When I've got the deer in sight of my longbow, I try to remain as quiet as possible, too. No use spooking your kill.*

After assessing the situation for several minutes, they stepped forward in unspoken agreement and began moving down the side of the valley. Tim took care with his footing; the last thing he needed was to twist an ankle on the way down. The carcasses they passed at the valley's edge were driest—no doubt older kills that had been moved away—while those closer to the middle remained fresher. Skulls ranging from tinier than Tim's head to as large as a boulder poked up from the sands.

Several minutes in, they spotted a dark form lying in a clear area ahead. As they neared they could see the form was Eklan, unconscious and supposedly unattended on a flat stretch of stone.

"Careful," Tim said.

"I know," Bria replied, hastening her step. Tim glanced left and right as they moved, expecting a krevur to appear from the shadows at any moment. The way remained tantalizingly empty. *It can't be as easy as this, can it?*

Bria reached Eklan and knelt by his side. Tim noted the rise and fall of the big man's chest as Bria tilted her brother's head and patted his cheek. His eyes opened. Eklan blinked once, twice, gaze moving in and out of focus before he struggled to a sitting position.

"Where are—" he began, but stopped as he took in the surrounding skeletons. "No," he said, rising onto his feet with a slight waver. "This is bad. Very bad."

"Then let's go," Tim said, turning.

"Too late," Eklan responded, just as Tim saw the first krevurs materialize from the shadows of an enormous ribcage. "We're in a nest."

Well, I didn't exactly expect anything different. I knew all along Eklan was just bait.

Three krevurs appeared. Three became six, six became a dozen. They appeared on all sides, materializing in the dawn, their numbers increasing to more than thirty, slavering as they surrounded their prey. A part of Tim's mind wondered how he and his companions could possibly serve as a satisfying meal for the enormous pack.

The forefront of his mind, however, was preoccupied with the immediacy of the situation. It had been bad enough when their group tangled with twelve krevurs on the plateau. This was far worse. *No time to waste.* He unshouldered his knapsack and reached inside. "Eklan? Bria?"

They looked at him.

"Get ready to run."

27

B oblin was getting ready to do some running of his own. He eyed either side of the canyon walls, trying to think quickly. *We need to scale upward. It's the only way. Down here, we'll only last so long.*

Soon, more immediate concerns occupied his attention. The krevurs rushed forward in a cluster at the same time that several more eggs cracked open, revealing additional spiders. An infant arachnid launched itself onto Jend's chest. The elion fell to the ground, wrestling with the beast, holding its snapping mandibles away from his face. Boblin and Celia spun back-to-back, Boblin using his sword to fend off a krevur's attacks, Celia taking on a pair of baby spiders.

As the group fought for their lives, it seemed to Boblin that time slowed. Far overhead, rays of light from the rising sun hit the strands of spiderweb above their heads, causing the dew upon them to sparkle. *Strange, how the mind can note something so deadly and yet think of it as beautiful.*

He paused, blade halfway through the krevur's neck as gouts of the lizard's blood pumped out onto the canyon floor before him. *That's it. The strands from the spiderweb!*

He jerked his blade free from the krevur's body and grabbed Celia by the arm. "The web," he said. "We can make a rope from it."

She glanced from him to the web and nodded. "I'll cover you."

Boblin ran to the edge of the web, Celia standing guard behind him to take on anything that came their way. He began slashing the silken strands. Meanwhile, Ken squared off against the giant spider, darting from one side of the canyon to the next, moving constantly in an effort to distract and confuse it. Several crossbow bolts sprouted from the creature's head, but it would take many more of Ken's arrows to even have a hope of bringing it down. At the same time, Jend wrested the infant spider from his chest and joined Hanqar, who was stomping every egg in sight before any of them could birth more of their mother's hideous children.

Boblin spat on his hands, using the saliva to keep the web from sticking to his palms, and began braiding its thick strands together. There was a ledge about twenty feet above his head. If they could climb even that high, they would be out of immediate harm's way. From there, he could launch a boomer and blow the cursed monstrosity of a spider into its next life.

Boblin wove the fibers hand over hand, noting the power of their tensile strength, each strand roughly the circumference of his thumb. With the far end of the web already connected to the ledge, he soon placed his hands around the new-formed rope and pulled tight to ensure its durability.

"Almost time to go," he said to Celia.

Ken hastened to join them. The hulking spider moved far more slowly now that most of its eyes had sprouted Ken's crossbow bolts. At Boblin's signal, Jend and Hanqar began retreating too.

The last two elions had almost reached Boblin them when the krevurs made their move, flanking Hanqar on either side, striking with vicious speed. One struck Jend with its tail, causing the elion to fly away and slam against the wall. The other krevur slammed Hanqar to the ground and took a bite from the elion's neck. Hanqar screamed, and the krevurs swarmed him, ripping, tearing, devouring. Boblin raced toward Hanqar, drawing his crossbow, knowing as he did so that he was too late.

"Commander!" Hanqar screamed from within the mass. "Commander, *help me!*" His entrails were all over the place, and the krevurs were eating him, eating him alive, while the massive spider closed on the group, mouth open wide for fresh meat.

Everything around Boblin was chaos, Jend surging back to his feet, eggs cracking, krevurs snarling, Hanqar screaming.

They will die. We will all die, if we don't get higher.

"Climb!" Boblin shouted. He fired a crossbow bolt into one of the small spiders that lurched into his path. "All of you, climb, *now!*"

* * *

As dawn rose above the krevur nest, Tim pointed west, toward the shortest path leading out of the valley. "Go that way. *Run.*"

"Matthias—" Bria began, but Tim was already barreling toward the krevur pack. The beasts swerved toward him, seeing a tender morsel eager to enter their grasp. Tim raced toward the ribcage of a giant animal's corpse, its curved spokes arcing high into the sky, while at the same time he withdrew his first boomer and struck it alight. He threw it in a low underhand toward the first cluster of krevurs, where it exploded on impact.

Tim cut through the center of the blast, rock and stone shooting skyward in all directions. Around him, at least a dozen krevurs had been felled by the detonation, some blown apart completely, others lying prone in death. Those who remained unharmed took up pursuit in earnest, though, and Tim barely made it to the safety of the ribcage. He jumped toward an arch in the bone above his head, grabbing hold with both hands and swinging his legs up to wrap around it, narrowly escaping the snapping jaws of a krevur below him.

Tim stood up on the rib, a surface perhaps twelve inches wide, and began to make an ascent toward a higher position of safety. Behind him, a krevur jumped onto a lower section of the skeleton. When it closed the distance between them, Tim stopped and rolled onto his back. Careful to retain his precarious balance on the curve of the bone, he kicked outward, striking the krevur in the chest with the flat of his boot and knocking it back to the ground. He continued climbing, rising farther above the ground as the krevurs gathered on the valley floor beneath him. Some jumped straight upward, but Tim had reached a point of the ribcage where he was high enough to be out of their reach.

He looked west. Eklan and Bria were running out of the valley, the path before them clear. *Good.* He balanced the sack of boomers in front of him on the rib and pulled a firestick from his belt. Below him, two more krevurs leapt onto the lower portion of the rib and began to climb. Without the advantage of arms and hands to keep balance, they only made it halfway up before tumbling free. The weight of their movement caused the ribcage to shake, and Tim had just struck the firestick into flame when the sudden shift in the ribcage made the sack slide off. He thrust the safe end of the firestick between his teeth, freeing his right hand to make a desperate grab for the bag of boomers. His fingers snagged the leathery fabric and started to pull it back into his grasp, but he lost his balance in the process. He found himself hanging from the ribcage with his left hand, a flaming firestick between his teeth, a sack of boomers in his right hand, and boots dangling above at least two dozen krevurs. One made its first leap up, its mouth coming within inches of Tim's foot.

All right, Tim thought. *They want something to come down their way? I'll oblige them.*

He raised the open sack toward his mouth and spat the flaming firestick directly into it, where it landed in the middle of eight boomers. Without further delay, he dropped the whole sack into the middle of the krevur pack.

* * *

Hanqar's screams were so horrible that Boblin wanted to plug his ears and close his eyes, but he couldn't. His soldier needed him. Hanqar lay on the ground, one leg mangled beyond belief, his stomach torn open, the krevurs tearing into him with savage gusto. Boblin used his momentum to roll across the ground, picking up a spare crossbow shaft as he came back to his feet. He held the bolt in his fist, driving it like a spear into the eye of the first krevur that came for him.

Hanqar looked toward Boblin, arm outstretched, eyes pleading. Boblin jerked the bolt free from the krevur's eye and slammed it home into the brace of the crossbow. He aimed. Hanqar's eyes met his.

"Thank you," Hanqar said, and Boblin shot him in the head.

He turned and ran, the other elions scaling the wall before him. He leapt up, grabbing the last strand of web, as behind him a krevur missed Boblin's boot. Just then the spider came among the lizards, grabbed the same krevur that had just nearly killed Boblin, and dragged the kicking lizard into its mouth.

From the ledge above, Jend grasped Boblin's forearm and pulled him up the rest of the way. Boblin rolled over and looked down at the commotion below him where the spider, its infants, and all the rest churned in a mass of limbs and flesh. He wished Tim were here, so that the man could utter a single word and wipe every last one of those creatures from this cursed trench.

"Well done," Jend said, patting Boblin on the shoulder. "Well done, Commander."

Boblin wanted to vomit. *Well done? I just killed my own soldier.* Bad enough when Hugo had died, but Hanqar's death had been at Boblin's hands. He knew well enough it was the right decision—Hanqar had been beyond saving, with the krevurs eating him alive. The choice had been between an agonizing death or a merciful execution, and Boblin knew which one he'd have wanted for himself. The knowledge didn't stop the self-loathing that coursed through him.

"Climb," he croaked, getting to his feet. "We need to keep climbing."

And climb they did, grasping handholds where they could, leaving Hanqar's body behind in the nightmarish canyon below. *We've come to Malath already,* Boblin thought, *and we haven't even set foot inside Agrazab yet.*

* * *

The explosion rocked the entire ribcage. Tim hung on with both hands as debris blew upward. A shard of something—either rock or krevur bone—struck his temple. He climbed upward with all his strength, balanced on the ribcage yet one more time, and scrambled down into the gaping crater the boomers had left on the valley floor. His ears rang, and blood ran from the fresh cut on the side of his head.

Though several krevurs survived, most had been torn apart, and the survivors were either wounded or disoriented. Tim took off at a run through what remained of the nest, following Bria and Eklan's path, and reached the bowl of the valley at full tilt. He grabbed at chunks of stone to help himself scramble upward, and though his haste proved in retrospect to be unnecessary—not a single krevur pursued him—dallying served no purpose.

Outside of the basin, he looked north and saw a pair of figures far ahead of him. Tim continued running forward, ignoring a stitch in his side, closing the distance in steady but painful increments. Eventually, Bria turned around and saw him. She halted Eklan, allowing Tim to finish the distance at a stumble. He fell to his knees at the very end, breath coming in harsh gulps. Bria handed him her waterskin, and Tim drank deeply, disregarding conservation for the moment, water slopping over the sides and down his cheeks.

After permitting Tim several heartbeats of respite, Eklan reached out a hand. "I owe you my thanks and my life, Matthias."

Tim took the man's grip, returning to his feet. "You might revoke your thanks when we arrive at the City."

"I probably will, but it remains for now."

Together, they hooked back toward the cavern where Wurit guarded the horses. It was a short walk, and though they kept a wary eye out for further attack, the krevur threat seemed to have finally passed. For one, the explosion had killed a great many of them, and for another, the rising light of day seemed to put a halt to the lizard's activities.

"Rest here, Matthias," Eklan said when they reached the base of the ridge. "I'll go get them."

Grateful for the reprieve, Tim found a rock and sat with his back against the face of the ridgeline. He was almost weary enough to fall asleep, in spite of his surroundings. Bria sat beside him, sword balanced across her knees.

"Will your brother be okay?" Tim asked, tearing a strip from his shirt and holding it to his temple.

"Yes. He's survived worse."

"Good."

Bria looked at him. "That took real nerve, Matthias."

"It wasn't as if we had any other options."

She replied with a noncommittal grunt.

"What's that?" he asked.

She arched an eyebrow. "What's what?"

He imitated her grunt. "*That.*"

She said nothing, just gave him a long, level gaze. Her piercing blue eyes did not blink once. The rising sun glanced off her blonde hair, while around them the air was hot and the breeze hung still.

At last she spoke. "Are we going to get this over with?"

It was his turn to arch his eyebrow. "Get what over with?"

"*This.*"

And then she was kissing him.

* * *

Agrazab. City of Darkness.

As night fell, the elion stumbled to the gates, where he collapsed on the ground before a massive arch. He had arrived at last, with sun-chafed skin, cracked lips, and open sores upon his hands and feet. But it mattered not, for he was here and Uklith would see to him. He could feel the Demon-Lord's presence deep within the city, pulsing like a dark rose about to open and draw all manner of unsuspecting victims within.

He lay in the dirt, panting, feeling the coarse grains of sand against his skin. Overhead, the sun's last rays encompassed the west in a haze of reddish glory, much like the rivers of blood he knew would spring forth once he unleashed his master. A thick veil of darkness stole over the city and the surrounding dunes. He looked back the way he had come. The only marks in the rise and fall of sand dunes were his two footprints, leading right up to where he lay in the shadow of Agrazab's gates.

He felt a stirring from deep within the city, a malevolent presence both wakeful and watchful, and knew that his arrival had not gone unnoticed. He was, he supposed, the first being to set foot in Agrazab since Eklan Hamur's ill-fated quest. A voice spoke in his head, and it was stronger and more robust than ever.

I AM PLEASED, MY SERVANT. YOU HAVE TRAVELED FAR AND DONE WELL. COME TO ME FOR YOUR FINAL TASK.

With slow, pained movements, the elion staggered around the half-open gate and walked beneath the massive arch into the city proper. The passing of time had left much of Agrazab covered in dust and sand. As he made his way forward, he saw a thin film of grains ghosting over the cobblestones from the breath of a slight wind. Around him, the city's wooden buildings were dry and hollow, all else that had once lived here long since withered away. A foolish person might have wondered why the beasts of the desert—krevurs, scorpions, spiders, and more—had neglected to make Agrazab their home, but the answer was quite obvious. Uklith's presence pervaded every pore of this place, filling the air with unmistakable dread, assuring nothing would enter the gates of the city unless he, she, or it wished to serve the Demon-Lord.

Or, in the case of Tim Matthias, the elion thought, *those who would seek to stop Uklith.* He felt a laugh bubbling in his throat. Yes, Matthias might seek to stop Uklith, but the Warrior was far from success. Everything that followed would only allow him and his companions the illusion of resistance. Uklith's power had grown absolute, and even as those brave but foolish adventurers made their way west, the final plans for their demise had been set in motion.

Uklith's prison was in the center of the city. The elion had to pass through a series of inner gates before arriving at the palace in which Agrazab's kings of old had reigned, where Uklith had taken his crown. In this place, the elion felt his master's presence: cold, dark, and strong. He quivered as he made his way up the steps to the palace. He came to a long hallway inside the gates, where empty sconces lined the passage. Once torches had burned brightly here, illuminating all that walked these halls so near to the Demon-Lord. The elion knew that it was in this very corridor that the three Advocates had plotted Uklith's demise, and in doing so secured a fate worse than death for themselves.

He moved down the hall, drawn toward the high, arched gates at the far end like a magnetic filing to a lodestone. The tongue of Homdee, a power far stronger than iron or steel, had sealed these gates shut. A buzzing sensation rose in the man's head, pain escalating to a level nearing ecstasy as he reached the gates. Here he knelt, head bowed, as Uklith's voice came from everywhere and nowhere.

TOUCH THE GATES.

The man reached forward, placing trembling palms upon the gruesome mural before him, making himself into an offering at the altar of his dark god.

THE POWER—

The elion shrieked as a hideous presence swept down the corridor, tearing at his senses. He felt as though claws raked his body on all sides. It seized the power from within him, that latent reservoir he had absorbed from Zadinn's journal and carried with him all this way.

YOU HAVE GIVEN MUCH IN MY SERVICE, AND FOR THAT I GRANT YOU THIS GIFT: I RESTORE YOUR SANITY.

The elion screamed as agony without boundaries struck him. Lava poured through his veins, filling him with fire and pain so great that it seemed he should die.

He did not know how long it lasted. When it stopped, he found himself bent over on his knees, face to the ground, strands of hair dangling before his eyes. He raised his eyes to the gates before him, seeing everything around him as if for the first time.

And he remembered his name.

* * *

Outside the palace, in the remainder of Agrazab, the wind blew with increasing ferocity. Power pulsed outward from the palace, racing through the entire city, and a lone tower at Agrazab's northwest corner began to glow with an unearthly white light. Sand flew across the streets, while in the sky above clouds gathered for perhaps the first time in the history of this place. The air within

Agrazab turned unnaturally cold, and a jagged streak of lightning flashed from the sky's impossible, dark thunderheads.

The white light growing within the northwest tower spilled out from its topmost windows, racing down the sides of the structure in jagged, writhing streaks. Upon reaching the cobblestones of the streets, the tendrils crawled outward across the ground, soon illuminating the entire city in a frenetic, freakish spiderweb of incandescent flashes.

The inhabitants of Agrazab might be long dead, but their corpses remained, deep beneath the sands. The power unleashed by Uklith's newest servant coursed into these lifeless bodies. Malichons might be lacking in this world of late, but Uklith was master of death, and so in death, these citizens would serve his purpose.

The first indication came when a clawed, skeletal hand shot up from the ground, grasping at the sky with taloned fingers. Soon after, a body—once dead, now undead—rose from its tomb within the depths of the earth. More around it followed, bodies large and small emerging from the sands of Agrazab. Their bodies were an amalgamation of rotting flesh and exposed bones, desiccated from the many centuries of death, defying all natural laws in the service of their unholy master.

At last the skies opened up, water descending in torrents, rain where there should not be rain, filling the streets of Agrazab with water and intermittent flashes of lightning. The tower in the northwest corner was ablaze with light. The undead army had awakened, numbering in the thousands, as Uklith, Demon-Lord of Malath, lord of the underworld and bringer of death, prepared to deliver the final stroke in his bid for unending power.

28

The schooner bearing Quentiin, Trivian, and the soldiers from Eltern made landfall at dusk. During the afternoon, they had slipped in and out as able between the vessels in Kaarst's fleet, keeping distance from the other ships to avoid drawing attention, yet moving slowly enough so that they did not appear to be fleeing the scene of battle. During their retreat, they watched the fight on shore as it turned against the defenders, and though they were helpless to give the Legion any aid, they took solace in knowing they had deprived Vila Kaarst of his most powerful weapons. What would have been an easy advance for the Admiral would turn into a protracted siege, and sieges ultimately worked to the defenders' advantage. Those who remained behind the walls of Vonku's inner city were well stocked, well defended, and able to fight from a position of strength.

Beside Quentiin, Trivian rode at the head of the ship. He'd been quiet for much of the escape, using a spyglass to observe the battle in front of Vonku's fallen wall. Every time a Legion soldier fell, Trivian jerked in a barely perceptible response, jaw set tight. By the time the schooner neared shore, the battle had dwindled to columns of smoke on the horizon, the outline of Vonku silhouetted against the setting sun.

Quentiin watched the man. Trivian's hand shook as he tucked the spyglass away inside his jacket. He'd received a cut along his jaw in the fighting aboard Kaarst's brigantine, and when he stood to look at the empty line of forest before them, his shirt showed several holes from knife and dagger thrusts. The other men of Eltern bore similar marks of battle, some worse than others. They'd lost twelve men in the assault, but those that remained seemed harder for it rather than discouraged. *Good. They'll need that edge, I'd say.*

"Yer laddies did well," Quentiin said quietly into Trivian's ear. "They have much to be proud of."

Trivian nodded. "They earned their victory."

This marked their third battle, the first being the liberation of Eltern, the second being the taking of the schooner at Peltin. Though Vonku still faced a serious threat, this small band's actions had prevented the city's immediate demise. Quentiin wondered about Eltern's badge of shame, and what it would mean after all was said and done here.

The ship's hull ground against the sandy beach, lurching as it came to rest. Quentiin expected the corsairs in Vonku would remain in the outer city for the short term, selecting structures to burn in strategic fashion. They wouldn't light the entire outer city ablaze at once, but rather would stagger the fires to create a perpetual smokescreen. With plenty of flammable structure to go around, this tactic presented distinct advantages: for one, it concealed the corsairs' movements, and for another, it would make life uncomfortable for those behind the inner walls. Also, winds from the sea would blow the heat and flames inward, making it difficult for the Legion to stay on the parapets and filling the air with noxious fumes. It would be up to Trivian's group, along with Quentiin and the dwerions, to break the siege. They were a meager crew at best, given that Kaarst had two thousand corsairs in his fleet and putting the odds near ten to one, but this didn't present any more of a challenge than they had already faced in the preceding weeks. While Quentiin and the rest did not have the numbers to launch an all-out assault on the corsairs, they had enough resources to hatch a plan that would delay and frustrate the enemy.

The company left the ship and went inland to make camp, where they would no longer be visible from the coast. The grounded ship would still give away their presence, but this way they could obscure their exact location from Kaarst's search parties. Quentiin wasn't sure that Kaarst *would* send any corsairs to find them, but necessity dictated remaining cautious. He, Trivian, and Jolldo held counsel near the periphery of camp, looking toward the battle to the south once the soldiers had established a perimeter.

"We'll have to use the corsairs' tactics against them," Quentiin said. "They're burnin' the city as we watch. This will give Kaarst good cover against the Legion soldiers defendin' the inner walls, but it will also give *us* good cover against *them*."

Trivian nodded. "I don't see a way to break the siege from the start, but we can at least make their lives uncomfortable. We'll harry their flanks, never staying in the same place for long. The smoke will help us keep our numbers concealed, and they won't be able to anticipate how large or small our attacking capabilities are."

"Let's begin by scouting," Quentiin said. "Just the three of us at first. Kaarst's men are up against a more sizable force given the walls themselves, even if not in raw numbers, and they'll be doin' exactly what we ourselves are plannin'—launchin' flank attacks in quick bursts. These will just be diversion as they prepare for a larger assault, though, an' that's what we need to disrupt. If we can keep the corsairs on their toes as much as they keep the Legion on theirs, we'll keep the situation in balance." The best they could do was give Sendalion and his soldiers time. The Legion soldiers behind the walls had the resources to launch a counterassault, but they would never be able to do that if the corsairs kept them on constant defense. If Quentiin and Trivian could keep the pirates distracted, perhaps those within Vonku would have a chance to organize a retaliatory strike.

Quentiin took first watch atop a hillock, eating strips of dried meat and drinking from a flask of water. In the distance, fires guttered across Vonku. The wooded area of Quentiin's camp would make a good base of operations. Though they would need to travel several miles to launch their attacks, it would be better to keep their distance. Landing too close to a giant would only get them swatted.

Later in the evening, Jolldo joined him, sitting on a stump and gazing into the distance.

"How are the rest farin'?" Quentiin asked his friend.

"They're ridin' high, laddie. Victory at Eltern, victory in the bay, an' not a single dwerion lost yet. It worries me, though. That's a sizable force in that city, an' we've only come this far by playin' our hand carefully. We can't get overconfident."

"No, we can't." Their previous fights—fighting from the shadows of Eltern, taking on the corsair crew in the confined space of the brigantine—had been one thing, but entering pitched battle in the streets of Vonku would be something else entirely. The dwerions had lost comrades before, most notably in the Pit of Zadinn's slave pens, but that conflict was a year and a half gone, and they had to take care to remember the lessons they had learned from it.

"What about Matthias?" Jolldo asked. "How does *he* fare?"

Quentiin shook his head. "I don't know. The focusin' reservoir went dark."

Jolldo went still. "What does that mean?"

Quentiin grunted. "It could mean a lot o' things, laddie. Mayhap it fell out o' his pocket, for all I know. Or he might be reluctant to use it as they near Uklith."

"Or, he could be dead."

"He could *be* a lot o' things laddie—dead, victorious, wedded to a malichon—but there ain't any use dwellin' on that with what we have before us. We'll take care of our own, an' let Matthias take care of his."

Quentiin had wondered more than once if he should be at Tim's side, although going south instead of west had been the best decision at the time they made it. They had thought that a user of the Lifesource might be playing some part in the siege. In hindsight, it had been only Kaarst and his cannons, so instead of Quentiin aiding Tim in his quest against the Demon-Lord, he was fighting an unrelated war in Alcatune. In in the end, however, Quentiin knew he was where he belonged: defending his homeland, serving his king of old. In some ways, this was how it had all begun, all those years ago during the Icor Rebellion, when he made friends with a fellow Legion soldier named Daniel Matthias. That friendship had led Daniel and Rosalie to make their home in the Odow, and brought them into the conflict that ensued when Zadinn Kanas made his first foray into the South. Seen in that light, Quentiin supposed things had come full circle, for now he was home serving his king yet again.

"Fair enough," Jolldo rumbled in agreement, interrupting Quentiin's thoughts. "We've enough on our plates without servin' ourselves another course o' concern. Tomorrow?"

"Aye, we leave at daybreak, an' we'll see what this siege is made of."

They passed the remainder of the watch in silence, dawn long off, listening to the gentle sounds of the forest around them.

* * *

Sendalion stood in the king's throne room, Vinsor at his side, King Aras opposite them. A handful of other Legion men stood with them, gathered around a table bearing a map of Vonku. Sendalion had placed red stones on the parchment marking where he knew the corsair crews to be. Sendalion suspected Harggra and Trivian had most likely made landfall north of the city, but without any means for communicating with them, he had to proceed as if they were a non-entity.

"What's the final count of Legion soldiers?" he asked Vinsor.

"Nine hundred and thirty-one," the man said. Sendalion winced. The force had once been two thousand strong, but after their losses under Captain Yastlin's command and the subsequent retreat, they were down to half their previous strength.

Another soldier pointed to a red stone on the map. "That's our best guess where their main strength is gathered, Captain Seltor. We could take five hundred men, leave the rest behind the walls in reserve, and launch an assault."

Five hundred. Sendalion looked at the map. It was certainly a feasible strategy. The dots showed the corsairs spread across several locations, and a direct attack would be close to an even match numbers-wise.

But he had other factors to consider: the corsairs commanded the streets, and the camp the soldier had pointed out was positioned at the intersection of several alleys. Any approaching force would have to funnel through the narrow streets, with corsairs likely commanding the buildings on either side. If the Legion maneuvered their numbers into such a narrow location, the corsairs could cut them off at each end of the alley and launch all manner of unpleasant things—arrows, fire, burning oil—onto them.

Though Sendalion understood the fundamentals of battlefield strategy, he felt ill-equipped to make this decision. On one hand, he didn't think a direct attack was the best call, but on the other hand, he couldn't sit behind these walls and let Kaarst wear them down.

"No," he eventually said, recalling one of Yastlin's sayings: *the man who chooses the battlefield wins.* "We keep this battle on our ground, on our terms. We bring the corsairs to us." Better for his men to be the ones on the walls with the arrows and oil.

"How do you propose we do that, Captain?" King Aras asked.

Sendalion's heart thudded. This was hardly his first time in Aras's presence, but during the other times, he had merely been present to accept the orders others suggested. This time, *he* was the one making the suggestions, and what he was about to propose had the ability to shape the lives or deaths of many others.

"Your Majesty," he said, "everything we've discussed is predicated on several assumptions: first, the assumption we hold a position of strength behind these walls, and second, the assumption that Kaarst knows this and will employ tactics to winnow our strength. He has presented us with two options: either bring the battle to him and allow him to fight from the position of strength, or allow ourselves to remain on the defensive until the tide of strength turns in his favor. We cannot take his camp as it is currently situated, but waiting is not an option, either. We have to make Kaarst bring his strength to bear *now*, earlier than he had planned on doing, and use this to crush him."

Aras nodded. "Indeed, Captain Danris—but how?"

"We feign weakness. Undermine a section of the wall, so that when it crumbles it does so on our terms. When they take the bait, we will be prepared with traps in the streets. This assault will happen with or without us, and better for it to be at a time and place of *our* choosing."

King Aras turned away from the group, facing out a window toward the streets. Sendalion suspected he knew what the monarch was thinking: removing a section of wall would deprive them of their last line of defense against the corsairs. *He has to understand that this way will be far better, though.* Their numbers would only grow smaller as the attacks continued. At present, the Legion was as strong as it would be, and rather than split themselves across skirmishes on several fronts, their best bet was to bring the engagement about quickly in a place where the Legion could bring their superior training to bear.

Sendalion caught Vinsor's eye, and the other man nodded. *He knows it's a good plan—a risky plan, to be sure, but a* good *one.*

At last, King Aras spoke. "You have guided us well, Captain Danris. You brought the dwerions to us, you freed the men of Eltern, and you implemented plans that deprived Kaarst of his cannons. What you propose could ruin us all, and yet it is also our best chance of success." He drew up to his full height and gave a curt nod. "Proceed at will, Captain."

* * *

After the men left, King Aras remained alone in his throne room. So this was it. They would plant the bait and see if Kaarst took it. He thought back on the years he'd known Vila as a noble in the royal court. Exiling the nobleman had been perhaps the most painful thing Aras ever had to do; he'd considered the man a friend, had seen how much *potential* Vila possessed even from a young age. Yet Kaarst was arrogant, and though Aras had attempted numerous times to appeal to the young nobleman's better qualities, he had failed. With this failure came the most trying years of King Aras's reign, for Kaarst's exile ultimately led to the Icor Rebellion, which eventually grew into its own beast, engulfing much of the South. In exiling the nobleman, Aras had loosed a monster upon the world, and it was his duty to correct it.

Now Kaarst had returned, as Aras had always known he would, and a reckoning was at hand. When the first alarm bells rang—it seemed a lifetime ago, though it had only been a few weeks—the threat of Kaarst had felt prominent but distant. At the time, multiple layers of city wall and all the might of the Royal Legion had separated king from admiral, but here they were today, armed with no more than a flimsy line of defense and a plan that might erupt in their faces. Aras had to give Captain Danris credit, though. The man's plan was aggressive, but good. He'd rightfully pointed out the flaws in the more obvious options and crafted a fitting third choice.

The king wondered how much time would pass before he and Kaarst were in the same room together. He knew such an occurrence was inevitable, whether it be in person, if the fighting came to that, or when one of their bodies was brought before the other. He could feel the gap separating the two of them closing more and more rapidly, but whether it ended his life, or Kaarst's, or both, Aras only hoped his citizens did not suffer as a result.

* * *

Sendalion and half of his men stood before a section of wall that ran perpendicular to a narrow alley. It was perfect; if they undermined it here, the corsairs would be funneled into the tightest section of the inner city possible, just as an assault on Kaarst's camp would have forced the Legion into a similar position.

He wrapped his hands around the haft of a sledge and brought it down on the cobblestones with decisive force. Several chunks of stone sprayed into the air. Around him, members of his crew began doing likewise. The second half of their group had gone farther back into the alley with Vinsor to begin laying traps. Sendalion had instructed them not to start too close to the wall, as he wanted to draw the corsairs into the net before tightening the noose. He had commanded a cluster of Legion soldiers on a far side of the city to start an assault on a corsair crew, drawing them away from the area where Sendalion and the rest were working. They didn't want to chance their work being discovered.

Sweat flew from Sendalion's brow as he struck the cobblestones repeatedly. Once they'd cracked the outer shell of the streets, they would dig trenches to run beneath the wall, erecting large beams into them to keep the battlements propped up for the time being. When it came time to accelerate the wall's collapse, they would break the supports.

The soldiers worked late into the night, taking shifts as needed, working as quickly as possible without compromising their battlefield effectiveness. It wouldn't do to have their plan ready, only to be too exhausted to spring it. Meanwhile, above them the guards on the battlements kept a lookout over the smoldering fires on the far side, watching their homes burn before their eyes.

* * *

Kaarst watched his corsairs at work in his camp. Two crews were on the upper levels of nearby buildings, preparing arrow slits from which they could fire down upon an advancing line of Legionnaires. Meanwhile, groups on the ground filled holes with all manner of unpleasant, sharp objects before concealing them beneath false surfaces. Although Kaarst doubted the Legion's current commander would be foolish enough to strike the corsair camp, he had nonetheless ensured that if the soldiers did attack, it would work to Kaarst's advantage.

"Adm'ral."

Kaarst turned to see an elion corsair behind him, a swathe of bandage covering the left side of his face. Perhaps twenty pirates stood in a rough group behind the elion, faces covered in soot and clothes tattered. And…Kaarst wrinkled his nose. They had a distinct *smell* about them—all corsairs did, but these had an odor stronger than most. A crew from the countryside, then. They'd been arriving in small groups here and there, increasing Kaarst's numbers.

"Welcome back," Kaarst said. He tossed the elion a bag of coin. Those who had been sowing chaos in rural Alcatune these past few weeks had earned their pay. "Make yerself useful. An' do somethin' about that stench o' yours."

The corsair took the money with a grin. "Of course, adm'ral." He snapped a salute and turned to lead his men toward a nearby building. They'd taken over a number of the surrounding structures as good places to lay bedrolls and pass around a flask.

Leaving the corsairs to their work, Kaarst entered his tent, the firelight from outside casting an orange glow through the fabric. He wondered how many citizens Aras still had behind his inner walls. He suspected the king had evacuated most commoners to keep them out of harm's way as well as to ensure they did not hinder the Legion's movements. It was a pity, for Kaarst would have enjoyed hanging them along the sides of the streets to taunt Aras while the pirates moved inward.

Kaarst had instructed his people to minimize losses as they made their periodic strikes against the wall—nothing too aggressive, just easy attacks in and out. He didn't have any particular care for the well-being of the corsair crews, but it remained to their advantage not to overcommit at this time. He'd held some small hope that they could commandeer the catapults from the outer walls, but the Legion had not been so foolish as to leave them intact. *That* would have been a treat, for Kaarst to use the Legion's weapons against them, rolling the catapults through the streets and firing upon the inner wall. The retreating soldiers, however, had dismantled and burned the constructs. Kaarst had a group working on salvaging a few, but it would be several days yet before any were capable of working.

He kept Captain Yastlin's head mounted on a pike outside his tent. Kaarst remembered Yastlin from his days training with the Legion, for all men of noble birth had some Legion training and service during their youth. The head would not be visible to the soldiers manning the walls, more was the shame, but Kaarst kept it to amuse himself. It reminded him to look forward to the moment when Aras's head would be on a pike.

The tent flap rustled, and a breath of cold air crept in. "You again," Kaarst said. He didn't bother to look. The robed man had been increasingly present ever since they made landfall in Vonku. Kaarst wasn't quite sure where the man disappeared to, or reappeared from, but he had given up any such lines of questioning long ago.

"How goes the siege, Admiral?" the stranger asked.

"Slowly. Do you perchance have any more of that powder that gives the cannons their bite?"

The robed man shook his head. "You had but one chance with my gift, Admiral, and you squandered it."

Sooner or later, this man needed to die. For one thing, he was too insolent for Kaarst's tastes—it had been bad enough when the man treated himself as Kaarst's equal, but of late he carried himself as a *superior*, and such a slight did not go unnoticed. For another, the man was quite obviously dangerous, and while he did not present an immediate threat, Kaarst could not let him become one. He had already seen enough of the man's skills to know he could not directly overpower him, so he bided his time, but whether it were on the morrow or in a month, this man's fate was sealed.

"Surely there must be some way to weaken these walls and allow ourselves in," the admiral said.

"Oh, there is, I assure you." The robed man sat on a stool. "In spite of losing my cannons, you've done well, and your path to victory is shorter than you think. At the end of the week, the Legion intends to collapse their walls to lure you in. When that happens, I suggest you throw your full might against them."

"And be drawn into their trap? I think not."

"It's only a trap if you don't have the numbers for it."

Kaarst spat. "I *don't*. I would need at least four times our number to make such an endeavor feasible."

Something rustled, and it took Kaarst a moment to realize the robed man was laughing. "You shall have those numbers, Admiral. You might have squandered my gift of cannons, but as it happens, I have a new gift for you."

"Is there an army here I don't know about?"

"As a matter of fact, yes."

Kaarst turned sharply to look at him. "Where?"

The robed man stood. "Ready the assault upon Aras's move, Admiral, and I will take care of the rest."

As the man left the tent, Kaarst yearned to tear the robe away and see the man's face, just once, but he restrained himself. When the robed man's head was upon a pike next to Captain Yastlin's, and Aras's head next to both, Kaarst would have all the time he needed to gaze upon their features.

* * *

He left the camp, smoke billowing around him. None of the corsairs saw him. Even those who might have walked into the tent when he was speaking to Kaarst would have seen only their Admiral, raging at empty air. A few pirates stirred with unease, and one who was recovering from his injuries instead took a turn for the worse, breathing his last breath—this man *did* see something, the hint of a dark, cold silhouette before he died—but no other trace remained of the robed stranger's presence.

He hadn't always possessed the talent of remaining unseen, but he'd grown much stronger since things changed. He could do things he'd never done before, and at times the power grew intoxicating.

Still, to the task at hand.

He climbed a rise in a street, looking over the city of Vonku and facing west. Uklith's puppet had reached the City and triggered the reservoir. That was the signal for the robed man and for the servants in the North. Uklith's plan had many hooks in it, and they all needed to be set at once for the Demon-Lord to obtain what he desired.

The man knew Kaarst was planning on killing him, which was a shame. He'd have been content to leave the corsair admiral in peace, ruling over what remained of Alcatune, but now he would need to end the other's life when the time came. He doubted that Aras had any inkling of what lay under his city, just as Ladu had little knowledge of what awaited him in the North. In the west, Matthias had drawn close to his destination, and the timing was perfect. The Warrior would enter the city just as Kaarst launched his assault upon Vonku. In the North, the nobleman would do his part, encouraged by Jeb if necessary. It was best to have thinking minds behind Uklith's plans when possible, but in a pinch those without sentience could fill the crucial gap.

The robed man opened his mouth wide, breathing in the night air, steeling himself for the upcoming conflict. *Three points of a triangle, standing by.* When the fourth point came into play, that would be the end of it. *On that day, all the world goes dark.*

29

Ladu hid in the shadows, Tavin beside him, watching a group of undead shambling past their hiding spot. Endar Varuc drew more allies to him with each passing day, and the woodsman Jeb walked at the front of this particular group of newcomers, leading them in from outside the borders of the city. Ladu kept as still as possible, employing a slow rhythm of inhalation and exhalation to keep the sound of his breathing muted. While the average undead seemed to possess little, if any, self-awareness, they nonetheless responded with sharp aggression toward any being in their environment other than those sworn to the Demon-Lord.

The creatures walked with singular purpose toward the palace several blocks away. Groups had come and gone from the palace multiple times over the past week, entering and exiting surrounding buildings in a pattern that suggested a methodical search. Initially, Ladu had assumed the undead were rounding up individuals from hiding—and they'd certainly done so, Endar Varuc having hanged several captured citizens only the day before yesterday— but he now suspected they had intentions beyond simply clearing the streets. More than once, he'd seen undead returning to areas previously searched, suggesting they had some goal other than finding escaped refugees. Vinsor's shop was among the places the searchers periodically returned to, and in this regard Ladu and the Frontier Patrol had been fortunate that the undead lacked the acuity of a normally-functioning individual. Had Endar searched the shop, he would have thought to look for hidden entrances and likely have discovered the trapdoor to the cellar. Undead operated at a more basic level, without the intellectual capacity to consider looking under a rug.

After Vinsor's place had been searched a few times, Ladu had considered vacating it, but there seemed to be little rhyme or reason that governed where the undead went. Besides, Vinsor's shop had the advantage of being designed to conceal soldiers. The company had separated into two groups, one staying at Vinsor's, the other relocating to a blacksmith's forge on another street. Ladu and Tavin had remained in place, while Raisha and Faldon led the group at the forge. Should one of their companies be discovered and overrun, continuity of command would be maintained through with the others.

Beside Ladu, Tavin let out a sigh after the last of the undead disappeared around the corner. "What do you think?"

"They're looking for something," Ladu said.

"Something other than *you*?"

That much, Ladu supposed, was obvious. Endar wanted the emperor hanging from a gibbet. "If they were only looking for us, Endar would send search parties outside the city, too. For all he knows, we are long gone. There is something *within* the city he wants, and I would surely like to know what it is."

Tavin nodded. "It's time we got going, your majesty." He slipped away, Ladu behind him. They kept low as they moved through the streets, alternating between one of them advancing a block ahead before turning to cover the other as he caught up. By and large Galdon remained empty, but they could not be too careful as they returned to the relative safety of their hiding place.

Prudence proved its worth, too, when Ladu rounded the corner and found himself facing an unfamiliar man. The stranger did not move with the gait of the undead, but Ladu nonetheless seized him upon sight. He couldn't allow the man to let out a cry of surprise, even unintentionally, and alert others to their presence. Ladu pulled the citizen in close, one hand clamped over the man's mouth, and pressed a finger to his lips.

In response, the man hissed. He bit Ladu's palm. Grimacing, Ladu lost his grip, and his captive tore away from him. Spinning around to face Ladu, the man's eyes went wide in surprise as he recognized the emperor.

"You!" The word came out low and quiet, but there was no denying the aggression his voice. Drawing a dagger, the man leapt toward Ladu, who met the attack head-on, his own blade out as he turned the assailant's dagger away.

In a flash, Tavin tackled the man from the side, bearing him to the pavement. The man spat and writhed, elbowing Tavin in the stomach and trying to wriggle free, but by that time Ladu had closed in. He brought the hilt of his sword down upon the back of the man's skull, knocking him unconscious.

Ladu and Tavin looked at the man and exchanged a wordless glance. They'd just been dealt an unexpected stroke of fortune, for they now had a prisoner. Working together, they held the man between them, the tips of his boots dragging on the pavement. Ladu wondered at the stranger's display of intelligence—it was higher than that of the undead, but he had clearly moved in a manic fashion, as if possessed. *So, it appears we have those who, like Endar, remain fully competent, as well as the undead, but what of these, the crazed folk that exist somewhere in between?*

Outside Vinsor's shop, Ladu stopped and looked toward the top floor of the building diagonal to theirs. He made a signal with two fingers and they entered the shop quickly, careful not to spend too much time exposed. Inside, he and Tavin lowered the unconscious prisoner to the floor.

"Shall we send for Raisha and Faldon?" Tavin asked.

Ladu nodded. This was important enough to risk exposure. Moments later, the door to Vinsor's shop opened and Wayne slipped inside, having left his post in the other building at Ladu's signal. "Your majesty?"

"Go across town to retrieve Lady Varuc and Captain Kule," Ladu said. "We'll be questioning this man below."

Wayne gave a curt salute. "I will make haste, your majesty." After a cursory glance outside to ensure no threats had appeared, he left the shop as quickly as he had arrived, disappearing into the shadows of the adjoining buildings.

"All right," Ladu said. "Let's go."

They lifted the trapdoor and took their prisoner downstairs into the underground chamber, which was dimly lit by a set of oil lamps. Upon the trio's arrival, the others in the chamber made space, pulling back from the entrance. At the sight of the prisoner hanging between Ladu and Tavin, they brought forward chair to seat the man. Ladu and Tavin sat the man upright on the chair, binding his hands behind his back and lacing his ankles together.

"He doesn't appear undead, your majesty," one of the elions said.

"No," Ladu agreed, "he is something else entirely."

The man remained unconscious on the chair, head slumped against his chest. Ladu let him sit that way for several minutes, trying to assess if he knew this man from anywhere. He did not, he decided, but another elion soldier spoke up.

"I know this man. He worked in the market, but we had to revoke his seller's license on account of swindling customers. Half the coin he paid turned out to be fake; it hadn't been properly marked."

So he *was* a citizen of Galdon. That ruled out one theory Ladu had begun to form, which was that these strangers came from somewhere outside the city. He took a swig of water, then splashed some against the prisoner's face. The man twitched, eyes blinking. After a few moments of disorientation, he snapped into wakefulness, head coming upright as he took in his surroundings. He attempted to rise, seemed to realize that his hands and feet were bound, and lashed against the restraints, jerking with wild eyes and manic gestures. Flecks of foam appeared at the corners of his lips, reminding Ladu of a rabid dog.

"You will all die," the prisoner said, looking around the room at the soldiers. "We've prepared for this. You may fight for a time, but it will be futile in the end."

"*Everyone* dies," Faldon replied with a grunt. "No changing that, last I checked."

The man let out a high-pitched laugh. "Play with words if you wish. After Uklith has taken your eyeballs and removed your tongue, you will beg for him to end your life."

Ladu allowed him to rage for a few more minutes, and when the man's energy was spent and he was hanging limply from his bonds, the emperor took a step closer. "What's your name?"

"It doesn't matter anymore. Nothing matters anymore, with the advent of the Demon-Lord."

"Perhaps, but he is out west, and you are down here."

The prisoner smiled. "Is that what you think, emperor?"

"Thank you for the information."

The smile faltered. Still, Ladu didn't like what the prisoner's statement boded. *Uklith is nearer than ever.* The trapdoor above their heads scraped open once more, and Ladu's hand instinctively went to the sword at his belt, but it was only Faldon, descending the ladder with typical elion nimbleness, Raisha close behind him.

Upon seeing the newcomers, the prisoner bubbled with laughter. "Lady Varuc! What a pleasure to see you. Your brother told us to send you his regards. He has a special fate in mind for you. A pity you did not choose the winning side."

Wayne came down the ladder last, closing the trapdoor above him. Raisha ignored the prisoner's taunt and instead turned toward Ladu. "This presents an interesting opportunity, your majesty."

Ladu nodded his assent. "Give us your name, stranger."

The man shook his head, still caught in the throes of laughter. "I answer to none but the Demon-Lord, Ladu Jovun IV. The darkness is upon us, and you can do naught to avert it. I urge you, swear your fealty while you still have a chance to earn my master's gratitude."

"It seems to me that you answer to my brother as well as to the Demon-Lord," Raisha said. "Tell us what you know of Endar's plans."

"You could have joined Endar, did you know that, Lady Varuc? He was tired of being in your shadow, of being the lesser, of being the fool. Whatever happens to you, know that you brought it upon yourself."

Raisha's eyes grew hard. "Aye, Endar always *was* a fool. Does he really think Uklith will permit him more than a temporary status? The Demon-Lord is using him, just as he is using you, to achieve an end. When that end is met, you will find yourselves suffering the same fate as the rest of us."

The prisoner giggled. "Perhaps—but perhaps not, and either way, your end *will* come first. If that means it buys the rest of us no more than a few days, I will still take them, Lord Varuc."

"What is Endar doing in the city?" Ladu asked.

"Occupying it. Preserving it in the name of Uklith. Can't you see as much?"

"No. He is doing *more* than that. What are the patrols? What are they searching for?"

The man fell silent, mouth growing tight, and Ladu knew he was close to something. He pressed harder. "Uklith needs Endar to find something in the city. What is it?"

Faldon drew a knife and squatted before the man. He looked into the prisoner's eyes, testing the blade's edge against his thumb. Ladu allowed the moment to linger and then joined Faldon, crouching to face level with the prisoner. "What did he promise you that made you swear allegiance?"

The man spat, and it took all of Ladu's resolve not to flinch away from the spittle that landed on his face. "One does not *barter* with the Demon-Lord," the prisoner said. "His coming is inevitable. Better to be on his side than the losing one. The faith you have placed in Matthias is misguided. Even as his party approaches the City, they are but a fraction of those who set forth. They are tired and weary, and when they arrive, Uklith will crush them like roaches under his heel. The Warrior of Light might have been a match for the Dark Lord, but he has no chance of defeating the lord of the underworld."

"What Matthias does or does not do is of little concern to me at this point." Actually, it was *quite* a bit of a concern to Ladu, but any such topic would be a digression from the more immediate knowledge he sought. "I am more concerned with the here and now, and I demand you tell me what Endar Varuc is looking for in my city."

The man's eyes grew distant, and his voice dropped to a whisper. "Three points of a triangle. North, south, west, and when the circuit closes, the gates of Agrazab shall open."

Circuit? Ladu looked to Raisha and the Kule twins, but Faldon shook his head. *He has no more idea what that means than I do. Is it a weapon of sorts?* "A triangle?" he repeated.

"North, south, and west," the prisoner replied. "And the fourth shall complete the other three."

Ladu felt a chill at the nape of his neck. At first, he thought it merely a subconscious reaction to the enigmatic way in which the prisoner spoke, but then he noticed a slight fog in front of him when he exhaled, indicating that the temperature in the cellar had lowered.

"Are we the north? Are we the first point of the triangle?"

The man licked his lips. "You are—"

A gust of air blew in, entering through the vents that existed to provide air flow to the room. The oil lamps flickered, and shadows danced across the floor. Near the base of the prisoner's chair, the darkness coalesced, changing from dark patterns on the ground into tendrils of smoke that curled upward. Ladu drew back from the dark, careful not to let it touch him, and beside him Faldon did the same.

The smoke exploded upward in a black swirl around the man. Ladu caught a glimpse of the prisoner's face, pale with terror as the clouds consumed him. From within the dark, a scream began, so horrible that Ladu took another handful of steps backward. Thankfully, the smoke remained confined to the area of the chair. Next came a ghastly snapping of bones, punctuated by shrieks that escalated with each crack. The last thing Ladu heard was a slow sucking, and then the smoke dissipated. The prisoner's body remained tied to the chair, but it was no more than a lifeless, desiccated husk.

Ladu took a step toward the chair, but Tavin held out a hand to halt him. "Stand back, your majesty."

Tavin went to the chair, one hand on the hilt of his sword. The prisoner's skin had a blackened, crisp look, as if he had been scorched by an intense fire. The elion surveyed the body in its entirety before reaching out and touching the corpse. He rubbed his fingers against the skin. "He's not actually burnt—there's no ash. It's as if all the fluids in his body drained at once."

Ladu thought on this. The undead occupying the city often had a withered, decayed appearance—unsurprising since they were literally walking corpses. This prisoner's body displayed attributes of the undead, but to an extreme level, and it raised a troubling notion in Ladu's mind. They'd always assumed the undead had risen from their graves at Uklith's command, but this man had appeared to be possessed rather than an undead, just like the attacker on the balcony and those at Kule's wedding.

What if it's not possession at all, but a transitory state? Ladu did not doubt the bulk of the forces occupying the city had indeed been awakened from their graves by Uklith, but what he saw here concerned him greatly: the transformation of living people *into* undead.

"It's the last stage," Raisha said. "Isn't it, your majesty?"

Ladu nodded. The temperature in the room returned to normal, and the chill at the base of his neck had nothing to do with cold. As he spoke, shreds of memory returned, scraps of knowledge gleaned during the first war against Zadinn and unlocked by the sequence of events he'd just observed. "It starts with someone like Endar, one who swears allegiance to Uklith but retains his or her mental faculties. After a period of time, it begins to wear on them. This man was in the second stage when we found him, still coherent, but under the sway of possession. They deteriorate, they die, and when they rise, that's when they've reached the third stage, undead corpses at the Demon-Lord's command."

Faldon looked at the withered corpse. "What's this, your majesty?"

"Undead are on borrowed time, dark magic or not, and I think this is what happens when they have been wrung dry." Ladu crouched before the prisoner. "I think we just saw the entire process, but greatly accelerated." This was another disturbing example of how much Uklith's power had increased. The Demon-Lord could raise the dead, commandeer the living, start an occupation of a city many miles to his east, and now—

Is that what you think, emperor?

"That was him, wasn't it?" Raisha said. "He was *in* here. He killed that man."

Ladu nodded. "Yes, I believe he did."

"He's free?" Wayne asked.

A long moment of silence hung in the air before Ladu replied. "No, it hasn't come to that yet. If the Demon-Lord were free, we'd have much more to contend with than a single black cloud murdering one prisoner. It *does* mean time is short, though." He drew up and gestured to Faldon and Tavin. "Let's rid ourselves of this corpse."

They loosed the man from his bindings. His skin felt leathery, the bones rigid. Ladu thought of Tim and the group making their way across the desert, and imagined this was what a body would look like if it had lain under the scorching sun for a week.

Ladu and Raisha followed the elions carrying the dead prisoner back up through the trapdoor and into Vinsor's shop. While it might have been an unnecessary risk to go into the streets simply to dispose of a body, Ladu did not want anything touched by Uklith in their hiding place. For all he knew the Demon-Lord was watching them through the corpse's eyes.

Wayne cleared the way, acting as point. They moved six blocks south before dragging the body into an abandoned baker's shop and leaving it behind the counter. Ladu wondered how many more like this man were in the city. All else being equal, the primary advantage undead had was in numbers. They weren't like malichons, who had been vicious and intelligent, but they had enough force to overrun an enemy en masse. The idea of groups of undead answering to more intelligent patrol leaders presented a greater threat. It would only be a matter of time before a patrol leader chose to enter Vinsor's shop and conduct a more thorough search than before.

They left the baker's shop, sticking to the shadows when they could. Through observation over the past few days, they'd gradually learned the intervals at which the patrols emerged, and Ladu calculated they had perhaps an hour before the next set of patrols went out.

"Your majesty," Tavin said as they moved, "What do you suppose he meant by the three points of the triangle?"

Ladu had been considering this. *North, south, and west ... and the fourth shall complete the other three...*

"I think it's obvious," Raisha said. She counted off on her fingers. "Galdon. Vonku. Agrazab."

And when the circuit is closed, the gates of Agrazab shall open...

"Do we have any way of knowing what's happening in the other two places?" Wayne asked.

"No," Ladu replied. "Matthias and Harggra split the focusing reservoirs between them." As time passed, Ladu had begun to suspect that the corsair assault on Vonku was not related in any way to what they faced here. The South had never played into the Demon-Lord's previous designs. Ladu had, apparently, been wrong. He believed that Raisha's statement regarding the three cities was correct. *Vonku is involved in all of this, after all.*

"But what's the fourth point?" Wayne asked. "Wouldn't it be the east?"

It was the obvious conclusion, but they knew precious little of the Rendrivin Ocean, and furthermore, if the fourth point were the east, Ladu didn't know why the prisoner wouldn't have said so outright. He'd already identified the other three directions.

Raisha's face was grave. "Is it a focusing reservoir, your majesty?"

"I've been wondering the same, my lady. They found the book within the Erdrar Forest, and it stands to reason Zadinn left another weapon behind outside the Deathlands."

"If that's the case," Faldon said, "It becomes imperative we impede them, in spite of the fact that we have few resources for doing so. I don't know that we can maintain our defenses if they indeed discover a weapon."

"Yes and no," Ladu replied. They had drawn within the last block of Vinsor's shop. "We've already noted the undead possess little initiative of their own. The man we discovered this afternoon was likely a patrol leader, but even he was under Uklith's influence to a heavy extent. To this point, there is but one person in this city who, while sworn to the Demon-Lord, appears to be in complete command of himself."

"Endar," Raisha said.

"Yes. When we fought the sarchons in the Northern Mountains, Matthias encountered their queen. His killing her is what allowed the rest of us to escape. I wonder if Endar is the link that tethers Uklith to this area, and I wonder how strong the undead would be without him."

"You are suggesting an assassination?" Raisha asked. He detected the undercurrent of a waver in her voice, though she hid it well.

Ladu reminded himself that Endar was still her *brother.* "There are too few of us to engage directly with the undead, but if we remove their leader, they may fall. We know that when the undead conduct patrols, they only leave a minimal guard in the palace. It would be the best time to strike." He paused. He had already considered attacking early on but opted to wait and assess the situation further. With the new information from the prisoner, time was of the essence. "It may not be necessary to kill, only incapacitate..."

Raisha cut him off. "Thank you for your delicate words, your majesty, but spare me euphemisms."

"I will not do this without your leave, Lady Varuc. Do I have it?" *And if she says no?* But she wouldn't.

After a long silence, she affirmed his instincts. "We do what we must, Ladu."

We go by our first names, now. Interesting. "Captains?" Ladu looked at the Kule brothers. "Do you agree?"

The elions exchanged glances. "It's risky, your majesty," Faldon eventually said, "but we're walking a razor's edge regardless. It's risky simply hiding out here."

"Besides, we're the Frontier Patrol," Tavin added. "When in doubt, we take the battle to the enemy."

I guess the Jovun dynasty does participate in assassinations. My father would be disappointed.

"You're smiling, your majesty," Raisha said.

Not a fitting reaction to the seriousness of the situation, I suppose. Still, Ladu couldn't deny that he would enjoy an opportunity for some retribution.

"How will we get into the palace?" Raisha prodded.

Ladu's smile got bigger. "About that..."

30

*C*ommand an army, and those you lead will die.

Boblin had the watch. Two days had passed since they exited the gorge in the wake of the krevur attack. During that time, Eklan led them northwest through the Wastelands, thankfully without further incident, and now Boblin sat at the edge of their camp beneath the shade of a lean-to. He scanned the hot, dry landscape, Jend Argul's words echoing in his thoughts.

Some will be those whose names you barely know, and others will be lifelong comrades. The Maker seems to care little about who returns from one battlefield to the next.

Two were gone, Hugo and Hanqar, one a veteran, the other a recruit. Boblin continued his vigil, the silence of the Western Desert settling upon him.

How did you cope with it?

I resigned.

Boblin uncorked his waterskin and took a sip, facing west over the jagged Wastelands. In spite of everything, the Western Desert possessed a sense of splendor, so long as one ignored the fact that it remained intent on killing anyone who set foot in it. Behind Boblin, his fellow elions slept in their tents. As soldiers, they placed implicit trust in him, their battlefield commander. It had been that way for Boblin when he enlisted, a faith rarely spoken of outright, but which lingered at the back of one's mind through engagements small and large, in the thick of battle and during long watches at night. At the Fort of Pellen, Boblin knew from the start that the duties before him were simple: *hone your skills, keep your wits about you, and follow orders.*

The third bit kept coming back to him: *and follow orders.* A soldier took responsibility for completing an assigned task, and for doing so to the best of his or her ability, but as to whether that task fit into a larger plan—well, that was the *commander's* duty. When soldiers put their lives on the line, they did so trusting that the commands placing them into that situation meant something. When Jend Argul had ordered the Frontier Patrol to charge headlong into the malichon army during the Battle of the Deathlands, Boblin hadn't worried about whether the Commander's battlefield tactic was sound. It was *Jend's* plan, and that had been enough. Those who died on the slopes of the Deathlands did so knowing their deaths might buy the others enough time for victory. Could Boblin say the same for Hugo and Hanqar? Had they died knowing their deaths meant something, that they advanced a greater plan or purpose? The truth was, Boblin and Tim *had* no plan other than to find Agrazab, and as for what would happen from there, nobody knew. Seen in that light, the elions' sacrifices might well have served no cause, and the very thought made Boblin feel physically ill.

"Commander Kule?"

Jend's gravelly voice brought Boblin out of his thoughts. He made way for the older elion to sit beside him. Jend drew his sword, placing it across his knees and bracing his back against the lean-to.

"Jend." When Boblin assumed command eighteen months ago, he had once addressed Jend using his former title of *Commander*, and the elion had taken him aside.

Sir, Jend had asked, *May I speak freely?*

You're always welcome to speak freely, Commander.

No! Jend said. *With respect, sir, I am* not. *You command me, not the other way around. If the soldiers observe you deferring to me, they will transfer their respect elsewhere. You lead the Frontier Patrol and you must act it. The title of Commander is yours alone. If the emperor bowed to Tim Matthias, whom would the citizens truly swear their allegiance to? Whom would they trust? It is the same for you and me, Commander Kule. It may seem a minor thing, but to those in the rank and file, it matters a great deal.*

Beside him, Jend settled into place. "How goes the watch, sir?"

"Quiet. Ninety-nine of every hundred watches result in nothing more than boredom."

"Commander Virgil once pointed out there is a fine line between vigilance and paranoia."

Virgil had been Commander before Jend. "'The difference,'" Boblin quoted the late elion's words, "'is that those who are vigilant can react.'"

Jend grunted. "Exactly."

"It's what the Patrol always stood for, right? Vigilance. We anticipate threats when none may come, knowing that *if* they do, we are ready for it." Boblin paused. "At the moment, though, I feel I understand standing watch much better than leadership. Watching is simple. Direct."

"Might I speak freely once more, sir?"

"Proceed."

"Did you *expect* the command to be easy when you assumed it? Did you think leading soldiers was nothing more than a simple variation upon standing watch?"

"I—no, I did not expect it to be easy."

"I remember when I lost my first soldier. I felt much as you did, until Pellen Yuzhar took me to task and told me to stop pitying myself. With all respect, sir, such words made me a stronger commander in the long run."

The comment stung, but it was also true. Boblin had never made a business of lying to himself, and he wasn't about to start. "Point taken, soldier." He took another sip of water. "A question for you. How often did you have a plan?"

"Half the time, Commander, the only *plan* I ever had was for us to live just one more day. Even when I did have a plan—such as using a force of two thousand as bait to divert the malichons from Matthias—it carried its risks. The Patrol trusted me to do right by them, and I'll stand accountable for that, but when we succeeded, it wasn't because they trusted me. It was because *I* trusted *them*."

"When we reach Agrazab—"

"—we'll do what we need to do when the time comes around. Every one of us might die, but as far as planning goes, sometimes that's as good as it gets, sir."

Simple. Direct. Perhaps no different than standing watch. "One more thing, Jend. Take a drink of water. You'll need it."

Jend accepted the waterskin from Boblin and took a sip. "Sir?"

Boblin pointed. "Fifty body-raisers. In the sun."

Jend choked on the water—not in surprise, but in mirth. "Aye, sir." He wiped his lips, stood, and walked out onto the floor of the Wastelands. Beneath the scorching sun, he dropped onto his hands and began the repetitions.

"You're making Jend do body-raisers?"

Boblin turned at Celia's voice. She had come to relieve him of watch, and she stood looking from Boblin to Jend with an expression of curiosity on her face.

"Yes."

After a second, she turned to him. "In the sun? *Why?*"

"Because I'm the Commander, and because I said so."

Jend must have heard him, because as Boblin retired to his tent, he heard the elion's booming laughter echo across the camp.

* * *

The following evening, they entered Asheti's Dunes while riding beneath the night sky. Around them, the sharp rock of the Wastelands transitioned to the gentler rise and fall of dunes, and their progress slowed as the surer footing of stony ground gave way to shifting sands. Occasionally, Tim found evidence of the elion who had come this way before them—a footprint here, a scuffed trail there, the signs few and far between, and only in places the wind hadn't touched. At one point, Tim wondered if they might discover the elion's body—and such a blessing it would be to stop the threat before it ever reached Agrazab's gates—but no such event transpired. Besides, even if the elion *had* died, Uklith's manipulation of the undead meant he could have manipulated his servant's lifeless body forward, shambling toward its inevitable destination. Tim looked up to the sky, seeing it full of stars. The guardians of Agrazab looked upon this very sky before the rift to the underworld opened, and Tim's only assurance that Uklith remained trapped was that no rift had reappeared.

Beside him, Eklan spoke. "The moon's almost full. We're getting close, Matthias."

Tim saw the subtle way the big man's body tensed. Were Tim to hold the Lifesource, he was sure he would sense a deep, restless fear hidden beneath Eklan's hulking exterior. Though the man showed few outward indications of unease, Tim could nonetheless tell Eklan's fear increased the closer they drew to the City. He suspected Eklan felt as Tim would feel if he were asked to return to Zadinn's throne room and face the Dark Lord one more time.

"Thank you," Tim said quietly. "For leading us to the City."

Eklan grunted. "I make it that obvious?"

"No, but we've each been to Malath in our own way. It takes one to recognize one."

"Well, now we're going to Malath together." Eklan guided his mount around a stunted bush. "It's a bit late for thanks, Matthias, and it's also irrelevant. Neither of us wants to be here, but it's the job that has to be done. I could thank you for saving my life—twice—but those are simply the situations we've found ourselves in."

The situations we've found ourselves in. Tim had thought about this to no small extent over the past several weeks. It harkened back to something Zadinn Kanas had said when they faced each other before their duel. *You are a pawn, Warrior, a pawn on a chessboard of the cosmos.* In retrospect, everything that led to Tim and Zadinn's final confrontation had been due to events that forced Tim down a singular path. Because the malichons invaded his home, he discovered the North. Because he had been trapped in the North, they sought the Fort of Pellen. Because the Fort of Pellen fell, they fled toward the Mountains—and so forth.

Has anything I've done been truly of my free will? Even now, Tim only traveled toward the Western Desert because Uklith's servant had absorbed power that could set the Demon-Lord free, and Eklan only traveled because he'd decided he would rather return to Agrazab than have it come to him. More than once, Nazgar of the Kyrlod claimed that men's ability to make their own choices was the most precious gift the Maker had granted them, but how much of what transpired in the last two years had been Tim's choice, and how much had been the Maker's machinations?

Both you and I have been manipulated, Zadinn had said. *You were born, imbued with powers you barely understand, and then granted the mantle of the Warrior. But this is a joke and a lie, a crown of false gold. If you win, it will only be the beginning of a long and arduous task with neither thanks nor reward. Before long, a new threat will rise, and you will need to overcome it or die. And if you win that battle, still another danger will arrive, and another after that, on and on without end, as you fight wars for an omnipotent being with little sense of mercy or gratitude, on your way down a long road with little comfort at its finish.*

Zadinn had been right about one thing: *before long, a new threat will rise.* Well, the threat *had* risen, and Tim was riding out to meet it. If he won this battle, would there just be another after this? Would it ever end?

"I suspect the City will kill us all, Matthias," Eklan said. "We've never attempted something this futile before. Did you know we named these dunes after another of my party? After the spider killed Mygon, after we'd been fighting krevurs for days, Asheti's mind gave out. He saw this place and began crying, 'the dunes, the dunes!' He walked off and we never saw him again. In retrospect, perhaps he wasn't mad. Perhaps he was the sanest of all and left while he could."

"If this is so futile, why are you here?"

"If I'm going out, Matthias, I'd rather it be on my terms. What of you? Would you say it's futile?"

"It might be."

"Then why are *you* here?"

"Because it's the right thing to do."

Eklan let gave a mirthless laugh. "You are beyond naïve, Matthias, but I suppose there are worse things for a man to be. Besides, what do I know? Maybe that's what got you through the last time around. Still, I'll say this." He clapped Tim on the shoulder. "If I *do* go down fighting, I'd like it to be beside someone like you."

They made camp as dawn rose in the sky. The task had become routine: establish the perimeter, build tents, make a meager meal, and station a watch. As always, Tim welcomed the opportunity to climb down from his horse and move his saddle-sore limbs, but with Agrazab's figurative shadow looming before them, his thoughts returned to one of Eklan's earlier questions: *What do you intend to do about it?*

He'd faced Zadinn Kanas and found a way to succeed, but the challenge of Agrazab—of *Uklith*—dwarfed that of Tim's previous encounter with the Dark Lord. However powerful Zadinn might have been, he had been a man. But Uklith was more. He was the ruler of the underworld, the Maker's antithesis, a being older than time. In short, Tim was mortal, and Uklith was not.

So how does a man defeat a god? Eklan might be correct. This task could be the most futile goal a band of humans have ever set themselves upon, as useless as nine ants setting themselves against a human.

Tim had thought on this before, and as they drew nearer to the city, the question of how he might defeat the Demon-Lord grew more pressing than ever. The fact that Tim had not risked touching the Lifesource ever since their first encounter with the krevurs further exacerbated the problem. His ability to practice with the magic was critical to keeping his skills sharp and ready. Strength in the Lifesource came in much the same way as strength of the body; disuse weakened one's abilities. This assumed Tim could grasp the Lifesource once they entered Agrazab. He was counting on Uklith's presence to be so strong that it would obscure Tim, just as his presence had shielded Nazgar in the Mountains, but he simply did not know for sure.

In the end, Tim surmised, better to plan that upon reaching Agrazab, he would find the elion and do battle with *him* instead. At this prospect, Tim felt more optimistic. The elion had probably already reached the City, but the fact that Uklith was not yet free meant they must be waiting for something. The amount of power required to release the Demon-Lord from his prison would be incredible—even when Zadinn and Uklith joined forces, they had barely been able to create a crack between this world and Malath, and Tim doubted the elion's power exceeded Zadinn's. Perhaps the elion needed time to prepare—maybe a ritual of sorts?—and their very best strategy was to simply stop him.

The unknown variable remained in how much the City would set itself against them, and if the tales Eklan related were any indication, Agrazab had plenty of unpleasant surprises in store for the travelers. Whether they came into direct conflict with Uklith or not, they would still be close to his power, and Tim did not doubt the Demon-Lord would throw as many obstacles as he could against them. There were a lot of bodies buried in Agrazab, and it wasn't too much of a stretch to imagine they'd be fighting undead before long. *And if Uklith has more Assassins at the ready…*

Tim had been able to defeat two, but that victory had been made easier because he faced them separately—and he had ambushed one. Were they to face a whole host of Assassins in Agrazab—ones directing undead—well, they'd be in for a very difficult battle.

Outside his tent, he unbuckled his sword and held it before him. His mind went back to when he first found the weapon, after a malichon threw him against a glass case in the Floor of History at the Fort of Pellen. Tim had seized the sword because it was the only weapon available to him at the time, and— like everything else he'd reflected upon earlier this evening—he'd simply been reacting to the situation at hand. He looked at the green pommel stone, thinking of how it felt when he imbued the sword with the Lifesource, the blade an extension of himself and of his powers. He closed his eye, snapping into the first form Daniel had shown him, back when he was twelve years old.

If one good thing had come of abstaining from the Lifesource, it had been the realization that he should practice his blade forms as often without the power as with it. It was good to bring the sword back to the fundamentals he had always known. The practice felt clean and wholesome, because in some ways the Lifesource had become a handicap for Tim, and he was glad to be learning again without it. He'd also had Boblin begin teaching him ailar once more. These days, Boblin had mastered the art to the extent that he could best most soldiers other than Jend. Ailar had evolved over the years, but Tim found it interesting that it had started as a means of self-defense against an opponent wielding the Lifesource. It required the practitioner to operate in complete harmony with the world around him—apparently, to the extent of being able to read the micro-expressions and subtleties that indicated where an Advocate would strike next.

Tim snapped into the next sword form, eyes still closed, melding his training from Daniel with the techniques Boblin had shown him. He focused on his breath, on the sensation of the sword in his hands, feeling the balls of his feet upon the ground, using the tension in his muscles to flow from one stance into the next. He moved faster and faster, a sheen of sweat forming on his skin.

"Where did you learn the sword, Matthias?"

Sword over his head in a diagonal attack maneuver, Tim opened his eyes. Bria stood near his lean-to. He relaxed, lowering the blade so that the tip was pointed toward the ground.

"I don't think I ever asked you," she added.

"Daniel. My father."

She looked him up and down, and though her jaw was set as tight as ever, he now saw a softness in her eyes. "He must have been very good."

"He was."

She held out her hand. "May I?"

Tim hesitated, one hand still on the hilt of his sword. Since picking up the blade on the Floor of History, he did not recall anyone else handling it. It wasn't as if Tim would have disallowed someone from doing so, it had just... never happened. The blade had been through much with him: the encounter with the Hunter in the Korlan Forest, the vrawl's attack on the elion camp, the sarchons in the Mountains, the final clash with Zadinn Kanas.

Bria caught his gaze and averted her eyes. "Never mind. I shouldn't have asked."

"No." Tim held the sword toward her, hilt first. "It's fine."

This time she was the one who hesitated, but after a glance, she took it from him. Her fingers brushed against his. "Good balance," she said, hefting the blade. After a moment, she executed a near-perfect quarter turn, the blade snapping so fast that Tim felt a brush of air past his scalp.

"Who taught you?"

"Who do you think? Eklan." She mirrored the stances Tim had practiced, her form precise, her margin of error thin.

"He says we're getting close," Tim said.

Bria nodded, returning to a holding position. "I can feel it from him—he's more afraid than ever, but Malath will freeze over before he shows it."

"There's nothing wrong with being afraid."

"No, there isn't." She returned the sword to him, their fingers brushing once more as the hilt passed hands. "What do you plan to do when we get there, Matthias?"

How does a man defeat a god? "We'll ride into the city and see what's there. As to what happens after that, well…we'll take it as it comes."

She arched an eyebrow. "I would suggest a more concrete strategy, Matthias."

"Which would be…"

"We kill Uklith."

He smiled at her dry tone, but then sobered. "Eklan thinks we'll all die there. Do you think he's right?"

She paused, giving it serious consideration. "No."

"Why not?"

"Because I don't intend to let that happen. Neither, I suspect, do you."

"No," he agreed. "I don't."

* * *

During their second night on the dunes, they travelled beneath a starry sky. The sandy mounds stretched far and wide in every direction, a seemingly infinite field of sand and dust. Motes floated on the air every time the wind rose. The company rested more often than usual, and not just because the going was tough. An unspoken dread had begun to build in the group, and Tim suspected Uklith's encroaching influence. The Demon-Lord knew they were close and was actively working to wear the travelers down before they stood upon his doorstep.

Near midnight, they arrived at an oasis, the second one they'd come across on their journey, many leagues distant from the one where the krevurs attacked. Tim supposed presence of an oasis here was unsurprising, for those who had settled Agrazab would have wanted to be close to water. He expected to see more water the nearer they came to the city. They took their rest, replenished their water skins, and set out once more.

On the third night, the temperature fluctuated between an unnatural cold and a searing heat, reminding Tim of the juxtaposition between the former Deathlands and the North, where the temperature had behaved in a similarly erratic fashion. As they rode onward, tempers grew thin, disputes becoming more heated than normal, until everyone seemed to realize this was yet another of Uklith's machinations and henceforth guarded their emotions more closely. They passed an enormous shell from a creature that might have been a giant centipede, causing Tim to shudder at the thought of meeting something so threatening in the open, with its numerous legs and searching mandibles. A cluster of human skulls lay at the husk's base, leaving Tim to wonder who the victims had been. When the fingers of dawn reached into the sky, few words were spoken, and they passed the day at camp in still trepidation.

On the fourth night on the dunes, they came within sight of Agrazab. The city's walls loomed on the horizon, blacker than the surrounding landscape, laid out in a rough square with four squat towers at its corners. Tim had expected a sensation of unbridled evil to emanate from the place, but instead he found that Agrazab evoked much subtler feelings—a trace of unease here, the impression of being watched there, a loss of one's appetite and an urge to submit to the inevitable. Agrazab's was an evil that slept, but with one eye open. They stopped short of their destination, for much remained of the night, and they had agreed not to enter Agrazab in the dark. They decided to wait out the night outside the city, and move forward at sunrise, rather than walk Agrazab's streets in the shadows.

Tim stood facing the city as the group made camp, attempting to ascertain as much information as possible about Agrazab before they entered it. In truth, he could tell very little by observation alone, as its walls remained squat, square, and unadorned. Still unwilling to touch the Lifesource, he relied on the prompting of his instincts, muddled though they might be from the mixture of emotions Uklith's presence was undoubtedly forcing upon on them. The sound of soft footsteps against the sand caused him to turn as Boblin approached.

"Looks like we made it," Boblin said as they faced Agrazab's walls together.

"We'll go in at first light," Tim said. "Assess the lay of the streets, establish a forward presence."

"Do you know where Uklith is?"

"Yes, I saw the palace in my vision. It's in the center of the city. We need to find the elion as quickly as possible. That's the best way to end this. If we can't..."

Boblin shrugged. "When in doubt, launch an assault."

"Works for me."

Boblin handed Tim a flask. "Here. Help yourself."

"We should conserve water."

"It's not water."

"Ah." Tim took a swig. Whatever it was, it burned on the way down. "Where in Malath did you get that?"

"Eklan calls it his battle tonic, and I'm growing quite fond of it."

Tim sniffed the contents, and, gauging that a sip went a long way with this stuff, took another taste. He could already feel himself relaxing.

"You know," Boblin continued, "some of the texts we read at the Fort claimed the borders of the world were out this way. They said you'd get far enough and then everything came to a complete stop."

"That might be preferable to what we're looking at here."

"Do you figure you'll be able to use the Lifesource in there?"

"Whether I can or can't, I'm surely giving it a go if it gets bad enough. We'll probably reach a point where I've got nothing to lose by trying."

Boblin produced a second flask, uncorking the cap and tipping it to his lips. "By, the Maker, that's some good stuff."

"How are the elions holding up?"

"We'll manage. You go in there, do what you need to do. We've got your back. That's the way it's always been, and that's the way it'll always be." Boblin held his flask up. "Side by side until the end, right?"

"Aye," Tim clinked his flask against Boblin's. "Until the end."

31

They entered Agrazab as the sun rose, bloodred fingers of dawn stretching over the sky from the east. Before them, the once-massive gates of the City of Darkness stood ajar, held open by drifts of sand that had piled up over time. Tim imagined the malichon army all those years ago, streaming out of these gates as they prepared to wage war upon the hapless empire of the North. He saw traces of footsteps in the trail of sand in front of the group, fresh and not yet blotted out, and knew their quarry was close.

Agrazab's battlements were made of a deep, reddish stone. Tim wondered if it had been mined from the Wastelands. He touched the wall as they drew close, and when he pulled his hand back he saw a thin line of dust on his palm. The mortar between the bricks flaked off, having been subjected to endless waves of searing heat for hundreds of years. Even the doors had been made of stone, the better to withstand the elements than oak or other wood.

The gate's apex reached fifty feet high. Passing beneath it, Tim felt small indeed. Once inside the city, he saw a grid of cobblestone streets. In some places, the sands had drifted in to block entire alleys, and in other places the way remained clear. More than anything else, though, Agrazab exuded a sense of abandonment. At the height of its population, this city had been as large as Vonku, home to tens of thousands of people, and to be one of only eight people—nine, if Tim counted the elion they pursued—in this enormous, empty place felt strange to say the least.

Agrazab appeared both ordinary and extraordinary. Like all cities from Vonku to Galdon, the layout of the streets was confusing to the newcomers, but would have been innately familiar to any who had lived here for their entire lives. With the inhospitable desert surrounding its exterior walls, Agrazab was a siloed world, a self-contained bubble, and during its lifetime it had grown inward rather than outward. Tim saw buildings that had been built in places the original constructors most likely hadn't intended, some structures short and others tall, though none exceeded the height of the outer walls. As new ingress and egress paths had been created to access these developing structures, the result formed a haphazard conglomeration of streets with little rhyme or reason for the traveling company. The poorer residents would have dwelt near the outer gates, the wealthier ones close to the center, and so as the companions moved inward the streets become more structured, the building design became more calculated, the sense of order more prevalent.

Tim wondered what Agrazab had been like before Uklith's coming. He knew nothing of why the original settlers had made their home here or of what had caused them to stay when more bountiful lands existed to the east. Had they even known of such? Perhaps to them, the whole world had been desert, and they had simply settled in the middle of what they knew.

Not too far in, the group came to a fountain perhaps a hundred paces in diameter, with dozens of spigots around its rim. Though long-since dry, it had no doubt once supplied fresh, plentiful water from wells deep under the city. In Agrazab, water would have been the most valuable commodity, and Tim recalled from his visions that Uklith, after his arrival, had deliberately restricted and rationed its supply to control the people, thirst being the cruelest torment of all in this arid place. At the center of the fountain stood the statue of a man with scroll in hand. Three words had been etched into the stone at its base:

ALL MUST SERVE

"I believe he was the founder," Eklan said as the group stopped before the statue. "The scroll has a list of names on it, which I take to be the city's first census."

They moved deeper into Agrazab, aided in one part by Eklan's memory, in another part by what Tim knew from the visions he'd seen in the Erdrar. The air struck Tim's lungs with hot fumes, extracting moisture from the tiniest pores in the body, reminding him why they had done most of their traveling at night. *Still better than entering this place in the dark, though.* Uklith's prison, the former palace, stood at the center of the city—Tim had rarely known a palace that didn't stand at a city center—but they did not intend to go directly there. They had to understand Agrazab first, to be ready to fight in its streets, whether against monstrosities from the desert or against creations of Uklith's dark magic.

Midway between outer and inner city, they came to a rectangular building that had the sparse, militaristic appearance of a garrison. Sure enough, when Boblin and Tim entered the base floor, they saw an assortment of weapons hanging from the walls. Boblin took an axe and hefted it. A shading of rust graced the blade's edge.

"I think this is where we should set up," Boblin said. "It was already built with defense in mind. The walls will be thick, and the rooftop should give us clear avenues of visibility into the surrounding areas. If it comes to it, we can hold this place against fairly stacked odds."

The other members of the party filtered into the garrison, save for Bria and Wurit, who had already begun walking down the adjoining streets to size up avenues of approach. Jend cleared off a table and laid out a string of currently empty birchbark tubes. With Ken beside him, the two elions produced the remaining powder they had saved since the Fertile Lands and began to fashion a new set of boomers. Though they could make many more boomers from their supplies than Tim hoped would be necessary, he was beginning to adopt Boblin's mindset that more options for blowing up enemies was better than fewer.

After a cursory glance around the interior of the building, Eklan grunted his approval and left to join his sister and Wurit in the streets. At the back of the garrison, a ladder led toward the rooftop. Boblin climbed upward, threw a trapdoor open above his head, and Tim and Celia followed.

"This will do," Celia said upon entering the open space. The roof offered an unimpeded view in all directions, with chest-high parapets that provided an excellent crossbow rest as well as shielding to crouch behind.

Tim stepped up to the parapet. Below, he saw Eklan and Bria enter a neighboring building on the opposite side of the street. They were clearing the buildings in the immediate perimeter, ensuring that they did not conceal threats such as undead. Wurit kept watch outside the door. The small man looked left and right down the street, obviously uncomfortable being alone if even for a short time. Tim didn't blame him.

"I don't think we need to debate long and hard about where the elion will be, mate," Boblin replied. "He'll be in the palace, sure as the sun's shining."

Tim knew there wasn't any use pretending otherwise. One way or another, the palace was where he would end up. He could see it from here, due east of the garrison, at the rise of a short hill. Between the company and the palace, the more elaborate inner city took up sprawl, a flow of short domes and spired roofs. The palace was nothing special, an ordinary rectangular building, not even the tallest in the city—a distinction that belonged to a columnar tower in the northwest corner—which made for an interesting contrast to the way Zadinn's citadel had dwarfed the surrounding structures in his city.

It was surreal to think of the evil that resided within such an unassuming place. "I'll go," Tim said. "The rest of you stay here and keep this as a defensible fortification to fall back to. It doesn't do to risk all of us going to the palace."

"Correct on most counts, but it also doesn't do for you to go alone. I'll cover your back, and no arguments."

"Only if you bring along a flask of the good stuff."

"Done." Boblin turned toward his wife. "Captain Kule, the command is yours."

"Aye, Commander."

Tim could see Celia wasn't entirely happy about the arrangement—he suspected she would prefer to be going with them to the palace—but the hierarchy of the command and the logic of the decision overrode any personal preferences. He looked toward the prison one more time. Even without touching the Lifesource, he could feel malice exuding from its walls. The air around the building seemed to bend inward, as if it were soaking up the surrounding shadows to make its presence darker. In the streets in front of the palace, a shimmering dust devil rose, buffeted up on a surge of air before dissipating into nothingness.

"Should be easy, right?" Tim said. "We walk in, stick a sword in the elion's heart, and head back out. Nothing to it, really."

Boblin replied without missing a beat. "Exactly. That's what I figured, too."

* * *

The elion was not, in fact, inside the palace. He *had* spent most of his time there, but now that the Warrior had entered the City, it was time for the elion to attend to the task at hand. It didn't surprise him that the company had waited until daytime to enter the city. Even the elion, favored disciple of the Demon-Lord, didn't enjoy being in Agrazab at night. The powers Uklith released into the City all those years ago, killing its many residents, had left behind a lingering residue that grew more active after nightfall. The first evening the elion spent here, he'd seen many strange sights. Apparitions had appeared from thin air—some of which were harmless, others he feared were not—while chilling screams, the ghosts of all that had passed before him, echoed off the walls. At one point he'd seen a house with rivers of red running down the sides, and he had realized that the building itself was bleeding.

The elion stood at the base of the tower in the city's northwest corner, looking at the summit two hundred feet in the air. No sign existed of the strange storm of magic that had emanated from this place several nights ago during the awakening, but he knew its effects persisted. His body still thrummed with the energy of hastening Uklith's release, pulsing through his veins with each beat of his heart, his skin simultaneously hot and cold to the touch.

A winding staircase stretched before him. The elion began to climb, one hand on the banister for support, motes of dust swirling away from each of his footfalls. A musty smell hung on the air, like that of a sepulcher recently opened to the daylight. During his ascent, the elion stopped to rest often; so much of his body had expired in serving Uklith that he could only do so much so fast. Though the elion knew his mortal form would become useless soon, Uklith had promised him eternity beyond that, and therefore he placed little importance on when his physical shell would breathe its last. The stairs above continued their clockwise spiral, the better for any supposed defenders to maneuver against an attacking force—though as it turned out, in the end the citizens of Agrazab had little to fear from invading armies. No, they had fallen to a more sinister force.

At first, the elion wondered why Uklith had not sent one of the three Advocates to complete this task. Though unwilling servants, the Advocates would have been much more suitable than he knew himself to be. However, during the past few days the elion had spent in the palace, he'd observed that the same weakness which tethered Uklith to his prison also applied to the Advocates. They *did* have slightly more latitude and could venture into the surrounding streets for a short way, but they could not reach the city's far corner.

The elion paused three quarters of the way to the summit, looking out a window. Here, at a higher point than any other building, he could see over all Agrazab, and though he had no hope of seeing the Warrior from this distance, he could approximate the man's location. *What will your next move be, Matthias? Will you be foolish enough to take on my master?* What a sight that would be, to see the great Warrior of Light humbled before the Demon-Lord Uklith, one man's pride brought low before the ruler of the underworld. *You will serve, Matthias, just as we all serve, and your torment will know no bounds.*

He resumed the last portion of his climb, movements feverish and excited, stopping only when he reached at the massive door at the head of the stairs. He pushed it open. The elion entered a room twenty paces across, a well at its center taking up much of the space. The stony base of the well connected to a shaft beneath the floor, one that ran all the way into the earth below. A shimmering liquid filled it to the brim, glowing but with a shade of darkness at its core, and when the elion stepped up to the well he saw his reflection in the strange contents.

Few people had ever seen the Lifesource in its raw form. *This is it, the power that ran in the veins of the Advocates of old, what Zadinn Kanas possessed, what Tim Matthias currently possesses.* The elion knew that Matthias had experimented with these focusing reservoirs during the last few months, and that the man had been successful in fashioning some rudimentary ones. This well, however, was the largest focusing reservoir in all the world, and it belonged to Uklith.

The Demon-Lord had given clear instructions that the reservoir was to be left alone until the Warrior entered the city, but Matthias had arrived and the time was nigh. Though the elion was no Advocate, that was the beauty of focusing reservoirs, just as Tim Matthias had learned. They allowed one to access the Lifesource in its most tangible form, permitting anyone with the right knowledge to command it to his or her will. In this, the elion was little more than a mechanism of transportation. Before him the liquid within the well thrashed, light flashing against shadow. The elion touched the sides of the well, and the floorboards quaked, discharges in the air causing his hair to stand on end. He noted a faint smell of sulphur, coupled with an acrid tang that reminded him of hot stones after a long rain.

The world around him sprang into clarity, every fiber of his being attuned to what was happening before him. Beneath the pure layer of the Lifesource, the darker, malevolent presence emerged. Uklith had filled this well over the last two hundred years, extending his reach just enough to siphon away trickles of power at a time, all of which had slowly accumulated into that which lay before the elion.

It was all here, the key to Uklith's release, and the time was right.

The elion dedicated the final shreds of his power to the reservoir, and the incandescent light flared for an instant before black billows of smoke replaced it, rising from the depths, pouring over the sides. Dark tendrils filled the room, running along the floor and out the windows. Wreaths of shadow curled across the landscape, stretching from the tower's peak to the sands below.

And all across Agrazab, the undead heard the call.

* * *

Eklan thought he remembered this building. The ground floor appeared to be a tavern, with a long serving counter at the back of the room and short stools and tables covering the rest of the space. *After a long day's work in the sun, I suppose folks would just sidle up to the bar and order a pint of Demon-Lord. A rather dark blend of ale, I'm sure.* He made his way to the back of the room, where there was a door set in the wall. When he opened it, the opposite side revealed stone steps leading down into darkness.

"What's that?" Bria asked.

"There's a set of tunnels beneath the city," Eklan replied. "Near as I can tell, they connect all of Agrazab. Most buildings have entrances like this one on the ground floor. My best guess is the tunnels were used during sandstorms or times of intense heat."

Bria looked down the shaft. "Spend much time using them when you first came here?"

"Hardly. The aboveground parts of this city were terrifying enough."

He closed the door and they proceeded to check the upstairs level, which he guessed had been the living quarters of the former tavern's owner. The top floor turned out to be as empty as the ground level, little more than a handful of barren rooms and the occasional piece of long-unused furniture. *No undead, no Assassins, no giant insects. That's one building secured.*

In a room with a bed and cracked washbasin, Eklan looked out a window and saw Tim, Boblin and Celia atop the nearby garrison. Boblin and Tim were heading back down to the lower level as Celia took up a position facing east, crossbow readied.

"Next building?" Bria asked. Eklan gave one more glance around and nodded his agreement. His sister went down the stairs first, leaving the building and joining Wurit in the street.

As Eklan passed the serving bar, something caught his eye and gave him pause. He wasn't sure how he'd missed it before. Motioning Wurit and Bria to wait a moment, Eklan stopped and picked up a scrap of red cloth from behind the counter. Sure enough, he saw the unmistakable embroidery in the corner.

R.H. Reidell Hamur. *It's one of Reidell's kerchiefs.*

Eklan looked around. The last time they were here, it had been in the midst of a frantic scuttle to escape Agrazab, and most of his memories came in a hazy blur. They'd been running through the dark of night, noises of all sorts echoing through the streets. There had been only three of them left by that time—himself, Reidell, and Darmet, and they had stopped to rest in the garrison's shadow. Eklan remembered how an unnatural cold had seized the air, and the next thing they knew, Darmet was gone, vanished without a trace. Then had begun the rush, half search, half escape. Had Reidell been standing here, in this very spot in the tavern, when his mind broke? Eklan could not say. His memories remained a jumble of fear and confusion.

Eklan...

He turned his head. Had that been Reidell's voice? No, Agrazab was playing tricks on him. Though not yet dark, he wouldn't put it past the city to have a daytime apparition or two up its sleeve. But still—the *kerchief* wasn't an apparition, was it? No, it was quite real, and he now held it in his hand.

He examined the space behind the serving bar, looking for any other sign of his brother or perhaps of Darmet. Reidell's legs hadn't given out immediately—that part had come after, during their slow, tortuous return journey across the Western Desert—but he had indeed lost his sanity within the city first, and at that point Eklan had been more or less on his own. *I failed you, brother.*

It still amazed Eklan that he had returned at all. They should have been easy victims on the journey back east, one man exhausted and the other insane, and yet they reached their destination whole, neither having fallen victim to the krevurs or to any of the other obscenities from within the deep gorge along the Mygon Path. He remembered a vivid dream one night in which they *had* been attacked, a gigantic centipede climbing out of a crevasse, but an old, bearded man had stood before the two travelers to protect them, hands held up, a shimmer of purple fire streaming from his palms to hold the monster at bay.

Memories caught in the past, Eklan reached the door leading to the tunnels and pushed it back open.

Eklan...I'm still here, Eklan...

His breath caught in his throat. Upon opening the door, his suspicions slid away, though the fact that this happened more easily than normal was lost on him. He did not even notice the faint buzzing in his ears, so transfixed was he by the words drifting up to him.

You can still save me, the part of me that never left this place...

A part of Eklan's mind spoke up, warning this was impossible, this was not something to be trusted, but he ignored it. It was *indeed* possible, was it not? Reidell had lost his mind here, but did it not stand to reason that something had taken it—and if that were the case, could Eklan not retrieve it?

Hurry, Eklan. Time grows short.

Eklan stepped onto the landing, leaving the door ajar. Dust swirled into the air as he placed his foot on the first stair leading downward. Shadows from within reached up to envelop him, caressing his face with their touch. He took his next step, and then one after that, as the gentle crooning beckoned him onward.

Make me whole again...

He reached the base of the staircase, one hand against the wall for support. He'd come on this journey to aid Matthias, knowing the inevitability of what they faced but determined to do his part, but *this*, the opportunity to save Reidell, held more purpose for him than any other objective. With his brother at his side, the two men could do anything, could face anyone—even the Demon-Lord of Malath. Yes, this was what Eklan had come here to do. It was time for him to face whatever held Reidell's mind and defeat it, freeing his brother to become whole again.

A tiny light rose in the middle of the passage, perhaps the size of a fist, hovering in midair. Eklan could feel Reidell's presence radiating from the orb. A soul was such an intangible thing, and yet here one was, suspended in the dark before him, little more than a dozen paces away. Eklan stepped forward, unaware of the black ooze that had begun seeping around his feet, climbing its way over the tips of his boots and lapping at his ankles. He reached out, unaware that the buzzing sound had risen to a crescendo in the background.

Closer, brother, closer...

The ooze touched his calves, so cold it made him jerk backward. Something within Eklan flickered, and he saw the reality of his situation—that there was no orb in front of him at all, but instead a malevolent, all-consuming shadow. He tried to step back, but the oozy liquid on the ground held him in place. The shadow swept forward, and this time Eklan heard the buzzing quite well indeed, and within it he recognized the voices of those who had been lost in Agrazab: Yoric, Darmet, Reidell, and still more, others he did not recognize but who must have come here at some point. Uklith had absorbed their essences one and all, hundreds of victims that had come into his grasp over the centuries, and though Eklan did not know it, those essences fueled the reservoir to the northwest, victims that Uklith had assimilated in order to facilitate his release. Eklan heard a voice again, but this time it was not Reidell, and it made him scream in terror.

WE MEET AGAIN, EKLAN HAMUR.

No! he cried back. *You won't have me!*

The voice carried a hint of amusement. *DO YOU THINK YOU HAVE ANY SAY IN THE MATTER?*

You did not win last time, and you won't this time.

OH, BUT THAT IS THE BEAUTY OF IT, EKLAN. YOU VOWED I WOULD NEVER HAVE ANOTHER CHANCE TO TAKE YOU, AND YET HERE YOU ARE. IN THE END, I ALWAYS GET WHAT I WANT.

He reached backward, fingers clutching the banister. He pulled at the railing, the upper portion of his body still mobile, and yet his efforts proved useless. The lower half of his body felt cold, so cold, and a part of him wondered if it was even worth it to try—he was so tired, and was it not useless? Would Uklith not win in the end? Should he just submit, and let fate take its course?

May the Maker help me…

THE MAKER CANNOT HELP YOU NOW.

But someone else did.

For the second time that day, Eklan's trancelike state dissipated as he felt Bria wrap her arms around his torso. She stood on the steps above him, face intent, one portion of her gaze on Eklan, the other on the monstrous, liquid blackness before him.

"Bria!" he shouted. "Don't step onto the floor!" The ooze was all about him, and he feared if she touched it, she would be trapped just as he was.

"I know," she replied through gritted teeth. "But help me help you."

They heard Uklith's laughter. *ANOTHER HAMUR, IS IT? YOUR FAMILY IS SUCH A JOY. COME, BRIA HAMUR, ENTER MY EMBRACE.*

"Eat a boomer," she said. "*Literally.*"

The next thing Eklan knew, Bria had pulled a stick from her belt and struck it aflame. Without a moment's hesitation, she threw it into the shadow.

They heard a wordless scream of pain. In such close proximity, the blast should have killed them, but Uklith's shadow absorbed the majority of the force, muffling the effect of the concussion—though that didn't stop Eklan's ears from ringing. In front of them, the shadow shattered, as if it had possessed tangible substance, right before the surrounding walls collapsed in a massive cloud of sand and stone. The resultant heap of rubble stopped just short of where Eklan lay, and he felt the capability of his lower extremities return. Holding onto Bria's arm, he dragged himself back to the staircase. They lay on the steps, regaining their breath.

"I can't believe that worked," Eklan said, looking at the collapsed hallway before them.

"Explosions always work," Bria said, hoisting herself back to her feet and helping him do the same. "Let's go."

* * *

Tim and Boblin moved back downstairs, leaving Celia at watch on the wall, and joined Jend and Ken on the first floor. The two elions stood before a tabletop full of partially completed boomers, a set of fuses running from each birchbark tube, Jend holding the tubes, Ken slicing the ends of the fuses to complete each device.

"They're shorter," Tim said, looking over their boomers.

"After Commander Kule launched one from a crossbow, it opened our minds to a new set of possibilities," Jend said. He hefted his crossbow and placed a boomer into the arrow slot. It fit perfectly. "We can fire them as projectiles."

"With these, we have enough power to level most of the buildings on the opposite side of the street," Ken added. "'Ware the enemy that comes looking for us."

Maybe that's what we should do, Tim thought. *Crater the palace.* Well, if there was one thing elions were good at, it was blowing things up. They had once rigged their own home to explode, and *that* took dedication to the cause.

"Here," Boblin said, handing an empty tube to Tim. "Make yourself useful. It's your fault that our stock of these grew so low. You used half of what we had left to blow up a krevur nest."

With delicate focus, they set to work finishing off the construction of the boomers before them, each one sized to double as crossbow ammunition. Tim and Boblin planned to set out within the hour, after the others returned from their investigation of the surrounding buildings. There was no use in wasting daylight, and if for whatever reason their search for the strange elion bore no fruit by dusk, they intended to once again vacate the city and camp outside the walls overnight. Though Tim doubted proximity would make a difference if Uklith started attacking them, he nonetheless figured staying outside the city was a safer course of action.

They'd only been working for a few minutes when a muffled explosion sounded from across the street. Tim was first to the window, keeping a narrow profile to minimize the potential target he might represent, the elions staying low behind him with swords drawn. He saw a cloud of dust waft from the windows of the building that Eklan and Bria had been searching. A few moments later Bria and Wurit staggered from the door, Eklan propped upon their shoulders between them.

Trusting Celia to cover him from above if necessary, Tim pushed the garrison door open and rushed outside, lending his assistance to carry Eklan across the street. The man was conscious, but clearly disoriented.

Once they were safely back inside the garrison, Eklan shrugged his helpers off and slumped against the table. His breath came in deep gasps. "I hate this karfing place." He paused between gulps of air to spit on the ground. "Never again."

"What happened?" Tim asked.

"Uklith," Bria responded. "Not in the flesh, or in full strength, but it was him, there in the tunnels."

"In the tunnels?"

Eklan pointed to a door at the back of the garrison. "There's an entrance right there if you're interested." He was visibly shaken, the first time Tim had ever seen him in such a state, and his face was pale. "I thought it was Reidell, but it was *him*. He put me into a trance, and he almost took my soul."

"And I used my last boomer," Bria said.

Jend gestured to the table. "I think we have you covered on that count, ma'am."

"All right," Tim said to Boblin. "Let's finish these up and go. If Uklith's in the tunnels, we need to move soon."

Bria looked at him. "And the plan is…"

"Boblin and I are going to the palace. If we can find the elion, so much the better. If that doesn't work"—he drew his sword— "we'll move to the backup plan. Not that I'm sure what that is yet."

She tossed him a sack of boomers and then slung one over her own shoulder. "I'll be your backup plan, Matthias."

"That works."

After they finished tying off the remaining boomers, Tim stepped out the door, Boblin and Bria behind him. The air hung still in the dusty streets, creating an uneasy sensation that the company stood in the eye of a storm. Tim took the lead, the overhead sun causing beads of sweat to spring out before long. Moving with quickened pace, Tim could feel time growing short, stretched taut underneath him like a violin string on the cusp of snapping. Just one more crank, one more turn of the knob, and all would come apart in a violent rush.

The streets grew wider the closer they came to the city's center, the buildings more elaborate and spacious. They also noticed the occasional statue, some of which appeared to be councilmen wearing ceremonial robes like the man at the fountain, while others looked like soldiers or knights of old. Soon they could see the palace, a squat building with turrets at each of its corners. Tim realized that the palace imitated the greater design of Agrazab, which was its own square structure with a tower at each junction of its four corners. As Tim kept his attention focused on the palace, Boblin and Bria held the rear guard, eyes on all sides to cover the territory. The urge for Tim to seize the Lifesource grew stronger than ever, but he held off.

In spite of Agrazab's well-to-do center city, several buildings had crumbled into ruins near the palace, though whether from the wear of time or from the powers unleashed when Uklith was imprisoned Tim could not say. A gust of wind brought a swirl of sand through the street, sending a previously fallen statue of a knight holding a broadsword rolling across his path.

MATTHIAS—

Tim halted. The voice was laced with waves of evil, and it caused his bones to vibrate. Behind him, Boblin and Bria stopped as well, looking at him with curious expressions. "Did you hear that?" Tim asked.

"Not a peep," Boblin said. "It's the wrong time to start hearing voices, mate. I always *did* know you were a step or two away from cracking, though."

"Funny. It was Uklith."

When he spoke the name, a horrible, cold laughter filled Tim's ears, so strong it made him cringe. He could tell that Boblin and Bria heard *this* voice, for they staggered as well, raising hands to cover their ears.

IT IS TIME, WARRIOR. WITNESS IT BEGIN.

The ground shook. In the northwest corner of the city, Agrazab's largest tower suddenly belched enormous billows of black smoke from its turret. Wreaths of dark cloud poured out the upper windows and down the sides, violent lights flashing from within the shadows. Even though he was not touching the Lifesource, Tim nonetheless felt waves of it oozing from the tower, dark and malevolent, a well of magic long pent-up and now unleashed with a single stroke.

The lightning flashing from within the tower snapped into a blinding, vertical column of white, stretching upward into the heavens. And with this strange eruption of magic, the wind gusted strong and violent, blowing a howling maelstrom of sand right at the three companions.

"Well," Boblin said, "that's not good."

The sandstorm slammed into them, filling the world with dust and stinging grit, and Timothy Matthias feared that the end had well and truly come.

32

The attack on Vonku's inner city came at dawn. A phalanx of corsairs charged toward the walls, letting out a ragged battle cry as they emerged from the smoke of the surrounding fires. Sendalion could see that the assault was halfhearted at best, no more than a diversionary feint. For one, a true attack would have begun several hours earlier, when the defenders' senses were dulled by the waning of a long night's watch, and for another, the charging pirate crew possessed little in the way of siege engines. It was just another of their winnowing tactics, meant to keep the Legion on edge but no more.

The better to get the corsairs to overcommit when they aren't planning on doing so.

On the walls, Sendalion's fellow soldiers swarmed to the defense, giving every impression of rallying to the cause. The first attack wave of corsairs threw climbing ladders against the wall, raised their weapons in the dim morning light, and began to scale the constructs. On either side of Sendalion, archers let fly with rounds of arrows. The barbed shafts struck the climbing corsairs, who either died outright or were thrown from their ladders by the impact of a direct hit. Near Sendalion, a grappling hook latched on the parapet, and he promptly cut its rope free with his sword.

Two more attack waves followed. Sendalion saw the corsairs at the back of the phalanx part to make way for a catapult, which crawled forward with wheels creaking. Though it was nowhere near as powerful as the catapults the defenders had burned in their retreat—Sendalion suspected this one had been hastily built during the last day—it was still large enough to deliver the sizable boulder nestled in its launch basket.

Maybe they are serious. Good thing we are, too.

At the appearance of the catapult, the corsairs abandoned the ladders, which had served their purpose of distracting the Legion while the pirates brought the device into position. The construct ground to a stop, facing the parapets. A corsair stepped up to the winch, but immediately fell to the ground with a dozen arrows sprouting from his body.

For a moment, everything hung still, the only movement the curls of smoke in the street. Then the fallen corsair's arm shot up, hand bloodied from where he'd grasped at the first arrow to strike him.

He released the catapult's catch.

"Cover!" Sendalion yelled.

The defenders split in two. The massive stone slammed into the parapets, the force of its collision throwing Sendalion against the nearest wall. The breath rushed out of him.

Get back up.

He struggled to his feet, those around him doing likewise. In front of them, chips of stone had fallen from the face of the battlements, and the corsairs on the ground were lifting a new boulder into position. Several of the archers regained their bearings quickly enough to fire arrows into the group, but this would only delay and not prevent the next launch. More of the corsairs' climbing ladders clattered against the wall, again to divert the Legion's focus from the catapult.

When the second boulder struck, a massive section of the wall to Sendalion's left gave way, collapsing in an inelegant jumble of bricks, mortar, and dust. Sendalion almost fell into the gap but managed to grasp a corner of stone and cling to safety. Outside the battlements, the attacking corsairs halted, visibly surprised by their unanticipated success. No properly reinforced wall should have fallen so quickly. Still, the breach had left the streets of inner Vonku open to them, and though the corsairs may not have intended it, they found themselves with a clear and unexpected avenue of success.

The hesitation did not last long. The corsair at the head of the crew, seeing a ripe opportunity, raised his cutlass and let out a battle cry. The enemy surged forward, almost tripping over one another in their haste to be the first inside the inner city.

Sendalion moved into position, signaling the group on the opposite section of the broken wall to do the same. When the corsairs entered the breach, the soldiers manning the walls carried forward the cauldrons of boiling oil they'd kept standing by. The first man to look up toward them cried out in alarm, seeing the trap, but he was too late. The Legion dumped the blazing contents of their cauldrons on the corsairs' heads, and though Sendalion knew he shouldn't relish the sound of their screams, a part of him couldn't help but feel a sense of grim satisfaction. These were the corsairs who had burned the *Steadfast*, who had killed Captain Yastlin in the bay, and who had butchered the young men of Eltern and Sevilin. It was past time, he thought, to be getting some payback.

* * *

Kaarst watched the crew charge into the breach. The oil would get the first ones, that much was obvious, and the Legion surely had additional trickery planned for those who made it into the streets on the far side. Kaarst stood in an alley a safe distance from the fighting, the robed man at his side, listening to the wails of ill-fated pirates and smelling the scent of burned flesh. Several corsairs stumbled back from the breach, covered in oil and quite literally boiling alive. The sight of melted skin and exposed bones caused Kaarst's stomach to turn in spite of his best efforts to prevent it. He'd seen many grisly things in his time, but siege fatalities were the worst.

"I would like some assurances," he said to the robed man. A lot of his corsairs were about to die, and though he had little care for the lives of individual men, he didn't want to lose a significant portion of his fighting force in an ill-advised endeavor.

"You shall have your reinforcements, Admiral. Commit the remainder of your corsairs and I will take care of the rest."

"All well and good, but we have reached a juncture where I need more than your word."

For a moment, the robed man said nothing. He turned to face Kaarst, though his features remained concealed within his hood as always. "Do you recall the first time we met, Admiral?"

Kaarst had been imprisoned in a ship's brig, as a matter of fact. The robed man had occupied the only other cell, and when the guards came down to deliver each captive a crust of moldy bread, the man had lifted a finger. The next thing Kaarst knew, both guards were hemorrhaging blood from their eyes, ears, and mouths. The memory made the scene of dying corsairs currently in front of Kaarst seem pristine by comparison.

"One snap of my fingers is all it would take, Admiral. I am *not* your enemy, but we can't dally anymore. Send the corsairs in."

Kaarst began to draw sword from scabbard—this fool's time was done—and stopped.

A trickle of blood had dripped from his nose.

"Do it, Andre," the robed man said softly.

Kaarst slammed the sword back home in its sheath. With one more glance toward the slaughter happening in front of the inner city, he stepped out of the alley and returned to a ring of his corsairs standing back from the action.

"Nerrliv," he called. His first mate, newly christened now that Grizzlen was no longer of this world, turned toward him.

"Aye, Adm'ral!"

"Send the crews in. It be high time to claim our prize!"

Nerrliv faltered. "It surely be a trap, though, Adm'ral, do ye not agree?"

"It only be a trap if we let it, me hearty! We have the goose's golden egg before us, an' anyone not brave enough to seize it will be facin' a ripe floggin'! Send the crews in!"

"Which crews, Adm'ral?"

Kaarst wiped his nose. The blood had dried. He smiled. "All of them, matey. Send them all."

* * *

Ladu held his breath against the stench, placing one hand over the next, climbing the rope in the dark. He looked toward the light overhead, willing it closer with every inch. The harder he exerted himself, the deeper inhalations he needed to take, none of which were pleasant in his current environment. Below him, an elion gagged.

Well, we are *inside a latrine.*

Ahead of the emperor, Tavin Kule was the first to reach the summit of their climb. Once clear of the pit, the elion turned to help Ladu the rest of the way, pulling him past the lip of the privy's seat and onto the floor of the washroom. While Ladu did not consider the washroom to be pleasant-smelling by any stretch of the imagination, it was certainly better than *that* place he'd just climbed from.

Raisha arrived next. Ladu *did* have to suppress a smile at the expression of disgust on her face. He was beyond impressed that she had agreed to come in the first place, and she deserved no small amount of credit for stepping up to the task. *She's the last person I would have expected to be agreeable to wading through a tunnel of hisht.* His respect for the woman had grown considerably since Endar's betrayal.

Faldon came next, then Wayne, who was followed by a string of several more elions, exiting the latrine one at a time. The group numbered twelve in all.

"One of your more interesting ideas, if I may be so bold as to say, your majesty," Faldon noted.

"It got us inside the palace, though," Ladu replied.

"It certainly did," Raisha said, and Ladu could see she was resisting the urge to spit. She wore pants instead of her usual dress, for obvious reasons, and had a sword buckled about her waist. The elions had been training her in combat techniques these past few days.

At the front of the room, Tavin cracked the door open to reveal an empty corridor. On the opposite side of the hallway a new door opened, revealing another dozen elions who had entered their washroom in the same way as Ladu's group. If all had gone according to plan, similarly sized groups of elions would be entering the palace via its other wings. The bulk of the undead were currently out in the city, performing one of their usual searches, and Ladu intended to use this opportunity to press an assault on the throne room.

With the Kule brothers in the lead, the twenty-four companions moved as quietly as possible, doing their best not to draw any attention. They left the top floor without incident, and though they did find themselves face-to-face with a pair of undead on the next level, Faldon and Tavin dropped them with a dual twang of crossbows before the creatures could raise an alarm. Many parts of the palace remained unfinished; some were in fact still open to the sky above, while others were completed rooms without any purpose or function yet. Ladu's group had entered palace's eastern wing, the second-highest level next to the north tower, and as such they would need to descend several more floors before reaching the level of the throne room.

Not too far into their progress, a vibration rattled the corridor. Ladu halted and looked up to see a ceiling chandelier shaking.

"Your Majesty?" Raisha asked. "What was that?"

"I don't know," Ladu replied, but it reminded him of the earthquake that had occurred during the Battle of the Deathlands, and he did not care for the gnawing sensation it created in his stomach. A second vibration came, this one much stronger, and this time a crystalline extension from the chandelier fell free. The fragment struck the flagstones, shattering.

"It's coming, your highness," a cold voice said. Ladu looked toward the far end of the corridor as Endar Varuc stepped forward. Faldon and Tavin drew their bows tight again, but held fast at Ladu's signal.

Endar came fully into the light. "Time is short." A rustling sound came from behind him, and a group of undead appeared at his back, an air of anticipation hanging over them. "I must admit to my foolishness, as I should have discovered the reservoir much sooner. It was with us the whole time, though not like Agrazab's or Vonku's. Uklith is quite resourceful, I must say. What will it be, your majesty? Sister? Death or servitude?"

Ladu heard another sound, this one behind him, and risked a glance over his shoulder. A cluster of undead filled the corridor behind them, trapping Ladu and the elions between the two groups. In total there were at least sixty enemies, far more than the size of Ladu's small company.

Endar held a hand up, and both groups of undead held still. "Your majesty?"

Ladu gave Endar a polite nod. "Lord Varuc, at this time I would be more than happy to discuss the terms of your surrender."

Endar laughed. "So be it." He dropped his hand, and the undead beside him rushed forward. Faldon let loose a shot, but Endar quickly disappeared behind the swarming mob, and the arrow instead buried itself in one of the many undead. The group from behind attacked as well, and all around Ladu steel rasped against scabbard as the elions drew their swords. As the first line of attackers struck, Ladu tried to catch one last glimpse of Endar, but the nobleman was gone, the only indication of his recent presence a cold laugh hanging over the corridor.

* * *

"Quentiin!"

Jolldo was shaking him awake. "Hurry up, laddie! It's started!"

Quentiin blinked his way into wakefulness. There had been a time when he'd lived a soldier's regimen and could rise in an instant, but that time had faded, and it took him a few moments to gain his bearings. He rolled from his cot, slipping on his boots and belting his sword.

When he left his tent, he saw Trivian and the soldiers donning garb in the morning light. To the south, the fires burning in Vonku's eastern quarter had flared up. Giant, billowing clouds of smoke rose into the sky, thick and full as the flames raged underneath. *So much for us keepin' a low profile today.* Two days of harrying maneuvers, though successful, had left the company in need of some rest. They'd been planning on pulling back for the next day or two, both to allow themselves to recuperate and to keep the corsairs off balance regarding the timing of the attacks, but that looked as if it were no longer an option.

Quentiin placed a spyglass to his eye, gaze drawn toward a concentration of flames in front of Vonku's inner wall. As the image sprang into clarity he saw that a section of the wall had collapsed, hordes of corsairs streaming over its edge. He cursed, handing the glass to Jolldo. "The walls have fallen, laddie."

After a glance, Jolldo gave a curt nod. The dwerions gathered in a cluster behind them—Briiga, Yagglem, Vellgo, Harrlin, and all the rest, standing by and ready to do their part. For the moment, the mist hung low on the ground, having not yet dissipated in the morning light. Eltern's soldiers stood close together, clad in whatever secondhand armor they had managed to gather over the course of the past few days. Many bore scrapes and injuries from the skirmishes they'd conducted, and more than one had dark circles under his eyes. Some of them held blades with rust and chipped edges. For the most part they waited in tense silence, marked by an occasional word between friends or the scuffle of boots upon the ground. The slightly rank smell of fear pervaded the air.

"Going to be a lot more of them this time," Quentiin heard a soldier murmur. Like many of the others, the stubble on this one's cheeks had taken several days to accumulate. *That puts the laddie at what—fifteen? Sixteen? Not many summers, that one.*

Trivian, who'd been standing just slightly apart from the rest, looked up at the boy's words and narrowed his eyes. "Aye, there will be."

The boy shied back.

"What does that mean to you, soldier?" Trivian asked.

The boy swallowed. "That the enemy will need a lot of graves to bury their dead,

Commander."

The lad makes a point.

Trivian looked over the group. In a matter of moments, he appeared to stand taller than before. He kept his gaze steady, his jaw firm. "It's an ill-kept secret that the men of Eltern are considered outcasts—secondhand, under-trained." His voice did not waver. "When a soldier goes to Eltern, it's not a badge of honor but of shame. Today, though, I ask you to look at the soldiers standing beside you. It is *we* who broke the siege of Vonku, who sank Vila Kaarst's ship, who made it possible for our brothers and sisters behind the city walls to fight one more day. Now our comrades need us again, for the enemy is at the gates and closing in. We are still men of the Legion, and on this day, we will do it proud. We will do the name of Eltern proud. We will do *ourselves* proud. And yes, soldier, our enemies will need many graves to bury their dead."

Trivian drew his sword and raised it above his head. "Men of Eltern! Men of the Legion! We ride to war!" Swords cleared their sheaths, rasping free of their metal guards, glinting in the morning light. The small band raised their weapons high above their heads, letting out a war cry that rang across the hills. As one, with Quentiin and Trivian in the lead, they swept out of the camp across the plains, toward to the city of Vonku and the battle beyond.

* * *

Jeb staggered up the stairs, clutching one hand to his stomach. His belly felt large and bloated, as if something within was trying to claw its way out. He gritted his teeth against the agony, at one point collapsing against the wall to regain his breath before resuming the climb. All that time spent searching the streets, trying to understand Uklith's mandate, when it had been *him* all along. He emitted labored grunts of pain with every step. A moment later he tripped, falling on the staircase and skinning his kneecap on the stone. When he pulled himself back up, he saw a trickle of blood running down his leg, but that was a small matter compared to the horrific burning sensation surging through his body.

Not long ago, he'd *felt* the reservoir trigger far to the west. He hadn't known what it meant at first. Shortly afterward, he felt a strange sensation growing in his gut, and it was then that he realized there was a power welling up within him. It must have happened when the Assassins killed him. They'd given him the gift of the Lifesource, the same that fueled the other undead, and in doing so they had given him a purpose to serve even in death. It was an honor, he knew, and yet it *hurt* so much. He could feel Uklith pressuring him upward, toward the doorway at the head of the staircase, the highest possible point of the palace. He grasped the banister and pulled himself up the last few steps. *So close.* When he reached the watchtower's door, he leaned against it with his shoulder. It creaked open and he stumbled onto an open platform, which the elions of the Frontier Patrol had built so they could look out over the city of Galdon below. Energy spent, Jeb slumped against the windowsill, looking at the land before him.

Galdon had come far in the eighteen months since Zadinn's demise. Jeb had spent little time in the city—he hadn't exactly been welcome here, not after what transpired in the Pit—but he found that it looked quite beautiful. It was here, on the verge of dying his second death, that Jeb the woodsman regained a bit of his former clarity. In his final moments, he wondered if things might have turned out differently.

Was it even worth it to live, after all it took to do so?

The last wave of pain hit him, far beyond the magnitude of anything that had come before. Jeb screamed, his voice echoing beyond the tower and across the city. He placed his hands over his belly. For the barest of seconds, he saw a blinding light, tinged with black at its center, seeping between his fingers.

He thought of a man who had died because he held a crust of bread.

And then he knew no more.

* * *

Ladu ducked as an undead swung a battle-axe toward his head. The edge of the weapon clanged against the wall, causing chunks of stone to clatter to the ground. He drove his sword through the creature's flesh, hearing the dry and bloodless *crunch* as his blade passed through its decaying form. Ladu came back up into a standing position, pulled his blade free, and the creature slumped to the ground.

Chaos reigned all around as elions fought a battle on two fronts. Raisha held her blade firm, using the techniques she'd been shown to drop enemies who came close. Faldon and Tavin worked in tandem, keeping the rear guard unified. Wayne remained by the emperor's side, one eye on Ladu's enemies and one on his own. They were faring well enough against the undead, but Ladu didn't care to think of what the long term looked like. He expected them to break free from this group soon enough, but he supposed Endar would be calling the undead back to the palace, at which point the elions' enemies might run them over on sheer numbers alone. He feared the forces in the other palace wings had been similarly ambushed, giving their group little hope of receiving any assistance.

The ground rumbled once more. Endar's words before disappearing indicated that the nobleman had finally discovered the weapon he sought for Uklith, and Ladu worried it was getting put to use. However, he had more immediate concerns before him. Ladu pulled to the side as a crossbow bolt flew past his cheek, clattering against the stones not a foot away from him. Ladu turned and met the attack head-on, seeing the undead who had fired the shot coming in close. Ducking beneath the creature's guard, he cleaved its arm free. Its desiccated limb, still holding the crossbow, clattered to the floor—and then the undead was upon Ladu, jaws snapping toward his neck. The emperor returned the favor by plunging his knife into the creature's neck.

With Wayne backing him up, Ladu slashed left and right, forward and back, slowly and surely cleaving his way through the group. Eventually they reached a side room, forcing their way inside with the rest of the elions behind them. The rearguard came into the room last, slammed the door shut and lowered a bar across it. The group found themselves in a wing of the palace where windows overlooked the rest of the structure. Outside, a series of rooftops led to the throne room, and beyond it, the north tower.

Ladu took a head count. They'd lost three elions in the fighting, and even though one was too many, they were relatively well off given the circumstances. Plenty of undead remained on the opposite side of the door, but the elions had the strategic advantage of choosing to either exit the building through the windows or take the battle back to the hallway when ready.

"Orders, your majesty?" Raisha asked.

Ladu was about to respond when yet another jolt, this one stronger than the preceding ones, practically knocked them onto their knees. "What in the name of Malath—"

Outside the window, the north tower erupted into a blinding column of white light. Thin veins of darkness spiderwebbed from the column's center, though they grew stronger as the heartbeats passed. The spire of power traveled high into the clouds, where it curved just slightly to the west.

Toward Agrazab.

"What is it?" Wayne breathed.

North, south, and west. And we're the north. Ladu felt a chill run down his neck. "It's Uklith's prison—that is, the power that will unlock it."

"Has Matthias failed?"

Ladu shook his head. "I don't know. Regardless, it's incumbent upon *us* to succeed." He moved to the window. "I need to get to the throne room. Our task remains as it always was: Endar is the head of the serpent, and we must cut it off. Captains Kule—you have the command. Take the battle to the hallways. Join the crews from the other towers if you can. Whatever it takes, keep the undead from the throne room." He opened the window and drew his sword from his sheath. "In the interim, I'll deal with Lord Varuc myself."

* * *

Thick smoke billowed through the streets of Vonku, so heavy and cloying that Quentiin could only see a few feet in any direction. Waves of heat from the fires lashed at him. Several blocks back, they'd entered their first engagement after encountering two-score of Kaarst's corsairs. The battle had been short but violent, Eltern's soldiers outnumbering the corsairs, but Quentiin knew things would get much more difficult from here.

In the smoke ahead, he heard several booming noises, followed by the screams of dying men. At first he wondered if some cannons had survived the sinking of *Innocent's Blood*, but dismissed the theory. If Kaarst had any cannons remaining, he'd have used them much sooner. Besides, the sound didn't quite fit. Moments later they rounded a corner, where they saw a crew of corsairs laboring to fit a boulder into the basket of a catapult.

Ah, Quentiin thought, *now the breach makes sense.*

Any Legion defenders that might have once been on the walls were long gone, no doubt having retreated farther into the inner city. Quentiin could see that the narrow gap in the walls nonetheless slowed the corsairs' advance, and a not-insignificant pile of bodies indicated their progress had been hard won.

Meanwhile, the catapult crew appeared to be doing their best to widen the gap. Quentiin led a charge against them, and upon seeing their new attackers, the crew released the stone. It sailed through the air, slamming into the wall and breaking free several more chunks. The battlement buckled just a hair more, but for the most part held firm. Sword in hand, Quentiin met the first corsair—an elion, even rarer among corsairs than dwerions. The tall, willowy figure attacked Quentiin blade-to-blade, steel ringing across the burning landscape.

The two combatants danced across the rubble on the streets as around them Jolldo, Trivian, and the rest surged in to overwhelm the other members of the crew. Elion dexterity was not restricted to Boblin Kule and his comrades, and Quentiin's opponent kept him on the defensive, pressing Quentiin to take one step after another backward and away from his companions. The elion drew blood when the edge of his blade brushed against Quentiin's shoulder, and Quentiin felt his back scrape the stone of a nearby building. *Karf.*

Looking for an avenue of escape—the last thing Quentiin needed was to be in a corner of his opponent's making—he glimpsed the opening of an alley just a few steps away. Ducking a blow, Quentiin moved toward the narrow space, where he would be able to use the elion's height against him. He caught another overhead blow with a two-handed grip, sliding the elion's blade away with a growl, and managed to step all the way into the alley. The corsair grinned, seeing this as a retreat, and swept into the narrow space in front of Quentiin.

Quentiin caught him in mid-stride, stepping in low and slamming the force of his body into the elion's gut. As the corsair stumbled in surprise, Quentiin followed through by ramming his blade through the elion's heart. Blood fountained out of the corsair's mouth, his grip going limp, and he slid free from the end of Quentiin's blade. Quentiin stood still for a moment, breathing heavily, raising a hand to touch the wound in his shoulder. The cut ran just beneath the surface of the skin, barely more than a nick. *I can handle a few more o' those, if it comes to that.*

A warning flickered at the back of his mind. Quentiin spun and saw a form staggering from the shadows at the back of the alley. The man seemed drunk, and Quentiin hesitated in confusion, but when the figure stepped into the light he saw that it was undead rather than human, a feral mess of dirty clothing and wild hair, eyes rolling in manic patterns, a stream of drool running from its jaw. Quentiin whirled his blade, taking the creature's head from its shoulders, and the decapitated body tumbled to the ground.

The head rolled to Quentiin's feet. Its flesh was withered, lips peeled away from the gums to bare the teeth. Only sparse strands of hair remained on its head. *What in the name o' Malath are undead doin' here in Vonku?*

He inspected the corpse more closely, second-guessing his assessment, but even as he did so he recognized the irrationality of his denial. This was an undead, no doubt about it, and it had just emerged from the shadows of Vonku.

Footsteps sounded from the far end of the valley. Here, smoke filled streets just as in the rest of the city, meaning Quentiin could only see so far. Soon, though, a moment came when the vapors parted, and through the veil Quentiin saw a cluster of ragged forms staggering forward, moving slowly but gradually picking up their pace.

Quentiin stepped from the alley and into the open street, where Trivian and the rest had cleared the space around the catapult. Trivian had the flush of victory on his face, but when he saw Quentiin's, the exultant light in his eyes slowly dissipated.

"What is it?" Trivian asked.

"Undead," Quentiin growled, pointing toward the alley. "Stand fast."

"You can't be serious. There's no such thing as undead."

Quentiin pointed. "Then what's that, laddie?" The first wave of walking corpses appeared from the alley, no longer moving with a shuffling gate, stirred by the presence of flesh and driven by lust for blood. Upon seeing the creatures, some of the Legion soldiers cried out in fear.

"I see," Trivian said, tightening his grip on his blade. "May the Maker preserve us."

* * *

The robed man stood before his giant cauldron, which he'd placed in the tombs deep below Vonku. The cauldron had been with him for some time, albeit with it a fair number of unpleasant memories. Still, what had been a burden would now be used to his advantage. He held his hands before the reservoir, feeling energy crackle in the depths. Ripples spread across the tomb floors, echoing past the coffins that had long since burst open, disgorging their inhabitants to roam Vonku's streets.

He had used the powers in the cauldron to raise the dead, not just in this tomb, but all the dead in Vonku, securing his promise to Vila Kaarst that the corsair admiral would have all the bodies he needed. Kaarst had been correct that committing an assault on the inner walls would merely be walking into a trap—but with over a thousand walking corpses risen, he'd have more than enough soldiers at his disposal to overrun Aras's meager defenses. The man's robes fluttered as wind rose, impossible in the tomb's confined quarters, yet here nonetheless. The Lifesource shifted in his hands, vying upward as it built up momentum. Despite having walked this world and several others, the robed man had never before seen such magnitude of power as this unleashed. The other two reservoirs had already been triggered, and this, the last, would complete the triangle. One piece remained, but he expected Uklith would have that well in hand.

The man drew the power into himself. It would have destroyed most mortals, as it had the woodsman Jeb, but the robed man was not a mere mortal. He supposed he had been, once upon a time, but those days were long past. No, he had become so much more during this past year, and he reveled in it.

The Lifesource surged through his veins, channeled from the reservoir, and he released it upward, where it blasted a hole through the roof of the tomb. Atop a tower, underground, it mattered not; power was power, so long as one had the capacity to direct it. A shaft of light pierced the clouds above him, a storm of blinding energy that rocked the heavens. He could *feel* it tearing at the boundary between worlds, not successful quite yet, but building in momentum and strength until it would be. And when that happened, all the underworld would pour forth.

* * *

The three columns converged in the skies above Agrazab, coming together at the apex of the City's northwest tower. The City's focusing point was the primary, the others secondary and tertiary. Directed by Uklith's hand, the energies surged into a maelstrom of madness, weakening the bonds of the Demon-Lord's prison, hastening his release. It was a power no one mortal could hope to stop, and as the wind whipped through the streets of Agrazab in a frenzy of chaos and sand, a dark noise floated on the breeze, and it was the sound of Uklith's laughter.

33

Tim covered his eyes as the sandstorm engulfed them, shielding his face with one hand, sword held in the other. Coarse grains pounded his skin, thousands of tiny pebbles stinging with every minuscule impact. He was dimly aware of Boblin and Bria behind him, also crouching against the encroaching madness, while the tower's blinding light cut through the haze of the whirlwind.

The attack came soon enough. A bony, claw-like hand clutched Tim's ankle, fingers curling around his boot. He turned his back against the wind, peering through slitted eyes, and saw a skeletal arm reaching up from the ground. The sands beneath him parted, revealing a withered head atop a decayed body, as one of Uklith's undead soldiers emerged from the depths. Tim pulled his boot from the creature's grasp and struck, beheading it before it could stand upright. The undead was but the first of many. Around the trio of companions an increasing number of creatures appeared, some climbing out of the ground like the previous one, others from within the buildings, and still more from the sandstorm.

Tim, Boblin, and Bria bared their blades, coming together with backs against each other, facing outward. As the undead surged forward, the three friends sliced and thrust, dodged and retaliated, cleaving torsos in half and striking heads from shoulders. The elements abated for a moment, allowing Tim to count at least two dozen of the creatures surrounding them, and then the winds picked up once more. The whirlwind's only saving grace was that it hindered the undead's advance, slowing them so that they could only attack in groups of two and three. Above the trio, the heat of the tower blasted down, its fiery skyward column casting all of Agrazab in an otherworldly incandescence.

Behind Tim, Boblin fitted a boomer into his crossbow and fired, sending the boomer directly into a large cluster of the creatures to their rear. The undead exploded in all directions, limbs and bones flying apart in a spectacular fireball. Bria danced on the balls of her feet, skewering two undead in the same thrust of her sword. A crosswind parted the wall of sand again, and Tim caught a glimpse of undead filling the street, each one practically climbing over the others in its attempts to reach the embattled companions, already swelling into the gap created by the boomer's blast. As the maelstrom closed once more, Tim felt his arms growing heavy, his body aching, and he knew that at long last the time had come. With a column of pure magic erupting into the sky behind him, there was no better time than the present. Tim closed his eyes, opened his mind, and for the first time in weeks, filled himself with the power of the Lifesource.

A tidal wave of energy filled him, his blade erupting into a tongue of green fire. The world sprang into crisp clarity, every fiber of his being on alert, vitality surging through his veins. With blade held in one hand, Tim opened his other palm and unleashed a column of green fire that blasted through the waves of undead not ten feet away. For a moment he tensed, fearing Uklith's presence would come crashing down upon him—but nothing happened. As he'd hoped, the sheer amount of power radiating from the focusing reservoir acted as a buffer, Tim's presence but a candle beneath a bonfire, and he breathed a deep sigh. For the first time in a long while, he felt whole again.

"About time," Boblin said. "Now what?"

Tim lowered his blade. "This way."

He drew on more of the Lifesource and *pushed*. A wave of energy shot outward, creating a narrow gap in the line of encroaching undead. With Tim in the lead, the companions ran through the opening in their enemies, Bria setting off a boomer to cover their backs. Though many undead disintegrated under Tim's onslaught, plenty remained to oppose them. The trio found themselves in the middle of a gauntlet of walking corpses, all of which struck at them with an assortment of weapons and gnashing teeth. The mass of bodies pressed inward, threatening to crush Tim and the other two, and then they burst free of the mob. They diverted course into a narrow alley, where Tim gestured Boblin and Bria to enter an adjacent building. After unleashing another column of fire to slow any pursuit, he followed them inside.

They had minutes at most. They slammed the door shut, lifting a long beam and placing it crossways to create a barricade.

"I suggest the rooftops," Bria said. "It will keep us above most of them."

Tim nodded. It wasn't by any means a foolproof plan, and he suspected some of the undead would find their way onto the rooftops as well, but they would ford that ravine when the time came. In front of them, the door shook as the first cluster of undead threw themselves against its frame. Without further ado, the companions hastened to the upper floor. Boblin threw open a window, and they heard guttural sounds floating up from the street below. When Tim stuck his head outside, he saw a group of Uklith's automatons looking toward them, arms raised in a futile attempt to seize their out-of-reach quarry.

Boblin went first, reaching outside and grasping the lip of the roof over their heads. He gave it a hefty test pull once, ensuring it wasn't a flimsy gutter that would break free at the slightest addition of weight, and hoisted himself upward.

"Those karfing elions make it look so easy," Tim said to Bria.

She shrugged, then followed Boblin's lead without any trouble, leaving Tim standing alone. From below came the sound of glass shattering on the first floor.

Fine. She makes it look easy, too.

Tim pulled himself out the window, while Boblin and Bria reached down from the rooftop to hold his forearms and pull him the rest of the way. The surface of the roof had an easy pitch for stable footing. Once fully atop it, Tim stood to assess their surroundings. They were six blocks from the palace, with five to six buildings comprising each block. Though not all of the buildings around them were constructed in as forgiving a manner as this one—some roofs looked very steep indeed—at least they stood close enough together that it would be relatively easy to cross between them. The companions moved forward quickly, leaping from their current building to the next, as behind them Tim caught glimpses of the undead crawling into the ground floor of the first structure through a broken window.

Near the end of the first block, where they would need to contend with a larger gap between buildings, an attic hatch flew open on a building behind them and a group of undead swarmed outside. Tim stopped. "Keep going," he said to Boblin and Bria. To their rear, an undead that had climbed onto the other building's roof lost its footing immediately, tumbling to the streets below. Three more drooling creatures replaced it, coming for Tim with mouths wide and weapons ready.

Tim closed his eyes and focused, filling himself yet again with the Lifesource's surging waves of strength, and held up both hands. A massive, green ball of fire danced between his palms, and when the first undead leapt across the gap, Tim unleashed the fireball toward the far structure's load-bearing walls.

The effect was spectacular. After a rush of green fire, the entire rooftop imploded in a mixture of shingles and dust, taking a score of undead with it. The one undead that had managed to cross the gap still came forward, and Tim blew it apart with a casual gesture. The expenditure of so much magic dropped him to his knees, one palm on the rooftop. After taking a few deep gasps to catch his breath, he stood once more, noting the half-collapsed building and the mob of undead clustered around it. He turned with the intention of following Boblin and Bria.

The attack came from nowhere. An invisible hand slammed into him, throwing Tim back toward the opposite building. Momentum carried him across the shingles in a roll, and he landed against the last remaining fragment of rooftop.

What in Malath?

He caught a glimpse of a tall figure in black robes standing on a rooftop to his left—a building perpendicular to the route he, Boblin, and Bria had been running. His opponent struck again with another wave of magic that threw Tim across the remaining segment of roofing. Tim retaliated, sending a blast of flames toward the robed figure. He felt the roof disappear from beneath him, and he tumbled off the edge toward the street below.

* * *

The lone undead stopped in the middle of a narrow gap between two buildings opposite the garrison. Celia kept her crossbow sighted on the creature, staying as low as possible behind the lip of the wall. It hadn't seen her yet. The undead raised its nose, sniffed the air, and moved forward again with a shambling gait.

Beyond the alley and in the street, outside the undead's line of sight, two bodies of its comrades lay. Celia had dropped them not ten minutes ago, when they'd appeared in the wake of the spectacle in Agrazab's northern quarter. The city's northwest tower blazed with fire, inky black at the column's center, though much of it was hazy through the whirling sandstorm encompassing the area. Thankfully, the streets in front of the garrison remained clear for the time being, the chaos not having yet reached them.

The sun bore down on Celia with merciless heat. She raised a level hand to her brow, both to aid her vision and to shield herself from the worst of the glare. The undead seemed to be doing little more than aimlessly wandering, but she still wasn't about to suffer its presence any longer than necessary. Just a few more steps, and it would be in range.

The creature poked its head out of the alley, turned its gaze to the right, and spotted the bodies of its companions. It let out a mangled shriek. Theologically, Celia knew Father Anelion would argue that the undead did not possess souls or emotion, but she sure heard a lot of anger in that cry. The undead began a loping run out into the open. Celia pulled her trigger and her bolt struck the undead in the head, dropping it mid-stride.

A small cloud of dust rose as the creature's body hit the ground. Nothing happened for perhaps a minute, and then the door of the garrison opened and Jend stepped into the street. Checking that the scene was clear, Jend made his way to the corpse and pulled Celia's arrow from its head. The elion looked toward her, snapping a salute of acknowledgment.

Celia's gut told her that many more of these creatures would be appearing soon. It was easy enough for her to reason these were the bodies of citizens Uklith had killed in his last stroke before imprisonment. Agrazab had once held a population in the thousands, and if every one of those corpses were to rise at once...

Behind her, the trapdoor creaked open. Eklan Hamur emerged. "How is it so far?" the big man asked, voice a whisper. He kept low, on hands and knees to remain out of sight.

"Manageable enough, but they're rising faster. I also think the sandstorm's getting closer."

"I expected as much. Agrazab has awakened."

Celia rose just enough to confirm Jend was on his way back toward the garrison. She looked toward the wall of sand once more, wondering yet again if it truly was coming toward them or if it was just her imagination. After counting the buildings between herself and the maelstrom, she had to conclude the former. The storm had advanced one block, and it seemed to be moving more quickly.

"There's two more," Eklan said, causing her to look to the south. A pair of undead stumbled out of the shop in which Eklan and Bria had encountered Uklith's presence. Jend, still in the streets, quickened his pace into an all-out run. She shifted her position, raising her crossbow to take aim—

A flicker of motion drew her gaze back north, toward a section of street upon which the sandstorm would soon descend. No less than a dozen undead had appeared, two of which were still pulling themselves out of newly opened holes in the ground. Behind them, the sandstorm whipped itself into a frenzy, accelerating as it advanced, a swirl of undulating patterns at its center. After a moment Celia realized they were not patterns at all, but the forms of undead, ready to rip and tear their way past the elions' defenses.

Focus. She released her first arrow, taking out the group's leader. It fell to the ground, tangling several others with it, but the rest pushed forward. Below her, Jend tore the garrison door open and rushed inside, while behind him three more undead emerged from beneath the cobblestones of the streets themselves. Celia thought this to be the most disturbing sight of all, that of a half-decayed corpse pushing out of its grave and back into the sunlight. It was as if the underworld was giving birth to a parody of life. The undead weren't nearly as smart as malichons, but they were more numerous, which brought a host of problems with it.

She selected the target nearest the garrison and fired. Eklan slipped back through the trapdoor in order to help bolster the defenses below. Seconds later, the sandstorm struck. Celia dove onto her belly, keeping her face down and wrapping her arms over her head to protect her eyes, ears, and mouth. The whirlwind washed over her, rocking her body with full gale force. The onslaught lasted perhaps a minute, after which the winds died and the sands settled. Celia lifted herself back up to see a thin layer of grit covering the rooftop's surface. To the north, the spire still burned bright as ever. She assumed it was a Lifesource reservoir of sorts, but that was Tim and Boblin's business, for she had more pressing matters in front of her. In the wake of the whirlwind, an entire mob of undead had stumbled into the streets, and it appeared—whether through Uklith's direction or some other sensory capability—that they knew exactly where the elions were taking refuge. As monsters large and small, young and old, male and female, focused on the garrison, Celia flipped open the trapdoor.

"Get a second archer up here," she said. "We've got company."

* * *

Boblin leapt across the gap between buildings and hit the next rooftop, still running. He had his sword and his crossbow strapped crosswise on his back, leaving his hands free to grab purchase as necessary. Behind him, Bria kept pace, landing in a crouch to properly absorb the force of her landing. He seized her wrist, pulling her to shelter behind a turret right before it exploded in front of him. Splinters, shingles, and glass flew in all directions.

The robed figure moved effortlessly across the rooftops, at times appearing to float, its clothes a swirl of darkness. Every so often Boblin caught a glimpse of pale skin as it waved a hand to cast one of its spells. At first, Boblin had thought it was an Assassin, but as it came closer he saw that it didn't appear to have quite the right build. For one, it was shorter, and for another, it was shaped more like a regular human and less like a hulking giant. Assassin or not, the creature was making Boblin's life very unpleasant at the moment.

He and Bria took off running once more as two subsequent explosions caused sections of the rooftop to crumble away on either side. He'd seen Tim fall from the previous building, but didn't have time to consider the implications of what it meant. Besides, the man was a karfing Advocate, and he had probably manufactured cushions from the air before landing. If anything, Boblin wished their adversary would leave them alone and go back to bothering Tim. The Warrior was the real threat to Agrazab—Boblin was just background scenery.

In front of them, an egress window opened and a group of undead burst out. Boblin pulled twin knives from his belt and jumped forward, sliding across the rooftop on his knees with arms outstretched to either side. He passed between a pair of the creatures, taking out both with sideways strokes of his blades. When he returned to his feet, he came around in a turning side-kick, knocking a third undead back through another window. It fell through in a shatter of glass. Beside him, Bria struck a boomer and tossed it into the now-open egress hatch; a moment later, the entire rooftop rocked as the boomer took out the remaining undead.

Boblin risked a glance toward their pursuer and *felt* it looking at him. Using what Nazgar had taught him, he jumped. A thunderclap sounded in the space where he'd just been standing, and Boblin knew for certain that the spell would have dropped him dead had he remained in place. He sensed the figure's frustration, but figured it served it right. *Leave us alone and pick on the Advocate instead, why don't you?*

The next spell flung Boblin and Bria to opposite sides of the roof. Boblin's momentum sent him all the way off the edge, and he made a desperate grab for a drainpipe. As his hands grasped the pipe, he dangled over the street, his boots inches above the undead in the alley. The creatures milled and rustled, reaching toward him. One grabbed his foot and Boblin kicked outward, shaking it free at the same time as he pulled himself toward the rooftop's relative safety.

He'd almost made it when the wall in front of him erupted outward and an undead leapt out, wrapping arms around Boblin's torso. One of Boblin's hands slipped free from the drainage pipe, forcing him to hang on one-handed, the creature clinging to him, swinging wildly over the mob below.

The undead struck a knife into his side, but Boblin's chainmail diverted the tip of the blade, leaving his skin bruised rather than punctured. He elbowed the undead in the skull, striking twice before it fell away to land amid its companions and be ground to dust under their feet.

Boblin regained his grip, and this time succeeded in pulling himself to the rooftop. As he lay on his back, catching his breath, he felt a cold wave wash over him. He looked up and saw a whirl of robes. Their onetime pursuer, now on the rooftop *ahead* of Boblin, finished crossing the gap. Behind the robed stranger, Bria's body hovered horizontally in midair, motionless as if she were sleeping on an invisible bed. Cords of black smoke bound her body. The robed figure proceeded toward the palace, Bria's floating form following.

Boblin struggled up to give chase, but Bria's captor snapped toward him, hand stretched outward. This time, Boblin did not successfully dodge the spell, and an invisible force slammed into his chest. He flew across the entirety of the roof, striking another egress hatch. The glass shattered beneath him and the world went dark.

* * *

When Tim went over the edge, he hit the side of a half-collapsed building, breaking his fall. Hands grasped and clutched at him, an entire mob of undead on the street below seeking to drag him into their midst. He'd dropped his sword in the fall, and it lay buried beneath hundreds of trampling feet in the dust of the streets. He had but a few moments to gain his bearings before the mob succeeded in tearing him free of his ledge. Tim landed on the cobblestones of Agrazab, a legion of howling faces pressing in around him.

He issued a blast that knocked away those undead closest to him, next summoning his sword. The blade blazed to life with green fire and flew to his hand. When he caught it, he drew up to full height, positioned on the balls of his feet, and delivered strokes to creatures on all sides. There were so *many*, an entire city of undead, and he knew more were still rising.

Tim jumped back toward the collapsed building, using the Lifesource to propel himself upward, landing on the sloped angle of rubble. A pair of undead followed him, but he beheaded them in a single stroke. He continued climbing upward, lungs and limbs burning from exertion, unleashing one more column of fire before jumping back onto the rooftop he'd fallen from. Once out of the mob's reach, he stopped to rest. He'd been drawing on vast amounts of the Lifesource since the conflict began, having either incinerated or rebuffed over a hundred undead, and the strain was beginning to take its toll. It was like the time he'd unleashed an entire wave of power against the vrawl in the Northern Mountains, only that had ended in a span of seconds, whereas today he had been maintaining high amounts of the power for a much longer, sustained period. It couldn't last. He drained a skin of water, noting that the desert sun and its heat had further exacerbated his exhaustion. He heard several detonations in the distance—perhaps boomers, perhaps the robed individual with the Lifesource—but remained where he was. Whatever was happening, it would have to take care of itself while he regained his strength.

He allowed himself a few meager minutes of respite, as much as he dared, before returning to his feet. His strange nemesis was nowhere in sight, though Tim still took care to proceed with caution. He followed the same line Boblin and Bria had taken, noting the damage to several rooftops as he moved forward. Far ahead of him and near the palace, he thought he caught the hint of a swirl of robes before they vanished, descending off the rooftop to the streets. Next, he saw Boblin's boots sticking out from a broken egress hatch and hastened his pace. The elion lay in a tangle of shattered glass, unmoving.

Tim rushed to his friend, lifting Boblin's wrist. After feeling the faint beat of a pulse, he pulled Boblin from the rubble. Moving an injured soldier was rarely a wise course of action, but under the circumstances it was better to revive Boblin than to risk a passing undead making a meal of him. When Boblin did not move or waken, Tim splashed water on his face.

The elion jerked, eyes opening wide. "You karfing Advocates. Blowing things up left and right...one of these days, mate..."

"Did you get a look at its face?"

"No. But I think it took Bria."

"Come on." Tim hoisted Boblin to his feet, wrapping the elion's arm around his shoulder, and together they staggered across the rooftop. Every so often Boblin listed to the side, but with each step they took he seemed to grow clearer-headed and more alert. He also cursed more, which Tim took for a good sign.

Looking ahead, he saw a turret that looked as if it would provide a decent view of the surrounding area. When he kicked open the door, an undead lurched into the sunlight, but Tim waved his free hand and sent it flying against the back wall. Its body managed to splatter and crunch at the same time, not a sound Tim wished to hear again.

Inside the turret, Boblin shrugged off of Tim, standing on his own once more. He grasped a banister and led the way up a short staircase into a small, circular room ringed by windows. He leaned against the wall, blinking, and drew in a breath. "Well?"

"I have an idea who it might be," Tim said. "When the three Advocates sealed Uklith in prison, they surrendered their free will in order to do so. I think that's one of them out there, doing Uklith's bidding all these years later."

Boblin winced. "An undead Advocate? *That's* not comforting."

"They would have been very powerful sorcerers in their time. The Academy's best."

"And what in Malath do you suppose is going on with the focusing reservoir?"

Tim had been thinking for some time on this as well. He looked toward the tower of fire. Two other streams had joined it, he noticed, trailing from the distance to form a tri-section above their heads, the apex of which had become a spinning orb of fire. Deep within the orb, blackness shimmered. "Quentiin went south because we suspected the Lifesource might be at play in the attack on Vonku. I think multiple reservoirs have been triggered, and they're converging here. It would take an unbelievable amount of power to free Uklith, and that's exactly what we're seeing."

Boblin turned to Tim. "It runs through all living things, yes? The essence of a person's life is bonded to it. Meaning Bria might be—"

"A sacrifice to deliver the final burst of the energy. Or perhaps a vessel to inhabit. His current body might have failed him."

"This is bad."

"Aye. It's time to split up. I'm going into the palace. You get back to the others."

Boblin nodded, looking back toward the orb of power in the sky. "It stands to reason that if one leg of a tripod goes, the whole thing collapses, right?"

"You're thinking—"

Boblin hefted a boomer. "I may not understand the Lifesource, but I understand *these* quite well. You go to the palace, mate. Keep Uklith distracted as long as you can. Me? I'm going to destroy a focusing reservoir."

34

Sendalion pulled a lever, and in front of him the walls on either side of the al-ley collapsed onto the incoming corsair crew. Dust and stone fell inward. To the west, he heard shouts and cries as Vinsor's crew similarly rained weaponry down upon another corsair group, trapping their enemies in a gridlock of ar-rows and burning oil. The smoke and flames had grown so thick he could only see a few feet ahead, forcing him to navigate off memory alone, eyes stinging, nostrils clogged with the acrid smell of a city put to the torch. The Legion had long since abandoned the battlements, sticking to their plan of triggering traps to cover their retreat, slowly but steadily winnowing the enemy down. One ob-servation, however, nagged at Sendalion: while it seemed the Legion had felled a fair number of corsairs, Kaarst's overall numbers did not seem to be decreas-ing. Sendalion began to worry that their calculations had been dramatically wrong, and that Kaarst's crews numbered far more than originally anticipated.

Right on cue, a new corsair crew emerged from an adjacent street, parting the curls of smoke and descending upon Sendalion's company with savage ferocity. The Legion met their enemies blade to blade in the narrow quarters, and Sendalion wished he had some of Vinsor's archers to provide cover. He moved in low and quick, raising his sword overhand to meet his first opponent, their weapons clashing at the hilts. Sendalion brought his elbow forward into the corsair's chest, driving him against the side of the alley. The corsair tripped on the bed of an overturned cart, losing his balance, and Sendalion drove his blade through the man's neck with a *crunch*.

He drew back, preparing to face the next threat, when a massive jolt shook the ground. The world rocked, throwing Sendalion to the side. He had no time to recover, because a sudden light pierced the cloying haze. To the south, a massive pillar of white light shot into the air, rising high above the city to disappear into the clouds. Both sides halted at this unexpected development,

Legion and corsairs alike staring upward in confusion and surprise. As the light grew stronger, the combatants shielded their eyes, and it felt as though time hung suspended. Sendalion saw a thin vein of darkness running through the pillar's core, pulsing like a living thing.

Then somebody—Sendalion couldn't say who—decided they were better off fighting than staring, and in the space of an instant the combatants sprang at one another's throats once more. Sendalion dodged a blow from an axe directed toward his shoulder blades, retaliating with a kick into his newest opponent's midsection before taking the man's head from his shoulders. Fighting in the surreal, unexpected light, the Legion pushed back against the pirates, a mass of bodies jostling for supremacy in a mixture of sweat, grit, blades, and blood. This time, the Legion found themselves well and truly outnumbered. Sendalion tripped on the very same cart he had used to his advantage not a minute ago, losing hold of his sword when he hit the ground.

Above him, a corsair pressed down, bracing hands high overhead, battle-axe poised to descend. Then the corsair jerked, the barbed shaft of an arrow protruding from his chest. As Sendalion pushed back to his feet, more arrows hissed into the alley from the far side, finding targets among the pirates. One projectile shot past Sendalion close enough to draw blood from his shoulder and landed between the eyes of a dwerion corsair not six paces to his left. All around him, enemies fell to the ground, some with multiple barbs sticking from their corpses. Sendalion looked down the alley and saw Vinsor Dalin lowering his longbow. The man caught Sendalion's gaze, giving a brief but firm nod, and Sendalion saluted back.

When it was done, Vinsor came forward, his crew of archers behind him. He clasped Sendalion's hand in a firm shake, and Sendalion gave him a weary smile. "None too soon, Dalin."

"My pleasure, Captain." Vinsor looked upward, brow furrowing as he studied the phenomenon in the sky. "This is an interesting sort of daylight we're fighting in, wouldn't you say?"

"Aye, I *would* say. Come on, let's find ourselves a rooftop. I'd like to get a better view of what we're dealing with."

Vinsor followed Sendalion's lead, the two men entering a nearby building and climbing to its upper level. Upon reaching the rooftop, Sendalion stopped in mid-stride, staring south. The enormous spire of light rose high into the sky at the far side of the city. It was the strangest sight he had ever seen; the power seemed so *raw*, so real, he could do nothing but stare with slackened jaw. The wind whipped his clothes, blowing his cloak in frantic motions, the column of light before them blazing with the intensity of the sun.

It was that power, the *Lifesource*—Sendalion was sure of it. Aras had suspected its involvement all along, and after everything Sendalion had seen, he did not doubt for a moment that Kaarst might have struck a deal with someone versed in the mysterious power. Movement caught his eye and he peered toward an alley below. At first, he thought it was a column of corsairs advancing, but a closer glance told him their gait did not seem quite right. The group appeared to shamble forward, none too graceful, and they did not have the same *feel* as corsairs.

Sendalion turned toward Vinsor. "When you were moving through the streets, did you think there were far more corsairs than expected?"

"Aye, I thought so indeed, Captain. We brought down our fair share, but there always seemed to be more."

Sendalion handed him a spyglass. "Take a look at that."

After a moment's glance, Vinsor lowered the tube and looked at Sendalion. "What in Malath are *those*?"

Their visibility hadn't always been superb when triggering the traps on the corsairs. Seeing the group below, Sendalion suspected they might not have been *fighting* just pirates. During plenty of their engagements, the smoke had been too thick to properly make out any features, and after collapsing buildings and pouring boiling oil, they hadn't exactly stopped to examine the bodies afterward. "Have you ever heard stories of undead?"

Vinsor snorted. "Yes, but—"

"There's a karfing column of magic shooting up to the sky, for the Maker's sake. Are undead really that far out of the question?"

Vinsor swallowed. "It would certainly explain the numbers. How many do you think there are?"

"I don't know—hundreds? Thousands?"

In tandem, they looked toward Vonku's palace. Undead or not, the hordes below were converging upon it. "Come on," Sendalion said, drawing his sword once more. "We need to get to the palace."

* * *

Tim selected a quiet section of streets to return to ground level. He moved quickly but silently, hopping to successively shorter buildings, finishing by climbing through a window on the upper level of a small structure. Upon entering, he found himself in a simple bedroom. Whereas plenty of the buildings they'd gone through in Agrazab had been shops, inns, or soldier's quarters, this place was clearly someone's home, and it gave Tim pause. He wondered who the former residents of this house had been, and if they were out among the undead that he'd been fighting on this day. *How much of their previous lives do undead recall? Are they cognizant of their bodies, but unable to control them, riders on a terrible journey in which they have no say?* If so, it would be the worst kind of damnation possible—and that, he supposed, would be what Uklith liked about it.

Tim left the building and stepped into the street, which remained empty of undead. He found the quiet to be eerie and disturbing. During the past hour, he'd been in the midst of so much chaos that it felt unnatural to be standing in silence. Dust rose from the cobblestones around him, creating motes in the air. Here, he felt suspended within a single timeless instance of Agrazab, as disconnected from the rest of the city as Uklith's prison was separated from the world.

He stood in front of a short wall surrounding the palace proper. After looking both ways, he grabbed his first handhold and began climbing. He paused, reflecting upon the irony of it all—here he was, fighting at the very edge of the world against the greatest evil to threaten mankind, and yet it all came down to the most classic, fundamental notion of those tales he'd loved as a young boy: one lone man, climbing the palace wall to save the lady within.

Stories might have their place in this world, after all.

Tim reached the peak of the wall and vaulted to the far side. He landed in an area that could only have been an inner garden, back when the water in the city's wells had been plentiful. The place was now as dry and dead as the rest of the city, but he could see the skeletons of shrubs and other vegetation lying in withered clusters on either side of the path. Farther in, he saw a dry fountain, similar to the one they had passed in Agrazab upon first entering the city. Above his head, the spinning orb of darkness hung at the convergence of the three points of power, and it sent a chill down his spine. He wondered what Nazgar would say if he were here. *Probably something enigmatic that would neither offer comfort nor direction.*

After a moment, he chuckled. True enough, wasn't it? As much as he'd appreciated the Kyrlod's guidance, Nazgar often left Tim with more questions than answers. Here he had been these past weeks, wondering how he could take up this impossible task without Nazgar to show him the way, forgetting all the while that even when Nazgar *had* been here, his advice had been minimal at best. *I have to do this by myself, but when it comes right down to it, it's the only way I've ever done it.*

So get on with it, and make it happen.

Tim Matthias, Warrior of Light, filled himself with the Lifesource and moved toward the interior of Uklith's palace.

* * *

Quentiin and Jolldo fought side by side. The undead army pressed forward, more creatures emerging from nooks and crannies in the city each passing minute. Trivian Seltor stood farther down the line, a Legion soldier guarding his flank. Several alleys back the company had made a stand against the enemy, doing their best to stem the tide, but the steady crush of automatons ultimately forced them to abandon their post.

They moved in search of a new place to hold high ground, and it was clear to Quentiin that Sendalion and Vonku's other defenders had done their diligence in preparing the city. The paths they traveled had been arranged to funnel any attackers through the narrowest gaps possible. Streets that did not serve a strategic purpose had been barricaded outright, and plenty more had been turned into ready-made traps to spring upon their enemies. The defenders stood outside the mouth of an alley, within which the undead were squeezed into a narrow line of advance. Behind Quentiin, Yagglem and Briiga wrestled a stone into the basket of a catapult they'd commandeered during their retreat. They would have time for one shot, two at most, before they'd need to torch the construct and withdraw from the area.

Above their heads, the column of fire shot into the sky, arcing northwest, which did not surprise Quentiin in the least. The power was, without a doubt, streaming to Agrazab. Quentiin *did* have to appreciate the subtle irony. He'd gone south in the event Uklith's dark magic might have some involvement in Kaarst's assault, concluded the two conflicts were unrelated, only to discover at the final hour that their fight here likely had dire consequences for Tim to the west.

"Hold fast!" Yagglem called, the boulder settling into position. The undead surged forward. In response, Trivian guided his men backward, skillfully leading the Legion men toward safety and away from the line of fire. Quentiin fell back, joining Yagglem and Briiga at the catapult, hand poised above the lever.

"Fire!" Quentiin roared, and they released the stone. It flew through the air right toward the alley's mouth, a near-perfect shot that clipped the corner of a building. The upper half of the structure collapsed, raining rubble and dust as the catapult's boulder landed in the center of the undead. Quentiin saw a splatter of limbs before the remainder of the enemy boiled from the opening like ants from a disturbed hill. *This is what we get when every grave in the city awakens.*

The dwerions and Legion fell back. Quentiin tossed a torch onto the catapult. He didn't expect the undead could actually use the mechanism against the Legion—the creatures were too elementary for that—but the flames and smoke could work to the defenders' advantage. And then they were running yet again, forcing themselves between the gaps in a field of waist-high stakes that Sendalion and Vinsor's crews had planted many nights ago. Though an incredibly useful mechanism for slowing down attackers, it worked as much against Quentiin's group as it had against any of the corsairs that had gone before. Quentiin saw many of the spikes tinged with blood, no shortage of bodies lying amid the pickets. He squeezed between a pair of stakes, ducking and twisting, diving and turning, his comrades doing likewise. When they pushed free on the far side, he turned to see the undead throwing themselves against the makeshift spears. Many impaled themselves within the first few feet, but for every one that was stopped in this fashion, two more pushed just a bit farther inward. To make matters worse, Quentiin's group pressed up against blockaded alley, their backs literally against a wall, with perhaps a hundred paces of stakes between them and a raving mass of limbs and bodies that just would not stop.

"Quickly," Quentiin growled. They had no more than thirty left in their company, and at least five times as many undead raging toward them. They had gained themselves a few minutes at most, but he intended to make them count. He and Trivian exchanged a glance of unspoken agreement and began piling up wreckage to build a short wall between themselves and the stakes. The first batch of undead had made it halfway through the field, and the soldiers had to work quickly. They removed the barricade behind them and placed it onto the pile of wreckage in front of them, both giving themselves a means of escape as well as adding to their last line of defense. They sweated and strained in the confined space. Quentiin thanked the Maker that undead did not appear intelligent enough to handle ranged weapons. It was one small blessing countered by the fact that the small company was about to get overrun in close quarters. The undead covered three-fourths of the distance now, pushing faster and faster through, the outer row of stakes so burdened by bodies that the spikes began snapping off, which only accelerated the pace at which the remainder could advance.

The first wave pushed forward, a spike inches in front of Quentiin's face breaking free. An undead staggered out, swinging its cutlass wildly, the blade passing inches above Quentiin's head—

The dwerion surged upward, head-butting the creature square in the face and picking it up over his head. "Light 'em up, laddies!" he roared, throwing the creature back into its companions. "Burn them all, the Maker help us!"

And with the hastily constructed barricade acting as a temporary shield for themselves, the company threw torches onto the cedar-picket stockade, setting the tinder ablaze. An angry line of fire leapt to life. Dozens of dark forms twisted in the resulting conflagration. One staggered over the barricade to land at Quentiin's feet, rolling on the ground in a flaming husk. Quentiin stamped the fire out and looked over the burning field.

"That should slow 'em for a bit," Jolldo growled from behind.

With enough of the path behind them cleared for the dwerions and soldiers to push through, they formed a line into the next street, which led uphill toward a small rise. At the top of the hill, they paused, able to see over most of Vonku's interior. They stood at the exact center of the conflict. Behind them, the column of raging light rose high into the sky, while ahead a winding column of undead and corsairs beset the main gates of Vonku's palace. Legion soldiers on the palace walls shot arrows and poured oil, culling attackers from the column, but Kaarst's ghastly fleet continued pressing forward nonetheless.

Everything centered on the gates. While a unified attack against one section of the palace would not win any awards for subtlety, Kaarst had the numbers to succeed with such a blunt approach. Even if Quentiin and the rest could arrive in time, they would add but a drop to the bucket. Still, Quentiin had come to defend this city, and that was exactly what he planned to do.

Trivian caught Quentiin's gaze and nodded. This was what they were here for, no matter how it turned out.

Down the street from which Quentiin and the rest had emerged, the first undead broke free. Some had the shattered hafts of stakes dangling from their midsections, but the creatures appeared impervious to any wounds except those that left them anatomically unable to function. Trivian led the soldiers in a quiet but hurried retreat down the far side of the hill. There, they found a side street free from the commotion, angling for an approach that would allow them to get inside the walls and join Sendalion's soldiers.

Quentiin risked a glance toward their rear, but the undead had not yet crested the rise. The soldiers disappeared into the alley, and he allowed himself to hope that they might have escaped the creatures' notice. Buildings rose high on either side of the group, though not high enough to cut off the sight of the spire of power reaching toward Agrazab. Though it was tempting to pause and rest, they did not stop for fear of their pursuers finding them. Every so often they saw signs of previous conflicts in the form of charred buildings, broken windows, or the bodies of Legion men and corsairs alike lying where they had fallen.

Perhaps midway to the palace, they rounded the corner into a new alley and came upon a corsair crew who had apparently decided to take a reprieve free from prying eyes. There were eight pirates, four lounging against the wall and passing a bottle, three clustered around a pile of coins on the cobblestone, and one who lay flat-out unconscious on a pallet of grain-filled sacks. Were it not for the circumstances, the scene might have been comical. The first corsair to see the Legion soldiers leapt to his feet, swaying as he pulled his sword from his belt in an exaggerated, drunken fashion. By the time he had his guard up, Quentiin had already run him through.

The soldiers and dwerions swept into the street, dispatching the corsairs in a sharp blur of axes and swords, but the delay had not been one they could afford. Only moments after their victory, they heard the thump of many feet coming their direction. The company had not, it seemed, been successful in their attempts to evade the undead behind them.

"Let's get out o' here," Quentiin said. Even as he spoke, a wave of undead came into view behind them, perhaps a hundred yards away, closing fast. For a split second he considered the merits of standing their ground, but given the enclosed space of the alley and the sheer number of enemies bearing down, he knew they had to flee. They would choose their battleground at a different location.

Trivian took the lead, pointing them toward the exit at the opposite end of the street. But he had just ordered the first line of soldiers to begin marching when the voice of a child cried out.

Quentiin froze. The voice had belonged to a young girl. "Stand fast," he said, and the group halted.

Trivian met his gaze, and the girl cried out again. This time they both looked upward. The sound had come from the uppermost level of a building to their left. Quentiin cursed, drawing his blade. They had less than a handful of heartbeats before the undead would be upon them.

"Let's go," he said to Trivian. To the rest of the group, he said, "Hold the alley."

He started toward the door of the building, but Trivian stopped him with a hand on his shoulder. "No."

"Like Malath, laddie."

"I'll do it myself. The rest of you go."

Quentiin opened his mouth, but Trivian cut him off. "Dying here serves no purpose. Get free, go to the palace. Serve the king."

Jolldo stepped forward. "Laddie—"

Trivian raised a hand. "This bill is long overdue," he said softly. "I will take care of it, Quentiin Harggra. You continue."

Quentiin remained silent but a moment, then nodded. *Every man has the right to make choices such as these.* "To me, laddies," he said to the rest of the group. "We make for the palace."

* * *

Jend Argul threw his weight against the garrison door. Outside, undead scratched and clawed, trying to find their way in. Above, Ken had joined Celia on the rooftop, and Eklan and Wurit were in the process of barricading the windows. A creature thrust its arm through a gap between the boards, hand grasping at open air, fingers flexing. With a decisive swipe, Eklan cleaved the undead's limb from its body. Wurit quickly placed a board across the gap, bracing it against those already in place.

Jend felt the door shake against his back. He dug his heels into the ground, putting every ounce of energy into holding the frame closed. Another *thump*, and his boots skidded across the dirt floor, just an inch, leaving tiny furrows behind. "Hurry," he said.

Eklan came forward wielding a giant crossbeam. He wedged it into place behind the elion and Jend stepped away, drawing a breath of relief. His thigh muscles ached, his limbs trembled. *I may be getting old for this.*

"How long do you suppose this buys us?" Wurit asked.

"It certainly won't last forever," Jend replied, "but any time it *does* buy, I'll take." He climbed to the roof, arriving just as a boomer detonated over the streets. Celia stood on the roof's far corner, lowering her crossbow. From the opposite corner, Ken tossed her a new boomer before raising his bow once more.

Jend drew an arrow from his quiver and advanced to take position midway between the two elions. In the street below, undead boiled in a throbbing mass of limbs and weaponry. A group pressed against the barricaded door below, and Ken was firing his most select shots toward that group, doing everything possible to trim the numbers throwing their weight against the company's hastily constructed defenses. Nearby, a cluster of detached limbs and torsos lay in the dirt, clearly the work of Celia's boomer. She raised her crossbow and took aim again, firing into the nearest concentrated mass of undead. The boomer detonated on impact, sending the corpses flying in several directions along with a small blossom of fire.

Jend released an arrow, but even as it dropped two undead—the shaft traveled through the head of the first and into the chest cavity of the next—he saw they would soon have a new problem. The corpses were piling so high that every undead that climbed atop those before it came just a bit closer to the rooftop. And though the creatures were only perhaps halfway to reaching the company, there were enough of them in the streets that the bodies would make the mound high enough sooner or later. When that happened, all the barricades below would do the elions no good, for the undead would be able to climb a mountain of their slain comrades and overwhelm the small band of defenders. *I hope Matthias and Kule have a good plan going,* Jend thought, *because I am fresh out at the moment.*

* * *

As the last of the Legion men exited the alley, Trivian Seltor slipped inside the building. Though the undead were not far off, he imagined he was safe enough in here. The creatures' focus would be on pursuing Quentiin's group rather than on chasing one man into an abandoned house. Upon entering, he saw plenty of overturned furniture in the dark, indicating a conflict had recently taken place. When he reached the back of the room, he saw a man's body lying in a pool of blood behind a countertop, the puddle of red still fresh, a sword inches from his outstretched hand. The man wore the drab brown clothing of Vonku's peasantry.

From above, the cry sounded a third time. A second voice laughed, and something *thumped*. Trivian pushed his way up a staircase, coming across a second dead man. At the summit of the steps, a woman's body lay in front of a closed door. Rough, coarse laughter came from the other side.

I was sent to Eltern because I heard two children crying.

He was no longer at Eltern, though. He'd traveled from the outpost, across the seas, and now he was back in Vonku, where he'd earned the badge of the Royal Legion and sworn to serve. It was here that he'd made a grievous error, and his company had paid the price. Today another child was crying, and it was time to make things right. He knew Quentiin Harggra would have stayed here, had Trivian asked him to do so—but Trivian Seltor could not allow anyone else to pay his debts.

He slammed his shoulder into the door, forcing it open, and entered the room with sword drawn. Three corsairs stood inside, one by the door and two on the far side. The latter two held a struggling girl of no more than ten between them. One had forced her to the ground, holding her by the strands of her hair, while his companions laughed.

The corsair by the door turned as Trivian appeared. The pirate brought his sword up in a hasty defense and the two blades clashed, steel on steel ringing in the enclosed space. Trivian ducked his enemy's retaliatory strike, and then killed him with sword to heart. The corsair's eyes went wide in shock and pain, and he issued a gurgling rasp as Trivian jerked his weapon free. *And good riddance to you.*

Hot, white pain exploded in Trivian's midsection. He looked down to see the tip of a blade protruding from his stomach. Time gelled around that moment, Trivian sliding onto his knees as the corsair who had struck him from behind pulled the sword free. Trivian cried out in spite of himself, glancing at his belly to see blood running in a deep, thick river. Sword still in hand, Trivian spun on his knees and brought his weapon around in an arc. Above him, the corsair blocked the blow with ease, giving a contemptuous flick and knocking the blade free from Trivian's hand. The weapon clattered to the floor with a leaden sound. From the corner of his eye, Trivian saw the girl attempt to pull free from the third corsair's grip. In response, the burly man cuffed her on the side of the head and sent her sprawling. She cried out, raising a hand to the spot where he had struck her.

"Stay where ye be," the corsair said to the girl. "You an' I ain't finished."

The second corsair, still standing above Trivian, drove his blade into Trivian's shoulder, forcing the Legion man onto his back. He placed his boot on Trivian's neck, applying a slow, steady pressure. Already numb with pain, Trivian could only gasp and gurgle.

"I'm goin' to gut ye like a pikefish," the corsair said, "but ye'll still live long enough to watch us. How does that sound, mate?"

Trivian wrapped his hands around the man's ankle, attempting to wrest him off balance. The man freed himself with an easy kick, knocking Trivian's arm back to the ground. He stamped down on Trivian's hand, hard, and Trivian felt his knuckles shatter. The corsair thrust his blade into Trivian's stomach once more, twisting, and Trivian screamed in agony.

The pirate stepped away. Trivian hadn't ever thought it possible the body could bear such pain. He'd been stabbed twice in the stomach, once in the shoulder, and his left hand was a mangled mess. A rushing sound filled his ears, but through it all he heard the two corsairs laughing as they turned away from him.

Not on my watch. Not while I draw breath.

Trivian Seltor climbed to his feet, pressing his broken hand against his stomach, holding his insides together as blood leaked through his fingers. He staggered to his sword, picking it up in his good hand. Neither corsair noticed, standing with their backs to him. The girl sobbed, the sound of her voice driving Trivian onward, giving him strength and purpose to continue. Every fiber of his being screamed for him to stop, to collapse and die, but he would not allow it.

He came upon the second corsair from behind, aim clumsy but still true, and brought his blade down upon the man's clavicle. Though Trivian no longer possessed the strength to finish the blow and take the corsair's head off, the damage was done. The corsair fell to the side, bright blood spraying as he raised his cutlass in defense. Trivian struck his wrist, this time successfully completing the stroke and separating limb from body. Blood gushed from the stump, and the sound of the corsair's screams brought Trivian nothing but satisfaction.

The last pirate released the girl, coming for Trivian instead. He pushed Trivian back against the wall, sticking his blade through Trivian's unwounded shoulder and into the wood, pinning the Legion man in place.

"Ye don't give up, do ye?" he asked, face close to Trivian's. His breath was hot and rank, and when he smiled, he showed a set of yellowed teeth on decaying gums.

"You're right," Trivian said, "I don't."

The corsair stiffened in surprise as Trivian shoved his belt knife into the man's heart. Trivian twisted the blade for good measure and pushed his attacker away. The corsair fell to the ground, twitching in death throes, as Trivian pulled the sword free from his shoulder and from the wall. He wavered, strength ebbing fast, knowing he had mere seconds left on his feet. He came into position over the second corsair, who still breathed, albeit with one less hand and blood running from his neck. Trivian Seltor looked every inch the angel of avenging justice, tall and dark, face implacable, covered in countless wounds.

The corsair looked up, fear and pain showing on his face in equal measure. "Mercy," he said. *"Please."*

Trivian lifted his sword, meeting the man's eyes. "No."

He held the tip of his sword over the other's heart, but having no strength left to deliver the blow, he fell forward, using the weight of his body to drive the weapon home. The corsair shuddered beneath him and went still. Trivian tumbled to the side and onto his back, looking up at the ceiling.

The girl came into view above him, wide-eyed, face framed with beautiful hair. Drying tears trickled down her cheeks, but when she looked at him, she smiled.

See, he thought, *things aren't actually that bad. And it doesn't hurt nearly as much as I thought it would.*

"Hello, miss," he said through cracked lips. "What's your name?"

"Vanya," she said. "Vanya Lerindell, my lord. And yours?"

"Trivian Seltor." He managed a smile. "But I'm no lord, I'm afraid."

"I'll get you help, my lord."

"No." It was too dangerous for her, too late for him. The tears returned to her eyes. "Listen to me, Vanya. I don't have long left."

"Anything, my lord."

The immediacy of her need gave him the strength to continue speaking. "Hide until this battle is done. After, make your way to the king's palace and ask for Quentiin Harggra. After that..." He swallowed to work moisture back into his voice. "Grow. Become a woman and *grow old*. It won't always be easy, but you will do it, and you will make yourself proud, and you will know it meant something. Promise me that."

Her tears fell on his bleeding chest. "Don't go."

"Promise."

"Yes," she whispered. "I promise."

Trivian laid his head back. It was finished, and he'd done what his comrades before him had also done: traded a life so that an innocent could survive. He let the Maker take him, up and away from his wounded body. Vanya Lerindell closed the lids of his eyes, placing a kiss upon his brow, and Trivian Seltor entered the world of harmony, where all men of true heart, courage, and above all, kindness, would find themselves one day.

35

Tim placed his hand over the footprint in the sand. He was getting closer to Bria and whoever—whatever—held her captive. Above him, the focusing point raged in all its brilliance, the spinning orb of darkness at its center juxtaposed against the radiant light. A gust of wind blasted past him, disintegrating the footprint and whipping his cloak. Through the Lifesource, Tim felt a malevolent darkness exuding from Agrazab's palace, evil layered upon evil, an eternity of pain and suffering mingled with the oily taint of Uklith's amusement. That very same darkness coursed through every undead roaming the city, fueling them with execrable purpose, and Tim suspected that the Demon-Lord meant for these unholy armies to cover the earth as the malichon armies once had, burning cities and feeding upon their victims, with Uklith's dark presence over all.

Within the Lifesource, a trio of smaller presences hovered in front of Uklith's, one closer to Tim, the other two deeper inside the palace. It was the three Advocates, two men and one woman who'd given up everything to stop the lord of the underworld, unwittingly bound to Uklith's service. *A punishment for their deed of saving the world.*

What if the same fate as theirs awaited him? Or worse, awaited Bria? His hand shook as he removed it from the footprint.

In spite of the evil the building contained, its short, squat shape made for an unassuming presence. Agrazab's rulers before Uklith, whoever they had been, had not lived a lavish lifestyle. The palace served function first, hunkering behind the surrounding walls to withstand inevitable sandstorms raging through the city, its thick walls preserving a cool interior to provide relief from the merciless heat. As Tim approached the steps, he saw rows of long-dried dirt indicating where trees might once have grown, offering shade to those who climbed the stairs, though the vegetation had long since died.

Most of the structure had been made of adobe atop a stone foundation. Upon reaching the apex of the stairs, Tim looked up at the arched doorway. There was nothing there, he realized, just a plain set of gates without so much as an ornament or crenellation to mark the significance of what lay beyond. This observation unnerved him more than anything else. He might have expected gargoyles or wicked sculptures, but this was simply the doorway to a long-abandoned palace.

He pushed the gates open, stepping into the dark interior. A draft of cool air blessed his skin, and Tim knew that even though this place did not look like much from the outside, staying in here would have offered the royalty true bliss. A long-faded tapestry hung to his left, and a row of wooden pedestals stood to his right. Behind him, the dim light coming through the door showed dust motes dancing in the air. Tim remained in the entrance for several heartbeats and the let the door close, plunging him into momentary blackness.

The attack came, just as he had expected. Within the corridor, a burst of purple fire blossomed, shooting straight toward him. Tim dove, the stream of fire striking the closed door behind him, causing a curtain of sparks to rain down. As he hit the ground, he flicked his hand and the pedestals along the hallway leapt into green flame, providing illumination once more. He saw a swirl of robes at the far end of the corridor. An invisible force lifted him into the air, slamming him against the opposite wall. Tim opened his palm, issuing an opposing stream of green fire, and the two columns clashed in the corridor's center in a frenetic merging of light. He felt the impact run up his arms, the same as if he'd struck an opponent's blade during a sword fight, and he planted his feet, putting mind and body into the battle.

Tim's opponent pushed, and Tim felt his limbs begin to shake—this one was well versed in the Lifesource, and must have been a true titan of power in their day. So it went, two combatants on opposite sides of the corridor, powers matched, first the balance shifting toward one, then the other, sometimes a foot gained, other times a foot lost. Tim could only hold this stalemate for so long. His physical body would work against him, for he would grow weary, while matters of the flesh were of much less import to his undead opponent. They might be well matched in the Lifesource, but Tim's endurance would fail much sooner.

Tim could, however, use the Advocate's momentum to his own advantage. He allowed the undead to advance his position, resisting just enough to ensure the Advocate was putting all its strength into the effort. As the Advocate neared, he saw her features and recognized this one was Shelendel. When she had covered three-quarters of the distance, Tim released the power. He dove to the side, as beside him the column of fire blasted into the ground. It struck a pedestal, causing it to erupt in fragments of wood and glass. Shelendel stumbled, off-balance from the unexpected lack of resistance, and Tim rolled back up to unleash a new wave of fire, striking her in the chest. For a moment Tim thought the flames would consume Shelendel, but the licking tongues of green fire winked out, revealing her standing with hunched posture, gathering herself to recover.

Tim came all the way to his feet, sword blazing in his hands, but as he brought his blade down for an attack Shelendel produced her weapon, a sword of purple fire. The two swords struck in the middle of the hallway, blade against blade, magic against magic. Tim spared just enough time for a glance beyond Shelendel's shoulder, hoping to see Bria's form hovering in the air as Boblin had described, but she was nowhere to be seen. He had no time for further thought, because Shelendel brought her blade around, and when the two weapons struck, multihued sparks showered to the ground. The weapons clashed a third time, raking against the side of the wall, causing flakes of mortar to tumble to the ground. In the dancing light of the blazing pedestals, the two opponents' shadows leapt large and full against the nearby wall, bigger-than-life replicas, as they vied for supremacy within the Demon-Lord's lair.

* * *

Boblin yanked his blade free from the undead. The creature fell to the ground, Boblin pressing his back against the stone wall behind him, as before him a mass of the creatures pushed and grasped, each struggling to be the first to reach him. The next one to break through came for Boblin with hands outstretched. Boblin kicked outward in defense, his boot striking the creature in the chest, knocking it back into the clutches of its comrades.

This was a right enough state of affairs. At least thirty undead clustered in the street, jostling like a sea of angry ants, their movements sometimes clumsy but always ferocious. It was a curious juxtaposition, how they moved so slowly yet remained so deadly, unintelligent in the singular sense but functioning with a unified purpose in the aggregate. Boblin held his sword in one hand, swinging the weapon to behead the next corpse, and tore a boomer from his belt with the other hand. He struck the fuse, holding it before his eyes as the tiny strand of wire sparkled.

The automatons slowed, their attention focused on the brightly burning wick. "That's right, mates," Boblin said, "take a good, long look." He slung the boomer to the ground, rolling it into the center of their cluster. As the undead turned to watch this new element in their midst, Boblin took off running. Heartbeats later the boomer exploded, shooting a fountain of dirt and stone into the air, sending corpses flying all directions. The concussion knocked Boblin from his feet, but he turned the momentum into a roll and sprang back up. He risked a glance over his shoulder and saw that half of the undead had survived the blast.

In front of him stood a crumbling wall. Boblin doubled his stride and leapt toward it, catching the top of the ledge with his fingers. One hand slipped free, knocking loose a waterfall of dirt and pebbles before he regained his grasp and swung upward. On top of the ledge, he rolled onto his back, staring at the sky and regaining his breath. The focusing reservoir's enormous column of light remained high above him, as if mocking his attempts to reach it. Well, he'd cross this city and make it to that tower if it was the last thing he did, and from there he would turn it into a karfing crater. *And good riddance to it.*

He staggered to his feet, feeling the structure waver under him. At the far edge, where a partially collapsed portion hung lower to the ground, an undead clambered up and came toward him. Boblin chose his footing carefully, wary of a collapse at first, before deciding a collapse was *exactly* what this wall need-ed. He leapt down the opposite side, into an empty alley, and threw his shoul-der against the wall. The structure buckled. Boblin rammed it again, throwing his entire weight into the blow, and the wall tumbled in a cluster of bricks and clay. The lone undead fell off, landing betwixt its companions as the mountain of rubble descended upon them.

As Boblin resumed his run, a shadow passed overhead. He glanced upward and noticed that the spinning orb had grown more malevolent, a rotating ball of darkness writhing with palpable purpose. When the shade came upon him, he felt his limbs grow weak and his heart flutter. His fingers become cold, his breath misty, and then he was back in the sunlight, where he skidded to a halt and looked back. That sphere was the gateway to the underworld, of that

Boblin was sure. If what he'd just felt was but a taste of what was to be unleashed, time was far too short.

He pushed his way into yet another abandoned inn, rushing through the common area and up the stairway. On the second level he reached a long hall full of bedrooms. He selected one in the middle of the corridor, inside of which there was nothing more than a mattress on a bed frame, covered in dust. Boblin wiped grime from a window and pushed it open. So far, the alley remained clear. He took a deep breath, forcing himself to relax, the quivering sensation of adrenaline dissipating.

His momentary reprieve ended when he heard explosions. Boblin leaned out the window, discerning the garrison against the city's backdrop. Another flare of light blossomed as one of the figures on the roof—Celia, judging from the way she moved—unleashed another boomer. Undead rushed toward the garrison, waves upon waves, climbing over the mounded bodies of their comrades, pressing in against the defenders. Boblin uttered an oath and raced back to the ground floor of the inn. He burst into the street. He looked over his right shoulder, toward the focusing reservoir and moon of darkness, and then over his left shoulder, where his wife and fellow elion soldiers fought their battle against innumerable enemies.

He narrowed his gaze, taking a final glance at the spire of Lifesource energy. "I'm not done with you yet," he said. But he had to help the others first.

Boblin spun on his heel and ran toward the garrison.

* * *

Fire and smoke filled Vonku's streets. By the time Quentiin and his companions reached the central square in front of the palace garrison, the defenders had long since fallen to the tide of undead. Bodies of friend and foe alike littered the streets, lying at intervals like broken puppets, some with arrows protruding from them, others missing limbs. In spite of it all, the palace on the opposite side of the garrison remained whole and unbroken, a single unblemished bastion in contrast to the death and ruin throughout all other parts of Vonku. Quentiin didn't let the building's pristine appearance fool him, though. A line of corpses ran up the steps and through the garrison gates, one of the oaken doors hanging ajar, the other shattered outright.

He led the soldiers across the open space in a rush, as behind them the undead spilled into the mouth of the square, fanning out with the intention of overwhelming the small company. As Quentiin ran, he cursed his short stride. He'd rarely felt the limitation as keenly as today, which had involved almost nonstop running. Up the steps he went, stumbling over the last one but remaining upright, and then he was through the open doorframe, seeing bodies strewn within. He climbed the steps to the battlements, Jolldo by his side. Behind them, the last of the soldiers into the garrison threw the remaining door shut and began filling the gap with any obstacles at hand.

Upon reaching the parapets, Quentiin looked out across the inner courtyard. Body upon body of Legion soldiers lay in the sunlight, one long column of resistance stretching up to the palace. The Legion had made a valiant stand here, falling one man at a time, each soldier placing himself between the enemies and the king, committing the ultimate sacrifice in service of Vonku. And, it appeared they might have failed.

"What next, laddie?" Jolldo asked.

"We do what we can," Quentiin said, gesturing to the empty battlements. "We man these walls once more, and hold as long as we must."

At his command, the men of Eltern took to the battlements, taking up the positions their comrades had died defending. They seized crossbows, longbows, swords, and oil, filling the parapets, and for the first time that day they stopped running, instead turning and standing their ground. Below, the rabble of undead surged forward, but the sudden hail of arrows halted them. Quentiin smiled. These men had run long and hard, and they'd now earned a chance to fight back, a chance to stand and serve their king as they had always wanted too—not from the outpost of Eltern, but from the walls of Vonku.

He looked up at the ever-prominent reservoir shooting into the sky. He knew it traveled west, toward Tim and Boblin. He wished he had a way of knowing how the others fared, but he had to settle for trusting in the best.

Quentiin turned to Jolldo, placing a hand on his friend's shoulder. Before them, the corsairs and undead continued forward, advancing in spite of the burning pitch and projectiles raining down. "Hold the line, laddie," he said. He began running yet again, for what felt like the hundredth time that day, this time down the far side of the battlements and into the courtyard where the bodies of good Legionnaires lay left and right. Blood covered the cobblestone path, and wind whipped through the streets.

A cluster of bodies lay in front of the palace's broad stone steps. Seeing a familiar glint in the sun, Quentiin raced forward, pulling one body off the group, and then another, to reveal Vinsor Dalin's form amid the rubble. At first, he feared his friend dead, but after a moment saw a faint rise and fall of the man's chest. After another moment, Vinsor's eyes fluttered open. He looked up to the sky, flinched at first and reached for his weapon, but Quentiin stayed his hand.

"Easy," he said. Moving Vinsor's body with care, he cleared the rest of the rubble off his friend. "How bad is it?"

"Bad enough, but I'll live."

Quentiin looked from him to the interior of the palace beyond. "How fares the king?"

"I don't know. When they came upon us, there were so many. I thought undead were just stories, but—"

"They're not. There's dark magic at work here, laddie."

"Who is it?"

"Uklith. He's touched the North before, and today it appears he's touched the South." Quentiin pointed toward the focusing reservoir shooting into the sky. "Do you see that, laddie? It's raw Lifesource power. Those are the bonds keeping Uklith sealed in his prison. That's what we're fightin' against—not Vila Kaarst, not his corsair lords, but against the Demon-Lord of Malath."

"But what designs does he have on this city?"

"Not just the city. He has designs on all the world."

Vinsor nodded, swallowing, following Quentiin's gaze. "Go, friend. Hurry. Time is short. Danris is with them. I don't know if they live, but if they do…"

"I know." Quentiin nodded toward the battlements. "Jolldo and the dwerions are in position. For now at least, they'll hold the line. If they fail—" He took a blade from a fallen soldier, handing it to Vinsor. He hoped it would serve the Legion man better than it had its former owner.

When Quentiin rose to his feet, Vinsor pointed to a tower on the main palace, at the top of which Alcatune's flag fluttered. "That's directly above the king's chambers. If they're retreating, they'll head there. Go with the Maker, friend. Go with all our hopes."

When Quentiin reached the base of the tower, the flag above him looked a lonely sight, perhaps reflecting the struggle of those within the palace. How many remained, he did not know. How many undead assailed them, he did not know. But neither number mattered, for Quentiin was here, and whether it meant facing one foe or a hundred, he would do his duty. Around him, still more bodies littered the grounds, lying in irregular, broken heaps. However, he had nothing to achieve by following the trail of those who had passed before him. If he had any hope of gaining the upper hand, it would be from *ahead* of the fight, not behind it.

He looked at the face of the tower. Though he shared Boblin Kule's distinct lack of fondness for heights, at times like this such preferences mattered little. He could see plenty of handholds in the grooves of the stones, and while it may not have been ideal, it would work. Quentiin Harggra grasped the edge of the first stone, hoisted himself up, and began to climb.

* * *

Emperor Ladu Jovun IV made his way toward the palace, the wind whipping past him as he climbed over the rooftops. He struggled for balance, putting one foot forward and then the other, alternating between handholds. All the while he kept an eye out to his left and to his right, cautious for signs of an attack, his free hand on the hilt of his sword. *Almost there.*

In the tower behind him, he caught a glimpse of Faldon, Tavin, and Raisha turning away from the window. Moments later he heard the sounds of battle resume from within, clashes of steel against steel rising alongside shouting voices. A new gust of wind caught Ladu and he wobbled, almost losing his footing before he grasped a crenellation for support. Though the palace remained half-finished, the throne room was complete, and he knew without a doubt that Endar Varuc waited there. This was what the man had wanted all along: to sit in the emperor's seat, to rule, making this kingdom his, even if it meant servitude to the darkest of masters.

The radiance of the focusing point blinded Ladu, and he thought of Jeb the woodsman—the traitor who had lived as a slave in the time of Zadinn's kingdom, transformed into a pillar of energy accelerating Uklith's release. *The last time, armies from the west did us in, but this time it was our fellow people.* The threat had come not from Malath, but from the likes of Endar Varuc, Jeb the woodsman, and those who had risen from their graves. And that was worth reflecting upon, for when it came right down to it, Zadinn had also been a threat from within, a student from the Academy of Naxish who fell prey to his own evil before seeking Uklith. When Zadinn went west and raised the malichon army, it had been but one example of the ways in which Uklith corrupted, and the possession of men such as Jeb and Endar was another. *Would we have anything to fear at all, if not for the darkness in our hearts?* Perhaps that was the point. Uklith might be the embodiment of evil, but he had only ever gained power by tapping into the nuggets of darkness that resided in all men and women. It was *people* who gave the Demon-Lord strength, who allowed him a foothold in this realm, and not the other way around.

Ahead, Ladu saw the skylight marking the throne room's peak. At the same time, an undead appeared from behind a turret, claw-like hands reaching, jaws clacking. From the undead wafted an odor of decay that had become all too familiar of late, and the creature set upon Ladu in an instant. Ladu tried to raise his sword, but the undead bore down on him, wrapping its arms around Ladu's midsection, and the blade slipped from the emperor's hand. The weapon clattered out of reach, skidding down the slope before coming to rest against an overturned shingle. Bringing its teeth toward the emperor's neck, the undead snapped its jaws shut. Ladu held his forearm against the creature's throat, keeping it at bay by a hairsbreadth.

The creature's breath was hot and rancid on Ladu's face. It let loose an unearthly howl as tattered shreds of its clothing whipped in the breeze.

Who were you in life, before all this began? What goals and aspirations did you have? Do you even understand what purpose you serve in death?

The impact of his fall on the rooftop jarred Ladu's senses and left him winded. A pain jabbed his right shoulder blade, which had borne the brunt of the fall. He pushed the discomfort to a distant corner of his mind, wrapping fists around the creature's tunic and holding it tight in their struggle. Eyes on the handle of his weapon, Ladu tried to use the pitch of the roof to slide toward the blade. The undead attempted another bite, its teeth coming so close to Ladu's cheek that hot saliva dripped upon his skin. He pressed his forearm harder against the creature's throat, pushing it farther back and opening a gap between their two bodies. In a desperate, quick move, Ladu twisted, reached a belt-knife at his side and pulled it free. He drew it across his opponent's throat, quick and hard.

When the blade passed through the flesh, the skin parted in two like an ancient roll of parchment, blood spurting. The creature gave a rasp and collapsed, the weight of its body coming down atop him. Ladu rolled to the side, pushing the creature away and watching it tumble off the roof. The tower behind Ladu had gone silent, and he suspected the Kule brothers had taken their battle elsewhere.

After retrieving his blade, he had just reached the skylight when another undead came against him. The attack slammed Ladu and the creature down against the structure. Their combined weight shattered the glass, causing shards to rain down to the floor as emperor and undead fell through the gap. They landed on the chandelier suspended over the throne room. Ladu lost his breath from the impact. Several of the fragments of glass had cut him, and his blood dripped to land on the floor far below. This time, Ladu kept his grip on his sword, and as the chandelier swayed beneath him, he had just enough room to slam the base of his pommel stone against the undead's head. The dislodged creature fell, grasping Ladu's ankle as it passed. Ladu dangled from one hand, the undead suspended beneath him. Endar stood on the ground, watching with a cold, quiet smile upon his face.

Kicking the undead with his free foot, Ladu dislodged it. The creature fell to the flagstones in a splatter of limbs as Ladu used the momentum of the swinging chandelier to launch toward the far wall. He slammed against the tapestry, grasped the edge of the fabric, and used its resistance to slow his descent.

Ladu landed in a corner of the palace floor. At the center of the room, Endar Varuc looked up, first to the chandelier, then to the broken skylight, and then back to Ladu. Ladu wrapped both hands around the hilt of his sword, holding it in the en garde position, moving fully to his feet. One final undead rushed at him from the side, but this time Ladu was ready. He whirled, taking its head in one clean stroke. After that, it was just him and Endar, standing alone in the throne room, staring at one another from a distance of thirty paces.

Emperor Ladu Jovun IV narrowed his eyes. "Hello," he said. "I'm back."

36

Endar Varuc spread his palms, displaying a sleek grin. He brought his hands together in a slow, steady clap, a hint of malice in his eyes. "Well done, Emperor."

Ladu stepped forward. "What did you hope to accomplish here? What do you gain by joining Uklith in his fight against us?"

Endar Varuc laughed, no longer the timid, wavering nobleman Ladu had once known. "Power—isn't that what it's always about, my friend? Power, and the ability to use it as I wish?"

"If you think the weight of the crown means only power, you are sorely mistaken." *They come every generation, those who do not realize the monarchy is as much burden as blessing—that the one doing the leading often finds himself or herself following.* Ladu imagined the subtleties of such reflections were beyond the likes of men such as Endar Varuc, and more to the point, beyond the interests of the one Varuc had sworn to follow. "Can't you see it's never ended well for those who served Uklith? Zadinn, Isanam, Elson and Kaiel Tulak. The Demon-Lord never delivers upon his promises, Endar."

Endar's smile never wavered. "Oh, I see plenty. Eighteen months hardly counts as a victory when compared to Zadinn Kanas's two-hundred-year reign. Did you actually think you *won*? No, Ladu Jovun, you lost when Zadinn overthrew your father, you lost when you became sealed in crystal in the Mountains, and though you might have gained a temporary reprieve this past year, you will now lose again."

In a simultaneous motion, both men raised their swords and swept toward one another. Whatever incompetence Endar once appeared to suffer, it slid away as a snake shed skin. His ineptitude had been a façade like everything else. Endar moved through the forms with ease, the two opponents whirling around, up and down the room, the clang of their steel echoing in the otherwise silent chambers.

Ladu followed the patterns of old. He understood little of how sword work had changed in the last two hundred years, but knew his own training well. He leapt onto the dais, landing near the throne. As they battled in front of the chair Varuc longed to possess, the throne's jewelry sparkled in the chandelier's light.

"Where are your elion guards?" Endar asked as their blades met, edges pressing near the hilt. They stared into each other's eyes from across the gap between the steel. "They have not failed you, have they?"

As if in response, sounds of conflict echoed from the corridor, shouts and cries mingled with the falling of bodies. "*Oh*," Endar said. "I believe I have my answer." He kicked Ladu in the midsection, knocking him from the dais.

Ladu had anticipated this. He positioned his fall by tilting his shoulder toward the ground, using the impact and leverage to spin into a backward somersault. Spreading his arms wide, he rose back to his feet in time to block an overhead strike.

At the start of the fight, Ladu had noticed something about Endar's sword, an observation he pressed to his advantage. He used a flurry of attacks, creating a constant circle around the other man—right, left, forward, back, his movements even and controlled. He aimed his blows not to kill, but to maximize the range of Endar's defenses. Endar Varuc might have trained, might have understood the principles of combat, but in selecting his weapon he had made one crucial mistake, and Ladu intended for it to be the man's undoing. Endar's eyes narrowed in confusion as he observed the emperor's tactics. He hadn't quite guessed the game yet, and Ladu had no intention of showing his hand.

"Stalling?" Endar asked after a moment. "Perhaps you hope to delay me until your friends arrive—but what about when *my* allies arrive?"

You'll see soon enough, Ladu thought, but did not reply aloud. Ladu was sweating from the exertion, as was Endar, and that was what Ladu had been waiting for. He returned to the dais, jumping in front of the throne yet again. Endar leapt up to join him, blade swinging in a wild fashion. Ladu ducked, dodging this last attack easily, and kicked Endar in the gut. He brought his blade around, and though Endar blocked the swing, Ladu saw what he'd been waiting for: the slightest slip of the handle in Endar's grip.

"Do you think being a ruler is merely about jewels and wealth?" he asked. "There is more to being emperor than sitting on a throne of gold, than possessing diamonds and sapphires. It's about understanding that fundamental laws govern our world, and that you are not exempt from them. Tell me, how long have you studied the sword?"

Endar hissed, and for the first time Ladu saw the man looking frightened. "Long enough."

"Then why are you using a jeweled hilt?" With a sudden flick of his wrist, Ladu sent Endar's blade flying, leaving the usurper standing before him wide-eyed and empty handed. "Your palms *sweat* in combat. They grow moist and slick. The sword you used was ornamental, and never meant for battle."

Ladu lifted his sword, its hilt wrapped in good leather, the same fabric used to make the jerkin of the hardiest farmer. For leather, not jewels, belonged in an emperor's hands. Ladu thrust his sword into Endar Varuc's stomach, propelling him backward. Endar stumbled, sprawling over the arms of the throne, looking up in pain and despair as his life-blood gushed forth. His mouth worked in soundless shock.

"Get out of my chair," Ladu growled, pulling his sword free. He gave the would-be usurper a push. Endar Varuc's lifeless body rolled off the dais, tumbling to the stones of the floor.

* * *

A line of elion soldiers raced down the hallway ahead of Raisha, dealing death to any undead that came close. Blade in hand, she followed them.

A week ago, she would have scoffed at the idea that she would actually be in *combat*. There were guards for that sort of thing. She was not a complete stranger to dueling, as the realities of hiding from Zadinn's malichons all those years had required her to acknowledge that some level of self-defense was necessary, but she had only ever handled a weapon to an extent suitable for keeping up appearances.

Well, the time for appearances was past, and the time for survival was here. Ladu had given her the choice of remaining behind, and she almost took him up on it, but then she had thought of the two elion guards who had died protecting her in the palace when Endar's betrayal first occurred. She had to do right by them, if nothing else.

So she had come.

The soldiers had been fighting a pitched battle throughout the palace, having lost many, yet killed many more. They almost reached the throne room but were forced by a new group of undead to turn a corner into a dead-ended corridor. They found themselves with backs to the wall, the enemy pressing forward. The bodies in the corridor served as an obstruction to the undead's advance, and perhaps that was what the small company needed most. However, it would not bode well for Raisha and the elions if they remained trapped here.

"Where's your brother, Faldon?" Raisha asked the elion captain.

"Close," Faldon replied. "At least, I hope so."

Tavin had gone to the other tower to gather the troops who had infiltrated the palace. Raisha thought it likely they had encountered similar resistance in their effort to join forces, and their arrival might well be delayed or not coming at all.

In front of them, an undead broke through the ranks, cleaving a Frontier Patrol elion in two and stabbing another before it Faldon struck it dead between the eyes.

Far too close for comfort. "What are our options, Captain?" Raisha asked.

The group of undead withdrew, then surged forward, like a tide retreating before advancing. Faldon cursed. Raisha pressed her shoulder blades against the wall's stones. *Nowhere to go.*

A battle cry sounded as a fresh group of men and elions swept into the corridor, none too soon. Tavin Kule led the charge, slamming into the flank of the undead, the soldiers behind him bringing weapons and skill to bear upon the rabble of automatons.

At the sight of the reinforcements, Raisha felt a swell of relief. She raised her sword with renewed confidence, and together the two groups made short work of the undead filling the passage.

Their task was far from finished, though. Without pausing after their victory, they raced down the last hallway and toward the throne room's door, where, as everywhere, they saw signs of death and carnage—overturned pedestals, torn tapestries, bloody walls, and broken armor. Though the throne room's arched gates remained shut, they heard voices and steel on the opposite side, and soon came a muffled gasp of pain. The elions threw themselves against the doors with desperate urgency, but Raisha feared they might be too late.

When the barricade burst open and the company flooded into the room, they saw Emperor Ladu Jovun IV sitting alive in his throne, blade in hand, weary but safe. Blood dripped from the weapon's tip, landing against the flagstones a drop at a time. Before the tired, victorious emperor, Endar's slain form lay on the steps in a broken heap.

She looked at her brother's body. *When did it go wrong for you, Endar? Would that this had ended differently.*

"Your majesty," Raisha said. "Are you hurt?"

Ladu looked up at her. Raisha had always found his rugged features and calm confidence to be attractive, though she didn't want him to know he held those cards on her *just* yet. Maybe soon. "I am well enough," he said. "But we are only halfway through this ordeal, I'm afraid."

Above Ladu, the broken skylight revealed the world above. The strange, awesome spire dominated the sky. When Raisha looked at the power streaming across her field of vision, she saw something new: a tinge of black shadow running along its edges.

"How go the affairs of the palace?" Ladu asked.

Faldon gave the reply. "The undead are cleared from most corridors, but I think—"

"Yes, there are many more to come. They'll only begin rising faster, I fear."

An elion from the Frontier Patrol stepped forward. "I saw it when we entered the western tower, your majesty. From every avenue and every street, they draw closer. The entire city is under siege."

"All we can do is hold our own," Ladu said. "The rest, I fear, may be up to Matthias."

Matthias may have already failed, Raisha thought, but that was a distant concern. Their battle was here, to protect Galdon, and they would hold as long as they could.

* * *

Pure, raw Lifesource power erupted in the corridor, frantic waves of energy slamming into the walls, ceiling, and ground. Before Tim, Shelendel moved in a swirl of robes, her blade clashing against his. Tim suspected that deep within a corner of the Shelendel's mind, she remained fully aware, albeit unable to control herself. Uklith would have *wanted* her to remain sentient, to suffer as she watched her body serve the one she'd fought so long against. It would be the purest form of vengeance.

Shelendel raised her hand, palm wide, and the next attack blasted a hole in the wall behind Tim, blowing it outward. Bereft of support, the ceiling above teetered precariously. Shelendel jumped through the air, reversing their positions to land in front of the hole she had just created. Tim unleashed a buffet of compressed air to knock the undead Advocate through the jagged opening into the room beyond.

A rush of wind followed. The torches winked out, plunging everything into darkness. Tim reached out with his senses, but almost immediately a new source of light blossomed within the room. The blast struck him directly in the chest, throwing him against a stone wall. He smelled his burned flesh, and in response used the Lifesource to wash away the most immediate of the pain. He knew he was lucky that he had not been killed outright. He rolled to the side, and a new jet of light slammed into the wall where he had just been. Chunks of dirt and stone rained down.

Tim pushed himself onto his knees, placing a hand to his chest, and felt a hole in his clothing and scorched skin beneath. Before he could rise, the light of Shelendel's blade flared above him, a purple line of raging flames. Tim raised a hasty shield, and though he was not fast enough to completely deflect the attack, what would have been a fatal stroke instead struck his side. Blood gushed and Tim fell face downward, teeth gritted.

He found himself moving too slowly. Diverting his focus in the Lifesource, he used half of his power to keep his shield in place, the other half to call his sword to him, the weapon blazing into existence as it rose back into the air. A wave of fire splashed against Tim's barrier, creating coruscating pillars of light. One more assault and the shield would surely fail, leaving Tim little time to come up with other options.

As he came to his feet and caught his sword, the ceiling groaned. Tim stepped deeper into the corridor, using the Lifesource to will the ensconced torches back into life, providing him a better view of the passage. Shelendel stood before him, wreathed in robes, floating on an unseen breeze with sword in hand. Knowing he had but one chance to finish this, Tim released all of his latent power, piercing the bubble of his shield. The resultant shockwave created a visible ripple in the air. The final brace holding wall and ceiling in place gave away, and Tim jumped back as rubble descended on Shelendel.

Tim staggered, his energy spent, the blade in his hand winking out. He leaned against the nearest wall and took a series of deep, ragged gasps; he'd expended considerable power already, and he didn't think it boded well for what lay ahead. He watched the pile of destruction for at least a minute, wary that Shelendel might rise again, but the mound did not waver. He eventually knelt by the stones that had buried her and placed his hand upon the rubble, closing his eyes.

Be at peace, Shelendel. It was the very least she deserved.

He took several gulps from his waterskin and splashed water on his worst wounds. He flinched at the agonizing sensation, but knew it would be better in the long run. Pushing the fatigue aside, he resumed his journey down the corridor, arriving at a set of doors that opened onto a balcony. From the balcony, he looked down into a much larger room—perhaps a ballroom, as the ornate floor suggested. Tall glass windows ringed the circular area, sunlight filtering through the panes and filling the space with a dusky glow. Tim stepped to the edge of the balcony, looking toward the far end of the domed room. He caught a flash of golden hair, and sensed Bria's presence in the Lifesource. After she disappeared, a high, cold laugh echoed through the space, seeming to come from everywhere and nowhere.

Tim tore a strip of cloth from his robes, binding it around the wound in his side. He stepped over the edge of the balcony into the open air, catching himself on an invisible layer of power. With tendrils of magic wrapped around him, he floated to the ground.

* * *

Sendalion Danris led the remaining members of the Royal Legion down the hallway. They'd fought three-quarters of the way to the King's throne room thus far, and now the last stretch remained before they would have to turn and make their final stand in the king's hall. He'd left many comrades for dead behind him, Vinsor Dalin among them, and he suspected his own final reckoning drew near. He'd failed his king—the city had fallen, and that blame lay upon Sendalion alone. However, he would hold his head high until the last, no matter what the result.

Around him, his companions were weary from battle. They'd fought well, every one of them, but even the best of intentions mattered little against overwhelming odds. He reflected ironically that, in serving less than one week in command of the Royal Legion, he might in fact hold the record for the shortest tenure as captain.

Sendalion ducked a blow from a corsair's cutlass, and the blade thunked into a wooden post above him, sending splinters down. As the corsair attempted to pull his weapon free, Sendalion dove beneath the man's reach, coming up with weapon in hand. The corsair was tall and lean, with jewelry studding his face and tattoos on his neck and shoulders. His weapon still stuck in the post, the pirate let out a muffled oath of frustration, right before Sendalion drove his blade through the man's neck.

The throne room waited. Without pause, Sendalion ran down the last corridor with his comrades, breath coming hard, perspiring heavily, the air thick with the scent of death. But when he pushed open the chamber doors and stumbled inside, he saw he was too late.

Admiral Vila Kaarst stood in the center of the throne room, a cluster of corsairs around him. The admiral held his sword in an outstretched hand, the long tip of his blade leveled at King Aras's throat.

Sendalion skidded to a halt, his thoughts of barricading the door gone. The battle was over, as suddenly as it had begun.

"Greetings, Captain," Kaarst said with a smile upon his face. The tall, dark-haired admiral wore a set of flowing robes. He had beady eyes and a narrow nose.

"Your majesty—" Sendalion began.

"It's all right, Captain Danris," the king said. "You fought well, better than most would have in your place."

"Oh, but that's your problem, your majesty," Kaarst said. "You forget the only measure that truly matters is that of success. The captain here may have fought a valiant battle, but he still lost."

"I don't expect the subtler nuances of principle to make an impression on you, Admiral," Aras responded. "You gave up any shred of understanding such things when you forsook your family's name."

"Philosophize all you wish, but this will be *my* kingdom, Aras. Truth be told, my first inclination is to kill you, but I wonder if it would be better to let you suffer, and have you watch as I remake your land?"

"Touch the king and die," Sendalion said.

Kaarst laughed. "Captain, the futility of your threat is beyond pathetic. As I've already said, you've lost, plain and simple."

"And what did you do to gain that victory?" Aras asked. "I've seen those fighting alongside you."

Behind Sendalion, the rest of the corsairs clustered in the room, alongside the final members of the Royal Legion. They did not fight, but instead stood and watched the scene before them.

"You condescend my fellow folk of the sea?" Kaarst asked.

"No, you know what I mean. I speak of those who walk with you—the undead, risen from their graves. This is not a natural war, and all know it. What dark magic have you brought to my city? I feared a threat had come from the North, from the one known as the Warrior, but this darkness comes from *you*, and from the forces you have allied with."

Kaarst curled his lips in a sneer. "It's none of your concern. Let us finish this." The admiral gestured for the corsairs to relieve Sendalion and the Legionnaires of their weaponry. He lowered his blade from the king's neck. After the appearance of deliberate, careful consideration, he backhanded Aras across the face.

Aras's head snapped to the side, flecks of blood flying from his lip. Sendalion tensed, resisting every urge to disarm the nearest corsair and take a swing for Kaarst's head. Such a move would be death, and while he didn't like his chances regardless, he decided to bide his time and wait for the right moment.

King Aras straightened, returning his gaze to Kaarst. A trickle of red ran down his chin.

"I've wanted to do that for a long time," Kaarst said.

"If you've traveled across the seas, murdered these men, and razed this city simply to strike me in the face," Aras said, "your priorities are sorely misplaced."

Kaarst laughed. "Amusing, your majesty. Since you seem desirous of forcing my hand, though, let's continue. Captain Danris, step forward. I believe you have led the resistance against us."

"Only during this past week. It was Captain Yastlin before that, but your corsairs struck him down, so I'm the one you must contend with."

Kaarst nodded to the corsair nearest Sendalion. "Bring the captain with us. The rest can remain here, but it's only fitting that the leader of the Royal Legion receives his just payment at the same time as the king. To the top of the tower."

The corsair grasped Sendalion from behind and gave him a callous shove. A pair of corsairs seized Sendalion and Aras, forcing them toward the tower stairwell. They took the winding stairs one step at a time, Sendalion keeping his eyes open, knowing if there were to be a chance for escape, it needed to come sooner rather than later. But in the enclosed interior of the spiral staircase, and with the king nearby, there was precious little he could think of to do, and so he simply went up the stairway, toward the top of the tower. They emerged upon the flagstones under an open sky, where only the vast energy jutting into the heavens was above them.

"Do you see that, Kaarst?" Aras asked. "That's the foul magic you've unleashed upon my city. I'm still not sure you appreciate the gravity of what you've gotten us into."

"I'm still not sure you appreciate the immediacy of your demise," Kaarst replied. "Leave me to worry about my partnerships. You'll be long dead."

The corsairs prodded them into the center of the rooftop, where Sendalion and Aras stood side by side, looking over the city below. The smoke, fires, and everything else Sendalion saw reminded him of the ultimate fact he had failed. *Perhaps Kaarst was onto something. For true, I may have fought long and hard, but in the end he's the one victorious, and mayhap that's all that really does matter.*

"I'm going to enjoy making those you once ruled suffer," Kaarst said. "When you go to your grave, go knowing this kingdom is no longer yours. Go knowing that everything I said to you those many years ago still holds true. It isn't truth or honor that wins in the end, it's power, and I would much rather be the one wielding it."

The king shook his head, his eyes large and sad. "Where did I go wrong, Andre?" he asked softly.

"That name no longer means anything to me," replied Kaarst. "*Nothing* you gave me means anything anymore, my father."

* * *

At last, the undead broke onto the rooftop. Celia had known it was coming, but it didn't mean she had to like it. Still, it was the situation in front of them, and she'd deal with it as it came. The first creature pulled itself up over the parapet, half its face missing, the open bones of its jaw protruding in the sunlight. The little skin that remained showed open sores, raw and chapped from the wind, cracking under the heat. The creature came with a swirl of sand behind it, a halo of grit surrounding its figure. Its breath sounded like a loose rattle, reminding her of chains clinking in the cold and dark of a dungeon.

She met the undead head-on, blade running through it with a dry *crunch*. The undead was but the first of several, though, and three more immediately took its place. The company drew back from walls that teemed with undead, putting their backs against each other to create a tight circle of defense. Celia wondered how many boomers remained, and for one chilling second thought maybe they should save the very last one for themselves.

The undead in front of her jerked, a bolt punching through its head, the tip of an arrow protruding from its desiccated skin, stopping inches in front of Celia's eye. She pushed the body away. She looked toward the opposite rooftop, and there she saw Boblin, lowering his crossbow and winking at her from across the distance. And, for the first time in a long while, Celia smiled.

* * *

Boblin watched the embattled company atop the garrison. There were plenty of undead to go around, and it looked as though he had arrived none too soon. He eyed the mound of bodies, which the creatures had used to gain their footing from ground to roof. There were far too many for him to make a difference by simply taking on those on the rooftop. No, he had to employ another means, one that would attack the literal root of the problem.

He rummaged in his belt, coming up with yet another boomer. He'd developed a distinct fondness for the things based on how well they'd served the group these past weeks. He struck the fuse, feeling it flare into the familiar sparkle of light, and fit the projectile into his crossbow. He raised bow to shoulder and took careful aim.

He pointed farther down the line, toward the base of the mound that had swelled to the roof and pulled the trigger. The boomer arced through the air and landed low in the hill of corpses, shredding the bodies of those already slain. The pile shifted, buckling just a little as Boblin fired his second shot. After the third, the pile started to collapse inward, filling the void left by the eruptions. *Just think, I'm making dead undead even more dead.* There were worse things, he supposed, to do with one's time.

Boblin raced forward and leapt, clearing the gap between the other rooftop and his, the ground passing underneath him in a rush, and landed on the dusty stones next to his wife.

"Took you long enough," Celia said.

"I stopped for ale and cheese. It wasn't very good, though."

"And Tim?"

"He took it into his head to go into Uklith's palace and start a fight. Karfing crazy, if you ask me."

"At least he's doing something useful."

Boblin grunted. "Believe me, *we're* going to do something useful too. We'll all probably die, but that's how the cards are stacked today. See that focusing reservoir? Gather round, folks, because it's high time we rid ourselves of it."

"And how do you propose to do that?" Eklan asked.

"The old-fashioned way. A really big explosion."

Eklan looked toward garrison's bottom floor. "You're not suggesting…"

"I am. We'll make use of the tunnels. I spoke to Tim about them before we separated. Uklith's presence *was* in the tunnels, but I don't think he'll be in there anymore. More likely he has drawn back to focus on the palace. We'll encounter undead, but those we know how to deal with, and it's better than staying exposed on this rooftop."

Boblin flipped the trapdoor and clambered down. The door leading to the street bulged inward, its oaken boards creaking as the undead from outside continued pressing against it. He doubted the defenses there would last long. All the more reason to do this quickly. He shuffled to the back of the room, found the door leading to the tunnels and flung it open. He looked into its dim interior. *At least it will be cool down there. I've had enough of this Malath-scorched sun.*

The others made their way down, just as the windows erupted inward. The first undead thrust the upper portion of its torso through, grasping at the edges of the sill. Boblin raised his crossbow and, in an almost negligent fashion, shot it in the face. He knew another would soon replace it, but it felt good. He needed to do something to blow off the tension. "Okay, let's hurry."

He led the way down the stairwell, Celia and Eklan behind him, Jend and Wurit behind them, and Ken holding the rear. As they did so, all Malath broke loose in the garrison, the undead forcing their way inside. Ken slammed the door closed behind them, but Boblin knew it would gain them minutes at most. He pulled a long-unused torch from its sconce and lit it, the flickering flames casting a weak illumination on the steps into the darkness below. In spite of Tim's assurances that Uklith had *probably* vacated the tunnels, Boblin nonetheless felt a twinge of unease. Leaving the Demon-Lord's presence—or lack of it—to chance was a large risk indeed.

He ran down the stone steps, reaching the floor as the undead resumed pounding. "Let's leave them a surprise." He placed a sack of boomers near the door and seized a fuse. He wound it to the end of the bag with Ken's aid and let it trace to the base of the stairs. At the very least, the detonation would kill a fair number of undead, but with any luck it would collapse the entrance to the tunnel, securing their escape.

With the trap in place, Boblin and Ken moved to the base of the stairs where the rest of the company had gathered, ready to move farther into the tunnels. They were none too soon, for the doors behind them erupted inward with a crash. Boblin touched his torch to the end of the fuse and then they were racing away, feet slapping against the ground. He took one final glance over his shoulder as the flames raced upward, into the sack of boomers. They detonated, the force of the concussion knocking the company forward at the same time it blew the undead backward. Though the blast did not block the entrance, it nonetheless slowed the enemy's advance, causing rubble and dust to rain down.

Boblin jerked to the side. Beside him, Ken stumbled as the bracing against the nearest wall disintegrated in a shower of dirt, stone, and wooden beams. The rubble descended directly upon Ken, and the sound of the collapse was followed by the audible *snap* of a bone breaking.

In the clearing dust, Boblin saw Ken buried to his waist, face white with pain. "Not good, Commander," the elion said through clenched teeth. At the head of the stairs, over the rubble at the entryway, the undead began forcing their way into the tunnel. *If only it had caved in completely, stopping them…*

"Time for some quick decisions," Ken said. "Give me a boomer, Commander."

Boblin ignored him, lifting the first beam away from the pile, but Ken brushed him away. "It won't do you any good, sir. My leg is broken, well and good. Now, before it's too late, *give me a boomer.*"

Command an army, and those you lead will die.

Again, so soon? *Will it ever stop, or must I keep losing them?* The reality of the situation was unavoidable: Ken's leg was broken, he was buried, and they had minutes before the undead came into the corridor. Even if they managed to free the elion, Ken would barely be able to move on one limb.

"I made Hugo a promise," Ken said. "I told him I would win this. It's looking as if I won't be there for the end, but I want to do my brother the justice of giving it my all."

Boblin drew a boomer from his sack and handed it to Ken. "I'll stay with you."

"No, you won't. You may want to, but it's not the right call. You need to bring down that reservoir." As the party stood there, Ken lit the boomer in one quick motion, the fuse burning brightly as he held it before them. "You really should be running."

* * *

After the company left, Ken stamped the fuse out. It wouldn't do any good to have it detonate before the undead arrived. No, that had just been theatrics to get the commander and his group away from here. Boblin Kule meant well, but he was young and still learning.

In front of Ken, the undead broke free, first a hand coming through the dirt, then a whole body. A second creature emerged, then a third. Above, the light from the building pooled down the shaft, illuminating Ken where he lay in the rubble. *So this is where it ends.* He'd been through much over the years—malichon patrols, the battles in the North, the quest for the Army of Kah'lash. But all soldiers met their end one way or another; it was one of the things taken as a given when signing up for the job. And, to tell the truth, his heart hadn't been in it since Hugo's death. Ken had been only half of a whole, and it was high time he joined his brother. *Besides, as far as ways to go, this one isn't half bad.*

They had bought nearly two years of peace with their last struggle, earning their people the right to freedom. Ken had never been prouder than on the day he stood with the other elions, celebrating their first hour of freedom in the North.

Ahead of him, the undead drew closer, looking upon this victim in their midst with curiosity. He could almost see their limited brains trying to process what was happening here, this man buried with a strange protrusion in his hand as he looked up toward them. No, he didn't suppose they fully understood—but they didn't have to. He lit the fuse once more. What remained of the wire was very close to the stub. It was good, for as they clustered all around him, Ken Rindar closed his eyes.

We bought two years, years that were nothing like those that came before. Hopefully, this buys two hundred more.

The fuse reached its end, and all the world disappeared in the bright light of sacrifice and salvation.

37

Sendalion watched King Aras of Alcatune face his son, Admiral Vila Kaarst of the corsair fleet. "It's been a long time, father," Kaarst said. "Many years have passed since we last spoke, you and I."

"You have much to answer for, Andre. The death of an innocent man, years of war and bloodshed in Icor..."

Kaarst smiled. "You revoked my claim to the throne, yet here I stand, ready to ascend to it anyway. Given a second chance, I'd make the same choices all over again."

Sendalion had heard stories of the man close to Aras, the exile who had started the Icor Rebellion, but it had always been difficult for him to separate which were facts and which were legend. As he looked closer, he saw Aras's features reflected in Kaarst's face. Both men had the same eyes, the same angular chin, the same build—and yet there was also an inherent contrast there. Where Aras's features were proud and regal, Kaarst's were cold and cruel, two people cut from the same cloth yet grown into different men. The father ruled the kingdom, the son the seas, one using his position to inspire and the other to terrify, two sides of a coin brought together to face one another on this wind-whipped rooftop.

The corsair behind Sendalion struck the backs of his thighs, knocking him to his knees. Sendalion willed himself to keep his head high. He had few illusions about what was coming next, but he sure as Malath planned on meeting it with an even gaze. He looked toward the bay, where the remnants of Kaarst's fleet lay scattered across the waters.

Kaarst placed a hand on Aras's shirt collar, dragging the king to the tower's edge. "Look upon your city, father. See what I have made of it." He spun Aras around to face Sendalion once again. "And look upon the captain of your armies. It's time for you to witness the first execution. We'll bring your men up here and slit their throats. You can watch their blood spill onto the flagstones, and after the last one, we'll kill you, too." He snapped his fingers. "Bring the rest of the prisoners up. We'll gut them and throw their bodies from on high."

Sendalion attempted to rise, determined to meet his end standing, but the corsair beside him would not allow it. The man forced Sendalion back to the ground, hand on Sendalion's shoulder, knife drawn. He pressed the blade's edge against Sendalion's throat.

"Go on, your majesty," Kaarst said. "Tell the captain it will be all right. Tell him what you told me when I asked you if mother would live."

"We did the best we could for her, Andre. The bone sickness is not merciful."

"And now, neither am I."

"Better she died with your love than live to see what you have become."

Kaarst struck the king. "I did it for *her*, father! It was more than you did, sending her to that mystic in the outer city, that fraud with his tales of a new treatment..."

"The palace physicians told me there was no hope, Andre! That she had a week at most! I saw a chance for help, and I took it. Better a shred of hope than none at all!"

"It didn't work, father. That doctor was not an innocent man. He failed mother, and I killed him for it."

"And you claim to serve her memory by raising the dead against our city? You've betrayed everyone: your country, your blood, humanity itself. Or—" Aras paused. "Is that what you think? By following one who can raise the dead, that you can raise *her*?"

"Enough," Kaarst growled. He pointed toward Sendalion. "Kill the first one, and make it hurt."

"I'm sorry, Andre," Aras said.

"Not good enough, father."

The corsair beside Sendalion flexed his grip, digging the blade in. Sendalion felt the first drops of blood form.

Thwock.

A bolt took the corsair between the eyes. He fell over, knife clattering to the flagstones. Sendalion reacted without thinking, surging to his feet and grabbing the fallen weapon even as the next corsair turned toward him. He drove the blade deep into the other man's throat, twisting and sending a gout of bright red gushing forward. *It won't be the blood of my comrades and I that stains these stones. It will be yours and that of your men, Kaarst.*

Sendalion caught a flash of movement and saw the admiral move toward the king. At the same time, Quentiin Harggra, still holding the crossbow he'd fired, struggled over the lip of the tower and into view. As Quentiin landed on the rooftop, King Aras threw himself against Kaarst, slamming him into the side of the parapet.

Sendalion tried to come to the king's aid, but corsairs swarmed onto the rooftop before he could do so. One attacked from the side, bearing him to the ground. Beside him, Quentiin roared and leapt into battle, sword held high. Sendalion wrestled with the assailant who had tackled him. He'd lost his weapon again in the fall, so he head-butted the corsair. The men grappled to and fro, and in a surge of momentum Sendalion reversed their positions so that he was on top. The corsair tried to bring a blade upward, but Sendalion's chainmail shirt turned it away. Sendalion wrapped his hands around the corsair's throat, throttling his life from him.

The trapdoor burst open. Quentiin was already in motion, leaving his last opponent on the ground. The first corsair through the door poked his head up, and a second later it was gone, Quentiin having cleaved it from his shoulders. As the decapitated body toppled back down the shaft, the line of prisoners on the stairs rose into action, turning on their captors as a bloody battle ensued.

Beneath Sendalion, his opponent's struggles subsided. Sendalion rose and saw Aras and Kaarst teetering on the brink of the parapet. The admiral pulled a knife from his robes. Sendalion leapt into motion, knowing he had only seconds—

—Kaarst slid the blade into the king's stomach, burying it to the hilt. King Aras wavered, placing his hands against his son's chest to keep himself upright.

"Please," the king said.

"Please what?"

"Forgive me."

The king of Alcatune pushed his son over the parapet.

* * *

Quentiin turned away from his fallen opponent and saw the knife go into Aras's stomach. He ran toward the king as fast as his stubby legs could carry him, heaving his bulk across the rooftop. Sendalion was three strides ahead of him.

Aras pushed Kaarst off the roof. The corsair admiral fell away without a sound, and then Aras began to topple, too. Sendalion reached him first, wrapping his arms around the king and pulling him away from the parapet to safety. Sendalion gently lowered Aras onto his back on the flagstones.

Quentiin reached Sendalion's side. The king looked up toward the two of them. Pain showed in his eyes, equal parts physical and emotional, the anguish of what he had just done to his son a figurative twin to the literal knife in his abdomen. The wound was deep and red. He breathed in shallow gasps, his gaze glassy.

"You've done well, Captain Danris," Aras said, voice weak.

"Hold on, your majesty." Sendalion said. With Quentiin's aid, he began binding Aras's wounds.

Quentiin grunted. "We need a healer."

Sendalion looked toward the trapdoor. "It's not far to Talladora's chambers. She is probably under corsair guard, but I think we have this well enough in hand. I won't be long."

As Sendalion took off, Quentiin looked at the binding. Aras's wound was grave, but he had seen enough on the field of battle to know the slight but important difference between fatal and near-fatal. He saw a chance here—not a great one, but a chance nonetheless.

The king grasped Quentiin's hand. "So you are the dwerion."

Quentiin could tell that the words came at great struggle to the man, but it was good for him to continue. It would keep Aras's mind on the real, the tangible, and that was what mattered most at this point. "Aye, yer majesty. Once a Legionnaire, always a Legionnaire. Focus on the sound o' my voice, on the feel o' the stones beneath yer back. Ye'll survive this yet."

"What is this dark magic around us, Harggra?"

"It's bad, yer majesty, far worse than anythin' I saw in the North. It's Uklith, an' his reach has grown long. Our hopes lie west."

Aras drew a long, shuddering breath. "Is Matthias up to the task?"

"That ain't an easy question to answer, but yes, yer majesty, if there's one man I trust to do right by us, it's Tim Matthias."

* * *

Tim landed on the flagstones of the ancient ballroom. He looked around, searching for enemies. For a long moment all remained silent. Tim pursed his lips, examining the room's ground level doors. It was difficult to say for sure which one Bria had gone through. All of the exits appeared identical, and he'd only caught a glimpse of her before she disappeared. He reached out with his senses, searching further, feeling a deep, pulsing ball of evil. Uklith was close, pressing at the edges of his prison, straining for release.

YOU THINK TO CHALLENGE ME?

"It's not something I'd *think* of doing," Tim murmured, "but I didn't really have a choice."

At a slight hint of movement from above, Tim looked up. Two more robed figures appeared, one from the right side of the balcony and one from the left. They glided forward, dark waves of energy radiating from them. Tim tensed, the wound in his side throbbing. He'd known this was coming, but he'd hoped he could at least face them one at a time.

The undead Advocates stepped to the edges of the balcony, looming over either side of Tim. Static discharge filled the room, causing Tim's hair to stand on end.

The Advocates struck. Jagged spiderwebs of lightning shot from their hands. The air crackled, and Tim had no choice but to meet both attacks at once, lifting one hand to his right and another to his left, unleashing his own fire.

This has no good ending. Either I die here, or I have to kill two more heroes. Or worse, they turn Bria and me into two more of Uklith's servants, just like them.

The shards of power met in the air above Tim's head, a vast, interlocking confluence that filled the entire ballroom with incandescent light. The stones beneath Tim's feet shook as he gritted his teeth, planting his boots firm and bracing himself, pushing in equal and opposite directions against his opponents. The heat singed his skin, and he felt blisters forming on his knuckles and forearm. It was nearly impossible to divide his attention between the attackers, yet divide it Tim did, knowing he had no choice.

The web of Lifesource writhed, one of its errant spokes blasting against a far section of the balcony, blowing away a chunk of flooring. The balcony sagged as the railing collapsed, and though Tim's lightning intersected that of the Advocates perhaps twenty feet above his head, he felt the struggle in the same manner as if he was in an arm-wrestling match, strength against strength, straining his physical muscles as well as that of the power surging through him.

The frenetic flashes of power illuminated their features, Amalar and Gardellin, legends of old whose former selves remained somewhere behind those dark, empty eyes. Rather than fixating on who they'd been, heroes of a former age, Tim concentrated on how he might bring them release, how he might end their torment, for death at his hands was far better than enduring further servitude to Uklith.

The sagging balcony gave out, and Tim felt the point of intersection in the lightning move back upward as the balcony's resistance became no more. The power climbed skyward, blasting open a window. Shards of jagged glass rained down as the sandstorm from outside blew in, blinding Tim's vision in a whirlwind of dust and grit. He continued the battle via his remaining senses, seeing the conflict only as occasional flashes of light from within the hazy whirlwind.

The world cleared in time for Tim to see Amalar appear in front of him, landing on the ground, his magic a whirl of blue lightning. Amalar raised his hand, a wave of energy rushing toward Tim. With no choice but to meet his opponent head-on, Tim retaliated, sending his power across the gap, and the two combatants clashed once more.

However, after fighting first Shelendel, then facing Amalar and Gardellin together, Tim had used so much power that his stamina could not last. From the start of this engagement, the Advocates had purposefully been wearing him down, knowing he was battered and weak from his first fight, pushing him to his limits and holding there.

Eventually he felt his strength go out and he fell to his knees, weariness washing over him. The Lifesource bled from him in the same way that the cut in his side leaked blood.

Amalar stepped forward. He did not draw his weapon, but rather reached out and placed his hand upon Tim's head. His touch was *cold*.

YOU HAVE A STRONG SOUL, WARRIOR, a voice said. Uklith. *I WILL ENJOY BREAKING IT.*

And Tim's worst fear was realized, that what waited for him here was not death, but the same fate the three Advocates had suffered: eternal enslavement, bound to Uklith's will.

Terror clawed into his throat. His heart froze. *Fight it!* Tim resisted, pushing outward—

His mind went blank.

* * *

Boblin felt the earth shake after Hugo detonated his boomer. The tunnel behind them collapsed in its entirety, cutting of further pursuit. He led his companions forward, crossbow slung across his back, holding a torch aloft to light the dusty corridor. It would have been easy to become lost in the catacombs, except Boblin *felt* the reservoir above him, like a whirlpool in the middle of an ocean, drawing everything in its proximity toward its maw. Even for one as unattuned to the Lifesource as Boblin, the sheer magnitude of power was palpable. Every time Boblin came to a corner, he felt a subconscious tug in one direction or another.

This was a strange network of tunnels, to say the least. Every so often they opened into larger rooms, one of which appeared to have been an underground market containing carts and tables scattered across a broad, open space, another with rows of pews that had perhaps been a chapel in times before a darker deity had made his mark upon this place. It appeared that as much of Agrazab's city existed belowground as aboveground, allowing its citizens to conduct their lives away from the sun's withering oppression when necessary. Farther along the way, they eventually stumbled into what could only be a tomb, where rows of coffins lined the walls. Boblin felt the reservoir's pull from the far side of the room, and so he led the group past the resting places of Agrazab's denizens from long past.

The skin at the nape of his neck prickled, but it wasn't until he saw one of the coffins quivering that his stomach lurched. A skeletal, dusty hand reached out from a crack in the lid, and Boblin froze. The other coffins began rattling as well. The one nearest burst open, its cover flying upward. An undead surged from its resting place. Boblin met the creature with the end of his blade, ramming the weapon deep. The undead's flesh gave a sturdy *crunch* as it fell back into its resting place.

Boblin pulled his blade free, looking at his companions. It seemed Uklith's presence had left the tunnels—which was all well and good—but they had now stumbled upon something else.

"So *this* is where they come from," he said. *By going underground, we haven't escaped the undead—we've entered their lair.*

More creatures clambered from their coffins, most of them nearer the entrance the group had come through. Unsure if they had been spotted yet,

Boblin and the others continued moving toward the far exit, walking slowly, careful not to bring unwanted attention upon themselves. When they reached the far door, Boblin raised his crossbow and pulled the trigger. The boomer flew forward, erupting amid a cluster of undead, sending fragments of bone and flesh in all directions. Boblin slammed the door behind them, bracing it with an attached sidebar. They had contained this group at least, but there would be many more. There were probably tombs upon tombs down here, brimming with undead prepared to surge forth. And Boblin supposed that Uklith, for all his lack of a tangible presence down here, knew what the group was up to. The Demon-Lord would fuel the creatures' strength, sending them after the company in fiercer pursuit than ever, hoping to prevent them from reaching their destination.

Boblin took the lead once more, and the small company resumed their flight.

* * *

Tim hung in the cosmos, suspended in starlight. A wave, blacker than black, appeared before him. It shimmered and undulated, advanced and retreated, before reaching toward him.

A SOUL IS SUCH A MALLEABLE THING, WARRIOR. YOU LEARNED THAT IN THE NORTHERN MOUNTAINS.

Tim raised his defenses, trying to repel the darkness. The wave of blackness hissed, pulling back, but Tim feared he could only slow, not stop, its advance.

THERE ARE MANY WAYS TO CLAIM A SOUL. FIRST, THERE ARE THOSE WHO SEEK ME OUT, SUCH AS TAAZVIN. THEY ARE AMUS-ING, BUT OFTEN INEFFECTIVE.

Tim grew conscious of his physical body, observing himself from without, kneeling in the dust before the undead Advocate.

NEXT, THERE ARE THE CONVERTS. THEY ARE THE MEN AND WOMEN WHO CLING TO THEIR PRINCIPLES, BUT ONLY SO LONG AS IT IS CONVENIENT TO DO SO. WHEN ADVERSITY STRIKES, WHEN I GIVE THEM CAUSE TO QUESTION THAT WHICH THEY BE-LIEVE, THEN THEY ABANDON THEIR PRINCIPLES AND TURN TO ME. THEY ARE MY FAVORITE, FOR CONVERTS ALWAYS SERVE WITH THE MOST ZEAL.

In the physical world, Amalar wrapped his fingers around Tim's skull. Cold, dark flames curled from his palm and enveloped Tim's head. Tim thought, perhaps, if he could but reach forward—grasp Amalar's ankle, perhaps, anything to disrupt the other's concentration—

Uklith spoke again and Tim's mind returned to the cosmos, to the energy threatening to overwhelm him. *LAST, WHEN I NEED TO, I CAN ALWAYS TAKE A SOUL BY FORCE.*

The wave pushed forward yet again. Tim felt his resistance begin to crumble, Uklith's presence seeping into him. At the same time Tim saw that his body, still kneeling before Amalar, was fully wreathed in cold tendrils of power. Tim wanted to scream—for he had failed—but he had no mouth to do so, not here in this unending darkness.

Without warning, Amalar jerked, head snapping back as the undead Advocate gave a hideous cry. Flames erupted from every orifice of his body, blasting from his eyes and ears. His hand fell away from Tim's body, the shadowy tentacles winking out, and the wave of darkness in the cosmos receded. As Tim's mind returned to his body, his senses coming back to him, he heard Uklith's wordless shout of frustration.

Tim fell from his knees onto his side. Above him, the tip of a fiery red sword stuck from Amalar's chest. After a handful of heartbeats, the Advocate's body slipped from the blade, landing on the ground in a charred husk. Gardellin stood over the corpse of his companion, red sword in hand as he drew its hood back. He met Tim's eyes, his gaze full of sad sentience, and—

The awareness in his eyes disappeared, Uklith reasserting his control over the body as quickly as he'd lost it. Gardellin began shaking, moving in jerky, awkward movements as the Advocate within tried to fight back. He took a halting step toward Tim, sword half-raised to attack.

Tim moved as quickly as he could, rising to his feet, but his movements felt feeble and clumsy at best. Grunts and gasps came from Gardellin's throat, a rasping and guttural sound that Tim eventually recognized as words.

"Kill me ... KILL ME ..."

Recalling what he'd seen in the vision below the cottage in the Erdrar, Tim wrapped both hands around the top of Gardellin's head. Fire leapt from Tim's hands, and Gardellin lurched beneath his grip. Tim willed his presence into Gardellin's mind, helping Gardellin turn the tide against Uklith's control, willing him to be his own man again.

Uklith's dark and oily presence slid away once Tim and Gardellin joined forces. Gardellin shrieked from the agony of the flames, but the pain helped, for Uklith felt it too. The Demon-Lord's touch fled, and Tim released his grip.

Silence. Tim and Gardellin stood facing one another for three heartbeats. Then Gardellin collapsed in a swirl of robes. He looked up, a man fully in control once more, but one who should have been long dead. And since Uklith's presence had been the only thing sustaining him for centuries, he did not have long to live.

"Who are you?" Gardellin whispered to Tim, his words raspy and strained. "How long has it been?"

"Two hundred years," Tim said. "I'm Tim Matthias, the last Advocate, the Warrior of Light."

"Zadinn Kanas?"

"Defeated."

"By your hand?"

Tim nodded.

"Well done," the Advocate said. "Well done, Matthias." He appeared to summon his remaining strength, swallowing to work moisture into his voice, and pointed toward one of the doors. "Go, but remember what you have learned of Homdee. You have released us, Warrior, and for that … *thank you*."

His eyes fluttered closed as he slipped into death's welcome embrace, his suffering ended at last.

* * *

Boblin aimed his crossbow and pulled the trigger. Celia stood at his right side, Jend at his left. The boomer flew forward and landed at an intersection between tunnels. Undead parts flew everywhere, the concussion echoing in the enclosed space.

Breathing heavily, Boblin began a backward retreat, eyes on every opening in the tunnel. Here in the dark and shadows, it was karfing hard to tell where the next attack would come from. He drew a hand across his face, wiping perspiration from his brow. The leftmost passage shuddered and collapsed, no doubt weakened by the explosion. At least it meant one more avenue of attack would be closed off.

"We have to be getting close," Eklan Hamur said from his position at the front of the group.

"We'd better be," Boblin replied. He was down to his last set of boomers, which he needed for the reservoir, and he didn't like the thought of using sword and shield down here. The catacombs were dim, their only source of light coming from the torches they held in their hands. Shadows danced and writhed with every step the company took. He felt the power of the reservoir all around them, the earth's very core thrumming like a plucked violin string. The amount of energy was almost too massive for him to comprehend, but he supposed it took quite a bit of effort to open the gates of Malath.

They turned down a new passage with Boblin keeping his eyes trained on their rear. This time a lone undead staggered into view, bereft of its comrades. Upon seeing them, the creature hissed. It had an open ribcage where its stomach should have been, revealing a pink flutter of lungs as it breathed.

The undead raised a massive broadsword in a two-handed grip. Eklan swung his own sword in response, cleaving the creature straight through its midsection. The top half of the undead's body tumbled to the ground, its arms grasping and waving. The pink of its lungs still fluttered as the company moved past. It stared at Boblin with rolling eyes, froth bubbling from the corner of its mouth.

At last, the passage ended at a pair of massive stone gates. Iron bindings held the doors shut, and even in the faint light, Boblin saw the door's edges quiver with the power behind it.

Eklan braced his hands against the doors and pushed the two halves inward. They creaked and groaned, opening to reveal a winding set of steps leading upward.

"All right," Boblin said, "this is what we came for."

Jend Argul raised a hand, and Boblin stopped. "What is it?"

"It's time we discussed the plan from here, Commander," Jend said. He pointed down the hallway they had just come from. "The underground's crawling with these undead."

"I hadn't noticed."

"You'll need time to destroy that reservoir of power up there—time you won't have if the undead are right behind you. I'll stay here and slow them, sir."

Boblin felt cold. *Why does this keep happening? Did they only come here to die?*

Well, hadn't they all come here to die, when all was said and done?

"It's the most strategic course of action," Eklan rumbled. "The more time we buy down here, the better you will be able to focus on destroying the reservoir, Kule. I'll stay with Jend."

After a moment, Wurit took his place beside the other two. "Me, too."

"This isn't your command, Jend," Boblin said. "The orders are mine to give."

Jend placed the tip of his sword into the dirt, hands on the pommel. "Very well. What are your orders, Commander Kule?"

Boblin looked at the two men and one elion standing in a line, then to Celia. She gave the barest nod, and he felt a taste like ashes in his mouth.

"Hold the line," he said. "Celia, with me."

Jend gave a crisp salute. "As you say, sir."

Jend, Eklan, and Wurit turned at the base of the stairs, facing outward to the tunnel. And Boblin, with Celia at his side, began to ascend.

38

Tim stumbled along the hallway, one hand holding his sword, the other braced against the wall. His palm left a red smear on the wall as he moved. Blood had soaked through the bandage on his side, and he'd had to wrap it with fresh cloth before moving on.

Nearing the end of the passage, he took another long drink of water to slake his thirst. There he saw her, Bria Hamur, on the ground before a set of high, arched gates. She lay with eyes closed, golden hair framing her body, so still that he felt his heart freeze. A mural covered the gates, depicting a conglomeration of anguished souls buried in a mountain of bodies, faces turned toward a robed figure far above them. It was a grisly sight, to be sure, but Tim expected nothing less from a depiction of Malath.

He knelt and placed an ear to Bria's chest. After a moment he detected the rise and fall of breathing. She lived, for now. *Uklith hasn't gotten his sacrifice yet.*
WELCOME, WARRIOR.

The voice was so powerful, Tim could not tell if he heard it aloud or in his head. He grasped Bria's hands and dragged her back from the entryway, determined to get her as far from the Demon-Lord's prison as possible.

"You're too late," Tim said to Uklith. "Your sacrifice is denied you."

A rolling tide of laughter came in response—dark and cold, powerful and resonant. The sound made Tim's bones vibrate as it filled the room and echoed off the walls. It was the certainty of one victorious.

YOU SEE FLAWS WHERE NONE EXIST, WARRIOR. I HAVE NO NEED OF THE WOMAN, NO NEED OF AN ELION SERVANT. THEY SERVED BUT ONE PURPOSE: TO BRING YOU BEFORE ME.

Tim felt the Lifesource rise unbidden within him. Something grasped the power forcibly from within his body, sending tendrils of light from his fingers and into the door in a coruscating rainbow of light. It reminded Tim of the first time he'd touched the Barricade, back when the power rolled from him in ways he neither understood nor controlled. Before him, the waves of magic changed from green to black. With a slow *creak* a seam appeared in the center of the arched doorway, revealing absolute darkness writhing behind it.

No. Could it have been that simple?

From above, Tim felt the three separate points of power slam into him, one from each focusing reservoir. For he, the Warrior, was the fourth and final reservoir, the one necessary to merge the others. His body rose into the air, and through him a stream of energy coursed into the gates of Uklith's prison—

—and they sprang open.

ALL ACTIONS SERVE ME IN THE END, WARRIOR.

A scalding sensation seared his veins, and Tim screamed as he pushed back, resisting Uklith's control. Tendrils of shadow seeped from the gates, accumulating in size and speed. He reached deep within himself, identifying each of the three separate reservoirs, and struggled to separate them. Before him the dark wisps had become an enormous cloud, billowing in all directions, consuming the entire corridor.

He gritted his teeth, latching onto the convergence within him, and *tore* at it. The motion was neither gentle nor painless, but it worked, and he ripped himself free from the power. He fell to the ground, the three points of light winking out behind him as the Lifesource fled his body. He looked up, seeing the awful darkness before him.

What have I done?

He staggered back, moving to protect Bria, right before a tendril of shadow wrapped around her ankle and jerked her forward. The darkness took her, absorbing her.

She was bait, plain and simple. Uklith just needed a way to get me inside the palace. The elion drew me across the desert, and Uklith used Bria to close the net. And now, he imagined, all the world had been lost with the opening of Uklith's prison.

Despair washed through him, so powerful he might have stopped right then, given up outright, if not for the thought of Bria.

I might have lost everything else, I might have doomed all humanity—but there is still a chance I can save her.

All the world for her.

The Warrior of Light grasped his sword. It flared into existence with green fury, and Tim leapt forward into the infinite darkness.

* * *

Eklan Hamur stood next to Jend Argul, hands wrapped around his sword, listening to the sounds of undead coming growing closer. The memories of this place had tormented him these past years, filling his nightmares as he hid in his cottage in Keldur. The dreams had come at least once a week, sometimes more, causing him to awaken in a cold sweat of dread. All along he'd feared that the City would find some way to draw him back into its embrace. Now he was here, and the nightmare was real. But it might be for the best, for a man should face his demons before he died.

"I've been in a lot of tight spots in my day," Jend said. "I have to admit, this is one of the worst."

"You don't say," Eklan murmured.

A cluster of undead came into view. *It's a small group, only six, but what about the next group? And the one after that?* Well, he'd deal with them as they came.

The six undead attacked.

* * *

Boblin's legs ached. One at a time, the tower's stairs wound ever higher. Every so often he and Celia passed a window, which gave them a glance of the outside world. Outside, the focusing reservoir had changed direction, aimed downward into the palace, joined by the beams from the South and North, pointed directly where he knew Tim to be.

"I think we need to hurry," Celia said, and Boblin nodded.

They picked up their pace, arriving at a closed door at the top of the tower. Boblin shouldered it open and stopped, looking upon the scene in awe. A massive well sat in the center of the room, filled to the brim with a source of pulsating, liquid light. The column rose from the well into the sky, first disappearing into the clouds, and from there descending into Uklith's palace at an angle. This was it, pure, raw Lifesource, so tangible Boblin could reach forward and grasp it, though he doubted that would be a wise idea—incineration came to mind. For a moment, he completely forgot the sack of boomers in his hand.

A voice spoke from the corner, bringing him back to the present. "Hello, Boblin."

He blinked. He should know that voice…he could not quite place it, but it tickled his memory. From around the far edge of the well, an elion stepped into view. Boblin had thought this elion long gone, for the last time he'd seen him had been in the dark of Malath's Teeth.

Kaiel Tulak, however, was apparently quite whole. Beside him, Celia drew her sword. Kaiel, weapon bared as well, took another step forward.

"Still doing what you do, Tulak?" Boblin said. "I'd have thought you'd take your chances to cut free after Zadinn discarded you."

Kaiel's eyes narrowed. "Once sworn, always sworn."

"I don't believe you felt that way about your oaths to the Frontier Patrol."

"This is different. I died long ago, in fact, but that matters little to the lord of Malath."

Upon closer inspection, in the light of the focusing reservoir, Boblin saw Kaiel was not *entirely* whole. Large chunks of his flesh were missing, no doubt torn away when the sarchons devoured him, but it appeared enough of him remained for Uklith to power yet one more undead back into his service.

"Did you know I was the first to rise?" Kaiel asked. "The first of this generation's undead, called back to fulfill my purpose."

"You should have stayed in your grave like a decent corpse," Boblin replied, moving forward to meet Kaiel. Their blades clashed in the center of the room.

* * *

A great cold surrounded Tim, engulfing him in an icy grip and squeezing the air from his lungs. Every fiber of his being screamed for release as he struggled to free himself, but in the darkness had no reference point from which to judge his progress. He was thrown forward, striking hard stone as he landed on hands and knees. His vision flared, for a moment filling with blinding light, before his sight slowly but steadily returned. His mouth was dry, his tongue swollen.

His head pounded, but in spite of the ache he soon comprehended something else—for when he placed his hand to the bandages on his side, the dressing fell away to reveal smooth, unmarked skin beneath. Whatever he had passed through had healed him. Even the burn on his chest was gone, though the tattered shreds of his tunic remained.

Tim stood. He remained disoriented for a moment, the world spinning as he got to his feet. After a few breaths, things righted themselves and he could focus again. He moved his hand back to the comforting hilt of his sword.

"Welcome to my humble abode, Warrior. I decided some minor healing was the least courtesy I could extend to you."

Tim turned and found himself facing the tall, dark-haired man from his vision below the cottage in the Erdrar forest. Uklith stood with a sardonic smile on his face. His dark eyes provided a notable contrast to the pale hue of his skin. Tim looked the Demon-Lord up and down, appraising his features. "Zadinn Kanas had no sense of originality, I see."

Uklith stepped forward, one hand resting on a stone basin beside him. A shimmering, radiant substance filled the well, casting an interplay of light and shadow upon his features. "I don't recall the last time someone made a joke in my presence. You are a unique specimen, Warrior."

Tim touched the hilt of his sword once more. "And when was the last time someone drew a weapon in your presence?"

"Trust me, they died screaming, but you won't be so foolish. You've made an interesting observation, Warrior. Over time, Zadinn Kanas did indeed come to resemble me. It was a simple consequence of our close relationship. However, he is no longer here, and you are. As such, it's the relationship between *us* that should concern you most."

The Demon-Lord took another step forward. Tim assessed the room. It was small, forty paces across, and completely bare save for a stone basin atop a dais. Except—

Tim's breath caught. At the back of the room Bria Hamur lay in the shadows, her golden hair spilling upon the floor. *Still unconscious, but at the very least alive, thank the Maker.*

"Oh, don't thank the Maker," Uklith said in a whisper. "He doesn't spend much time in this room, I'm afraid."

Tim's skin tingled.

"Yes, Warrior, I can hear your thoughts. Nothing escapes me in this place. I've had plenty of time to assert my control here, small realm of mine though it may be."

Tim nodded toward Bria. "Let her go."

"Why?"

"You have what you need. Leave her out of the rest of it."

"There are *many* more things I still need, and I suspect she will be helpful in ensuring your compliance."

Tim opened his mind and sought the Lifesource. He didn't hold the power, not quite yet, but he needed it ready on the instant.

Uklith clucked, shaking his head, and Tim felt the light that had been the Lifesource wink out. "Warrior, Warrior. You know I *have* to deny you that. At the very least you could have been willing to exchange a few pleasantries first. Then again—" he pursed his lips, looking thoughtful. "I don't recall you behaving any differently when you met my Advocate in the North."

Tim said nothing, returning Uklith's gaze.

"Better," Uklith said. "*That* is more reminiscent of the Kyrlod." He issued a drawn-out sigh. "Do you know I watched it all from here? Come, stand closer. I won't hurt you—to the contrary, I welcome your presence."

Uklith stood aside, and after careful consideration, Tim stepped forward. He looked into the shimmering basin.

"It's all I've had, these long years," Uklith continued, "the only thing left to me." He waved a hand over the waters, and Tim saw Boblin Kule climbing a set of winding stairs, Celia at his side. "My spyglass into the world. I could observe—and, from time to time, exert my influence."

"But only through exploiting evil in the hearts of people with a capacity for it."

"True, but don't you see that is the beauty of my power? We *all* have a bit of darkness inside. You…" Uklith shook his head. "Oh, you were one to watch, Warrior. I was there with you in the Mountains—prodding you, encouraging you—and you were so close, could have realized such power. Zadinn would have been nothing compared to you."

"As I remember, he and I were evenly matched."

Uklith raised a finger. "Good point—but you *did* win. Something to ponder."

"What do we do now?"

"I suppose we must watch the world crumble together." Uklith stood before the basin. "We'll see it all from here."

"Wouldn't you rather go out and exert your influence?"

"I'm afraid I can't do that quite yet."

Tim raised an eyebrow. "You have your freedom, and yet all you can do is watch?"

Uklith gestured once more to the room around them. "Do I look free to you, Warrior? I'm trapped here, same as ever. The only difference is that you're also sealed in here with me." He tilted his head toward Bria. "As is she."

This time, Tim shook his head. "Uklith, Demon-Lord of Malath, ruler of the underworld—and yet you tell me, after all this, you are *still* a prisoner? I suppose even the all-powerful have limits to their power."

"You know nothing. You and I have only just begun."

Tim stepped back, trying to piece it all together. There was something missing here, something he needed to poke his finger at.

"Yes, Warrior," Uklith breathed. "Think it through. You are marginally more intelligent than most of your kind."

Zadinn Kanas left a piece of himself in one of his journals. Not much, but a nugget of power. The first undead to rise sought out the journal—

"Kaiel Tulak, to be exact," Uklith interjected. "An old friend of Boblin Kule's. You *did* see him at the Fort when you were first captured, but only long enough for Kule to deliver him an intriguing insult. Had Boblin seen the same vision as you, he'd have identified the elion right away."

And Kaiel traveled west. To free Uklith. Except that—

"He didn't come to free me at all. Kaiel thought that was his task, I won't deny that, but as it happens, I lied to him. As I said, Warrior, I just needed to get *you* here."

"Yes—you've said so already. But you tried to stop me."

"Did I?"

"Taazvin. The Assassins in Keldur."

"Oh, I appreciated Taazvin's zeal, but he acted quite on his own. As for the Assassins, well, you needed a guide. I only let Eklan Hamur survive the first time so that he could lead someone with the proper power here. But he was reluctant to return, until the Assassins presented him with the reality of the situation."

Because Eklan did not agree to lead us until after the Assassin attacked—and Kaiel was simply bait to draw me west. West, so I could stand in that chamber and become the fourth focusing reservoir.

"But you're not free yet?"

"Not in the slightest. I do see how you may have misconstrued events, but that business outside the room wasn't about releasing me. It was about capturing you."

Tim's mind skipped back a few paces. "You drew Eklan out here the first time so he would know the way to lead me. Why did you care? Zadinn Kanas was at the height of his power. I wasn't even on this side of the Barricade."

"But you're here now. I plan ahead, Warrior. I knew I might need you."

"*Might*. An interesting word."

"The rewards of being omniscient."

Tim shook his head. "I don't think you are. You sent an Advocate to conquer the world. You didn't know if he would succeed, so you put a backup plan into motion. Eloquent, to be sure, but hardly omniscient."

"And your point is?"

Tim pointed to the basin. "You say you can exert your influence on all the world, on the darkness in our hearts, and I suppose that's true. But you just admitted that everyone already possesses the darkness to begin with. You did not *create* that darkness, you only enhanced what existed to begin with. In admitting as much, you've revealed your greatest weakness."

Uklith spread his palms. "Do go on."

"You *can't* create. Influence, yes, but create...no. Only the Maker can do that."

"I tire of you saying his name in this room. Besides, look upon my armies. Look upon what I *have* created."

The basin shimmered, and Tim saw waves of undead surging through the tunnels, clambering over one another, snarling and grasping. Tim shook his head. "No, that's exactly the point. They're corpses. You've animated them, to be sure, but they are not alive. You imitated life, but didn't create it, because you aren't the Maker and never will be. The best you can ever hope for is to be a worthless mockery of him."

Uklith hissed, nostrils flaring, eyes gleaming. He bared his teeth in a snarl, flicking a hand toward Tim. Tim flew across the room to slam against the wall. His headache, which had subsided, returned when the back of his head struck stone.

Tim slid to the ground. *I've made you angry. Good.* "Admit what you and I both know," Tim said. "The Maker will be around long after you've passed into dust and everyone has forgotten your name. *That*, and nothing more, will be your legacy."

Uklith snapped his fingers, and in response Tim felt pain blossom in his gut, great enough to make him imagine a creature was trying to claw its way out from inside of him. He tried to stand but doubled over after his first attempt.

"Free me," Uklith said. "Free me, or I will peel the skin from your bones and consume your flesh."

"No."

Uklith crooked a finger, and Bria rose into the air from the back of the room. She floated on her back, eyes closed, to hover in front of him. Tim tried to surge to his feet, but an invisible grip held him in place.

"Then I will hurt her first," Uklith said, voice a snarl. "I will carve out her liver and make you eat it."

Tim reached for the Lifesource once more. He knew Uklith had cut him off, but he had to try. If there was even a chance...

It felt as though a smooth, invisible wall existed between him and the power. Tim could sense the Lifesource, lingering just on the other side, so close and yet unattainable. He *pushed*, but the wall did not yield. At the same time, in the physical world, Tim attempted to rise again, pushing against the invisible cords still holding him. His mind and body were trapped, and Bria was at Uklith's mercy.

"Why?" Tim asked through gritted teeth. "Why do you need my help?"

"*Because I can't do it myself!*" Uklith growled, and Tim could see clearly that the Demon-Lord was infuriated by his own impotence. The vise holding Tim in place tightened, squeezing until he thought his blood vessels would burst. Uklith seized a fistful of Bria's hair in his hand, jerking her head down and leaving her neck exposed. He opened his mouth wide, revealing a forked tongue and serrated teeth.

"You fell in love, Warrior," he said. "That's why she's here, because you're pathetic enough to sacrifice yourself, but you'll *never* sacrifice her, and therein lies your weakness."

The air at Tim's windpipe cut off. As an invisible, steady pressure began building on his throat, a faint line of spittle formed at the corner of his lips. Dark spots floated before his eyes, and he looked at Bria's face. If he was to die, she would be the last thing he looked at.

"Zadinn Kanas succeeded for two hundred years, Warrior, where you will fail, all for one simple reason: *you fell in love*. It's an aspect of your vaunted Maker, and it is your greatest weakness."

Tim made one final, desperate grab for the Lifesource, still without result. The mention of Zadinn's name, though, made his memory flicker.

We were evenly matched, Tim had said.

Good point, Uklith had replied, *but you* did *win. Something to think upon. Why?*

He slipped to the ground, consciousness almost gone. He perceived just enough to feel the impact when Uklith gave him a contemptuous kick in the ribs. A spray of blood flew from his mouth.

I defeated Zadinn. Our powers were evenly matched. Until...

Something had shifted. Tim remembered that quite clearly, and to this day he didn't fully understand why or how that had happened. He'd been facing Zadinn, equally and oppositely opposed, and then—

I released the Lifesource. I assumed I would die, but I saw dying as better than destroying the world.

Zadinn hadn't cared about destroying the world, though. He would have laughed while doing so. Because—

Because Zadinn didn't have anyone he cared about, while I refused to destroy the world because I did. And with that, the balance of power shifted. To me.

You say it's a weakness, Uklith? I think that might be your greatest lie of all, and you're willing to kill me before I realize the truth of it. The truth is that it's anything but a weakness.

Tim had been wondering why Uklith was so intent on needing *Tim's* power to free him. Because if Zadinn and Tim possessed equal power, wouldn't Zadinn have freed Uklith? But Zadinn hadn't, because Zadinn couldn't.

The very same truth that allowed me to triumph over Zadinn is why Zadinn did not have the power to break the spell of Homdee, and it's why Uklith can't either. It's why Bria is here now. I love her, and it's a power Uklith will never have. It's why he hates us and fears us.

Because he can't love, and we can.

Tim blew away the barrier separating him from the Lifesource. The power surged back into his body, and at once everything changed—he could breathe again, could stand again. Most importantly—

He could fight again.

"I hope you were listening to all that," Tim said, and he struck.

A wave of fire washed over Uklith, tearing him away from Bria. Tim gave her a gentle nudge, removing her from the center of the room and from the conflict. The fires Tim had thrown at Uklith shimmered and dissipated, leaving the Demon-Lord standing in their wake. The man's—creature's—face was cold and hard, the beads of his eyes blazing, his jaw set in fury. He raised his hands, and Tim saw long, black tentacles curling from the Demon-Lord's fingertips. A circle of black flames rose from the floor, surrounding them.

"You think to best me in my domain?" Uklith asked.

"Yes, I do."

The two combatants met in the middle of the room, trading physical blows as well as blows of power. The ground quaked and dust tumbled from the ceiling. They ended up atop the dais, Tim with his back to the stone basin and its reservoir of Lifesource power.

Uklith's fingers closed on Tim's throat, burning where they touched his skin. The Demon-Lord showed his serrated teeth once more. "This *isn't* my domain, though. My domain lies behind you, behind the focusing reservoir I used to enter this world."

Tim stumbled against the edge of the well. He tumbled backward, and at the last moment reached out to seize Uklith's tunic.

He struck the waters of the reservoir. Shimmering droplets of power absorbed him, and Tim felt the world shudder.

A veil has parted, he thought.

And then a blinding flash of light consumed everything.

39

Boblin crossed blades with Kaiel Tulak. The elion danced before him, dodging and twisting, pulling back and lunging forward, as beside them the focusing reservoir raged. A wind rose from the well, whipping about the room and gusting so hard he found it difficult to remain balanced. From the corner of his eye, he saw Celia move forward, flowing on her feet to enter the combat. As she did, two more undead emerged from the shadows, so she spun to face the new threat, leaving Boblin and Kaiel to continue their duel.

Outside, the sandstorm surged through Agrazab's streets, lashing a swirl of dust against the window, scouring it with beady grains. Some swept through a crack in the glass, whipping over Boblin and slicing thin lines of blood across his skin. Kaiel smiled, seeing the drops of red drip on Boblin's forearm. "We've come a long way from the Fort, you and I," Kaiel said. "Yet here we are, dancing the same dance as always."

"It's too bad there aren't any sarchons this time around. I'd enjoy watching you get eaten again."

"Oh, I think not. This time, I'll see *you* eaten, from the inside out as the Demon-Lord devours your very soul."

Boblin jumped back, dodging a slice aimed at his chest, and felt a whisper of air as the edge of Kaiel's blade passed over his skin. His back touched the wall. Cornered, he feinted left and dove right, rolling toward the center of the room. As he rose to his feet in a fluid motion, his shoulder touched the reservoir, and the pure energy radiating from it and scorched his skin. He flinched, the cloth of his jerkin burnt away, his shoulder raw.

Kaiel smirked. "Careful."

On the other side of the well, Celia came up between her opponents, thrusting a sword through the first one's neck. The undead fell backward, and as she jerked her blade free, she took the creature's weapon from its hand. Breathing heavily, a sword in each fist, she turned to face her second opponent. Meanwhile Boblin moved to the side, away from the reservoir to face Kaiel once more. He was tired—from the long battle aboveground, from the flight through the tunnels, from the climb up the stairs, from it all. With aching legs, weary arms, and heavy eyelids, his movements were not as quick as he would like, his attacks too clumsy and his retreats too slow. Kaiel, however, remained fresh.

As fresh as an eighteen-month old corpse can be, that is.

Kaiel's next attack caught Boblin on his uninjured shoulder. The blade passed through Boblin's skin and out the far side, tip tinged red with blood. The pain drove Boblin to his knees, his back so close to the focusing reservoir that he felt the breath of heat once more. He gasped. The sword fell from his hands, clattering to the ground. A drop of sweat slid from his forehead and into his eye, burning and causing his vision to blur.

"Any last words, Kule?" Kaiel asked.

Boblin met Kaiel's gaze. "Yes. I've got you right where I wanted you."

He spun and clamped his right hand around Kaiel's sword-wrist, then turned it clockwise, sealing his grip and using the leverage to rise back to his feet. It was a classic ailar move, and Kaiel should have known better, but Boblin would take his blessings as they came. Boblin levered Kaiel's arm forward, knocking him off balance. He brought his left palm around in a hammer blow against Kaiel's elbow, breaking the bone. Kaiel cried out.

"For the last time," Boblin said, "I *told* you I'd kill you." He seized Kaiel's tunic and drove the undead elion headfirst into the focusing reservoir. Kaiel did not have time to scream. Buried in the light up to his waist, Kaiel's body bucked wildly in a strange, jerking motion. Boblin's knuckles brushed the edge of the light. The fire burned, but he forced himself to stay in position for another long minute. He pulled Kaiel Tulak free. The top half of the elion's body had been charred beyond recognition. All that remained was a crusty skeleton, the skull with eye sockets empty, mouth open in its final scream. Its teeth glistened white in the light. For good measure, Boblin cut Kaiel's head off, just to be sure he *stayed* dead this time.

Beside him, Celia caught her opponent's neck crossways between her two blades. She pulled her arms back outward with a clean sweep, beheading him as well.

By the Maker, there's enough heads rolling around in this tower for us to play a game of kick-stone.

"Was that a smart plan?" she asked, nodding toward the gaping wound in Boblin's shoulder.

"No," Boblin said, clamping a hand against it to stem the flow of blood, "but it worked."

He felt very woozy. The next thing he knew, he was wavering and falling back to his knees. Celia rushed to his side, knelt beside him and tore strips of cloth to bandage the wound.

"Come on," she said. "We're almost there."

Boblin nodded, swallowing. "Aye, let's get this done." She tied the bandage off, and he reached forward to pick up the sack of boomers. He struggled to his feet, moving past the window toward the focusing reservoir—and froze when he caught a glimpse of the sky outside.

Waves of power rolled off the top of the palace where Tim and Uklith fought, creating a dancing, shimmering mirage of coruscating light in all colors. That was nothing compared to the sky, though, where a giant vertical slit had appeared above the city. The edges of the crack rippled with jagged streaks of red light, spiderwebbing to the far horizon.

Boblin looked from the seam in the sky, to the palace, and back to the seam. The crack grew steadily wider, the darkness within becoming more pronounced. It roiled like a living thing, and Boblin saw shapes clamoring within—shapes in unbearable agony, begging to be released. He thought he even heard a faint chorus of screams.

"Are we too late?" Celia whispered.

"I don't know."

* * *

Bria Hamur opened her eyes. She lay on her back in a tiny room. At first, she had no bearing on her location. Gradually her memories returned—fighting undead in the streets, running across rooftops, the hooded figure in pursuit, and then—

Nothing.

She touched her head, expecting it to feel tender from whatever had rendered her unconscious, but there was no pain. No bruising, no soreness, as if she'd done nothing more than awaken from a long nap. She put a hand to her waist next and found she had no weapon.

Not good.

She stood and saw it: a well of shimmering, radiant light on a dais at the center of the austere room. An orb of darkness spun at the light's core, trailing tendrils of shadow. Of more immediacy were the two unconscious men hovering above the reservoir of power. They lay on their backs as if sleeping on invisible mattresses. The first figure was a young man, dark-haired and pale-skinned, wearing a plain black shirt and trousers with a gold belt cinched around his waist. The other figure was Tim Matthias.

Bria looked around the small, circular room. It had no doors, windows, or exits, and its drab, brown stone walls were completely empty. She stepped closer to the two forms. A thin line of power ran from Tim to the stranger, like a rope tethering their bodies together. Only, the end stretching from Tim was of pure white light, while that from the stranger was deep and dark. A glowing bead hovered where the two halves met in the middle. As she watched, the bead slid just an inch toward Tim, extending the dark half of the line closer to him.

Is that Uklith? She looked around once more. *No doors, no exits. Are we in his prison?* The bead of light moved another inch toward Tim, but stopped, and after a moment of quivering, slid back the other direction. *He's fighting back, wherever he is.*

The ground beneath her feet shook, a shower of fine dust descending from the ceiling. She placed a hand on the edge of the well to steady herself. The shaking subsided, but after no more than a heartbeat of peace, a new tremor shook the room, throwing her to the floor. Bria landed on the palms of her hands. Risking another glance toward the rope of light, she saw that Tim had lost whatever ground he'd gained.

A crack formed on the far wall facing her, beginning as a jagged hairline that rapidly widened. On the far side she saw a mass of writhing and tormented bodies, an entire pack of undead trying to claw through the seam.

Malath is opening.

An undead stuck its arm through the opening. Its long, crusted fingers curled around the edge, using it as a handhold to pull itself forward until head and torso emerged. Bria's hand instinctively went back to her belt, even though she'd already checked for a weapon. She scanned the room and spotted Tim's blade lying on the ground, recognizing it by the green pommel stone. She dove for the sword just as the first undead came through the crack. It rose to its full height on tottering legs, arms extended, and stumbled toward Tim with jaws clacking.

Bria met it halfway, placing herself between the creature and Tim's body. She took its head in one clean sweep, and its body collapsed to the ground as quickly as it had risen. Behind the first creature, two more pushed their way through the still-widening rift. Bria balanced on the balls of her feet, blade held in the ready position, guarding Tim's floating body.

"You're going to owe me for this, Matthias," she said. "I hope you're worth it."

* * *

Jend pulled back as an arrow bounced off the curve of the stairway near his face. In front of him, the undead filled the stairwell to the brim, the mass of their bodies serving as the greatest hindrance to their advance. The stale, rusty scent of their bodies filled his nostrils. They could no longer hold this level, and the time had come to pull back. They'd already been pushed at least a quarter of the way up the tower, maybe farther, and it was becoming harder to slow the mounting horde.

Shoulder to shoulder with Eklan and Wurit, he backed up the steps. An undead pushed forward, flailing at them with its weapon. Jend brought his blade down, shearing its hand from wrist, and the undead screeched. The skin over its face was leathery and cracked, wisps of white hair sticking in odd tufts from its scalp. The creature's eyes rolled in its sockets as, bereft of its weapon, it fell in an ungainly tangle of limbs.

The curve of the stairwell hid the retreating trio from of the undead for a moment, and Jend leaned against the wall, resting his sword. "We go slow. Give ground only when we have to. Every minute buys Kule more time to destroy the reservoir."

Eklan nodded, broadsword held in two hands. Jend wondered if he looked as bad as the other two did. Eklan and Wurit were covered in bruises, cuts, and dirt. Resuming the retreat, Jend took another step. Something rope-like snaked around his ankle. Before Jend could react, the rope jerked forward and pulled him from his feet. He landed on his back, the force of the blow driving the wind from him as he felt himself being pulled down, back around the curve of the stair. The stone steps scraped his skin. An undead pulled at the opposite end of the bola, the rope of which had wrapped tightly around Jend's ankles and entangled his feet. A mass of the creatures reached for Jend as he came into view, mouths working ceaselessly. They were going to devour him, and he'd be alive when it happened.

Eklan lumbered into view, swinging his massive sword, mowing through ranks of undead like a scythe through wheat. The big man roared a challenge as Wurit grasped Jend's shoulders, pulling him back to safety. Jend sat up, grasped a knife from his belt, and leaned forward to cut through the strands—one, two, and then he was free, rising back to his feet.

In front of him, Eklan Hamur was bodily thrown back by the sheer weight of the undead pressing upward. One of the undead skewered Eklan's bicep with the jagged tip of its spear, and a bright gout of red sprayed. This time Jend was the one who leapt into action, coming forward to save the other. He threw his belt-knife, striking the undead between the eyes, and it tumbled out of sight down the stairwell.

Eklan's face was tight, one hand over the wound. A tiny fountain of blood continued spurting, and Jend feared the weapon had struck the big man's artery. If so, he could have minutes to live at most.

"I guess that's it," Eklan said through gritted teeth.

"No," Jend replied. Though they'd dealt with it in different ways, Hugo and Ken's deaths pained Jend as greatly as they had Commander Kule. Jend understood the cold necessities of battle, but today, he'd simply had enough. *We've lost too many already, but Malath will take me before we lose another.* He unwound his belt, fashioning a tourniquet for Eklan's arm and wrapped it around the big man's bicep. He ratcheted it tight as possible and put Eklan's injured arm around his shoulder. Wurit stepped forward, bracing Eklan's opposite arm over his shoulder, and supporting their comrade between them, the two warriors stepped back. From below, more undead surged into view.

"Keep climbing," Jend said. "All of us, or none of us."

His companions nodded.

* * *

An all-encompassing darkness surrounded Tim, so cold he thought his bones might shatter. It was absolute agony. When he tilted his head back to scream, he found he had no voice to do so. He thought back to when he'd faced the second Advocate in Uklith's hall, when he'd floated in the cosmos before the black cloud. Then, he had escaped the darkness, but now it had found him once more and his heart wavered. When the dark cloud retreated, Tim found himself on hands and knees on a field of red sandstone. A gust of wind blew red dust across his knuckles. His throat felt choked and dry, and he no longer had his water skin to slake his thirst.

Am I back in the Western Desert?

Tim stood, dusting off his pants and looking around. A jagged, harsh wasteland surrounded him, a series of mountainous ridges against the horizon and an expanse of cracked stone before him. Black vines, thorns poking out on all sides, snaked across the landscape and twisted into crevasses. He looked up and saw that the sky above him was not of his world, not by any stretch of imagination. A mass of black clouds writhed far overhead. Where they separated, they revealed the sky beyond to be a mixture of pale blue and deep red, with lines of darkness stretching to connect one set of colors to another. A ceaseless interplay of lightning flashed, but without any accompanying sound of thunder.

He had no water and no weapons. He turned and saw that he stood near the edge of a great fissure. A chorus of sounds emanated from somewhere within. Tim approached, one cautious step at a time, moving with trepidation until he could look at last over the edge.

The sheer walls descended impossibly far. What he saw at the bottom of the chasm, easily a thousand feet below, made him sink to his knees in despair. A million tortured souls writhed in the depths, wailing and crying out for an end to their suffering, an end which had been denied them for millennia as they languished in perpetual damnation. The horrific sound combined the cries of all races: humans, elions, dwerions, and more, races that had come long before, lost in the annals of histories dead and gone.

A sob escaped his lungs. This was the most awful thing he had ever encountered, and he feared the sight and sound of it all might drive him mad. Because Tim Matthias knew exactly where he was, and it terrified him to no end.

He was in the bowels of Malath itself.

* * *

"Stand back."

In the room at the top of the tower, Celia obliged Boblin's request as he finished tying the fuse on the end of the boomers. He dropped all of the boomers into his bag and cinched the drawstring.

Outside the window, the rent in the sky had grown to unimaginable proportions. Scintillating shades of white rippled alongside erratic flashes of blue and green, purple and gold, red and black, all the colors of the Lifesource swirling in a terrifying blend around the otherworldly darkness threatening to surge forth. From within the palace, a nimbus of light had sprung up, surrounding the building with a domed shield. Boblin suspected this indicated Tim still held ground, but as with the barrage of power assaulting the shield from the heavens, he could tell the defenses were inevitably weakening.

It's fascinating, in a way. We've always thought of Malath as below, and Harmea above, but it appears Malath now descends from above and Harmea protects from below. Here in Agrazab, where Uklith reigned supreme, all Boblin and the rest had once held to be unassailable truth found itself under assault. That observation, perhaps more than anything else, scared him to no end.

At the moment, he had more pressing matters to occupy his attention. Where the light from the sky struck the city streets, he saw rustling and unrest as more undead came forward. They were the heralds, the forerunners. Whatever was to emerge from that awful abyss in the sky was sure to be a thousand times worse.

Boblin struck the fuse, throwing the boomers toward the reservoir.

As soon as the bag left his hands, he sprinted and dove as far from the well as possible, arms outstretched to land beside Celia. She pulled him into a rough shelter she had made beside a small table, though in truth Boblin expected this to matter little once the detonation occurred.

The boomers erupted on contact with the reservoir. Boblin braced for an impact, but none came. The explosion was more than evident, even as the sack vanished into the blinding light, but it had no effect at all. A second after the detonation flared into existence, it disappeared, and Boblin found himself and Celia staring at a completely unchanged reservoir.

"Well," he said, "that didn't work."

* * *

Tim forced himself to turn away from the sight of so many tormented souls. He summoned the Lifesource, his only small comfort in this place of suffering.

Is this what happens when we die? Is it no more than this?

The lightning in the sky grew more frantic, while the ground rumbled, a vibration of pebbles and soils that increased in violence to become a great earthquake. The earth rose beneath him, forming the side of a great mountain lifting higher and higher. Tim tumbled backward down this sudden slope, which grew jagged contours and sudden outcroppings as it reached for the lightning in the sky. At the peak, a vast, dark cloud appeared, a maelstrom that increased in size. It writhed and twirled like a living thing, tendrils reaching forth.

YOU HAVE MY THANKS, WARRIOR. The words came from everywhere and nowhere, filling Tim's ears. *THE VEIL HAS BEEN TORN, AND HERE I REASSUME MY RIGHTFUL THRONE.*

The dark cloud parted, and Tim saw a pair of red eyes form at its center.

I've seen you before.

It had been outside the camp in the Northern Mountains, shortly after his first encounter with Zadinn Kanas, after he destroyed the vrawl with his ring of power and Nazgar reprimanded him. He had slept and dreamt of a dark cloud with red eyes at its center. And again, when he became fevered underneath the mountains, Tim had awakened in the tunnels before facing the sarchon queen. Just for a second, he had thought he saw a wisp of cloud and heard a chorus of voices, but it vanished, and he presumed it nothing more than a fever-dream.

YES. I HAVE BEEN WATCHING YOU ALL ALONG.

Beyond the rise of the mountain, beyond the cloud, a slit emerged in the sky. Tim saw a bright blue beyond, the sky of his world.

YOU HAVE MY THANKS, WARRIOR. WITNESS THE END, BROUGHT ABOUT BY YOUR OWN HAND.

The Demon-Lord's laughter boomed great and loud, a thunder that would never end.

* * *

Celia moved toward the focusing reservoir, its glow illuminating her face. Lights played across her battle-worn features, and she had a curious look in her eyes.

"Don't get too close," Boblin said.

"No," she replied. "I think we've been going about this wrong. I think you need to *use* it, not destroy it."

"Use it?"

"That's what reservoirs are—latent wellsprings of power, accessible by those who don't even have the Lifesource within. Uklith might have usurped this one, but that doesn't mean you can't wrest it back from his control."

Boblin gave a desperate laugh. "Me? Fight *Uklith?*"

She looked through the open window, toward the slit in the sky beyond and the powers hammering down on the palace. She had the slightest smile upon her face. "I think he's a little distracted."

By the Maker, she might be right. But I've never been able to tap the reservoirs before. It doesn't come to me as it does others. I focus on the tangible, the real. If Quentiin had been here, perhaps he could have done it. He seemed to have at least a small affinity for such things.

But there wasn't anyone else here. It was up to him.

The door to the top of the tower thudded open, and Jend and Wurit staggered inside, Eklan Hamur hanging between them. The big man's face was ashen, his eyes half-closed. Boblin saw the tourniquet about Eklan's arm and knew the wound was serious. Jend and Wurit didn't look much better. Beaten and bedraggled, covered with wounds, they had clearly fought to their limit. Jend's sword hung in his hand, and every feature in his face bespoke weariness. Wurit hefted the door closed, just as Boblin heard an undead throw itself against the opposite side.

"We held as long as we could, sir," Jend said. He and Wurit deposited Eklan on the floor near the wall. Boblin couldn't even tell if the man was conscious or not. He looked back at the reservoir. Celia was right—if it was the last thing he did, he'd seize this power and turn it upon itself.

The door shook again. "You're going to have to hold a bit longer," Boblin replied to Jend. "We're not quite done here."

Jend pulled himself together with visible effort. There he stood, Jend Argul, the greatest warrior Boblin had ever known, beaten to within an inch of his life, knowing quite well what came next. "Aye, Commander Kule."

Boblin saw Eklan's lips moving and heard the man's barely audible words. "Sword," Eklan croaked. "Give it to me. I'll die with it in hand."

Wordlessly, Wurit handed him a big blade. Eklan tried to rise, failed, and settled for grasping the weapon between his hands as he sat against the wall, blade pointed outward at the failing defenses.

Boblin looked over the company. "Celia Kule has the command."

He sank to his knees before the focusing reservoir and reached toward it, closing his eyes.

40

Bria pulled the blade free from the undead's body. She kicked over the next creature to come at her, sending it sprawling back down the dais steps. In front of her, the crack in the wall had widened enough to permit undead through two at a time, though they often stumbled over each other, hindering their movements. She'd already slain near to a dozen of the creatures, the bodies of which lay across the room. After encountering each pair, she usually had several minutes to catch her breath before the next two arrived; however, her periods of rest were growing shorter and shorter, and every so often, the entire room shook, sending perpetual clouds of dust down upon her. Some of these quakes were only slight tremblings of the earth, but others were strong enough to throw her onto her face. At first she'd feared the crack in the wall led to the underworld, but upon closer inspection she saw it led back into the palace hallway. At the end of the day, she was just as likely to die, but she'd rather do so knowing she was in her world rather than in Malath. And on that note…

Above her, Tim and Uklith still hung suspended, the rope-like line connecting them burning brighter on Tim's end and darker on Uklith's end. At the beginning, though the bead alternated sliding to one side or the other, it had always returned somewhat close to the middle, but no longer. Now, even though Tim's side managed to gain ground at times, it was losing the larger battle, held to a quarter of the length at most. Even so, she believed that if she could keep Tim alive long enough, he might have a chance to win.

Another undead made its way through the crack. Each creature seemed to move more quickly than the previous one, and they were becoming harder to kill. This time, her sword bounced off the creature's leathery hide with her first strike, and it took a second blow for her to plunge her blade between its ribs. As she did so, she tripped backward, landing on the steps and losing her grip on her weapon. The undead loomed over her, the blade still sticking from its midsection, and raised a two-handed mace above its head, chains rattling at its far end. As it brought the weapon down, Bria rolled out of the way and the studded ball landed on the stones beside her. She swept her leg outward, drawing the undead's feet out from under it, and the creature fell. Using her momentum to rise, she grabbed the creature's mace. The weapon was hefty, indicating just how strong these creatures truly were, but it didn't stop her from bringing it around and crushing the other's skull.

She retrieved Tim's sword as the room shook again, a more violent quake this time, throwing her backward on the dais to strike the stone well. She looked up and saw cracks running across the ceiling. The center of the structure sagged inward with an ominous *creak*, and she thought uncomfortably of the thousands of pounds of dirt and stone above their heads. *One or two more like that, and we're all buried alive. Except for the undead, who will be buried dead.*

The first time she tried to get to her feet, the quaking threw her right back down. She was successful the second time and found herself standing near Tim's face as his body hovered level with her head. The seam leading to the tunnels widened just a little more, and three undead rather than two pushed their way inside this time. *There's more of them, they're getting faster and stronger, and I'm only getting weaker.*

She looked at Tim, hoping to catch some glimpse of where he was, but his face betrayed nothing. She saw only his closed eyelids and the straight line of his mouth. His hands lay clasped upon his stomach as if he rested on a funeral bier, and but for the slow rise and fall of his chest, she might have feared him dead.

She had hated Tim upon first sight—not for who he was, but for what he represented. He had come to open wounds not yet healed and done so with an arrogant calmness. Over these last weeks, though, she had grown to understand him. Wielder of power and destiny though he might be, he was still just a man. She'd seen him roll beneath the scorpion on the Mygon Path without hesitation, the fear on his face making evident his knowledge that he was fighting without his greatest weapon, the same as if a master swordsman were forced to fight a duel with only a dagger in his non-dominant hand. The Sheels of the world might have fled that fight, but not Tim. Later in the Wastelands, he had stayed behind in the krevur's nest, relying on a half-concocted plan that by all rights should have ended in his death.

And he had followed her captor to this darkest of places, placing himself against a nemesis whose power dwarfed his own. For *her.*

She had heard Eklan ask Tim the other night: *Why are you here?*

Because it's the right thing to do.

He was not a complex weaver of plots, not a sorcerer pulling strings behind the scenes. He was a simple, direct, and honest man, and wherever he was, he'd fight this battle with every fiber of his being.

In the meantime, she would protect him for as long as she breathed.

"The Maker be with you," she said softly. She placed a kiss upon his lips and turned to face the next group of undead.

* * *

Tim fought his way up the mountain, toward the cloud above. Howling winds whipped to and fro, every gust threatening to rip him from his precarious perch, but he continued climbing. Every handhold he grasped tore at his skin, leaving it cracked and bleeding. In the sky above him, threads of blackness leaked through the vast rent, exiting this world and entering the next.

Grit stung his eyes. Thorns snaked from the ground to hinder his approach, but he burnt them away with merely a thought. As much power as he held, though, he knew it was nothing compared to the dark maelstrom he approached one step at a time. As he neared the summit, he recognized the stones beneath his feet for what they truly were: skulls of all races, thousands upon thousands combined to form this dark, terrible mountain. They crunched under his boots, some grinding into dust, others rolling down the slope. A legion of souls had died to form this mountain, yet it was not enough to satisfy the Demon-Lord's tastes. His hunger was insatiable, his desire for dominance unquenchable.

YES, NOW YOU UNDERSTAND. I HAVE BUILT THIS DOMAIN OVER MILLENNIA, DRAWING TORMENTED SOULS INTO MY DARK EMBRACE, BUT I WANT THEM ALL, THE SOULS OF EVERY WORLD. THEY SHALL BE MINE, UNTIL ETERNITY BECOMES MY SLAVE. I WILL SUNDER THE GATES OF HARMEA AND ASSUME MY RIGHTFUL THRONE OVER ALL EXISTENCE.

Tim reached the edge of the peak. A landslide of skulls descended upon him, burying him up to the waist, rooting him in place.

YOUR END IS MY BEGINNING.

Tim filled himself with as much of the Lifesource as he could muster and hurled it at the Demon-Lord. The power ripped from him with such ferocity he screamed aloud, a funnel of green light stretching from his hands and stabbing into the clouds. He held so much power that he expected his body to turn to ashes and dust, enough to have slain Zadinn a hundred times over, and he threw all of it at the Demon-Lord. The clouds merely absorbed the magic, rustling as if laughing.

I DO NOT DENY IT, AN IMPRESSIVE DISPLAY OF POWER, BUT IT TRULY MATTERS NOT, FOR YOU ARE ONLY A MAN, AND I AM ETERNAL.

The Maker save us. Bring salvation, for this is beyond anything any mortal was meant to face.

HE WILL NOT AID YOU, WARRIOR. HE HAS FORSAKEN YOU.

Tim used the Lifesource again, screaming once more as the next torrent of power ripped forth. Again, the clouds absorbed the barrage without impact. Behind him, he heard the whisper of tortured souls from the chasm as they made their way up the hill.

THEY CLAMOR FOR RELEASE, AND THANKS TO YOU, THEY SHALL HAVE IT.

Tim saw dark shapes floating forward, some of them recognizable as humans, elions, or dwerions, others completely unknown. One floated past him, its touch cold, before rising into the air toward the rent.

WOULD YOU LIKE TO SEE WHAT HAS BECOME OF THOSE YOU LED, WARRIOR?

A section of the sky peeled back, and Tim saw a vision stretched across the heavens. Boblin knelt before a well of power, Celia and Jend beset on all sides by undead, Eklan Hamur lying against the wall and perhaps slain.

The vision flickered. Quentiin fought in the streets of Vonku—buildings around him aflame, smoke billowing—surrounded by clamoring hordes that looked to be a mixture of undead and corsairs.

The vision flickered again. Ladu was cornered in a section of the palace in Galdon, an arrow sticking from his midsection, an undead climbing onto him with jaws opened wide.

The vision flickered a final time. Bria Hamur stood in the room where he had left her, a semicircle of a dozen undead in front of her. She looked left and right as she tried to anticipate from which angle the next attack would come.

THEY WILL ALL DIE.

* * *

Boblin knelt before the well. He closed his eyes, attempting to find the inner calm Tim spoke of. He reached with his mind toward the reservoir, even as he heard the sound of the door breaking inward.

Tim described accessing the Lifesource as standing in a room and reaching behind a veil. Boblin imagined the room in his mind, veil fluttering in front of him, envisioning the reservoir behind it, filled with glowing light. He stepped toward the veil...*close...careful...*

He felt the fabric between his fingers, heard the rustle, pulled it aside—and Hanqar's body, bloodied and broken, tumbled through the veil to land in his arms. Boblin stumbled back, staring in horror at the elion's mangled flesh.

Command an army, and those you lead will die.

Hanqar's dead face turned toward him, and his lips moved. "Why did you fail me, Commander?"

Boblin dropped him, and the body flickered and changed into that of Hugo, then of Ken, all of whom who had placed their trust in him and paid the final price for it.

Boblin's eyes opened and he found himself in front of the reservoir, tears wet on his face. Celia and Jend formed the primary defense in front of him, blades flashing as fast as the eye could move. At least ten undead were in the room, moving with quick, deadly force past the bodies of their comrades and toward the soldiers. At the broken door, more pressed inward. The companions had moments at most before they'd be overrun.

He looked back toward the reservoir. *Give me something, a sign, anything. How can I use you to save us?*

* * *

Eklan Hamur curled his hand around his blade. By the Maker, he was weak. *This is it. Agrazab has me at last.*

In front of him, undead clambered into the room, a wild mob of crazed, manic creatures. Jend Argul took the right, Celia Kule the center, and Wurit the left—

—Eklan saw it coming and tried to cry a warning, but the sound came only as a muffled grunt. An undead thrust a spear forward, driving it through Wurit's neck with a definitive *crunch*. Blood sprayed in all directions and Wurit tumbled over, dead before he struck the ground. Their defenses wavered, and the final wave of undead closed in upon them.

* * *

Tim saw Wurit fall, for the vision had flickered back to Boblin and the company in the tower. Wurit hit the ground with a spear through his throat, sightless eyes staring upward. The defenses crumbled on the flank he had been guarding, undead pushing forward with relentless intent, with Boblin exposed in front of the focusing reservoir as he tried to tap its energy.

ONE BY ONE, THEY FALL.

Tim filled himself with the Lifesource, preparing to strike again at Uklith.

WHY DO YOU CONTINUE TO TRY? YOU KNOW IT IS FUTILE. IT'S THE STORY OF ALL YOUR COMRADES, WARRIOR—THE ELION IN THE TOWER, THE DWERION IN THE STREETS, THE EMPEROR IN THE PALACE, THE WOMAN IN MY CHAMBERS. IF THERE IS ONE THING THAT AMUSES ME THE MOST, IT IS THOSE WHO CONTINUE TO FIGHT THINKING IT MEANS SOMETHING. IT IS THE GREATEST JOKE OF ALL, FOR IN THE END, ALL PURPOSES SERVE ME.

Tim felt the power swell within him and took one more glance at his friends.

Perhaps it is futile.

So why do *we continue to fight?*

He hesitated, the Lifesource tingling in his veins. Uklith's taunts had become almost predictable by now, and yet—

If our efforts truly are futile, why does Uklith bother saying so? He is fixated on reminding me that we can do nothing against him, but Uklith is the master of lies. Could it be…that we are close to something he is afraid of? He is trying to overwhelm us with despair, and yet if our loss was truly inevitable, he wouldn't try so hard to make us lose hope. Our hope, our stand, terrifies him. Because…

Uklith's presence slammed into Tim. Had he not already been buried to his waist in the landslide of skulls, the force of the blow would have ripped him from the mountain. As it was, it merely caused him to sway in the wind. Blood blossomed from dozens of minor wounds that appeared from nowhere. Yes, Uklith was indeed trying to divert Tim's train of thought, he was sure of it.

Because it's not about whether we defeat him. It's the fact that, even if we lose this battle, he's afraid hope will continue to exist. Uklith wants to reign supreme, but he's already as much as admitted that fundamental evil exists without him, and that he merely influences the evil that we already possess. It doesn't matter if we die. What matters is that, as long as there is evil in the world, there will still be someone, somewhere, who is willing to stand against it.

And as long as that is the case, Uklith will never win.

Tim unleashed his power—not toward Uklith, but toward the seam in the sky. He had already realized his power alone against the Demon-Lord would never be enough, but that didn't matter, because Tim had *never* stood against Uklith alone. He'd always had others by his side, and now, it was his time to stand by theirs.

He directed his energy toward Eklan Hamur first, where the big man lay against the wall on the cusp of death. Tim still couldn't heal people. No, he feared that skill would always be beyond him, but that didn't mean he couldn't help. *Come on,* he thought toward the man, using his power to give Eklan energy. *It's up to you. Fill the flank Wurit lost.*

* * *

Eklan felt a deep power rise into him. For a moment, his pain washed away, and his thoughts returned with sudden clarity.

Aye, this might be the end indeed. But by the Maker, I'll meet it on two feet.

He slowly but surely dragged himself into a standing position, blade in hands, and stumbled forward to join the defense.

* * *

NO! Uklith roared, slamming into Tim again. Tim felt as if strips of skin were being flayed from his body. Droplets of blood spattered in all directions. He gritted his teeth and roared, because he knew that he was not truly in his body, he was only here in the mind, and that his mortal form was still in the room with Bria. Uklith might make him feel like he was being torn to shreds—and doing a good job of it—but it was an illusion, a lie like everything else.

Tim redoubled his efforts, pouring power into Eklan Hamur. The big man stood up, sword raised, and faced the undead.

I've figured it out, Tim said to Uklith. *I've figured you out. So watch this.* He directed his attention toward Celia next. This approach was subtler, not quite what Eklan had needed, but something else. *Hurry, Celia*, he thought. *Boblin needs you.*

* * *

Boblin opened his eyes again, pounding his hand on the ground in frustration. He saw Celia draw back from the battle, Jend filling the gap where she had been. She knelt by his side, hand on his shoulder. He looked at her, feeling the pain evident across his face.

"I can't do it," he said. "I'm too weak."

"No, you aren't," she replied, shaking her head. "Far from it. Boblin Kule, you are the strongest elion I know."

"I keep seeing Hanqar. Hugo. Ken. They all died."

"They were willing to die because they believed in you, and the way you inspired them is your strength, not a failing. Think about the reservoir differently, though: have you ever succeeded in using a focusing reservoir by meditating?"

"No, but—"

"Yes, I realize that's how Tim describes it. But he's also always said the Lifesource is a tool, and men use tools in different ways. How do you use a sword? How do you use *your* tools?"

In front of them, Jend Argul and Eklan drew back. The lighting storm outside the window shadowed the terror on their faces. The undead came ever closer.

"Swords are simple. I pick them up."

Celia cupped his face in her hands. "This can be simple too, Boblin. So go—and *pick it up.*" She kissed him and rose, drawing her sword. She turned to face the end.

Boblin looked at the reservoir. It had *burned* Kaiel, incinerating him, and he'd simply assumed it would do the same to him. But Kaiel had been undead, a perversion of the Lifesource, and Boblin was quite alive.

Well, it might still kill me, but we're probably dead either way. Boblin stood up, plunged his hands directly into the shimmering light, and felt the power flood into him.

* * *

The hill of skulls buried Tim up to his neck. He saw Boblin place his hands into the reservoir, saw waves of Lifesource surge through his friend, turning the elion into an enormous conduit of energy.

THIS MEANS NOTHING, Uklith said. *YOU WILL STILL LOSE!*

Tim felt the Lifesource trickle out of him. He had spent his powers and had nothing left. He supposed Uklith would still enter the world, for the rent in the sky was growing, but Tim had done his part. He thought of Nazgar, wondering what the Kyrlod would say to him if he were here. *Would you have any advice for me, old friend? Any last words?*

Then he saw it: a campfire, the night before his battle with Zadinn. *I only have one thing left to teach you,* Nazgar said. *There is an ancient magic called the tongue of Homdee. There are many spells of Homdee, but tonight I give you only one. The Banishing Spell.*

And he thought of Gardellin, lying outside Uklith's chambers. *Go, but remember what you have learned of Homdee.*

Back in Agrazab, the power of Homdee had been the only thing strong enough to even *slow* Uklith. Tim knew little of the magic. But before Tim's final battle with Zadinn, beside the campfire, Nazgar had taught him one spell.

The Banishing Spell will rid you of any enemy, no matter how powerful. It removes him from your world, from reality, and sends him to an empty void, a place of darkness…forever.

Every spell of Homdee had a price: the caster must suffer what he or she inflicted. *The Advocates gave their souls for this cause,* he thought. *But even they had a release at the end.*

It didn't matter, Tim supposed. Nazgar had not given him the Banishing Spell to use against Zadinn. Even then, the Kyrlod had known other tasks lay before Tim. Perhaps that was why Tim was here—he'd been brought to this point, given this knowledge, for one reason alone.

To use it now.

Eternal darkness…for both of us…forever.

He realized he was laughing madly.

* * *

Boblin rode a wave of fire.

His eyes remained shut, but in his mind, he still saw the room around him with full clarity. He stood before the reservoir, arms outstretched, his body imbued with an awesome light, practically vibrating with the energy coursing through it. He could do anything—*anything*. Level mountains. Raise the dead. It was intoxicating and terrifying. Boblin walked a knife's edge between complete control and absolute incineration.

The undead swarmed into the room. Boblin directed a wave of fire toward them, blasting through one after another. The creatures disintegrated before the onslaught, turned to naught but dust motes on the wind. He saw Celia, Jend, and Eklan throw themselves to the ground. A vast wind whipped around him, and jagged streaks of energy shot into the sky. He saw the rent ever widening, felt unspeakable evil about to pour forth, and Boblin knew what he had to do: he had to sever the portal's connection to this world. *Cut the city off, cut Uklith off.*

Boblin felt the entire layout of Agrazab at his fingertips, seething with suppressed malice and evil. He felt the central palace, where Uklith's malevolent presence was concentrated. He knew Tim was still in there, perhaps deep underground, along with Bria.

I'm sorry. Boblin struck the outer walls first. Brick and mortar flew as Boblin ripped the foundations out from underneath them. Fountains of earth and stone erupted skyward as the battlements collapsed, caving inward in a ceaseless cascade of destruction. Boblin pulled the power ever closer, dragging a maelstrom of destruction through the streets, sundering buildings and undead alike, until he reached the palace.

Tim had known it might come to this. Boblin brought down all his power like a hammer from above, cracking the squat walls and raining absolute destruction upon the Demon-Lord's onetime residence.

And now for the very last bit. Boblin drew the Lifesource back toward himself, bringing it into a spinning vortex centered directly above his head, the only radiant light in a sky that had otherwise gone dark. He looked up at it.

May the Maker preserve us.

Boblin turned the power of the reservoir in on itself. The well shook with a titanic impact, and a sphere of brilliant light erupted. Everything in view disappeared, consumed utterly by the blinding brightness. Boblin felt his body flung across the room like a rag doll before he struck something solid and heard a disturbing *crunch* from one of his bones.

He opened his eyes and caught one last glimpse of Celia. She smiled at him.

And then the entire tower collapsed beneath them.

* * *

Tim thought of everyone he had lived for. He thought of Daniel Matthias, practicing the sword in the peaceful afternoons of the Odow. He thought of Rosalie, gentle and caring, showing him how to harness their horses and till the earth. He thought of Boblin, of Quentiin, of Ladu and Jend and Nazgar. And he thought of Bria, of the way her golden hair cascaded down her shoulders, the easy grace of her smile, the firmness with which she spoke, the bravery she displayed, the gentle wisdom she shared.

Goodbye.

The Warrior of Light erupted from beneath the mountain of skulls. He rose into the air, hovering over the slope of the mountain, facing up toward the black cloud which roiled and threatened and despaired, but which would never, ever take their world.

Because Tim would not allow it.

He looked over the chasm of anguished souls as winds buffeted him from all sides. He raised his face toward the darkness, filling his lungs with air.

"Laiscete oin sperenze," he cried out, and the voice that came from his lungs was not just his, but that of a hundred thousand—the voices of his friends and his comrades, of the souls in the chasm behind him, of all peoples. It was the voices of all those he surrendered himself for. *"Vu chentre!"*

The black cloud wavered.

No... the voice said, and it was no longer titanic, no longer powerful. It was thin, reedy, and terrified. *You fool...you utter, pathetic, fool...do you know what price you will pay?*

"Yes," Tim said, "and I pay it gladly."

The seam in the sky above their heads slammed shut with a clap of thunder.

It was but a heartbeat before another seam opened, this one different from the first, for on the other side it revealed nothing but cold, endless darkness. He heard Uklith wail, saw the cloud swirl upward and away, into the crack, gone forever.

Thousands of feet below Tim, a second seam opened, this one for him, and he felt himself pulled forward, unbidden, into that which awaited him. When Tim had first passed between his realm and Malath, he had never thought he would experience a greater feeling of loneliness and isolation.

He had been wrong.

The Warrior of Light tumbled into the rift. The darkness consumed him and the gap closed, locking him into his prison for all eternity.

41

Quentiin Harggra led the last sortie against the corsair horde. They'd slowly but steadily retaken the palace, a painstaking floor at a time, and next moved into the streets. The city still burned around them as they pressed forward, but the tide of the battle was nonetheless turning in Vonku's favor. He had left King Aras in Talladora's capable hands, Sendalion Danris at the king's side, Aras entrusting Quentiin to this final task.

Buildings burned and smoke rose as Quentiin and the soldiers with him pressed against corsairs and undead alike. For every new fire that arose, they put at least two out.

The ground underneath Quentiin suddenly shook. All eyes turned to the sky, toward the reservoir of power raging high above. Soldiers and corsairs watched as, for the first time that day, the reservoir's energy appeared to abate. The column inverted, gradually at first, then with increasing speed, until with a final, cataclysmic *boom* it disappeared. Quentiin felt a shockwave of air rush outward, and though he kept his balance, he saw several others lose their footing.

An unnatural quiet followed. When Vonku's defenders took up the battle again, the corsairs, already on the verge of defeat, either broke and fled, or surrendered entirely. And so it was that the people of Vonku held the city once more—a ruined city, an embattled city, but a city nonetheless.

Quentiin sheathed his sword and led his small company back to the palace, picking up other survivors on the way. When they entered the throne room, Quentiin saw Sendalion standing before a table with maps on it. The tall man looked up at the dwerion. For a long moment they stared at each other, the silence stretching between them.

At last, Quentiin gave a curt nod. "It's finished, laddie."

Behind Sendalion, Vinsor Dalin hobbled forward on a crutch, his broken leg set with planks of wood. He gave a crisp salute, which Quentiin returned.

Sendalion gave a deep sigh of relief. "Very good. Well done, all."

"The king?"

"He will live."

A ragged cheer arose from the assembled Legionnaires. Many men of El-tern, Quentiin noted, were among the survivors. *Aye, as I thought. The name shall no longer bear the burden of shame, but rather be a badge of honor. If not for the outcasts, if not for the rejects, this city would not stand today.*

"Sir?" a voice said, and Quentiin turned to see a Legionnaire step forward. "There is a girl at the palace gates. She is asking for you by name."

Quentiin looked at Vinsor and Sendalion. Both appeared as confused as he. Quentiin nodded. "Send her inside."

After a moment, the crowd of soldiers parted, and a small girl came for-ward. Her hair was streaked with dirt, and her face was smeared with ashes and dust. She also bore some spots of blood—though, Quentiin suspected, not hers. She stepped toward him, bare feet shuffling on the flagstones, and he crouched to face-level with her. "Aye, lass. What is it?"

"He told me to ask for you, Master Harggra."

"Who?"

"Lord Seltor."

Ah...

Quentiin took her hands. His large, meaty palms engulfed her diminutive fingers, and he drew her into a gentle embrace. "All will be well, lass. Tell us, what of Lord Seltor?"

"He died saving me, Master Harggra."

Quentiin closed eyes. *Too much death. Will the requisite sacrifices never end?* The room around him fell so silent, he quite clearly heard a teardrop splash on the flagstone. With great effort, he raised his head again, looking in her eyes and brushing the tears from her cheeks. "Don't cry, lass. When a man such as Trivian Seltor swears his oaths, he does so for the sake of those such as you. He does so not so that you will cry, but that you might smile." Quentiin stood and looked at the assembled Legionnaires. "His name will not be forgotten. Isn't that so, men?"

They responded with a uniform stamp of their feet on the ground, a pounding of fists against breastplates. A warrior's acknowledgment.

We mourn what we have lost, but we will also cherish what we have saved. The battle is won, now let the healing begin.

* * *

Tim floated in darkness. He saw nothing, heard nothing, felt nothing. The time that passed might have been but seconds or millennia. He did not know. He might have thought he'd be terrified, but instead he felt a strange peace. He had done what he needed to do, at great cost to be sure, but some fees had to be paid. The world would continue, his friends would go on. They would endure, and time would move forward into the next generation.

So be it.

When Tim saw the bright light, he thought it a hallucination, but realized the contradictory nature of such an idea, for in this endless limbo there was nothing to hallucinate about. The light came toward him, a pinpoint growing broader to fill his vision. With it, he began to feel human again. The sensation in his limbs returned, the tingling of life. Tim felt a warm glow of hope, muted but not vanquished.

He heard the rushing sound of wind—

—and found himself in a room, seated in a chair at the end of a long table. A hooded figure sat on the far side. Faint illumination came from above, not from a torch, but from an unrecognizable domed instrument hanging from the ceiling. It shone with a light from within. *Another reservoir of the Lifesource?*

"Hello?" Tim said.

Silence replied. Tim considered rising to his feet but thought better of it. The stranger drew his hood back to reveal an old man with white hair. The figure raised his face to the light. He had a long beard and wise, kind eyes. When he saw Tim, he smiled.

"Hello, Tim," said Nazgar of the Kyrlod.

* * *

Good karfing riddance, I hate this place.

Boblin lay on his back in the rubble, staring skyward. Every inch of his body seemed to hurt, though he knew that his wounds were merely superficial. He'd shielded himself and his companions during the collapse, using the last dregs of Lifesource energy to wrap them in a protective bubble. It hadn't stopped the odd beam or two from giving him a bruise, and it certainly hadn't prevented the wind from getting knocked out of him. A greater elion than

Boblin would have counted his blessings and been grateful, but Boblin Kule felt he'd earned the right to complain, and he planned to enjoy every karfing moment of doing so.

Above the survivors, the sky had returned to normal. Again, a wiser elion might have been grateful, but as far as Boblin was concerned, that just meant the Malath-blasted heat had returned. He'd rather enjoyed the shade, truth be told.

He rose to his feet, looking at the ruins of Agrazab. The City of Darkness had been leveled to a large field of rubble. He turned to the east, facing the Desert and the world beyond, where the horizon shimmered with the heat of day.

Celia rose next, stumbling over the wreckage to stand by his side. He took her hand in his, their fingers intertwining. A light breeze gusted over them, and Boblin raised his face toward the blessed coolness. Eddies of dust and sand swirled at their feet.

To their side, a beam shifted away from a pile. Eklan Hamur emerged, the tourniquet still around his arm. He reached back into the pile and pulled Jend Argul free. The four comrades stood together in the tower's ruins.

"Well," Boblin said after a moment. "That was interesting."

"What of Matthias and Bria?" Eklan asked.

The palace of Agrazab was gone, Boblin had absolutely ensured that, and it didn't bode well for the other two—he knew that to be a grim truth. But they had to go and see.

"Let's find out," Boblin said, and the four companions began making their way through the ruined streets.

* * *

Tim stared at the Kyrlod. Nazgar sat on the opposite side of the table, hands folded, face betraying nothing. The silence stretched between them until Nazgar spoke at last.

"Hungry?" A bowl of porridge appeared on the table in front of Tim. Tim eyed it cautiously at first, until Nazgar cleared his throat. "I don't deny it is somewhat common fare, but I think you'll appreciate it nonetheless."

"Ah." Tim took up the spoon and began eating. "Thank you." He attacked the meal, filling his stomach eagerly. *A few minutes ago I thought I'd never eat again.* Between spoonfuls, he took a moment to look back up at Nazgar.

"What happened?"

Nazgar arched an eyebrow. "To me, or to you?"

In spite of himself, Tim couldn't help but laugh. "Both, I suppose. But by all means, start with yourself."

"By the time I met you, very few Kyrlod remained. We are blessed, or perhaps cursed, with an intimate knowledge of our futures—not in the way I perceive the futures of others, which are often hazy and subject to change, but with great clarity. We know where we need to be and what we need to do. To be certain, some things did surprise us—my brother Ragzan's betrayal, for one. As for Ragzan, I doubt he anticipated his demise at Zadinn's hands. For what it's worth, I suspect he only ever opted to serve Zadinn in the hopes of escaping a different fate.

"As for myself, I'd seen my path end at Zadinn's citadel, and beyond it, a vacuum that I knew to be my death. Believe it or not, after many years of servitude, the thought of dying becomes a welcome rather than a fearsome notion. It was rest, and I was ready for it."

"What's it like?" Tim asked. "Death? Harmea?"

"Rest assured, you will experience it for yourself someday. Beyond that, I will say no further, for it's not the story I have come to deliver. Suffice it to say, I would have chosen to stay, but was informed I still had work to do." Nazgar leaned forward, eyes intent. "This was something I did *not* expect. All I'd been led to believe during my years of service was that my path ended with you—but I learned, to no small surprise, my work in your world was in fact just the beginning. Just…preparation."

"For?"

"Even I cannot answer that question in its entirety, for I do not know, but I have learned this much: just as your world exists, other worlds exist, countless realms side by side, each largely unaware of the rest. Harmea and Malath underpin all these realms, a pair of hubs that all realities share. They are called by different names in different places, but they always distill down to the most fundamental of truths: good and evil. In each realm, these two forces wage their struggle. Upon my death, I was given the task of traversing all these worlds." His face showed the touch of smile and a hint of wonder as his eyes grew distant. "I've seen many of them, though not all, and each is more exotic than the last. The Lifesource, the very blood that fuels Harmea in Malath, also exists in all places—but, like the great war, it manifests itself in a fashion unique to each realm." Nazgar pointed to the dome above their heads, which emitted a strange, harsh light. "In some worlds, people have harnessed the Lifesource so thoroughly, integrated it into their lives so regularly, that they would not know how to live without it. In other worlds, folk have shunned the power entirely."

"Are we in one of those other realms?" Tim asked.

"I had work to do here."

"How did I come here? I thought I banished myself for eternity."

"Ah." Nazgar gave his knowing smile again. "Yet another matter in which I have been surprised of late. Do you remember what I first told you of Homdee?"

"The caster must suffer what he inflicts."

Nazgar ticked off a finger. "Correct. Homdee's consequences have prevented its widespread use. However, the power has certain … safeguards in place. You already answered one mystery for yourself this evening: how did you defeat Zadinn?"

"I refused to let the world burn for the sake of our battle. I surrendered myself, and in doing so, shifted the balance of power in my favor."

"Quite unknowingly, of course. Think on today, when you cast the spell against Uklith. *Why* did you cast it?"

"To destroy Uklith."

Nazgar spread his arms wide. "What good would destroying Uklith do? As you and he discussed at length, evil exists and will continue to exist. Malath will continue to exist. Why not recognize the futility of it, and leave well enough alone?"

"Because…" Tim paused, thinking before continuing. "Regardless of Malath, if Uklith had been set free, he'd have subjugated our world, and remade it in his image."

"In truth, you did not cast the spell to destroy Uklith. You cast it to *preserve* your world, and, I daresay, your friends and those around you. Therefore, the consequence of the spell—the purpose for which you cast it—reflected back on you and—"

"Preserved *me*," Tim said. *Is it really that simple?* He felt a slow, great swell of relief begin to grow in his chest.

"Exactly. That, Tim, is one of Homdee's most exquisite attributes. Anyone who had cast that same spell with the intent of destruction, with the intent of causing suffering, would indeed have had an awful fate visited upon them. But you cast it to save others, and in doing so, saved yourself."

"What happened to Uklith?" Tim asked.

"He, I suspect, is far beyond our help. He is gone, and not likely to return."

"Is there any precedent for this?" Tim asked. *What are the theological consequences? As long as there has been the Maker, there has been the Demon-Lord.*

"Actually, yes. Uklith lied in more ways than one, and his most fundamental lie was to present himself as the eternal antithesis to the Maker. Far from it. Go back far enough, and Uklith was only a demon who gained enough power to assume the helm as lord of the underworld. He personified evil, but he was not evil itself. It will not be long before a new entity assumes command of Malath, and I have little doubt about who it might be."

The tone of Nazgar's voice and the look on his face gave Tim a chill. "What do you mean?"

"It seems we are ever connected, Ragzan and I. Having died but months before myself, Ragzan found himself in a Malath unhelmed, a Malath from which Uklith—still sealed in Agrazab—had long been separated. Ragzan now walks the same realms I traverse, sowing discord and strife, reveling in it. *He is the reason I was sent back*, for he defied fundamental laws separating the realms, and in doing so risked bringing ruin to them all. He was in your world but recently, orchestrating several events with the hope of furthering Uklith's ascension to power. Fortunately, thanks to you and your friends, he failed. But he will try again."

"Do you know how to stop him?"

"I do not."

"I see." Tim pushed the empty bowl of porridge away. "I'd be remiss if I didn't thank you again. So, what must I do next?"

"For the moment, Ragzan is my concern and not yours. His incentive for returning to your world was Uklith's gambit for power there. Barring that, he may pursue other goals. For now, Tim, you go back. Your task is what it has always been: be the Warrior, stand ready, and know you have friends by your side. And Tim?"

"Yes?"

"It was good to see you."

Tim smiled back. "It was good to see you, too." Behind him, a slit in the air opened, showing the room that had been Uklith's prison in Agrazab. Bria Hamur stood on the other side, though from the looks of things it didn't appear she could see the doorway connecting her to Tim.

Tim rose, but before he crossed the threshold he paused. "I have one more question. Do these other realms have Warriors, too?"

Nazgar nodded. "They do. But like Harmea and Malath, they are not always called by the same names, and, like the Lifesource, they manifest their purpose in ways unique to each place."

He gestured to the room around him. "Who is the Warrior in *this* world?"

"That was two questions, not one."

Tim looked at Nazgar closely. The Kyrlod's face had an odd expression. "What happened to him?" Tim asked.

"They killed him," Nazgar replied.

"Oh." Tim paused. "I see."

He turned and stepped through the doorway.

* * *

He opened his eyes in midair, right before he fell on top of Bria. They hit to the ground together with a muffled *thump*.

"Sorry," he said, rolling off her.

"Welcome back, Matthias."

He looked about himself. The bodies of undead lay strewn in all directions. There had to be at least two dozen corpses, with the last several lying halfway through a crack in the wall. Bria must have been holding them off.

"Took you long enough," she said, handing him his sword. "Nice work, anyway."

Tim buckled his sword belt about his waist. Most of the room had collapsed around them—indeed, it looked as if Bria had retreated to the center of the dais as destruction rained down.

"Both of you vanished," Bria said. "You'd been floating in the air for some time, and then the ceiling started caving in. I'd just pulled you to safety when your body disappeared."

"It's a long story," Tim said. "I'm much happier to be back here, though."

Behind Bria, where a section of the roof had collapsed, it had done so in such a fashion that it left a pile of rubble leading to an opening above their heads, just enough for a person to squeeze through and return the streets of Agrazab.

"Why were you still waiting here?" he asked. "Looks like you had a way out."

She shrugged. "I knew you would be back."

He took her hands in his. And then he kissed her.

* * *

They stepped out into the sunlight. Tim paused for a moment upon seeing the destruction all around them, Agrazab leveled, the City of Darkness no more. The desert air hung hot and still.

"From now on, I'm leaving the Lifesource to you, mate."

Tim turned to see Boblin standing behind him, along with Celia, Jend, and Eklan, all bearing the dust and scrapes of battle. They looked absolutely terrible—though Tim supposed he probably looked pretty bad himself.

"Water?" Tim asked, holding out a skin.

"Forget the water," Boblin replied. "Where's the ale?"

"You look at me as if I brought any."

"I look at you because I know you did."

"It's gone."

Boblin grunted. "I figured as much. Well, what do you have for us?"

"Uklith's gone, Nazgar's back, and there's an evil sorcerer who can cross worlds who will probably show up here sooner or later."

"The usual, then."

"Aye."

They made their way back across the city. Once they exited what would have been the outer walls, they returned to the lean-tos where they had sheltered the horses with water before entering the city, intending to return to the routine of resting in the sun and traveling at night during their long journey back east.

"You know," Tim said as they settled in the shade of a lean-to, "it would have been nice if you'd left some power in that reservoir."

Boblin who had been cutting a slice of bread from a loaf in his lap, paused. "Excuse me?"

"I'm just saying, I could have used it to return us to one of the other reservoirs that had been triggered—the one in the North, for example. It would have made for an easy journey back."

Boblin *hmphed.* "You've got to be kidding me. I save our skins, practically burn myself into a flake of ash, and you're complaining that we have to walk back. One of these days…"

"I'm just pointing it out," Tim said.

Boblin threw the loaf of bread at him.

42

"King Aras of Alcatune," Emperor Ladu said. "Well met, Your Majesty." Quentiin watched the proceedings before him. It had been easier than he thought to convince Aras to come North, once Talladora proclaimed the king fit for travel. Rather than being resistant to the idea, as Quentiin had feared, the king was quite open to it. Quentiin supposed that, after seeing his own city beset with undead, Aras understood Ladu better. Galdon's recent battle against the undead notwithstanding, Ladu had fought and lost against an invasion from Malath two hundred years ago. Aras, having seen how close his kingdom had come to that very fate, now had a better appreciation for those in the North. And Ladu, for his part, had a thing or two to learn from Aras. The emperor meant well, but he was young and inexperienced. Quentiin didn't think northerners and southerners would ever *truly* understand each other, but at the very least they could grow closer.

The emissaries from Keldur had come to the palace too, arriving several days before Quentiin's group arrived. The Keldurians arrived in a Galdon as beset with battle as Vonku, though Quentiin decided Vonku had seen more in the way of fire and destruction. Galdon, for what it was worth, hadn't had much to destroy to begin with, and in their case most of the fighting had been concentrated closer to and within the palace. The story was much the same here: undead and reservoirs. The reservoir here, like the one in Vonku, had inverted upon itself before disappearing. Quentiin wondered what to make of it all. His small reservoir connecting him to Tim remained dark, and each day he looked anxiously to the west for any sign of his friend.

"Thank you for welcoming me into your kingdom, Emperor Ladu," Aras replied, inclining his head. "We have much to discuss. But first, an apology. The truth of the matter is, I feared the powers at play here in the North. I did what I thought was right by my people, urged caution of this land, and yet the last few days are proof indeed that we are more together than separate in this endeavor. You are not our enemies, and you never were."

"You humble me with your words," Ladu replied. "I, for my part, confess I did too little to understand you. The only other outside ruler I encountered before you was one who enslaved my entire people, and it did not precondition me to trust other people in positions of power. For that, I was wrong, and you have my apologies."

Quentiin had to stifle a chuckle. *Politics at its best. They could just say, I was wrong, you were wrong, let's move on an' share a pint—but that wouldn't let them make such flowery speeches, would it?*

The discussion continued for some time, both sides more agreeable than they might otherwise have been to make concessions to each other. The gist of it was sound enough: North trusted South, South trusted North, individuals free to make their homes in one land or another, so on and so forth. The details were more particular than that, but Quentiin was happy to ignore them. One of his first orders of business had been to appoint someone else to his diplomat's post. He was well and gladly rid of those duties.

The sound of footsteps jerked Quentiin awake from where he had been standing with eyes half-shut, a standing doze that he had perfected during long hours of sentinel duty in the Royal Legion. He'd been dreaming of ale.

His disgruntlement at being so rudely awakened from the sweet, savory pint dissipated when he saw the expression on Faldon Kule's face. The elion had just entered the room, and his eyes were bright.

"Your majesties," the elion said, a smile splitting his face. "They have returned."

* * *

The journey across the desert had gone easily enough. The krevur packs were much smaller because of all the ones they killed in the nest, and those that remained proved less a challenge given that Tim was freer to use the Lifesource as a deterrent. That wasn't to say they didn't have their challenges. They'd gotten into another tight spot with a scorpion on the Mygon Path, but made it through well enough. Therefore, though the journey was not without incident, they entered the North well and whole, staying north of the Fertile Lands and opting for a direct path back to Galdon.

As Tim rode Rookwind underneath Galdon's gates and into the city streets, he saw the telltale signs of a battle that had ended. The elion scouts at the outpost had already told them of the siege of Ladu's palace, and that King Aras of Alcatune was here, too,

Better that they be talking than starting a war. Tim hadn't truly thought it would come to that, but he felt far better knowing the men were at last working to bridge the divide.

He would have preferred a hot bath and warm meal as a first order of business, but they could hardly make time to do so. Word spread quickly that Tim Matthias and his companions had returned, though their company was smaller than it had been before. They had names to add to the list of the Frontier Patrol's fallen, and it was with heavy hearts that they would do so.

At the garrison, the companions dismounted before entering the palace. Tim patted Rookwind's neck. "You did well, friend." It had been a long, arduous journey for these horses, and they'd borne their duties and their riders well. *Rookwind, you've earned a lifetime of carrots and then some. Enjoy it.*

Inside the palace hallway, Tim saw shredded tapestries and allowed himself a wry smile. They always seemed to be the first casualties in battle, those tapestries, never long for the world once the swords, arrows, and torches began flying.

Silence greeted the company when they entered the throne room. Faces turned toward them in expectation. When Tim and his company came forward, the sound of their boots upon the flagstones was unnaturally loud.

Emperor Ladu stood near the base of his dais, on equal footing with King Aras. Quentiin stood in the small audience before them, and the dwerion gave Tim a curt nod, showing the hint of a grin at the corner of his mouth.

"Welcome back, Warrior." Ladu paused, and when he spoke again, he did so in a tone that was much less formal, and with a hint of wry humor. "I don't suppose there is a good way to ask how a battle against a dark god went, is there?"

Tim bowed, and rose smiling. "It went well, your majesty. Uklith is defeated."

Celia, Boblin, and Jend followed suit beside Tim, dipping a knee before Ladu bade them stand.

Eklan and Bria had hung back, but Tim waved them forward. "Your majesty," Tim said, "I'd like you to meet the man who showed us the way to

Agrazab, and his sister who joined our cause. Without them, we would have failed. This is Eklan and Bria Hamur, of Keldur."

"Aye," a voice responded, and an emissary from Keldur stepped forward. "You do our village proud, brother and sister—both of you."

It was a moment before Tim registered who he was looking at: Reidell Hamur, the third Hamur sibling, looking healthy and whole. Tim thought the throne room had been silent before, but that was nothing compared to now. Eklan and Bria stopped in mid-stride, Eklan with his mouth open, Bria with a tremble in her lip.

This can't be real, Tim thought. *Can it?*

But it *was* real. The flagstones beneath his feet were solid. The air he breathed was fresh. The power of the Lifesource thrummed through all.

"Reidell?" Bria whispered. Her eyes glistened.

He held his arms out. "It's me, sister. My mind walks in shadow no more." The surreal moment broke, the reality of it solidified, and the three siblings embraced.

The last clutch of power Uklith had in this world was his hold upon Reidell's mind. Gone for good. The City is broken, and the Hamur family is free.

The discourse among the group continued, until Ladu dismissed everyone from the room except for Tim, Boblin, Celia, Eklan, Jend, Quentiin, Sendalion, Aras, and Raisha. As for Lady Varuc, Tim saw Raisha brush a kiss against the emperor's cheek. Ladu tried, and failed, to hide a smile.

Curious. I think we may have an empress soon.

Each group related their respective tales: Tim of the long journey to the City of Darkness, Ladu of the revolt in the north, Quentiin of Vila Kaarst and his corsair hordes. They continued their conversations late into the night, sometimes joyful, sometimes tearful, but always content. The great, dreadful danger was past, and Tim's heart was light. Whatever challenges lay in their future—and from Nazgar's words, challenges there would be—what mattered most was the group in this room. At this moment, folk of both North and South stood together for the first time in thousands of years. They had been two worlds divided, but now they were united.

And for the moment, that was all that mattered.

Epilogue

Tim stood in an alley of Vonku, the cauldron before him crumbling into dust. It wasn't the first time he'd seen the Cauldron of Souls disintegrate. He just hoped, as he relinquished his hold on the Lifesource, that the Cauldron *stayed* gone this time.

Tim had started near the site of Jeb's corpse in the north, visiting the reservoir to ensure it was not just dormant but actually destroyed. These reservoirs were things of great power, and after seeing what they'd done, he had to be sure that they could never again be used to open a portal to Malath. *And, going forward, I'll be more careful with the any reservoirs I myself create.*

"This is where you grew up?" Boblin asked, looking around at the streets of Vonku.

"For a time," Tim replied. Vonku had been his first home, long ago. It had made him into a southerner, had inspired him to serve in the Legion. That service had never come, of course, but now he had a different duty to fulfill.

"It's prettier when it ain't burned to the ground," Quentiin rumbled. He and Boblin had accompanied Tim on his journey here. It seemed only fitting that they finish this long quest together. With the destruction of the last reservoir, Tim was looking forward to some much-deserved rest—with Bria Hamur for company, of course.

They left the city, opting to camp in the hills north of Vonku. As evening fell, they reached the crest of a hill in the countryside, overlooking the ocean to the east. Rays of light from the setting sun behind them cast a red glow upon the waters. Boblin gave a low whistle of amazement at the sight. Tim didn't think the elion would ever get over how vast the ocean was. Boblin had never seen the sea while growing up in the wastelands of the North. It was beautiful indeed, with red-gold light dancing on the waters, the crashing of surf in their ears, and the scent of salt on the breeze.

At first they sat in silence, simply appreciating the scene before them. Moments like this, after all, were a part of why they fought so hard for freedom.

Eventually, Quentiin broke the quiet. "What do ye know about Ragzan?"

"He was—is—Nazgar's twin brother," Tim replied. "Zadinn used his blood to open the Barricade the first time, in fact. He's gone, though. Nazgar said he's left this world, focusing on other things."

"But he'll come back," Boblin said.

Tim nodded. "This world made him. If he has an opportunity for power, whether here or somewhere else, he'll take it."

"Ever feel like we're just gettin' moved around on somebody else's chessboard?" Quentiin asked.

You are a pawn, Warrior... Zadinn's words came back yet again, still haunting Tim.

Boblin gave a snort, but it was one of agreement, not derision. "The thought has crossed my mind."

Tim picked up three stones. He handed one to Boblin and one to Quentiin, keeping the third for himself. "Yes, me too. But we are settling this question once and for all."

"A rock knows the answer to my questions about destiny and free will?" Boblin asked.

Quentiin gave a rumbling laugh. "I've heard some say that ye have the *brains* of a rock, laddie. Mayhap this one is a smarter rock than you."

"Close your fists," Tim said. "Don't show anyone whether you are holding the stone or not. Stone in your hand, you believe we're here because we choose to be. Empty hand, you believe that we're here because we were forced to be. We open our hands at the same time, agreed?"

The other two nodded, and there was a shuffling of hands as they concealed their decisions.

Tim held his fist out in front of him. Boblin and Quentiin did the same. "Ready?" Tim asked.

They opened their hands.

Each of which held a stone.

It's long past time that I stopped worrying about lies an evil man told me in a citadel. The power to make our own choices is the greatest gift the Maker granted us.

"Ragzan may come someday, but when he does, we'll be ready for him," Tim said. "The three of us. Right?"

"Indeed," Quentiin replied.

"I wouldn't have it any other way," Boblin said.

Tim drew his sword, sat, and placed it across his knees. "That's what I thought." With that, the three comrades sat on the hilltop in silence, side by side, looking over the ocean as the sun set behind them.

www.ingramcontent.com/pod-product-compliance
Lightning Source LLC
Chambersburg PA
CBHW070827260626
47170CB00007B/2291